Praise for S. Andrew Swann's Moreau Novels:

"The private eye tiger hero is a tough, serious minded, but often sentimental character who really makes this story of secret plots, assassins, drug dealers, and political intrigue work. One of the more interesting blends of mystery and SF." —*Science Fiction Chronicle*

"An entertaining hard-boiled detective novel set in a gritty, relatively near future. . . . If any book was meant to be made into an action-adventure movie, this is it." —*Locus*

"An enjoyable mix of a hard-boiled detective novel with near-future science fiction." —*SF Site*

"Here is the printed page equivalent of an action movie: a novel as vivid as a cinema blockbuster. . . . Swann has superb technical skills . . . the particular details and variations that he comes up with are inventive and neat. More importantly, he has a style that makes the action leap off the page. Many SF writers who have more famous names could learn a great deal from Swann." —*The New York Review of Science Fiction*

"An exciting and inventive adventure." —*The Denver Post*

DAW Novels from S. Andrew Swann

MOREAU OMNIBUS

Forests of the Night
Emperors of the Twilight
Specters of the Dawn

S. ANDREW SWANN

DAW BOOKS, INC.

DONALD A. WOLLHEIM, FOUNDER

375 Hudson Street, New York, NY 10014

ELIZABETH R. WOLLHEIM
SHEILA E. GILBERT
PUBLISHERS

http://www.dawbooks.com

DAW Book Collectors No. 1266
DAW Books are distributed by Penguin Group (USA) Inc.

First Printing, August 2003
1 2 3 4 5 6 7 8 9

DAW TRADEMARK REGISTERED
U.S. PAT. OFF. AND FOREIGN COUNTRIES
—MARCA REGISTRADA.
HECHO EN U.S.A.
PRINTED IN THE U.S.A.

Introduction

Twenty years ago I had the idea for a story. I wanted to write a hard-boiled detective yarn. Something very noir that would come across in sepia and shades of gray. It was a time of Reaganomics, cold war paranoia and cyberpunk, which flowed rather seamlessly into the environment I was envisioning—dark, urban, and threatening. There would be twisted conspiracies, clients with mysterious motivations, crooked politicians, all the elements you need.

The problem was, the main character insisted on being a Bengal tiger, an eight-foot-tall predator complete with fur, claws, and tail. He also wanted to be a private investigator.

This was a bit of a departure for the genre. But Nohar didn't want to go away. I had a tiger in my head that wanted to be Jack Nicholson in *Chinatown*. So I wrote about Nohar Rajahstahn on a creaky used Olivetti typewriter.

And, at first, the story didn't work.

All through high school I worked on various drafts, collecting carbon copies and rejection slips. The manuscript swelled from a short story, to a novelette, to a novella. Editors wrote back little notes on how the background overwhelmed the story and how the plot overwhelmed the characters. All of which should have told me something.

However, at the time, I was too inexperienced to realize *what* it was telling me. I shelved Nohar and went on to try my hand at other things.

For another six years or so, I continued to write, and continued to remain unpublished. I kept writing short stories that kept getting rejected and, at some point during my extended undergraduate college career I made pact with myself—I was going to publish *something* before I graduated, or I was going to give up on this whole writing idea. And, since I didn't *want* to give up on the whole writing thing, I tried to seriously analyze what it was I was doing wrong.

That was when I had the first major epiphany of my writing career: *I wasn't a short story writer.*

It comes as a shock to some new writers that a short story is, in many ways, a more difficult form than a novel. It requires a disciplined focus similar to what's required to poetry. Telling a complete story in four thousand words is a feat worthy of respect and admiration, because it is a hard thing to do.

The reason that new writers come to short stories first is because they are short. The typing is done sooner, and the object of creation is easier to manage.

Novels seem so unwieldy by comparison. A marathon rather than a sprint.

But some people are sprinters and some aren't. There are stories that can be told in the short form, and some that can't. And if your creative diet, like mine, consists of novels rather than short stories, more likely than not the story ideas you produce will be novel ideas. And if you try to write a novel idea into a short story, it won't fit.

It was one failed novel later when I realized that was the case with Nohar's story. It had kept getting longer because it wasn't a short story. The background overwhelmed the story and the plot overwhelmed the characters because so much was shoved into such a small space that it left no room for the characters to breathe, much less think their own thoughts or have their own motives. What I had was a novel outline disguised as a very long short story.

I decided to try and do Nohar justice this time. I pulled out the yellowing carbons and started writing. On a computer this time.

I hadn't really shelved the story though. It had been with me ever since I started, and I never even referred to the original draft. The image I had in my head was much better than what had made it to the page in that first attempt.

Much more made it into Nohar's world this time. The wars that created the moreaus, his family history, a personal relationship, a pet cat. Other characters came out of nowhere, like Evi Isham and Angel, both of whom insisted on having their own books. The space allowed me to think a little more deeply about Nohar's place in the moreaus' world, and the moreaus' place in ours.

People have said that I wrote an allegory about race relations, though I think what I did was considerably simpler—I imagined the average human being having to coexist with an eight-foot-tall, intelligent anthropoid tiger with canines the size of his thumb. I imagined street gangs made up of fast-breeding rodents that die of old age by eighteen. I imagined genetically engineered weapons with human intelligence. The world that results in wasn't allegory, it was just human nature.

Welcome to Nohar's world. . . .

S. Andrew Swann
February, 2002

FORESTS OF THE NIGHT

This is for John, Heather, and their kid(s?)

Acknowledgments

Thanks to a number of people who left their mark on this manuscript. To Dan Eloff, who knows he got me writing again, and to R. M. Meluch, who doesn't. To the members of the Cleveland SF Writer's Workshop, who helped me get the burrs and toolmarks off this novel. To Stacy Newman, who offered to proof this. To Anastacia H. Brightfox, for naming one of the characters. And thanks to Amy, who, if nothing else, helped to give me something to write about.

Tyger! Tyger! burning bright
In the forests of the night,
What immortal hand or eye
Could frame thy fearful symmetry?

In what distant deeps or skies
Burnt the fire of thine eyes?
On what wings dare he aspire?
What the hand, dare seize the fire?

And what shoulder, and what art,
Could twist the sinews of thy heart?
And when thy heart began to beat,
What dread hand? And what dread feet?

What the hammer? What the chain?
In what furnace was thy brain?
What the anvil? what dread grasp
Dare its deadly terrors clasp?

When the stars threw down their spears,
And water'd heaven with their tears,
Did he smile his work to see?
Did he who made the Lamb make thee?

Tyger! Tyger! burning bright
In the forests of the night,
What immortal hand or eye
Could frame thy fearful symmetry?
                    —WILLIAM BLAKE

Chapter 1

"One day, Nugoya, you're going to screw the wrong person." Nohar Rajasthan raked his claws across the seat of his booth, wishing it was Nugoya's face. Like the rest of *Zero's,* the vinyl on the seat was flashy, shiny, and cheap. The seat shredded.

Nugoya grabbed the collar of the black jacket that was draped over his left shoulder, shaking his head. He looked human, but only at first glance. A close examination of the graying Japanese would reveal joints large beyond normal human proportions and muscles that snaked like steel cable. The light above the booth glinted off the chrome irises of Nugoya's artificial Japanese eyes. "I hire you to find my girl. You find me a corpse. A corpse is worthless. I owe you nothing."

Nohar shouldn't have had the bad sense to let Nugoya hire him. It was becoming hard to contain his anger. "Expenses, and four days of legwork."

Nohar shouldn't have trusted a frank. Japan had been one of the few countries to ever defy the U.N. ban on the manipulation of human genetic material. The INS had tight restrictions on letting human frankensteins into the country and those that made it here found that they had few, if any rights. That kind of bitterness tended to turn people into assholes—and Nugoya didn't need any help on that score.

Even moreaus like Nohar had a constitutional amendment in their favor.

"I owe you nothing. I should ask back the thousand I paid you. You are an arrogant cat. Were we elsewhere, you would have to show some respect, and pay for your failure." Nugoya held up his mutilated right hand. It was missing two fingers.

Nohar was already scanning the rest of the bar. He picked out Nugoya's people easily. They were all moreaus—a human would not be caught dead working for a frank.

"Twenty-five hundred, Nugoya. Pay me."

It was Tuesday, two in the morning. There were only a half-dozen other people. The civilians—all human since they were downtown—were giving Nugoya's booth a wide berth. No surprise, since two of Nugoya's soldiers were hovering near the table. One was a tiger, like Nohar. The other was a dark brown, nearly black ursine that couldn't quite stand upright even with the relatively high ceiling. Nugoya had a vulpine manning the bar, and a trio of white rabbits sat near the entrance. Nohar knew there was a canine somewhere out of sight, probably in the kitchen. Nohar could catch a hint of the dog's scent.

"You failed. No money."

Nohar told himself that he should just walk out of there. Shut up, leave, and cut his losses. He didn't.

"I found the bitch, peddling her ass on the side for the flush *you* hooked her on. I don't know if it was cut with angel dust or drain cleaner, but her last trip splatted her all over Morey Hill. It's *your* fault she's dead."

Nugoya's jaw clenched, and Nohar could smell his anger. Nugoya stood up. His jacket slid off his shoulder, revealing his artificial left arm and some scarring on his neck. "How dare you, *an animal,* presume—"

That was enough. "And what are you, Nugoya, but a half-pint, half pink sleazeball?"

Nugoya sputtered something incomprehensible. Probably Japanese.

Nohar was glad he was the one facing the rest of the bar. He could feel all hell was about to break loose. Why couldn't he keep his damn mouth shut? One more try at being reasonable. "I just want my money, Nugoya. You aren't going to shake me down like one of your girls."

Nugoya's problem was he couldn't ever be anything but a small-time pimp. He wasn't human and he wasn't a moreau, so neither world would let him have more than a few scraps of the power he thought he deserved.

"I will not take any more insolence. Leave or I will have you removed."

Nugoya motioned with his left arm at the other tiger and the bear. The tiger started moving forward. The bear reached under a table and took a hold of something large and presumably deadly. He kept it out of sight of the patrons.

"It's insolence to think the world owes you respect because some defunct Jap corporation built you like a disposable radio."

That did it. Nugoya had a killer ego, and could only take a little needling before he jumped. In his prime, a Japanese corporate samurai could take Nohar in a fair fight. Nugoya's ego would never let him admit that he was well past his prime. Tokyo was nuked by China a long time ago, and Nugoya had been sitting on his butt for longer than that.

The frank ripped the table from the wall and threw it to the side. The advancing tiger almost tripped over it. Nohar stayed seated and Nugoya went for his neck. Nugoya was fast, faster than any normal human, faster than most moreaus.

Nohar was faster.

As the other tiger manhandled the remains of the table out of his way and the bear pulled out a Russian-make assault rifle, Nohar's right hand shot up and clamped on Nugoya's mechanical wrist. At the same time, Nohar wrapped his left arm around Nugoya's right arm. The frank's three-fingered hand ended up clamped under Nohar's armpit. Nohar had his forearm levered under Nugoya's upper arm, his hand resting on the shoulder.

Nohar pushed down and heard the bone crack.

Nugoya yelled, washing Nohar's face with his sour breath, and tried to escape. But Nohar had lifted the frank off the ground by the mechanical arm. Nugoya didn't have the leverage.

Predictably, one of the civilians screamed.

"That will heal. If I did that to your other arm, who's around to fix it? Call off the muscle."

Nugoya showed some reluctance, so Nohar bore down on the broken arm. Nohar could hear the bones grate together. Nugoya shook his head violently and screamed something back at his people in Japanese. The tiger stopped moving, and the bear set the rifle down on the ground.

The tiger slowly drew his gun from a shoulder holster and dropped it.

"You're dead, Rajasthan."

"Hundred years we'll all be dead. I just want my money."

It was a standoff. Nohar had Nugoya as a shield, but there were six of Nugoya's people between him and the door. The rabbits weren't an immediate problem, the press of exiting civilians were pinning them by the door. The bartending fox had pulled out a shotgun, but he had the sense not to point it at his boss. Even so, Nohar couldn't move away from the wall without exposing himself.

He might be 260 centimeters tall and weigh 300 kilos. He might be able to whip anything but that bear and a few franks in a fair fight. But guns were guns.

Nohar stood up, lifting Nugoya by his mechanical arm. The little pimp barely gave his torso cover. Nohar would have preferred kevlar—he would have preferred not being there in the first place.

Nohar could smell the canine, stronger now. The other tiger's nose twitched. The bear started turning toward the bar. The civilians were gone.

So were the rabbits.

What?

Nugoya was still yelling. "Dead!"

The tiger turned toward the entrance. Nohar was smelling it now, too. The copper odor of blood. Rabbit blood. It had drifted in from the open door to the empty bar with the algae smell from the river. Nugoya stopped yelling.

The fox started turning around to face the long mirror behind the bar. The canine's smell was rank in the bar now. Nohar began to realize the dog might not be one of Nugoya's people. The fox must have heard something because he was raising the shotgun toward the mirror.

"Let me down!" There was the hint of panic in Nugoya's voice and more than a hint of it in his smell.

Someone turned on a glass jackhammer and the mirror for the length of the bar exploded outward in a wave, from left to right. It was some sort of silenced submachine gun. The vulpine got in the way of at least three shots, and large chunks of fox flew out over the bar. The shotgun went off, blowing away a case of Guinness that was sitting behind the bar. The fox fell half over the bar and bled.

The smell of cordite, beer, and melted teflon wafted over. Whoever was shooting was using glazer rounds. If the internal injuries didn't get you, the blood poisoning would.

The other tiger was ducking for cover in a booth across from Nohar and Nugoya. There wasn't cover for the bear. All the ursine could do was reach back for the rifle and hope the guy with the machine gun missed.

The bear was bending over. Nohar had an unobstructed view of the assassin jumping out of the broken mirror and on to the bar. Canine. A dog with a shaggy gray coat that tagged him as an Afghani. The dog wore a long black coat over a black jumpsuit that bulged with the kevlar vest he wore under it. The gun was small, the silencer was twice as long as the weapon itself. The clip was the length of the dog's forearm.

The bear was intimidating, but size was the bear's downfall. What was terrifying on the battlefields of Asia was a deadly handicap in the small confines of the rear of *Zero's*. The ursine couldn't turn around fast enough to shoot the canine.

The canine emptied a burst into the bear's back and Nohar got a good look and a good smell of the inside of the bear's chest as the ursine splatted on to the ground.

The tiger had a problem. His gun was on the ground, by the rifle. Nohar could smell the bloodlust rising from the other cat. *No,* Nohar thought, *you don't jump a guy with an automatic weapon.* But the cat was already hyped on adrenaline and Nohar could see the muscles in the tiger's haunches tense, even under the human clothing.

The dog was waiting for the tiger to pounce. Three bullets hit the cat before it got halfway. Blood sprayed the wall and the tiger slammed into a booth, smashing a table and scattering glassware.

Then the dog turned his attention to Nohar and Nugoya.

Nugoya was thrashing like a fish out of water. "Get me out of this, you have your money, you have three times your money—"

The dog licked his nose. The smell of his musk made Nohar want to sneeze. "Drop the pimp."

Nohar didn't argue.

Nugoya hit the ground and collapsed, cradling his arm. He turned toward the dog. "Hassan . . ."

The canine shook his head. "Too late. You were warned last time."

"Can't we deal—"

"No. You knew the rules. Do not tread on our business. Flush is our business. We say who sells, and who to."

Nugoya staggered to his feet. "I needed the money to keep my girls supplied. You're charging too much—"

"Others will be quite glad not to get off as cheaply as you." The canine fired one shot that hit Nugoya in the face. The pimp's head jerked back hard enough that Nohar heard the neck crack. Nugoya fell backward at Nohar's feet, looking upward with only half a face.

Only one chrome iris looked up. The other eye had become electronic shrapnel buried deep in what was left of Nugoya's brain.

Nohar looked up from the corpse, and at Hassan. "Me now?"

The dog shook his head and raised his gun. "Not today. This was
a lesson. Lessons need witnesses."

Hassan began backing away, keeping his eyes on Nohar.

When Hassan reached the door, he gave the carnage a brief in-
spection. Then he looked back up at Nohar, who was still standing
by the rear wall. "Advice, tiger. Next time be more careful who you
work for."

No shit.

It took all of fifteen minutes for the first police to descend on
the party side of the flats. In twenty minutes the east side of the
Cuyahoga River was illuminated by a wash of dozens of flashing
blue and red lights. Even though Nohar was the one who called in
the shooting, he had to sit on his tail in the back of a very cramped
Chevy Caldera sedan. At least the pink uniforms didn't cuff him—
not that they hadn't tried, but this far out of Moreytown they didn't
have cuffs that would fit him. They simply deposited him in the
back seat and kept their distance.

Nohar squirmed to get his tail in a comfortable position and
looked out the windows facing the river. Not much to see, water for
a few hundred meters reflecting the police flashers. The water terminated at the concrete base of the West Side office complex. The
office buildings were so dark at this time of night that they seemed
to be trapezoidal holes cut in the night sky, revealing something
blacker behind it.

There wasn't much else to watch out the other window. The
forensics people were all in *Zero's*. He'd end up talking to Manny
later anyway. Not that there was anything to discuss. It wasn't like
he was on a case any more.

Twenty-five hundred dollars. Gone. The first of the month was
at the end of the week, and he only had about two hundred in the
bank. Served him right for working for a pimp.

Nohar had his pride. He didn't want to have to ask Manny about
his old room—

He shook his head. Things would work out. They usually did.

A soft rain began to fall. It broke up the reflections on the river.

Nohar heard the scream of abused brakes. He turned around to
face the entrance of the parking lot. A puke-green dodge Havier that

was missing one front fender jumped the curb and skidded to a halt in a handicapped parking spot.

It had to be Harsk.

Indeed, Irwin Harsk's bald head emerged from the driver's side door of the unmarked sedan. Harsk stormed out like an avalanche. Many standards of pink beauty escaped Nohar, but some forms of ugly transcended species. Harsk's black face resembled a cinder block.

It had been only a matter of time before Harsk got involved. He was the detective in charge of Moreytown. He had jurisdiction over anything involving moreaus, and, by extension, any product of genetic engineering. In the case of the shoot-out at *Zero's* that covered the victims, the suspect, and the witness.

This obviously didn't please the detective.

Harsk stood a moment in the rain, looking over the scene—the ambulances, the forensics van, Manny's medical examiner's van, the seven marked and two unmarked police cars. Even over the twenty-meter distance between them, Nohar could hear Harsk grunt.

After giving the scene the once-over, Harsk targeted a lone uniform who was standing by the door to *Zeros*. Harsk looked like he wanted to unload on someone. The cop by the door was the unlucky one. Nohar supposed Harsk chose his victim because of the cup of coffee the guy was drinking. Harsk walked up to the guy, and even though Nohar wasn't great at reading human expressions, the way the poor cop bit his lip and gave forced nods indicated that Harsk wasn't having a nice day and was doing his best to share the experience.

Harsk pointed at the Caldera that Nohar was sitting in and yelled something that Nohar couldn't quite make out. The cop shrugged and tried to say something, and Harsk cut him off. Harsk grabbed the guy's coffee and pointed back into *Zero's*.

Nohar wished he could read lips.

The cop went inside and Harsk started walking toward the Caldera. He took a sip from the uniform's coffee and grimaced. He looked into the cup, shook his head, and dumped it on the asphalt.

Harsk walked up to the door and opened it. "Rajasthan, how did I know you'd be involved in this crap?"

"Deductive reasoning?"

Harsk grunted. "Get the fuck out of that patrol car. The city just bought those and we don't want you shedding on them."

Nohar ducked out the door and stretched. The misting rain

started to dampen his fur immediately. He wished he had worn his trench coat to the meeting. "No apology for treating me like a suspect? I didn't *have* to call this in."

"Be glad that some downtown cowboy didn't shoot you. Half these kids are just out of the academy and tend to shit if they see a moreau. This ain't your neighborhood. What the fuck are you doing here?"

"Nugoya was a client."

Harsk looked at Nohar. "So when are you going to start selling yourself to the flush peddlers?"

Nohar had his right hand up, claws fully extended, before he knew what he was doing. Harsk's face cracked into an ugly grin. "Do it, you fucking alley cat. I would love to put you away and get you out of my hair."

Nohar took a few deep breaths and lowered his arm. "What hair?"

A lithe nonhuman form left *Zero's*. The moreau wore a lab coat and carried a notebook-sized computer, the display of which he was reading.

Nohar called out, "Manny."

Manny—his full name was Mandvi Gujerat—looked up from the display, twitched his nose, and started across the parking lot toward Nohar and Harsk. Manny was a small guy with a thin, whip-like body. He had short brown fur, a lean, aerodynamic head, and small black eyes. People who saw Manny usually guessed he was designed from a rat, or a ferret. Both were wrong. Manny was a mongoose.

Manny reached them and Harsk interrupted before Nohar could say anything. "Gujerat, what have you got on the bodies?"

Manny gave Nohar an undulating shrug and looked down at his notebook. "I have a tentative species on six of seven. The three bodies outside were all a Peruvian Lepus strain. From the white fur and the characteristic skull profile, I'd say Pajonal '35 or '36. They all have unit tattoos, and some heavy scarring. Infantry, and they saw combat."

Manny tapped the screen and the page changed. "The bartender was definitely vulpine. Brit fox, Ulster antiterrorist. I think second generation, but I can't be sure. The British ID their forces under the tongue and most of the fox's head is gone.

"The tiger—" Manny looked at Nohar briefly. "Second-generation Rajasthan. Indian Special Forces.

"The bear, I would guess Turkmen, Russia, or Kazakhstahn.

That's only on my previous experience in ursoid strains. Her species—"

"Her?" asked Harsk.

"Yes. I think she was a parthenogenetic adaption. But as I was saying, *her* species isn't cataloged. She's either a unique experiment, or one of the few dozen species that fell through the cracks during the war. From the corpse, for all I know, she could be Canadian."

Nohar snorted.

Manny shrugged again. "I supposed you already have a file on the one engineered human. But his strain checks out against what we have on Sony's late human-enhancement projects. The one we have here underwent a massive reconstruction after some major trauma. The hardware in his body was worth a few million when there were people who could make and install the stuff."

Harsk nodded. "Any leads on the suspect?"

"Some hairs from the mirror check out as canine. From that and a description, purebred Afghani, Qandahar '24. Attack strain, one the Kabul government 'discontinued' after the war."

"Enough. Rajasthan, I'll get your statement from the uniforms. Get out of here before you attract more trouble. Gujerat, dump the rest into the precinct mainframe." Harsk started to go toward *Zero's* and paused. "The *Moreytown* precinct."

Manny nodded. "Where else?"

Harsk left.

Manny folded up the computer and twitched his nose. "So, stranger, what the hell are you doing at this bloodbath?"

"Bad sense to let Nugoya hire me—"

"Let me guess. Female Vietnamese canine who shot herself so full of flush that she thought she was avian? The one you asked me to ID for you?"

Nohar nodded.

"I know you don't like my advice—"

"Then don't give me any."

"—*but* something dangerous is going on. I don't think you want to be involved, even tangentially, with anything that has to do with the flush industry."

Nohar leaned against the Caldera. His fur was beginning to itch. "Sounds like you know something you think I don't."

"Something's in the air. The DEA is crawling all over downtown, and the gangs in Moreytown are acting up. Most of the bodies I'm looking at the past few weeks are young, second-generation street kids."

"I can handle myself."

"So I worry. You were once one of those second-generation street kids."

"I can handle myself," Nohar said a little more forcefully.

Manny backed off. "Anyway, we do have to stop meeting like this. When are you going to come back and let me cook you some dinner?"

You've been trying to get me back there for fifteen years, Nohar thought. "I'll make it over one of these days."

"The door's always open."

"I know."

Manny turned and started back to *Zero's,* where a gaggle of pink EMTs were trying to manhandle the ursine's corpse out the door.

Nohar sighed.

"I know," he whispered to himself.

Nohar uselessly turned the collar up on the irritating pink-designed jacked and headed for his car. There wasn't anything left for him to do here.

Chapter 2

Nohar's apartment had holes in the wall, a leaky roof, a sagging floor in the kitchen, and wiring that hadn't been up to code when it was put in forty years ago. However, the place had one redeeming feature. Someone had installed a huge stainless-steel shower that Nohar could fit into. Four in the morning was a god-awful time to take a shower, but Nohar wanted to get the city off of him—as well as pieces of bear and Nugoya.

Nohar stood under a blast of warm water, feeling the grit melt off his fur. Through the open door of the bathroom, he listened to the news coming off his comm and tried to forget the fiasco he had left downtown.

". . . major demonstrations through the Economic Community. However, despite public pressure and threats of violence, the European parliament followed through on its vote to eliminate most internal restrictions on nonhuman movement. The French and German states are braced for a massive influx of unemployed nonhumans from the rest of the economically troubled European nation.

"The French and German interior ministers issued a joint statement condemning the parliament's decision to outlaw screening across internal borders."

Nohar sighed. The pinks in Paris and Berlin were worried about a few thousand moreaus—relatively benign moreaus for the most part. The EEC had a few combat designs in reaction to the war, but it never produced many moreaus. Most of their nonhumans were designed for police and hazardous industrial work.

The European parliament probably would still have considered their moreaus as not better than slaves or machines if the Vatican hadn't screwed everything up with the pope's decision that moreys had souls. The EEC was still dealing with the repercussions of that, even fifteen years after the production lines stopped.

"In a related story, a car bomb exploded in Bern, Switzerland, today outside of the Bensheim Genetic Repository Building. No injuries were reported, and no one has claimed responsibility. Damage to the Bensheim building was estimated at a quarter of a million dollars. The Bensheim Foundation issued a statement to reassure their clients that no damage was done to their inventory of genetic material which is kept in an undisclosed location. The building that was bombed housed only administrative offices. The Foundation says that this will in no way affect its worldwide collection and distribution of semen.

"Dr. Bensheim himself issued a statement from Stockholm deploring the attack, and saying, 'the right to reproduce is fundamental and should not be denied on the basis of species.'

"In local news . . ."

Nohar turned off the water and leaned his back against the cool metal wall of the shower. He couldn't get that two and a half grand out of his mind. How the hell was he going to pay the rent—how the hell was he going to eat? He knew too many moreaus who lived out on the street, and he had already done time there himself.

Nohar slid the shower door aside and Cat looked up quizzically. The yellow tomcat was curled up on top of the john and was looking annoyingly serene. Sometimes Nohar thought there was something to the idea that you shouldn't have pets too close to your own species.

Nohar turned on the dryer and Cat made a satisfying leap out the bathroom door. Served the little fuzzball right for not having the sense to worry about where his next meal was coming from. After a few minutes, Cat peeked around the doorjamb and gave Nohar a peeved expression.

Nohar allowed himself the luxury of standing in front of the dryer until his entire body had aired out. Who gave a shit what this month's utility bill cost. Moot if he couldn't pay it. He needed the time to relax. He was too tense to think rationally.

". . . buried tomorrow. Graveside services to be held at Lakeview Cemetery. The police have no suspects as of yet, and the Binder campaign has yet to issue an official statement other than appointing Congressman Binder's legal counsel, Edwin Harrison, as acting campaign manager.

"Former Cleveland mayor, Russell Gardner, expressed sympathy for his opponent and said that he did not to intend to make rumors of alleged financial irregularities in Binder's fund-raising a campaign issue.

"Binder finance chairman, Philip Young, could not be reached for comment."

Nohar turned off the dryer and walked out of the bathroom. He collapsed on the nearly dead couch in the living room. There was the sound of protesting wood and permanently compressed springs. He shifted on his back, and Cat ran up and pounced on his chest. Nohar winced as four *cold* little feet kneaded his fur. Cat curled up to take a nap.

Nohar lifted his hand to push him off, but a loud purring made him stop and simply pet the creature.

". . . more violence on the East Side today. There was an apparent clash between nonhuman gang members on Murray Hill—"

Only newscasters and politicians still called it Murray Hill. It was Morey Hill now, had been for nearly a decade. Nohar sighed. The guy on the news couldn't bring himself to say the word morey—or even moreau. Nohar looked at the guy on the comm. Pink—what else—slick black hair, a nothing Midwestern accent, dead gray eyes, all the animation of a cheap computer graphic. The bodies on the screen behind him were more lively.

"—fifteen dead, all of various species, making this the most bloody incidence of cross-species violence since the 'Dark August' riots of 2042. Local community leaders have expressed concern over the latest escalation of violence in the nonhuman community . . ."

To prove the point, the newscast started to show clips of interviews with said "community leaders." Nohar snorted, with the token morey exception—Father Sean Murphy, a Brit fox who defected to the Irish Catholics, one of two ordained morey priests in the United States—the "community leaders" were all human.

The newscast then went into the obligatory human fear/responsibility versus moreau poverty/empowerment segment. Same shit, different day. Nohar closed his eyes and listened for something interesting to come on.

Nohar woke to the sound of the comm buzzing for his attention. Grayish daylight streamed through the windows. The comm's display was still on the news channel. More gang violence, even worse this time. It barely registered on Nohar that it had gone down only three blocks from his apartment. Flashing text informed him he had slept through two other calls and nearly eight hours.

The incoming call was from Robert Dittrich. Nohar called out to the comm. "Got it."

The newscast winked out and was replaced by a red-bearded human face. "I wish you'd put on some clothes before you answer the phone."

Nohar growled. "What the hell do you want, Bobby?"

"Tough night?"

Nohar closed his eyes and sighed. "What do you think?"

"Heard about Nugoya. Tough break—"

"Tough all over. What do you want?"

Bobby coughed. "If you're going to be like that. I was going to give you the background I hacked on Nugoya—"

"Great, real useful."

"Did anyone ever tell you that you can be a real asshole at times, Nohar? As I was saying—" Bobby paused. Nohar didn't interrupt. "As I was saying, I was going to you that data when the Fed landed on my doorstep."

Nohar sat up, fully awake now. Cat tumbled off his chest and ran off into the kitchen. "Shit. You in trouble?"

Bobby laughed and shook his head. "No, apparently I'm still clean. As we all know, everything I do on my computer is perfectly legal."

Nohar shook his head at that.

Bobby went on. "Wasn't me at all. They were asking about you. That's how I heard about Nugoya and last night."

"Me?"

"Yes, thought I'd call you. They wanted to know about your politics, of all things." Bobby put his hand to his forehead and chuckled. "They had this *babe* with them. Was she a hard case—"

"Skip the commentary. What were they looking for?"

"Some hired gun, I think. Named Hassan. I think they wanted to know if they could link the two of you."

"An Afghan canine and an Indian tiger—do they know how silly that sounds?"

"The war's been over for eighteen years. Things change. Just wanted you to know the Fed's interested in you. I got to go. Still want the data on Nugoya?"

"Keep it."

"Don't let the Fed screw you."

"I try to avoid it."

Bobby's face winked out and the news came back on.

Wonderful stuff to wake up to. Not only was he broke and one day closer to eviction, but now the FBI was curious about him.

The comm was talking about dead politicians. Nohar told it to shut up.

There were still two messages on his comm, waiting for his attention. One had been forwarded from his office—

Maybe it was a client.

Yeah, real likely, and maybe a morey would get elected president. Nohar told the comm, "Classify. Phone messages."

"two messages. july twenty-ninth. message one, ten-oh-five a. m. unlisted number—"

The voice of the computer was a flat, neutral monotone. Nohar never understood the urge people had to make computers sound like anything but. He told the comm, "Play."

Nohar didn't like calls that didn't ID themselves. People who called from unlisted locations generally had something to hide.

This caller definitely had something to hide, the screen came up a generic test pattern. This guy either didn't have a video pickup, or had turned his camera off.

"I hope to reach you, Mr. Rajasthan." The voice that came over the comm sounded like it was at the bottom of a well. It sounded bubbly. The words oozed. "I have need of the service of a private investigator. Please meet me at Lakeview Cemetery today at one-thirty p.m. This is not something I can discuss on a phone. I look for you by the grave of Eliza Wilkins."

That was the end of the message.

"Damn. It *was* a client."

"instructions unclear." The comm thought Nohar was talking to it.

Nohar told it, "Comm off," and the comm shut off obligingly.

It was a client, and a damn secretive one at that. Nohar didn't trust the situation one bit. There was little he could do about it. Nohar was so low on cash that he would have to at least meet the guy—

Nohar suddenly realized that it was already fifteen after one.

It took him two minutes to dress and another five to call Lakeview and get a plot number for Wilkins. Nohar did it with the video off, because if they saw he was a moreau it would have taken five times as long.

The first thing to greet him as he walked out into the misting rain was the acrid smell of burning plastic. The smoke made his nose itch. He realized the smell was coming from a burning car up by the traffic barriers.

Across the street from his apartment was an abandoned bus. There was a fresh graffiti logo on it. "ZIPPERHEAD—Off The Pink."

Another gang with it in for humans.

He walked up Mayfield, toward the cemetery, passing a knot of pink cops at the traffic barrier. Apparently this was the latest violence the news was going on about when he woke up. The fire was burning a prewar Japanese compact, an ancient Subaru. The car was wrapped around one of the concrete pylons. The way the thing had gone up—was still going; the cops were letting it burn itself out in the middle of the street—it had to have been wired with explosives. Inductors might explode, but they don't burn very well.

The cops didn't stop him—any other part of town and they probably would have on general principles.

The car wasn't all. It had been a busy morning. A block past the cops, things got ugly. Upwind of the burning plastic, Nohar could smell the scent of someone, multiple someones, who had bought it nasty. He smelled blood, fear, and cordite. The victims smelled canine.

He rounded the old cemetery gate—sealed by a solid four meter concrete wall behind the flaking wrought iron—and headed down toward Coventry. When he turned the corner, he could see the medics loading body-bags—three vans' worth of body-bags. Canine had been a good guess. Nohar caught sight of one of the victims before the black plastic was zipped over the face. The body was a vulpine female with a small caliber gunshot wound to the right eye. One of the hispanic medics saw him looking over. There was the fresh smell of fear from the pink.

Another day, Nohar would have ignored it. Today, however, he had just had a case blow up in his face, the Fed was taking an unhealthy interest in him, the record July heat and the misting rain were making his fur itch under his trench coat, and—if his luck held—he was going to be late and miss his potential client. Today he was in a particularly bad mood.

Nohar could not resist the urge to smile.

Some moreaus don't have the facial equipment to produce a

convincing smile, but Nohar's evolved feline cheeks could pull his mouth into a quite perceptible arc. The same gesture also bared an impressive set of teeth. Predominant among which were two glistening-white canines, the size of a man's thumb.

The poor guy didn't deserve it. Nohar could tell he was nervous enough just *being* in Moreytown. He didn't need to have a huge predatory morey looking at him like he was lunch.

Nohar didn't hang around for the reaction. He was still running late. Two blocks further down, at the intersection of Mayfield and Coventry, was the only open gate on this side of Lakeview Cemetery—seemed appropriate that it was into the Jewish section.

When he reached the right monument, "Eliza Wilkins, 1966-2042, beloved wife of Harold," it was thirty-two after. He was in time for the show. A funeral was progressing below him.

He was out of sight of most of them, and it was probably a good thing. They were planting someone of consequence, and from his vantage, it was pinks only. He thought he saw a morey in the crowd, but—damn his bad day-vision—it turned out to be a black pink with a heavy beard.

Not a morey in the lot, and the *whitest* bunch of pinks he had ever seen. Especially under the canopy. There, he figured on fifty people who got to use the folding chairs, at least another fifty standing back under cover, and a hundred or so milling about beyond some sort of private security line in back of the paying customers. Even with his poor eyesight he could make the types. The pinks who knew the corpse were obvious, they wore their money—he could see the glints of their shoes and jewelry whenever they moved—and they were, with few exceptions, white. The pinks who wanted to know the corpse were just as easily made, and they were closer to the normal mix of human coloring, a few blacks, orientals, hispanics. The black cops were totally out of it, with their cheap suits and their attention on everything but the service. The private security goons—they were white—were better dressed than the cops and were intent on keeping the flow of riffraff behind the tent. Then, the back with the crowd, were the vids. Cameras and mikes at the ready . . .

Some of the riffraff—mostly blacks and orientals—were carrying signs. Looked like a full-fledged protest was going on. The vids were paying as much, if not more, attention to the riffraff than to the service. Nohar wished he could make out more of the signs, but the best he could do was read the occasional word. Lots of isms,

"Racism," "Sexism," "Speciesism." The signs that weren't isms seemed to mention capital-R Rights.

The Right to what, Nohar couldn't read.

Nohar wondered who had died—irritating, because he thought he had heard something about this, and the job his anonymous client had in mind probably involved the stiff. Perhaps the guy left all his money to some morey squeeze and they needed to track her down.

Nohar heard a truck, and hoped it wasn't security. The pinks might take offense at a morey walking around the human part of the cemetery. But instead of security, Nohar saw an unmarked cargo van. A Dodge Electroline painted institution-green. It was windowless, boxy, cheap, and either remote-driven or programmed. It wasn't the kind of vehicle Nohar expected to see in a cemetery. It pulled on to the shoulder and backed toward him. When it stopped, the rear doors opened with a pneumatic hiss.

The smell was overpowering. His sensitive nose was suddenly exposed to an open sewer. Nohar was enveloped by the odor of sweat, and bile, and ammonia. Even a pink would've been able to sense it.

He had no idea what this guy was supposed to look like, or who he was—but Nohar did *not* expect another frank. They were supposed to be rare. Despite that, what the opening door revealed *couldn't* be anything *but* a frank.

And a failure at that.

Once Nohar's eyes had adjusted to the nearly black interior of the cargo van, he could see it. The frank was vaguely humanoid and had a pasty white color to its rubbery skin. Its limbs seemed tubular and boneless, and its fingers were fused into a mittenlike hand. It wore a pink's clothes, but its pale bulk was fighting them. Rolls of white flesh cascaded over its belt, its collar, even its shoes. Glassy eyes, a lump of a nose, and a lipless mouth were collected together on a pear-shaped head. Its face seemed incapable of showing any expression. It seemed that, if the clothes were removed, the frank would just slide down and form a puddle on the ground.

The frank also massed more than Nohar did though it was a meter shorter.

Whatever gene-tech had designed this monstrosity had screwed-up big-time. Until now, Nohar could never quite fathom the reason for the pinks' horror at the franks. It seemed bizarre to him that humans, who took all the genetic tinkering with other species in stride, were so aghast when someone tinkered with their own. If this was a sample of what happened, Nohar could begin to understand. *Maybe*, thought Nohar, *pink genes didn't take kindly to fiddling*.

The voice was the same as the one over the comm—deep, bubbly, and, somehow, slimy. "Are you the detective, Nohar Rajasthan?"

Briefly, Nohar wondered if he needed the money this badly—he did. "Yes."

Nohar began to feel warmth coming from the back of the van. Nohar realized that the frank had the heat on in the van, all the way. Back where the frank was sitting it could be fifty degrees. An unpleasant sound emerged from the frank's mass. It could have been a belch. "We have fifteen minutes before van goes to next stop, forgive. I need to smuggle myself out. Have to keep meeting secret."

Nohar shrugged. "Then you better get on with it."

At least the frank took Nohar's appearance in stride. In most of the directories it didn't mention that Nohar was the only moreau in the city with a private investigator's license. For some people, his address wasn't a big enough clue. Of course a *pink* detective would have a problem with this guy, even more so than with Nugoya. At least with Nugoya, a pink could pretend the guy had been human.

"What kind of job? Surveillance or missing persons?"

Nohar heard flesh shifting as the frank moved. "Do you know who is being buried down the hill?"

Chalk one up for obvious conclusions. The stiff was involved. "Rich, human, lots of friends."

Another ugly sound emerged from the mass of white flesh. It might have been a laugh. "The dead man is a politician. His name is Daryl Johnson. He is the campaign manager for twelfth district congressman, Joseph Binder."

Nohar was wondering about the frank's weird accent when he realized that the frank had ducked his first question. "What's the *job*?"

"I must know who killed Daryl Johnson."

Nohar almost laughed, but he knew the frank was serious. "Outside my specialty." So much for the money he needed. "I don't mess with police investigations—"

"There is no police investigation."

Nohar was getting irritated with the frank's bubbling monotone. "I work with moreys. I don't work with human problems. You got the wrong P.I."

"Binder pressures the police, they close the case. I need to know if someone in my company is responsible for Johnson's death . . ."

Nohar looked straight into the frank's eyes. That usually unnerved people, but the frank was as expressionless as ever. "Did you hear what I said?" It took Nohar a while to realize that the reason he didn't like the frank's eyes was because they didn't blink.

"Let me finish, Mr. Rajasthan. You are the only person I can contact for this job. For obvious reasons, I am unable to hire a human investigator—"

"No solidarity shit."

"Practical matter. No qualified human is willing to talk to me. My company is Midwest Lapidary Imports. We're privately owned. We import gemstones from South Africa. The board is formed of South African refugees—"

"All like you?"

The frank showed no offense at the question. "Yes, like me. We retain contacts in the mining industry—" Nohar got a picture of the South African gene-techs trying to create a modified human miner. Hell, maybe the frank's appearance wasn't a mistake. For all Nohar knew, this guy was perfectly adapted for work in a five-mile-deep hole. Nohar stopped musing and waited for the frank to get to the point. "To succeed, the owners of Midwest Lapidary Imports, MLI, need to remain hidden, unnoticed, private. The company will not survive if our existence is widely known.

"With Johnson's death there is the possibility that one of our number is behind the murder . . ."

Nohar sighed. Learn something new every day. A bunch of franks were importing diamonds from South Africa, probably illegally. The pinks would just *love* that idea. The Supreme Court was still debating if the 29th amendment even covered the franks. No one knew yet if the franks were covered by the Bill of Rights, the limited morey amendment, or nothing at all. Before the pinks in this country had even locked down the legal status of engineered humans, here were a few, acting just like eager little capitalists. "You said Binder's blocking the investigation. What are you worried about?"

"One kills once, one kills again. You have no idea what it would mean if one of our number is directly involved in a human's death. The company is a worthy project, but someone may commit atrocities in its name. I cannot, nor can anyone else, abide our secrecy, our existence, if one of us kills to further our ends."

"How is your organization involved?"

"The police call it a robbery-murder because there are over three million dollars in campaign funds missing from his house—"

"Sounds plausible." Nohar realized that he was just leading the frank on. He had some natural curiosity, but there was no sane way he could touch this case.

The frank's bulk groaned and rippled as he leaned toward Nohar. The heat and stench that floated off of the frank's body almost made Nohar wince. "I am the accountant for MLI. The three million that is missing is never there. Campaign records the police use are wrong about this. The money comes from MLI, and *should* be there. But I handle the books and such a sum never leaves our accounts, or, if it does, it returns before the sum is debited.

"I do not go to the police. For now I must retain the secrecy. I can be wrong. I cannot damage the company until my suspicions are proved correct. I can't work within MLI. I have no idea who of my colleagues are involved. And I am closely watched—"

Nohar stood up. "I don't deal with anything involving murder. I have to walk from this one—find an out-of-towner."

"I have a five thousand retainer, and I will pay five times your usual rate, another five thousand when you complete the job successfully."

Nohar froze, his usual rate was five hundred a day. *No,* he told himself, *it's a bad job all over. You don't get involved with killings. You don't get involved with pinks. You don't get involved with things bigger than you are.* Against his will, he found himself saying. "Double the retainer."

It was a ludicrous request. The frank would never go for it. He'd be able to walk away clean.

"Agreed."

Damn it. "Plus expenses."

"Of course."

Nohar had trapped himself.

"Time closes in on us." The frank handed him an envelope. Ten thousand. He'd been anticipated. "Start with Johnson, work back. Do not contact anyone at MLI. I'll contact you every few days. Get any information about MLI through me. We have a few minutes. Any immediate questions?"

Nohar was still looking at the cash. "Why is a bunch of franks backing a reactionary right-winger like Binder?"

"*Quid pro quo,* Mr. Rajasthan. The corporate entity will see its interests served in the Senate. The fact that we're of a background

Binder despises is of little consequence. Binder doesn't know who runs MLI. Anything else?"

"What's your name?"

Nohar heard the engine start up again. As the door closed with its pneumatic hiss, Nohar heard the frank say, "You can call me John Smith."

The ugly green van drove away, leaving a pair of divots in the grass. The ghost of the frank's smell remained, emanating from the money Nohar still held in his hand.

Once he took the money, he did the job. No matter what.

No matter what, damn it.

Nohar put the money in one of the cavernous pockets of his trenchcoat. Now that he was on the job, he pulled out his camera, slipped in a ramcard, and started recording the funeral.

Chapter 3

The ATM was half a block from Nohar's place. To his relief, it appeared to be working. At least the lights were on. He stopped in front of the armored door, and, under the blank stare of the disabled external camera, he pulled his card and slipped it into the slot. The mechanism gave an arthritic wheeze and he feared it was going to eat his card again. Fortunately, the keypad flashed green at him. He punched in his ID number while the servos on the lensless camera followed his every move.

The door slid aside with a grinding noise and he ducked into the too-small room. When the door shut behind him, he finally felt comfortable with all that money on him.

The chair the bank provided was too small to sit on. The best he could do was to lean against it and hunch over, hanging his tail over the back of the seat. Besides, somebody had pissed all over the damn thing.

There was a short burst of static, and a voice came through one of the intact speakers. "Welcome to Society Bank's Green Machine—bzt—Mr. Noharajasthan. Please state clearly what transaction you wish—"

The voice was supposed to be female human, but it was tinny and muffled. Nohar interrupted. "Deposit. Card Account. Ten thousand dollars."

"Please repeat clearly."

"Deposit. Card Account. Ten thousand dollars."

"Please type in request."

Great, the damn thing couldn't hear him. He typed in the transaction on the terminal.

"Is this a cash transaction?"

It didn't believe him. "Yes," he said and typed at the same time.

A drawer opened under the terminal. Unlike most of the ATM, it seemed to be in perfect working order. "—bzt—please place paper currency in the drawer. There will be a slight pause while the bills are screened."

Nohar placed the two packets of bills in the drawer. Nohar knew that the note of surprise he heard in the ATM's voice was in his own head more than anywhere else. "Your currency checks as valid. Thank you for banking with Society, Mr. Noharajasthan. The current balance on your card account is —bzt—ten-thousand-one-hundred-ninety-three-dollars and sixty-five cents. You may pick up your card and receipt at the door. Have a nice day."

Nohar left the ATM and turned up the collar of his coat against a sudden burst of more intense rain. He typed in his ID again at the keypad, blinking twice as water got in his eyes. The ATM released his card and the receipt. As he pocketed the items, he noticed a couple of ratboys hanging around across the street.

An ATM in use attracted vermin.

The two ratboys were crossing the street. Nohar had hoped that his appearance would have put them off. Apparently, they were too zoned or too stupid, perhaps both. As they closed he could smell that they were probably on something. Itching for a fight. both of them.

"Kitty."

"*Pretty* kitty."

Nohar decided to ignore them. All he wanted was to get home and shuck his wet coat. He walked down the road past them.

The damn rodents didn't seem to know any better. They cut around in front of him, blocking his path.

"No, no, *wrong*, kitty." This rat was a dirty brown, shiny black in the rain. His nose seemed to twitch in time to his spastic tail. He wore an abbreviated leather vest and denim cutoffs. He was taking the lead in this idiotic display. "Doncha know who we are?"

This was more than enough for Nohar. "You're two rodent wetbacks too stoned for your own good. You're future road kill if you keep this up."

The big one—well, the relatively big one, maybe 70 kilos, mostly fat—didn't like that. "We the Ziphead, man, and you better up some bucks for that. We rule here . . ."

This was nuts. These guys were Latin American cannon fodder. Honduras, Nicaragua, Cuba, Panama, all the Central American countries went for quantity and quick reproduction. Huge standing armies from zero—most of the rats were never even trained to use their weapons.

Two of those, those jokes, were trying to face down someone whose genes had gone through a multibillion dollar evolution simulation to produce the elite troops of the Indian Special Forces. Nohar had no special training, but it was still ludicrous.

He smiled, teeth and all. He couldn't take this seriously. "Ever occur to you I just made a *deposit?*"

Fearless Leader was put out. "You don't fuck with us—stray— we'll *shave* you."

"We vanish what don't give us respect—"

"*Stigmata de nada.*"

Stupid and stoned. That last line only made sense to them, and they found it uproariously funny. Nohar stepped to the side and left them to their inside joke.

"Fucking stray." Snick. Bigboy had pulled a weapon, sounded like a knife. Nohar slowly turned around. Bigboy had a switchblade out and was showing the world that he couldn't use it. It was long, pointed, and had no edge to speak of. Bigboy was swishing the thing like a baton. Wide slicing arcs that, had they connected with anything solid, might raise a welt and would probably sprain Bigboy's wrist all to hell. "Teach you some respect. I'll have your tail for a belt."

Nohar stowed the comments. He spread his legs apart and bent down, lowering his center of gravity. He thrust his left arm, claws forward, in a defensive posture, while his right arm hung back behind him, hand cupped to slice at any opening Bigboy gave him. He growled, deep in his diaphragm. The sound didn't make it out of his throat.

Bigboy was oblivious in his advance. Fearless Leader had a little more brains and hung back. Bigboy was reeking of excitement and adrenaline. Fearless was almost as jacked, but he was beginning to realize he might have bitten off more than he could chew.

Bigboy swung one of his wide, predictable arcs. Nohar caught Bigboy's wrist with his left hand, remembering Nugoya, and smiled at the rat. Nohar's right hand swung forward in a well aimed sweep that left four light trails of blood on Bigboy's overlarge gut.

"Listen, ratboy, I *could* have pulled you into that sweep. We'd have a nice view of your intestines— Drop the knife."

The knife clattered to the ground. Nohar stepped on it and let Bigboy go. Fearless was still backpedaling. Fearless didn't seem to get the point, he was still on his line of bullshit. "Your pussy bastard ass is mine."

Fearless was reaching behind, into the waistband of his cutoffs. Nohar knew instinctively that the rat was going for a gun. Nohar was about to jump Fearless—he could clear the distance easily before the rat got his hand untangled from his pants—but the action was broken by a burst of high-pitched rapid-fire Spanish from down the street, by the old bus.

They all turned that way to face a snow-white female rodent. She wore the same abbreviated leather vest and denim cutoffs. Her naked tail was writhing, and she sounded pissed. Nohar immediately pegged her as a superior. Bigboy and Fearless seemed to forget about him and began talking back to her in Spanish as well. All babble to him, he just hoped she was cussing the fools out.

Cat-and-mouse is not a smart game to play when you are the mouse.

The three rodents were talking among themselves, and Nohar began to slowly withdraw from the rodent fiasco.

Nohar had nearly gotten to the door to his apartment. Bigboy and Fearless had slunk away, but the white one stayed.

"Rajasthan!"

The white rat was addressing him directly. She wasn't making any threatening moves, so Nohar stopped and waited.

"You are a lucky cat, son of Rajasthan—"

How did she know, how could she— "What do you—"

"I speak! You listen." The force of the rat's voice actually made Nohar stop his question in mid-breath. The tiny rat's body could produce a voice that would intimidate a rabid ursine. "The finger of God has just touched your brow, son of Rajasthan. Those that control want your life for their reasons. They buy you much tolerance."

The rat paused, and for once Nohar had nothing to say. She just stood there, staring at him with eyes that looked like high-carbon steel. Nohar turned toward his door—

"Pray you that God doesn't forget you, Nohar. If the blessing is lifted, Zipperhead will have you."

Nohar punched the combination on his door. He had given the rats enough of his time.

"*I'll* have you, Nohar."

As Nohar ducked inside, the white rat added. "You, or someone you love."

He slammed the door shut. It was a shame. She hadn't been bad-looking. Her triangular face ended in a delicate nose—but she was a die-hard creep just like her idiot subordinates.

She also wore cheap pink perfume. Why would a morey wear that kind of crap?

Nohar had hurried away from the smell as much as the spiel. He took a few deep breaths of relatively clean air before he started up the stairwell.

The humidity was making his door stick again, and it took him a few seconds to unwedge it. The damn thing was heavier than it should have been because it had a steel plate in it, a relic of the previous tenant. Nohar would have questioned the wisdom of sticking an armored door in a wooden door frame.

Cat ran up to the door and immediately began rubbing against his foot. "So you hungry or lonely?" Nohar asked the yellow tomcat as he picked it up. A loud purr from under his hand told him to figure it out for himself. Nohar pushed the door shut with his foot and ducked into the living room. Cat started butting his head into Nohar's chin, and, after glancing into the kitchen to check Cat's dishes, Nohar decided Cat wasn't hungry.

"Sorry I took so long, I got distracted by the local color." Cat closed his eyes as Nohar scratched him behind the ears. "But, lucky us, I got one hell of an advance from a client before the first of the month."

Cat started grooming Nohar's thumb.

"Yeah, right. Look, you little missing link, I have to put you down so I can get this damn pink clothing off. So don't start mewing at me—"

Nohar put him down and Cat started mewing.

He undressed and looked at the comm. Two messages waiting now.

"Comm on," he said to the machine as he started peeling clothing off of his damp fur.

"comm on."

Nohar reclined on the couch. Cat took up a perch on his chest and purred.

"Classify. Phone messages."

"two messages. july twenty-ninth, three-oh-five p.m. from detective irwin harsk, calling from—"

"Play."

Static, then Harsk's bald black head appeared on the screen.

"Sorry I didn't catch you, Nohar." There was a smile on Harsk's face and Nohar couldn't decide if it was ironic or sarcastic. "I thought I'd tell you that another little red light is flashing by your name. The DEA computer has this 'thing' about large cash transactions. Ten thousand dollars? The Fed is curious, and so am I. We're watching you, so—on the off-chance the cash is legit—remember to withhold your income tax."

That was damn quick, even for the Fed. The DEA must have a tap on the ATM down the street. It was irritating, but not that surprising. Harsk knew he was clean, but he'd let the Fed wonder just out of a sense of perversity. The comm was asking if he had a reply.

"Yes. Record," Nohar cleared his throat., "Harsk, don't call back until you have a warrant. End. Mail. Reply."

Nohar closed his eyes and clawed the back of the couch. He told the comm to play the earlier message without really paying attention to it. He wasn't looking directly at the screen when he heard a husky female voice.

"Raj?"

"Pause!" His eyes shot open and he turned to look at Maria Limon. The call had come in close to two in the morning, during his meet with Nugoya. In the pressure of the moment, Nohar had forgotten to call Maria and cancel their date—

This wasn't the first time either. Nohar had a sinking feeling.

She was at a public phone. He could see the streetlights behind her. There was frozen shimmer on the screen where the lights were reflecting off the black fur under her whiskers. Apparently the Brazilians had been more creative with their moreaus. She'd been crying. Nohar doubted his tear ducts could be triggered emotionally.

Maria's golden eyes, her pupils almost round, seemed to level an accusation at him.

Cat tilted his head and gave Nohar a curious look.

"Replay."

Static, then Maria's face reappeared on the screen. Nohar watched as one delicate black hand wiped away the moisture on her cheek. The hand fell and she looked directly at Nohar.

"Raj? I'm sorry about this. I should have the guts to face you, but I can't. You'd say something and we'd end up shouting at each other, or fucking each other—or, God help me, both—I can't do this anymore. I still care for you, but if we keep seeing each other, I won't—" Maria's voice broke, and more tears came. Maria was a strong person. Nohar had never seen her cry before. "Good-bye,

Raj, I have to leave while the memories are still worth something to me."

Maria's face vanished as she broke the connection.

Nohar felt like someone had just kneed him in the balls, and he was feeling his stomach drop out just before the pain came.

They had known each other for only two months. It shouldn't have been a surprise. He had been expecting something like this all along. She was right.

Cat must have sensed some of his agitation, because he started butting his head against Nohar's face and licking his cheek. Cat stopped after a few seconds and regarded Nohar with his head cocked to one side. Cat's expression seemed to be asking him what was wrong.

Nohar stayed quiet for a long while before he told the computer to put the message into permanent storage. He tried to call Maria, but her comm was locking out his calls. Maria would want a clean break. He could probably talk her out of it once, maybe twice, more. She didn't want him to.

He spent a few moments in relative silence, stroking Cat and listening to the high-frequency hum of the comm.

Instead of turning the comm off, he called up Maria's message, and paused it. He paused it where the claw on the index finger of her right hand had caught a tear. The small sphere of liquid was nestled between the hook in her claw and the pad on her finger. It refracted the unnatural white of the streetlight behind her, causing arcs of light to emerge from one golden half-lidded eye. It was the kind of image that made Nohar wish he had a scrap of romance in his soul.

Chapter 4

After a while, Nohar decided he had better things to do than stare at Maria.

"Load program. Label, 'Log-on library.' "

"searching . . . found."

"Run program."

Maria's face disappeared as the computer started the access sequence. It showed the blue-and-white AT&T test pattern as it repeatedly buzzed the public library database, waiting for an open data channel. It was close to prime time for library access. It took nearly fifteen minutes for the comm to lock onto the library's mainframe.

Even when the Cleveland Public Library logo came up, there were a few minutes of waiting. The screen scrolled messages about fighting illiteracy, and how he should spend his summer reading a book. Nohar knew that a few thousand users on a clunky time-sharing system at the same time tended to slow things down, but it still seemed the delay was directed at him.

He shifted on the couch, trying to become more comfortable. Waiting always made him aware of his tail.

Two minutes passed. Then, with a little electronic fanfare, the menu came up—though you couldn't quite call the animated figure a "menu." The library system called their animated characters "guides." The software was trying too hard to be friendly. It verged on the cute.

The "guide" facing him on the screen wore a sword strapped to his side, and was in the process of contemplating a human skull when he seemed to notice Nohar's intrusion. The effect was spoiled by a glitch in the animation. A rolling blue line scrolled up and down the screen, shifting everything above it a pixel to the left. Nohar sighed. He had no desire to spend his time with a manic-depressive Dane. Especially after that call from Maria.

He spoke before the prince had time to object. "Text menu."

The only library "guide" he liked was the little blonde human girl, Alice.

The text menu came up and the first thing he did, despite Smith's admonition to start with Johnson, was to conduct a global search for information on Midwest Lapidary Imports. He wanted some sort of handle on his client's employer, which was also the home of the alleged suspects.

There was only a fifteen second pause.

The computer came back with the report, "Three items found."

Nohar shook his head. Only three? With a *global* search? That meant there were only three items in the entire library database that even mentioned MLI.

Nohar played the first item and got a newsfax about diamond imports, legal and illegal. The focus on the article was how hard it was to keep track of the gems. It had a graph that dramatized the divergence between the gems known to have come into the country, and those known to be in circulation. In the last fifteen years, a hell of a lot more gems had been in circulation than could be accounted for. It was, in fact, causing a depression in the diamond market. The article blamed the Fed and new smuggling techniques. The least likely smuggling method Nohar read about was casting the diamonds in the heat-tiles on the exterior of a ballistic shuttle. Midwest Lapidary was only mentioned peripherally in a list of domestic diamond-related companies at the end of the article.

The second article was actually *about* MLI, but it was only barely informative. It was from some subscriber service and was just a sparse paragraph of electronic text. MLI, a new company, incorporated in 2038. Wholesale diamond sales. Headquartered in Cleveland. Privately owned. Address. That was it. Smith was right about these guys keeping a low profile. Nohar pictured most new corporate enterprises announcing themselves with trumpets and splashy media campaigns. It looked like MLI was trying to hide the fact it even existed.

The third item was a vid broadcast from December 2, 2043. The broadcast was dated. The guy with the news was still following journalistic fashion from the riots. Grimy safari jacket, urban camo pants, three-day-old stubble, sunglasses. The outfit had nothing to do with the story. The guy was standing in a snowdrift outside a pair of low office buildings faced in blue tile. Nohar recognized a stretch of Mayfield Road behind the buildings. The guy was only a few miles to the east of Moreytown.

Hmm, Nohar thought there was a prison there.

The guy was trying very hard to have the voice of authority. "I am standing outside the offices and the laboratory of NuFood Incorporated. Today, came the surprising announcement that NuFood had been bought by a local diamond wholesaler, Midwest Lapidary. There had been speculation that NuFood had been on the verge of bankruptcy when it sold its assets and patents to Midwest Lapidary for an undisclosed amount. Shortly after the sale, NuFood's two hundred employees were laid off in what Midwest Lapidary called in a press release, 'a streamlining measure.'

"NuFood, you may recall from a Special Health Report earlier this year, is the company with patents on the dietary supplement, MirrorProtein. While NuFood has had success creating synthetic food-products resembling natural items, which the human body cannot process, it has had continuing problems with the FDA in getting its products approved. Sources say this created the financial difficulty that led directly to the sale of the company. No one from Midwest Lapidary could be reached from comment."

That was a big help.

So Smith was right. He needed to start with Johnson and work back. Johnson was Binder's campaign manager, so Nohar did a global search using both his name and Binder's.

The pause was closer to a full minute this time. His tail fell asleep. Nohar stood up to massage the base of his tail. Cat took the opportunity to jump up on the couch and snuggle into the warm dent in the cushions.

The screen flashed the results of the search. Over six thousand items, more like it. No way he could peruse all of it on-line, so he slipped in a ramcard and downloaded the whole mess of data. He leeched nearly fifteen megs in half that many minutes.

He now had his own little database on Binder and his campaign.

By five, his examination of the public information on Binder gave him no reason to alter his first impression of the guy as a right-wing reactionary bastard. It seemed Binder had something bad to say about every group or organization that didn't count him as a member; women, foreigners, liberals, intellectuals, blacks and hispanics, Catholics, the poor, the homeless, pornographers, the news media—the list was endless. Despite the vitriol that coated every word the man uttered, three groups in particular gained his very special attention. In order of the invective he threw upon them, they were: moreaus, franks, and all their genetically-engineered ilk, whose rights he was actively involved in trying to repeal; homosexuals, whose sexual preference Binder seemed to rank primary in his personal list of mortal sins; and the U.S. federal government—the only place Binder and Nohar seemed to touch common ground—whose propensity for spending money was only equaled by Binder's impulse to slash any spending program he could lay his hands on.

Nohar found it hard to believe he was investigating the murder of this guy's campaign manager.

The data on Daryl Johnson was more scattered. Nohar couldn't get a fix on his beliefs. All he got was the fact that Johnson was loyal to Binder and had been with the congressman since the state legislature. He had been recruited out of Bowling Green in the autumn of 2040. The same time as most of Binder's inner circle. Johnson's three classmates were: Edwin Harrison, the campaign's legal counsel; Philip Young, the campaign finance chairman; and Desmond Thomson, the campaign press secretary. Johnson graduated at the age of twenty-three, late. Apparently because of a shift in his major, from chemistry to political science. A bit of a jump. That would make him the ripe old age of thirty-nine when he died.

Not so ripe, Nohar corrected himself. This guy was human, so thirty-nine was barely on the threshold of middle age. Thirty-nine was better than the life expectancy of some moreys.

He was a little more familiar with the situation he was dealing with. That was all. His client wanted to find out if MLI was behind the Johnson killing. So far, he didn't have any connection between the two, other than Smith's assertion that the missing three megabucks came from MLI.

Time to start making some calls. Thomson looked like a good choice. The press secretary would be used to talking to people, if not actually to saying anything.

If he was going to talk to a pink, he'd better put some clothes on. He snorted. Clothes were a needless irritation that wouldn't have been necessary on a morey case. Getting dressed, just to make a phone call, was just plain silly.

He pulled a button-down shirt from a small pile in the corner of his bedroom. The storm had reduced the light in the apartment, so

Nohar couldn't quite make out the color of the shirt. It was either a very light blue, or a very off white. Nohar put it on, claws catching on the buttons, and decided to forgo the pants. The comm was only going to show him from the waist up, as long as he didn't stand up.

He ducked into the bathroom and looked in the mirror. Pointless, really. What did a pink know about grooming anyway? Still, Nohar licked the back of his hand and ran it over his head a few times, smoothing things out.

After that, he sat on the couch, shooing Cat away. He set the comm to record and told it to call Desmond Thomson at Binder campaign headquarters. He routed the call through the comm at his office so his credentials would be shown up front.

Oddly enough, though it was only a little after five, no one at Binder headquarters seemed to be answering. After nearly a minute of displaying the Binder Senate campaign logo, the comm at Binder headquarters forwarded his call to Thomson's home. Nohar shrugged. It didn't matter as long as he got through to Thomson.

Thomson surprised the hell out of him by being black. In fact, Thomson had been the bearded pink that had tricked Nohar's eyes into seeing a morey in the crowd at the funeral. Thomson's hair and beard were shot with gray. He had the bearing of a pro wrestler and the voice of a vid anchorman. "Mister," Thomson's gaze flicked to the text on his monitor, "Rajasthan?" Thomson's voice had begun on a high note, indicating some surprise at Nohar's appearance. However, by the end of Nohar's name, the tone of Thomson's voice had become smooth, friendly, and utterly phony.

"Yes, Mr. Thomson?"

"I am. I see your call has been forwarded from our campaign headquarters. I presume you wish to talk to me in my capacity as Congressman Binder's press secretary?"

The man talked like a press release, and Nohar couldn't get over the fact that Thomson was black. It made about as much sense as having a Jewish spokesman for the Islamic Axis. Nohar nodded.

"I would like to ask about your late campaign manager—"

"Of course. I'll help as much as possible. We've been quite free with what we know about the tragedy. However, things are quite chaotic in the organization with the loss of Mr. Johnson. We've had to give the whole campaign the week off so we can sort out the mess. So my time is limited. I'm sure what you need has already been told to the police or the press."

Nohar could smell a brush-off coming from a mile away. "I only have a few questions. They won't take long."

"Would you mind transmitting your credentials?"

Either Thomson didn't trust the label from Nohar's office comm, or he was politely looking for an excuse to hang up. fortunately, Nohar's wallet with his PI license was sitting on top of the comm and he didn't have to stand up to get it. He slid his license into the fax slot on his comm and hit the send button. Thomson nodded when he saw the results. "I can give you ten minutes."

At the length this guy spoke, that wouldn't give Nohar much. "When did Johnson die?"

"I am given to understand the time of death was placed sometime in the middle of the week of the twentieth—"

"July twentieth?"

"Of course."

"When was the last official contact with Johnson?"

"As we have informed the police, he attended a political fundraiser Saturday the nineteenth. He didn't come in to work the following week—"

"Didn't this strike anyone as odd?"

Thomson was undoubtedly irritated by Nohar's interruptions, but he hid it well. "No, it is an election year. It's common for executive officers to be pulled away from the desk for trips, speeches, press, and so on. Johnson was the chief executive under Binder, he often did such things on his own initiative—"

"Do you know what he was doing?"

"No. If it wasn't dealing with the media, it was not my department. Now, if you don't mind, the time—"

It didn't feel like ten minutes to Nohar. "One more thing."

Nohar thought he heard Thomson sigh. "What?"

"About the three million dollars the police believe was stolen from the campaign—"

Thomson interrupted this time. "I am sorry, but I do not have the authority to discuss the financial details of the campaign."

Ah, Nohar had finally run into the brick wall. "I am sorry to hear that. You see, I have conflicting information. I simply want to know if the three million was physically in Johnson's possession, in cash—"

"I said, I can't discuss it."

Try another tack. "Who has access to the campaign's financial records?"

Thomson was shaking his head. He even grinned a bit, showing a gold tooth that had to be decorative.

"Me, the legal counsel, the campaign manager and his executive assistant, and the finance chairman, of course."

"Thank you."

Thomson chuckled. "I'm afraid they can't help you. No one but Binder has the authority to release confidential financial data. Except, of course, disclosures required by law."

"Or a subpoena," Nohar muttered.

"I would call that a disclosure required by law. Now, as I said before, my time is limited. I really must go."

"Thanks for your help," Nohar said, nearly choking on the insincerity.

"You're welcome. It's my job," Thomson replied, just as insincere, but much more professional.

The line was cut and Nohar was left staring at a test pattern.

Nohar ran through the record of the conversation a few times. It irritated him that Thomson was right. Nothing was in the conversation he wouldn't be able to get from the police record or the news. Reviewing the tape didn't tell Nohar anything more, other than the fact Thomson lived in a ritzy penthouse overlooking downtown—Thomson's home comm faced a window.

The comm told him it was fifteen after. It was time to call Manny down at the pathologist's office. Nohar wanted to set up a meeting for tonight. One he hoped would be more fruitful.

Chapter 5

During the night, the rain turned into a deluge. Nohar didn't feel
half as uncomfortable under the sudden thunderstorm as he
had in the misting drizzle in the cemetery. The dark violence of it
suited him.

Coventry suited him.

The three block area was a ragged collection of bars close to the
East Cleveland border. It was far enough away from the heart of
Moreytown to see the occasional pink in the area. As always, there
were two patrol cars, the riot watch, one on either end of the strip.
Nohar passed one of them at the intersection of Coventry and Mayfield, and, while it was too far for him to see it, he knew its twin
was parked in the old school parking lot, three blocks away.

Like Nohar's neighborhood, Coventry was blocked off from car
traffic by three-meter-tall concrete pylons left over from the riots.
Graffiti wrapped around the rectangular blocks, as if the strip were
trying to escape its arbitrary confines by oozing through the gaps.

The rain hadn't slowed things down. Ten-thirty at night and the
street was packed with the backwash of Moreytown. The downpour
couldn't remove the omnipresent smell of damp fur.

Nohar made his way down the center of the old asphalt strip. He
passed canines, felines, a knot of rodents in leather vests and denim
briefs—he avoided the slight scent of familiar perfume—an unfamiliar ursine, a loud lepus shouting at a rapt vulpine congregation.
The people around him only made the briefest impression. A few
shouted greetings. Nohar waved without quite noticing who they
had been.

His destination, *Watership Down*, was one of the few bars on the Coventry strip that was actually owned and operated by a morey proprietor—Gerard Lopez, a lepus. The reason Nohar chose to frequent this particular bar, out of the two dozen on the strip, was the high ceiling. This was one of the few places he could get fully toasted and not ended up bashing his head into a ceiling fan or a light fixture.

Nohar entered the bar, shook some of the rain out of his coat, and took his regular seat, a booth in the back that had the seats moved back for people his size. The table was directly underneath a garish framed picture someone had once told him was an original Warner Brothers' animation cell. It was a hand drawn cartoon of a gray bipedal rabbit in the process of blowing up a bald, round-headed, human. Lopez had mounted a little brass plaque under the picture. It said, "1946—Off the Pink." Even if it was a joke, Nohar was glad that most humans didn't come down to Coventry.

Manny was waiting at the bar. He bore down on Nohar's booth carrying two pitchers of beer. Alert black eyes glanced over Nohar as the quick little mongoose put the pitcher on the table. "Nohar, you look like hell."

Nohar's mind had drifted off the case and on to Maria. He was at once irritated and defensive. Manny was the only real family Nohar had. The mongoose had come to America with Nohar's parents, and had been there when Nohar's mother had died. When he was younger, Nohar had resented him. It was still hard for Nohar to accept Manny's concern with good grace.

It had taken finding his real father to allow Nohar to appreciate Manny.

"Maria dumped me." Nohar poured himself a beer and downed it.

Manny slid into the opposite side of the booth and chittered a little in sympathy. "That's hard to believe. After the last time I saw you two together, it looked like you finally found the right one."

"I thought so myself. Always do."

"Do you want to talk about it?"

"I want to talk to an M.E., not a psychiatrist."

Manny gave his head a shake and poured himself a beer. "Are you sure you want to talk business right now?"

Nohar glared down at Manny. "I didn't ask you to meet me for a counseling session." Nohar reined in the outburst. "Sorry. Been a tough day. Did you bring the database?"

Unlike Nohar, Manny couldn't form a smile, but between them

a nose-twitch on Manny's part served the same purpose. Manny took a notebook-sized case and put it on the table and flipped up the cover. There was a pause as it warmed up.

"What happened to your wallet computer?"

Manny gave a brief shrug. His voice held a tone of resignation. "The Jap chip blew. It was a prewar model, so the county couldn't replace it. So, I got this new bug-ridden Tunja 1200. Soon we're going to be back to manual typewriters and paper records . . ."

Manny's head shook, accompanied by a high-pitched sigh. In a few seconds, the screen began to glow faintly and the keypad became visible. "I updated it from the mainframe after you called. Do you have a name for the stiff you're looking for?"

Nohar poured himself another beer. "Yes, but this isn't a normal case—"

"But you want records for a stiff, right?"

"The name's Daryl Johnson."

Manny's whole upper body undulated with a momentary shrug. "Off hand, I don't remember that name. What species?"

"Human."

Manny froze; the sudden absence of motion was eerie on the mongoose. "What?"

"I need the complete forensic record on the murder of a man named Daryl Johnson."

"What the *hell?*"

Nohar could see him tense up. He could almost see the vibration in Manny's small frame. Nohar could smell Manny's nervousness even over the smell of the beer. "You *can* access those records?"

"Nohar, you said *human,* you said *murder.*"

"I said it wasn't a normal case."

Manny was silent. His black eyes darted from Nohar to his little portable computer and back. Nohar was a little surprised at his reaction. They'd worked together and had shared information ever since Nohar had gotten his license.

But then, until now, it had simply consisted of Nohar making sure the moreys he'd been hired to find hadn't ended up in the morgue.

After nearly a full minute of silence, Manny finally spoke, "Nohar, I've known you all your life. You don't ask for trouble anymore. You've never interfered with a police investigation. You've *never* messed with pink business."

"You slipped, you said the 'p' word." Nohar regretted it the instant he said it. Manny had to work with humans. He was one of perhaps a half-dozen moreaus in the city with medical training, and they would only let him cut up corpses. Only morey corpses at that. Manny was always open to the accusation of selling out, being pink under his fur. Nohar just rubbed Manny's nose in it.

"Forgive me if I don't want to see you mixed up in something that might hurt you."

"Sorry. It's just a case. An important one. I'm trying to find out who killed him."

Manny closed his eyes. His voice picked up speed. "You are trying to find out who murdered a human? You know what'd happen if word got on the street? You know what happens to moreys that get too close to humans—"

"I still need your help."

Manny made an effort to slow down. "I'm not going to change my mind, am I? I'll call up the file, but first—" One of Manny's too-long hands clasped Nohar's wrist. "Remember, my place is as far from Moreytown as you can get."

Nohar nodded.

Manny held Nohar's gaze for a brief moment. Then Manny looked down at his computer and started rapid-fire tapping on the screen. For a terminal with no audio, Manny handled it very efficiently. His hands were engineered for surgery, and their gracefulness permeated every gesture.

He did, however, have to hit the thing a few times to get it to work right.

Manny's nose twitched. "I don't believe it. The file's inactive. It's barely a week old."

"The police are under pressure to drop the investigation."

Manny looked like he was about to say something, but apparently thought better of it. "Fine, well, we have the autopsy report, list of the forensic evidence, abstract of the scene of the crime, a few preliminary statements from the neighbors, as well as the witness who found the body, etcetera. Pretty complete record. Compared to most I've seen."

One of Manny's lithe hands dove into a breast pocket and pulled out a ramcard and slid it into the side of the computer. Nohar briefly saw the rainbow sheen of the card reflected in a small puddle of beer on the table. "I'm running off a copy. Do me a favor and make a backup. Occasionally they *do* monitor access to the database."

Nohar nodded when Manny handed him the card. Nohar slipped it into his wallet, next to the as yet unexamined card from his camera, the pictures from Johnson's funeral. "could you tell me how Johnson died?"

"It's all on the card I gave you. He was shot in the head. Through his picture window. Splattered his brains all over his comm—oh, *that's* interesting . . ."

"What?"

There was the hint of what might have been admiration Manny's voice. "Are you familiar with Israeli weaponry? Thought not. The forensics team found the remains of two bullets, from a Levitt Mark II, fifty-caliber." A slight whistle of air came from between Manny's front teeth.

"So?"

"Came out of Mossad during the Third Gulf War. It was designed for a single sniper, and, like most designs they came up with, it's made to keep the sniper alive. The bullets are propelled by compressed carbon dioxide. It can't be heard firing by anyone farther away than fifteen meters or so. The ammunition is made from an impact-sensitive plastic explosive impregnated with shrapnel. It's intended as an antipersonnel weapon. I haven't seen an impact wound form one of these since the war. The Afghanis favored them for night raids—Nohar, what the hell have you gotten yourself into?"

"I don't know."

Nohar knew Manny was tempted to try and talk him out of it. However, Manny wouldn't try. Nohar hated when Manny got into surrogate-father mode, and Manny was too aware of that fact.

Such meetings usually ended with them spending a few hours discussing innocent bullshit over too many beers. This time they finished the pitchers in relative silence. Nohar wanted to reassure Manny he wasn't in over his head. But it would have been a lie. Nohar had trouble with lies, especially with Manny.

So, at eleven-fifteen—an early night for them—they walked to the south end of the strip, and the lot where Manny had parked. The rain had intensified, finally chasing the moreys inside. The abandoned trash-strewn asphalt reminded Nohar of pictures of the Pan-Asian war. It was the view of a city waiting for a biological warhead.

They rounded the pylons on Euclid Heights Boulevard and Nohar caught sight of the other cop on the riot-watch. Nohar wondered what it would be like, to come to work each day, to sit and wait for something to explode. The cops would have to be on rotation. Someone on permanent assignment would go nuts.

The cop looked at them as they passed, two unequal-sized moreys huddling through the rain. There was a flash of lightning, and Nohar saw the cop's face. The pink looked scared. In that instant he saw a man, a kid really, no more than twenty-two—young for a human that was, most moreys who made it into their twenties were well into middle age. The pink kid would have no idea what he would do if Nohar and Manny decided to do something illegal. He could imagine he sensed the smell of fear off of the kid, even with the car and the rain between them.

They passed the police car and walked into the parking lot of the old school. Nohar couldn't help but feel sorry for the cop. No one deserved to be placed in that kind of situation unprepared.

They stopped at the van and Manny spoke for the first time since they'd left the bar. "I can't talk you out of this, but my door's open if you need it."

"I know." Nohar was uncomfortably reminded of last night.

Nohar told himself that there was not reason to except things on this case to go bad like that. Hell, he'd been paid a hell of a lot up front, things *couldn't* go that badly this time.

At least it didn't look like he was going to be stiffed again.

Manny got into his van, another Electroline. In the dark of the storm, away from the streetlights, the van reminded Nohar of the frank in the graveyard. Both vans were the same industrial-green, the same boxy make, and had the same pneumatic doors on the back. The only difference—Manny's van had a driver's cab and "Cuyahoga County Medical Examiner" painted on all the doors.

As Manny drove back toward downtown, Nohar supposed the van's markings had a deterrent effect on car thieves.

"I said, a *fifteen* by *fifteen* grid with times *three* magnification!"

"instructions unclear."

Nohar almost shouted something back at the comm. Instead, he took a deep breath and stroked Cat a few times. *There are a few things,* he thought, *more fruitless than getting angry at a machine.* Shouting at it was just going to overtax the translation software.

"Display. Photo thirty-five. Grid. Fifteen by fifteen. Magnification. Times three."

This time the comm did was it was told.

Photo number thirty-five was a good, panoramic shot of the seated parties at Johnson's funeral. It was the one picture that had a full facial on everybody. The haze had helped by diffusing the July sun. The indirect lighting eliminated stark shadows, and would help in making the attendees, especially those to the rear, under the tent.

He had enlarged it enough. Most of the faces were clear, which was good. Nohar did not want to wait half an hour while his cheap software enhanced the picture.

Now for the grunt work. "Move. Grid. Left five percent."

One box on the grid now enclosed a face.

He told the program to print it and a portrait of a funeral attendee started sliding out of the comm's fax slot. One down, forty-nine to go.

Nohar spent two hours getting identifiable portraits from the one picture. Most of them, he knew, would offer no useful information. However, the procedure calmed him. It was something he had done hundreds of times before.

The routine was so automatic that his mind kept traveling back to Johnson's murder.

According to the autopsy, the time of death was somewhere between 9:30 p.m. on Tuesday the twenty-second, and 10:30 a.m. on Wednesday the twenty-third. The body was discovered by a jogger who noticed the broken window around noon on the twenty-fifth. There was a violent thunderstorm Thursday night, washing away a good deal of evidence. Presumably, this was why no evidence was found of the party or parties who allegedly stole the three million the campaign finance records said should have been there. Well, that wasn't quite right. The police *thought* the finance records said the three million was there. However, before the cops folded, they only had a brief perusal of the campaign finances over the weekend. Apparently the records never left Binder's headquarters.

The autopsy also said Daryl had been having a good time before someone slammed a mini-grenade into the back of his head. Nohar read at the time of death Daryl had a good point-oh-two blood alcohol, traces of weasel-dust in his nose, as well as a few 'dorphs lying undigested in his stomach. To top it off, he'd shot his wad into somebody in the twelve hours previous.

Seems he died happy.

Nohar pictured him at the comm, riding his buzz, watching some party film or other, air-conditioning going full blast. Daryl might be giggling a bit. Then the sniper takes up his position. The sniper is hiding somewhere. The ballistic evidence gave an approximate trajectory giving a field of fire at the back of Johnson's head. Five houses across the street fit the bill, all occupied, no witnesses.

Perhaps the sniper uses a driveway between those houses across the street.

It's night, to give the sniper cover. Night makes sense. Daryl's been partying. The sniper knows the alarm is off because Daryl is home. He can see Daryl through the sight. The sniper aims at Daryl's head, which might be bobbing to the beat from the comm. The sniper squeezes off a shot. The shot explodes, vaporizing the picture window.

The sniper squeezes off shot number two.

Daryl is sitting in the study, facing his comm, when his head gets blown away by the second exploding projectile belonging to the sniper's Levitt Mark II. It hits six centimeters from the base of the skull—dead center, according to the autopsy.

It hits from behind him, through the picture window in the living room, through the dining room, and through the open door to the study.

The cops found remains of two Levitt bullets. One set in Daryl's head. The other set by the picture window.

There was a problem with this sequence of events.

It was those two words. "dead center."

Daryl Johnson should have turned to see what the noise was.

For Nohar, that was a big problem. Daryl was shot in the back of the head. Nohar couldn't see someone so jazzed-up he'd be oblivious to twenty square meters of glass *exploding* directly behind him—now that he thought about it, the whole damn neighborhood was oblivious. What the autopsy listed shouldn't have zoned Daryl out that bad. Even a reflexive jerk toward the noise, no matter how fast the sniper got the second round off, would have put the shell toward one side of the head or the other.

Also, what was a nine-to-five working stiff doing that jazzed in the middle of the week? Given the time of death, Daryl was doing some heavy partying for a Tuesday.

Finally, even in Shaker Heights, a house standing open like that, two or three days without the alarm or a window, and nothing *else* ripped off? That didn't ring true.

The final portrait ejected from the printer.

Nohar stretched and got to his feet. His throat hurt from all the commands. Someday he was going to have to fix the keyboard. Despite the overstuffed cushions on the couch, his tail had fallen asleep again.

Nohar rubbed his throat and decided he needed a beer. He ducked into the kitchen. As he ripped the last bulb of beer from its envelope, he realized how hungry he was. The only food in the fridge was a plate of bones, and the last kilo of hamburger. Nohar only briefly considered the beef bones, even though a few looked fairly meaty. He grabbed the lump of hamburger and tossed it into the micro as he snapped the top off his bulb.

The cold brew soothed the raw feeling at the back of his throat, leaving a yeasty taste in his mouth. One of the few decent things pinks did with grain was turn it into booze.

Outside the dirty little kitchen window, the storm was worsening. The thunder rattled the glass in its loose molding.

Nohar drank as he watched the lightning through haze glass and rippling sheets of water. If Smith was right, and there never was any three million, why was Johnson killed? What was Johnson doing Tuesday night? Why didn't Johnson, or anyone else, respond to the shattering picture window—

Ding, the burger was warm. Nohar dropped the empty bulb into the disposal and washed his hands in the sink. He pulled the meat out of the micro, and spent a few seconds finding a clean plate. The hamburger leaked all over the plate as soon as he began unwrapping it. The blood-smell of the warm meat wafted to Nohar and *really* reminded him of how hungry he was. He ripped out a red, golfball-sized chunk from the heart of the burger and popped it into his mouth, licking the ferric taste from his claws.

Another thing the pinks did well, picking their domestic prey animals.

Cat was suddenly wide awake, mewing and rubbing against Nohar's leg. Nohar flicked a small gobbet of hamburger toward the other end of the kitchen. Cat went after it.

Nohar ate, standing at the counter by the sink, looking out the window, thinking about Daryl Johnson. Occasionally he flung another chunk of meat away, to keep Cat form distracting him.

Chapter 6

The rain broke Thursday morning and the sun came out.

Nohar barely noticed. He spent a few hours attaching names to the faces he had excised from the funeral picture. The only real interesting aspect of that drudgery was the fact that Philip Young, the finance chairman, had not attended the funeral.

He spent wasted effort trying to get a hold of Young. He tracked down an address and a comm number, but Young wasn't answering his comm. Neither was his computer, which was irritating. He called Harrison, but the legal counsel's comm was actually locking out Nohar's calls.

Nohar had never talked to the lawyer before.

Thomson's comm was also locking out Nohar's calls.

That left Binder. Nohar knew *that* would be hopeless. He tried anyway, going as far as calling Washington long-distance. The guy manning the phones was polite, condescending, and totally useless. Binder was somewhere in Columbus, raising money and campaigning, and the only way to talk to him would be to have a press pass or a large check.

Nohar didn't know if it was because he was a morey, a PI, or because they were hiding something. Nohar would lay odds on all three.

No need to be frustrated yet, Nohar told himself. There were a lot more people employed by Binder than the executive officers. Someone out there knew Johnson, and would hand him a lead.

He scanned through the items he had downloaded from the library yesterday. He was looking for a likely subject to hit. Predictably, the picture that caught his eye was a photo-op at a fund-raiser.

Behind Binder, with the upper crust of his campaign machine, there was an extra player.

Nohar leaned forward on the couch. "Magnification. Times five."

The picture zoomed at him. The resolution was excessively grainy, but he could see the extra person in the gang of four. To Binder's right were Thomson and Harrison, to his left were Young and Johnson—and Johnson's executive assistant. Johnson's assistant happened to be a woman. The picture implied a lot about them.

Nohar ran a search through his Binder database with her name, Stephanie Weir. Every time the software found something with Weir in it, there was Johnson. They seemed inseparable.

Now, here was someone who'd know about Johnson.

But would she talk to him?

He almost called her. However, when he thought it through, he realized this wasn't going to be one of those cases he could run from the comm. He had already seen how easy it was for the pinks to shut him out over the phone. He was at enough of a disadvantage as it was. He'd do this in person.

He should wear his suit for this. He hated it with a passion, but he was going out to the pinks' own territory. They had their own rules. He opened the one closet and took out the huge black jacket and the matching pants. He hesitated for a moment.

Maria wasn't here, but he could smell her tangy musk.

Nohar snatched shirt, tie, and shoes, and slammed the door shut. The memories didn't stay in the closet. He did his best to ignore them as he dressed. The relationship was over. It was only going to be a matter of time before he found one of her tops. She always left them here in hot weather.

He was still thinking about her by the time he got to the tie. The difficult ritual of getting the black strip of cloth properly wrapped around his neck was a welcome distraction. While he did so, he tried to force his mind off of Maria and on to Weir.

Nohar left the apartment comparing Maria's black jaguar fur to the long raven hair Stephanie Weir had in her pictures.

He had to walk three blocks to his car, because of the traffic restrictions. It was parked outside his office—actually a glorified mail drop—on the city end of Mayfield Road. It was a dusty-yellow Ford Jerboa convertible. Nohar wished someone would steal it. It was too old, too cheap, and for Nohar, too small. He could fit in the little thing, but the '28 Jerboa had a power plant that could barely push around its own two tons with Nohar on board.

He unplugged the car from the curb feed and tapped the combination on the passenger-side door, the one that worked. With the door open and the top down, he stepped over the passenger seat. Nohar eased himself behind the wheel, slipped some morey reggae into the cardplayer, and pulled away from the curb.

Shaker Heights was a different world. It was only separated from Moreytown by a sparse strip of middle-class pink suburbia. It could have been on the other side of the city. Driving into Shaker required some effort, since most of the direct routes were blocked off by familiar concrete pylons. In keeping with the neighborhood, these barriers were faced with brick and sat amidst vines, bushes, and tiny well-kept lawns. Nohar actually had to drive into Cleveland proper before he could weave his way into Shaker.

He expected to be stopped by the cops at least once, but he wasn't. Could be the suit. It didn't lessen the tension he felt. The roads were smooth and lined with trees. Not a morey in sight. The cozy one-family dwellings stared at him from behind manicured lawns.

Stephanie Weir lived in one of those intimidating brick houses.

Nohar pulled the Jerboa up to the curb in front of her house. Brick, one family, seven rooms, a century old or so. It was the kind of building that reminded Nohar how young his species was.

Come on, he told himself, *a few questions, nothing major.*

After saying that to himself a few times, he climbed out of the car and stretched. Before he realized what he was doing, he had reached up and started clawing the bark from the tree next to his car. No matter how good it felt, when he noticed himself doing it, he stopped. He hoped the Weir woman hadn't seen. It was embarrassing.

He shook loose bark from his fingers and walked up to the house. He pushed the call button next to the door and waited for an answer.

A speaker near his hand buzzed briefly, then spoke. "Damn, just a minute." There was a very long pause. "Who do we have here?"

Nohar tried to find the camera. "My name's Nohar Rajasthan. I'm a private investigator. I'd like to talk to a Ms. Stephanie Weir."

Another long pause. "Well, you got her. You have any ID?"

Nohar fished into his wallet and held up his PI license.

"Stick that into the slot."

A small panel under the call button slid aside. Nohar tossed it in.

Nohar stood and waited. He was tempted to push the call button again. But, without warning, the door was thrust open. Nohar had to suppress an urge to leap back. Weir offered his license back. "What can I help you with, Mr. Rajasthan?"

Pronounced it right her first try. Nohar was relieved, and a little puzzled, not to smell any fear. He was also grateful Weir didn't wear any strong perfume. She had an odd smile on her face and he wished he was better at reading human expressions. "I'd like to talk about Daryl Johnson."

Weir bit her lip. "Complicated subject. You better come in."

Nohar watched her walk away from the door before ducking in and closing it behind him. He could stand in the living room and not feel cramped. He wondered what she did with all this space. A comm was playing in the background. He recognized the voice from his research, ex-mayor Russell Gardner, Binder's opponent.

". . . is in a crisis. Our technological infrastructure was fatally wounded when Japan was invaded, as surely as if the Chinese had landed in California. For nearly a decade my opponent has been leading a policy of government inaction. For twenty years our quality of living has been degrading. There are fewer engineers in the United States now than there were at the turn of the century—"

"Sit down." she motioned toward a beige love seat that looked like it could hold him. "I was just about to fix myself a drink. Want one?"

Nohar sat on the love seat and wriggled to get his tail into a comfortable position. "Anything cold, please."

Gardner went on as if he had found a new issue.

". . . space program as an example. It's been four decades since a government program—a program since disbanded for lack of funding—discovered signals that are still widely believed, in the scientific community, to be an artifact of extraterrestrial intelligence. NASA's nuclear rockets have been sitting on the moon ten years, waiting for the launch and we are losing the ability to maintain them. We've lost the ability to maintain cutting edge tech . . "

Nohar wasn't interested in the political tirade. Instead of listening, he wondered why the pink female was acting so—relaxed wasn't quite the word he was looking for.

Weir walked into the kitchen and Nohar's gaze followed her. He enjoyed the way she moved. No abrupt motions, every move flowed into every other seamlessly. He watched as she stretched to get a glass from a cabinet. The smooth line of muscle in her arm melded into a gentle ripple down her back, became a descending curve toward the back of her knee, and ended in the abrupt bump of her calf.

She said something, and Nohar asked himself what he'd been thinking about.

"What did you say?"

Weir apparently assumed the comm was too loud. She called out, "Pause." Gardner shut up. "I said I've been waiting for you to mention it."

Nohar felt lost. "Mention what?"

She returned with two tumblers and handed one to him. He couldn't read the half-smile on her face. "Well, I'd picture a detective jumping all over me for not being more broken up about Derry."

"I was just trying to be tactful." That was a lie. The fact was, Nohar had been so nervous he hadn't even noticed. He took a drink, hoping it was something strong. It turned out to be some soft drink whose carbonation overwhelmed any taste it might have had. At least it was cold.

"I guess I'm not used to tact." She sat down in an easy chair across from him. He could identify her natural smell now, somewhere between rose and wood smoke. He liked it. "So, let's talk about Derry."

Nohar took another long pull from the glass. It did little for him but give him a chance to think. "Could you describe your relationship with him?"

"We weren't that close. At least, not as close as it was supposed to look. I suppose you've gotten the intended message from all the photo-ops and the social events. All window dressing, really."

"Meaning?"

"Just what I said. It was supposed to look like Derry was hot for me when he could really care less about women. It was all an elaborate game. I was supposed to cover up one of Binder's political liabilities." *Now* Nohar could read her expression. The hard edge in her voice helped.

"Daryl Johnson was gay?"

She nodded. "I got recruited by the Binder campaign right out of Case. Major in statistics, minor in political science. So I can go to parties and look cute. All because Binder is too loyal to fire his chosen, and is too right-wing to accept a homosexual on his staff. Publicly anyway."

That was amazing, even though he had some idea how extreme

Binder was. "That attitude's bizarre." He had to restrain himself from adding, "Even for a pink."

"You don't know the man."

"You put up with that?"

That brought a weak smile. "Selling out your principles pays a great deal of money, Mr. Rajasthan. Until he died, anyway."

She noticed they both had empty glasses. She got up. "Can I get you a refill? Something a little stronger this time?"

Nohar nodded. "Please—"

He didn't like questioning good fortune, but he was beginning to wonder why she was so open with him. "What was playing on the comm?"

"One of Gardner's speeches. Sort of self-flagellation."

Odd way to put it. "Are you still *with* Binder organization?"

She stopped on the way to the kitchen and shook her head. "Binder's legendary loyalty doesn't apply to the window dressing. After all I put up with—you know, someone even started a rumor I was a lesbian."

"Are you?"

Weir's knuckles whitened on her glass. Nohar thought she might throw it at him. The smell Nohar was sensing was powerful now, but it was more akin to fear and confusion than anger. The episode was brief. She quickly composed herself. "I'd really rather not talk about that right now."

Nohar wondered what he'd stepped in with that question. Pinks tended to lay social minefields around themselves. Nohar wished had had a map. "Sorry."

She managed a forced smile. "Don't apologize. I shouldn't have snapped at you. I've never been very good around people . . ." She sighed.

Nohar tried to get the conversation back on track. "I'm supposed to be here about Johnson. Not you. What *do* you know about Johnson? What kind of enemies did he have?"

Nohar watched covertly as she walked to the kitchen and went from cabinet to cabinet. "I suppose his only enemies would have been Binder's enemies. He had been with Binder since the state legislature. Straight from college. Loyal to a fault. A big fault considering Binder's attitude toward homosexuals. I never understood it, but I wasn't paid to understand. Young and Johnson were already an organizational fixture when I came on the scene."

"Were they—"

She came back with the drinks. "I really shouldn't talk about it.

It's Phil's business. But he shouldn't have snubbed the funeral. After fifteen years, Derry deserved more than Phil worrying about someone figuring out the obvious."

"Could you tell me about what Johnson was doing the week he died?"

"I didn't see him the week he died. I think Young mentioned him seeing some bigwig contributor."

"When was the last time you *did* see him alive?"

"A fund-raiser the previous Saturday. On the end of his arm as usual. He left early, around nine-thirty." She lowered her eyes. "You know what the last thing he said to me was?"

"What?"

"He apologized for consistently ruining all the dates 'an attractive girl' should have had." She lifted her glass. "To the relationships I should have had." She drained it.

The way she was shaking her head made Nohar change the subject. "Can you tell me why Johnson would have three million dollars of campaign funds in his house when he was killed?"

Weir looked back up, her mouth open, and her eyes a little wider. "Oh, Christ, in cash?"

"According to the police report's interpretation of the finance records, yes."

Weir got up from her chair and starting pacing."Now I'm *glad* they let me go. There's no legitimate reason for having that kind of money in a lump sum—"

"Why would he?"

"Could be anything. Avoiding disclosure, a secret slush fund, illegal contributions, embezzlement—"

"Could this have to do with Binder pressuring the police to stop the investigation?"

"I heard that, too. Sure. That's as good a reason to pressure his old cronies in the council and the police department as any."

Nohar stood up and, after a short debate within himself, held out his had. "Thank you for your help, Ms. Weir."

Her hand clasped his. It was tiny, naked, and warm, but it gave a strong squeeze. "My pleasure. I needed to talk to someone. And please don't call me Miz Weir."

"Stephanie?"

"I prefer Stephie." Nohar caught a look of what could have been uncertainty cross her face. "Will I see you again?"

Nohar had no idea. "I'm sure we'll need to go over some things later."

She led him to the door and he ducked out into the darkening night. Before the door was completely shut, Nohar turned around. "Can I ask you something?"

"Why stop now?"

"Why are you so relaxed around me?"

She laughed, an innocent little sound. "Should I be nervous?"

"I'm a moreau—"

"Well, Mr. Rajasthan, maybe I'll do better next time." She shut the door before Nohar could answer. After a slight hesitation, he pressed the call button.

"Yes?" said the speaker.

"Call me Nohar."

Nohar sat in the Jerboa and watched the night darken around him. He was parked in front of Daryl Johnson's house, a low-slung ranch, and wondering exactly why he'd acted the way he did with Weir—with Stephie. He really couldn't isolate anything he'd done or said that could be called unprofessional, but he felt like he'd bumbled through the whole interview. Especially the lesbian comment—"I don't want to talk about that right now." Nohar wondered why. She was willing to talk about anything but, even seemed reluctant to let him leave.

The night had faded to monochrome when Nohar climbed out of the convertible. He decided the problem had been Maria. Thinking about that was beginning to affect his work.

Nohar watched a reflection of the full moon ripple in the polymer sheathing that now covered the picture window. The scene was too stark for Shaker Heights. The moon had turned the world black and white, and even the night air tried to convey a chill, more psychic than actual. From somewhere the breeze carried the taint of sewer.

The police tags were gone. The investigation had stopped, here at least. Nohar approached the building, trying to resolve in his mind the contradictions the police report had raised.

He stood in front of the picture window and looked across the street. Five houses stood in line with the window and Daryl Johnson's head. Similar ranch houses, all in well-manicured plots, all well lit. The specs for the sniper's weapon said it weighed 15 kilos unloaded, and it was over two meters long. None of the possible sniper positions offered a bit of cover that would have satisfied Nohar.

Chapter 7

It didn't rain on Friday.

Philip Young still refused to answer his comm, so Nohar donned his suit and went to see the finance chairman in person. Philip Young's address was in the midst of the strip of suburbia between Moreytown and Shaker. It was close enough to home that Nohar decided to walk. By the time he was halfway there, his itching fur made him regret the decision. When he had reached Young's neighborhood, Nohar had his jacket flung over his shoulder, his shirt unbuttoned to his waist, and his tie hung in a loose circle around his neck.

Young's neighborhood was a netherworld of ancient duplexes and brick four-story apartments. The lawns were overgrown. The trees bore the scars of traffic accidents and leaned at odd angles. Less intimidating than Shaker Heights—Moreytown, only with humans. He still received the occasional stare, but he wasn't far enough off the beaten path for the pinks to see him as unusual. Only a few crossed the street to avoid him.

Nohar felt less of the nervousness that made his interview with Stephie Weir such an embarrassment. Nohar was well on his way to convincing himself he might just be able to get Young to give him some insight on that three million dollars. His major worry was exactly how to approach Young about homosexuality. Pinks could be tender on that subject.

Nohar stopped and faced Young's house with the noontime sun burning the back of his neck. Young should be home. The staff had the week off because of Johnson's death.

Gnats were clouding around his head, making his whiskers twitch.

He wondered why the finance chairman—who presumably guided those large sums under the table—lived here. This was a bad neighborhood, and the house wasn't any better off than its neighbors. The second floor windows were sealed behind white plastic sheathing. The siding was gray and pockmarked with dents and scratches. The porch was warped and succumbing to dry rot. It was as much a hellhole as Nohar's apartment.

And the place *smelled* to high heaven. He snorted and rubbed the skin of his broad nose. It was a sour, tinny odor he couldn't place. It irritated his sinuses and prodded him with a nagging familiarity.

Why did Young live here?

Young was an accountant. Perhaps there was a convoluted tax reason behind it.

Nohar walked up to the porch with some trepidation. It didn't look like it could hold him. He walked cautiously, the boards groaning under his weight, and nearly fell through a rotten section when his tail was caught in the crumbling joinery overhanging the front steps. Nohar had to back up and thrash his tail a few times to loosen it. It came free, less a tuft of fur the size of a large marble.

After that, he walked to the door holding his tail so high his lower back ached.

The door possessed a single key lock, and one call button with no sign of an intercom. Both had been painted over a dozen times. Nohar pressed the button until he heard the paint crack, but nothing happened. He knocked loudly, but no one seemed to be around to answer. He had the feeling Young's directory listing was a sham, and Young lived about as much at his "home" as Nohar worked at his "office." He carefully walked across the porch to peer into what he assumed was a living room window. The furnishings consisted of a mattress and a card table.

So much for the straightforward approach.

Nohar undid his tie and wrapped it around his right hand. He cocked back and was about to smash in the window, when he identified the smell.

The tinny smell had been getting worse ever since he had first noticed it. Nohar had assumed it was because he was approaching the source, which was true. However, he had been on the porch a few minutes and the smell kept increasing. What had been a minor annoyance on the sidewalk was now making his eyes water.

The smell was strong enough now for him to identify it. He re-

membered where he had smelled it before. It had been along time
since he'd watched the demolition of the abandoned gas stations at
the corner of Mayfield and Coventry, since he had watched them dig
up the rusted storage tanks, since had had smelled gasoline.

Instinct made him back away from the window and try to identify where the smell was coming from. His tie slipped from his claws
and fell to the porch.

The smell was strongest to the left of the porch. It came from behind the house, up the weed-shot driveway.

The garage—

Carefully, he descended the steps and rounded the porch. He
walked up the driveway toward the two-car garage and the smell
permeated everything. His eyes watered. His sinuses hurt. The smell
was making him dizzy.

The doors on the garage were closed, but he could hear activity
within—splashing, a metal can banging, someone breathing heavily.
He slowed his approach and was within five meters of the garage
when the noise stopped.

Nohar wished he was carrying a gun.

The door shot up and chunked into place. Fumes washed over
Nohar and nearly made him pass out. Philip Young faced him,
framed by the garage door. Nohar knew, from the statistics he had
read, Young was only in his mid-thirties. The articles had portrayed
him as a *Wunderkind* who had engineered the financing of Binder's
first congressional upset.

The man that was looking at Nohar wasn't a young genius. He
was an emaciated wild man. Young was stripped to the waist, and
drenched with sweat and gasoline. Behind him were stacks of wet
cardboard boxes, file folders, papers, suitcases. Some still dripped
amber fluid. Young's red-shot eyes darted to Nohar and his right
shook a black snub-nosed thirty-eight at the moreau.

"You're not going to do me like you did Derry."

Nohar hoped his voice sounded calm. "You don't want to fire
that gun."

The gun shook as Young's head darted left and right. "You're
with them, aren't you? You're *all* with them."

Young was freaked, and he was going to blow himself, the
garage, and Nohar all over the East Side. "Calm down. I'm trying to
find out who killed Derry."

"*Liar!*" Nohar's mouth dried up when he heard the hammer cock.
"You're all with them. I watched one of you kill him."

Young was off his nut, but at least Nohar realized what he must be talking about. "A moreau could have killed Derry and I never would have heard about it. Why don't you put down the gun and we can talk."

Young looked back at the boxes he'd been dousing. "You understand, I can't let anyone find out."

Nohar was lost again. "Sure, I understand."

"Derry didn't know he was helping them—what they were. When he found out, he was going to stop. You realize that."

Young was still looking into the garage, Nohar took the opportunity to take a few steps toward him. "Of course, no one could hold that against him."

Young whipped around, waving the gun. "That's just it! They'll *blame* Derry. People would say he was *working for them*—"

Young rambled, paying little attention to Nohar. Nohar worked his way a little closer. He could see into the garage better now. His eyes watered and it was hard to read, but he could see some of the boxes of paper were filled with printouts. They looked like payroll records. One suitcase was filed with ramcards.

Young suddenly became aware of him again. "Stop right there."

Young's finger tightened and Nohar froze. "Why did 'they' kill Derry?"

The gun was pointed straight at Nohar as Young spoke. "He found out about them. He went over the finance records and figured it out."

"You're the finance chairman. Why didn't you figure it out first?"

Mistake. Young started shaking and yelling something inarticulate. Nohar turned and dived at the ground.

Young fired.

Young screamed.

Nohar was looking away from the garage when the gun went off. He heard the crack of the revolver, immediately followed by a whoosh that made his eardrums pop. The bullet felt like a hammer blow in his left shoulder. The explosion followed, a burning hand that slammed him into the ground. The acrid smoke made his nose burn. The odor of his own burning fur made him gag.

Young was still screaming.

The explosion gave way to a crackling fire and the rustle of raining debris. Nohar rolled on to his back to put out his burning fur. When he did so, he wrenched his shoulder, sending a dagger of pain straight through his neck.

He blacked out.

* * *

The absolute worst smell Nohar could imagine was the smell of hospital disinfectant. As soon as he had gained a slight awareness of his surroundings, that chemical odor awakened him the rest of the way. Before he had even opened his eyes, he could feel his stomach tightening.

"Someone, open a window!" It came out in barely a whisper.

Someone was there and Nohar could hear the window whoosh open. The stale city air let him breathe again. Nohar opened his eyes.

It was what he'd been afraid of. He was in a hospital. It was in the cheap adjustable bed, the awful disinfectant smell, the thin sheets, and the linoleum tile. It was in the odor of blood and shit the chemicals tried to hide. It was in the plastic curtains that pretended to give some privacy to the naked moreys lined up, in their beds, like cattle in a slaughterhouse.

Nohar hated hospitals.

Nohar turned his head and saw, standing next to the window, Detective Irwin Harsk. The pink was as stone-faced as ever.

"Am I under arrest?"

Harsk looked annoyed. "You *are* a paranoid bastard. Young blew up, you're allegedly an innocent bystander. Believe it or not, we found two witnesses that agree on two things in ten. Give me some credit for brains."

"Why *are* you here?"

"I'm here because you're giving me problems downtown. I'm supposed to be some morey expert. They expect me to exercise some control over you. I don't like jurisdictional problems. I don't like the DEA staking out half of my territory. I don't like the Fed. And I don't like outsiders pressuring me to bottle something up. I don't like Binder. I don't like Binder's friends—"

Nohar struggled to get into a sitting position and his shoulder didn't seem to object. "What?"

"A bunch of people who think they're cops are trying to dick me around. They want me to keep you away from Binder's people, or bad things will happen. Like what, I don't know. I'm already as low as you get in this town." Harsk slammed his fist into the side of the window frame. "Hell, Shaker's screwing around the ˚Johnson killing for Binder. They *deserve* you."

Harsk looked like he needed to strangle someone. For once, Nohar was speechless.

"Look," Harsk said, "I'm not going to do their shit-work for them. But you're on your own lookout. I just want to avoid the bullshit and do what someone once laughingly described as my job." Harsk walked to the door and paused. "One more thing. The DEA has a serious red flag on your ass."

With that, Harsk left.

Nohar watched Harsk weave his way between the moreys, and didn't know what to think. He'd always pictured Harsk as constantly dreaming up new ways to screw him over. Maybe Harsk was right, he *was* paranoid.

He felt his shoulder. The wound didn't seem to be major. The dressing extended to the back of his neck, which felt tender when Nohar pressed it. He pulled back the sheet. There were five or six dressings on his tail. That, and a transparent support bandage on his slightly swollen right knee, was the only visible damage.

Considering how close he was to Young when the nut blew himself up, he'd gotten off light.

"Damn it." Nohar suddenly remembered Cat. He didn't know how long he'd been out, and Cat only had half a day's food in his bowl when Nohar left.

He looked up and down the ward. No doctors, no nurses, not even a janitor. Harsk had been the only pink down here and he had already left. Nohar knew when, or if, hospital administration finally got to him, there would be a few hours of forms to fill out. Just to keep the bureaucracy happy.

To hell with that.

He swung his legs over the edge of the bed and gently started putting pressure on his right leg. It wasn't a bad sprain. It held his weight. He stood up slowly and felt slightly dizzy. He was alarmed until he realized it was still from that damn disinfectant smell. Breathing through his mouth helped.

There was a window between his bed and the next one. The fuzzy nocturnal view—Nohar wished he could kill the lights in the ward so he could see better—of the skyline told him he wasn't far enough down the Midtown Corridor to be at the Clinic. That meant he was at University Hospitals and only a few blocks from Moreytown. He was probably in the new veterinary building.

Lightning flashed on the horizon.

Nohar looked at the bed on the other side of the window. In it was a canine who had an arm shaved naked inside a transparent cast. He—like Nohar, the canine was naked and not covered by a sheet—was watching Nohar's activity with some interest. The canine spoke when he saw he'd caught Nohar's attention.

"You blow up?"

It was hard placing the accent, but defiantly first generation. Probably Southeast Asian. Nohar began looking for exit signs as he answered.

"Yes."

"Pink law's bad news. Best eye yourself, tigerman—"

Nohar was barely listening. He'd located the exit. "Sure. You have the date?"

"Fade side of August two. Saturday is five minutes from nirvana."

Thirty-six hours. He must have been drugged.

That was it. He was leaving.

The canine was still nattering. Nohar thanked him and started toward the exit. Most of the moreys here were asleep, but a few watched him leave. There were a few comments, mostly of the "Skip on the pinks" variety. He did get one sexual proposition, but he didn't pause enough to register the species or the gender the offer came from.

He slipped out of the wardroom, the glass doors sliding aside as he passed, and found himself in a carpeted reception area. There was a waiting room, and a nurse's station across from it. No one in sight. The elevators and the stairs were directly across from the doors to the ward. All he needed to do was cross between the station and the waiting room. Once in the stairwell he could make it to the parking garage.

He limped across no-man's-land and nearly made it to the stairwell.

The elevator doors opened without any warning. He was caught right in front of the elevator. If it hadn't been so damn silent, he might have had a chance to duck to the side.

The last person he expected to see in the elevator was Stephie Weir.

As the doors opened, she took a step forward and her motion ceased. Nohar thought he must have looked as surprised as she did. Neither of them moved. They stood there, staring at each other, until the doors started closing again.

Realizing he was about to blow his escape, Nohar jumped into the elevator. He called out, "Down. Garage level," and pressed the button for the garage level just in case the thing didn't have a voice pickup. Nohar hoped no one else in the building would want to use this particular elevator in the next half-minute.

Stephie was staring at him. Nohar waited until he felt the car moving downward, then he asked, "What are *you* doing here?"

The question seemed to break her out of shock. She lifted her gaze. "I want to know what happened to Phil. I was waiting down there two hours until Detective Harsk—Christ, what are you doing with no clothes on?"

That damned pink fetish. "Avoiding bureaucracy."

"What the hell are you talking about? *You're naked!*"

"Not until they shave me."

The doors on the elevator opened and Nohar held his breath. They had made it all the way to the garage. Again, no one in sight.

Nohar turned to Stephie who looked and smelled of confusion. "If you want to talk about what happened, you better come with me."

He stepped out on to the cold concrete. He finally felt comfortable breathing through his nose. The only strong smells down here were the slight ozone smell from the cars, and Stephie's smoky-rose scent.

She choked back a few monosyllables and started walking after him. "Just tell me why, please."

He almost gave her a curt answer, but he decided she deserved something of an explanation. "I need to get back home. Checking out and getting whatever the explosion left of my clothes could take a long while, and they might just decide they want to keep me for a day or two. Besides, I hate filling out forms. They can bill me."

"What's so important?"

"I don't have anyone to feed my cat."

That got her. "You're not kidding, are you?"

Nohar shrugged and started toward the entrance of the parking garage. His claws clicked on the concrete.

She called after him. "Where's your car?"

"I suppose it's still parked outside my office."

"You're going to—" She paused. "Of course you intend to walk home like that. Come back here. At least let me give you a lift so you won't get arrested."

Nohar turned around. He didn't know what to make of the offer. "Can I fit in your car?"

"A Plymouth Antaeus? What it cost, you better fit."

"Sure you want to do this? My neighborhood—"

"Screw your neighborhood. We need to talk about Phil."

Nohar silently agreed they needed to talk about Phil. He allowed himself to be led to the brand-new Antaeus.

Chapter 8

The Antaeus pulled up behind the Jerboa, splashing a deep puddle by the curb. The barriers prevented Stephie from driving any closer to Nohar's apartment.

When Stephie parked, she turned to face Nohar. She seemed to be making an effort to keep her gaze fixed on his face. "It doesn't sound like Phil."

"It's what happened."

"The cops called it a suicide. Detective Harsk said Phil *shot* you."

Nohar reached up and rubbed his left shoulder. "Can *you* explain what happened?"

Stephie turned toward the windshield, shaking her head. She was silent for a few seconds. Finally she said, "He bought that house so he could have a separate address."

So, it *was* a sham. "He lived with Johnson?"

"Five years now." She still looked out the window. A street lamp shone through the cascading rain and carved rippling shadows on her face. She spoke slowly and deliberately. "I can't believe Phil would kill himself."

Nevertheless, that's what Young had done, as surely as if he had pointed the gun at his own head. Nohar could still picture Young saying they all—Nohar presumed Young meant moreys—were with *them*. Nohar suspected *they* were in MLI.

"How'd he feel about moreys?"

"I don't know—" *Very few people do*, thought Nohar. "I didn't talk to him much. I knew him mostly through talking to Derry." She sighed. The sound seemed to catch in her throat.

After an uncomfortable long pause, she changed the subject. "I don't think Derry's death *would* make him . . "

"What would it take?"

"More, just . . . *more*." Stephie turned and looked Nohar in the eyes. Her expression seemed to show bewilderment and she smelled of fear, nerves, and confusion. "Do you think I'm a bad person?"

What the hell brought that on? "Of course not, why?"

"I feel terrible about what I said about Phil snubbing the funeral—"

Nohar restrained the immediate impulse to ask her why she was telling him that. Instead, he tried a close-lipped smile. "We all say things we end up regretting. It doesn't mean we're thoughtless."

"It's not just that. My whole life has been a hypocrisy—"

"You don't mean—"

"I know exactly what I mean. I never even was a Binder supporter—I despise the man." She sucked in a shuddering breath. "Me, Phil, and Derry—we were all playing the twisted charade. All of us hiding because Binder was signing our paychecks."

"What were you hiding?"

The look in her eyes changed for a moment. Nohar felt like he had let his mouth make a major mistake again. Instead, she smiled, even let out a little laugh.

"I was hiding myself, I guess."

Nohar realized he was only going to get that cryptic comment. He nodded and opened the rear door to let himself out into the rain. The damp soaked into his fur in a matter of seconds.

"Thanks for the ride." Nohar didn't know why he felt obliged, but he added, "I'll give you a call later on, if I find out anything."

Nohar shut the door and she looked like she still couldn't quite believe he was going to walk home without any clothes. "Nohar?"

He paused and looked back into the Antaeus. "Yes?"

"Forget it, never mind . . ."

She shook her head and drove the Antaeus into the darkness without an explanation.

Nohar stood and watched it go for a while, wondering.

Moreytown pressed around him. He had three blocks to go, so he started walking. He was safe from the cops here. Moreys were so casual about clothing that trying to enforce pink exposure laws in Moreytown would be impossible. His lack of attire would only be noted because of the rain, and the time of night. Now all he had to worry about were how many eyes had seen him with the pink female.

He nearly made it home—

A ratboy bumped into him.

No, they wouldn't be that stupid.

He was on the wrong side of the street. He was between the abandoned bus and a boarded-up pizzeria. His usual alertness had failed him, and he realized the hospital smell was still clogging his nose.

The familiar-looking ratboy, brown fur and denim cutoffs, rebounded from Nohar's side. "Lookee—"

Now Nohar could catch the rat's musk. The ratboy was flying a wave of excitement, reeked of it. It was Fearless Leader, and he was jacked about as far as a rat could go.

"The stray just ruffled my fur!"

Footsteps, two sets one end of the bus, two at the other. Subordinates. From the look and smell of it, Fearless' boys were jacked worse than he was. Bigboy was there, and he snicked a blade. Nohar should have taken the knife when he had the chance.

Bigboy made a few ineffective waves with his switchblade. "Let's shave the kitty pink."

A chain rattled from the other end of the bus. "Teach some respect for the coat."

Great, they *were* stupid.

So much for the Finger of God.

Fearless Leader pulled a gun, a twenty-two. Fortunately, he wasn't doused in gasoline. "We don't like pink moreys. We goina mark you. You move and we veto your pretty kitty ass."

Nohar always held his fighting instinct under iron control. Both nature and the Indian gene-techs had designed his strain for combat, for hunting, for the spilling of blood. Almost always, that part of his soul was at odds with his conscious mind. Nohar thought of it as The Beast.

When Fearless pulled the gun, Nohar felt a shock of adrenaline. His heart began to pound and he felt the rush in his ears and his temples. There as the anticipatory taste of copper in his mouth. His breath like a blast furnace in the back of his throat.

The Beast wanted out. It was scratching at the mental door Nohar always kept locked.

Nohar opened the door and let The Beast take over.

The night snapped into razor-sharp monochrome. The smells

erupted into a vivid melange. He could hear the ratboy's heartbeat as well as his own. Time crawled.

The Beast roared.

Nohar roared. The sound bore no trace of his speaking voice. It was a scream of rage that tore the skin from his throat. The ratboys hesitated at the sound. Fearless smelled of fear now, fear that told Nohar he had never seen a morey turn wild before.

Nohar's left arm, the one with restricted mobility, shot out toward Fealress' gun hand. Nohar grabbed the weapon and turned it toward the ground. There was a snap of bone before the gun blew a hole in the side of the bus. Fearless Leader had some control. No scream.

Not until Nohar's right hand, sweeping upward with the claws fully extended, caught Fearless between the legs. Nohar didn't simply rake his claws across Fearless' body. His claws came up, point first, and when they bit flesh, jerked up, hooked forward, and partially retracted. Fearless Leader screamed when Nohar lifted him up. Nohar's claws were hooked into the flesh of his groin.

Nohar was jacked higher than the rats now. Fearless Leader's 50 kilos weighed nothing. Fearless slammed into the bus through a broken window. The gun was still in Nohar's left hand. Fealress' hand was still holding it, reaching through the bus window. Nohar yanked the gun away. There was another crack.

Bigboy was now within reach, swinging his knife. Nohar pivoted and the knife missed. Nohar's cupped right hand aimed for the eyes as Bigboy passed. Bigboy slipped in the rain before the claws hit him. Lucky. The claws sank in behind the ear and tore off a flap of skin down the left side of Bigboy's face.

Nohar's left arm blocked a chain coming at his head. It wrapped around his forearm. He pulled that rat toward him and upward. He sank his teeth into the weapon arm. A toss of Nohar's head disarmed his attacker and dropped the rat off to his right. Into the same puddle that had saved Bigboy's eyes.

Two others. They spooked.

Leader in bus. Bigboy huddled in doorway to pizzeria, trying to hold half his face on. Chain trying to stop the bleeding, hand limp, muscle severed. Fight over.

Slowly, Nohar shut the door on The Beast.

The comedown was hard. He began shaking. The rats didn't notice. They had their own problems. That fifteen seconds of savagery had jacked him higher and faster than these ratboys had ever thought of going. The crash would've killed them.

Nohar stumbled across the street and to the door of his building.

When he staggered into his living room, Cat hissed at him. Nohar was covered in rat blood. He wobbled into the kitchen, opened a cabinet, and spilled Cat's food all over the counter.

It would have to do, for now.

Nohar dragged himself into the bathroom and slumped into the shower. He turned on a blast of cold water.

Dipping into his reserve as a bioengineered weapon had its price.

When Nohar woke up, the shower was still going full blast. Cat was asleep on the lid of the john, and the only remains of the night's activity was the taste of blood in his mouth. The bandage on his shoulder fell off the moment he moved. It revealed a puckered red wound where they had dug out Young's bullet. There was a shaved area around it the size of his hand. The flesh was a pale white, contrasting with Nohar's russet-and-black fur. Nohar quickly looked away from it. The skin made him uncomfortable.

The support bandage was still there. At least he hadn't aggravated the injury to his knee. That was good because there was no way he was going to end up in a hospital again.

He stood up, killed the cold water, and hit the dryer. He barely noticed when Cat spooked. Nohar stood under the dryer and shook. He tried to tell himself it was his unsteady knee, but he was too adept at spotting bullshit. He knew it was a reaction to loosing The Beast.

All moreys dealt with The Beast in one form or another. Some, like Manny, lived with it without it making so much as a ripple in their psyche, the techs having let a basically human brain mute the instincts they weren't particularly interested in. Then there were moreys like Nohar, who bore the legacy of techs playing hob with what nature gave them. This was only the second time he had let out The Beast with no restraint. Nohar was grateful nobody had died.

He had enjoyed it too much.

He saw in himself the potential for becoming another type of morey. The one who gave himself over to The Beast and reveled in the bloodlust. The one like his father—

"No," he said to his reflection as he left the bathroom. To his practiced ears, it sounded like a lie.

Forget the rats, he told himself. He still had a job to do. Even if it cost him two days, his run-in with Young had given him something besides a gunshot wound and a sprained knee. If Young was not totally out of touch with reality—no mean assumption—Nohar now had some idea of how Daryl Johnson was killed, if not why.

First things first—he went to the comm and turned it on. "Load program. Label, 'I lost my damn wallet!' Run program."

"searching . . . found. program uses half processing capacity and all outside lines for approximately fifteen minutes, continue?"

"Yes." It was going to take him that long just to run through his messages. While his cards and Ids were being canceled and re-ordered by the computer, he perused the backlog.

There were no phone messages on the comm, but a pile of mail was waiting in memory for him.

It was early in the morning on Sunday the third. Predictably, bills predominated in the mail. He'd have the comm pay them off as soon as it was done with his lost wallet program. There was the usual collection of junk mail. However, for once, there was something more than those two categories in his mail file.

"John Smith," his client, had been true to his word to keep in touch. Two days after their meeting, he had left a voice message for Nohar to meet him in Lakeview Cemetery, for noon on Saturday—when Nohar had been zoned in a ward at University Hospitals. About twelve hours after that little bit of mail, Smith apparently found out what had happened. The slimy voice carried little emotion. "Mr. Rajasthan, I regret this incident with Binder's finance chairman. I am unable to meet with you personally, but I finance your medical expenses when I hear what happens to you—"

"Pause." Nohar was having trouble following the frank's heavy accent. Nohar, living in the middle of Moreytown, had to deal with, and understand, an incredible variety of unusual accents. A Vietnamese dog not only had an Asian accent, but a definite canid pronunciation. The problem with the frank was more subtle. Nohar didn't think it was a South African accent—even if that *was* one of the few countries to have defied the long-standing United Nations ban on engineering humans. Nohar promised himself he'd press the frank a little more closely about his origins next time they met.

"Continue."

"—I hope this does not prevent you from the discovery of Daryl Johnson's murderer. I increase your fee to reflect your current difficulties. I call to set up meeting when you are released from hospital. There you tell me what you discover."

It took Nohar a few seconds to figure out exactly what the frank meant.

The next item in the mail file was from Maria. Nohar was afraid to play it. Then he cursed himself and told the comm to play the damn thing. It was the same husky voice, much calmer this time. Nohar wished he could see her face. "Raj, I thought you deserved a more civilized good-bye. I still can't meet you face-to-face, and for that I apologize. I just want you to know it isn't your fault. We're incompatible. Maybe it would be easier for me to deal with your wholesale contempt for everything if you weren't such a decent and honorable person."

There was a pause as Maria took a long breath. "I am going through with it. You were right about the money—you always are about things like that—but I'm going anyway. California is a lot more tolerant, and the few communities there aren't just glorified slums the humans abandoned. I know you can't appreciate this, but God bless you."

Nohar sat, her voice still ringing in his ears, remembering. He had the comm store the message and sighed.

"instructions unclear."

He had sighed too loudly. "Store mail. Comm. Off."

She had been wrong about one thing. He *could* appreciate the blessing. Especially after their last argument, the night before he had stood her up for that fiasco with Nugoya—

It had started when she suggested they both move to California. Of course, there was no way they could afford it. She brought up God, and Nohar went off. That damned little bit of pink brainwashing infuriated him. Especially when a moreau spouted it. Religion, pink religion, wasn't just a form of mind control, but the primary justification for people like Joseph Binder to consider moreys worse than garbage. Why should a morey believe in God, when people like Binder said they were abomination in His eyes?

Maria was a devout Catholic and Nohar had been drunk enough to think he might be able to talk her out of such stupidity. How could she be secure in her belief when she only had a *soul* by dispensation of some sexagenarian pink in a pointed hat? A decision that had more to do with politics than divine inspiration.

Why couldn't he keep his damn mouth shut?

Worse, all his money problems had evaporated with the ten thousand Smith gave him. Maria's message had come in yesterday. Knowing her, she had left town by now.

Chapter 9

Nohar parked the Jerboa in front of Daryl Johnson's ranch. He stayed in the car. Shaker Heights still made him paranoid about cops. It was early Sunday morning and he suspected the slow-moving bureaucracy at University Hospital was just now discovering him missing. Shortly afterward, the cops would be notified. Nohar didn't know exactly what would happen then. He was a witness to Young's explosion—they *should* want a statement from him. But Binder was pressuring the cops. Binder probably wouldn't want any real close investigation of Young's empty house, or the records Young had destroyed.

At least Nohar's investigation, such as it was, was progressing. He had checked the police records again. The air-conditioning *had* been going full blast when Johnson was blown away.

Nohar yawned and raked his claws across the upholstery of the passenger seat. He spent a few minutes picking foam rubber as he looked at the sheathing covering the picture window. His watch beeped. It was eight, Manny would be answering his comm.

Nohar took the voice phone out of the glove compartment and called him.

"Dr. Gujerat here. Who—" There was a pause as Manny must have read the text on the incoming call. "Nohar? Where in the hell are you? I got to the hospital during nocturnal visiting hours. You were gone—"

Fine, his disappearance had been discovered that much earlier. "Manny, I'm fine. I need to ask you something—"

"Like the percentage of untreated bullet wounds that become

gangrenous? Damnit, you weren't in the hospital just to be inconvenienced."

Nohar shook his head. At least Manny wasn't saying, "I told you so." Even though he'd been right about getting involved with pink business.

"I needed to feed Cat."

"Great, just great. I won't even tell you how silly that sounds. You couldn't have gotten me to do that?"

Nohar thought of the ratboys. "No, I couldn't."

Manny sighed and slowed his chittering voice. "I know how you feel about hospitals, but you can't avoid them forever. Things have gotten a lot better. They don't make mistakes like that anymore—" Nohar knew Manny stopped because of the ground he was treading. *Thanks for reminding me,* Nohar thought. He was about to say it, but, for once, he managed to keep his mouth shut.

"You better promise to come over and let me look at that wound. There are a lot more appropriate things to die of."

"Promise."

"I know you didn't just call to say hi. What do you want?"

Nohar caught the dig at him. It was unlike Manny. Manny really was worried about him. "Before I ask you, promise *me* something."

"What?"

"When this is over, we get out together. No business, no corpses."

There was a distinct change in the quality of Manny's voice that made Nohar feel better, "Sure . . ."

Damn, Manny was almost speechless. "I wanted to ask you about the time of death. How accurate can that be?"

Manny found his professional voice. "Depends on a lot of things. The older the corpse, the less accurate. Need a good idea of the ambient temperature and the humidity—"

That's what Nohar wanted to hear. "What if they were wrong about the temperature? Fifteen degrees too high."

"Definitely throw the estimate off."

"How much?"

"Depends on what they thought the temperature was to begin with."

"Thirty-two at least."

Nohar could hear the whistle of air between Manny's front teeth. "Nohar, the time of death could be put back by up to a factor of two. If the humidity was off, maybe more."

"Thanks, Manny."

"You're welcome, I think."

Nohar hung up the phone and looked at the ranch. All the little nagging problems with Johnson's death— And it was so damn simple.

Problem—it took much too long for the local population to notice the gaping hole if it had been shot when Johnson was shot. Solution—the window was shot out long after Johnson was dead. Probably during the thunderstorm that Thursday, so few people would have heard the glass—real glass, expensive—exploding and none would recognize its significance.

It had taken Young to make Nohar think of that. Young said he had seen a morey kill Johnson. "One of you," he said. The only way Young could have seen the killer shoot Johnson was if he, the killer, and Johnson were all more or less in the same place when Johnson died. If the assassin was in the house, he could have offed Johnson with one shot—no need for a shattering window to draw Johnson's attention. Johnson could have remained facing the comm, oblivious enough to be shot dead center in the back of the head.

Because no alarm, no break-in. That meant Johnson let him in. With a Levitt Mark II? Not likely.

Johnson let in someone else—one of *them*—and that person let in the assassin. Yes, Johnson let in someone. Perhaps to confront the person with whatever he had found in the financial records. Young lived in the ranch with Johnson, but no one was supposed to know that. So Young would be hidden from the guest. Maybe in a darkened bedroom, looking out a crack in the door.

The guest—maybe one of the franks from MLI—talks to Johnson in the study. The frank leaves the door open, so the assassin can sneak into the living room and set up the Levitt. The door to the study must remain closed except for the last minute, to give the assassin a chance to prepare. Young would only see the gun when the frank opens the study door to give the morey killer a field of fire.

The one shot gets Derry Johnson in the back of the head. Young is in shock. The frank and the morey clean up a little and leave.

It must have been Saturday night, after that fundraiser Young and Johnson had departed early. That would explain Johnson's state, and why no one could finger Johnson's location during the week. Young wasn't thinking right. He freaked, packed his stuff, and ran out to his empty house.

The corpse was left in an air-conditioned, climate-controlled environment, until the morey with the Levitt blew away the picture window on Thursday. The storm ruined the traces of the assassin in the living room. The killing became an anonymous sniping. The time of death shifted to Wednesday and nobody got the chance to plumb the inconsistencies because Binder clamped down immediately.

Neat.

But why didn't Young call the cops?

Something had freaked Young. If Stephie was right, something beyond Johnson's death. From the way Young acted, it was something linked to the financial records. Something Johnson saw and Young didn't.

Nohar looked back at the broken window. The police ballistics report was based entirely on the assumption that both shots came from the same place. Now the second shot, the one that blew the window out, no longer had to be in line with Johnson's head. The field of fire at the picture window was *much* wider. The sniper no longer had to be crouching in one of the security-conscious driveways across the street.

Nohar stood up on the passenger seat of the Jerboa and looked for good fire positions. He scanned the horizon—lots of trees. The Levitt needed a clear field of fire; crashing through a tree could set off the charge in the bullet. Nohar kept turning, looking for a high point, above the houses, behind them, without a tree in the way.

Feeling a growing sense of disillusionment, Nohar parked the Jerboa next to the barrier at the end of the street. He had been pounding pavement and checking buildings for most of the day. Evening was approaching and, while he had found a number of buildings both likely and unlikely to hold a sniper, he was little closer to discovering where the sniper had shot from. He was afraid he might actually cross the path of the gunman and not recognize it.

Fire position number ten was inside Moreytown, which was a plus as far as likelihood was concerned. Nohar figured you could drive a fully loaded surplus tank inside Moreytown and the pink law would give it just a wink and a nod.

The name of the building was Musician's Towers. It was a twenty-story, L-shaped building, supposedly abandoned since the riots. Good spot for a sniper. Hundreds of squatters in the place, but there weren't likely to be any *witnesses*.

There had been a halfhearted effort to seal it up. It'd been condemned ever since a fire took out one wing—as well as the synagogue across the street. Most of the plastic covering the doors and windows had been torn off ages ago.

He slowly approached the doorway, on guard even though it was still daylight. The entrance hall was in the burned-out wing. The hall went through to the other side, looking like someone had fired an artillery round all the way through the base of the building. He had to climb over the pile of crumbled concrete in front of the entrance, debris that came mostly from the facade on the top five floors.

White sky burned through the empty, black-rimmed windows at the top of the building. That was the place for a sniper.

Above the gaping hole that led into the building someone had spray-painted, "Welcome to Morey Hilton."

Inside, the heat became oppressive. Nohar was nearly used to the itch under his shirt, but in the sweltering lobby—it might have been because of the still lingering smell of fire—he had to take it off. He leaned against the hulk of a station wagon someone had driven into the lobby, waiting to become acclimated to the heat.

No sign of the squatters yet, but Nohar doubted any lived near the first floor. That would be a little too close to the action. The empty beer bulbs scattered across the floor, the occasional cartridge from an air-hypo, the fresh bullet pockmarks, marked the lobby as a party spot for the gangs. Not to mention "Zipperhead" painted on the side of the station wagon. Hmm, Nohar corrected himself. *Gang*—singular. Lately, the one gang seemed to be it. He didn't know exactly what to make of that. There had been at least five gangs around when he had been running with the Hellcats. But that was a long time ago—the years before this building burned up—and Nohar really didn't want to think about it.

He decided he had waited long enough and went straight for one of the open stairwells. The winding concrete stairs were swathed in darkness, and Nohar's view became colorless and nocturnal. Here, the heat was even worse, and the smell of fire was overwhelmed by the aromas of rust, mold, and rotting garbage. The stairs were concrete, but every other footstep fell on something soft.

Nohar tried ignore the garbage and think like a sniper. The face of the burned-out wing was pointed at the target, so the assassin would take a point amidst the wreckage. Few squatters in the remains of the fire—

Nohar hit floor ten and had to pause because he thought he'd come across a corpse. A lepus was curled in a fetal position in the corner of the tenth-floor landing. An acrid odor announced the fact the rabbit had soiled—him, her? Nohar couldn't tell in the dark—itself. As he approached, the rabbit's twitching showed it was still among the living. An air-hypo cartridge lay on the ground.

A jacked rabbit—might have even been funny if it hadn't been so obvious the rabbit was on flush, and having a bad reaction. Nohar knelt next to the rabbit. She—Nohar could tell now—wasn't wearing anything. Filth covered her dark fur. He felt a wave of anger when he didn't see the hypo. That meant one of two things. Either someone had done her, or had stolen the hypo. In both cases they'd left her on her own like this. Scenes like this made Nohar think the fundamentalists might be right and moreys were an abomination in the eyes of whatever deity.

It was flush, all the classic symptoms. Near catatonia, chills, dehydration, voiding the bowels, rolling up of the eyes, shallow breathing, slight nosebleed. She was lucky. In truly severe reactions, the nervous system went. Then he *would* have found a corpse. She'd been through the worst of it, though. What she needed now was light and water. The darkness tended to perpetuate the hallucinogenic effects of flush. She could be psychologically unable to move long after the physical effects had worn off.

Nohar picked her up. She weighed nothing. She was a small morey to begin with, and she was skinny as well. He hoped the squatters still kept those rain barrels up topside.

On the burned-out wing, with the exception of the concrete facade, the top three floors were gone. Nohar carried the rabbit out of the stairwell and into the open air of the seventeenth floor. Nohar saw the orange plastic barrels immediately. Good, the occupants still collected rainwater. He looked at the shivering rabbit, silently asked himself what he was doing, and lowered her face gently into one of the cleaner barrels.

The moment the water brushed the side of her face, her ears picked up. Good sign. They stayed like that, Nohar holding her face just above the water, the rabbit curled up with her neck resting on the edge of the barrel, for close to fifteen minutes. The only thing keeping Nohar from giving up on her brain-lock was the gradual improvement, and the fact she did seem to be drinking a little.

There had to be a better way to deal with this, Nohar thought. He wasn't a trained medic. He was following the home procedure for a bad flush trip. It was a lot easier with a toilet handy—the running joke was, the comedown in the head was the way the drug got its street name.

A sputtering came from the barrel. Nohar hoped she wouldn't

vomit. "Listen to my voice." Nohar tried to sound reassuring. "It was a bad trip, but you're coming back. It wasn't real. You can relax now. It's important to untense your muscles, slowly—"

After a decade plus, the lines came back with surprising ease. She didn't say anything as he talked her down, and Nohar counted himself lucky she wasn't a screamer.

"*Let go, damnit!*"

A wide foot made a hollow slap on Nohar's chest, announcing the fact she had regained some contact with reality. Nohar didn't think letting go of her was a good idea, but the rabbit had suddenly erupted into thrashing motion from near paralysis. She was saying something in Spanish, and from the tone of her voice, it wasn't very pleasant. Good intentions only went so far. He set her down next to the barrel. She was panting, and a little unsteady on her feet.

Nohar rubbed his shoulder. It was tightening up after the stress of holding the rabbit above the barrel. He knew he was asking for it, but he said it anyway. "Are you all right?"

She looked up. She had a scar on one cheek that turned up her mouth in a quirky smile, as if she enjoyed some private joke at his expense. "Don't do no favors, Kit."

"Name's Nohar." He shrugged and started walking toward the windows on the south wall.

He got to the windows, began looking for Johnson's house, and immediately realized the limitations of his vision. The houses were mere blobs.

Nohar turned back to the rain barrel and saw the rabbit, apparently recovering out of sheer cussedness, doing her best to clean herself off with a rag. Oops, not a rag, he had left his shirt over there. Oh, well, the shirt was too hot anyway.

"Hey, Fluffy—"

She glared at him.

"Better at giving favors than receiving them?"

"Name's Angel. Fuck you."

"You owe me something for that shirt you just wasted."

She looked at the dripping cloth she'd been wiping herself with. "Yeah, you and every Ziphead this side of nirvana."

"Your trip an old debt coming home?"

"Wow, Kit, you have a grasp of the obvious that's worthy of a cop." She stood up—most of the filth-out of her spotted brown fur—walked over to the window and slapped the wet shirt across his midsection.

"Your shirt."

Nohar wrung out the shirt and tied it around his waist. "Thanks, Angel— Can you help? I need someone with better vision than I have."

Angel sighed. "What you want?"

"I need to find a window overlooking a ranch house with a shot-out picture window."

"You say shot?" A real smile overcame the ghost of the scar.

"Yes. I can't pick it out—"

She shook her head. "Kit, I didn't know the cops were hiring—"

"I am not a cop!"

Angel stepped back, still smiling, showing a pair of prominent front teeth. "Sore point? What are you then? What you looking for?"

"I'm a private detective. I'm trying to find a sniper."

She laughed and said, "I can tell you who. What I get?"

It took Nohar half a second to realize she was serious. He closed the distance between them in an instant and grabbed her shoulders. There was a brief adrenaline rush, but he contained it.

"Tell me."

"Not for nothing."

"What do you want?"

"You played the savior, play it all the way. I want protection. You're a big one, Kit. Keep Zipheads from expressing me to nowhere again."

She had him. He'd gone to the trouble of saving her life. Now, he had to make it worth something.

Nohar looked into her eyes and she stopped smiling. "I will, if you tell me two things. First, why are they after you?"

She shrugged. "Made stupid mistake. I tried to keep Stigmata, my gang, going after the Zips moved in. Didn't know then that they were backed from downtown. My clutch didn't fall off the map; so got erased."

Nohar could live with that. "You on flush—or anything else?"

"Do I look stupid?"

He told himself not to answer that.

He might as well play the samaritan while he could. "You get the couch."

Chapter 10

Nohar didn't see any rats when he parked the Jerboa across from his office. He hoped that meant Fearless Leader and his cronies were laying low. Even so, he was nervous, and Angel was more so. He gave her his shirt—dragged on the ground when she wore it—and had her hold her ears down.

With ears down and her body covered, she could pass for a deformed rat.

It was the longest three blocks Nohar had ever walked.

They got to his apartment, and no ambush was waiting for them. Nohar breathed easier once he managed to unwedge the warped door and close it behind them.

Cat ran up, as usual, and seemed puzzled to find one of Nohar's shirts moving under its own power. When Angel lowered a hand, Cat shied away and hissed, but the moment she stopped paying attention to him, Cat attacked the end of her foot that struck out from under the edge of the shirt.

"Ouch! Shit, Kit; put a leash on it."

"*His* name is Cat. If you have an argument with his behavior, you have to take it up with him. He doesn't listen to me."

Cat backed up, crouched, shook his ass back and forth, and pounced on Angel's exposed toes.

Angel jerked her foot up and Cat tumbled back into the living room. She twitched her nose and snorted. "You think that name up by yourself?"

Angel unbuttoned the shirt and took it off. She tossed it so it landed on Cat. Cat found the shirt more absorbing than Angel's toes, and he started rolling across the living room floor buried inside it. Occasionally a paw would come out and swipe at the air. Angel made for the couch. Nohar went into the kitchen and filled a bottle of water. When he returned with it, she took the bottle and started drinking greedily.

By the time she'd finished her first bottle, Nohar had already made the trip for the second one. She drank this one more leisurely, and her story came out.

Angel had seen the sniper on the twenty-fourth, the stormy Thursday. "Ancient history now," she said. Stigmata still had a few loyal holdouts at the time. By then, though, the Zips had confined Stigmata's turf to the tower. War was about to break out all over. Everyone knew that. The Zips were going to vanish the remaining gangs. Only three were left—Babylon, Vixen, and Stigmata. According to Angel, Vixen's last shred of territory was the strip of Mayfield Road between Kenelworth and the concrete barrier, and Babylon was hunkered down in an enclave somewhere on Morey Hill.

Everyone was edgy. There was always someone watching, hidden behind a wall of rubble in the lobby. Angel, and the rest of them, wanted the chance to take some ratboys down with them. The twenty-fourth was her watch and Thursday was the night all hell broke loose. Angel thought Stigmata must've been the first of the mopup because the Zips must've realized there were only six members left.

The Zips weren't subtle about it. They announced their presence by having a burning station wagon rocket into the building. She told him car wrecks were a territorial symbol for the Zips. The wagon was loaded with explosives and went off in the lobby. Not enough to do any major damage, but enough to spook the whole building and knock Angel out before she could get warning upstairs.

She was only a few minutes, just long enough for her and the ratboys to miss each other. The rats had made their way upstairs and she could hear gunfire and fighting above her. The Zips had left three as rearguard to catch stragglers. Two brown males and a white female hung around the open stairwell. Angel said she wanted to be sure of taking down one particular rodent. They didn't know she was there, the fighting covered her noise and the garbage covered her smell. She aimed her Nicaraguan ten-millimeter at the white one's head. Their leader, Angel said.

She was about to lay a slug right between the white rat's eyes when the canine showed.

"This guy was a chiller, Kit. Should've seen that righteous weapon."

From Angel's description, that "righteous weapon" had to be a Levitt. It was two meters long, with a scope the length and twice the diameter of Angel's forearm. The canine was carrying the weapon in one hand, a tripod in the other.

The newcomer was out of place at the scene of a gang war. The way Angel described him, the genetechs that designed him were at least as advanced as the ones who produced Nohar's stock. That made the canine Pakistani or Afghan.

Nohar had a bad feeling that he had met this canine before.

Angel described a dog with the domestic veneer removed. The canine was lean and had a shaggy gray coat, prominent snout, green eyes. He stood about two meters and massed about 100 kilos. Angel said he looked mean enough to take a bite out of a manhole cover.

"He had a raghead accent. Walked right to Terin—the white one—and asked, 'Is the roof cleared?' Ain't going to forget him. You could smell my people getting whacked up topside, and I smell *him* when he passes me. He was getting off. The blood was turning him on something fierce.

"She calls him Hassan, Hazed, Hazy—something like that."

Damn it, it *was* Hassan. The same morey who offed Nugoya. Nohar shook his head. What the *hell* did a small-time pimp and a gang war have to do with Daryl Johnson and the franks running MLI?

"There's this mother of arguments between Terin and the pooch. The raghead is blowing my shot, standing right in front of me—"

"What were they arguing about?"

"Fuck if I know, Kit. Terin's pissed for some reason, like the dog is treading on her territory. She also rants about her best people being dragged off to the four corners of the country—hell and gone, she said. Dog's frosty, though—think he's got the handle on the Zip's supplier, guns and drugs. Terin can mouth off, but not do much. Pissed her good.

"After blowing off steam, she leads him up. There goes my shot. I might've written myself off to get Terin, but I wasn't about to give it up for two goons. I laid it low. Not that I wasn't tempted when they tossed Hernandez out a window, but not much I could do. I waited them out, hoping for another shot at Terin. Didn't happen."

Nohar was sitting on the floor across from Angel. Cat, half wrapped in the shirt, had tired of his game and had come to rest by Nohar. Angel was chugging her third liter of water.

"Thy caught up with you."

"Inevitable. They knew all of us. Snatched me by surprise—five to one, they like that kind of odds—up the Midtown Corridor. Wasn't in Moreytown so my guard was off. Was last Thursday—end of the month—the day after Vixen bought it."

Nohar remembered the burning Subaru and the dead foxes, both Wednesday.

Angel was still talking. "Surprised they didn't vanish me then and there. Upset I'd survived, more upset I had been at the tower when the raghead dog showed—someone saw me book outta there an' told the Zips. Terin wanted to know if I had told people, told her to fuck off. Pissed her good. Took me back to the tower an' pumped me with flush. Someone calling the shots said look like an O.D. That really pissed Terin. I could tell she wanted to off me painful. Must've been Friday when they left me. What day is it?"

"Sunday."

Angel yawned and stretched out on the couch. She barely filled a third of it. "Well, I'm getting some real sleep."

She fell asleep instantly.

They should have pumped another into her—but that would have looked like murder—and they were trying to make it look like an O.D.

Why? Because she'd seen the canine?

Again, what the hell did Zipperhead have to do with Daryl Johnson?

Nohar had a nasty thought—another morey uprising?

He shuddered at the idea. He'd been through that once already, when he was in the Hellcats. His own father had been shot, deservedly, by the National Guard.

"Don't let it be a political killing," Nohar whispered to Cat.

The express mail people had left a message for him. He'd have to come pick up his package of ID replacements, they didn't deliver to his neighborhood.

Nohar let Angel sleep when he went out. Once he got most of his wallet replaced, Nohar realized there was nothing for his guest to eat. Nohar did some hasty shopping down by the city end of Mayfield Road, around University Circle.

Then, now that he had a card-key replacement, he stopped at his office.

The Triangle office building was a crumbling brick structure that was still trying to fight off the advancing decay from Moreytown. The brick looked like a patchwork from the many attempts to remove graffiti. It was getting dark, and the timers had yet to turn on the lights inside. There was just enough light to give Nohar a slight purple tint to his vision. He climbed the stairs in the empty darkness. Nobody else was around this late on a Sunday.

His office lived in the darkness at the end of a second floor hallway. It didn't even have a number to distinguish it. The door was simply a fogged-glass rectangle with a basic card-key lock. Nohar ran his key through the lock and the door slid aside with a slight puff of air.

The room was barely big enough to hold Nohar, even though it only contained two items of furniture—a comm that was a few generations out of date, and a file cabinet that was older than the building it lived in. Nohar knelt down and punched the combination on the padlock that held the bottom drawer shut.

"Comm on."

There was a slight change in the quality of light in the room as the screen activated. This comm was mute, the synth chip had burned out a decade ago. He made sure the forwarding list was up to date, and got a bit of a surprise in the mail—a note from Stephie Weir. She'd found his listed number. It had been forwarded to his home comm while he was out. He played her message.

"Nohar, I need to talk to you. Can we meet for lunch tomorrow at noon? I'll be at the *Arabica* down at University Circle."

That was it. At least the joint she picked for the meet wasn't adverse to moreys. Although Nohar wasn't a great fan of coffee or coffeehouses, the college crowd seemed a little more tolerant.

He wondered what she wanted.

Nothing more interesting on the comm, so he opened the file drawer. It was nearly filled by a dented aluminum case, about a meter long by a half wide. The electronic lock on the case had long been broken, and there were scorch marks on that side. There was a painstaking cursive inscription on the lid that contrasted with the ugly functionalism of the box itself. The inscription read, "Datia Rajasthan: Off the Pink."

He pulled his father's case out of the drawer. The lock had been broken for nearly a decade, ever since Datia Rajasthan had been gunned down by a squad of National Guardsmen. Nohar'd gotten it a few weeks later when he split the Hellcats.

Nohar opened it. The seal was still good. The lid opened with a tearing sound as the case sucked in air and released the smell of oil. Nohar looked at the gun. The Indian military had manufactured the

Vindhya 12-millimeter especially for their morey infantry. A pink's wrist couldn't handle the recoil. It was made of gray metal and ceramics, surprisingly light for its size—the barrel alone was 70 centimeters long. The magazine held twelve rounds. There were three magazines in the case, all full. A dozen notches marred the composite handgrip.

He held up the gun and cleared it, checked the safety, and slid a full magazine in. The magazine slid home with a satisfying solidity. The Vindhya was in perfect condition, even after ten years of neglect. The weight was seductive in his hand.

Nohar had practice with guns before it was a felony for a morey to own a firearm, but he had never even taken this one out of its case.

There were two holsters in the drawer. He left the combat webbing and removed the worn-leather shoulder holster. Nohar had never worn it, but he tried it on now. It fit well, comfortably, and that disturbed him.

One final item—a file folder containing a sheet of paper and a card for his wallet. Both items were pristine, the card still in its cellophane wrapper. It was the gun's registration and his license to use it. They were still valid, despite the ban on morey firearms. He'd gotten them a year prior to the ban.

He put the card in his wallet, holstered the loaded gun, and, hot as it was, put on his trench. Nohar had brought the trench coat despite the fact there had been little threat of rain. He had brought it to hide the gun. He pocketed the two extra magazines and put the case back in the drawer. As he locked the drawer up again, he told himself he was never going to fire the thing, but he knew, if he'd really believed that, he would have never opened that drawer.

Nohar left the office, the gun an oppressive weight under his shoulder.

Angel was awake again when Nohar returned with the groceries. She began cursing in Spanish the second he opened the door. Nohar had thought he'd get back before she woke up. After an experience like she'd been through, she should have slept like the dead.

"We had a fucking deal, Kit—" More Spanish. "You don't leave me alone like that."

He ducked through the living room and into the kitchen, shucking the trench as he went. Cat followed Nohar, and the food, into the kitchen.

"You listening to me, Kit?"

The dry cat food was still covering the counter where he had spilled it last night. Nohar had forgotten the mess. He set down his bag and picked up Cat's dish. After rinsing it off, he swept about half the spilled food off the counter and into the dish. When he put it down, Cat pounced on the bowl, oblivious to the fact that it was filled with the same stuff that was on the counter.

Nohar decided he could afford the waste and brushed the rest of the spill into the sink and turned on the disposal.

Angel was leaning against the door frame. She looked a lot better. She had taken a shower, returning her dirty brown coat to its original light tan. Her ears had perked up, though even with them she was still over a meter shorter than Nohar.

She was jabbering in Spanish, and Nohar knew she wasn't saying anything nice.

He asked her what she wanted to eat.

She walked into the kitchen and looked into the bag. She was still angry, Nohar could smell it, but her tone was softening. "And I thought you *weren't* a cop."

"I'm not."

She squatted next to Cat. She was calming down, and Nohar began to realize exactly how scared she must have been when she woke up here alone. Angel was someone who wouldn't like being scared. It would screw with her self-image.

Angel was looking at Nohar's left armpit. "What about the sudden artillery?"

Nohar had forgotten the Vindhya. "Just because I have a gun—"

"That righteous? That fine? Something that worthy goes for 5K at least. Tell me you bought it."

She tried to pet Cat, but Cat was eating and couldn't be bothered. When Cat hissed at her, she stopped.

Nohar began putting away the stuff he'd bought, tossing a half-kilo of burger into the micro for himself. "I didn't *buy* it. My father brought it over from the war. Got it when he died."

She stood up. She wasn't argumentative anymore. She seemed to have gotten it out of her system. "Knew your sire?"

"It's not unheard of."

"Only morey *I* heard of with a set." She intercepted a bag of tomatoes he was putting in the fridge. "Even the rats make kids with a needle, and they're as common as fleas on a Ziphead. How'd two modified *panther tigris* ever get together to make you?"

The micro dinged at him and he pulled out the burger. Angel's nose wrinkled. She was vegetarian.

"Mother and Father were in the same platoon. He led a mass defection. The entire company of tigers, even the medic. Of all the cubs he must've made, I was the only one to track him down afterward."

From her expression he could tell he'd talked too much. "Hot shit, that *is* a Vind twelve. You're talking about the Rajasthan Airlift. You *knew* Datia—"

"Yes, I knew him, I don't want to talk about it."

Nohar took his food and ducked into the living room.

Angel followed, with her tomato. "Datia's a legend, the first real morey leader—"

Oh, that was great. A true leader. Nohar whipped around to face Angel. Cat was there to pounce on a spilled hunk of burger. "Datia Rajasthan was a psychopath. He needed to be gunned down, and if you so much as mention him one more time I am gong to hand-feed you to the Zips one piece at a time."

Angel just stared at him.

Nohar sat on the couch, ate a handful of hamburger, and turned on his comm to the news.

Chapter 11

Monday morning was breaking into a steel-gray dawn when the Jerboa pulled up in front of Young's shadow house.

"Wake up, Angel. We're here."

The rabbit, who'd looked like an inanimate pile of clothes until Nohar spoke, stirred. "Kit? Time is it?"

"Five after." Nohar stood up and stepped over the nonworking driver's side door. Young's house was the worse for wear. The garage had gone up like a bomb. The only remains of it was a black pile of charred debris at the end of the driveway. The house itself had caught. Nohar supposed some burning debris had landed on the roof.

There was a yawn from behind him that seemed much too large for the rabbit. "Five after what?"

"Six." The fire had gutted the house to the basement. The windows looked in on one large, black, empty, roofless space. The two neighboring buildings—Nohar hoped they had been unoccupied—had caught, too, but had escaped with relatively light damage.

"Six, Kit, this is no sane time to be awake—"

"You said that when I woke you up."

"Could have let me sleep—"

Nohar shook his head. "Not after that tirade yesterday."

Angel hopped over the door. She was dressed in an avalanche of black webbing and terry cloth that used to belong to Maria. The only clothing Nohar had for her. Somehow Angel had gotten the castoffs to fit her with a shoelace and a few strategic knots. The problem was, she smelled like Maria. "Couldn't wait till a decent hour?"

"Quit complaining. If I had a safe place to file you, I'd do it. For now, Your along for the ride."

Angel yawned again. Her mouth opened so wide it seemed to add twenty centimeters to her height. She shook her head and her ears flopped back and forth.

"So, what we doing here?"

Nohar started walking down the driveway. He could smell the gasoline. Even now, after at least one night of rain, there was still no question of arson. "I want to see if anything made it through the fire."

They passed the rear of the house, and the damage was much worse. The entire rear wall of Young's house had collapsed. The siding was sagging and puckered and bowed in the middle. Angel was only a few steps behind him. "Hope you're not talking architecture. This place is worse than the tower."

Nohar wasn't talking about architecture.

There's a difference between a supervised, methodical destruction of a body of records—Nohar was pretty sure Young was trying to torch, judging by the volume, close to everything in the Binder campaign finance records—and the accidental combustion Young had initiated. Something would have survived.

Apparently he hadn't been the only one to think so. He walked up to the spot where the garage used to be. The charred remains were in piles that were much too neat, and it looked like someone had gone through the ashes with a rake. "Damn it."

"What's the prob?"

Nohar waved at the garage, and expanded the gesture to take in the entire backyard. The rear lawn had been turfed by truck tires to the point that no grass was left. "Someone beat me here. Whoever it was, shoveled up everything Young didn't torch."

Nohar wasn't expecting to find *the* piece of evidence, but it would have been nice to find *something*. Angel was walking around the backyard, wide feet slapping in the mud. When he had looked for clothing for her, Nohar couldn't find a damn thing that even resembled a shoe for a rabbit.

"What am I looking for?"

Nohar was surprised Angel wanted to help. He supposed she was bored. "It was mostly paper. Some might have blown to the edges of the property where our trash-pickers missed it."

That was a bit of wishful thinking. The plot was bare of even normal garbage. Nohar supposed the people with the truck had grabbed everything that had even a slight chance of having been part of the records. They had a full weekend to work in. They were very thorough. Nohar wondered if they'd been the cops, or Binder's people, or MLI, or—

Nohar looked up from the edge of the driveway he was examining. "Angel? Do the Zips have any workings with a congressman named Binder?"

Angel's laugh was somewhat condescending. "Must be kidding. Zips and politics? Me becoming president'd happen sooner. All Zips want is a free hand to deal their flush."

Nohar shrugged. A connection seemed unlikely, but he couldn't deny the fact that there was a connection—somewhere. Hassan was involved with the Zips, and it looked like Hassan killed Johnson. But Hassan wasn't working for the Zips. If anything, it looked like the other way around.

"Were the run-ins with the other gangs because of the drugs?"

"Don't know about other folks, but my clutch was into protection—When you do, you have to protect people you charge. Both Zips and flush were pretty dangerous." She sighed. Her ears drooped. "Too dangerous for us."

She turned to face him. Her scar fighting the frown she wore. "Could've used someone like you back then, Kit."

Nohar didn't have a response for that. So he went back to his fruitless search.

By nine they had combed every inch of the property at least twice. The only result was part of a letter-fax Angel had found halfway across the street. It had been written by a gentleman named Wilson Scott, presumably to Binder or someone in the campaign. They only had the bottom half, so Nohar didn't know. It could be totally unrelated.

The letter went into detail on "the late morey violence." It got pretty down on the moreys, talking about moreys offing pinks, moreys taking hostages, morey air terrorism, and other generally alarmist topics.

Sounded like something somebody wrote during the riots. It was dated the tenth of August. Nohar wished he had a year to go with it. He also wished Scott didn't have a habit of writing in sweeping generalities.

With just half a hysterical polemic, the morning seemed to have been a waste of time. They didn't even had an address for Scott.

*   *   *

Nohar took Angel to his office with him. He wanted to make a few phone calls, now that people in the Binder campaign weren't on vacation. He would have liked the less-cramped atmosphere of his apartment. However, he figured the more he kept Angel away from Moreytown, the better off they both would be.

Even with Angel, the office wasn't more cramped. He lifted her up, and she fit on top of the filing cabinet, out of the way—and out of view of the comm . . .

Not that he intended to use the video pickup. He was going to try and bull through to the one living member of the Bowling Green gang of four he had yet to talk to. Edwin Harrison, the legal counsel.

Nohar's funeral picture had him sitting right next to Binder, front row, center. With Daryl Johnson's death, Harrison would be the most powerful man in the Binder organization, after Binder himself. In fact, Nohar remembered news off the comm had him as the current acting campaign manager.

The top, or close to it.

He killed the video pickup and hoped he could reach Harrison before anyone realized who was calling. Nohar also engaged in a slight electronic legerdemain. The outgoing calls he had been placing from his apartment had all been piped through his comm in his office. This was the listed one, his professional voice, so to speak. This was the comm everyone was locking out.

However, the process worked in reverse. He could pipe calls from the office through the unlisted comm at his home. They wouldn't be locking that out—yet.

It turned out to be easier than Nohar had expected. The strained voice and the strained expression on the secretary—from the obvious makeup, and the hair perfect as injection-molded plastic, she would fall into Stephie's category of window dressing—made it obvious she'd been operating the phones too long. Nohar could see lights blinking on the periphery of the screen. She had at least a dozen calls coming in. The way her eyes darted, she had at least four on the screen.

Nohar asked for Harrison. Her only response was, "Hold on, I'll transfer you."

The screen fed him the Binder campaign logo and dry synth music as he waited for Harrison's secretary to pick up the phone. It was a long wait and Nohar had to restrain the urge to claw something.

The call was finally answered, not by a secretary, but by Harrison himself.

Edwin Harrison had to be the same age as Young and Johnson. They had all been contemporaries out of college about the same time. But Nohar knew pink markings well enough to see the graying at the temples and the receding hair as some indication of premature aging. Harrison bore the slight scars of corrective optical surgery—Nohar had a brief wish his rotten day-vision could be corrected as easily—distorting his eyes. Under a nose that had been broken at least once, he had a salt-and-pepper brush of a mustache. There was no real way to estimate height over the comm, but Harrison looked small.

Harrison's shirt was unbuttoned and his face looked damp. The man was rubbing his cheek with one hand. Nohar figured he'd been shaving, a pink concept the moreau didn't understand.

Nohar found his polite voice. "Mr. Harrison—"

Harrison sat down in front of his comm. "Whoever you are, if you want to talk to me, you better turn on your video pickup. I can tell the difference between a voice-only phone and someone with a full comm who just doesn't want to be seen. I have no desire to spend a conversation with a test pattern when you can see me perfectly well."

So much for polite.

Nohar just hoped the guy was too long-winded to hang up immediately. He did as requested.

Harrison's reaction was immediate. In the same, level, conversational tone of voice, he said, "Holy mother of God, it's a hair-job."

Hair-job?

Nohar hadn't heard moreys referred to as hair-jobs in nearly a decade. "Can we talk?"

"Mr. Raghastan, correct?"

Nohar hated it when people mispronounced his name, even if it was only a generic label for that particular generation of tigers. Nohar nodded.

"I am sorry, but I have a very busy schedule. If you could make an appointment—"

So you can ignore me at your leisure, Nohar thought. *Not without a fight.* "I only have a few questions about Johnson and the campaign's financial records."

Harrison seemed to be indecisive about whether he wanted to be evasive or simply hang up. "I am sure you know any financial information that isn't a matter of public record is confidential. I can refer you to our press secretary. I am sure he can—"

—*brush me off as well as anyone in the campaign,* Nohar thought. "No, you don't understand. I don't want specifics." *A lie,* Nohar thought, *but there's little chance of getting specifics out of you, right? Right.* "I was just wondering how thorough Young was in torching the records." Harrison looked pained. "I am afraid I can't discuss Young. We are still dealing with the police on that matter."

Probably true. Trying to cover things up, no doubt.

"Your headquarters was closed down last week. I suppose Young just waltzed in and took what he wanted?"

From Harrison's expression, Young *had* just walked in. It also looked like Young had done a lot of damage.

"How many years back, five? Ten? Fifteen?"

From Harrison's face, fifteen.

"How much were you able to salvage?"

Harrison looked puzzled. "Salvage?"

Binder wasn't the one with the trucks. Nohar supposed there was little harm in telling the lawyer, and it might jar something loose. "I was under the impression you were in charge of the trucks that carted away the remains of the fire."

That got Harrison. "I am sorry. I really must go—"

I bet you must, Nohar thought to himself. He wondered exactly what kind of illegal crap was in those records that could turn Harrison white.

Harrison regained his composure. "I should tell you. Stay out of this—it doesn't involve you, or your kind."

As the connection broke, Nohar said, "But it does. More than you know, you little pink bottom feeder."

If *he* could pick up that much from Harrison's face, Nohar decided the lawyer would never win a jury trial.

There was a snore, and Nohar saw that Angel had fallen asleep on top of the filing cabinet. Instead of waking her up and leaving, he leaned against the wall and thought.

All that talk—well, all *his* talk— about Young had shaken loose a doubt. He was missing something, a big something.

Young's motivation.

It just wasn't your standard grief reaction to torch the finance records of your employer. Nohar could, even with Stephie's doubts, believe Young blew himself up over lost love. But why the records?

Slowly, it began to dawn on Nohar that he was missing the obvious.

True, Johnson and Young had been lovers, fifteen years, above average for any relationship, pink or otherwise. Young saw Johnson's killer—the morey canine Nugoya called Hassan—he probably saw Johnson get shot. *But Young never called the cops.*

Not only didn't he call the cops, but Young actually covered for the missing Johnson. Stephie said Young had mentioned Johnson was out with "some bigwig contributor."

Then, after a few weeks, he blows himself up.

Someone very purposefully removed almost every trace of the records Young had torched. If the motive for Johnson's assassination was in those records, the odds were they had been carted away by the people responsible for Johnson's death. There were four ways they could have known what Young had been trying to destroy. Binder's people, Young himself, or the cops could have told them. All unlikely.

Or, they told Young to destroy the records.

"You're not going to do me like you did Derry."

Fear. Young was scared when he said that. He was talking paranoid. "You're *all* with them." Moreys, he was talking moreys and—something else. Franks? MLI? Whoever *they* were, *they* were in charge of Johnson's death—and Young.

Young was afraid of *them.* Young was also pathological about Daryl Johnson taking the fall for something.

"Derry didn't know he was helping *them*—what *they* were. When he found out he was going to stop. . . . People will say he was working for *them.*"

Why that fear for Johnson's rep? If Young cared that much, why wasn't he at the funeral?

Guilt.

Nohar triggered Young's suicide: "You're the finance chairman. Why didn't you figure it out first?"

Then, blam.

Of course Young knew what was in the finance records. Nohar felt like an idiot for not realizing sooner. *Young* was the one to let in the canine assassin with the Levitt Mark II. Young was in a conspiracy with *them.* Somewhere there was a trail in the records. Johnson had found it and had confronted *Young* with it.

The two of them were close, but Johnson was going to put a stop to it, whatever *it* was. Young couldn't let that happen—no, not quite right, *they* couldn't let that happen. *They* hired the morey. *They* killed Johnson. *They* probably just told Young to turn off the security and leave the door open so *they* could explain things to Johnson. When Young blew up, *they* made sure the records vanished.

No way Young could call the cops. Whoever was handling Young must have forced him to go on, business as usual. Go into work, go back to his shadow house. All the while, guilt ate Young up. He felt responsible for Johnson's death.

The whole charade of blowing out the picture window was to cover *Young's* tracks. To give *Young* an alibi.

It was working so well—up to the point Young torched the records.

That seemed an act of desperation, and not just Young's desperation—

Nohar had a bad thought.

Thomson had mentioned Johnson's executive assistant, Stephie, as having the same access to the financial records as the gang of four. That was obviously just the "official" slant on things. After all, Stephie described herself as window dressing. What if *they* didn't know that?

That worried Nohar.

What if *they* thought Johnson's executive assistant knew something, and just weren't sure enough to go to the lengths they went with Johnson?

What if she was being watched?

Could it be a coincidence Young went ballistic the day after Nohar talked to her?

Could it be a coincidence that the white rat's—Terin's—"Finger of God" seemed to have lifted?

He called Stephie. No answer.

It was ten-thirty, an hour and a half before he was to meet her. Damn. Nohar clutched the filing cabinet and started deep breathing exercises. His concern had triggered the fight-or-flight reflex, the adrenaline was pumping. He wanted to fight something. It was still too soon after those Ziphead rodents behind the bus. Something inside him was responding to the pulse, the adrenaline, the stress—

He fought it off.

Nohar couldn't let his control slip like that.

He had barely brought himself back under control, when the comm buzzed.

Nohar told the comm. "Got it."

The comm responded.

Smith had the video on. He was as eldritch as ever. The glassy eyes still stared out of a flat, expressionless face in the center of a pear-shaped head. Moisture glistened on the rubbery-white skin. On the monitor, Nohar got a chance to examine Smith from a closer perspective than he really wanted to. The pear shape of the frank's head, Nohar now saw, was caused by a massive roll of flesh that drooped over the frank's collar. The roll of fat obscured any neck or chin the frank might have had. The frank was totally hairless, too, no hair at all, anywhere. No pores Nohar could see. The frank could have been a white polyethylene bag filled with silicone lubricant.

The reason the frank didn't blink was because he didn't have any eyelids.

Smith also didn't have any nostrils.

No ears either.

The frank was calling from an unlisted location, and the lighting only picked up the frank's white bulk, nothing of the background. "I am glad I see you mostly unhurt from when you go to Philip Young."

"Thanks." Nohar immediately noticed Smith's weird accent again. It was not Afrikaans. "Your message said you paid the hospital."

"It is a legitimate expense of the investigation."

"You want a progress report."

The frank attempted a nod, sending the flesh of his upper body into unnatural vibration.

Nohar told the frank what he knew and what he thought he knew. How Johnson was killed, who was involved, and, of course, the as yet nebulous why. Nohar had convinced himself, despite Young's unreliability, that the reason lay in the now-destroyed-and-or-missing financial records of the Binder campaign.

"Excellent progress in such a short time."

"Now let me ask *you* a few things." Nohar knew he had jumped into the case prematurely, and what bothered him most wasn't his involvement in a pink murder, or even his involvement with a murder, period. What bothered him was the absence of information on his client and his client's company.

"I render what aid I can."

"First, you're worried about MLI being involved in the killing, and you told me you're an accountant—what's in the campaign records that could have connected back to MLI?"

"Only our heavy financing of the Binder campaign. A connection our board informs me will be severed as of our last payment—the three million Binder is missing and we are not. Our only contact with the Binder campaign is our money and suggestions on appropriate votes to take on the issues before him."

Nohar snorted. Having a bunch of franks telling Binder what to do bordered on the absurd. "You dictated the way he voted in the House?"

"He never votes against us. Our support is based on his closeness to our views."

That *did not* ring true. A frank's views being close to Binder's? Binder was a little to the right of Attila, was for the sterilization of moreys and probably the outright extermination of franks.

However, the finance records *were* the only connection between MLI and Binder. That gave credence to Smith's suspicion someone in MLI was behind the killing. Since the money trail had been sitting tight that long—fifteen years back, the way Harrison acted—if the motive was in the records it was in some incredibly obscure financial tidbit where Johnson never would have seen it in the first place, or it was in those "suggestions on appropriate votes."

"Second, I want to know where you and the other franks at MLI *really* come from."

For the first time Nohar saw what could be the remotest trace of expression on the frank's face. *Close to a nerve.* The bubbling voice seemed just a little strained when Smith responded. "I told you. We come from South Africa—"

"South Africa never signed the U.N.'s human genome experiment ban—but it's just one non-signer of at least two dozen that have the technology. One of a half-dozen that uses it. That isn't an Afrikaans accent."

Smith let out a sound that could have been a sigh. "I do not know if I am glad or not I hire such a perceptive investigator."

"Don't compliment me on noticing the obvious."

"I am afraid this information I cannot give you."

"Oh, great—"

The sigh, it *was* a sigh, came again. "Please, I explain. Our origin must remain private. Just as we must remain unseen ourselves. It is for the company's survival. If MLI has a murderer, or murderers, in its midst, such secrets are public. But my loyalty will not permit such knowledge until I know if the guilt is there. If you can't pursue this without that information, I will let you go with the money you have earned."

Good, you have an out. Nohar stood there, staring. He told himself he was going to say to hell with it. Drop the whole mess then and there. . . .

He thought of Stephie.

He couldn't.

He had never ditched anything in the middle.

"You know you're hobbling me when you withhold information."

"I am sorry."

"I need copies of those 'suggestions.' "

"They're on file. I get them. At ten-thirty Wednesday night we meet in the cemetery."

"Comm off."

What in the hell did he think he was doing?

He should have dumped the case when he had the chance.

Chapter 12

The walk past the city end of Mayfield was nerve-racking for Nohar. His sudden concern for Stephie had hit a few buttons. He was passing Ziphead territory with Angel. He felt the gun was all too obvious under his green windbreaker, even though when he chose the jacket it had seemed up to the job of concealing the Vind.

It felt like there was a target strapped to his back and the weight under his arm didn't really help.

There were nor rats around, hadn't been since yesterday. That was becoming suspicious. There were always rodents around in Moreytown, even in daylight.

The streets were bare of them.

There was new graffiti under the bridge that separated Moreytown from the Circle. It was under the sarcastic, "Welcome to Moreytown." It read, "The Zipperhead rules here." The Zip graffiti was becoming too ubiquitous.

Nohar remembered the too-common slogan, "Off the pink," from the riots. A decade later, that slogan—Datia's slogan—had passed into general usage as a stock antiauthoritarian comment.

Nohar wondered if the people who used it habitually were consciously aware it was a call for human genocide.

It felt like he was in the Hellcats again and everything was about to explode into brimstone and shitfire. The feeling didn't leave after they passed the concrete pylons demarking the end of Mayfield Road.

The pink universe of Case Western Reserve University was only a few blocks from the farthest extension of Moreytown. The border was marked by the sudden shift into decent landscaping.

Angel turned toward him. "You feel safe, Kit?"

"No."

"Feel the shit's about to go ballistic?"

"You, too?"

"When the players absent all of a sudden, you know the situation is going to ground zero on you."

Nohar shrugged. "I've got a meeting to go to."

"Right. Whatever it is, it ain't us."

Nohar let it go with an insincere nod. He knew Angel didn't believe that. Neither did he. He didn't believe in coincidence. He thought it pretty damn likely the absence of Zips had a hell of a lot to do with them.

They made the coffeehouse at a little after twelve. The aroma of exotic, rare, and engineered coffees overwhelmed Nohar's sense of smell—at least it removed Maria's ghost-odor from Angel's clothes.

It was a college lunchtime crowd, with only one other morey—at least he and Angel weren't the only ones—a graying red vulpine who was engaged in a chess game with a black pink. Some of the patrons gave the new pair a few stares. Nohar, being a rather singular morey, got more than his share. Nohar was relieved to see Stephie in the back. She had chosen a table with enough room for him to maneuver around.

Nohar walked straight to the table and sat down. Angel hovered a second at the counter, until she seemed to realize she didn't have any money. Stephie was looking at Angel, but she directed her question to Nohar. "Who's your friend?"

"She's a lead from the Johnson killing."

"*She?*"

Sometimes pinks weren't quick on the uptake when it came to morey gender. Nohar supposed it had to do with the lack of prominent breasts.

Angel turned a chair around and sat on it backward. She rested her chin on the back, and scratched the base of her scar—her nose twitched. "Name's Angel, Pinky. Kit here's my bodyguard."

"Ah, hello. My name's Weir, Stephie Weir."

Odd, Nohar thought, now she *was* acting like he'd expect a pink to around morey. It was usually one of three things—fear, condescension, or this vague nervousness that was now spilling off of Stephie in waves.

"You wanted to talk. What about?"

She took her eyes off the rabbit and looked at Nohar. "I've been offered my job back—"

Nohar gave her a close-lipped smile. "Congratulations—"

Stephie interrupted him. "—aren't in order. It was conditional I didn't talk to you. That kind of job security I don't need. I've been let go once, like excess weight on a ballistic shuttle. I'm not going to be blackmailed into helping in a cover-up."

Angel chuckled. "Good for you, Pinky. Fuck the PTB."

Stephie looked confused. "PTB?"

Nohar felt his claws digging into the table. He untensed his hand and tried to stare Angel into shutting up as he explained. "P. T. B. Powers that be. Terminology from the riots— When did you get this offer?"

"After I gave you the lift from the hospital. It was waiting on my comm when I got back home. I never liked Harrison that much." She smiled now. "I called his house the minute I got the message. I got him out of bed at two in the morning to cuss him out and tell him what to do with his offer. He gave me a raise twice. I told him, at this point, not even if I supported Binder."

That nagged at something. The Binder campaign was riddled with that kind of inconsistency. "I want to know why the campaign has people like Thompson, Young, and Johnson in it."

"I never probed too deeply into that. I told you I was just window dressing. It was a money thing. I admit it. I sold out. They needed me for Derry. Anyway, there are precious few women in my age-group that are for Binder. Those that were might have had some principles."

He appreciated the fact she wanted to tell him about Harrison's offer. It also reminded him about his worries earlier today. "Who'd you tell about our meeting?"

Stephie shrugged. "No one, not even Harrison—though I was tempted to tell him he was too late with his little job offer. Just to make him stew."

Angel beat Nohar to the question. "Why not?"

Nohar glared at her as Stephie answered. "It's *my* business. Why should I have told him about it?"

There's the anger again, Nohar thought, *just like that lesbian comment.* It was laced with confusion, too, but less of it. It felt like she had come to some sort of decision.

Oh, well, let Stephie be pissed at the rabbit. "Stephie, you told no one?"

"Right."

"Not boyfriend, girlfriend, family, your mother?"

"I said, no one—" She gave a weak smile. "Not even my non-existent boyfriend."

Now Nohar had reason to worry. Young's self-destruction and the Zip attack on him had been just too well-timed.

"Someone found out. You're being watched."

"What?"

Nohar glanced at Angel, and gave Stephie the story. Nohar briefly wondered if he should be doing all this exposition in front of Angel, but she *was* involved in this—however tangentially—and she was getting the short end of it as well.

After the brief rundown, Stephie looked thoughtful. "You might be right. I think Phil could handle the strain of losing Derry. But if he thought himself responsible. If he actually *was* responsible . . ."

Stephie shook her head. "But I *do not* understand why you think the black hats from Phil's conspiracy are watching *me*. Of all people, I am—was—the least significant person in the Binder organization."

Angel dived in again. "Pinky, do *they* know that? Overheard your story, and the whole point was to make you look like honcho's squeeze *and* his second. Like, this is what pissed you in the first place, right? You just *looked* high-mighty when your *real* job was to make mister rump-ranger look like an upstanding pink hetro."

Angel was crude, but right. Nohar jumped in before Stephie could say something to Angel. "As Johnson's 'executive assistant,' you 'officially' had access to all the finance records Young torched. *They* might not realize your only function was to cover for Johnson's homosexuality. Also, Young started destroying records, not right after the murder, not when the body was found, not even right after the funeral. Young waited till nearly two weeks after the killing—"

Nohar leaned in for emphasis and tapped the claw of his index finger on the table. "He waited until the day after I talked to you."

"I see what you mean—"

"Hey, Kit. You smell something?"

Nohar looked at Angel. He was finally about to tell her to shut up, when he smelled it too. If it wasn't for the coffee, he would have noticed it immediately. Someone was wearing a very distinctive perfume. Nohar remembered the first time he had smelled it—in front of the ATM in Moreytown. It belonged to a female white rat.

Terin.

The Zipheads were here.

Nohar looked to the front. The front door was closing. As it did, the waft of sickening perfume died out. The fox was still the only other morey in evidence inside the coffeehouse.

"Terin?" Nohar asked Angel.

"Terin," she agreed.

The only change in the street was the car parked in front. It was a black ailing Jerboa, like Nohar's. Older and not a convertible. The windows had been painted black on the inside. Nohar heard the door slam on the car, and saw a hunched form run away from the vehicle. Nohar couldn't tell if it was pink, morey, or one of the Ziphead rodents. But Nohar remembered the Zips' trademark.

The driver was running away—

"Stephie, get down!"

Angel had already dived under a table. Nohar didn't wait for Stephie to reach cover on her own. He circled his left arm around her chest and slammed her against the far wall behind the table, putting him between her and the windows. His right hand went for the Vind.

For three seconds, Nohar felt real stupid.

Then the car exploded.

The windows weren't glass. They were some engineered polymer. They didn't shatter so much as tear and disintegrate. Then the air blew in carrying the heat and smoke of the blast. The pinks were yelling and screaming. Thankfully, Stephie wasn't one of them. Her face was buried in the fur of his chest.

The sounds began to fade as Nohar became too aware of his own heartbeat in his ears. He felt his pulse behind his eyeballs and in his temple.

He tried to fight it.

Nohar turned as soon as he realized there wasn't going to be a secondary explosion. He wasn't surprised to see four rodents diving through the now-open windows. The pinks didn't know squat. They had all hit the ground. The members of the gang advanced on the patrons, jumping overturned tables, kicking aside chairs.

Nohar was back in the riots again, watching one of Datia Rajasthan's terror runs on the pinks.

He was breathing heavily. Against his will, he could feel his time sense telescoping. Things were slowing down. His head throbbed as the adrenaline started kicking in.

A black rodent with a sawed-off shotgun was diving straight for their table. The room was hazed with smoke, and his eyes stung and watered, but Nohar knew Blackie was aiming at them. Nohar jumped to the side, hoping to draw Blackie's fire.

Nohar assumed he was the target.

He was wrong.

Blackie kept going straight for Stephie and leveled the shotgun at her.

The Beast kicked the door wide open, roared, and pulled the gun.

The Vind 12 slid out of its holster like it was on greased bearings. His thumb had clicked the safety as it cleared his windbreaker. He leveled the Vind about twelve centimeters away from Blackie's head and pulled the trigger.

The report deafened Nohar.

It did worse to Blackie, who had started to turn when he realized Nohar was armed. The bullet caught Blackie in the face, under the right eye. Datia's bullets weren't the standard Indian military teflon-coated armor-piercers. They were twelve-millimeter dumdums, strictly antipersonnel. The bullet carried away half of Blackie's head out of the back of his skull.

Time was moving incredibly slowly. It seemed there was a full second between each heartbeat, but Nohar knew his heart was running on overdrive and trying to jackhammer out of his rib cage. His nerves were humming like an overloaded high-tension wire.

He had whipped around to face the other Zipheads before Blackie hit the ground. The rodents, who had been about to lay waste to the pink population, were all looking in his direction. One of them had an Uzi nine-millimeter. The rat had been facing the wrong way, and as only now swinging the gun toward Nohar.

The Vind was already pointing in Uzi's direction.

Three shots in rapid succession. One for each heartbeat in the space of a second. Nohar's aim wasn't great. The first shot went high. Nohar corrected and the second went low, taking out Uzi's right knee and knocking the rodent sideways—sending the gun sailing over the counter. Third correction got Uzi right in the chest as the rat was spinning. The shot took Uzi off his feet and slammed him down nearly two meters back toward the smoking window.

There was a pop, it sounded like someone breaking a light bulb. Someone rammed what felt like a white-hot knife into Nohar's right hip. The warmth spread down his leg, soaking into his fur.

The rats were unfreezing.

One had a familiar-looking twenty-two revolver. Wasn't Fearless. As Nohar turned, the popgun fired again. Nohar felt a breeze on his cheek, brushing his whiskers as a supersonic insect grazed his neck. The Vind swung at the rat with the popgun and Nohar saw one of the Zipheads had a forty-four. Forty-four had a nice, expensive Automag. Problem was, the rat must have been used to revolvers. He seemed to have forgotten about the safety.

The Vind stopped on the dangerous one and unloaded four rounds as Twenty-two popped off another shot that missed.

Forty-four got it in the gut twice, once in the neck.

Twenty-two ditched his gun and ran for the window, diving.

Nohar had a perfect shot and three bullets left. He almost pulled the trigger.

The door creaked shut on The Beast. Reluctantly.

The front of the *Arabica* coffeehouse was now obscured by smoke from the burning car. Pinks were making for the exits. Nohar's hearing was coming back and he could hear the fire alarms wailing. The sprinklers came on.

Unlike most everyone in the room, with the exception of Angel, Nohar had been through shit like this before. It wasn't over.

"Angel, you still with us?"

A table turned over and Angel climbed out. "Yeah, Kit."

"Grab Blackie's shotgun, cover our rear."

"Gotcha."

Stephie, like most of the other pinks, had yet to react. She was still staring at the rodent whose head had done a halfways vanishing act in front of her.

"Stephie, rear exit."

She turned toward Nohar with a blank expression. The crash was already hitting him. He didn't need to deal with this. He grabbed her and shook her a little too hard. "You know this place, where's the back door? They're only hesitating because they didn't expect a gun in the crowd!"

Angel had the shotgun. She was leveling it at the windows. "That Vind ain't a gun, it's a howitzer. Kit, I got two shots—and the way this shotgun's been treated, lucky if it don't blow up."

"Exit!"

Stephie was finally getting a grip on herself. She started back to the rear of the place. Nohar was grateful. She wasn't one of those pinks that suddenly collapse at the sight of blood and violence. And thank whatever deity, she didn't suggest waiting for cops.

"Here."

The rear of the shop was, for the most part, covered with old sacks and bags that used to hold coffee. At this end of the store, the bean smell overrode even the smoke. Stephie pulled aside one of the bags. Behind it was a short hallway with a public comm and restrooms, terminating in a fire exit.

They piled in, Nohar first. For the first time since he had broken free from the adrenaline high, he realized the hole in his right hip was more than minor. The engineered endorphins were wearing off. Felt like someone was holding a hot iron on his leg. "Stephine, you drive here? Where'd you park?"

"Lot behind the building. Were they after *me?*"

Nohar pressed himself against the fire door and peered through the one small pane of cracked yellow glass. "Blackie went straight for you. The Zips are hooked into the Johnson killing."

"If they've been watching, they know my car."

"Pink has a point. Zips are real fond of burning transport." Angel paused because the chaos in the front room had just upped a notch. Nohar thought he could hear the sound of distant sirens. "We best vanish ourselves, quick."

Nohar had been scanning the parking lot, looking for the Antaeus. The huge Plymouth was hard to miss. Especially with the rat fumbling over the open hood to the power plant. Nohar grunted. His temple was pounding and there were little flashes of color interfering with his peripheral vision. Keeping his concentration focused while he slid the downside ride from that violent high was giving him a migraine.

"Bad news, you're right. They're wiring the car. Angel, cover me and be quiet."

"Gotcha, Kit."

Lucky, lucky. They were lucky because the Mad Bomber didn't quite seem to have a handle on what he was doing. Lucky because there weren't any other rats in the back. Mad Bomber was supposed to be the rearguard. Apparently the Zips gave him too much to do.

Nohar didn't rely on stealth, but Bomber seemed oblivious. Nohar closed the space between him and the rat in five running steps—each lumbering step drove a spike into his hip—and leveled the gun at the back of Bomber's head. By then, the rat knew something was up.

Mad Bomber was in the process of turning around. Nohar cocked the Vind and clucked his tongue at the rat. "Car has a wonderful finish, I wonder if you'll see the brains leave your head in the reflection?"

"Wha?" The wave of fear that floated off the rat was gratifying.

"Undo it, now. Or we're walking and you're on permanent vacation."

"Yeah . . " The rat started taking things out of the power plant. Too slow, the sirens were getting louder.

"Remember, fifteen seconds and you're going to start the car."

Bomber hurried, ripping other things out of the power plant. Nohar hoped the rat knew the wires he was pulling.

Mad Bomber finally came out with what looked like an Afghani landmine. It had Arabic markings on it.

Bang form behind them.

Angel called back as the smell of cordite and blood drifted over. "Kit, that's one shot. Hurry up, pink law's coming!"

Nohar kept his eye on the rat. It was becoming hard to keep his vision focused. He had all his weight on his left leg. "You heard the rabbit, hurry up. That sound back there was your backup."

"Done, it's done . . "

Mad Bomber was shaking now. Nohar could see why he didn't get the job of diving in on the pinks. The rat couldn't handle it. He was going to die. Not from the cops or another gang's guns. He was going to die from his own stupidity—or the gang would kill him itself. Nohar waved the two females over.

"Some advice. Quit the gang before you make a fatal screwup. Take the mine, stand over there."

Nohar motioned with the gun and Mad Bomber did meekly as told. Angel ran up, Stephie in tow, and leveled the shotgun at the rat. "Shell left, let me vanish the ratboy."

At east she asked. "Self-defense, no preemptive strikes." The migraine was getting worse.

"Fine with me, Kit. Saves the ammo."

Stephie eased behind the wheel and Nohar hustled Angel into the passenger side. Bomber was still blubbering under the stare of the Vindhya, but he managed to say something. "You said I would start the car . . "

"I lied."

Nohar dived into the back seat. The fire in his hip totally blacked out his vision when he hit the seat. As Stephie floored the Antaeus, the door slammed shut. Nohar heard the cables tearing out of the metered feed. He hoped they had some jumpers in the trunk or they'd only have one full charge to go on. A car this size didn't go far on one charge.

They were topping sixty klicks per as they jumped the curb on to the Midtown Corridor. Nohar's sight came back a little as he watched the destruction from out the rear window. Smoke billowed out from the car in front of the *Arabica*. Black, brown, and white rodents were bugging out of the place, heading toward Moreytown. All attention was riveted on the coffeehouse, or the flashers coming from the east. Except—

Two moreys in an off-road four-wheeler, the kind of thing you needed to drive into Moreytown past the barriers. With the speed the Antaeus was going and his pain-shot vision he could only make the types. White rodent, grayish canine. Terin and Hassan, had to be. Terin was aiming what had to be military binocs at them.

Nohar gave her the finger.

Stephie called back to him. "Where are we going?"

After telling Angel to make sure they weren't being followed, Nohar gave her an address on the West Side that, in Manny's words, was about as far from Moreytown as you could get.

With luck and a pink driving, they might not get stopped by the cops.

Chapter 13

Nohar woke up somewhere on the Main Avenue bridge. Someone had bandaged his hip. Maria's clothing was pulled tight on his leg and seemed to have stopped the bleeding.

The Antaeus was tailing a three-trailer cargo hauler out the other side of downtown Cleveland. The car was surrounded by the towering structures of the West-Side office complex. The sun glared off the acres of mirrored glass—it felt like they were traveling through a giant microwave. Nohar's eyes hurt. It felt like someone was squeezing them in time to his pulse. Nohar's blackout had lasted nearly fifteen minutes, and his migraine was still sending streaks of color across his field of vision. His hip still throbbed.

He tried to focus out the rear window, but his vision was too blurred to make out any details on the cars behind the Antaeus. He did a self-inventory and found himself in less than ideal shape. He had bled all over the back seat, despite Angel's—at least he hoped Angel had done it, Stephie shouldn't have stopped the car—field dressing. The twenty-two had only grazed his neck, opposite his bad shoulder, but the shot that clipped his right hip felt like it had ripped out a good chunk of meat. It felt like someone was running a drill bit in the joint. Between that and the sprained knee, his right leg was nearly immobile.

He didn't remember doing it, but somewhere along the line he had cleared, safetied, and holstered the Vind. Stephie was still driving. Angel still had the shotgun. Fortunately, Angel wasn't stupid and kept the gun down in the foot-well out of sight of neighboring drivers. Armed moreys usually didn't even get a warning from cops. . . .

Angel was the first to notice him revive. "Kit, how you doing back there?"

"I'll live." Nohar tried to get into a sitting position. His groan got Stephie's attention.

"Nohar, I've been trying to tell Angel here that we've got to get you to a hospital. She stopped the bleeding, but—"

"No pink hospitals."

"Pinky, Kit's in charge. He said West 58th, we do West 58th. You don't break command structure if you wanna live."

"Nohar, you're wounded."

He grunted and finally shoved himself up into a sitting position. He could feel the bones grinding together in his hip. "Don't worry about me. We're going to the house of the best combat medic that was ever in the Afghan theater. Be worried about someone following us."

Angel turned around and wrinkled her nose. "Moreys this far west shine, Kit. We've not been stopped only 'cause Pinky's driving. The off-roader with Terin in it paced us halfway up the Midtown Corridor. Quit when they figured we were headed downtown."

"Stop calling me Pinky."

"Hey, Kit, we got a sensitive one here—"

The byplay was getting on his nerves. "Angel, did anyone ever tell you you don't know when to shut up?" Nohar's vision was still blurred, but the colors weren't washing over as badly. He thought he caught a hint of a smile play around the edge of Stephie's mouth. He wondered exactly what kind of conversation the two of them had been having while he was blacked out.

"Sorry, Pin—I'll quit. What's your name again?"

Stephie made an abrupt lane change that shot them around the left of the cargo hauler. They rocketed out in front of the truck to the blare of its horn. "The name is Stephanie Weir. I would like it if you call me Stephie."

"Sure, Stephie . . ."

The Antaeus pulled off the bridge and on to Detroit Avenue. In the space of one city block the glass monoliths gave over to old brick warehouses with dead windows. Even the few places that were in use were aged black. They passed the first Ohio City marker and they were in Manny's neighborhood.

Nohar pointed to the side of the road, next to a whitewashed building that held an unnamed bar that was just opening. "Pull over."

"What?"

"We pull over and wait for our shadows to catch up with us."

"Kit, I told you they pulled—"

"Angel, the Zips aren't the only ones in on this."

Stephie pulled over. "Now what?"

"We hunch down, out of sight."

"If you say so." Stephie crouched in the foot well with Angel. Nohar eased back into a prone position.

Nohar looked back the way they had come. At the height of lunch hour, in this part of town, traffic was dead.

It only took half a minute for their shadow to show up. An unmarked industrial-green Dodge Electroline, programmed or remote-driven, was moving down Detroit. It paused, hazards on, directly across form them and stayed there for nearly a minute. Then it accelerated and took the next right. Nohar figured it was about to perform some sort of search pattern.

Angel shook her head. "What now? And where did that come from?"

"Now, we walk and avoid the pattern that remote is running."

Stephie was pulling herself out of the foot well. "What about your leg?"

"I'll manage—"

Nohar felt a little more warmth ooze down his leg. He pressed the bandage and tried to get adequate pressure on the wound. "Van's from Midwest Lapidary Imports, I think. The company involved in this mess."

He pulled the shirt tight and winced. "Ditch the shotgun, let's go."

He hobbled out and his leg nearly buckled. In the daylight, his leg was soaked from the hip down, and his denim pants were beginning to adhere to his fur. He could put weight on it, but the bloodstains could be seen from a block away. Nohar was getting the feeling any halfway decent search would turn them up. They were too damn conspicuous.

He just hoped nobody called the cops on them.

He led the way through a vacant lot across the street from the bar, down an alley between two warehouses, through someone's cracked-mud backyard, across a narrow brick dead-end street, through a gaping hole in a rusted chain link fence, over the rotting ties that were the only remains of the abandoned train tracks, and finally into an alley that led behind some residential garages.

When he stopped, he had to look down to make sure his leg didn't end in a ragged stump. Angel spoke.

"Lady above, Kit. You know this place better than my runners knew Moreytown. And this place is solid pink—"

Nohar paused a second to catch his breath. "Angel, the divisions aren't clear as they seem to be when you're in Moreytown. I used to *live* up here."

Stephie asked, "Open housing policy?"

Nohar snorted and rubbed his leg. "Call it no housing policy and a relative absence of lethal anti-morey violence. By the way, we're here."

Nohar hooked a thumb at the rear wall of the garage they had stopped behind. Carved in the wall, amid a host of childish doodles and vertical claw marks, was some blocky lettering. "Nohar and Bobby, 2033," The threes were carved in backward.

Stephie was tracing the old carving. "Who was Bobby?"

"First and only pink friend—Let's get inside."

Nohar limped off around the garage. Manny's van was gone. Manny probably wouldn't be back until late afternoon or evening. When Nohar thought about it, he had probably contributed a lot to Manny's current caseload.

The side door was locked—in this neighborhood, predictable. Nohar rang the call button. He was right. Manny wasn't home. Angel and Stephie were rounding the side of the house. He called out to them. "This place has an old key lock, if you check the loose clapboard under the vehicle feed in the garage, you'll find a spare."

Nohar didn't add the "I hope" he felt. It had been nearly fifteen years since he'd had occasion to use the spare key. Luck was with them. Stephie came back with the key in hand.

Nohar let them in.

It was close to seven-thirty and they were all waiting for Manny in his living room .Nohar sat on his windbreaker to avoid leaking blood on the furniture, while Stephie and Angel watched the news off the comm. News wasn't great. The attack on the coffeehouse resulted in three dead—all rodents—and the local news called it a morey gang war. Great.

Even better were the reports of similar, and more deadly, incidents on the fringes of morey communities in New York, Los Angeles, and Houston. All had the car bomb tie-in. All Honduran rats.

Reports were still coming in, they said, about unconfirmed attacks in San Francisco, Denver, and Miami. Everyone made connections back to the "Dark August" of 2042. Eleven year anniversary of the first riots in Moreytown, also on a Monday, August 4. Nohar didn't need the reminder.

What really freaked the pinks was the obvious coordination between all the incidents. Same gang name. Same M.O. The Zips could have done no damage whatsoever, and the pinks would still freak.

The mall in New York was the worst. All four Zips there had automatic weapons, and the car bomb was a bit nastier than most. The vids had panned with loving attention to every body-bag.

Angel had overheard Terin complaining about her best people being dragged to the four corners of the country. While all the attacks were violent and bloody, the news never mentioned more than four rats involved in any one attack. Thirty rats, max. All heavily armed, supplied with explosives, and timed to the minute.

Terrorism staged to be a media event.

The whole situation made Nohar sick to his stomach. "A decade out of the hole, and a bunch of psychopaths push us back in."

Angel stared at the screen. For once, her wiseass attitude was gone. "Kit, hell the Zips trying to do? Why?"

"Wish I knew."

"Binder's moreau control bill is going to make it through the House."

Angel turned toward Stephie. "Huh?"

"The bill shuts down moreau immigration and starts mandatory sterilization."

Nohar shut off the bodies on the comm. "We're on the wrong side of another anti-morey wave. The riots all over again."

Angel let out a nervous laugh. "Come on, Kit. You were there, this ain't nothing like the riots."

Stephie responded for him. "All you need is some media terror and Congress will jump on the bandwagon. It seems almost engineered to push Binder's legislation."

The front door interrupted their conversation. A very tired-looking mongoose entered the living room. Manny glanced at Stephie, then Angel, and finally Nohar. He seemed beyond the ability to register surprise. He was still wearing his lab coat, and a ghostly odor of blood, death, and hospital disinfectant was following him.

"You stupid bastard, why aren't you in a hospital?"

Nohar was still wearing the Vind, but from Manny's attitude, more concerned than angry, Nohar knew Manny hadn't connected him with the rodent attack yet. Guiltily, he didn't explain.

Manny released a whistling sigh from his front teeth. "I wonder what would happen to you if I wasn't a medic. Can you walk?"

"I got here, didn't I?"

"That's not what I asked. How long have you been sitting there?"

Manny had a point.

Nohar tried to get up, but a shivering wave of agony rippled up the entire right side of his body. He collapsed on the floor, pulling the bloody windbreaker after him. Both women underwent a brief panic, but Manny shooed them away as he pulled out a sheet and laid it on the floor. It took all three of them to help roll Nohar on it.

"I hope you've already written off the clothes . . ."

Manny walked out of the living room and in to the kitchen where he kept his medical equipment. Manny came back with a loaded air-hypo and a medical bag. He set the hypo down, next to the sheet.

"Introduce me to your friends." Manny started shredding Nohar's jeans with a pair of scissors.

Nohar tried to ignore the pain of the clotted blood tearing out his fur. "Angel, Stephanie Weir, the doctor doing violence to my pants is Manny, Mandvi Gujerat."

Manny nodded. "Pleased, I'm sure."

Angel twitched her facial scar. "You were really a combat medic?"

Manny had laid open Nohar's pants leg and was examining the remains of Maria's shirt that still bound the gunshot wound. "Five years in the Afghan frontier before New Delhi got nuked—You, Stephanie? Hand me those forceps." Stephie removed them from the bag. Manny took the forceps from her and used them to start peeling away the outer layer of the makeshift bandage. "Nohar, if it wasn't for that engineered metabolism of yours—"

Manny shook his head at the mess of Nohar's hip. "No, forget it, I'm not going to get through to you anyway."

Manny stood up. "I'm going to wash up. I've got to do some cutting and stitching on this obstinate lump of stupidity." He looked at Angel. "You know, when this bastard was six, he broke his arm and forced me to set it myself? A compound fracture yet . . ."

Manny left the living room and soon there was the sound of running water from the kitchen. Stephie looked at Nohar. "What is this with you and hospitals?"

Nohar looked down at the gory mess on his right hip and suppressed a shudder. "I don't trust them—"

Manny came back, pulling on a pair of gloves. "Yes, he'd rather trust himself to my floor. Who needs a sterile environment?"

Manny turned to Angel. "Pick up that hypo I brought in here?"

Angel did as she was asked. Manny turned to Stephie. "It's probably a futile gesture, but would you tie on my mask?"

Stephie tied the conical face mask around Manny's muzzle, muffling his voice. "Angel, can you handle that thing?"

Angel nodded and there was a mumble behind Manny's mask that sounded like, "Doesn't surprise me."

In a louder voice trained to be heard from behind a jaw immobilized behind the restrictive mask, Manny told Angel to empty the cartridge into Nohar's arm. Angel rolled up Nohar's right sleeve, there was a slight sting, and the world floated away.

Chapter 14

Nohar had an intense fear he would wake up in a hospital.

However, no disinfectant assaulted him when he awoke. He could smell alcohol, a much sharper and cleaner scent. There was also the faint coppery rust smell of his own blood. There was the dry dusty smell of old cloth and paper.

And the nearby was the smell of roses and wood smoke.

Nohar opened his eyes.

He was in the attic. His old room still had no air-conditioning, and should have been hotter than Hades—but the omnipresent rumble and the breeze through his whiskers told Nohar the old ventilation fan still worked, pulling a crosswind through this two–room insulated oven. His eyes quickly shifted into nocturnal monochrome.

Her scent had betrayed her presence. Stephie Weir was asleep in a claw-scarred recliner across from Nohar's bed.

He gave the room a brief scan and was thankful Manny wasn't overly sentimental. The chair and the bed were the only remains of his old furniture. The attic was now a haven for boxes, old luggage, and older clothes.

Nohar's gaze lit on the small end table that jutted out the side of the antique headboard. After a decade and a half, the table was still familiar. Nohar remembered the scratches that marked its surface. His name and idle crosshatches had clawed through five layers of paint to reveal the black finish underneath. The desk lamp was still clamped to it, still with three or four knots of electrical tape holding the cord together.

Orai's picture was still in its cheap gold-plated frame, cocked at an obsessively perfect forty-five degree angle toward the bed. Its lower edge rested in a groove worn in the last two layers of paint. The gold was flaking and rust spots dotted the gray metal beneath. The glass was hazy with dust and, in the dark, Nohar could barely make out the picture.

Nohar sat up on the edge of the bed—his hip objected, but only slightly—and turned on the desk lamp which, to his surprise, still worked. Now he could see the picture. In it, Orai was in her combat harness, but unarmed. She was center frame and holding up one end of an American flag. The other end was being held by some friend from her unit. In the background he could see the Statue of Liberty and part of the Manhattan skyline. Orai and her friend, both tigers, were smiling, totally oblivious to the show of teeth. Orai was already beginning to show her pregnancy. The writing on the old picture was faded a bit, though the picture itself was still in good shape. It read, "Rajasthan Airlift—March 2027."

Nohar sighed.

He realized Stephie was awake now. She was leaning forward in the recliner, probably trying to get a glimpse of the picture. Nohar didn't know what to feel about that. It was a personal part of his life. But Stephie was just sitting there. She seemed to know it was his decision to tell her . She didn't ask.

Nohar realized he liked this pink woman.

He handed her his childhood icon. "She's the one on the left."

Stephie took the picture. "Who is she?"

"My mother. She was already pregnant when the company defected. Her name was Orai."

Stephie's eyes raised from the picture. "You used the past tense."

Nohar was about to evade the question, but why shouldn't she know? He cleared his throat. "Died when I was five, just old enough to remember. She'd gotten inseminated, wanted to give me a little brother or sister. She'd saved for the procedure since getting to the States. Things went fine. Then, three months in, she went for a prenatal checkup—" Nohar sucked in a breath. "Those *damn* idiots at the Clinic—do you know what Pakistani gene-techs had done with feline leukemia?"

Stephie shook her head. The color drained from her face.

Nohar went on. "Those doctors didn't know either. They misdiagnosed a Jaguar, put him in with the other felines, including Orai." Nohar's voice cracked a bit. He brought it under control. "They *could've* quarantined the Jaguar. But they don't give moreys private rooms. Every feline in the ward started dying. *Then* they knew. She was near to term. She died miscarrying two cubs—"

Nohar fell silent. There wasn't much left to say. He closed his eyes and tried to remember when he had told anyone that story in full. No one came to mind. Not even Manny, though Manny knew the story well enough.

The smell of smoky rose was suddenly very close, and Nohar felt a tiny naked hand on his cheek, brushing his whiskers. He opened his eyes and saw Stephie's face, close to his own. Her breath was warm on the skin of his nose. Her eyes were liquid green nothing like the eyes of a cat—visible whites, tiny round pupils.

Nohar had never realized how alien human eyes were.

Her lips parted in a whisper. "Lord, how you must hate humans."

Nohar shook his head. "No, no hate. Not for people."

The hand left and Stephie replaced the picture, in its groove and at its forty-five degree angle. She did it in one fluid motion, stretching across Nohar to replace the picture. Again Nohar found himself admiring her muscle tone and her economy of movement.

She sat down next to him on the bed. The springs barely noticed her weight. Her nervousness was back. Just like at the table at the *Arabica*. She shook her head and looked up at him. Nohar wished once again that he was better at reading human expression.

"Nohar, would you tell me, who's Angel?"

Back to business. "I told you, she's a lead. She saw the sniper—"

Stephie was shaking her head again. "Not what I meant. I want to know who she is *to you*."

Huh? Maybe not. "What? Only met her yesterday— We sure as *hell* aren't lovers. If that's what you mean."

Stephie turned a bright red. She clenched a fist that made her knuckles whiten. "I'm sorry, forgive me. I didn't mean to offend—"

Nohar got a sensation he often got when talking with humans. There were two different conversations here. Stephie was, he felt, about to bolt off somewhere and cry. He didn't want to be responsible for that, even if he didn't understand what was going on. He placed his hands on her shoulder. Nohar didn't know how to do this gracefully, so he just told her the truth. "I *wasn't* offended. But the idea of having relations with that little twitch is ludicrous."

Nohar could tell Stephie almost laughed. She was still flushed.

"Why ask?"

Nohar could sense a slight tensing of her muscles under his hand. "Angel was bragging all the time while you were unconscious. I just wondered, you're such different . . ."

Ah. "Different species? I'd admit, me and her, it would be unusual, but not unheard of."

"Isn't that bestiality? Would it be possible?"

"Some human taboos, like nudity, can't wash with moreys for practical reasons."

Stephie was still looking up at him, and Nohar realized he'd only answered half the question. "And, uh, some morey characteristics came out the other end of the labs remarkably similar. I think it might be linked to bipedal . . ." He trailed off.

Great, no *he* was getting embarrassed.

Stephie had a questioning look in her eyes. The flush was fading. "Who *do* you have, Nohar?"

Nohar thought of Maria. "No one, anymore."

"You're lonely, aren't you?"

He would have objected, but he had trouble lying to people he felt something for. He nodded. "You?"

They faced each other, on the bed. He was feeling her breath on his nose again. No longer warm, hot. Beads of perspiration were forming on her forehead. Her voice was a whisper. "My nonexistent boyfriend." She tried to laugh, but it died. "No girlfriend either."

"Why did you get so upset when I asked if you were a lesbian?"

"Too close to what I was feeling."

They were very close now. He could feel her pulse under the hand that still rested on her shoulder. It was incredibly rapid, like her heart belonged to a kitten or a small bird. His heartbeat was racing to catch up with hers. Her sweat was beginning to lend a tang to the air that was alien to him, one he liked. What was going on had dawned on him gradually, and a small part of his mind was screaming at him, asking him what the hell he was doing. It wasn't the time for that question.

Her alien—human—eyes were staring deep into his own. "You saved my life. Have you ever heard of Chinese obligation?"

Nohar had. "I'm responsible for you now."

She sucked in a shuddering breath, and her lips touched his. He had seen kisses in human videos—but a feline skull and lips didn't move the right way for it. Even so, he tried. He let her small lips part his mouth and felt her amazingly smooth tongue alight on his own, caress one of his canines, and withdraw, to be felt, briefly, under his nose. When her eyes opened, the nervousness was gone.

Nohar, what are you doing? He ignored the questioning voice because he needed her, human or not. He moved his hand up from her shoulder and undid the bonds that were keeping her hair in a ponytail. He nuzzled the top of her head, thankful not to smell any heavy chemicals, and began to groom her hair. The taste and texture of her human hair was different from Maria's fur. The ritual perhaps seemed as strange to Stephie as kisses did to Nohar.

When Nohar had cleaned her hair, he began to move to her ears and the back of her neck. He expected the taste and feel of naked skin to repulse, but it was quite the opposite. The sweet acidic taste of her sweat and the smooth surface of her walnut-colored skin was beginning to excite him.

The questioning voice shut up.

By the time he had reached her shoulders, he realized she did have fur, of a sort. Tiny, downy hairs were scattered over her arms and her back. Somewhere along the line, he didn't know where, her blouse had disappeared.

They both reclined on the bed as Nohar worked his way down her body. He groomed both her arms. Her skin broke into a burning flush under his tongue. He cleaned the small puddle of perspiration that pooled between those odd human breasts. When he cleaned her breasts, she began to moan loudly. Nohar thought he was too rough, so he lightened the pressure. Stephie immediately responded by locking her hands in the fur on either side of his head and pulling his face back down.

He worked his way down her abdomen. She continued to urge him lower with her hands—

Humans kept their hair in the strangest places.

When Nohar could no longer restrain himself he rolled over on his back, ignoring the pain in his hip, and pulled her on top of him. She drew him in and shuddered, arching her back.

Nohar added his voice to hers.

It took them a long time to expend each other.

Nohar awoke.

He could still smell Stephie—between them they had drenched the bed with their scent—and he realized it wasn't a dream. Now was the time to ask the question. He opened his eyes and whispered, "Nohar, what the hell are you doing?"

The desk lamp was still on. The small fluorescent tube was now overwhelmed by the morning light. Stephie was curled up next to him. Her head rested on his chest, spilling her black hair across his upper body. It contrasted with the areas where his russet stripes faded to near-white. In the sunlight, where his color vision reached its optimum, he could appreciate the similarity of their coloring. Her black hair and golden-tan skin formed a near-perfect match to the shading of his stripes. They both had green eyes—

He had been perfectly prepared to blame last night on the emotional pit he had fallen into. But when he considered the way he was watching the light from the window curve its shadows around her tailless rear, he couldn't blame that night on any temporary condition.

Stephie stirred, and turned to face him. "Morning."

"Do you realize how much this complicates things?"

He could feel her twisting the tip of his tail between her toes as she spoke. "You're as romantic as five lanes of new blacktop."

"Please, I'm serious."

Her foot was going up and down the undamaged length of his tail. "I know." She rolled over and sat up, looking down at him. "Is this going to be it?"

Nohar tried to answer the question, but his thinking process was a mess. "Damn, I don't know how I feel about it. What prompted you to—with a morey—why *me?*"

Nohar damned his mouth, it was still running away with him. At the worst times. He'd just parroted one of the five stupidest questions anyone had ever uttered in any situation.

Stephie closed her eyes. "Don't ask that. I don't know *why.* Until I met you, I didn't think I could care for anyone—male *or* female."

She exhaled. Nohar didn't interrupt her. She was quiet for a few seconds. Then she opened her eyes and looked at him. "You've asked me twice, I might as well tell you. I *was* a lesbian—for about four months at Case Western I was the most radical bull-dyke feminist lesbian you could want. It didn't do a damn thing about my inability have a relationship with another human being. I was posing as much as Phil and Derry ever were."

She idly ran her fingers through the fur on his abdomen. "Then I met you. I was set to be lonely for the rest of my life, and you screw everything up. After I met you the first time, I couldn't wait to see you again. All during that drive from the hospital I desperately wished you were human. Last night I decided I didn't care."

Nohar knew the kind of repulsion most humans held for moreys.

Stephie had to be feeling even more confused than he did. He didn't know what to say. "I *should* dump you. For your own good."

There was a hopeful note in her voice. "Why don't you?"

Nohar thought about Maria. "I may be stupid and self-destructive, but I'm *not* going to do that to you."

Stephie gave him a hug that made him forget moreys weren't supposed to get involved with pinks.

He left Stephie to clean herself up and hobbled down to breakfast. As loud as they had been with each other, there was no question Manny and Angel knew what had gone on with him and Stephie last night. They didn't mention it.

He walked into the kitchen and found Angel watching Manny with rapt attention. Manny was involved in one of his passions, cooking. Angel actually seemed interested in Manny's omelete-making procedure. She wasn't even wrinkling her nose as Manny started adding raw hamburger to the cooked sausage. They both seemed to avoid watching his entrance.

"Found a disciple, Manny?"

Manny added the sausage/hamburger mixture to the omelette in the large skillet and folded the eggs over perfectly. "Don't make fun of an appreciation of good food, even if she's never heard of olive oil."

Manny got out a platter and let the omelette slide out on to it. Angel was trying to act spellbound. "Doc, how you keep the eggs from sticking?"

"You just have to remember to start with a cold pan—"

Stephie came down, interrupting what might have been an endless speech—Nohar had always seen Manny's cooking as obsessive. Nohar noticed, with some pleasure, Stephie wasn't put off by the lack of clothing on him and Angel. Stephie, however, was fully clothed, and she'd worn the outfit long enough that it was beginning to broadcast her scent on its own, even over the sausage.

Manny cut his omelette speech short. "What will you have? We have a vegetarian and a carnivorous version."

"Could you do both?"

"No problem—"

Nohar and Angel had the same reaction. "In the same omelette?"

Chapter 15

Stephie sat on the recliner as Nohar searched the boxes in the attic for something to wear. Nohar's mind had drifted back to MLI, Binder, Hassan, and the Zipheads. Somehow they were connected and he still had no easy way of fitting the pieces together.

"The answer has to be in those financial records."

Stephie sighed. "I know. That's the third time you said that."

Nohar pulled out a relic of his gang days, from before he'd left school—and Manny. It was an old denim Hellcats jacket. It still fit and it was big enough to hide the Vind when he wore it. "Are you sure that you never saw or heard anything that would help me?"

She shook her head. "I don't care what they wrote down on my job description. They never let anyone near those records. It was a tight little group, the five of them. Even though Derry trusted me, no one got into the inner circle who wasn't there back in '40."

"Trusted you?"

"Yes, not to screw up the campaign machine. He knew me from my radical phase at Case. It's a right little community, even for the ones who are still in the closet. I managed to convince myself that I was helping him out. Found out it was Binder's idea much later. By then I was used to the life-style."

"Why didn't Binder just let Johnson go?" The potential for a media explosion was even worse with Johnson in the campaign, than if he left under a cloud.

"I don't know. Derry never expressed any great love of Binder, but he also never gave any indication of ever being willing to re-

sign. Believe me, I tried to talk to him about it. He was always evasive about why he stayed."

"What about Young and Thomson?"

"Young was never willing to talk about anything but business. I
think he resented me. Thomson, I don't know, he's slick and never
says an ill word about Binder or the campaign—but he acts like he
knows some joke the rest of the world doesn't."

Still batting zero for hard information.

Nohar pulled out a T-shirt. It was the only black one, but it had
a yellow smile-face on it. Stephie repressed a giggle.

Nohar frowned as he pulled out the most intact set of jeans.
They'd still been using the human model for morey clothes when
they'd made it. The seams on the legs were split so his legs could
move, and there was a slit in the ass for his tail. He pulled them on.
"And nobody ever discussed Midwest Lapidary, or morey gangs?"

"You must be kidding." Stephie had reached over and pulled the
Hellcats jacket off of the bed. The denim covered her legs like a
blanket, and she ran her fingers over the embroidery. "How come
you get to ask all the questions?"

Nohar pulled the shirt over his head. It ended up twenty centimeters short of his waist. "What do you want to know?"

Stephie looked up. Her fingers traveled over the demonic feline
form that graced the back of the jacket. "Well, you called Bobby
your first and only pink—"

Nohar felt like he'd gotten blindsided by a baseball bat. "No.
That's not—I mean . . ."

She laughed. "I'm sorry. I didn't want to sound accusatory." Stephie stood up, leaving the jacket on the chair. "I was just wondering who Bobby was."

Nohar was still recovering. "Bobby, Bobby Dittrich. I met him
when I was trying to make it through high school We were both sort
of misfits—Though as we got older, he fit in more and more, and I
fit in less and less . . ."

He lapsed into silence.

Stephie walked up and put her hand on his arm. "Are you okay?
Did I hit another bad memory?"

He shook his head. "No, not at all."

He grabbed the jacket and hobbled down the stairs. He was
wondering why he hadn't thought of it sooner. Stephie was following, "Where are you going?"

"I have to call Bobby."

"Are you sure it's the time to look up old friends—"

Nohar didn't answer until he got down to the comm. "I think he might be able to help me."

He switched off the news. "Move it, Angel—"

Angel said something unkind in Spanish as she moved off the couch. "Damnit, Kit, you *could* ask."

She stalked off to the kitchen, probably to take out her aggression on some poor vegetable. Nohar ignored her as he called the number for Robert Dittrich. It buzzed once, then he got a test pattern as the home comm forwarded the call.

"Budget Surplus, can I help—" Bobby displayed a rapidly growing smile of recognition.

Nohar was happy to see a friendly face.

"Christ, what's going on with you? The Fed is looking for you—"

"I need your help as a prime hacker."

"You *know* I *never* engage in illegal activity—" Bobby winked.

"Can you help?"

"Come down, we'll talk."

Stephie's car was out of the question. Everyone—the cops, the Zips, MLI—everyone would know it on sight. Nohar called a cab.

Angel didn't object when Nohar left. She seemed a little resentful. Nohar supposed he'd been a little too curt with her, but he had other things on his mind.

The cab that showed up on front of Manny's house was an anachronism. It was a prewar Nissan Tory. The thing was almost as big as the Antaeus, but the huge hood covered batteries and a power plant that took up nearly half the car's volume. Nohar got into the back of the cab before he realized it had a driver.

A black human woman, her hair dyed red and strung into dreadlocks, was staring at Nohar with a wide-eyed expression. Nohar decided it had been too much to ask them to send a remote into this neighborhood.

"Shee-it." She was articulate, too.

"Don't tell me, you've never given a ride to a morey before."

"Dispatch didn't tell me no—"

Nohar slipped his bank card into the meter and tapped out his ID on the keypad. In addition, he typed in one hell of a tip. He could afford it. "Welll, I didn't tell *them*. Is there a problem?"

She saw the numbers come on her display. She spent a few seconds composing herself. "Sorry *Mr.* Rajasthan, didn't 'spect someone like you 'sall. Where you going?"

Money was a great equalizer.

Budget Surplus was a dirty little marble-fronted warehouse that hugged a nook between—really under—the Main Avenue bridge, and one of the more obnoxious mirror-fronted towers of the West Side office complex. It took more than a little creativity to find the grubby dead-end street that was the only access to the building.

The cab pulled up and Nohar typed in a hundred, on top of the tip. "Will waiting for me be a problem?"

The cabbie shook her head. "No problem at all. Take your time."

Nohar stepped out of the yellow Tory and felt like he'd been abandoned at the bottom of a well. One side was the warehouse, one side the black-dirt underside of the bridge, the other two sides flat sheets of concrete forming the foundation of the office building—whose doors would open on more wholesome scenery.

When Nohar entered the building, it no longer seemed small. The interior was one huge room. Windows made from dozens of little square panels let in shafts of bright sunlight. Despite the sun, the corners of the building were covered in darkness. Standing in the light, Nohar found the shadows impenetrable. Endless ranks of metal shelving dominated the space, tall enough to barely give clearance to the slowly rotating fans hanging from the corrugated ceiling.

Nohar heard the slight whine of an electric motor. Then Bobby's wheelchair made a sudden appearance through a gap in the shelving that was invisible from Nohar's vantage point. The shelf Bobby rounded held nothing but oscilloscopes ranging in age from the obsolete to the archaic. Bobby wheeled forward and thrust his hand in Nohar's direction. Nohar clasped it.

He released Nohar's hand and maneuvered the chair around. "Let's talk in my office."

Nohar followed the chair as it wove its way through the acres of shelving. He smelled the omnipresent odor of old electronics—a combination of static dust, ozone, transformers, and old insulation. Shelves held dead picture tubes, keyboards, voice telephones, spools of cable—optical and otherwise—and rows and rows of nothing but old circuit boards. Mainframes were stacked against the walls like old footlockers filled with chips and wire.

Bobby's office was defined by four shelves that met at right angles with a single gap in one corner that would have been difficult to detect if Nohar wasn't looking for it. The shelves of electronics tended to camouflage themselves, any open space looking over more of the same. The illusion was of endless parallel rows, when the reality—demonstrated by their erratic maneuvering—was anything but.

His suspicions of the eccentric layout were confirmed by a rank of four monitors behind Bobby's desk. The monitors were connected to security cameras looking down on the floor. The arrangement of shelves resembled nothing so much as a hedge maze.

Bobby whirred behind his desk—a rusty cabinet trailing optical cable, it had the Sony logo on it—and motioned to a chair that was another chunk of technoflotsam. Nohar sat down. It was hard to get comfortable, buttons in the armrests dug into his elbows.

"We shouldn't be bothered here. Now you can tell me what's going on."

Nohar told Bobby what was going on.

An hour later, Bobby leaned back in his wheelchair and shook his head. "I thought the shit had hit the fan with Nugoya. I guess there's shit, and then there's *shit*." .

Nohar had almost forgotten about his run-in with Nugoya.

"You picked the right politico to involve in this." Bobby whirred around the desk toward one of the shelves. The shelf he picked was dominated by a large bell jar-looking thing; it sat on a sleek black box. Nohar recognized the box as an industrial card-reader. "Even though all politicians are slime."

"Why the right one?"

Bobby parked himself next to the bell jar, and drew a metal cart from another invisible gap in the shelving. Three different processor boxes rested on the cart. There was an ancient Sony that was held together with duct tape. On top of it was a more compact Tunja 2000. On a shelf, by itself, was a huge homemade box. Frozen rainbows of ribbon-cable snaked from box to box.

"Can't get more right than Binder—" Bobby snickered. "Hate Binder. Wish you were investigating *his* absence from the mortal coil."

"Why?" Nohar could understand Bobby's dislike for Binder. But Nohar had never heard him express a political view on anything before. Legislation had always been irrelevant to Bobby.

"Need a license to hate a politician? Give you just an example— last session in the House, he led a vote to scuttle NASA's deep-probe project."

Ah, the space program.

Bobby pulled a small blue device from a shelf. Nohar got up and walked over. The device had AT&T markings on it, a pair of LCD displays, and a standard keypad. It could have been a voice phone, but there was no handset. Instead it had five or six different jacks for optical cable. "Those probes have been sitting on the moon—would you plug this in?"

Bobby handed him the end of a coil of optical cable and indicated a small plate on the floor. The plate had old East-Ohio Gas company markings. Nohar reached down and lifted it. Under the plate was a ragged hole in the concrete. Half a meter down was a section of PVC pipe running under the concrete floor of the warehouse. A hacksaw had a cut a diamond-shaped hole in the pipe, and a female jack had been planted amidst the snaking optical cable. Nohar knelt down and made the connection.

Something Bobby was working on, probably the blue AT&T box, made a satisfied beep.

"Thanks, I have trouble getting down there myself. Where was I? Oh, yeah, Binder's shortsightedness. His group of budget nimrods in the House have been stalling the launch for nine-ten years. Finally decided maintenance was too expensive, so they're going to dismantle the project. Forget the fact they would have *saved* money in the long run by launching on schedule, *and* we would be getting pictures back from Alpha Centauri by now, and the Sirius probe would have started transmitting already—"

Nohar shrugged. "My concerns lie closer to home."

"Yeah. My friend, the pragmatic tiger." Bobby snapped a few more connections. "Worst bit is, he started as a liberal."

"You're kidding."

"Nope, kept running for the state legislature as a civil libertarian, government-for-the-people type guy. Lost. Kept losing until he shifted to the far right and got elected. Never looked back. Children—can we say 'hypocrite'?"

"Enough of that—*The Digital Avenger* is now online."

Bobby flipped a switch and a new rank of monitors came to life with displays of scrolling text. Inside the bell jar, lasers were carving the air into a latticework of green, yellow, and red light. "Now what kind of system do we want to run our sticky little fingers through?"

First things first. "Any information on MLI you can dig up."

"As you wish—" Bobby pulled out a keyboard and rested it across the arms of his wheelchair.

He paused for a moment. "Another thing about Binder. With just a little tweak of government finances, we might have caught up to the technology that got wasted with the Japs—"

"I thought you were an anarchist."

"Don't throw my principles at me when I'm drooling over bio-interfaces nobody this side of the Pacific knows how to install. Besides, the engineering shortage is degrading the quality of my stock."

There was hypnotic movement in the bell jar as the holographic green web distorted and a blue trail started to snake through the mass. Bobby noted his interest. "Like the display? You ever hear a hacker refer to the net? That's it. My image of it, anyway. The green lines are optical data tracks, the yellow's a satellite uplink or an RF channel, red's a proprietary channel—government or commercial—the few white ones are what I and the software can't figure out—whoops, close there, someone's watching that one." The blue line took a right angle away from a sudden pixel glowing red. "Nodes are computers, junction and switch boxes, satellites, office buildings, etcetera. Jackpot!"

Bobby smiled. "Anyone ever tell you credit records are the easiest things in the world to access?"

The blue line had stopped at a node, which was now glowing blue and pulsing lightly. Text was scrolling across three screens as Bobby's smile began leaving his face. "You gave me the right name?"

"Midwest Lapidary Imports."

Bobby sighed. "Never as easy as it looks." He typed madly for a minute or so, then he typed a command that faded the blue line back to the neutral green. Bobby shook his head. "MLI doesn't exist."

"What are you talking about?"

"No credit records—"

"Check *my* credit. Someone is making deposits to my account."

More mad typing and colored lights. Bobby ended with a whistle. "You want to loan me some money?"

"Did you find anything?"

"Just daily cash deposits to your account, untraceable. Thirty kilobucks, plus . . ."

Nohar was speechless. He hadn't had the time, lately, to check the balance on his account. After a while, he said, "Check somewhere else."

"If you say so. I have an in at the County Auditor's mainframe." The blue trail snaked out again, and headed straight for a small nexus of red pixels and lines in a corner of the bell jar. Just before the blue line hit the nexus, it turned red itself. "Isn't that neat? But I am telling you, you *can't* have a company without a credit record.

Economically impossible. Even the most phony setup in the world is going to be in debt to someone, you can't—"

Bobby paused as the new red line pulsed and text scrolled across one of the screens. "Okay, I'm wrong, you can."

"What?"

"I just downloaded the tax info on MLI." The scrolling continued. "Shit."

Bobby remained silent and the scrolling eventually stopped. The new red line faded. Bobby hit the keyboard again and numbers scrolled across another screen, and stopped. Bobby was looking at the display with his jaw open. Nohar looked at the screen. No more than columns of numbers to him. "What're you looking at?"

"The third line. The net assets they reported to the County."

"Eighty thousand and change, what's so great about—"

"Those figures are in *millions*."

Time for Nohar's jaw to drop. Eight—no, *eighty*—billion dollars in assets. Bobby started scrolling through the information. "And forty thousand mega-bucks in sales and revenue— With no credit record? Someone is playing games here."

These guys were having billion-dollar turnovers from gemstones? Maybe he was in the wrong line of work. This was one set of rich franks.

"And Christ is alive and selling swampland in Florida—these guys have never been audited."

"So they play by the rules."

Bobby shook his head. "You dense furball. That has nothing to do with it. The Fed assigns auditors for anything approaching this size. And those auditors aren't paid to sit on their hands. They're paid to dig up dirt—"

"So why hasn't MLI been audited?"

"Beats me." Bobby studied the screen. "It ain't normal. For some reason, MLI hasn't raised a single flag in the IRS computers. They don't pay too little, or too much—and that is damn hard to do. They even have this little subsidiary, NuFood, to dump money into so they can smooth out their losses. Know what I think?"

"What?"

"It's all a fake and they have a contact in the Fed telling them what their tax returns should look like."

Nohar shrugged. "So what are they spending their money on?"

"I can give you a list of real estate from the property taxes." This was accompanied by a few keyboard clicks and scrolling text on one screen. "There's records of withholding, I can give you a list of employees and approximate salaries." More clicks, another scrolling list, "That and a few odd bits of equipment they depreciate. Not much else, sorry."

Nohar was looking at the names scrolling across one of the screens. He was hoping he might glimpse a name he'd know. No luck on that score.

"The main thing I want to know is how they were paying Binder—"

Bobby shrugged. "Public database at the Board of Elections, no sweat. But there's a solid limit on the amount of individual and corporate contributions, even for a Senate race. I can't itemize the public record, but all the illegal shit ain't gonna be there."

The blue rail began snaking its way through the net.

Bobby had just raised another question in Nohar's mind. The cops had at least one look at the finance records that told them that the three million was in Johnson's possession. However, Smith said all the money was from MLI—and that wasn't legal. Nothing in the police report he'd read had mentioned it. From the campaign end of things, the money had to have looked legitimate—to the cops at least.

More names were scrolling past Nohar on the last screen. Again, Nohar watched it for names he knew—and, suddenly, he got lucky. Nohar stared in widening fascination at the scroll. It was almost too fast to read at all. He was only picking up about every tenth name, but that was enough.

Except for the label on it, he was looking at a copy of MLI's employee list.

Bobby stopped clicking and in the periphery of Nohar's vision, the blue line faded. The room was silent for a moment. The only noises were the slow creaking of the ceiling fans, the buzz from the holographic bell jar, and the high-frequency wine of the monitors.

"What do you see?"

Nohar was smiling. "Can you cross-reference the MLI employee list with the Binder contributors?"

"Sure thing, compare and hold the intersection." Tap, tap, tap.

"Why don't you have a voice interface on this thing?"

"Silly waste of memory. My terminal smokes about twenty megahertz faster than anything else because I don't bother with the voice. Besides, some of the shit I pull with this thing is best conducted in silence— Bingo!"

A third list was scrolling by on the last monitor. "Hell, I missed that. Good thing you were paying attention. The intersection set is the entire MLI payroll. Every single one of MLI's employees made a contribution close to the limit . . ."

Bobby had stopped talking. Nohar was beginning to smell anger off his friend. "What is it?"

"The contributions from Midwest Lapidary cover sixty-five percent of Binder's treasury. These guys *own* Binder. I knew he was corrupt, but *this*—"

Now it made sense. Binder's finance records held the key—but it now made even less sense for MLI to be behind the killing. Their investment in Binder was incredible. MLI was probably going to lose all that hard-bought influence.

Then, Nohar remembered what Smith had said—MLI's connection with Binder was to be *severed*. That was right before the attempt on Stephie. He still didn't believe in coincidence, and sever was a sinister verb. Nohar wondered if the other people in the Binder campaign were all right.

"You've got a rat's nest of innuendo here."

Nohar looked at the three lists. Only the last portion of each was shown on their screens. On the left was the list from the public contribution records. In the center was the withholding list from the County Auditor. To the right was the list of the names that intersected the two other lists. Something bothered him—

"How many people are on the withholding list?"

"Eight thousand, one hundred, and ninety-two."

The employee list had finished with an endless list of T's—Tracy, Trapman, Trevor, Troy, Trumbull, Trust, Tsoravitch . . .

"This is alphabetical?"

"Yes, you seeing something?"

"There's something about this list of names. It seems unnatural somehow. I can't put my finger on it."

Bobby hit the keys again. "Perhaps if I ran some pattern-analysis software on it—"

A brief summary replaced the list on the screen. Bobby read a couple of times. "Blow my mind! There are—get this—exactly 512 names for sixteen letters of the alphabet. 512 starting with A, 512 starting with B, same thing for C, D, E, F, but no G's, 512 H's, 512 I's, no J's or K's. There's L, M, N, O, P, no Q's R through T, then nothing till the end of the alphabet. Talk about unnatural patterns—"

"It's all fake."

Chapter 16

Nohar stayed with Bobby until it was nearly noon. After Bobby had found those unnatural patterns, he had started dumping tax and credit info on individual employees. All the employees they had checked had no credit record and overpaid their taxes. None of them took more than the standard deduction, no investments, no losses, no dependents. The credit record was an anomaly, since the employees they had checked had all been homeowners without a single mortgage among them.

One of MLI's employees was named Kathy Tsoravitch. She allegedly lived in Shaker Heights. Her address gave Nohar something to check, to see just how phony the MLI employee list was.

The Tory was still waiting for him when he left Budget Surplus. The cabby had been leaning back and listening to the news, looked like it was going to be a profitable day for her. Nohar got in the back.

"'Kay, where to now? Back to the 'hio city?"

"No, Shaker—"

She shrugged and started off east. She was a talker, and started going off on recent news events. The Ziphead attacks, a bomb on the Shoreway, and so on. Nohar let her, all her passengers probably got the same treatment.

When they pulled up outside an empty-looking one-family brick house, there was still thirty dollars left on the meter. Nohar added another twenty and told her to wait.

Nohar got out and quickly walked up the driveway to get away from immediate observation. He wasn't dressed for the neighborhood. The clothes made him look like a hood.

The back of the house was as closed up as the front. Shades were pulled at every window. There wasn't the ubiquitous ozone smell by the empty garage. It hadn't been used in a while. The backyard had withered in the summer sun. It was too yellow for Shaker Heights.

Nohar stood in front of the back door of the house. The lock was a clunky one with a non-optical keypad. The door probably led to the kitchen, but he couldn't tell because a set of venetian blinds blocked his view. He tried the door. It was locked.

He stepped back and raised his foot to kick it in, and he had an inspiration. He lowered his foot and typed in zeros—five of them, enough to fill the display—and the enter key. The keys were full-traverse and a little reluctant to move, but Nohar managed to force them to register.

In response to the dipshit combination, the deadbolt chunked home.

It made a perverse sort of sense that someone on the MLI payroll never bothered to reprogram the deadbolt combination when it came from the factory.

He opened the door and went inside Kathy Tsoravitch's house.

The door *did* lead to the kitchen—a pretty damn empty kitchen. He let the door close behind him as he surveyed the nearly empty room. No furniture except the counters, no stove, no micro, no fridge, not even light spots on the linoleum tile floor to show where they should be. The only appliance was a dishwasher built into the base cabinets. He turned on the lights and the overhead fluorescent pinged a dozen times before coming on full.

He walked over to the sink and his left foot slipped. He looked down and saw that one of the linoleum tiles—some faded abstract geometric pattern on it—had come loose from the floor in a small cloud of dust. The adhesive as no more than crumbling yellow powder. He slide it across the floor with his foot and it hit in the corner of the room, shattering into a half-dozen brittle pieces.

He stopped at the sink. Its stainless steel was covered with a thin layer of dust. He turned on the water. There was a banshee scream from the plumbing, and a hard knocking shook the faucet. It sputtered twice, splattering rust-red water speckled with black muck, and settled into a shuddering stream. Nohar killed it.

He opened drawers, but there wasn't much to see. One drawer held a five-centimeter-long mummified body—a mouse or a bat.

The house was empty. The place had the same smell as the boxes in Manny's attic—dry and dusty. Any odor with texture to it had faded long ago to a nothing-smell. Even the little mouse corpse smelled only of dust.

There was a newspaper—a real newspaper, not a fax—lining a drawer. He pulled out the sheet. The date on the paper was January 12th, 2038, fifteen years ago. The headline was ironic, considering Bobby's view on recent events. According to the paper, NASA had just gotten appropriations to test the nuclear engines for its deep-probe project. The original plan was to have a dozen probes going to all the near star systems. Now, fifteen years later, Congress was going to scuttle the project before the first one was even launched.

The end of the Pan-Asian war was news, even two years after the fact. The paper had a rundown on the latest Chinese atrocities in occupied Japan. It also contained the latest 2038 reshuffling of the boundaries within a balkanized India. The Saudis had finally killed off their last oil fire, and found their market gone along with the internal-combustion engine. Even the sheikhs were driving electric. Israel hadn't yet been driven into the sea, but most of the occupied territory was now radioactive. Russia signed peace treaties with Turkmen and Azerbaidzhan—finally. And the INS released new figures on annual morey immigration. In 2037, it topped at one-point-eight million. Putting the new, 2038 moreau population at over ten million. The United States had the largest moreau population in the world—with the possible exception of China from which no figures were available.

A candidate for the state senate named Binder was adding his voice to the growing concern about moreau immigration. Bobby was right about Binder's radical shift. Binder spoke before the Cleveland City Club about the moral imperative to allow moreau refugees across the border. Poor tired huddled masses and all that. Five years later, Moreytown would explode into an orgy of violence, and Binder would be in the House as the congressman from the 12th district of Ohio with promises to ban moreau immigration altogether.

He balled up the depressing paper. It crinkled and disintegrated like an old brown leaf. He dropped the remains and kicked the pieces away as he entered the living room.

The living room had wall-to-wall carpeting, an old comm, nothing else. Nohar walked to the comm, kicking up dust and loose pieces of carpet. Wroth a try. "Comm on."

It must have heard him. He could hear a click from inside the machine. Nohar looked over the relic as it began to warm up . It was a Sony and that meant old, at least five years older than the paper. Probably came with the house.

The picture was wavy, and the "message waiting" signal had carved a ghost image into the phosphor. The voice the comm used was obviously synthetic. It tried to sound human, but it sounded more fake than Nohar's own comm. "Comm is on."

At least the commands were standardized. He asked it for messages, and there were one hundred and twenty-eight of them. The comm's memory was filled, and had been for quite some time. Each new message was erasing an older one—stupid system, Nohar's home com erased anything more than a month old to avoid memory problems.

Nohar wondered what kind of messages were waiting on the comm. It was clear now the intended recipient didn't exist.

"Play."

Static, then a digital low-resolution picture with every tenth pixel gone to volatile memory heaven. "Kathy Tsoravitch, I with—bzzt—in person. Even so I wish to give my personal—bzzt—for your generous contribution—bzzt—"

Hell, it was Binder. Saturday, July 29th. The last night Stephie had seen Johnson alive.

Nohar smiled. She had last seen Johnson at a fundraiser—that Saturday. On that same night, Binder was thanking the nonexistent Kathy Tsoravitch for her generous contribution. A contribution that must form part of that missing/not-missing three million dollars.

Now he had something to play with. He wondered how well Thomson or Harrison could stonewall if he threw this in their faces.

However, this was only one message. He played the next one. "Play."

"My dear friend, K—bzztTsoravitch. Even though I am unable to thank you in—bzzt—I am giving you my personal promise that I will jus—bzzt—your confid—bzzt—I intend to fulfill my promises of law and order—bzzt—waste in government, and humane laws to promote huma—bzzt—and I am glad there are still people like you in this—bzzt—"

Someone named Henry Davis in Washington D.C. Nohar didn't believe in coincidence. The first two messages were thanks for political contributions—

"Play."

Berthold Maelger from Little Rock, Arkansas, a month ago. Thanks for helping his run for the Senate, appreciating the fact transplanted natives still took an interest in Arkansas politics. He promised his best to try and eliminate pork-barrel politics and to legislate the Hot Springs federal moreau community out of existence.

"Play."

Prentice Charvat, Jackson, Mississippi, same week as Maelger. Running for the Senate. Nohar knew him. The vids portrayed him as the most abrasive and vocal anti-morey congressman in the House. He let it be known he wouldn't stop at sterilization. He wanted to deport moreys—by force if necessary.

Nohar played every single message. With a few exceptions for junk calls and wrong numbers, the entire message queue consisted of thankful politicians. The queue went back for nearly two years. Even with the repeats, Nohar must have counted ninety different congressmen—only two or three Senators—that owed Kathy Tsoravitch thanks for her contributions.

Between taxes and donations, it was a good thing Kathy didn't exist. Her salary barely covered her expenses.

Nohar walked back to the cab, dazed. He let himself in the back and sat in silence for a few minutes. The cabby didn't seem to mind, though after a while she asked, "We gonna sit here, or you got somewhere else in mind?"

"Get on the Midtown Corridor, go to the end of Mayfield. There's a parking garage behind the Triangle office building."

She nodded and started gabbing again as the Tory left Shaker. Nohar was ignoring her. Zips or not, cops or not, he had to empty his apartment. There were things he needed to wipe off his comm, there was the remaining ammo for his gun, and, of course, there was his cat. He was going to have to take Cat over to Manny's since he didn't know when, or if, he'd get back to his apartment again.

Fortunately, there was more than one way in.

They rounded the Triangle and Nohar saw his Jerboa. His car was now a burned-out effigy at the base of the pylons under the old railroad bridge. He thought he caught some movement around the abandoned bus, but his vision wasn't good enough to make it out.

The parking garage was a block away and behind the Triangle. It had its own street. Two-lane blacktop ran under a bridge straight to it. Nohar's office cardkey let them in. He told her to go to the fourth level and park. There, he put forty dollars on the meter. "Wait for me until that runs out."

"Sure thing."

Nohar got out of the cab and walked to the barrier at the edge of the fourth floor and looked out. The garage was a relatively new addition to the Triangle, but it was old enough to predate the expansion of Moreytown into what used to be Little Italy. Now, Moreytown surrounded the garage on three sides. For four floors, the openings in the sides of the structure were covered by chain link and barbed wire. However, years had atrophied security, and one corner of the chain link on the fourth floor had been pulled away from the concrete.

Nohar looked out of the hole now. No sign of the Zips yet. A meter away and down was the tar roof of a neighboring apartment building. The piercing smell of the tar made his sinuses ache. The building blocked his view of the street, which was good. It meant anyone on street level couldn't see him.

Nohar straddled the lip and ducked under the gap in the security fence. He reached over with his good left leg. His left foot hit the tar roof and slid a little. The tar was melting in the heat. He was glad for the boots he'd found at Manny's, tar'd be impossible to get out of his fur.

Nohar eased himself across the gap, trying to be gentle to his injured leg. He brought his right foot down on a clay tile on the lip of the roof. The tile was loose and his leg slipped. His foot followed the tile into the narrow gap between the building and the garage. He managed to hook his claws into the fence to avoid falling.

The tile exploded on top of a green trash bin below him. The sound was like a rifle shot.

For a moment Nohar could sense a target strapped to the back of his head. Once it was clear no one was going to appear at the sound, he could move again. Staying to the rear, to avoid being seen from Mayfield, Nohar crossed the connecting roofs to reach his own building, which was a floor taller than its neighbors. Five windows with wrought-iron bars stared across the roof at Nohar. He made for the rearmost one.

The bars were connected to iron cross-members that were bolted to the brick wall. However, security maintenance was even more lax here. The bolts were resting in holes of crumbling masonry and the whole iron construction came loose with a slight pull on Nohar's part.

The window was painted shut, the glass was missing, and a black-painted sheet of plywood had been nailed over it from the inside. He stood up on a wobbly right leg and kicked in the plywood with his left foot. The plywood gave too easily and Nohar had to catch himself on the window frame. It almost broke off in his claws. Tight fit, but he managed to lower himself through the opening he made. He briefly considered replacing things, but if cops or Zips were around, he might need to leave in a hurry.

He was in a broom closet at the end of the fourth-floor hallway. The sheet of plywood had landed on a double-basin sink and Nohar had used it as a step to get down from the window. The sink was now at a forty-five-degree angle from the horizontal, and rusty water was beginning to pool across the hexagonal tiles on the floor.

Nohar made for the stairs.

As he descended, the odor of tar receded. He became aware of a familiar perfume—

The Vind came out. Nohar backed toward the wall and crept down the steps. He rounded the landing, sliding under the window to the street, and pointed the gun down toward the third floor. No one. There was the ghost smell of blood—

He was getting a sick feeling.

Bottom of the stairs, nobody in the third-floor hallway. Three meters away, his door was ajar. The frame was splintered, proving Nohar's belief in the uselessness of an armored door in a wooden door frame.

No sounds. The perfume was still ghostlike, but the blood was stronger. Nohar flattened himself against the right side of the door frame and pointed the Vind through the opening as he pushed the door open with his foot. Blood, feces, the burning smell of terror filled his apartment—

Nohar covered all the rooms in record time, but the bastards were gone.

They had left Cat in the shower. Nohar found his pet, strips of skin removed from the back and chest, lying in a pool of blood, urine, and feces. They'd hadn't even the decency to kill the animal before they left it. Cat had bled to death, limping around the stainless-steel pit.

Shaving is a different thing to a morey than it is to a human. To a morey it is a gesture of hatred and contempt. Removal of hair is still the basis of it, but the skin is often removed as well. Survival is rare.

The Zips couldn't find Nohar, so they had shaved Cat.

They left a message on the mirror for him, in Cat's blood. "You next, pretty kitty."

Nohar put his fist through it.

Chapter 17

Nohar wanted to kill something.

It was an effort for him not to listen to the adrenaline and finish trashing the apartment. What was worse, every time he thought of Cat, he couldn't help picturing Stephie—

He tried to calm himself by making a methodical inventory of the damage. The Zips had wrecked his comm, along with most of his apartment. They had shredded his clothes out of spite. The couch was dead; it had been ailing to begin with. The kitchen was a disaster. It looked like the Zips had been trying to burn down the building.

But they had missed the two extra magazines for the Vind. Those were where Nohar had left them, on top of the cabinets in the kitchen. The rats weren't particularly thorough, just violent.

Once he made sure the ammo was the only thing he could salvage, he took a sheet—one they had shredded—and wrapped Cat's stiffening body in it. The blood soaked through immediately, and Nohar wrapped him in another sheet, and finally stuffed him into a pillowcase. He didn't know what he was going to do with the corpse, but he couldn't leave it here.

On the way back to the cab, Nohar had the gun out. He hoped Zips would show themselves, but the way was clear through to the garage. He holstered the gun as he closed in on the cab.

The cabbie interrupted him before he could get in the back. "What hit your hand? No, don't want to know—stop right there."

Now what?

"No shit, piss, or blood in the back of my cab. They lemme

drive, but I clean it up." She got out of the cab and walked around to the back and popped the trunk. She pulled out a first aid kit. "'Spect one hell of a tip for this. Come 'ere."

Nohar hadn't bothered dressing his right hand. It hadn't seemed important. There were several deep cuts on the back of it, from punching the mirror.

The cabbie cleaned off the wound and tied it up.

"There—what's in the bag?"

"A dead cat."

"Won't ask if that's a joke. Put it in the trunk."

What now? Nohar got in the back of the cab and tried to think clearly, putting his heads in his hands.

"Where to now?"

"Sit tight for a minute. We're still running off the forty bucks I gave you."

"Sure 'nuff."

Damn good thing Angel didn't want to be left alone in the apartment.

Should have ditched things when he had the chance. Now he was waist-deep in shit river no matter what he did. Ziphead had a serious in for him. *Guess the limit for rodents in this towns topped off at six—*

He shook his head. That kind of thinking didn't help. He wanted to claw the upholstery, but it wasn't his car.

The Zips had trashed his comm, that was bad. If Terin knew what she was doing, she would have dumped the call record and read or copied the ramcards before her muscle scragged them. The Zips would have his Binder database. That was public info, not too bad. They had all his photographs. Again, something he could live without.

But now they had the forensic data base, and that was bad. Nohar didn't want to think what could happen if they figured he had a contact in the Medical Examiner's office.

Worst of all, he had no idea what messages had been waiting for him.

Nohar cursed under his breath. He was looking out the cab's window, across the garage and the bridge. He was looking at the Triangle office building—

Wait a minute. He had another com! It the calls were being forwarded—and most of them were—there would be a copy on the comm in his office. Did the Zips know about that? Were they watching his office? Did the gang even know he had an office?

"So, you want a big tip?"

She turned around and gave him a look ranking that as a stupid question.

"Like to make a quick hundred?"

"Nothing illegal?"

"No." Nohar pulled out his card-key to the Triangle. "You just go to my office and pick up my messages."

The cabbie only took a few seconds to make up her mind. She took his key and left the garage.

She took her own sweet time getting back. It gave Nohar some more time to think. As Angel would say, things were beginning to look like they were going to ground zero on him.

The Zips' nationwide spree of violence made things loom large. MLI's pet congressmen were as ominous, and scared him more than the Zips—especially if MLI was as reactionary as Binder. He wished Smith wanted to have the meet tonight. Nohar didn't want to wait for tomorrow.

The cabbie came back with a ramcard and sat back behind the wheel. "Like you, but I'm nearly off shift. Last ride, where to?"

Nohar told her to drop him off downtown, near East Side. He was going to pay press secretary Thomson a visit.

He had the cabby drop him off next to the lake.

Nohar walked out on a pier, carrying Cat. He picked a chunk of crumbling asphalt and placed it into the pillowcase. After making sure the knot was tight, Nohar picked up the bundle and looked at it. It was a shapeless mass, but blood had seeped through and the outline of Cat's body was becoming visible in red. "Good-bye, you little missing link."

He walked up to the end of the pier and looked over Lake Erie. There was an overwhelming organic stink from the reclamation algae that hugged the shore. He spared a glance to the light-green plants that shimmered slightly in the evening sun light. Then he tossed his package over the water like an ungainly shot put. Cat hit the water about five meters out, splattering algae. He watched as the pillowcase ballooned up with trapped air, then slowly sank with the weight of the asphalt, pulling the algae in behind it to cover the surface of the water again.

He looked back behind him.

A few blocks away were the massive East-Side condos. On top of one lived Desmond Thomson, Binder's press secretary. Nohar was angry enough about recent events to not even consider how the pinks would react to him. He needed to take this out on someone.

Thomson would be a convenient target.

Nohar started walking toward the condos. The sun was setting, coating the windows of the buildings in molten orange. As Nohar walked toward the building, he amused himself by picturing Thomson's reaction when he unfolded the conspiracy MLI represented, and how deeply the Binder campaign was involved. It wasn't something you could hide, once someone knew what to look for.

Nohar smiled. When this got out, the vids would have a field day. Bobby had been right, Binder *was* the congressman to involve in this.

As Nohar walked into the valley between the ritzy condominiums, reality set in. These were security buildings. How did he think he was going to get in to talk to Thomson in the first place? Bad enough, being a morey. But he was dressed like a gang member and he was armed.

If he walked into one of these lobbies, he'd be lucky if security didn't shoot him and claim self-defense. Nohar got as far as the front door to Thomson's condo before he realized his chances of talking to Binder's press secretary was somewhere between slim and none.

For one of the few times in his life, Nohar wished he wasn't a morey.

He was sitting on the biggest political scandal of the century and he couldn't even confront someone with it. He felt positively useless. What now, he asked himself. Sit here all night and wait for the guy to leave for work? Go back to Manny's?

He thought of Stephie waiting back there and decided to call it a day.

He turned away from the door and smelled something.

Pink blood, and canine musk. Nohar turned back to the door and looked through the glass, into the lobby. There was a guard station in a modern setting of black enamel, chrome and white carpeting. Nobody was behind the desk. That wasn't procedure. The whole idea of security in ritzy places like this was to be high-profile. There should be a pink guard there.

Nohar tried the door. Locked.

He tried to buzz the desk. A guard wouldn't let him in once he saw him, but the guard would have to come to the desk to see who was buzzing. Nobody showed.

Nohar looked deeper into the lobby because he thought he saw some movement. It was an elevator door. It was opening and closing, opening and closing, again and again.

The doors were blocked by a blue-shirted arm on the ground, extending out from the inside of the elevator. The arm belonged to a pink, and in its hand it held a large automatic.

"Shit." Nohar could barely produce a whisper.

There was the echoing squeal of tires from his right. Nohar turned that way and faced the exit of the condo's underground parking garage. A green remote Dodge Electroline shot out and bore to the right so hard it jumped the curb and almost ran Nohar down. Nohar jumped and his back hit the lobby door with a dull thud.

The van shot by him, accelerating, going east.

It made no sense to do so, but Nohar drew his Vind and started chasing the van. Five seconds after he started running his limp had gotten bad to the point where he was in danger of toppling over. There was no way he was going to catch the van anyway. Not unless he shot out the inductor or a tire—and that would be pointless when he didn't know who was inside the vehicle.

Nohar holstered the Vind and began massaging his hip.

Something behind him exploded. A tearing blast that made Nohar immediately turn around, jerking his wounded leg. The shot of pain he felt was forgotten when he saw what had happened.

The top of Thompson's building had erupted a ball of flame that was being quickly followed by rolling black smoke. Nohar felt a hot breeze on his cheek as he heard the distant bell-like tinkle of cascading glass. There was a secondary explosion and the floor below belched black smoke through shattering windows.

Nohar had chased the van three or four blocks away from the condos. He still backed away involuntarily. Within seconds, the top of the cylindrical building was totally obscured by thick black smoke. Nohar was starting to smell the blaze.

It was the choking smell of melting synthetics and burning gasoline.

Nohar was stunned. He stared at the burning building until, a few minutes later, five screaming fire engines blared by him. By then, the entire top three floors were belching out smoke like a trash can that had caught on fire. Nohar backed into an alley. Cops would be arriving soon, and he didn't want to be questioned.

Nohar found a vantage point on a fire escape. At that point, a dozen fire vehicles surrounded the condo, twice that many cop cars. The vids had showed, like a flock of carrion birds. Three helicopters arrived in tight formation and aimed foam-cannons at the top of the building.

The copters pulled a tight turn, carrying them over Nohar. They were flying low and the loud chopping of the rotors made his molars ache. More smells hit him, ozone exhaust from the choppers, the dry-fuzzy smell of the foam—it made him want to sneeze—above it all, the choking, nauseating smell of the burning building. Up there, with all the synthetics, the smoke was probably toxic.

Streams of foam from the cannons cut through the air in precise formation. Three thin bands of white flew from the copters in parallel ballistic arcs, expanding as they went, until all three hit the building as one stream. Nohar watched the foam hit the east side of the building and smash through a window on the top floor. The stream displaced volumes of smoke, and after a short pause, white foam began cascading out windows, dripping down the sides of the building.

Desmond Thomson, MBA, press secretary for the Binder campaign, had lived on the top floor.

Nohar doubted Thomson lived anywhere anymore.

Chapter 18

Nohar waited for the chaos at Thomson's condo to die down before he walked out on the street again. Harsk had called him a paranoid bastard, but he didn't want to deal with cops. Being this close to blatant arson, Nohar doubted he'd be let alone. Nohar had the feeling if he got too close to the cops now, he'd be hung out to dry.

He hung by a public comm, painfully aware of Angel's comment, "Moreys this far west *shine*." He was glad rush hour was long over. The pinks had abandoned downtown Cleveland for another day, and the cops were involved elsewhere. The only pink Nohar had to worry about was an oriental rent-a-cop staring at him from the lobby of the Turkmen International Bank. The pink's suspicion was ironic. The pink was probably a Japanese refugee—during the Pan-Asian war Japan and India would have been on the same side, and both had been nuked into a similar fate.

Species before nationality, Nohar guessed.

The cab pulled up. This time, better neighborhood, the cab company sent a remote Chrysler Areobus. Nohar got into it, to the visible relief of the pink rent-a-cop. The van was brand new. Nohar could still smell the factory scent form the upholstery. No one had pissed in this one yet.

"Welcome to Cleveland Autocab. Please state your destination clearly."

The computer started repeating itself in Spanish, Japanese, Arabic—

"Detroit and West—" not too close to Manny, just in case— "63rd. Ohio City."

"Five point seven five kilometers from present location—" Nohar would have walked if not for his leg and the neighborhood. "ETA ten minutes. Please deposit twenty dollars. Change will be refunded to your account."

Nohar slipped the computer his card, punched in his ID, and deducted the twenty dollars. There was a slightly overlong pause while the computer read his card.

"Thank you, Mr. Rajasthan."

The cab rolled out onto the Midtown Corridor, passed through downtown, and got on the Main Avenue bridge, heading west. Night had wrapped itself around the West-Side office complex. The buildings had shifted from chrome to onyx. Traffic was dead with the exception of Nohar's cab and the endlessly running cargo-haulers.

The cab reached the Detroit Avenue off-ramp—

The cab passed it, still doing 90 klicks an hour.

What the hell? "You missed the exit."

The computer was mute. Nohar tried typing on the keyboard provided for passengers. It was dead. So was the voice phone sitting next to it. Nohar began to worry about that pause over his card.

The cab passed the Detroit on-ramp, and two cars pulled off the ramp to follow it. Even in the dark, with his vision, he knew their make. Late-model Dodge Havier sedans.

Unmarked police cars were always Dodge Haviers.

Stupid. Of course the cops would put a flag on his card. They were probably going to have Autocab dispatch send the cab straight to police headquarters.

As if the cab was reading his mind, once it had picked up the shadows it took the next off-ramp, circled around under the bridge, and got back on the bridge—going east, cops in tow.

If he was going to do something, he'd better do it quick.

Now he wasn't so glad he'd gotten a new cab. An older cab would have been fitted with a seat and controls for a driver. This cab's interior was totally filled with pseudo-luxury passenger space. Nohar had little chance to override the controls.

He got down on one knee and felt around the carpet between the forward two seats and the passenger console. When he found the edge, he clawed it up. There had to be a maintenance panel in here. The cab had no hood, and the design people didn't have hatches on the outside to mar the plastic-sleek lines of the vehicle. The only other place for a maint panel would be under the damn cab, and if that was the case, Nohar would be in trouble.

Nohar held his breath until he saw the maint panel under the carpet. It had a keypad, and a red flashing light. A breach would alert the cab's dispatcher. Nohar looked back at the two Haviers behind him. Alerting dispatch wouldn't be a very big problem.

Nohar unholstered the Vind, wishing for the standard teflon-coated rounds, and fired a point-blank shot at the keypad. The gun bucked in his hand and the keypad exploded under him. Little plastic squares with numbers on them went everywhere in the van. It set off the car alarm. He looked back at the cops and saw them activate their flashers.

Where the keypad had been was now a smoking rectangular hole. The sour odor of burning insulation filled the cab. The magnetic lock had only been on the maint panel for the deterrence value. The dumdum had scragged it. Nohar hooked his hand into the remains of the keypad and pulled out the panel.

From the light of the flashers, he could tell the cops were pulling up next to him. He kept low. If the cops had heard the shot, they wouldn't hesitate to blow his head off.

Under the maint panel were the electronic guts of the computerized driver. Now he had to think fast. The sky was suddenly visible out the side windows. He was passing over the Cuyahoga River. The three cars were hitting downtown Cleveland, and soon after would be at police headquarters.

The circuit boards were labeled and color-coded. Nohar pulled the one labeled "RF Comm." That should cut signals from dispatch—he hoped.

The Haviers were pacing the cab, one on each side of the center lane. The second the three cars hit downtown, the cab pulled a hard left—against the light. There was a skidding crunch as it clipped one of the Haviers on the inside of its turn. Nohar was thrown against the right wall. He grunted as the impact reawakened the wound in his hip.

It seemed he'd done two things in addition to cutting contact with the Autocab dispatcher. He had activated a homing program— the cab was no longer heading to police headquarters. It was probably returning to Autocab itself—and the collision with the Havier showed that he had cut the cab's ability to pick up the transponders of other cars.

He heard the long blare of horns and the screeching of brakes— Fuck the cover—the sides of the cab wouldn't stop a bullet any-

way. Nohar sat up so he could see what was gong on. The cab had
run a red light without stopping. The cab wasn't picking up on
transmissions from the lights anymore. Or the street signs—it was
accelerating. Nohar had blinded the robot cab as well as deafening
it. It was following the streets from its memory.

Nohar looked behind him. Only one Havier was following—the
one the cab had violently cut off wasn't in sight. The cop had to
slow to weave through the chaos the cab had left in the previous intersection.

More horns, another crunch. Nohar was thrown flat on his back.
Now his hip sent a crashing wave of pain that made his eyes water.
Somehow, he managed to keep hold of the circuit board. He saw the
front windshield split in half and fall out onto the road. Nohar staggered up and looked out the back. The cab had plowed through the
front end of a slow-moving Volkswagon Luce. The Luce spun out
and almost hit the pursuing cop.

The cab must have been moving over a hundred klicks an hour
now. He was actually losing the cop. Even so, he wondered if
pulling the circuit board had been a good idea.

He turned around to see where he was going. Down the road
was a row of sawhorses dotted with yellow flashers. The city was
digging up another chunk of road—

The cab's brain had no idea the flashers were there. They were
topping one-twenty. . . .

Nohar slammed the circuit board back home and dived for one
of the rear chairs, trying to get a seatbelt around himself. The cab
suddenly knew what was ahead of it and how fast it was going. The
brakes activated, almost in time.

Whack, one sawhorse hit the front. The flasher exploded into
yellow plastic shrapnel. The rest of the sawhorse flipped over the
top of the cab. There was an incredible bump, thrusting Nohar into
the seat belt. The belt cut into his midsection as the nose of the cab
jerked downward. The front-right corner of the cab slammed something in the hole, and the rear of the van swung to the left. The left
rear wheel lost pavement and the van tumbled into the hole. It
rocked once and stopped on its side.

The seat belt and the brakes had saved his life. The cab had hit
the hole only going thirty or thirty-five klicks an hour. Nohar was
lying on the left side of the van, which was now the floor. Nohar
was still for a moment, letting the fires in his right leg fade to a dull
ache.

After the cops were done with him, Autocab would probably

want his balls for breakfast. Hell, it was their own fault—a remote that gets disabled like that ought to stop.

Nohar unbuckled himself and smelled the dry ozone reek that announced the inductors had cracked open and melted. The cab was dead. Nohar stumbled out the remains of the windshield. Outside was knee-deep mud that smelled of sewer and reclamation algae. Nohar faced the round, three-meter-diameter, concrete mouth of a storm sewer buried in the wall of the hole. He didn't hesitate. He knew providence when he saw it.

He limped into the echoing darkness under the streets.

It seemed like an eternity in the colorless dark, slogging through the algae, listening to the echo of his own breathing, unable to smell anything but the sour odor of the water. The only redeeming feature of his slog through the storm sewers was the fact the air was cool. The water itself was cold, and after a while his feet had numbed to a dull throbbing ache that matched the pulse in his hip.

For once he was worried about Manny's admonitions about infection.

The one big problem he was facing now was that not only had he lost the cops in the sewers, he had also lost himself. From the Hellcats, he knew every inch of the storm sewers under Moreytown. But, of course, he had no idea where the storm sewers were under downtown Cleveland. He had lost his sense of direction a while ago, so he was going upstream—had to be away from the river or Lake Erie. The direction was somewhere between east and south. Eventually he would find an inlet and get his bearings.

The few times he was tempted to go into a smaller branch off of the main trunk he was following, he decided against it. While the trunk was arrow-straight, and an obvious subterranean highway for the cops to follow, he would have plenty of warning before pursuit caught up with him. The slight phosphorescence from the algae was enough light for him to see a couple meters in any direction, the pinks would need a flashlight—that would give them away a hundred meters before they ever saw him.

It was also the only route that gave him enough clearance to stand upright.

Nohar's time sense was screwed. He'd gone for what seemed like hours without sign of pursuit. He kept glancing at his wrist, but his watch was still with whatever Young's explosion had left of his clothes at University Hospitals.

After an interminable period, the world began to lighten. At first Nohar thought it was pink cops with flashlights. However, even though the light let some blue back into his monochrome world, it was much too dim for pink eyes.

He drew the Vind and slowed his approach to the light ahead. It wasn't an inlet. It was a line of holes, large and small, that had been drilled through the concrete wall of the storm sewer. He ducked under a small one that was halfway up the wall, and crept up on a large ragged hole he might fit through.

A glance through the hole only showed him a metal-framework scaffold that was draped in opaque plastic from the other side. The tiled floor outside came to Nohar's waist. Under the scaffold he saw a jackhammer, a small remote forklift, a portable air compressor, and someone's hard hat hung up on one of the struts forming the scaffold. Nohar holstered the Vind and hauled himself up with his good arm.

He climbed in, crouching under the scaffold. He paused and looked back over his shoulder. He sensed something was wrong, even though he didn't hear or smell anything. He turned around, kneeling on his good knee, and leaned slightly back out the hole. He was waiting the split second for his eyes to readjust to the darkness beyond.

He heard a splash and his hand went for the Vind. A hand shot out of the darkness, much too fast, and grabbed a handful of T-shirt and fur, while a shoulder hit him in the right thigh. He wasn't well balanced and the way his leg was, it buckled immediately.

Things were going too quickly. He barely had time to recognize the arm belonged to a pink. Nohar tumbled through the darkness and splashed into the green algae water. His hand had only gotten halfway to the Vind.

His head went under for a moment . . .

Nohar came up sputtering. His eyes had adjusted to the darkness. Facing him, and pointing his own Vindhya at him, was a pink female. She had short, dark hair—black as the jumpsuit she wore. She was only 160 centimeters or so, *maybe* 50 kilos. Despite her size, the way the cords stood out on her wrists as she held the 12 millimeter told Nohar she was prepared to take the massive recoil of the weapon.

"FBI." One hand left the gun, whipped a pair of cuffs at him, and was back bracing the Vind before Nohar could react. "I am placing you under arrest. You have the right to remain silent . . . "

The cuffs fit.

As she mirandized him, noticed something. Her eyes, pupils dilated all the way, were reflecting light back at him. Her pupils glowed at him. He hadn't noticed at first, since a lot of morey eyes did that.

Pink's eyes did not have the catlike reflection.

She was a frank.

He stared at this small woman who held the Vind like it was a Saturday night special, and he realized he was scared shitless.

Chapter 19

Nohar didn't know much about human standards for such things, but he was pretty sure that this frank agent was the "babe" the Fed sent to Bobby. He went with the agent quietly. He had no desire to test her capabilities. Despite a probable resisting arrest charge, he could claim he'd pulled the circuit because he'd thought they were Zipheads out to kill him. Wouldn't convince the cops, but it was enough to keep the charges down to reckless endangerment, discharging a firearm, and whatever Autocab wanted to lay on him.

She called in on her throat-mike and wasted no time getting him to the surface. Despite the long walk alone with the agent, Nohar smelled nothing from her that made him think she was worried about him escaping. He noticed she put on a pair of chrome sunglasses as soon as they left the underground. They didn't seem to affect her vision at all, even though it was close to midnight. They came out by the shore of the Cuyahoga River, in the Flats close to *Zero's*. There was still a ghostly smell of carnage to the place.

The pink law was there, in force. A few dozen uniforms had scrambled down to the shore and taken up positions covering the exit from the tunnel. They seemed almost disappointed when Nohar didn't come out, gun blazing.

She led him up the rise next to the river, toward the congregation of parked black-and-whites. The pink cops gave her a wide birth and Nohar detected a slight odor of fear from them. He wondered if the uniforms knew the agent wasn't quite human.

She ignored the uniforms and headed right for the one puke-green Havier. Harsk was sitting on the hood, drinking a cup of coffee that smelled synthetic. She smiled, first time her face showed something other than a hard, expressionless mask. It stopped short of being a sneer.

"Detective Harsk, when I say I have the target in custody—the target's in custody. I was assigned to this for a reason."

Harsk grunted and got to his feet. "Isham, don't dick me around. I don't tell the Fed how to blow its nose. Don't tell me how to wipe my ass."

So her name was Isham. Nohar had thought he detected a slight Israeli accent.

"These men would be of better use elsewhere."

Harsk was steaming. Isham's smile was widening. Nohar wouldn't be surprised if she could smell Harsk's irritation herself. Harsk grabbed Nohar by his good arm and addressed Isham in a tone of forced civility. "I appreciate you helping us with your expertise." That was a blatant lie, Nohar could tell. "But I am still going to do things by the numbers. Especially with moreys. Especially after yesterday."

For a brief moment they were both hanging on to his arm. Harsk had a firm grip. He was strong for a pink. But Isham's hand felt like a steel band. When her hand left—it didn't release his arm so much as vanish—there was an ache where it had been. He suspected she had left a deep bruise there.

Harsk squeezed him into the back of the unmarked Havier, algae and all, and slammed the door shut. Soon Nohar was headed to police headquarters.

The two DEA pinks had fallen into a good-cop, bad-cop routine and didn't seem to realize they were stuck in the middle of a cliché. The bad cop was the fat one. His name was McIntyre. Good cop was a cadaverous black man named Conrad. From every indication, both their first names were "Agent."

Nohar had already gone through the numbers with Harsk, who was, if not civil, at least businesslike and professional about things. These two acted like they were going for first prize at the annual asshole convention.

McIntyre was into rant number five. "We got you by the shorthairs, you morey fuck. There's over thirty grand in *cash* deposits to your account. You expect us to believe it ain't morey drug money? You suddenly get that kind of *cash*, in the middle of the burg with the biggest flush manufacturing center we've found to date—*and* you show up in a firefight with the biggest distributors. Tell us what's going down, tiger, because we're going to trace those bills no matter how well you laundered them."

So far, Nohar had gotten more information from the pinks than they'd gotten from him. Apparently, somewhere in Cleveland was a major flush industry. Somewhere, the DEA didn't know where, was the lab, or labs, that manufactured the flush for the drug trade throughout the center of the country. The Zips were the major dealers of flush on the street level.

Conrad was doing his variation on being reasonable. "We don't want you. We want the labs. Tell us where they are, or give us some names, we can work with. We can intervene with local judicial system, make it easy for you."

He had already protested his ignorance. So he ignored them and studied the acoustic tiles, silently counting the holes that formed abstract patterns in the white rust-stained fiberglass. He wanted to go home, forget about Zips, Binder, MLI. Worse, he was beginning to worry about Stephie. Someone torched Thomson. Of the people with access to the finance records, that only left Stephie and Harrison.

It was going to be a long night. At least he knew McIntyre was blowing smoke out his ass about the cash. If the money was dirty, they'd know by now, and he wouldn't be in an interrogation room at police headquarters. He'd be in a cell in the federal building. As it was, all they had was the fact any morey with that much cash had to be guilty of something.

When Nohar didn't respond, rant number six was on the horizon. McIntyre never got to deliver on the steaming invective he must have been considering. Harsk opened the off-white metal door and let in Isham, who was still wearing her mirrorshades. Harsk smelled angry. He pointed at the agents and hooked his thumb out the door. "McIntyre, Conrad, get out here. I have to talk to you."

McIntyre wasn't impressed. "We aren't done here."

"Out, *now!*" Harsk was pissed. The DEA pinks obviously didn't expect this from someone they saw as a local functionary. They collected their recording equipment and left.

That left him alone in the room with Isham. She skidded a key ring at him across the formica table. It came to a stop right in front of him. She indicated his handcuffs.

"Take those off."

She didn't wait for him. She turned around to face the large mirror on the wall opposite Nohar. She took off her sunglasses, knocked on it twice, and pointed back toward the door. "I'm waiting."

The comment wasn't addressed to him.

Nohar didn't want to be alone in a room with this woman.

He thought he heard a door open out in the hall. she had just dismissed the cops stationed behind the one-way mirror. By the way her head nodded and moved, he could tell she was watching the cops leave.

"Now we can talk in private." She turned around to face him and smiled. He finally saw her eyes in the light. They looked like pink's eyes at first, with round iris and visible whites. But there were few, if any, pinks with yellow irises, and none with slitted pupils.

"Aren't you going to remove those?"

He had forgotten about the cuffs. He picked up the keys and fumbled them off. "What's a frank doing working for the FBI?"

She put her sunglasses back on. Now there was no visual cue to her nature. But she was still not a pink. For one thing, she didn't have a scent. For another, her breathing was silent. This woman could be behind him and he would never know she was there.

She paused a moment before she spoke. "The executive isn't as picky about humanity as some people would like. IF it wasn't for the domestic ban on macro gene engineering, they'd build their own agents."

Nohar slid the cuffs and the keys back across the table. He tried not to let his nervousness show, but she could probably smell it as well as he could. "So they pick up whatever trickles over the border?"

"Let's get down to business. I want information."

Nohar sighed. "I told the DEA I knew jack—"

That evil smile widened. If she had been a morey, the display of teeth would make him fear for his life. "Those schmucks never dealt with moreys before. They're convinced all moreaus know each other *and* are involved in the drug trade."

She reached into a pocket and tossed a grainy green-tinted picture on the table. It showed a shaggy gray canine in desert camouflage. It had been taken with a light enhancer.

Even with the rotten resolution, there was no question it was Hassan.

"I am searching for a canine calling himself Hassan Sabah. Contract assassin, specializes in political killings. Started in the Afghan occupation of North India. Works for every extremist cause you can name. Japanese nationalists, Irish republicans, South African white supremacists, Shining Path social humanists in Peru—"

Every group she mentioned was punctuated by a picture dropped on the table: the car bomb that took out the Chinese political director in Yokohama; the hotel fire that killed three UK cabinet ministers in Belfast; the half-dozen Zulu party leaders hacked apart by machetes in Pretoria; the barracks of lepus-derived infantry taken out by a remote truck filled with explosives in Cajamarca . . .

"Hassan smuggled himself into the country last year with the Honduran boatlift. The Fed didn't know he was in the country until a native of Belfast living in Cleveland recognized this canine." Isham tapped Hassan's picture with one of her slightly-pointed nails. "He's in the country, and he's involved with the Zipperheads."

"Why aren't you talking to your tip?" Nohar had an idea why. A morey from Belfast meant a fox.

Isham flipped out another picture, confirming Nohar's suspicion. The picture showed a morey vulpine, very dead. The fox had a small-caliber gunshot wound, close range, right eye.

"She was our witness. Whelp fox from North Ireland. Had the bad luck to be in a street gang that called itself Vixen—I see you know what happened to Vixen. Never got the chance to contact her."

She leaned back and glanced, over her sunglasses, at the one-way mirror. Then, satisfied, she went on. "The Fed only has suspicions of what Hassan is doing. But it scares Washington. Joseph Binder's Senate campaign seems to be his latest target. The Fed thinks a radical morey organization is operating out of Cleveland. The terror attacks by the Zipperhead gang give credibility to the suspicion."

"You want information on Hassan."

"We put you and Hassan in the same area on at least three separate occasions. When Hassan killed a local pimp named Tisaki Nugoya. During the attempted assassination of Stephanie Weir, former assistant to the late Daryl Johnson. And the arson attack that killed Desmond Thomson."

"Hassan was there?"

"One of the security guards lived long enough to give us a tentative ID."

Maybe he could bargain. "What do I get for talking to you?"

Isham took off her glasses and looked at Nohar as if she was examining a corpse to determine the cause of death. "You'll get my good will."

The smile was gone. "Nohar, you are going to walk. Make me happy."

Nohar scratched his claws across the linoleum and decided he didn't want Isham as an enemy. "I'll tell you, but it's mostly second-hand . . ." He gave her the story, as he saw it, leaving out the MLI angle in deference to client confidentiality. Saturday the 19th, Young had let Hassan into Johnson's house. Johnson gets whacked by Hassan's Levitt. Thursday the 24th, while Stigmata is being wiped up by the Zipheads, Hassan takes position up on Musician's Towers during a thunderstorm and blows Johnson's picture window. Thursday the 31st, Young empties the Binder finance records, torches them, and himself, on the 1st. Monday the 4th, the Zips attack the coffeehouse. Hassan and Terin are together in the four-wheeler.

She completed the list. "Today, Desmond Thomson is a victim of a firebomb in his condo and Edwin Harrison's BMW explodes on the Shoreway—"

"Harrison's dead?"

"Haven't you followed the news?" Nohar remembered the cabbie mentioning something about a bomb on the Shoreway. "Him and twelve other commuters during the morning rush hour. So far, because of you, Weir is the only one to survive an attempt by Hassan. Do know where she is?"

"No." He didn't want to lie. He didn't know how far he could push Isham, but he didn't want to get Manny involved with this. "She gave me a lift to my old neighborhood. I don't know where she and the rabbit went after that."

Isham seemed to know it was a lie. "I want to know if you find out where she's hiding out. The Fed would like to put her under protection—"

The conversation stopped because a muffled yell was coming from the hall. It was McIntyre. "*What?*"

The room was supposed to be soundproof, but Nohar could hear the conversation if he concentrated. From the pause in Isham's speech, she was eavesdropping as well.

"I said," Harsk's voice, "the tiger walks. Your own fault. Screwed your own collar, if there *was* a collar to begin with. Acted worse than a couple of rookies."

"You can't talk like—"

"Maybe if I put it like this. *Fuck* you, *fuck* your little proprietary

DEA investigation, and *fuck* inter-agency cooperation if you're going to fuck up like this around here!"

"Detective Harsk—" That was Conrad.

"Shut the fuck up! DA sent the word. No prosecution on the coffeehouse, self-defense. None on the gun. Check your files, he's had a license since 2043. As far as recklessness is concerned, *you're* the glorified dimwits that stormed into Autocab dispatch and not only disabled the override comm, but the emergency shutoff as well. DA's position is, since you didn't identify yourself, and the emergency shutoff was disabled, Rajasthan was justified."

"You don't understand," Conrad again, "this is our first lead—"

"The charges from Autocab—"

Harsk almost sounded pleased. "*You* don't understand. You have shit. Autocab *is* going to press charges—*against you two*. It might come as a surprise, but not everybody likes to have the DEA walk in and take over. Not to mention the fact the Transportation Safety Board is upset with you. Cutting the override on a remote vehicle is a felony. Because you two goobers couldn't identify yourself to the suspect, the cab goes flying blind into traffic. You're lucky you don't face kidnapping charges. You're not too far from assault with intent."

"You don't really believe he thought it was the Zips—"

"*You unbelievable shits!* Just because it's a morey, doesn't mean you can forget all that bothersome civil rights crap. The collar *still* has to fly in court. You blew it. Now get the hell out of my station and back to your stakeout in Moreytown—or better, back to the rock you crawled out from."

"Your superiors are going to hear about this."

"What a coincidence, your superiors already have. A district chief named Robinson would really like a word with you two."

That ended the conversation. Nohar turned back to Isham. He was confused. "If DEA started this, why were you the arresting officer?"

"Only one with experience tracking moreaus. Trained by Israeli intelligence." The evil smile was back.

Harsk burst into the room. "Agent Isham, where the hell you get off dismissing the observing officers? It's against operating procedure for an officer to be left alone with a suspect—"

"I'm not one of your officers, and Rajasthan is no longer a suspect."

"Christ, woman, are you pulling this shit just to piss me off?

Nohar, you're walking. The DEA guys are fucked worse than a ten-dollar whore, and the DA doesn't want to press charges."

Nohar stood up. "Thanks."

"Don't thank me yet. Because of you, and Binder, I got internal affairs clamping down on my ass—even if it was those Shaker cronies of Binder's that dicked around the Johnson murder. This Ziphead crap has got City Hall in a panic, the vids are having a field day—And I got suspicions it's all because you stuck your nose where it don't belong. If it was my choice, I'd lock you up and never let you go.

"As it is." He turned to Isham. "If the special agent would kindly leave me and the tiger alone. Nohar, we have things to discuss, in private."

Harsk led him out of the interrogation room.

Chapter 20

Harsk's office was in the basement of police headquarters. It smelled of paper, dust, and mildew. When Harsk led him in, Nohar had to duck the pipes that snaked along the ceiling. There were two chairs opposite the rust-dotted green desk. They were water-stained chrome pipe with red-vinyl seats that were held together with silver-gray duct tape. Neither one looked like it'd survive him, so Nohar stood.

Harsk took a seat behind the desk. He picked up a cup of old coffee that had been sitting on one corner of the desk. It was one of many cups that occupied various open spaces in the room. Harsk took a sip, grimaced, and finished it.

"So, Nohar, you think you just walked out of all that crap because of a clean life-style and goodness of heart—"

Nohar wrinkled his nose. He thought he saw something floating in the coffee Harsk was drinking. "You're about to tell me otherwise?"

The left corner of Harsk's mouth pulled up. The closest the pink cop would ever come to a smile. He drained the cup and tossed it in the corner of the room, near a wastepaper basket that was awash in a tide of old papers. "Good. Your bullshit detector is working. I'm going to tell you *why* you're walking. It has little to do with the DEA's incompetence—"

Harsk opened a drawer and took out the Vindhya. "How many people know who your father is?"

That was the last thing Nohar expected to hear from Harsk. "What has that go to do—"

Harsk started taking out the magazines for the Vind. He arranged it all on the desk in front of him. "Everything, Nohar. If you don't see that, you're dumber than most people give moreys credit for. Do you realize what the Fed, much less those dimwits at the DEA, would do if they knew you were your father's son?"

"It isn't my fault who my father is."

Harsk gave Nohar a withering stare. "If that ain't a load of bull-shit, I don't know what is. There's a good chance that half the tigers descended from the Rajasthan Airlift were sired by him. You're the fool that had to track down your paternity. There's a few hundred Rajasthans out there that left well enough alone. You brought Datia's history on to yourself. Now you got to deal with it."

Nohar wished he had a good argument for that. He didn't. "What do you mean, if the Fed knew?"

"They don't, yet. I'll answer my first question for you. Perhaps a half-dozen people in the department know that Nohar is Datia's son. The DA's one. I'm another. All of us were at that last show-down at Musician's Towers. He held off a SWAT team with that gun." He motioned to that Vind. "When the Guard showed up, they torched the building to get him out."

Nohar didn't want to hear this. He was grateful that Harsk was a pink and couldn't smell the emotions off him.

"Datia was a dyed in the wool psycho who left about half his mind in Afghanistan. A lot of humans don't understand why hun-dreds of moreys followed the bullshit he spouted. Datia, at the end, didn't believe it either. Could've been anyone, though, That August was too tense, too hot, too unstable. Moreytown was primed, any-one could have touched the spark—A lot like it's been lately."

There was silence in the room. It stretched out for a long time. "What are you getting at, Harsk?"

Harsk shook his head. "You blind SOB. Do I need to spell it out for you? Six people in the department and two National Guardsmen were with your dad when he croaked. He mentioned you. His ram-blings are in the official transcripts. It's just that no one has cross referenced them yet. It is only a matter of time before someone in the Fed is going to see how closely this Ziphead thing was engi-neered to look like the riots, and look up your dad. Poof, all hell breaks loose."

Harsk stood up. "Does the word scapegoat mean anything to you? What you think McIntyre and Conrad would do if they knew this?"

Nohar felt the world slipping away from him. "They'd think I was . . ."

"—running the show, you shithead. It's damn lucky me and the DA know different. Though, if it wasn't for two things, I'd lock you up just to be on the safe side."

"What two things?"

Harsk sat back down. "Me and the DA think you'd make a great martyr. If you get locked up, or shot, or anything, and word got out of your parentage, that could be the spark that blows everything up again. Right now, we have to deal with the rats—that's enough."

Nohar could feel his own past bearing down on him. It felt like he had spent a decade running away from his own tail. "You said, 'two things.'"

Harsk turned the chair away from Nohar. "The other reason is your typical interagency departmental screwup. Agent Isham seized your weapon and didn't turn it over to property. Somehow the Vind got lost in the shuffle and never got tagged as evidence. You can't have a weapons charge without a weapon—"

Nohar looked at his gun, laid out on the table. He didn't need more of a hint. He holstered the Vind and pocketed the magazines. "Is that it?"

"Fucking enough, ain't it? Do me a favor and stop being one of my problems."

Nohar left Harsk's office.

When Nohar got to the lobby, dawn was breaking across a slate-gray sky. He was glad that they didn't make people pass through the weapons detectors on their way out.

The public comms in the lobby of police headquarters were in better than average condition—which meant maintenance spent at least one day a week cleaning off the piss and graffiti.

He called Manny collect, hoping to catch him before he left for work.

Angel answered the phone. "Fuck you be, Kit?"

"What the hell are you doing answering the phone? Nobody's supposed to know you're there—"

"Chill, Kit." Angel looked chastened. "Whafuck happen to you? Pinky's been up all night—" Nohar felt guilty for the way his spirit lifted when he heard Stephie was worried about him. "—and Doc's been riding a pisser ever since he got back last—Speak of the devil."

Manny came on the comm, pushing Angel aside. "Do you have

any idea how lucky you are? I told myself I shouldn't ask where that hole in your hip came from—I was just about out the door to do more autopsies on rodents you shot—"

"Sorry, only place I could go."

Manny sighed. "I know, and I can't well turn you away. I hear that no one is pressing charges."

"It *was* self-defense."

"Next time would you go through the process? Where are you? You look like hell."

"Is that a professional diagnosis?" Nohar was still coated with algae. He probably smelled like the pit, but his nose had long ago gotten used to it.

"When am I going to get the full story on what's going on?"

"You don't want to know if you like to sleep nights. How's Stephie?"

Manny shrugged. "Better than most humans around a group of moreaus. She's been asking me a lot of questions, about you mostly." Manny looked off to the side of the screen and lowered his voice. "Stupid question, but did you—"

"Yes." And he'd do it again in a minute. Manny took a few seconds to respond.

"Damn." There were a few more seconds of silence while Manny recovered. "Well, did you know that they've reopened the Daryl Johnson murder investigation? Internal Affairs got wind that the Shaker division dropped the ball on purpose. Congressman Binder might get called before the House Ethics committee. Half the cops involved rolled over on him. It's all over the vids."

"I got some idea of that from Harsk."

"My office is pissed. They've been given a court order to exhume Johnson's body, even it if wasn't the autopsy that got fugged."

They talked for about ten more minutes. The rest of the conversation consisted mostly of Nohar's stories of the DEA, and Manny's inquirers after his injuries. Neither of them raised the subject of Stephie Weir again.

Then Nohar called for a cab. He specified one with a driver.

Fifteen minutes later, a familiar Nissan Tory pulled up in front of the building. Same driver as yesterday—Autocab probably only had one.

"'Spected it was you."

Nohar climbed in the back and slipped his card into the meter. She pulled the cab away and started west toward the Main Avenue bridge. "Busy night. Clocked in this mornin' and, whoa, the rumors. Narcs bust into dispatch and take over a remote. They ain't no drivers. They trash the van with some poor fool inside it. Never trust those remotes . . ."

The patter went on and Nohar dozed off.

She woke him up when they got there, probably after copping a few dollars from the timer. He didn't begrudge her and gave her a fifty dollar tip. "Thanks. Any time you call you can ask for me special. Tell 'em you want Ruby. Shit, you're not bad—for a moreau."

Nohar stood in front of the whitewashed bar with no name and watched the Tory go. The heat was beginning to bake the early morning pavement, as well as the algae caked in his fur. But, for once—though clouds threatened—things were dry. He paused a moment where they had parked the Antaeus. The only trace of the car was one of his own bloody footprints on the asphalt.

He walked to Manny's and had barely limped up to the door when Stephie yanked him inside. Nohar followed, stumbling slightly. He could smell fear and excitement as she pulled him into the living room. Angel was there. Manny had already left for work.

Stephie was breathless. "They started broadcasting it five minutes ago. It's on all the stations. All over the comm—"

Angel pushed her away from in front of the comm. "Shhh—"

Nohar watched the newscast. There was a pink commentator standing in front of the video feed. "We are now going to see exclusive footage of the disaster. Tad Updike, our Channel-N weatherman for the Cleveland area was on the scene. We now give you the uncut video as we received it."

The commentator faded, leaving Tad Updike there, in a safari jacket. He *looked* like a weatherman, slick black hair, insincere smile. He seemed to be standing on top of one of the terminal buildings at Hopkins International Airport, on the far west side of Cleveland.

"—it promises to be another record scorcher. Today, a high close to 33, and the National Weather Service is announcing the third UV hazard warning this sum—*cut it.*" A plane was approaching, rendering Updike nearly inaudible "[bleep] damn planes, didn't anyone look at the flight schedu—"

The cameraman had panned to the plane, over Updike's right shoulder. It was a 747 retrofit, the huge electric turbofans clung to the reinforced wing like goiters. Something streaked up from the ground and hit the plane, behind the front landing gear—

A cherry-red ball of flame engulfed the lower front quarter of the aircraft. It was still over a hundred meters in the air. The nose of the 747 was briefly engulfed in a cloud of inky-black smoke. The right wing dipped and the camera started shaking as the cameraman tried to follow the plane. Updike was screaming. *"My God, someone shot it! Someone shot the plane—"*

The wing crumpled into the runway, pulling the nose of the plane into the ground. It skidded like that for a half-second and the camera lost the plane off the right of the screen. The cameraman overcompensated and swept the picture back to the right, losing the tumbling plane off to the left.

The picture caught the plane center frame again. The focus was fading in and out. In the meantime, the plane was skidding on its side down the runway. The left wing pointed straight up, reflecting the sun back at the camera. The image briefly resembled a chromed shark. The camera followed the plane as it twisted and started to roll. The left wing crumpled and the tail section separated, letting the body roll twice before it broke in two as well. The nose kept going the longest.

Updike's voice-over was useless, so the commentator took over for him as the camera panned over the trail of wreckage and bodies that was scattered over the length of the runway. "Casualty estimates are still coming in, but there are at least one hundred dead. It has been confirmed that among the dead is Ohio Congressman Joseph Binder—"

Nohar felt like someone just kicked him in the stomach.

"—Binder was returning to Cleveland from Columbus, where he was reorganizing his Senate campaign which has been in chaos ever since the assassination of campaign manager Daryl Johnson. Also, sources say Binder's return was to answer allegations that there was a cover-up involving the Shaker Heights police investigation of Johnson's death.

"The FAA will not comment on the possibility that a surface-to-air missile was involved in the crash . . ."

Nohar slowly sat down. Someone, it had to be Hassan, had killed a few hundred people just to kill Binder. Nohar could feel that events had steamrollered way past him. Everyone who had any connection with the Binder finance records was dead now—

With one exception.

Nohar reached out for Stephie, and pulled her into his arms. They watched the plane explode a few dozen more times.

*   *   *

Nohar turned off the water in the shower. He had finally gotten the baked algae out of his fur. He stepped out and unkinked his neck. Stephie was sitting on the john and drying her hair.

Nohar faced her, dripping, and asked, "What do you mean, I've been 'too hard on Angel'?"

Stephie looked down, shaking her head. Nohar cold tell she was smiling. She picked up a washcloth and cleaned off a steak of algae on the inside of her thigh that her shower had missed.

Nohar was getting impatient. "Come on—"

Stephie handed him a towel. "I just think you haven't seen how bad this has all been for her."

Nohar started squeezing the water out of his fur, wishing for a dryer. "Stephie, this whole business has been bad for everyone."

"I know. But she's taking it hard. I know she puts on a brave face—" *You mean an irritating, obnoxious one,* Nohar thought. "But she's scared, Nohar. Scared and alone." She stood up and helped him towel off. "She has nightmares."

"Look, she should have known better than to answer Manny's comm. And I'm sorry if her wiseass attitude get on my nerves."

"She's only fourteen."

Nohar sighed. "Stephie, for a morey, that's adult."

"Physically adult. She's still just a kid. How do you think you'd handle her situation if you were her age?"

That hit close to home. When he was that age, he was still with the Hellcats. Back then he was probably worse than Angel—

"What do you want me to do?" He mentally added, *fuck her?* He congratulated himself on not actually saying that.

"I think she needs some respect. She needs someone to show some confidence in her, reassure her. Most of all—" Stephie looked up at him, her hands knotted in a towel resting on his chest. "I think she needs you to like her."

"I do like her, sort of."

"She needs to know that."

Nohar shook his head. He supposed he had been treating Angel like a liability. Angel didn't deserve that. He changed the subject. "Stephie, I think we better get both you and Angel out of town."

She cocked her head to one side. "Is that necessary?"

"You're not safe in Cleveland. You're the only one left from the campaign that could have seen those records. Hassan blew that plane just to take out Binder. God help you if Hassan, or the people he works for, finds out where you are."

"Thougt you were an atheist."

Huh? Nohar mentally ran through what he'd just said. "Figure of speech. Anyway, we can't have you anywhere near me until this is over. I'll have Bobby reserve a car rental and a motel room somewhere. He can fudge the records so no one will see your name—"

"Why me *and* Angel?"

Nohar put his arm around her. "I want someone to be around to keep an eye out for you when I'm not there. Also, you pointed out, Angel needs a friend. You fit the bill better than I do."

"When do I leave?"

"Soon as possible. Sorry."

She turned around and started wiping the condensation from the mirror. "Why is Hassan killing everyone in the campaign?"

Nohar saw the two of them together in the mirror. She was so damn small. "I still think it's the campaign finance records—the Fed thinks some radical morey group is behind the killing. The *target* makes sense, but I'm not convinced."

"Why?"

"Daryl Johnson wasn't a terror hit. It was precise, to the point, with no collateral damage. Doesn't fit. There's a motive for Johnson's death beyond some ideology."

Stephie shrugged. "You're the detective. You talk to Bobby and I'll try and see if any of Manny's clothes fit me—"

She walked out of the bathroom, leaving behind the pile of her old clothes. He watched her naked back recede down the hallway and realized that she *was* adjusting well to living with a bunch of moreaus.

Nohar limped downstairs and headed for the comm. Angel was still stationed in front of it. She seemed to have a growing addiction to the news channels. She was flipping through the stations with the keyboard.

Morey this, morey that . . . The nonhuman population was getting top billing everywhere across the board. It wasn't just the Zipheads either now. Harsk was right about the summer being explosive. There were already reports of retaliatory human-morey violence from New York. A Bensheim clinic in the Bronx had been firebombed, killing three doctors and three pregnant moreaus.

He thought about what Stephie had said about being curt with Angel. "Angel, I need to use the comm."

Angel turned around, like she hadn't heard him approach. She looked a little surprised. "Sure, Kit."

Angel got up and Nohar slid in and started calling Bobby.

"Nohar?"

She called him Nohar? He turned around and Angel was looking at him, "What?"

"Do you mind when I call you Kit?"

Huh? "No, go right ahead—"

The comm spoke up, "Budget Surplus."

From behind Nohar heard Angel. "Thanks for not minding."

Angel left him alone with Bobby. Nohar watched her leave.

"What do you want Nohar?"

Nohar turned to face Bobby and explained his problem.

After he was done, Bobby nodded. "Simple enough. I'll get back to you in a few hours with some specific instructions. By the way—"

"What?"

"Are you ever going to want that data on Nugoya? It took a little effort to dig up . . ."

Nohar had totally forgotten about that. "What could I possibly want out of that now? He's dead."

"Well, Daryl Johnson's name pops up in it."

Nohar sat bolt upright, ignoring the protests of his hip. "*What?*"

Bobby displayed his evilest smile. "I *knew* that would get your attention."

Chapter 21

The wait while Bobby's electronic gears whirred into motion gave Nohar a chance to think. For the most part he thought about Daryl Johnson. He now had a connection, however tenuous, between Johnson and the Zipheads.

But then, there was so much junk in Johnson's system when he died, he had to be hooked on something. It was too bad flush addiction didn't show up on an autopsy unless they looked for it. That's what it must mean—had to be flush.

Bobby had traced one of Nugoya's financial threads and it led back to, of all people, Johnson. There were only two reasons why Nugoya would be receiving money from Johnson. Since Nugoya only pimped female morey ass. it probably wasn't sex.

Nugoya was offed for reselling the flush he got from the Zips. Johnson was buying that flush.

Was he? Nohar wondered. If he was, Young had taken all trace of that drug from Johnson's ranch. Bobby had only found three weekly payments—if it was the sign of an addict, it was a recent one.

Blackmail? No, the deposits were much too small for Nugoya's taste had he known anything damaging. There was plenty of information that was damaging. . . .

It was another piece of the puzzle that didn't quite fit.

The comm beeped. It was time for Bobby's ride to show up.

A familiar Nissan Tory pulled in front of Manny's house, Ruby again. It would be a long time before Nohar would trust a remote van. Nohar opened the front door and waved at the cab. Then he turned to Angel and Stephie. Stephie had somehow made some of Manny's clean clothes fit her even when the proportions were all wrong.

She still looked good in them.

"You both know what you're supposed to do?"

"Sure, Kit, no prob."

Nohar shook his head. He was trusting the rabbit, but he wanted to be sure she got it right. "Let me hear it."

Stephie and Angel looked at each other. Stephie cocked her head and motioned with the palm of her hand, Angel first. "Right, Kit, um, we go to the Hertz counter at the airport—"

"Hopkins."

"Lady above, I know that. There's a prepaid '51, ah—"

"Maduro, it's a black, General Motors Maduro sports coupe." Stephie gave him a critical look and Nohar reined himself in.

Angel rolled her eyes so the whites could be seen.

"Lemme finish the rundown, Kit. Paid for with Pink—Stephie's—new name." The little scar pulled into a smile at Stephie's expense. Stephie didn't seem to mind.

The name was Bobby's doing. He had programmed a shell identity over Stephie's card. It wouldn't fool a real close scrutiny. However, it would run up false data trail on any casual ID scan. It was a total software construct—Bobby didn't even need to see the card. The software would self-delete when its usefulness was expired.

"—then we blow to the other end of the country, and shack up together across the line in Geauga—she drives so pink law don't stop us. Woodstar Motel is in Chesterland, off highway 322."

"Good enough. I'll get word down as soon as the shit clears."

Nohar smiled at the rabbit, and, to his surprise, he got a full smile back.

He piled them into the Tory and paid Ruby. The cabby must have been getting used to moreys. She didn't even comment on Angel, who was buried in one of Nohar's old concert T-shirts.

Stephie mouthed, "I'll miss you," out the window as Nohar shut the door.

The cab drove west, toward the airport. Nohar was left alone in front of Manny's house. He kept looking down the road long after the Tory had passed from view.

He yawned, walked back into the house, and planted himself next to the comm. The chair still smelled of his blood.

Tonight was the meeting with Smith. He'd pretty much decided he was going to tell that blob of flesh to go straight to hell if he didn't get the full story on MLI. Things were too dangerous now to cater to his client's sense of secrecy. Smith's lockjaw might have already cost a few hundred people their lives.

He stretched and tried to make sense out of it all.

Johnson's death had an air of precision and forethought about it.

Staring with the 4th, the deaths in the Binder campaign were loud, messy, and seemed to fit into a nationwide spree of violence by the Zipheads. Violence that seemed engineered to resonate with the riots of eleven years ago. Up to and including starting the violence on the generally accepted anniversary date, August 4th. It was a coordinated effort by the Zips to scare the pinks shitless.

Nohar raked his claws across the armrest of the chair. The upholstery ripped.

The Zips weren't making sense. The Zipperheads were drug dealers, not terrorists. What kind of profit would there be in encouraging the pinks to clamp down? If there's a new wave of morey riots, nobody wins.

Somehow, it also seemed MLI was involved with the Zips. That made little sense either. It was also hard to deny. The rats'd kept showing up, ever since he'd discovered Hassan. He wouldn't be surprised if MLI was using those green remote vans to smuggle the rats back and forth. Especially after he saw that van shooting out of Thomson's building. There was also no denying that there was some higher authority than the Zips, represented by Hassan. From Angel it sounded like Terin was under somebody's thumb—her supplier?

Was it MLI?

And, even embedded in a wave of rodent terrorism, the deaths were going to focus everyone's attention on the Binder campaign. If there was some information buried in the campaign *they*— Young's nebulous *them*— were trying to cover up, this would be counterproductive—wouldn't it?

Nohar fell asleep feeling like he had forgotten something.

Manny woke Nohar up. He was home early.

"Where are the girls?"

Nohar yawned and sat up. "I sent them to a motel out of town, out of harm's way—"

"As opposed to you . . . and me."

Nohar was stung by that. "I've been trying to keep you out of this. That's why I sent them—"

Manny sighed and sat down on the couch, across from him.

Manny formed his engineered surgeon's hands into a peak before the tip of his nose. "Has it ever occurred to you that I don't want to be left out?"

Nohar didn't respond.

"Why do you think I told you you could come here if things got rough? Why do you think I help you with all those missing persons investigations? Why do you think I took that slug out of your hip?" Manny shook his head. "When you left home and disappeared with that gang, I knew there was no way I would ever talk sense to you. But I have the right to know what you get mixed-up in. I promised Orai I'd keep an eye on you."

Manny stopped talking. The only sounds now were the faint buzz of a fluorescent and Nohar's own breathing.

"I've already involved you in enough to lose your job—"

Manny cast a glance out the window, toward the driveway where the van was parked. "I was trained to save lives. Today, we had an emergency, the 747. So damn many bodies to identify. We need all the help we could get. *They dismissed me from the scene because there weren't any morey dead.* You think I really care about conflict of interest?"

Manny deserved to know.

Nohar told him everything, including the money, the frank, Hassan—everything. Manny didn't interrupt, didn't ask for elaboration. He just sat and listened. Nodded a few times. Fidgeted a little with his hands. Otherwise he let Nohar explain the last week—

By the time Nohar was done, the sky outside had turned blood-red.

Manny seemed to weigh his response before he said anything. When he spoke, it was in the even tones of his professional voice, as if he was describing a corpse he had dissected. "You're right. Your frank is not from South Africa. All their franks have been cataloged since the coup d'état in Pretoria. What you describe isn't anything *they* came up with, and it doesn't sound Israeli or Japanese. On the other hand, the way you describe Isham, it's pretty clear she's a Mossad assassin strain, something they co-opted after the invasion of Jordan. Hassan's Afghani, a strain they abandoned after the war, likes killing too much—"

Manny put his hand to his forehead and stopped talking. "I knew this would be bad. You should have seen that 747—"

"Are you all right?"

"I'll be fine, it's nine-thirty, you better read your messages if you want to meet your client on time. I'll drive you to Lakeview."

Nohar had forgotten about the messages he'd had the cabbie fetch for him. So much had happened since—

He turned on the comm and got the ramcard out of his wallet. He put it in the card-reader. He called up the messages. There was a predictable—and out of date—message from Harsk about how, if he turned himself in, things would go easier for him. In retrospect, Harsk wasn't lying. Then there was a message from the late Desmond Thomson, the press secretary.

Thomson's face was sunken, The skin looked hollowed out and the vid anchorman's voice had turned into the voice of a jazz musician who smoked too much. "I have no idea what your interest in this is. Whatever you've uncovered, I am supposed to request that you refrain from making it public until Congressman Binder's press conference tomorrow."

Damn, if Terin copied this message some time Tuesday night, when they wrecked his home comm . . .

He played the next message. It was John Smith, the frank, in the same unidentifiable location.

Light was glistening off the frank's pale polyethylene skin. The glassy eyes stared straight ahead. A pale, mittened hand adjusted the comm. Manny stared at the screen, fascinated by the figure of Smith.

"It is worse than I think before. We meet in Lakeview and we must go public. I discover it is not one individual responsible. The whole company is involved and condones the violence. I cannot let them do this, the organization is not supposed to physically intervene. MLI is corrupted and we must make it known who they are and what they do here. I bring all the evidence I can carry to the meeting tomorrow."

Nohar sat back. It looked like he didn't have to threaten the guy to get the full story.

Manny was looking at him now. "Didn't you say these Zipperheads had probably copied your messages off your home comm?"

Oh shit, Terin had that message! They knew the meeting was at Lakeview, *today*. They blew a 747 to get Binder. They'd certainly be willing to ambush the frank—if MLI hadn't dealt with him already.

"Manny, we got to get to Lakeview now!"

The green Medical Examiner's van sped down the Midtown Corridor. Manny drove.

Manny had wanted in. He was in, and God help him—Nohar

caught the thought and told himself what he had told Stephie, fig-ure of speech.

He almost missed telling Manny where to take the turn. It was the opposite side of Lakeview that he was used to using. Nohar yelled, and Manny skidded the van into the driveway of the Corri-dor gate. There was an immediate problem in that this was the Pink entrance, so the gate was closed and chained shut. Nohar's normal entrance was the gate on the Jewish section, which was rusted open.

It was ten-fifteen. They didn't have time to circle around East Cleveland to get to the right gate.

In a pinch, Manny's van could double as a rescue vehicle—a half-assed rescue vehicle, but a rescue vehicle—so, it had its share of equipment to deal with these situations. Nohar pulled a pair of bolt cutters and got out of the van. He walked up to the wrought iron gate and looked through.

No pinks, no security, nothing but darkness, graves, and the sur-real image of a tarnished-green bronze statue of a natural buck deer. It stared at the gate. Nohar cut the chain. They had twelve minutes to beat the frank. He pushed the gate open and waved Manny into the cemetery. The headlights targeted the statue, and for a moment it looked like luminescent jade.

Nohar jumped into the passenger seat—pain shot through his right leg—and started yelling directions at Manny.

Lakeview was a large place, and it was a good thing Nohar knew its layout by heart. They were racing through at the maximum safe speed, and it felt to Nohar as if they were crawling up the hill that formed Lakeview's geography. When they crested the bluff where President James A. Garfield resided in his cylindrical medieval tomb, it was ten-twenty.

They rounded the turn on the other side of the concrete barrier on the Mayfield-Kenelworth gate, and Nohar saw a familiar green van in the distance. *The bastard was early.*

Chapter 22

Smith's remote was pulling up to Eliza's marker, and the damn headlights were fucking with Nohar's night-vision.

"Manny—kill the lights."

There were still the lights on the remote, but they were pointed away from them. Nohar could start making things out in the gloom, like the pneumatic doors opening on the frank's van. The frank stepped out carrying a briefcase. Almost immediately, the remote drove away.

"Stop here." Nohar had a slight hope, maybe they'd be lucky and there wouldn't be an ambush. "Radio the cops."

Nohar got out and limped up to the frank.

Smith stood alone, clutching a briefcase to his flabby chest. Now that Nohar saw him standing upright, Nohar realized he was looking at a creature that wasn't designed for bipedal motion. The frank's mass seemed to slide downward, reinforcing the basic pear shape. He still smelled like raw sewer, but in the open air, Nohar could make an effort to ignore it.

Nohar stared into the frank's blank, glass eyes. "If I'm going to help you, Smith, you have to tell me everything, *now.*"

"Please, let us move. We tell everything to media. We must—"

Nohar put his hand on the frank's shoulder. Even under the jacket, a jacket much too heavy for the weather, Nohar could feel his hand sink in and the flesh ripple underneath. "You're going to tell me first. You've been using me, withholding information—if you'd told me about MLI up front, that 747 might not have been shot down."

Smith said something that must have been in his native language. It was low, liquid, and sounded like a dirge. Then he went on. "Do not say that!" There was the first real trace of emotion in the frank's voice, even if it didn't register on his face or in his odor. "They do not let me know what they do. You must understand, violence is anathema. Murder is unforgivable. They do this without me—"

Nohar shook his head. "What are they doing, and why are you out of the loop?"

"We must go—"

"Look, the cops will be here any minute. So calm down and tell me why you set me up in this mess."

"No, I do not intend, you do not understand—" More words in that odd sounding language. "When authorities find out what goes on, they will not let us go public. You must make this public." Smith handed Nohar the briefcase. "It is mostly in there. I tell you what is not."

Smith loosened his tie, and the roll of fat around his neck flowed downward. The frank was trembling, as if he was in pain. "You know our purpose is to support politicians. We do so fifteen years for the benefit of our homeland. I am not just an accountant, I am—" The frank let out a word that sounded like a harsh belch. "Perhaps the right term is political officer. I enforce our laws not to physically intervene. We do not engage in violent acts. To do so will prelude a war."

The frank sounded despairing. "Fifteen years in a foreign land is too long to do such work. Laws from so far away become less binding. I am supposed to prevent this. I fail. An operation has left its controls. They try to isolate me and accelerate things beyond safe limits.

The frank pulled a letter out of his pocket and handed it to Nohar. "This is the proof I find when I search our files. It is a filing mistake. I am supposed to handle the letters, but they cannot let me see this. The files are not their job and they make an error filing this paper too early. I do not know what other mistakes they make by keeping this from me—"

It was a letter from Wilson Scott. The same letter Angel had found at Young's. Only, this copy was intact. It went on mentioning moreys offing pinks, moreys taking hostages, morey air terrorism. It was dated August tenth—

This year.

"Oh, shit."

"English is a difficult language for us. We compose letters months in advance. But I am the one who is to deal with the outside world. I conduct the business. I handle the money. Without me it becomes easy for them to make mistakes of sending letters too early."

"They are telling the Zips what to do?"

"Yes. They do not pay in money, to avoid me."

Flush. Nohar shook his head. "But why?"

"They are impatient. They feel control progresses too slowly. They want our men in the Senate, and they can't wait—"

Nohar could see now. "They want to panic the pinks so anti-morey candidates like Binder get elect—"

He shifted the briefcase and the letter to his left hand. He had heard something moving out in the darkness. He started drawing the Vind. "Smith, there's a van right behind me. Get to it."

"But I have to tell you where—"

"Move!" Nohar could smell canine musk in the air now. Something was approaching, fast. Smith started running. The poor frank bastard seemed to have trouble moving. He was wobbling on rubbery legs. Why the hell would someone engineer something like that?

The bulk of the frank was moving toward the van when Nohar heard the rustle of some leaves above them.

It was no louder than the crickets or the gravel crunching under his feet. Nohar could smell a rank canine odor now—a wave of musk that overwhelmed the frank's sewer smell. The canine was riding a wave of excitement sexual in its intensity.

The smell hit Nohar too late, because the canine, Hassan, was already in the air, falling out of a tree and on to the frank.

Hassan landed on the frank. Nohar whipped around, aiming the Vind at the canine, but his knee and bad hip fought him. Smith hit the ground, his flesh rippling. The canine sank his right knee into the frank's chest and he was jabbing a rodlike weapon deep into the folds of flesh where the frank's neck should be.

Nohar fired. A hole appeared in the chest of Hassan's jacket. The slug carried the canine over a monument—Eliza's monument—to collapse behind it. Nohar ran up to the marker. The air near it was now ripe with the odor of burnt flesh as well as the frank's sewer smell. Nohar glanced at Smith, who lay on Eliza's grave, unmoving, eyes staring upward. There was a circular purple discoloration on the frank's neck.

Nohar rounded the monument, and Hassan wasn't there. He whipped around, dropping the briefcase to brace the Vind with both hands, and a foot came out of nowhere and hit his right hand. The Vind tumbled out into the darkness. Nohar kept turning to face Hassan. Hassan's jacket hung open now. He was wearing a kevlar vest. The dumdum had only knocked the dog over.

Nohar dived at the canine. Hassan spun sideways, letting Nohar pass over and slam into the ground. Nohar's right knee hit a low-lying monument and spasmed with an excruciating wave of pain, blurring his vision. He could hear and smell the canine approach. He dodged blind.

He went through a line of hedges and started to roll down a steep hill. He caught himself before he rolled all the way down.

Hassan hunched low, tongue lolling. He leapt over the hedge and started bounding over the monuments that dotted the hillside. Nohar knew he couldn't move that fast, even with a good leg. He braced himself defensively to receive the canine's charge. Hassan didn't seem to have a gun. Hand to hand, he had a chance to take the assassin.

Nohar felt his heartbeat accelerating. The adrenaline was kicking in.

Hassan passed him and Nohar tried to pivot to follow him. Nohar wasn't quick enough. He felt a kick slam into his lower back, above the base of his tail. He tried to roll with it, but the blow still sent him to his knees.

The Beast was roaring—

"Time for death, cat." A shaggy canine arm hooked around his neck, and there was a fiery tingle under his left armpit. He smelled his own fur burning.

He could feel the rush as The Beast was triggered. But he couldn't move. Hassan was using a stun rod—Nohar was paralyzed. When Hassan pivoted Nohar's body around on his bad knee, pain fogged his sight again. When he could see again, he was propped in front of an open grave. The canine arm began to choke him.

"Your final reward. Make your peace, cat."

Why didn't the sick bastard just shoot him and get it over with?

Manny said they were exhuming Johnson's grave. Apparently, they had. The open grave he was looking into was Daryl Johnson's less-than-final resting place. Lack of oxygen was making him begin to black out. The effects of the stunner were beginning to wear off, but his muscles felt like mush. He didn't want to have to smell Hassan's musk when he died.

Suddenly, there was a bright light. Nohar saw something—a bullet?—ricochet off Johnson's marker. They were both bathed in white light, their shadows extending forward into infinity. Hassan was quick, and the arm around Nohar's neck disappeared. Hassan's shadow jumped out of the light to the sound of another bullet.

Nohar's muscles weren't under his control He tumbled forward, into the grave.

He splashed facedown in an inch-deep layer of black mud. His whole body cramped up on him. The stunner had been military-style, not a street or a cop version. His muscles had been through a blender and felt predigested.

It took an interminable time for him to recover. As he fought to get his body under control, he could hear sirens in the distance. It certainly took them long enough. By the time he could get up on his hands and knees and look up, the grave was surrounded by Manny and three nervous pink medics. All backlit by red and blue flashers. They were about to climb down into the rectangular hole. Nohar waved them away and stood up. His right knee nearly buckled, and from the loose way it felt, the support bandage had torn off.

Standing, he cold reach the lip. It wasn't a good idea in his condition, but be damned if he was going to a hospital. He grabbed the edge, buried his left boot in the side of the grave, and hoisted himself up. His bad shoulder protested and he nearly slid back into the hole—but he clawed his way out.

There was some fear from the medic, but the strongest smell was coming from Manny. He was worried. Nohar tried to allay Manny's worries by walking—without any help—back up the hill, to where all the cops were. Manny followed. "Are you all right? What did he hit you with?"

Nohar answered through gritted teeth. The walk up the hill was sending daggers of pain through his knee and his hip. "I'm fine. Hassan was using a stun rod—" Nohar noticed a bandage around Manny's right hand. "What happened to you?"

Manny handed Nohar the Vind. "This thing has one hell of a kick."

Nohar stopped. "Oh, hell, Manny, your hand. You broke your fucking hand to shoot—"

"Calm down, it isn't like anyone's going to die from it."

Manny, Nohar thought, *your hands are your life.* "How's Smith?"

"Smith's dead."

They passed the broken hedge Nohar had fallen through and were on level ground again. "*Dead?* He only got hit with a stunner, I saw it."

Manny shrugged. "Then that's what killed him—"

There were a half-dozen black-and-whites parked around Eliza Wilkins' grave. There was also Manny's van, an ambulance, the predictable unmarked Havier, and, of all things, a black Porsche. The frank was still there, looking like an inert lump of flesh only vaguely molded into a humanoid form. Cops were all over, planting evidence tags and yellow warning strips. Harsk was yelling into a radio, alternately cussing someone out for losing Hassan, and trying to hurry the forensics guys. The only nonhumans were Nohar, Manny, the frank—and Agent Isham, FBI, who left the Porsche and walked toward him and Manny.

She still wore the shades. "Doctor Gujerat, I've cleared it with your office. We want you to make a field ID of the deceased."

Manny nodded. "No promises with just the equipment in the van—"

"Do it."

Manny gave an undulating shrug and walked toward the van. Nohar started to follow, but Isham grabbed his arm. "We talk, Mr. Rajasthan. Sit down, your knee will appreciate it."

Nohar found himself sitting on one of the cold granite monuments. She was right—taking the weight off his leg was a relief. It had been in constant pain. Isham pointed to the dead form of Smith. "So, who has Hassan killed this time?"

He didn't have any reason left to be recalcitrant. "He called himself John Smith. He's an accountant for a company called Midwest Lapidary Imports. Apparently the board of directors consisted of franks like him. Claim to be from South Africa, but they aren't."

Isham nodded. "Not South Africa. The frank's much too xenomorphic. Doubt his type is anywhere in the catalogs. Why did Hassan hit him?"

Client confidentiality was irrelevant now. "Until the killings started, MLI was a quiet little covert operation buying influence in Washington. The company has over eight thousand false identities they funnel the money through to avoid the limits on individual campaign contributions. The amount runs into the billions. Smith hired me to find out if someone in MLI was behind the Johnson killing."

"Was there?"

Nohar waved at the dead form of Smith. "The papers in the briefcase are evidence with which he wanted to go public. The MLI organization seems to have slipped out of the control of whatever government was backing them. They're in direct control of the Zips."

Isham lowered her sunglasses. "What government?"

"Hassan showed up before Smith told me. He implied that information isn't in those paper—"

Nohar turned to face the corpse. She was already watching. Manny had come out of the van with a large hypodermic needle. He was trying to take a fluid sample and do a field genetic analysis. He was kneeling over the body, removing the needle from the frank's doughy chest. As Manny withdrew the needle, odors erupted from the corpse—evil bile and ammonia smells. A few cops covered their mouths and retreated into the darkness. From somewhere behind him, Nohar heard the sound of retching. While the cops backed away, he, Manny, and Isham watched in horrified fascination as fluid began leaking from the hole Manny's needle had made.

Manny had ripped the frank's shirt open to get at the chest, and now, cloudy liquid was seeping from a tear in the otherwise featureless skin. The tear was widening with the pressure of the escaping liquid—Manny seemed to realize what was happening. He ran back to the van. Fluid was now pouring from the frank. The smell had driven back all the pinks, and Nohar's nose was numbing. The frank's clothes were soaked with the cloudy liquid, and there was a growing dark spot on the yellow lawn. Nohar thought he could see steam rising from the corpse.

The rip was no longer tearing open. The edges seemed to be dissolving. Manny was racing back with an armload of evidence jars. He was barely in time. The frank had already spilled half its mass on to the ground, and the pace of the dissolution was accelerating. Manny began shoving jars through the hole in the frank's chest— Harsk's eyes widened and he turned around, falling to his knees. Manny got three of the specimen jars into the body before holes began spontaneously erupting in the frank's skin. The skin dissolved like an ice cube in boiling water. Manny tried to get a solid piece of the frank's skin into one of the empty jars. He scooped it up, and it melted into more of the cloudy white fluid.

The body was gone. It left only a pile of clothes, a pair of pink dentures, and a pair of fake plastic eyes.

"Holy Christ." One of the cops was crossing himself.

Manny looked at the puddle surrounding the clothes where John Smith had been, and said, in a tone of epic understatement, "This wasn't normal frank."

Isham walked over to Harsk. She seemed to be listening to her earplug. "The Fed's taking this over, Harsk. National security."

Chapter 23

The trip to Metro General, down the Midtown Corridor and I-90, was a convoy. Nohar didn't want to go to the hospital. In fact, just the idea of it made him nauseous. But Isham was clamping down and the Fed was going to keep all the principals in one place. Manny's van was led by Isham's Porsche. The black-and-whites followed, and downtown they were joined by a group of five dark-blue Haviers.

The convoy converged on Metro General. The cops were shunted into quarantine, Isham shouting down Harsk's objections with talk about waiting for a delegation from the Center of Disease Control. Isham had most of the cops believing the frank was some bio-weapon delivery system.

Isham knew it was a crock, Nohar could tell, but it gave her a convenient excuse to lock up the local law enforcement. It was her show now. Nohar decided she could have it.

She didn't quarantine him. She wanted the cops isolated, and she didn't want him telling them about international conspiracies to control the U.S. government. She took him and Manny to the brand-new genetics lab on the fifth floor of the new Metro wing. The floor was dotted with her agents, and Manny was given lab assistants who were not on the normal hospital payroll. The Fed had dived in with both feet.

Isham spent a half hour in someone's day office, poring over the documents in the briefcase. She had Nohar sit across from her, getting graveyard mud all over some poor doctor's leather couch. Occasionally Isham would shoot a question at Nohar. The questions were instructive in themselves. A hundred and fifty members of Congress had received MLI's money. Over seventy had been supported enough to have a massive conflict of interest. Thirty-seven congressmen had received enough money to owe their careers to MLI. Half of these people MLI bought had made it into the various House committees. Three of them held chairs—including the chair of Ethics committee. There were records of outright bribes to dozens of people in the executive.

And all of this had been done indirectly.

MLI's money *did* come from wholesale dealing in gemstones—massive dealings. They moved so many rocks that the whole lapidary industry was suffering a depression. The devaluation of diamonds and lesser stones didn't seem to bother MLI's balance sheet. They simply moved more rocks to compensate. There was no sign of where their inventory came from, but its volume justified the eighty billion in assets MLI claimed.

In with the accounting information was a collection of letters.

Isham asked about a few of them. None came from MLI itself. They were all forgeries from the hands of MLI's nonexistent employees.

A Jack Brodie from South Euclid, Ohio, wrote to ask a California legislator to consider helping to eliminate federal morey housing in that state. Just a simple request from someone who contributed twenty-five grand to his campaign.

Diane Colson, allegedly living in Parma, Ohio, "informed" a committee member on House Appropriations of all the waste in the federal budget. In the military and NASA in particular.

There was that August 10th letter—Wilson Scott from Cleveland was urging support for Binder's moreau control package, "in view of the recent violence." The smoking gun as far as the Zips were concerned. The proof the violence was engineered to get certain people elected Senate.

Isham dispensed with most of this with a few questions. She seemed to be in a hurry to assimilate the information. She only slowed once, over a letter from the familiar name Kathy Tsoravitch, written to Joseph Binder back in the Fall of 2043.

Isham looked up at Nohar. Her sunglasses were off and her retinas cast an orange reflection back at him. "What's NuFood?"

Nohar shrugged. "A little R&D enterprise MLI bought out. My friend with the computer thinks it's only there to smooth out the loss column of their taxes. Some sort of diet food."

"Why a food company?"

Nohar really didn't care. It wasn't his problem any more. "Diversification?"

To his surprise, Isham actually laughed a little. Her laugh was as silent as her breathing. "They went to a bit of trouble to get this particular company—"

Isham slid the letter across the desk and Nohar glanced it over. Kathy was positively adamant Binder prevent NuFood's enterprise from being approved by the FDA. If he remembered correctly, MLI bought out NuFood only a few months after this letter.

Isham riffled through the papers. "NuFood's ten million in assets is barely a ripple in MLI's finances. The patents are nearly worthless. It doesn't seem to have an income at all."

"I told you it was a tax dodge. A money pit the IRS would buy."

Isham looked at length of computer printout. She seemed to be talking to herself. "They why would they be piping money into it *before* it failed?"

The comm rang. Even though it wasn't her office, Isham didn't hesitate. "Got it."

When the comm lit up, only showing black, she said, "Bald Eagle here. This isn't a secure line."

An electronically modified voice came back. "We have the go."

The caller hung up.

Isham smiled and gathered up the papers. "Well, I'll ask these franks about NuFood when we have them in custody."

She locked the case and gestured to the door as she put on her mirrored sunglasses. When Nohar stood up, his knee began throbbing again. He had to grab the door frame to help himself move outside. Isham walked by him and started down the hall. She paused to turn and say to him, "I'm afraid we're going to have to keep a close eye on you until this clears. You're probably going to be stuck here for a while."

"I don't have anything better to do at the moment."

Nohar hobbled down the corridor and collapsed in a chair in a waiting room across from the lab where Manny was working. Isham passed him, going toward the stairs. She looked at the redhaired FBI agent who was sitting across from Nohar. She pointed at Nohar and the agent nodded.

It seemed Nohar now had his own personal pet FBI agent. The agent didn't wear shades, a normal human—

Even with the pet FBI guy, for once, Nohar was thankful for the Fed. With all this, MLI was blown open. There'd be nothing left for them to cover up. The violence should be over. He was sorry for Smith, but Nohar was glad *his* part had ended.

The agent looked vaguely uncomfortable. Nohar wondered whether it was because he was guarding a morey, because the morey he was guarding was still covered with graveyard mud, or because FBI agents were trained to look constipated as a matter of course. Nohar yawned and struggled his wounded leg up on a table.

Manny came out of the lab across from the lounge, trailing another agent. He carried a black bag in his good left hand. "Seems to be my eternal duty to patch you up. Let me see that knee while the lab techs troubleshoot the chemical analyzer."

Nohar's agent walked up so the two FBI guys framed Manny like human bookends. Manny was ignoring the agents as he felt along Nohar's right leg. Nohar tried not to wince, but Manny knew when he got to the tender area. "Damn it, you should have gone to the emergency room."

"And make the Fed divide their forces?"

"Very funny." Manny slit the pants around the knee, which was swollen a good fifty percent. Even under the mud and the fun, Nohar could see the discoloration. "You need an orthopedic surgeon. You may have done yourself some permanent damage."

Manny reached into the bag and got out an air-hypo and slipped in a capsule. "This is a local—" Manny shot the hypo into the leg and the pain left Nohar's knee, leaving no feeling at all. Then Manny pulled out a hypodermic needle, a large one. Manny found the needle impossible to maneuver with his bandaged right hand and shifted it to his left. When he did, the color leeched from the face of Nohar's agent. "I'm going to drain this and put another support bandage around it. And if you don't see a specialist about this, I swear I will hunt you down, trank you, and drag you there myself."

Manny slid the needle home. Nohar only felt a slight pressure under his kneecap. Nohar's agent, however, began to look ill. The guy got worse when Manny started withdrawing blood-colored fluid from Nohar's knee. Manny filled the hypo, put it in a plastic bag, and repeated the process with another hypo. The agent turned away, looking out the window at the hospital's parking garage.

Manny sponged off Nohar's knee with alcohol and a strong-smelling disinfectant that made Nohar want to retch. As Manny scrubbed, Nohar tried to get his mind off the smell. "What's with the analyzer?"

"Every new piece of equipment has some bugs—" Manny

sounded like he didn't quite believe it. He looked up at the agent who'd accompanied him. The guy stayed expressionless. "Your client was one weird frank. If frank is even the right term—nothing to indicate the gene structure even has a remote basis on the human model. It looks like it was engineered from scratch. I don't know what we got here. There was no cellular differentiation in the samples I salvaged. Through and through this guy was made of the same stuff."

Manny pulled out a bandage, a white plastic roll this time, not clear. As he wrapped it tightly around Nohar's leg, he continued, "No organs, nerves, skeletal system . . . all I can think of to explain it is all the constituent cells are multifunctional, able to do duty as anything the body needs as it needs it."

That was just plain weird. "No organs? Nerves? It—he had to have a brain. He was intelligent. He talked to me—"

"His identity, his 'mind,' would be distributed in electrical signals over his entire body. Just as all the other functions would be diffused within the creature. Eating, excreting—probably reproduces by binary fission."

Manny stood up and watched the bandage fuse and contract in response to Nohar's body heat. Nohar was still having trouble accepting what Manny was telling him. "Smith was just a huge amoeba?"

"In essence. Though a multicellular one. Just looking at the little sample we have is fascinating. The gene-techs that built this thing were geniuses."

"Great— *Why* would someone build something like that?"

Manny produced his undulating shrug again. "I'm only making inferences from a limited sample. But these things would be incredibly tough. Having all their vital function distributed throughout their mass, there's very little you could do to hurt them. Fire, acid maybe—"

"So how the hell did he die?"

"Electricity. The stunner is intended to temporarily paralyze a normal nervous system. Neural paralysis to *this* creature rendered the entire mass inert. Once that happened, the mass dissolved, from the inside out."

Manny closed up the black bag and picked up the used hypos. "They have a set of showers here for the staff, use one. I left you some hospital greens that might fit you. I better see if they've 'fixed' the analyzer yet." He turned and started trailing his agent back to the lab.

As Manny started back down the hall Nohar called after him. "What's wrong with the thing anyway?"

"Nothing much." Manny sounded like it was pretty major. "We'd just started to catalog amino acids and the display keeps coming up backward."

Once Manny had disappeared back into the lab Nohar waved at his redheaded agent, who still looked a little queasy. "You heard. Doctor's orders—shower."

As Nohar limped toward the showers, he tried to talk to his agent. "So, what do you think of Agent Isham?"

He answer in a voice as colorless as he was. "She's a good agent."

Talk about your stock answers. "So where is she now?"

"I've been encouraged not to speculate."

"Loosen up. You sound like the voice-over for a hemorrhoid commercial."

That got him. Nohar could swear he got a ghost of a smile from the guy. He looked down at the agent who was afraid of needles. "You bothered by guarding a morey?"

The agent shook his head. "I've worked with moreaus before. It's what our division is trained for."

Nohar stopped in front of the doors to the changing area. "That's not what I asked you."

Now there was a smile. A small one. "I suppose not. perhaps I'm bothered, a little. This is my first assignment, and all the moreaus I've trained with were federal recruits. Mostly Latin American—"

"Never prepared you for a tiger?"

"They can't train you to deal with everything. I apologize if I've seemed remote. You're an important witness, not a suspect—"

"My *name's* Nohar Rajasthan. What do I call you?"

The agent held out his hand. "Agen—Patrick Shaunassy."

Nohar gripped it and decided there was hope for him. "Pleased to meet you."

Shaunassy gave Nohar's hand a healthy shake. "Ditto. You're going to be taking a shower here?"

"Like I said, doctor's orders . . ."

Shaunassy opened the door. "Well, once I secure the area why don't I go back to the vending machines and get us some coffee?"

Nohar usually detested coffee, but he was feeling the lack of sleep catching up with him. "Do that, I could use a few cups."

They entered the changing area and Shaunassy stopped him at

the door. Shaunassy made an economical search of the room and the shower stalls as he spoke. "Sugar, cream?"

"Both."

He checked the toilet stalls. "Anything to eat?"

"Hate hospital food."

He returned to the door and made sure it had a lock. "Lock this until I come back. Shouldn't be more than ten minutes. If you're in the shower, I'll wait."

Shaunassy left and Nohar locked the door as requested. Amazing, scratch an FBI agent and there might be a person underneath.

The changing area was a study in white. White plastic lockers with recessed keypads, white fiberglass squares in the ceiling, white tile on the floor, white fluorescents—the only things in the room that weren't white were the greens Manny had left folded on the bench, and the chromed fixtures in the showers. The glare was irritating, so Nohar killed the lights, letting his eyes adjust to the darkness.

The disinfectant was bad here. It was killing his sense of smell. He wished there was a window in here he could open.

He breathed through his mouth as he removed the latest set of clothes he had destroyed.

He got into a shower, turned on a blast of cold water, and let the mud melt off his body. He found himself thinking, not of the FBI or the whole MLI business, but of Stephie Weir. All he wanted, right now, was to be in that motel room in Geauga. He was exhausted and had had enough of this bullshit. He just wanted to hold somebody—her—and get some sleep.

There was thirty grand in his account. He wondered if it was worth it.

He killed the shower and stood there, dripping, listening to the drain gurgle and wondering why he had taken the case in the first place. Did he really, subconsciously, want to go to California after Maria? Did he just want enough money to leave this burg? And where was that coffee?

He stepped over to the dryer—he was going to be done before Shaunassy got back—and slapped the large button with the back of his hand. He was enveloped in a nearly silent column of warm air. His abused muscles appreciated it.

Nohar nodded off a bit.

He slipped against the cold tiles and woke up. He shook the sleep from his head and walked out to the changing room. He spared a glance out the little rectangular windows into the hall. He hoped Shaunassy didn't see the lights off and assume he'd left already. He decided he wasn't going to wait behind a locked door just for Shaunassy to get back. The disinfectant smell in here was getting to him.

He unfolded the bottom of the greens and pulled them on. They fit around his waist, and they came down to a dozen centimeters past his knees. Nohar still had to split the seam on the bottom of the right leg to fit around the swelling.

The top that went with the pants—came short above the waistline and both arms—looked just plain silly. Nohar left it. While the boots he had been wearing were still intact, he left them. His feet needed to air out and it felt good to give the claws on his feet a chance to stretch.

Still no coffee, damn it.

Nohar opened the door and was no longer immersed in the disinfectant smell. Now he could smell fresh coffee, the same synthetic-smelling stuff Harsk drank.

Nohar also smelled blood.

He grabbed his Vind from the pile of his clothes and ran— limped, really, the drug Manny had shot into him was keeping him from feeling his knee, but didn't make it work any better—down toward the vending machines, the waiting area, the labs. The first corner he rounded brought him to the vending machines—

Shaunassy was dead.

He had slid halfway down the wall between the micro and the coffee dispenser. His right hand had knocked over a brown plastic tray, scattering small bulbs of cream and packets of sugar into the widening pool of blood. Three cups of coffee had spilled on the linoleum tile floor. The edges of the spill mixed with Shaunassy's blood, pulling swirls of red to mix with the tan—

Nohar's heartbeat was thudding dully in his ears.

Nohar pulled him away from the wall. Shaunassy hit the ground with a boneless splat. His throat hung open and his shirt was drenched with red. He was still warm.

The canine's musk hung in the air.

Hassan had done this. Probably with a straight razor.

Nohar kept up his limping run to the genetics lab, his breath a furnace in his throat. Why? Why was Hassan doing this?

The hall smelled like an abattoir. The smell of blood seemed to adhere to the back of Nohar's sinuses.

Nohar passed another agent. This one was crumpled in the middle of the hall. Hassan had sawed through the windpipe and had held the throat open. Blood had splattered halfway up the walls. Nohar stepped over the body, and his left foot slipped in the agent's blood. He ignored it and kept running, his foot making little tearing sounds each time he pulled it away from the linoleum.

He took the safety off the Vind and cocked it. The blood smell was getting worse. There was no question in Nohar's mind that Hassan was heading for the lab.

Nohar took in a deep breath, sucking in the smell of blood. His heart hammered in his ears, his head, and neck. Nohar raised his left hand to his mouth and tasted Shaunassy's blood.

For the first time, Nohar willingly invited The Beast into his soul.

The Beast came out and sniffed the air. Blood, it smelled human blood from at least five different people. It smelled the discharge of someone's gun. It smelled an excited canine. It smelled blood from a morey—

From Manny.

Nohar would have roared, but he was stalking now. Hassan didn't know he was here. The canine had passed by the changing area and the room had looked empty, the disinfectant had covered Nohar's smell. Nohar closed on the lab. It formed a T-intersection at the end of the hall. Ahead were a pair of fire doors, an agent crumpled against them, one arm hooked through one of the crash bars. To Nohar's right was the lounge. An agent was sprawled across the table. To Nohar's left were the swinging doors to the genetic lab. He could hear someone moving in there. He could smell Manny's blood.

Things slowed down as the adrenaline kicked in. One of the doors was half open. And this time Nohar recognized the smell of gasoline—

He crept up on the open door and listened, smelled the air. Hassan was in the rear of the room, to his right—

He burst through the door. Hassan turned, very quickly. Not quickly enough. Nohar's first shot hit him. Hassan's right shoulder exploded into a shower of blood. The canine dropped the package he was carrying and spun off to the left. Nohar, still moving toward the rear of the room, followed with another shot. That one missed and hit a large piece of equipment—probably the chemical analyzer—the impact exploded a picture tube and caused the body of a dead tech to roll off it and hit the floor.

The third shot followed Hassan, missed again, and slammed into a stainless steel sink. Water shot up in a mini-geyser.

Nohar was moving slowly, dreamlike. Hassan took cover behind a large, stainless steel object, an oven or an autoclave. Hassan was drawing a gun. Apparently the need for the stealth of a razor was over. Hassan took too long to aim, and Nohar's fourth shot hit his cover. A white jet of steam blew from the side of the machine, hitting his gun arm. Hassan's wild shot hit the ceiling, taking out a light fixture, and his gun sailed into the middle of the room.

The gun slid and came to rest next to the corpse of another FBI agent, sprawled facedown in a pool of blood in the center of the room. Nohar looked up and Hassan was hidden behind something—a cabinet, the chromed oven, or the other lab-tech, who was slumped over a cart, giving some cover.

Nohar covered the door and backed toward the corner where Hassan had started. His foot stepped on something soft—

Manny.

Manny was facedown on the ground. The slashing wounds on his throat were multiple, violent.

Nohar roared. He screamed rage as he advanced on Hassan's cover—

"Cat—"

Where did that voice come from? Behind the lab cart?

Nohar pumped four shots at Hassan, through the corpse of the lab-tech. Blood sprayed the white lab coat and the cart rolled across the floor with the impact, bottles rattling. There was scrambling, perhaps the smell of canine blood.

Nohar walked up and kicked over the cart. The tech thudded on the ground and the glass bottles shattered. The smell of alcohol filled the room. Hassan had moved behind a counter, closer to the exit. "Cat, thirty seconds and the place goes up. We both go. Still time to leave."

Nohar replied by pumping a shot into the base of the counter. Cabinet doors under the sink splintered.

The canine bolted for the door. Nohar bolted after him, firing. He missed and hit the light switch. The fluorescents winked out as a few anemic sparks leapt from the wall. Next shot was an almost. He could see the shell slam into Hassan's back, pushing him through the door—But the bastard wore a vest. The third shot slammed into the door, blowing a perfectly circular hole in it.

Nohar slammed through the door after the canine. Hassan was still picking himself up from the impact in his back. He had rolled into the lounge. Three shots in rapid succession—

Hassan would be dead if the gun wasn't empty.

Hassan stood up and backed toward a window. He started to open it. "Ten seconds, cat. You can make it down the hall—"

Hassan warded off Nohar with a blood-soaked straight razor in his left hand. His right was trying to fumble open the window in time . . .

The Beast didn't give up that easily, and Nohar wasn't going to stop it this time.

Nohar shifted the weight off his bad knee and leapt at Hassan, claws extended, roaring. Hassan cocked back with the razor to slash at Nohar's neck, but he was wounded, using his off-hand, and he was trying to do too many things at once. In peak condition, he might have hit Nohar. Instead, his forearm hit ineffectively against Nohar's right shoulder. Nohar grabbed Hassan's neck with his teeth as the window gave way before his weight.

Hassan's blood was the sweetest thing he had ever tasted.

The lab exploded.

Chapter 24

The window was blown apart by the explosion. They fell onto the top floor of the adjoining parking garage.

Hassan's back slammed into a car below them. The fiberglass underneath them gave and Nohar felt his knee sink into Hassan's chest. Something inside it broke. The canine coughed up blood.

Hassan cocked back with the razor again. Nohar responded with a back hand slash. The fully-extended claws of his right hand hit Hassan's left arm, slicing open Hassan's wrist. The razor went tumbling into the darkness.

Nohar's teeth were still buried in the flesh of Hassan's neck and canine blood spilled into his mouth.

Hassan jerked underneath him. The canine's flesh ripped out of his mouth, and Nohar head a collarbone snap. Hassan spilled out on the concrete drive and backed away, toward the end of the garage.

Somewhere a pink screamed.

Debris from above began to rain down on them.

". . . cat." Hassan spat a gob of bloody phlegm at the pavement. He seemed to be laboring to breathe and his voice had a breathy, bubbling quality to it. Nohar thought a rib must have punctured a lung. "Too bad, you didn't go . . ."

Hassan paused to get his breath as Nohar jumped from the car and advanced. "To Geauga with everyone else . . ."

Nohar was barely a meter from the canine and Hassan actually smiled. How—no, he couldn't have. There wasn't enough time.

But where had the Zipheads been when Smith got hit at Lakeview? Where were they now?

Hassan had backed all the way to the railing. Behind him was only space.

Nohar—The Beast—roared and swung his right hand. He aimed at the soft part of the skin under Hassan's lower jaw. The claws, and his fingers, dug in through the skin under Hassan's muzzle. Nohar's claws pierced the skin and crushed Hassan's tongue against the inside of the jaw. Hassan's eyes went wide with shock. Warm blood streamed out of the wound, soaking Nohar's arm.

Nohar put his whole body into the follow-through. He grabbed hold of Hassan's jaw from inside the mouth and his arm continued the swing. Hassan's weight barely slowed it. The swing carried the canine out over the edge of the roof. He was actually thrown upward before he started falling. Hassan slid off of Nohar's hand and followed a near-perfect ballistic arc to the ground.

Hassan crashed into an ambulance that was in the process of pulling out of the driveway below. The roof caved in with his weight, and the siren and flashers—for some reason—kicked in. The ambulance slowed to a stop and a pair of medics piled out to see what the hell had happened.

The Beast retreated but didn't leave. Nohar was shaking as he ran through Metro General's parking garage. No one stopped him as he made his way down, even though his arm and his face were streaked with Hassan's blood—or perhaps because of it. Good thing. Nohar was in a dangerous state of mind. Even an innocent bystander who got in his way would find himself in trouble.

Manny's van was still where they had parked it less than an hour ago. It cut diagonally across three parking spaces and was surrounded by a flock of dark-blue Haviers. One of the Haviers' doors hung open. The agents from it must have rounded the building to see Hassan's splat.

Manny had never bothered to hide the van's combination from Nohar. Nohar punched it in, opened the door, and got in the driver's seat. The feed ripped out as he floored the van out of the Metro lot.

He could still taste Hassan's blood and it didn't do a damn bit of good. Manny was dead, pointlessly.

"WHY?"

MLI was finished. It was all blown open. *Why?*

Nohar smelled Manny of the driver's seat and he wished the Indian techs had made his strain able to cry.

He was already pushing the van at one-twenty klicks an hour when he hit the I-90 ramp. He was dodging slower-moving cars when he remembered this van had a siren. He found the switch and turned it on. He stopped dodging. The other cars were pulling to the side.

He maxed it out at one-fifty as he shot through the exit on to the Midtown Corridor.

Even blowing down the Corridor, going twice the speed limit, gave him time to think, time he didn't want. He didn't want to know Manny was dead. He wanted The Beast to handle it. That's what it was for, damnit.

However, invoking his bioengineered combat-mode didn't help him a bit when it came to dealing with the death of the closest thing to a father he had ever had.

He needed to hit Mayfield, and fuck the barriers. He put on the seat belt.

He shot past the city end of Mayfield and took a right toward the Triangle parking garage. Between the bridge over Mayfield and the one over the driveway, there was a small hill that sloped toward the tracks. Nohar left the driveway and shot the van over the mostly dead lawn, up the hill, and over the dead tracks. A Dodge Electroline wasn't intended to take that kind of grade, but the velocity carried it over. The van started spilling over the other side of the hill, only going seventy now, headed for the side of an apartment building.

Siren still going, Nohar skidded the van to the right. The rear left corner clipped the building as he bumped on to the crumbling Moreytown section of Mayfield. The van rolled to a near stop, scattering the nocturnal population off of the street.

Nohar floored it again, feeling the uneven road in his kidneys.

After the first block, he was going eighty.

He passed the abandoned bus going a hundred.

Third block, he was going one-twenty—

Three concrete pylons blocked the road ahead of him, each three meters tall. The hulk of the dead Subaru was still wrapped around the center pillar.

He pulled the van all the way to the left, on to the sidewalk. On one side was now a concrete wall to Lakeview, and coming up on the right, one of the pylons. Nohar hoped the gap was big enough.

The front end screeched and the van bucked forward with a crunch—

He was through.

He'd made it. There was now a wobble on the front left tire, and he'd left both front fenders behind him. But now he was shooting east down Mayfield.

He was back to going one-fifty when he passed by Coventry. The cop on the riot watch only took three seconds to decide to give chase. Good for him. Nohar saw the first 322 marker when he passed the minimum-security prison. So far, the cop was the only shadow.

As long as the cop didn't try to stop him.

The vibration from the front wheel was getting worse, but he didn't slow. Malls and suburbia shot by him, a ghostly gray blur under the streetlights. His headlights had been taken out by his squeeze through the barrier. He drove by his night-vision and the infrequent streetlights.

Some shithead going through an intersection didn't get out of the way. Nohar wove a tight arc around the vehicle without hitting the brakes, and raked the side of the van across the rear end of the new BMW. It spun out and hit a light pole.

Suburbia vanished in a wave of trees. The Cleveland cop was still the only shadow, and they were now three suburbs out of his jurisdiction. The streetlights vanished with the malls and the split-levels. The only light now was the van's red flashers, turning the world ahead into a surrealistic image in pulsing-red monochrome.

He hit the county line and could see the blurred lights of the motel coming up on his right. Bobby had chosen a fifty-year-old relic to stash the girls—all tarnished chrome and flickering neon. Nohar saw the lights when he was about a klick away from the hotel and cut the siren as he slowed the van.

When he passed the entrance, he spun the van into the parking lot. The van was going seventy. The first thing he saw in the parking lot was a Ziphead with a submachine gun. The rat was standing guard outside a familiar-looking remote van. Nohar aimed his vehicle at him.

The ratboy's reaction time was just too slow. He jumped to the side too late to avoid being hit. Nohar heard a burst of ineffective gunfire as the wobbly front tire bumped up over the rat.

The front end of Manny's van plowed into the side of the remote. The remote tumbled forward like it had been jerked on a cable, the sudden deceleration throwing Nohar against the seat belt.

There was the sound of shattering glass. Then more gunfire. He felt a wave of shots strafe the rear of the van. He heard more gunfire, not aimed at the van.

Where he hell was his Vind?

Nohar felt the bottom fall out of his world when he realized he had lost it somewhere in the fight with Hassan.

Something inside him smelled the rat-blood under the van and told him it didn't matter. He was the hunter, they were prey—

And Stephie was in there.

He loosed a subliminal growl as he popped the seat belt and tumbled out the driver's side door, away from the motel. When he hit the ground he shuddered in pain. He was beginning to feel his knee again. He let the pain jack up the adrenaline.

He took cover behind the van—most of the shots were coming from the hotel. He looked at where the shots seemed to be going and saw the Cleveland cop car. The cop was huddling down behind the front fender. The flashers were going, but a bullet had taken out the plastic covering them—the flashers were now giving off a stark white searchlight glare. The cop looked like he had taken a hit or two. Nohar recognized him. He was the pink cop who had looked so scared when he and Manny had passed him—the night all this shit started.

The whelp had better've called backup.

The ratboy who'd guarded the remote was a smear on the pavement. When he looked at the corpse, he could feel his time sense telescoping. The rest of the Zips were holed up in the motel. The Zips weren't paying attention to him yet. The cop must've rounded into the parking lot just after he had plowed in.

The wreck of the remote offered him some more cover. Nohar hunkered down and ran along the side of the wreck on all fours, right leg barely touching the ground.

The motel was simply a line of rooms facing the parking lot. The nose of the remote was only a meter in front of a door—the room next to the Zips. Nohar tackled the door, and the cheap molding splintered. He kept going, tumbling onto a twin bed. The legs on the bed snapped off and spilled Nohar onto a synthetic rug that smelled of mothballs, rug shampoo, and old cigarette smoke. The room was empty.

Nohar could hear the gunfire and the Zip's chittering Spanish through the thin drywall. He stood up and looked for a weapon.

The room's comm was bolted to its own table. His shoulder protested as he lifted it. The cable connection ripped out of the wall, taking a wall plate and ripping a hole up the drywall for nearly a meter before it snapped free. Knee shaking, he lifted the comm over his head—it had to weigh thirty kilos—and listened to the Zips.

One was near the wall. It sounded like he had a nine-millimeter. Nohar aimed the comm at that one—

The comm and attached table flew in an arc that intersected the wall. It hit dead center at a fake painting—some anonymous land-scape—and crashed through the drywall separating the two rooms. The mylar wallpaper tore away in sheets, following the comm through the hole.

Perfect hit on the rat—bandage on the face marked this guy as Bigboy—the side of the comm hit the rat in the face and the picture tube imploded, adding a small cloud of phosphor powder to the plaster dust.

The comm kept going, knocking away a table another rat was using for cover. The rat—dressing on his arm marked him as the one with the chain—turned to face Nohar. That was a stupid mis-take. The cop was still covering the picture window from behind the cop car.

The cop put a .38 slug through the rat's neck before the ratboy realized he had lost his cover.

The hole in the wall was a meter square.

Nohar jumped through without any hesitation. He aimed at the third rat, who was hiding behind a set of dresser drawers.

For a moment Nohar bared his entire flank to the cop, the kid had a perfect shot through the long-ago-vaporized picture window. Nohar didn't care.

Nohar landed on the third rodent, Fearless Leader. Leader had a revolver, a forty-four. An old gun but powerful. He tried to turn it on Nohar, but Nohar grabbed the ratboy's wrist—it was in a cast—and slammed it into one of the open drawers of the dresser. Then he crunched the drawer shut with his entire weight. The gun went off inside the dresser, blasting chunks of particleboard over the rat the cop had shot.

Fearless was looking at Nohar with wide eyes, going into shock. Somewhere, under the growling, Nohar found his voice. "So, 'pretty kitty's' next?" The rat tried to shake his head.

Nohar slashed Fearless Leader's throat open with his claws, opened the drawer, and removed the gun from the sputtering ro-dent.

The gunfire had ceased.

He could smell perfume coming from the bathroom, over the cordite. Nohar could also smell blood that didn't come from a rat. He gave the cop a great shot at his back as he bolted for the bath-room door at the rear of the motel room.

Somewhere, where his rational mind was hiding, he prayed to Maria's God he wasn't too late.

He kicked the door open, sending a piercing dagger of pain

through his right leg. Terin turned toward him. She was picking up a nasty looking assault rifle. It looked too big for her. It was certainly too big for the small bathroom. Terin couldn't sweep it to cover the door.

There was a bloody knife sitting on the sink. Something small and blood-covered was hanging in the shower—

"I'll give you the fucking Finger of God."

The first shot hit her in the chest, slamming the rat into the white tile wall.

The second got her in the face.

The third clicked on an empty chamber.

There was a weak sound from the shower ". . . way to go, Kit . . ."

Chapter 25

Angel's voice brought him back. The Beast didn't go back to its mental closet—the closet didn't seem to be there anymore—but it did let his rational mind take over. For the first time Nohar felt the full impact of what he had put his body through. Glass had been ground into his left foot. The falls and the leaping had strained his back. His knee couldn't hold his weight anymore. Any pressure on it was agonizing—

He grabbed the sink and pulled himself into the bathroom. He looked into the shower. Angel's hands were tied to the showerhead. Her feet didn't touch the floor. She was still conscious, and her face was recognizable. Terin had been working from the bottom up. Terin was experienced at shaving moreys—the process was supposed to be long, painful, and the victim was supposed to live up to and, hopefully, a little past the end.

Angel's legs had become strips of bleeding meat.

"Kit, you look like hell . . ."

Nohar gritted his teeth and knelt slowly to examine the damage. It was bad, Angel was probably in shock. He dropped the forty-four in the toilet and grabbed Terin's knife. He stood on his left leg and circled his right arm around, under Angel's armpits, as he cut the bonds on her hands. Her weight nearly toppled him over. He pulled himself along, out of the bathroom, with his left hand. The three rodents that had been covering the picture window didn't move. Every half-second the room was bathed in the searchlight glare of the cop's flashers. Nohar wondered where the cop was.

He laid Angel out on one of the twin beds. Her legs began to stain the white sheet. "I'm calling an ambulance—"

Her head was cocked toward the front of the room. "Only one?"

Nohar went to this room's comm, it was intact. He called emergency. "I need a half-dozen ambulances, Woodstar Motel off route 322 in Chesterland, humans and moreys—cops, too, some of these people are dead—"

The dispatch cop nodded. "What's the problem there?"

He didn't bother to hang up. He turned to Angel. Somewhere along the way he had screwed up, badly. "Where's Stephie?" He almost didn't get the words out. He was too afraid of the answer.

"Back in our room, last in line. Talked about having a hostage. Left a Zip with her . . ."

Oh, shit. If a ratboy was left with her, the bastard would probably kill her once he saw how the fight went. Nohar hobbled over to the picture window; still no sign of the cop. He reached and turned Bigboy over. The rat had been using an Uzi. Nohar grabbed the gun and crawled out the window. Once outside, he saw the cop. Fearless had got off one well placed shot. The cop was unconscious or dead.

Because of his knee, he had to advance on Stephie's room while leaning against the wall. His progress was agonizingly slow. He passed the wreck of the remote and the door he had busted in. He passed an unoccupied room. Slowly, he came upon the last in the line, the black GM Maduro parked in front.

He checked the clip on the Uzi. Good thing Bigboy wasn't spraying the cop. There were a few shots left. He hit the ground and scrambled under the picture window—the right knee was beginning to make popping sounds every time he moved—and rolled in front of the door.

With the feeling this was going to be it for him, he shouldered the door open and covered the room with the Uzi.

And there was Mister Mad bomber, looking like he was about to wet his pants. The rat's twenty-two thumped on the carpet.

Stephie was alive, and apparently unhurt. She had been stripped naked and tied to the bed. She turned her head toward the door when it burst open. She had never smelled so good to him.

The Beast wanted Nohar to shoot the rat. To Nohar's surprise, he still had control. Even though the mental door was no longer there.

"Kid, second chances are rare, use yours. Get out of here."

The rat carefully approached the door, where Nohar was still half-sitting, stepped over him, and ran into the night. Stephie's eyes were wide as she watched Nohar pull himself into the room and on to the bed. Nohar didn't waste time. He bit through the rope.

As soon as Stephie was free, Nohar found himself on the receiving end of an embrace that smeared her with blood. "God, what's happened to you—where's Angel?"

"Angel, I called an ambulance for her—and everyone else. They killed Manny—"

Stephie broke off the hug. "Oh, Christ, I'm sorry—"

"Can you find me something to use as a cane?"

The curtain rod was stainless steel, and not as cheap as everything else in the motel. It made a halfway decent cane. Stephie found a robe and followed him out to the parking lot. He asked aloud the question that had gnawed at him ever since he had smelled Shaunassy's blood—

"Damn it, why?"

He hobbled to the wreck of the remote. The power plant was still alive. The wheels were trying to drive it away despite the broken axle. He walked up to the vehicle. Green, just like Smith's van. Hell, it could *be* Smith's van. "The whole thing was *blown*. The Fed has *everything*."

He slammed his left fist at one of the dangling pneumatic doors. There was a slow hiss, and the door slid aside with the smell of leaking hydraulic fluid. There were guns and a dozen white plastic crates in back. Most of the crates had burst open. Little vials of red liquid rolled out the rear of the van. Hypo cartridges—flush, a few million dollars' worth.

The DEA would be happy.

Nohar leaned in and looked at the crates more closely. They were labeled. "NuFood Inc. dietary supplements—MirrorProtein(tm)"

MLI was using NuFood as a drug lab.

There had to be another reason for NuFood. The Zips had only come on the scene recently. MLI had been dealing with NuFood ever since MLI's inception.

MirrorProtein?

What was it Manny said about the chemical analyzer? They had been cataloging amino acids and the display was reversed. Nohar had thought the picture had been coming up backward.

What if it was the amino acids themselves that were coming up reversed?

"Stephie, do you know any biochemistry?"

Stephie was already at the Zips' room checking on Angel. *"What?"*

Nohar hobbled after her. His thoughts were flying, trying to remember things, put them into place. "This is important. Really important. Biochemistry, proteins, amino acids, what do you know?"

"Next to nothing." She had her hand on Angel's neck. "She's still alive—What the hell are you talking about?"

"I need to remember if we're based on levo or dextro amino acids . . ."

"Derry was the chemistry major. Where the hell are you getting this from?" Stephie was looking worried, as if she thought he had gone over the edge.

Far from it. Things were making sense. "I don't know if you'll understand this." He was racing to get it all out. "I lived most of my childhood with Manny—a doctor and an expert on moreaus. I got a biology lesson every time I asked a question like, 'Why am I different from the other kids?' "

Even to him he sounded like he was rambling. He slowed down. "You can't live like that and not pick up on biological trivia. Like the fact our amino acids all have their mirror image versions." He finally remembered. "Almost all the life in this world is based on levo amino acids—"

"So?"

Nohar shook his head. "Just tell the cops when they get here. You have to talk to an FBI agent—Isham. Tell her the franks aren't at MLI's office building. It's just a front, like everything else. If they're anywhere, they're at NuFood's R&D facility. Tell her the MLI franks are based on a *dextro* amino acid biology. Got that?"

"Yes, but—"

Nohar was hobbling back to the Maduro. He stopped at the remote. An Uzi wouldn't do much to one of the things Manny described. He looked in among the crates of flush and saw a pump shotgun. He'd take that, and hope.

He was beginning to hear sirens in the distance. Stephie ran after him. "Where are you going?"

"NuFood. This isn't over—"

He slumped up next to the car. "Did they wire the car?"

"No—"

"What's the combination?"

"Nohar, you can't! You're in no condition . . ."

"The damn combination!"

Stephie backed up a bit at Nohar's growled command. Nohar shook his head. "*Please,* God damn it."

Stephie heard the sirens now as well.

She stepped up and punched the combination on the driver's door. Nohar watched the numbers. She looked up at him afterward. She was crying. "You are not going to die on me."

Nohar hugged her with his good arm. "I don't intend to."

The Maduro had pulled out of the parking lot and was going down Mayfield by the time a convoy—Chersterland and Cleveland local cops, sheriffs from Cuyahoga and Geauga, six ambulances, two police wreckers, a fire rescue vehicle, and three Haviers—shot by going in the opposite direction. Everything but the National Guard.

Nohar drove by them going a sedate sixty klicks an hour. He was squeezed in the sports car, but the gentle ride of the undamaged suspension made up for it.

Everything came together for him when he saw that NuFood label. He had been right along. Despite the hyped violence, the morey terrorism, the Johnson killing came down to one little piece of information in Binder's financial records.

The precognitive letter from Wilson Scott was only part of it. That only proved MLI had a hand in planning the Zipheads' terrorism. MLI was trying to hide something else.

Their origin.

Johnson used to be a chemistry major. It made sense he would figure this mess out.

It had all started thirteen years ago. Midwest Lapidary would have approached Young, Binder's new finance chairman. It would have been a very tempting offer. Young took the offer, and the bucks poured into the campaign.

And Binder's position became more and more reactionary.

Over the next few years, other, similarly unpopular candidates had made some sort of deal with the shadowy diamond merchants working out of Cleveland—candidates that weren't supposed to win. Their positions would evolve as well.

Then, in 2042, morey communities across the country exploded into a week of riots and burning that took the National Guard to control. Led by the psychopathic rhetoric of a morey tiger named Datia Rajasthan.

The violence created a convenient wave of anti-moreau sentiment that catapulted most of MLI's candidates to office.

MLI had about seventy hard-core puppets in the House now, all incumbents. They only had a few men in the Senate, though, and a large percentage of their men, including Binder, wanted to be Senators.

The rogue agents in MLI, without Smith's knowledge, recruited the Zipheads to step in to create their own "Dark August." The Zipheads were happy to comply, considering the profits they made on flush on the street level.

Daryl Johnson knew or suspected all of this. At first he must have condoned it. You couldn't keep that kind of conspiracy secret from the campaign manager. The whole Binder inner circle must have known about the illegal financing. That's why it was so tight. Harrison, Thomson, Johnson, and Young stuck with Binder through his radical shift to the right. They *all* had been bought.

Johnson was the first to have second thoughts. Nohar suspected that it would probably have originated with the whole duplicitous situation with Stephie. It must have grated badly. He stewed for years. Even tried to drug himself out of an untenable situation.

MLI must have thought they had him under control because he was hooked on flush that they supplied—though indirectly. If he did anything to break the silence, his supply would be cut.

Three weeks before his death Johnson found a new supplier. Nugoya.

That wasn't what got him killed. The flush still came from MLI, they still controlled his supply even though Johnson didn't know that. What killed Johnson was *why* he was trying to get out from under the thumb of his supplier. Johnson's problem was curiosity. He thought too much.

He had thought too much about NuFood.

He thought too much about Kathy Tsoravitch's letter.

Johnson made the mistake of wondering, as Isham had just a few hours ago, why MLI would be interested in preventing NuFood from succeeding. Tsoravitch lobbied to prevent FDA approval. Denial of that approval bankrupted NuFood.

Whereupon, MLI bought out the company, and the patents.

Why?

The question must have nagged Johnson for years. Especially when MLI simply sat on the company. He might even have realized that MLI was using NuFood as its flush lab. A very expensive drug lab.

He finally figured out the real reason. When he did, he made his second, and last, mistake. He told Young. And Young had told the creatures running MLI—

That's when the shit went ballistic. That's why Young was so scared, as well as guilty. He *knew* MLI's secret—they would have killed him once he had served his purpose, IDing the people in the campaign whom Johnson had talked to, those who read the letter.

But Young toasted himself, so MLI had to use their agents— Hassan and the Zipheads—to waste anyone who could have read that letter.

All from Kathy Tsoravitch's letter, and her pleading that the DA reject NuFood's application to mass market their dietary supplements. Supplements that were based on synthetic proteins derived from the mirror image dextro amino acids. Proteins a creature based on a levo amino acid biology—like the fat pinks at whom the food would be targeted—couldn't metabolize.

Johnson had looked too closely at MLI's agenda. He saw Nu-Food, moreys as a hot issue to be counted on to get MLI's people elected, and the budget. And the letters about government waste always mentioned NASA.

Johnson must have seen the creatures running MLI—the humanoid things that could only be franks. Otherwise, Nohar doubted Johnson would have come to the conclusion he must have. Because the truth was quite a leap.

Nohar's Maduro had glided into the suburbs again. He began watching the left side of Mayfield. NuFood's R&D complex was at 3700 Mayfield, near the minimum security prison he had passed earlier. NuFood's plot was cheap property, little-traveled.

The conclusion was simple, if hard to accept. Johnson must have asked himself the same question as Nohar did when Smith told him MLI supported Binder.

Why were a bunch of franks backing right-wingers like Binder?

They weren't franks.

Why the hell were they involved with something like NuFood?

Johnson must have inferred what Nohar had told Stephie. These things were based on a dextro amino acid biology. Manny had discovered that from Smith's remains. Manny had known, but he had never gotten the chance to double-check the results. He never got the chance to make sure the analyzer wasn't broken.

That was what MLI had to cover up.

The prison came up on the left.

Nohar pulled the Maduro over and parked on the sidewalk across from it. NuFood was next to the prison's barbed wire topped chain link. It sat in the midst of a grove of trees and bushes that nearly hid the two lab buildings from sight.

They couldn't let anyone know they were based on a mirror image biology. It was because of that *they* needed NuFood. *They* literally couldn't live without it. Normal living things couldn't metabolize NuFood's products, but the converse was true. NuFood's production was the only thing *they* could eat.

No gene-tech, even as an experiment, would give their work such a bizarre handicap. Johnson would know that. It left one conclusion.

These things *weren't* bioengineered.

They had evolved naturally.

It was a fifty-fifty chance life on Earth ended up stabilizing around the one type of amino acid. Life elsewhere, if it evolved as it had on Earth, would end up stabilizing around one form or the other, dextro or levo. Same chance, fifty-fifty. Even odds. It was just bad luck, for everyone concerned, that these guys came from a planet that was based on the wrong type.

They were aliens.

Nohar hobbled across the street.

Chapter 26

The storm that had been threatening all night finally came as Nohar crossed Mayfield. It was a sudden deluge that washed some of the blood off of him. His makeshift cane was thumping an erratic counterpoint to the click of his claws. It was slow progress, but it was nearly three in the morning and there wasn't any traffic. The street was dead.

He made it across. To his right was the prison hiding behind its electrified chain link. Its yard was bathed in arc lights.

To his left was a line of shrubs and trees that almost hid an old, low slung, office complex from the street. Ahead of him, between the overgrown shrubs and the five-meter tall electric chain link, was a dirty-gravel driveway. It looked like a landscaping afterthought.

He began worrying about the pink guards at the prison. They weren't involved in this, but it wouldn't be good if they noticed a morey with a shotgun skulking just outside their grounds.

He limped a dozen meters down the gravel path, all the while cursing his knee and wishing he could move faster. He made it to a point where the hedges got sickly. He turned away from the prison and pushed through a small gap between the bushes. He immediately tripped over a rusted "No Trespassing" sign. He managed to land on his left side, but the fall still hurt his knee.

He was sprawled on a shaggy, uncut lawn, looking across at a parking lot of broken asphalt. The only light came from the arcs of the prison behind him. Half the NuFood complex was wrapped in glaring blue light, the other half in the matte-black shadows of the surrounding trees.

Two remote vans were parked in the lot, the only vehicles there. There were two buildings in NuFood's complex, both old two-story studies in metal, glass, and dark tile. The tiles had been falling off in clumps, helped by ill-looking ivy. The glass was sealed shut from the inside. A few panes were cracked and broken—real glass—allowing Nohar a good look at the white plastic that covered the windows from the inside.

Between the two buildings were an overgrown lawn and a crumbling driveway. A fountain was choked by an advancing rosebush—and even in the rain, he could smell the stagnant water filling it.

These guys weren't big on maintenance.

Nohar pushed himself up and got unsteadily to his feet. The makeshift cane sank about half a meter into the sod when he put his weight on it. He squished to the asphalt parking lot.

The remotes were parked next to each other. Nohar hobbled between them. He decided if the guards back a prison started hearing gunfire, the worst thing they could do was call the cops.

He eased himself down on the ground and looked under the chassis of one of the vans. The inductor housing was nestled in front of the rear axle. Nohar leveled the shotgun at it, the barrel a few centimeters from the housing. He turned his face away, closed his eyes, and pulled the trigger.

The blast popped the pressurized housing, and the air was filled with the smell of freon, ozone, and the dust from a shattered ceramic superconductor. There was a wave of heat as the housing sparked and began to melt

He did the same to the other one.

There went their transport. If *they* were still here, they'd *stay* here.

The guards back at the prison had heard the gunfire. Sirens began sounding behind him.

Nohar hauled himself upright and limped up the circular driveway to the first NuFood building. The door was glass and black enamel. Gold leaf on the glass announced this was indeed NuFood. Its slick modern logo was flaking off. A chain was padlocked around the handle, the one thing that looked new and well maintained.

Locks on glass doors made about as much sense as an armored door in a wooden door frame.

Nohar hunched up against the wall for support and raised the curtain rod. He put the end of the rod through the logo, shattering the glass—real glass again. There was another plastic sheet sealing the window. It tore away from the frame, loosing the bile-ammonia smell Nohar associated with Smith.

Bingo.

There was a crash bar on the inside of the door, halfway up. The plastic caught and bent over it. Nohar had to lean the curtain rod up next to the doorjamb so he had a hand free to knock the plastic out of the way. In response to Nohar's break-in, an alarm inside the building did an anemic imitation of the sirens at the prison.

Because of his leg, Nohar put down the shotgun and scrambled under the crash bar on both hands and his good leg. He sliced open his right palm on a stray piece of glass.

Once he pulled the cane and the gun after him, he pushed himself up to a standing position.

Inside, the place was much better maintained—and strange. He could smell *their* odor, as well as the odors of chemicals—there was a strong hint of sulfur and sulfur dioxide—and disinfectant that had a fake pine odor. The hall he was in was brightly lit with sodium lamps. They cast an unnatural yellow glow over the hallway. There were filters on the lamps that seemed to increase the effect. The floor he was hobbling along had been stripped to the concrete. It had been polished and felt slightly moist under his feet. Not water. It was damp with something more viscous that made it hard to keep his footing.

The first door to his right was open. He looked in and saw a storage area. The room must have filled half the building, both floors. It was stacked with white plastic delivery crates. It was lit with normal fluorescents, and to the rear was a rolling metal door that must open onto a truck-loading bay. Nohar could smell the flush—even through the packaging, there was so much of it—a rotten, artificial fruit smell, like spoiled cherries.

Nohar continued to limp down the hallway. The doors he passed on his left were new, solid, air lock doors. He looked through the round porthole windows, and saw clean rooms containing glass laboratory equipment filled with bubbling fluids. Here was the damn flush lab the DEA wanted. Nice sterile environment. The stuff must be real pure.

He kept walking, following the ammonia smell. *They* were here. He could feel it. He kept going down the corridor. It took a right turn near the far wall. More labs, older, not behind air lock doors. Nohar noticed familiar items that matched the genetics lab at Metro General. Especially the hulking form of the chemical analyzer. This had to be part of the food production, R&D anyway. Any real volume processing must happen in the other building.

Nohar rounded the corner and faced a stairwell, up and down. Same slick polished concrete. The sulfur and the ammonia were worse going down. That's where he went.

The steps went slowly, one at a time. Each step felt like he was going to slip and break his neck. As he descended, the atmosphere became thicker, denser. The sodium lights faded to a dusky red, and Nohar was beginning to feel the heat—the temperature down here must be around 35 or 40. The atmosphere was heavy with moisture that clung to his fur.

The heat and the heavy atmosphere were making his head throb. He could feel his pulse in his temple.

Down, he was in the basement. Here, there was no pretense at normal construction. The hall was concrete that had been polished to a marblelike sheen. All the right angles had been filled in and polished smooth, giving an ovoid cross section. The walls were weeping moisture that had the viscosity of silicone lubricant.

There were pipes and other basement equipment, but all had been molded into the walls. Nohar looked up and saw a length of white PVC pipe just above his head. Concrete had been molded around the ends where it came in through the wall so the wall's lines melded smoothly with the length of pipe. It looked like some organic growth. Nohar looked at one wall, and from the discoloration he could make out where the lines of the old cinder block wall used to be.

There was only one way to go. He followed the hall. He hobbled down and left the last of the yellow sodium lights, and entered the world of green-tinted red. The ammonia smell was very close now.

He rounded a very gradual turn in the hall. It felt like he was hobbling through a wormhole in the bowels of the earth. He completed the turn, and saw a perfectly round door. Out the door was pouring an evil bluish-green light and that bile-ammonia smell.

Nohar stumbled through the opening and covered the room with a shotgun held, clumsily, in his left hand. He didn't realize the floor was a half-meter lower than the floor in the hall until it was too late. His good foot slipped away. He tried to catch himself with the cane in his right hand, but the pipe was slick with blood from his palm and slid off into the room, beyond his reach. He slid down a steep concrete curve sitting on his bad leg. He heard a crack. A shiver of agony told him he was not going to walk again for a long time.

He did manage to keep a grip on the shotgun.

Through his pain-blurred vision, he realized that if there had been any doubt Smith wasn't the product of some pink engineer, one look at this room put all doubts to rest. The room was a squashed sphere nearly ten meters in diameter. Eight evenly spaced round holes were in the walls, doors like the one he had come through. In the center of the room was a two-meter-tall cone, molded of concrete, shooting up a jet of blue-green flame. From it came most of the oppressive heat in the room, and the smell of burning methane.

The wall had niches carved into it. Hundreds of them, all the same size, a meter long by half a meter high. They were concave, oval pits that angled down into the wall slightly. From nearly half of them came the glitter of MLI's wealth, diamonds, rubies, emeralds. Thousands, perhaps hundreds of thousands, of stones—

And, of course, there were Smith's kinsmen. The creatures that ran Midwest Lapidary. Four, in all, were facing him. They were wearing pink clothing, like Smith had. They all had the same blubbery white humanoid form that Smith wore.

"That's why," Nohar managed through gritted teeth. "The hit in Lakeview. Couldn't tell who he *was* over the comm . . ."

One of them addressed him in Smith's blubbery voice. "We do not do such things lightly. We must be certain of the right when we do such irrevocable acts. A waste you must be here—"

The pain in his leg was making him dizzy. He was beginning to feel cold, clammy. In this heat, he must be going into shock. "*Right?*" It was a yell of pain as much as an accusation. "I talked to Smith." Nohar caught his breath. "You were breaking your own rules when you cut him out of the loop." Nohar wished he had one of Manny's air-hypos.

"He is a traitor. He knows not that the mission is paramount. He clings to propriety as if we are in—" A word in the alien's language. "And not in this violent sewer."

Another one continued. "We do not allow ourselves to perform physical violence. The traitor does not understand our circumstance is dire and requires an exception."

Nohar was beginning to have trouble feeling his leg. The dizziness was getting worse. "End justifies the means?"

A third one, near the cone, spoke. "It is a waste. The tiger understands."

The first one—perhaps the leader, but Nohar was having trouble keeping track of these similar creatures—continued. "The traitor, perhaps, understands or suspects our plans when he hires you. It is intended you lead the new unrest—"

The one by the cone, "—like your father leads the convenient rebellion eleven years ago. The traitor anticipates us and hires you against us—"

"The traitor," one of them went on, "knows what kind of resonance there is when he hires you—"

"—Datia is a useful charismatic figure to keep unrest going, Datia's son is useful as well. A waste the traitor talks to you before us—"

The one by the cone bent—no, oozed—over to turn a valve that was recessed in a concave depression near its base. The flame sputtered out. "It doesn't matter. We go, take our supplies and begin elsewhere. We have done well to prepare for the time the plan is uncovered—"

Nohar shook his head too quickly. He felt faint.

He couldn't tell them apart. They all looked like Smith, all smelled like Smith, talked like Smith. "You guys blew it—"

"Who are you to judge? We achieve our end—"

"It was the vote to scuttle the NASA deep-probe project, wasn't it? It will hit the Senate after the election and you just couldn't wait . . ."

All the *things* stopped moving. They didn't say anything, didn't move. Nohar slowly raised the shotgun.

"Enough of your pet congressmen were supposed to win Senate seats to tip the scales on the vote. Then the shit hits the fan and MLI falls apart. You designed the whole thing to be uncovered eventually. The phony identities are just *too* damn phony. You want the scandal and the indictments that would follow to throw the Congress into chaos—"

Nohar paused to catch his breath. He couldn't feel his leg at all anymore.

They were regrouping to face him. He still had the shotgun covering them, and he hoped desperately it would do some good. "The Fed was about to follow up all your false trails. The DEA was about to find its flush manufacturing center. But you blew it. Forensics was not supposed to get to Smith's body that fast. There wasn't supposed to *be* a body. You tried to have Hassan erase that mistake. It was too late. I know, and now, the Fed knows."

That got them. They were looking at each other. One spoke, "Then we must end it—"

"End us—"

One of them headed back for the cone while another addressed Nohar. "We complete our original mission. We end ourselves. Nothing is left but speculation and pieces of paper. Without physical evidence, no probes are sent. Your violent races will not contaminate our star systems. We need those new worlds, you will not take them away—"

Nohar was leveling the shotgun at the one that was at the cone. "No, you're not getting off that easy. No suicides. And you call us violent. How many people have you managed to kill because of those probes? A tac-nuke on the moon would have done the same thing, and not killed anyone—"

"Law requires we act indirectly in covert activity."

Nohar gagged on that one. "*Law?* You screwed-up bastards—no wonder the only one of you with a shred of morality ended up a 'traitor.'"

It kept moving. They were going to flood the room with methane. Nohar pumped the shotgun and shot the creature. Bile and ammonia filled the air, and the creature was knocked back to the far wall. A chunk of the creature's translucent flesh splattered against the wall. But it didn't bleed, didn't even leak. The shot had passed right through it.

It stood up, none the worse for wear.

"Unnecessary display, such things do not hurt our kind. Useless since we end now anyway."

The thing went back to the valve and started turning. "You, and others, may know we originate from a different biology. But without us to examine, your ethnocentric culture never accepts the idea of an extraterrestrial culture."

Nohar lowered the shotgun.

What were they going to do, asphyxiate or ignite? Didn't matter, he was dead either way—his leg wouldn't let him move.

Chapter 27

The one at the valve had finished his job, and Nohar could hear the hiss of the methane.

The creature had half-turned toward him when Nohar heard a soft "phut" from the hole behind him. A small tube had planted itself in the folds under the creature's chin. There was a bubbling groan from the creature, and it raised a flabby white arm to the tube stuck in its neck.

Three more "phuts" and similar tubes embedded themselves in the other aliens. There was a shuddering moan from the first one. Its arm had stopped halfway to its neck. There was a tearing sound as the pink clothes gave way and the thing collapsed into a shapeless white mass. There was a clatter as its eyes, fake plastic orbs, rolled off the mound of shuddering flesh. A pair of pink dentures followed.

The others collapsed as well.

They weren't dead, so much as reverted to some natural state. They still moved, though in a shuddering, rhythmic fashion—occasionally throwing out a multitentacled pseudopod from their mass, only to be reabsorbed into the mound of flesh a moment later. They now *looked* like the amoebic form of life Manny had described.

Isham came through the hole behind Nohar and went to the valve on the cone, shut it off. She was talking to herself. ". . . cave dwellers, lots of heat vents and volcanic activity. Dim red-yellow sun, thick atmosphere, probably high gravity. They could survive very heavy acceleration. Could have ridden in on a nuclear rocket not much more advanced than our own. Gems are probably synthetic . . ."

Nohar hadn't realized how tightly he was holding the shotgun until he tried to drop it. His hands didn't want to move. "Damn it, Isham. Where did you come from, and what took you so long?"

Isham squatted and was looking at one of the quivering mounds of alien flesh. She poked it with the end of an air rifle she was carrying. The white flesh rippled like a water balloon. "We were staked out at Midwest Lapidary 'headquarters.' NuFood seemed too small to rate notice. Our team got word from the DEA. McIntyre and Conrad have been two steps behind the Zipperheads all night, ever since the rats jumped a cabbie at the airport. They radioed your message, and my team had to scramble all the way from downtown. I was point, got here about two minutes after you did—"

"What?" Nohar had spoken too loudly. He was suddenly out of breath and felt faint.

She activated her throat-mike. "Aerie, this is Bald Eagle—nest is clear, send the Vultures in with the cleanup. We need a local ambulance, with our own medics. Out."

She stood up and looked into one of the niches in the wall. She reached in and took out a diamond. It glinted red facets of light.

"I had to tape them just in case the drug killed them. Otherwise, their rapid decomposition would be hard to explain to Washington—"

"You were there." Nohar was fighting alternating waves of pain and nausea. "All that time?"

She tapped a lens hanging off her belt with the diamond and dropped the gem back in the niche. "Two meters behind you. All the way through the building."

Nohar sighed.

"That D amino acid information was vital. But you threw the tac-squad for a loop. We had stunners, but we wanted the 'franks' alive. And because of you, we discovered the trank we were using wouldn't have worked right on their biology—"

Nohar looked at the pulsing forms of the aliens. "What'd you use?"

"The only thing I had access to, flush. It's a symmetrical molecule. Probably use the same stuff, wherever they come from."

Talk about poetic justice. "What happens now?"

"The cleanup crew'll be here in about three minutes. They'll pack these things up. The Fed will take over the processing plant here, keep them alive. If we're lucky, these will lead us to any more covert cells these guys have set up in the country. You *do* understand this is a national security matter. These *are not* aliens. This didn't happen."

The Fed and its passion for secrets. It was becoming difficult to remain conscious. "What about the Zipperheads, and the politicians?"

"The DEA has the Zipperheads. They can have them. The MLI plot was designed to unravel, so we'll let it unravel. We've done extensive computer searches into MLI's background, much more thorough than your hacker friend. These things seeded a money trail that leads back to the CIA. It's going to look to the vids, and everyone else, like this was just another rogue Agency operation—"

Nohar sucked in a breath. "You're not really FBI, are you?"

Isham smiled. It didn't look like a grimace this time. "Only on loan."

"Just let the CIA take the heat for this?"

"That's what it's for. The CIA's designed to take the heat for the NSA, the NRO, and a half-dozen other organizations in the intelligence community. We'll gladly let them fall to the wolves to keep this bottled up. Justice will prosecute a good percentage of Congress, Congress gets to flay open the CIA. Executive hits Legislative, Legislative gets back at the Executive—"

Nohar leaned back on the curved concrete, ignoring the sudden dagger of pain that erupted from his leg. It was just too much effort to stay upright. "Checks and balances, right?"

"The way it works in practice anyway."

"What about NASA's deep-probe project?"

"Congress will scuttle them. The NSA will black-budget them, launch, and eventually, we'll find out where these things come from."

Nohar closed his eyes. It felt like he was losing consciousness. "We're going to do the same thing to them, aren't we?"

"Not my decision . . ."

Figured . . .

Nohar slipped into the darkness.

It was Friday, the 26th of August, and the weather was deigning to cool down a little. That, and it looked to be the first week of August with no rainfall. Nohar had just closed the deal on Manny's house, and he was feeling emotionally exhausted.

He sat down on a box in the center of the empty living room and looked at the comm. He wanted to call Stephie, ask her to go with him. However, he couldn't muster the courage—he'd been avoiding her ever since he made the decision to leave this burg. He knew if she said no, he wouldn't leave. And staying in this town would kill him. Too many memories.

He sat on the box in the middle of Manny's living room, realizing he was going to do to Stephie the same thing Maria had done to him. That decided it. He *was* going to call her.

He had just reached for the comm when someone at the front door rang the call button.

Their timing sucked.

Nohar grabbed a crutch and hoisted himself up to his feet. He was getting good at maneuvering with the cast. He managed to get all the way to the door without bashing it into anything. He didn't bother with the intercom. He just threw the door open.

There she was, carrying a huge handbag, smelling of roses and wood smoke.

Nohar fell into the cliché before he could stop himself. "I was just going to call you."

There was a half-smile on her face. "Oh, you were? I've been looking for you ever since you left the hospital. You moved out of your apartment—"

"Transferred the lease to Angel—"

Stephie nodded and patted him on the shoulder—the left one where the fur had come back in white. "You going to let me in?"

Nohar stepped aside and let her through. She surveyed the empty living room and sighed. It echoed through the house. "So you're moving out of here, too—how is Angel, anyway?"

"She's lucky rabbits are common. They had skin cultures to match her. The fur on her legs is white now, but she can walk. She got a job."

The concept seemed to shock Stephie. "As what?"

"Cocktail waitress at the *Watership Down*. A bar on Coventry—"

She pulled up a box and they sat down, facing each other.

"So how are you taking things?"

Nohar slapped his cast. "They had to weave some carbon fiber into the tendons, but the cast comes off in a month, and with a few months of exercise—"

She shook her head. "That's not what I mean and you know it. You're still blaming yourself for Manny, aren't you?"

That hit home. "If—"

Stephie put her finger on his lips. "I talked to Manny a lot about you. He was your father for five years, and because of school you ran away to Moreytown and joined a street gang. When your gang got involved with the riots and you found out what your real father was, you ran away from them. Now you're going to run away from this life, right?"

Nohar shook his head. "I can't live here anymore . . ."

"I suppose not. But you aren't going to run away from me. I won't let you."

They sat, looking at each other.

"I suppose not."

She smiled and shook her head. "At least he doesn't object. Well, I got myself a new job, demographics for Nielsen."

Nohar had a sinking feeling. He forced a smile. "Great. Where?"

"Santa Monica."

Nohar was speechless for a moment, and she seemed to enjoy his reaction. "You *knew* I was going to California?"

" 'California is a lot more tolerant,' " she quoted.

"Where did you hear that?"

"Those rodents had more than drugs and guns at that motel. The white one left this on the comm." She reached into the overlarge bag and pulled out a ramcard. Nohar noticed the bag kept moving when she took her hand out of it. The bag emitted a slightly familiar smell. "Seems to be a copy of whatever you had on permanent storage on your comm. I *was* going to give this to you when you got out of the hospital. But you slipped out without telling me. So I played it."

Nohar took the card wordlessly.

"That Maria is one stupid cat for walking out on you."

"No, she isn't."

The handbag was still moving. Nohar couldn't hold it anymore. "What the hell do you have in the bag?"

Stephie broke into a wide grin. "I still remember that line you gave me in the parking garage, about your cat."

Another thing Nohar wanted to forget. He sighed. "Yes?"

Stephie reached in the bag and pulled out a small, gray-and-black tabby kitten and handed it to Nohar. Nohar had to collect himself enough to cup his hands under the little creature. It barely fit on his palm. Nohar watched as it stumbled a little, disoriented, and circled around. Then, finding the new perch satisfactory, it curled up, closed its eyes, and began to purr.

Nohar stared at the little thing in his hands. "Damn it, Stephie. that isn't playing fair."

"I know."

She began scratching the little thing behind the ears.

EMPERORS OF THE TWILIGHT

Dedicated to Dan and Grace,
both of them, through whatever.

Acknowledgments

Thanks to Jane Butler and Sheila Gilbert, without whom this book would have remained, if not unwritten, definitely unpublished. Also a load of thanks to the Cajun Sushi Hamsters, you know who you are.

Chapter 1

At four-thirty in the morning on a snowless New Year's Eve, Evi Isham was naked on a penthouse balcony overlooking Manhattan. She was doing her best to beat the crap out of her weight machine, and the machine was winning. Even after gearing the bench press down to 250 kilos, the reps were still eating into her shoulders. She had just come back from Havana, her first vacation from the Agency, and her muscles had turned to mush.

Great thing to realize first thing on your birthday, she thought to herself. She was thirty-three, allegedly. She could be twenty-nine or thirty-six. She had picked December 31, 2025, as her birthday for simplicity's sake. No one actually knew her real birth date, but the INS didn't like blank spots in their forms.

However old she was, she couldn't slack off on the workouts like a teenager. At least she had three days to catch up before the Agency wanted her back.

She stopped at rep number twenty and grabbed a towel. She was damp with a light mist of perspiration and her breath fogged, leaving little trails of infrared on the air.

Evi walked to the corner of the balcony and looked at her adopted home. The Manhattan skyline cut a glowing hole in the night. The buildings accumulated toward the chrome-blue spine of the Nyogi tower. Red lights from the constant aircar traffic enveloped the city like hot embers. To her right, through the gap between two neighboring condominiums, she could see a forest-green light from the misnamed Central Park Dome. Beyond the luminescent city, the sky was a dead black.

A cold wind drew across Evi's skin, causing an involuntary shiver that seemed to shake open every pore in her body.

Thirty-three, she thought. She was settling down. She had a permanent address for the first time since the war. Even though she'd kept in top condition, it'd been over five years since the Agency had put her in a dangerous field mission. The only running she did was running the computer at the think tank. The only thing she chased now was lost page work and obscure reference texts.

She'd been here long enough that she already had one male resident hitting on her. Chuck Dwyer on the seventeenth floor had given her his apartment number and a raincheck in her second week here.

She'd even had a coworker invite her over for dinner. Dave Price wasn't quite in her department, but they kept bumping into each other. She'd been to his house in Queens and met about a dozen cats. If David hadn't been aware Evi wasn't human, it might have gone beyond dinner.

She was definitely settling down.

Some people would miss the action.

Such people were nuts.

Even though she had been bioengineered for combat, flying a desk was fine with her. Back in '54, when the Supreme Court finally gave the products of human genetic engineering the same rights the 29th amendment gave the moreaus, Evi had even considered quitting the Agency.

But, by then, she didn't have terrorists shooting at her anymore. One shitfire case in Cleveland and she was transferred to an advisory capacity. More than once she'd supposed that dropping her out of the field was someone's idea of punishing her for unearthing that mess.

As far as she was concerned, it was a promotion. For close to six years she'd been working in that think tank. The closest she ever got to "action" nowadays was writing reports about hypothetical alien invasions and less hypothetical projections on possible moreau violence.

She sometimes felt out of place as the token nonhuman expert in the midst of the academics, economists, and political scientists. But the job provided her with a decent living and a human identity. With a pair of contact lenses she could pass for a compact, muscular human, and the Agency helped her maintain that fiction.

Evi padded back to the weight machine and started to reconfigure it for a leg press. She flipped the cover off the keypad and punched in the resistance at 600 kilos. There was a long pause as she listened to the hydraulics of the machine adjust.

She straddled the bench, leaned back, and put her feet in the grips.

The weight machine was at the end of one arm of the L-shaped balcony. It was pointed toward the corner of the balcony and, beyond, toward one of a twinned set of condominiums that bordered the park. The condo she faced was a dozen stories taller, fifty years younger, and about five grand cheaper than the place Evi lived in.

She watched the front of the neighboring building.

No matter how early she got up for her workout, her penchant for exercising in the nude always drew a few spectators. She hadn't yet decided if she was bothered by it or not.

And, even though she had started her workout a half-hour early, apparently this morning was no different.

Four windows up and three to the left there was a peeper. He gave himself away with the high-spectrum glow from his binocs. She strained to focus on the guy. The peeper's blurred window shot into focus and the rest of Manhattan quashed itself into her peripheral vision. She saw his face, monochrome and sliced into strips by the venetian blinds in his window. She guessed mid-twenties with mixed Anglo heritage. She couldn't see anything of the darkened apartment behind him. He had supplied himself with a pair of military binocs, a pair of British Long-Eighties with night-vision attachments.

Evi's eyes watered and she closed them.

She did a few presses and opened her eyes and refocused on the peeper. December, and the guy was sweating. She could see the stains under his armpits, and light was reflecting off his forehead. There was something wrong about the guy, and not a standard New York wrongness.

She was working up an irritating sweat herself. Her ass was beginning to slide all over the plastic seat. That usually wasn't a problem, but apparently she'd slacked off a lot. She did three more leg presses and stopped to get a towel to lay on the seat.

When she stopped, she strained at her maximum to get a look at the peeper. That's when she noticed that the peeper had an earplug and a throat-mike. She'd missed it at first, because of the blinds and the shadows they were casting. The peeper was also talking to himself.

And while in Manhattan you expect all the pervs and scuzzballs to talk to themselves, this peeper was talking to someone else.

He wasn't subvocalizing, so Evi could watch his lips move. At a hundred meters plus it hurt to make out, but the old Japanese gene-techs had designed good eyes.

Evi didn't make the mistake of staring at the guy. That would have been a tip that she could see him, and the guy would clam up and dive for cover. Even her brief pause in the leg presses might have alerted him. She resumed pumping.

Fortunately the peeper seemed not to have noticed her pause. So, while the peeper was getting an eyeful down her leg press, she tried to read the peeper's lips.

The fact that he wasn't speaking English threw her for a second. It took her a moment to recognize the syllabication as Japanese. *Damn it.* Trying to lip-read a language that relied so much on inflection was close to hopeless. Then he nodded a little and slipped into Arabic. Evi was much more fluent in Arabic than she was in Japanese.

What the peeper was mouthing looked like, "Word is go. The package is on southwest balcony. Team one is the pickup. Two and three, stairs."

It didn't take a tactical genius to figure out what "the package" might be. And, while being raised within the Israeli intelligence community might have prejudiced her against anyone who spoke Arabic, it wasn't too far a leap to decide that the "pickup" wasn't anything pleasant.

She was on rep number twenty, and she had to blink a few times to clear her vision. Once she refocused and had a wider field of view, something glinted in her peripheral vision. At the same time, she heard a whirring chunk. The glint belonged to an open window on the top floor of the building next to the peeper's. The chunk, and the whir she was now hearing, belonged to the penthouse's express elevator.

No one but her was supposed to be able to use the elevator. The other penthouse was unoccupied.

Colonel Abdel, her first instructor and surrogate father, had given her a number of maxims, and near the top was "know your territory." She knew her building, knew its occupants, knew the sounds it made, and she knew that the elevator would get to the top floor in forty-seven seconds.

The French doors were around the corner of the balcony from her. Only fifteen meters separated her from her weapon.

The open window across the street glinted again, and something visceral made her vacate the weight machine and vault to the roof of the penthouse. Behind her something slammed into the bench she'd just left. She heard the crash of tearing metal and the siren wheeze of escaping hydraulic fluid.

"SHIT!" Evi screamed into the darkness. A sniper was firing at her, with something fifty-cal or better. She ran at top speed across the slick solar-collecting surface roofing the penthouse complex. She felt the wind of the second shot breeze by the small of her back before it shattered into the roof behind her. An explosion of ceramic powder dusted her legs as she dived behind the cover offered by the rectangular brick shack that housed the motors for the elevators and the central-air for the building.

She hunched up, shivering, against the brick wall. She could feel the wall vibrate as a third shot slammed into the other side of the shack.

"What the fuck is going on?"

She could hear Abdel telling her to ask questions later. When people weren't shooting at her.

The sniper let up, apparently waiting for a clean shot. She had been damn lucky she saw that glint. If the sight of the peeper hadn't primed her for trouble, she never would have paid attention to it.

That scared her.

What could she do now? The peeper was talking to a pickup team that must be in the elevator now. The team would be there in less than half a minute. The sniper had her pinned back here, and the peeper was spotter on the high ground, broadcasting her movements.

She forced the panic back and tried to think clearly.

In the elevator their radio would be blacked out for the duration. She looked up at the wall she was huddled against. The door to the shack was facing the sniper, but here, on this side, was a small window. She forced it open. There was a screech of twisting metal, but she was unconcerned by the noise. The pickup team in the elevator wouldn't hear it. The elevators in this place were plush, luxurious, and soundproof.

Inside the room, the only noise was the motor raising the elevator. The place smelled of grease and electricity. She stuck her head under the blackened girders that held up the whirring motor and looked down the shaft at the elevator. If their radios had been working, the emergency exit on top of the elevator would have been open.

The elevator was halfway up the shaft and the trapdoor was still closed. The radio blackout prevented the peeper from telling the team that she was about to land on them.

Whoever they were.

Evi looked at the cables stringing between the motor and the elevator. She didn't want to do this, but taking the offense was the only way she could gain control of the situation. She grabbed a cable and started lowering herself, hand over hand. Dangerous as hell if her grip slipped, but that was only par for the course.

She and the elevator met on the fifteenth floor of the twenty-story building. Her feet squished in the black filth coating the top of the elevator. Her skin was now covered in brown grease, making her wish for some clothes.

She crouched over the trapdoor and listened. She couldn't hear them, but she could smell them. Two of them, and they weren't human. She could identify the smell, canine, both of them. They were most likely Afghani-engineered dogs. Plenty of combat experience during the Pan-Asian war, would have gone merc when the Kabul government discontinued the strain.

She was glad the Japanese gene-techs had avoiding moreaus in mind when they designed her odor profile. Had she been human, it would have been *them* smelling *her*. But they hadn't smelled her or heard her. If she did her job right, they never would.

The trapdoor was just a panel resting in the roof of the elevator. When the sixteenth floor was passing by, she silently lifted it. She looked down, and her guess was right. Two Afghanis. Their shaggy gray fur was the tip-off. Both faced forward, pointing a pair of silenced submachine guns at the chromed door.

Their black noses began to twitch in unison and the one nearest her began to turn. Noise and stale air from the shaft were blowing in.

She straddled the trapdoor and grabbed the sides of the opening with both hands. She heard the metal crunch in her grip, and so did the canines.

The elevator reached floor number seventeen, and both dogs were turning around. *Too slow*, she thought. She shot her legs through the opening and wrapped them around one dog's neck. She hauled the dog upward, pulling with her arms. The other one wanted to shoot, Evi knew, but his partner was in the way.

She yanked the dog halfway through the trapdoor, giving herself some cover from dog number two. She ended up on her back on top of the elevator, the dog still thrashing. He faced her, sputtering white foam on her stomach as he whipped his head back and forth.

She grabbed the dog's muzzle and snapped it shut with her right hand. Blood and a piece of tongue splattered warmly on her thigh.

She used the dog's muzzle as a lever-arm to break his neck.

She unscissored her legs and rolled to the side of the elevator. The elevator passed floor eighteen. The corpse lay folded over the lip of the trapdoor. Its head looked back over the right shoulder as if it saw something interesting at the top of the shaft. Evi spared a look to her right, down the adjoining shaft. The neighboring elevator was down by the lobby, unmoving. She swung down and dangled by the side of the elevator.

She'd just cleared the top of the elevator when the second dog started spraying the roof with gunfire. The corpse shook like it was having a seizure, and the shaft rang with the sound of bullets ricocheting. She worried about the cables and the motor.

The dog ceased firing, managing not to hit anything vital. Evi stationed herself across from the trapdoor, bracing her feet in the metal strut halfway up the side of the elevator's exterior. She ducked low and listened. She heard the corpse thud back into the elevator, and suddenly the shaft was filled with the odor of gunfire. She listened. Soon she heard the canine pull himself out of the hole.

Nineteenth floor.

She waited a heartbeat and popped her torso over the edge. The canine was standing on top of the elevator and, predictably, looking up. She sank her right hand into the dog's crotch and lifted him up and off balance. She held on to the roof of the elevator with her left hand as she leaned her body back into the adjoining shaft. The canine had both hands on his gun, so he didn't have a chance. Evi felt the cables brush her hair as she flipped the dog over her. The dog tumbled headfirst down the neighboring shaft.

Inside the elevator, she heard the doors ding open: twentieth floor.

Below her, she heard the dog hit.

She vaulted to the top of the elevator and dropped through the hole. Her feet squished into the blood-soaked carpet. The canine that took the header had done quite a number on his partner. The inside of the elevator was ripe with the smell of wasted canine. She hit the emergency stop before the doors could close.

Evi gave herself fifteen seconds to examine the body.

The dog looked a little too healthy to be from the Indian frontier, so she guessed that he had originally been involved in Persia or Turkmen. Long time since the war, and the canine had since gone independent. The vest was vintage Afghani special forces, as was most of the dog's outfit. . . .

The gun was a different story.

She briefly considered running into her apartment for her own gun. The windows could stand at least one slug from her sniper's weapon. She decided she didn't have time—yet.

She grabbed the dog's gun and the radio that was clipped to one ragged ear.

She pulled herself back up through the trapdoor and maneuvered through the girders supporting the motor. She gave herself another few seconds to admire the gun. Very rare weapon, Japanese make, something that just wasn't seen anymore. It was hard to find Japanese *anything* after the Pan-Asian war. Weapons were unheard of. The small black Mitsubishi SG-2 was mostly plastic and ceramics. The only metal component would be the firing pin. Even without the silencer it was quiet as the devil.

She checked the magazine. Nine-millimeter, plastic tip, antipersonnel. No wonder the cables and the motor survived the dog's salvo. Full clip, thirty rounds.

The earplug she salvaged from the dog wasn't a human model, of course, but the plastic alligator clip that held it on was serviceable. She hung it off her earlobe. The speaker ended up facing the wrong way, but her hearing was good enough to make out the peeper's Arabic. ". . . team one, repeat, package is on top of the shaft. Over."

Then silence.

She ran through the door into the room adjoining the elevator shafts. She spared half a second to wonder what happened to building security as she rounded the green sheet-metal block of the main air-conditioning unit. The room was steaming from the building's forced-air heating system. It used the same ductwork as the air-conditioning.

She looked at the throat-mike and the radio connected to it. The throat-mike and the strap that held it on hung loosely around her neck. The radio itself was a small box that dangled between her breasts. On the box was a small recess with a row of four dip switches. They were the only controls. She figured they were the frequency pre-sets. It was a guess. The radio wasn't a familiar model.

She reached into the tiny recess with a slightly pointed nail and turned on switch number two.

". . . three to north stairs. Team one needs help delivering the package. The package is intact and unwrapped, repeat, package is intact and unwrapped . . ."

Long ago, she had trained her laugh to be totally silent. There were just too many things in combat that ended up striking her as funny. When the adrenaline was really cooking, she could get inappropriately giddy. She was sure that "unwrapped" must mean she was assumed to be, wrongly now, unarmed. However, unarmed or not, she certainly was unwrapped.

She stopped laughing. Abdel, during many training sessions, had told her that her sense of humor was going to kill her.

She set down the SG-2 and turned the bolts on one of the side panels in the massive air-conditioning unit. She was careful to avoid making undue noise. If team three was made up of more canines, their hearing was to be respected, even if the furnace in the basement would cover most of her noise. Another worry was her smell. She had been engineered to avoid, as much as possible, having a signature odor, but she was covered with grease and blood that would broadcast her location well enough. Still, she'd be descending and the air currents were upward. She'd be downwind of them most of the way.

The green panel came loose and she lowered herself into the ancient ductwork. She shimmied down a rectangular sheet-metal aluminum tube. The hot metal burned against her skin and seemed to do its utmost to amplify her every noise. The updraft of stale furnace air made her eyes water.

"Team three to post office, floor eighteen, no sign of package. Over."

"Post office to team three, team one is not responding. Assume they delivered to wrong address, you're to pick up the package now."

She hit a ceiling duct on the nineteenth floor. She trusted her sense of direction to get her to the north stairwell. She squeezed into a narrow transverse duct. By the time she got behind a grille overlooking a landing in the north stairwell, she was squeezing, gun first, through a tube that was barely a meter wide by a half tall. She couldn't back up. She had scraped her knees, hips, elbows, shoulders and nipples raw.

She got to the grate in time to see two canines rounding the stairs. Evi could tell the dogs were smelling something odd blowing out the vents.

She clicked the SG on full auto and sprayed the dogs through the vent, aiming high. Her aim was good. The first bullet caught the closest canine in the face. The dog's face exploded in a mist of fur, blood, and flecks of teeth and bone.

The other one was quick. He had seen the grating on the vent fly out and started firing immediately, but his gun was pointing the wrong way. She swept her gun on the dog. The dog swept his SG toward her.

She felt a spray of cinder block dust as the dog hit too high above the vent. That had been his only chance. She tracked her fire into the canine, plowing shots into his vest. She pulled up slightly as the dog fell back against the railing. The dog's gun ran away, firing into the ceiling, sending down confetti of broken fiberglass acoustical tile. He flipped backward over the railing as she clipped his neck with a shot. The canine merc tumbled down the center of the stairwell.

The peeper was going nuts over the radio. "Team three, come in, team three. Where is the package, where are you? Over."

Evi squeezed out of the vent with some relief. No one from team three was responding to the peeper. Only the two of them. She looked over the railing to see where the second dog had gone.

The corpse was folded backward over the railing on the opposite balcony on the fifth floor.

She flipped the radio to another frequency pre-set.

". . . two cross over to the entrance to the north stairwell. Package has not been picked up. Team four will join you at the door. Do not pick up the package until team four joins you. Package is now wrapped . . ."

That would be at least four dogs. Five if they had an extra in the lobby. This was getting messy. She'd gotten the four so far by surprise and an edge in the skill department. Time to change tactics.

Team four had to make it up from the lobby, and they wouldn't engage now until the two teams linked up. She had a chance now to get her emergency pack and her own gun.

She ran up the stairs, leaving an obvious trail of grease and blood, and slammed through the door into the hall. The hall ran between the two penthouse apartments, and it had a stairwell on either end. It was done up in mirrors and red carpeting. The elevator was open, still stopped on this floor.

She inched up on her door and punched in the combination. It was a risk, but she doubted anyone had made it up to the apartment yet. The lock chunked open. She shouldered the door open and dove into her apartment.

The peeper went nuts again. "The package is in the penthouse! Repeat . . ."

A shot from the sniper tore into one of the bedroom windows next to the French doors. The polymer held, the bullet now embedded in it. Evi's view of the sniper's building was now distorted and prismatic.

That was good, the sniper now had the same distorted view of her.

She kept moving, rolling through the door to her bedroom as the sniper hit the window again. Two slugs now sat in the center of concentric rainbows. The window began to make ominous creaking noises.

She dropped the SG and swept her arm under her bed. She came out with a black backpack.

Evi rolled to the corner of the bedroom and huddled behind the brick pillar that supported the end of the roof. It offered cover from the sniper. Another shot plowed into the window and it finally gave. The window snapped and sprayed pieces of itself all over the bedroom.

". . . repeat, package is in the southwest bedroom . . ."

She pulled her weapon out of the backpack. It was an IMI-Mishkov LR 7.62, an Israeli design for the Russian secret service. She snapped on the extension, lengthening the automatic's barrel by nearly a meter, and flicked off the safety.

The recoilless Mishkov only held six shots, standard 7.62 millimeter rifle cartridges. She used it because it was the longest-ranged and most accurate handgun in existence, even though the extension was so finely machined that the accuracy crapped out after only a dozen shots. As she shouldered the pack, she made a mental picture of the neighboring apartment building.

She silently thanked the sniper for clearing the window out of the way.

Then, with her heart in her throat, she rolled out from behind the brick pillar and aimed dead center, at the window four up and three to the left.

"Hurry, the package is moving . . ."

She fired at the peeper's window. As she rolled away from her firing position, she saw the venetian blinds close as the peeper collapsed against them. Red stains spread along the slats of the blinds. The peeper's windows weren't bulletproof.

"Now maybe you'll shut the fuck up."

She had a moment to hope that didn't go out over the air.

The sniper missed the one shot she gave him. The bullet tore into her bed. Water sprayed as far as the ceiling. She'd just decapitated the hit squad's command and control, partially blinded them as well, and she now had the evil things she kept in the pack for emergencies.

The sniper missed another shot. The slug embedded itself in another window.

She rolled back out into the hall, and the sniper finished off the window behind her. It wasn't until then that she began to feel the cuts from rolling over the broken window. The grease on her skin got into the cuts, making her feel like a feline moreau was using her for a scratching post. She ignored the pain and headed for the south stairway, carrying her emergency pack in one hand and the Mishkov in the other. Teams two and four would be storming up the north stairway. She didn't have much time.

The south stairway was concrete, functional, the mirror twin of its opposite number. On the nineteenth-floor landing there was a vent grating, exactly like the one she had shot two canines through. The duct led straight across to the other stairwell. She could even catch a whiff of the carnage there.

The vent was barely in reach. She set down the backpack and jammed her fingers through the grating, ripping it away, taking some of the wall along with it. She put the gun back in the pack and withdrew a small round grenade. She chinned herself up, wincing as she rubbed her nipples across the whitewashed cinder block wall. She looked down the vent, a straight aluminum tube down to a small rectangle of light, maybe thirty meters. She smelled canine blood, even over the forced air from the furnace. She listened.

They were trying for stealth, but there were just too many of them. Of course, there was the predictable pause by the corpse. There was a slight echo effect as she heard them through the duct and over the radio.

"Team two to post office, we've found team three. Returned to sender . . ."

She'd never been fond of explosives. They were messy, imprecise, and likely to involve people other than the intended target.

Her left arm ached. She raised the grenade in her right hand, pulled the pin with her teeth and made a quick estimate. She waited exactly one and a half seconds before she threw it through the vent. She dropped and rolled immediately. Two seconds later she heard the grenade hit the aluminum vent and roll half a second before falling out the other side. It was a close thing, but the alarm she heard over the radio told her that it had gone out the vent in the opposite stairwell and not into some side passage.

Teams two and four only had an instant to recognize the grenade.

The sound was deafening even though she was on the other side of the building. A belch of smoke came out of the vent preceding a pressure wave that made her ears pop.

Evi hated explosives, but sometimes they were indispensable as an equalizer.

The canine's radio now only broadcast static. She tried the other settings and their combinations. She only got silence. In the best case that would mean she had gotten them all. However, the safe assumption was that the team doing the hit had discovered that their communications were compromised and were running on radio silence.

In any event, the sniper was still out there. Also, despite their precautions—taking out security, using the penthouse elevator and the fire stairs, silenced weapons—the hit was no longer a secret. The fire alarm was going off, half the building would have just woken up, and the top of the building must be pouring out smoke.

Ten minutes and the NYPD, the fire department, and probably a car from the Bureau would be showing up. In twenty minutes, the Agency would take over the Bureau investigation on behalf of the Fed. In a half-hour the vids would be parroting an official statement about random moreau violence. It would be a bland, simplistic story that would fit the facts while remaining a blatant falsehood.

She had about that long to leave the building and come in from the cold.

She couldn't get caught up with law enforcement. Standard procedure for covert ops: get caught doing something a little to the left of legal, even by domestic forces—*especially* by domestic forces— the operative gets thrown to the wolves while the Agency cooks up a cover story, usually about rogue agents.

Sometimes she wished it had been the CIA that recruited her. They'd eat a little bad press to save an agent.

Her time sense told her it was four fifty-two in the morning.

Chapter 2

What the hell was going on? It had been nearly six years since she had been involved in anything really sensitive. Why was she suddenly targeted by a sniper and a team of Afghani mercenaries?

She was running at top speed down the south stairwell wearing only the backpack slung over her shoulder. Panic was still clouding her thinking. She wasn't ready for this shit.

She could hear Abdel telling her that no one was ever ready for it.

She decided that she had a minute, maybe a minute and a half, before the civilians heeded the fire alarms and started filling the stairwells. When she hit floor number seventeen, she left the stairwell and jogged down the hall. She could hear the civilians waking up behind their doors. In a few seconds, doors would begin to open.

She passed an intersecting corridor and saw a old man, forty-five, gray hair, towel around his waist. He wasn't looking in her direction. She smelled sweat, musk, and someone else in the room behind him. Then she'd passed the intersection.

Evi hoped Chuck Dwyer had given her the right apartment number.

She stopped at apartment 1712 and pounded on the door. She restrained herself. In her state it wouldn't take much to splinter the door frame.

Chuck Dwyer opened the door. Chuck was in the process of dressing, and Evi could smell a woman back in the apartment.

He couldn't hide his shock. He stood there, staring at a naked woman covered with blood and grease.

Evi didn't have time. She pushed through into the apartment, slamming the door shut behind her. Chuck was trying to squeak out a comprehensible monosyllable and not doing a good job of it.

"I'm using your shower."

She had to get the gunk off of her, or she had little chance of getting anywhere, past anyone. Chuck, still trying to talk, stared into her eyes.

Damn it! She'd forgotten about her contacts.

In his eyes she could see her own reflection, her own eyes. She could see her yellow iris and slitted pupil quite clearly, and Chuck was probably staring at the green reflective glow from her retinas. Cat eyes.

Chuck finally managed to say, "Y—you're a frank . . ."

Frank. In other words, frankenstein. Lower on most people's lists than the moreaus. Lower because her designers had the temerity to actually fiddle with the human genome. It had taken half a century for people in the States to achieve an uncomfortable acceptance of the engineered animals that kept pouring over the border.

An engineered human was still a horrifying concept.

Evi didn't even like the word. There should be a kinder word in general usage. Even the term moreau, arising from nearly the same source, sounded better.

It didn't really matter that Chuck knew. The penthouse was dead for her. Probably the whole of New York as well.

What really bothered her was the fact that a guy who was once actively trying to get into her bed was now looking at her as if she were a diseased animal. Better to not even try giving him an explanation.

"Chuck, does the woman in the bedroom live in the building?"

Chuck nodded.

"Take her back to her apartment. The police will be here soon and it would be good for you if you never saw me. Say you spent the night there."

She went into the bathroom and didn't bother to close the door. She didn't care what Chuck did. It was irrelevant what he told the cops. Her trail of grease and blood would lead to his apartment. Nothing Chuck could say would compromise her position.

She had told him the truth. His silence would be for his benefit.

Especially if the Agency was in the mood for disappearing some-one.

Three minutes under a cold blast of water and she didn't look like a refugee from a war zone. She hit the dryer and grabbed her pack off the john. In the pack was a one-piece all-purpose black jumpsuit. It was denim made from engineered cotton. It was faded gray in places and didn't look like a stealth number. Its one special aspect was the carbon-fiber monofilament microweaved into it. It would deflect a knife, and while it wouldn't stop a bullet, it could slow one down enough to save her life.

It was also broken in to the point where it didn't feel like it was sanding her skin off when she put it on.

There were a pair of her special contact lenses in her backpack. Unfortunately, during all the running and jumping, their case had popped open. The one brown lens she found had torn in half.

"Damn," she whispered as she flushed the lens.

She took out a pair of chromed sunglasses. If the cops saw her eyes, they would stop her. Her eyes could adjust to the light level. The only problem was that the sunglasses cut out the high end of the spectrum.

Chuck—and whoever the woman was—had split the apartment. Chuck had the New Yorker's sense of self-preservation.

Now all she had to do was get out of the building with the sniper watching. She doubted a wave of cops would deter the gunman, whoever he was.

The sniper didn't make sense to her. Unless he was supposed to pin her down for the dogs. But it sure *felt* like the sniper was doing his best to kill her. In which case the hit team swarming the build-ing was irrelevant and costly.

Evi had the feeling that if she hadn't seen the peeper, she'd be dead.

Who was behind it, and why the overkill?

She locked Chuck's door behind her and did Chuck a favor. She kicked it in. The door frame split, and the door swung open. Chuck would receive no embarrassing questions about how she got his combination.

Out in the hall there was a slight haze in the corridor that prob-ably only she could see. She could smell smoke coming from the north stairwell. The fire door leading there was flashing its red fire-warning lights. The scene behind its rectangular chicken-wire win-dow was white and opaque. The door was radiating brighter than the heat vents.

She sensed that most of the civilians had taken the stairs. The floor felt empty. The occasional apartment door hung open, and a few stragglers were heading for the other stairwells.

She'd wanted to take out the hit squad, not torch the building.

Evi hated explosives.

She hung back by the unusable exit until the last of the civilians filed away. She wanted to melt in with the civilians and evacuate out the stairs. But it was doubtful she could get by the cops before they realized her part in this chaos. Not to mention that there were at least a half-dozen felonies sitting in her backpack.

Her internal clock told her it was five-ten. The cops would be around the base of the building trying to figure out exactly what happened. The fire-rescue people would be here as well. Probably headed up the north stairwell. She hoped that if there *was* a team five, they had the sense to bug out when the hit went sour. A shoot-out in the lobby between dogs and the NYPD would complicate things for the fire fighters.

Once the floor felt empty enough, she went to the elevator shafts.

She pulled on a pair of black leather gloves as she stood in front of the chromed doors. Then she shoved her fingers into the gap and pushed the doors open. No elevator. The elevator for this shaft was home on ground level, with a dog on top of it.

Evi took some climbing line out of her backpack, hooked a cara-biner to the carbon-monofil-strengthened belt on her jumpsuit, looped the line through, and hooked the end of the line to a strut in-side the shaft. She tossed the rest of the line down the shaft and watched it unravel. The rope hit bottom without snagging on any-thing. She started rappeling down the elevator shaft.

She hit floor five and heard the gunshots and the screaming downstairs. There *was* a team five, and it was engaging the cops.

Pretty soon the SWAT team would arrive.

She landed on top of the elevator and looked down at the dog. Little blood, but quite definitely dead. This was going to be the last body they found, so she gave herself a chance to search this one. Ten minutes, tops. She already knew how he was outfitted. She wanted to know what else the dog carried. No wallet, no ID, but she didn't expect any.

The dog didn't have much. He had one ramcard, black and un-marked with the exception of a long number on the top edge. She pocketed it.

The dog also carried cyanide capsules. She let out her silent laugh again.

Ten minutes, her time was up. The gunshots were becoming more sporadic. From the sound, the dogs had a habit of spraying automatic fire. They were probably running low on ammo. With that thought, she spent an extra ten seconds retrieving the dog's weapon and a few clips. The Mitsubishi was a decent gun, and after removing the jumpsuit and the rope, she had room in the pack for it.

She kicked the remaining loop of rope off the top of the elevator and into the neighboring shaft. The elevator there was still stopped at the penthouse, so she could see all the way down to the water that collected in the shaft below the third sublevel.

She lowered herself over the side of the elevator, more dangling than rappeling now, toward the foul-smelling, stagnant water. Even in such a high-class place on the Upper East Side, she could see rats, real ones, small sleek and black, swimming in the muck down there. It didn't bother her much. She used to be squeamish, but that was before they nuked Tel Aviv.

She rested her feet on a girder that crossed the shaft a few centimeters above the water. It was slick footing. The girder was covered in brown slime that smelled of rotten algae. Evi unhooked herself and left the rope. She drew the Mishkov, sans extension, from the backpack and listened at the door. She heard only the faint echoes of the chaos in the lobby.

She shoved her left hand into the gap and pushed the left side of the elevator door open, using the right half for cover.

The garage was empty of people, human or nonhuman. Evi knew it as soon as the door slid open. Only empty ranks of expensive metallic-painted cars. No odor except for the faint ozone-transformer smell from the cars and a slight smell of smoke. Evi rolled out of the shaft, still expecting to be shot at. Nothing, but she couldn't count on it to last.

She had a brief unprofessional thought about her Porsche. She didn't go in that direction. If it wasn't wired to explode, it certainly had a tracking device in it. In any event, the sniper would start pumping shots into the car the second it showed on the street.

She headed for the far end of the parking garage. In the far corner, across from the entrance to the garage, there was a manhole in the concrete. That was what she was heading for.

The lights didn't reach far back. That entire end of the garage was swathed in gloom. Evi's eyes adjusted to the darkness as she moved toward her destination. As she left the influence of one light, another light began to resolve itself.

A sleek, metallic-blue General Motors Maduro sports coupe was parked back here. The power plant was emitting a barely visible infrared glow. It must have been operating no more than fifteen minutes ago.

And it was parked on the manhole.

She got unreasonably angry. She put her gun away and punched the driver's side window of the low-slung sports coupe. The plastic safety window cracked and collapsed into the car in hundreds of small pieces. The shock of impact started the aching in her overworked shoulder.

The garage echoed with the piercing sound of the Maduro's car alarm. That was a little much. The high-frequency resonance of the alarm made it feel like her enhanced ears were bleeding.

She pulled the parking brake, shifted the car into neutral, grabbed the wheel, and started pushing. Her first intent was simply to move the car off the manhole, but the alarm got to her. She ran down the center of the garage, pushing the coup down a gentle incline. She let go when the Maduro was going at a fair clip.

Right toward her own car.

She hit the ground as the coupe crunched into her Porsche. A bomb was set off by either a proximity or a vibration switch. The explosion killed the Maduro's alarm and set off every other one in the garage. She heard pieces of the black Porsche fall by her and skate across the floor. She looked up in time to see a momentary ball of flame engulf three cars.

The sprinklers came on.

Someday she was going to have to control her anger. But while she had wasted the Maduro, she had also saved the innocent bastard who would have gotten too close to her Porsche.

She had to vanish quickly now, before the firemen got down here to clean up the mess. She ran back to the manhole, hooked two gloved fingers in two separate holes and lifted the metal cover. She set it down, jumped into the darkness, and pulled it shut after her.

A nice thing about Manhattan, in her situation, was the fact that if you wanted to get from point A to any point B, you could do it underground. There was more architecture buried under Manhattan than there was under Jerusalem.

The manhole was access for ConEd, AT&T, Mann-Sat, and a few hundred other data companies to the main comm trunk into the building. She landed in the concrete tunnel and ran, being careful not to slip on the scum of ice that lined the bottom of the concrete tube.

It was five twenty-five. She had been awake nearly an hour. She ran down the comm tunnel, trying to piece things together.

It was obvious that the mercs weren't trained as a hit squad. Their vests and their tendency to spray their weapons made her think that they'd been an infantry unit. Maybe special forces trained for heavy armed resistance, not stealth, not hit-and-run.

Well-trained, expensive, and not what she would send in for an assassination attempt.

The sniper was a different story altogether. If she had stopped moving under the stare of that gun, she'd be dead. If the sniper had been alone, she'd be dead. If she hadn't broken routine by starting her workout a half-hour early, obviously before the sniper had reached position, she'd be dead.

Evi didn't like those kinds of ifs.

She stopped under a grate that was probably three hundred meters away from her entrance. She could hear, echoing behind her, sounds of commotion in the parking garage, probably firemen.

She climbed up a few rungs in the side of the tunnel and pushed the grate up and to the side with her right hand. She winced a little. The strain from the 250-kilo repetitions was getting to her.

The grate was padlocked to a bolt in the concrete, but water and corrosion had done most of her work for her. The bolt came loose from the wall.

She came out into a recess under the subbasement of the peeper's building. She was playing a dangerous game here, but she wanted to know who was trying to erase her. She gently replaced the grate, so, she hoped, the firemen and cops wouldn't hear.

She now stood in a rectangular concrete recess in the floor of the peeper's basement. The walls next to her snaked with cables of every description running from the tunnel to just under the level of the basement floor. To get to the basement proper, she had to push up against a white enamel panel that roofed the recess.

This panel was unlocked, and it levered up with a hydraulic hiss. Evi crawled out and closed it behind her.

This basement was cleaner than the one to her building. Stark white modular panels were everywhere. Air-conditioning, communications, heating, power, everything was behind square panels that were flush with the walls. All of it sat in a cavernous room indirectly lit by soft fluorescents hidden near the tops of the walls.

The elevator was easy to find. It was a newer maglev design, and the gigantic toroidal magnet housing filled half the basement. The elevator door was recessed nearly two meters inside the outer wall of the magnet.

There wasn't a keypad. So Evi called "Up?" in the hope that the elevator was voice activated. It was. The green up arrow lit above the door.

The elevator hushed into place with a tiny whoosh. The games she'd played in the shafts across the street wouldn't work here. No cables. No real shafts.

"Twenty-four," she said as she walked into the cylindrical elevator.

Ding. It heard her. The elevator's response had a slight English accent. "Going up."

Once she got to his floor, she'd be able to find the peeper's room. She would smell the blood.

She felt a brief two-G acceleration, and an even briefer deceleration. The doors slid open on a plastic-white corridor. The carpet was a stain-resistant splatter-brown pattern that made the walls appear whiter than they actually were.

She saw three cameras, covering the three axial corridors visible from her central location. She wasn't too concerned about them. This building wasn't very security conscious, as shown by her easy access. Also, the guards here would be lazy and probably paying more attention to the chaos across the street.

As she'd thought, she smelled the peeper's blood. Three doors down, she could tell. The door was ajar.

She ran up to the door and listened. Nothing. Evi wanted to take out the Mishkov, but the cameras were watching. She pushed the door open with her foot and tried to look casual for the cameras while still using the doorjamb for cover.

The blood-smell was ripe in the room. She'd plugged him in a major artery. Blood had soaked into the carpet by the chair, a pint or two, and the blinds on this side were practically painted. The British Long-Eighty binoculars lay on the ground by the chair, the slight green glow from the LCD eyepieces the only light in the room.

The peeper, however, was gone.

Evi ran in, carefully avoiding stepping in the blood, and checked all the rooms in the apartment. The apartment was empty of both bodies and furniture. The peeper's corpse was gone. Someone had to have taken it. Even if the peeper had survived, he certainly wouldn't be ambulatory. Evi grabbed the Long-Eighties. There was a ramcard in them. Maybe the peeper had recorded something useful.

She looked at the carpet by the door. She could see a faint bloody impression. A human shoe, size 14, large person, probably male. The nap was already returning to an upright position. It didn't *look* like the guy was carrying a body.

Evi felt her nostrils flare. She could barely see the blood on the brown carpet in the hall, but she could follow the smell. She broke into a silent run, bent over in a crouch, following the trail.

Chapter 3

She followed the trail of the peeper's blood with a growing in-credulity. The building here might not be as security conscious as hers, but she did pass a dozen cameras as she followed the smell of blood down a flight of stairs and into a parking garage adjoining the building. She couldn't believe someone carrying a corpse would have been ignored by the guards.

However, they had been. The peeper's remains had made it down the stairs, up three levels in the garage, and to a parking space reserved for apartment 2420. When she reached it, there was still the ghost-smell of burning rubber. The vehicle feed was still emitting some infrared.

That was it then.

What she had to do now was get to a public comm. Everyone who worked for the Agency had a number to call when the shit got real thick. She'd memorized hers a dozen years ago. She'd never used it before.

But then she had never gotten caught with her ass hanging this far out. The Agency would have to bring her in.

She walked out the front of the parking garage with a practiced air to make it look like she belonged. The ramp was out of sight of the sniper but on a street in common with her building.

Her guesses had been good. SWAT was there, and since the gun-fire had ceased, she assumed that they had mopped up the last of the Afghanis. The firemen were going in now, they'd been holding back because of the guns. She saw three unmarked Dodge Havier sedans, Bureau vehicles, parked down the street.

She turned down the street and started walking away from the scene. She wanted to stay and watch. It wasn't normal in the States to walk away from a knot of cop cars and fire engines. There was a perverse rubbernecking instinct in Americans that made anyone walking away from such a scene an object of suspicion.

She had to risk looking suspicious.

If she walked toward the chaos, like everyone else who was out on the streets this early, she would walk right under the sights of the sniper. She hoped he was going to cover her building until he was damn sure that she wasn't in it anymore.

She turned south on Fifth Avenue, crossing the street to the park side. The sniper was facing her building, the opposite direction, and on the park side of Fifth she'd be in the shadow of the peeper's building.

She wished it were a few hours later in the day and there was a crowd to get lost in.

She ran. She still had no idea if there was anyone else lying in wait for her. She had to get away and lose herself. She ran south, along the massive concrete wall that contained the park and formed the foundation of the "dome."

Only one other person was on this side of Fifth. A tall man in his mid-twenties, walking a nasty-looking, but apparently un-engineered, doberman. Before she reached the guy, she turned into the East 85th Street entrance to the park. Five steps under the dome and the temperature rose by a half-dozen degrees. Humidity stuck to her skin after the December chill in the street.

She kept running, hoping that she looked like a jogger.

Ahead, a new bridge spanned the street, and running across it was a man who instantly made her suspicious. Short, stocky, balding, gray mustache, and in his mid-forties. The build under the yellow jumpsuit showed constant conditioning; the jumpsuit was loose in the top, and Evi could swear that he was wearing a shoulder holster. It didn't look like he was jogging.

The man actually looked down and locked eyes with Evi for a moment.

But he kept running.

When she was under the bridge, she spared a look behind her. The dog-walker had just turned down 85th after her at a dead run. He was drawing a silenced automatic as he ran. The doberman was running, tongue lolling, and was halfway to her.

The embankment was too steep. She dived behind one of the pilings that held up the bridge. She could hear growling and claws clicking across concrete, getting closer.

The doberman was a trained attack dog. In some ways it was more dangerous than its intelligent Afghani cousins.

There was a crack as a bullet chipped away part of the piling behind her.

She got to her feet and listened as she pulled the SG from her backpack. The dog was almost to her position, and the guy with the gun was following. The dog reeked with excitement and blood lust, it was probably barely controllable in the best of circumstances. The guy was using the dog to flush her and give him a clean shot.

The SG cleared the pack as the doberman rounded the piling. She aimed an improperly balanced kick at the dog's nose. The contact was solid and she felt the soft tissues give, but the dog didn't back off or shy away. It should have, simply by reflex.

Instead, the doberman clamped its teeth around her right calf. The carbon monoweave kept it from breaking the skin, but it felt as if the dog were ripping her lower leg off. Evi lowered the silenced SG and fired a round into its upper chest. The bullet sprayed pieces of the dog on the sidewalk and knocked it over.

Despite a hole in its chest she could put a fist into, the dog stayed clamped on. It felt as if waves of fire were shooting up her leg. The dog was still alive and still biting down. A few more seconds of this and the monoweave would give. She lowered the barrel and wedged it between the dog's eyes. That's when she saw that the dog didn't have eyes. It stared back at her with a pair of slightly disguised video cameras.

She pulled the trigger and prayed for her leg. Parts of dog brain and circuitry flew away from her. Fortunately, the bullet missed her leg. She kicked and the dog's corpse fell off her leg, dead now. A dull ache throbbed in her calf in time to her pulse.

The dog's owner had rounded the piling and was covering her. She could now see he was armed with a silenced nine-millimeter Beretta. His face was permanently etched on her brain. Straight black hair, Japanese features, and irises so black that Evi couldn't see the pupils.

The gunman addressed her in perfect English that, had he been two decades older, she would have assumed was the benefit of a corporate education. "Do we go quietly, Miss Isham?"

He must have been kidding.

It was a contest to see who fired first, and she knew she was going to lose even as she started to raise the SG from the dog's corpse.

She was caught by surprise when the gunshot she heard wasn't the soft hammer of the nine-millimeter but a cannon shot from something forty-five caliber or better.

Most of the gunman's head evaporated. There was a soft crack as the Beretta blew away more of the dog. Evi rolled away as the gunman collapsed on the doberman. She whipped the SG around to cover the area behind her where the shot had originated.

Evi found herself covering the jogger in the yellow jumpsuit.

"Who're you?" She didn't fire, though every instinct was screaming at her to do so.

"Colonel Ezra Frey, USMC retired—"

Evi recognized the voice. *"Aerie?"*

Frey reached down and helped her up. "We better leave before the local law follows that gunshot. Too bad they don't make silencers for the old Smith and Wesson forty-four. Can you keep up on that leg?"

Evi nodded as she put away the SG. Frey holstered his weapon and started jogging off into the park behind the Museum as if nothing had happened. Evi followed, trying not to limp.

Frey had just thrown her a massive curve. He had been, she could tell from the voice, her controller in the field for the first eight years after the Agency recruited her. He was a few leaps upward in the Agency hierarchy by now. She hadn't heard his voice manning the Aerie since '53, nearly six years ago. Evi had never seen his face before, and, until now, she didn't have an alias for him other than Aerie.

Damn it all, what the hell was he doing here? He couldn't be with the hit squad, or she'd be dead . . .

It *couldn't* be a coincidence.

They jogged through Central Park for ten minutes before they spoke again. She knew they were hunting for a tail, either cops or black hats. None showed. The only people were the homeless who clogged the domed park, especially in winter. A good quarter of the ragged population were moreaus. Evi kept an eye out for heavy-combat strains, like the mercs that'd attacked her. She didn't see any. The moreaus they passed were, for the most part, rabbits and rats from Latin America.

The sky was lightening beyond the moisture-whitened surface of the dome, and other joggers were beginning to pass them.

"What the hell are you doing here?" Evi asked when they seemed clear of eavesdroppers.

"What happened back there?" Frey asked, avoiding her question.

"A hit on me. Afghani canine special forces. At least ten mercs. One human coordinator. A sniper, didn't see him. As well as the suit with the doberman."

"Christ." Frey shook his head, whispering to himself. "A fucking shitstorm. Price was right." Before she could ask him what he meant, he asked her, "Have you called in yet?"

There was such a desperate urgency to the question that Evi didn't prod him about what David Price might have been right about. "No, I just got out of there."

She didn't trust the situation. But the agitation she began smelling on Frey was hard for a human to fake. Especially since he kept a professional front that didn't let it show in his face or his voice. "This mess, I'm sorry you're stuck in the middle of it. I'll take you in, a safe house in Queens."

They jogged along a few more minutes, past an empty playground, in silence.

After a while, Frey asked, "What's the status of the hit team?"

"The sniper's the only one undamaged."

"Damn." Frey shook his head. "You didn't get a look at the sniper?"

She shook her head no.

"Gabe, you bastard," Frey whispered to himself, subvocalizing. Evi doubted if he knew she heard him. She restrained herself from asking who Gabe was.

After they left the dome and rejoined Fifth Avenue, she asked again. "What were you doing there, just when I needed you?"

Frey ran a hand through his slate-gray hair. They were waiting for the light, even though there wasn't any traffic. "Call it an embarrassing streak of curiosity." He removed a small plastic box from his pocket and she saw that it led to an earplug in his left ear.

"Police scanner," he explained. "You and the Afghanis caused one hell of a ruckus. I was on my way to see what it was."

Curiosity, hell, she thought, *you were running full out.*

What was he hiding?

Frey lived in a condominium close to Central Park South, about ten blocks away.

She got to his apartment, fifteen floors up, and the situation was still very wrong. Having Frey show up in the nick of time strained credulity.

Frey punched in the combination and let her in. "I'm going to put the call through. We have a secure line here."

She nodded as she walked into the apartment. It wasn't as large as her penthouse, but it could've been as expensive. The Agency tended to reward performance.

The impact of the sunken living room, with its modern black lacquer furniture and glowing holo-table, was ruined by stacks of white plastic boxes scattered at random.

One was spilling Frey's underwear on a couch.

Frey weaved through the boxes and headed for a flat, compact-looking comm hanging on the wall. "Pardon the mess."

Frey paused and said, "Comm. On."

The rectangle on the wall flickered and came on. Evi heard a seductive female voice from the glowing white screen. "Your comm is active, Colonel."

The voice was an artifact of the comm, but she could swear she heard the synthetic voice lick its nonexistent lips.

"Load program. Label, 'Secure Line.' Run program."

"Searching . . . I found it, lover."

Evi arched an eyebrow as Frey responded. "Love you, too."

Frey noticed her reaction and explained. "Security code requires the response." Then he shrugged as if it wasn't him that programmed the thing.

She decided that you really didn't know anyone until you saw his or her home life.

Frey looked at a text menu that had come scrolling up on the comm. He was shaking his head. "It'll take me awhile to contact the current Aerie. After I set up a meet to take us in, we won't have much time. Go in the bedroom and find yourself some protective coloring."

"Like what?"

"Cover that jumpsuit. Looks like Agency issue. It also shows off your physique. Any description of you is going to emphasize that. Not too many women built like you."

She supposed not.

She walked into Frey's bedroom and her ears picked up on his subvocalization. "Pity."

That almost made up for Chuck's reaction.

Everything still felt wrong. Too much of a coincidence. However, Frey couldn't be one of the assassins, or she would be dead.

If Frey had turned, he was after something else. She'd have to roll with it.

Evi looked around the bedroom. Black and red furniture, indirect lighting, no boxes lying around. She wasn't surprised by the mirror on the ceiling. Looked like it doubled as a holo projector, damn expensive. She wondered if the room came furnished, or if it was Frey's decor.

She slid aside one closet door, and she decided that it was Frey's decor.

Neatly hung up, taking up most of the space in the closet, were women's clothes. An incredible variety of sizes and styles. Cocktail dresses, negligees, evening gowns in red and black, blue jeans that no way could fit the Colonel, a peasant blouse in paisley, T-shirts, one executive suit, skirts, it went on. Some clothes were old, way out of style; some weren't. She could smell at least six or seven different women in the closet.

She wondered if Frey was going to make a pass at her, then shook her head. Things were going too fast, and her mind was beginning to wander.

Besides, Frey was too much the pro.

She found a few items that broke up the appearance of the jumpsuit. She wasn't going to lose the monofil. It had already saved her leg, though the bruise was getting tender and hard to walk on now.

She chose a leather jacket, removing a few of the chrome chains and studs so she could achieve a semblance of stealth in it. There was also a belt in the closet with a brushed-steel death's head on it. It seemed to go with the jacket. Lastly, she undid the velcro tabs that held the jumpsuit's integral sneakers on and replaced them with a pair of engineered-leather boots. The boots were black, like everything else she'd chosen, and had a fringe at the top.

She considered pulling one of the pairs of jeans over the monofil, but she didn't want to restrict her movement that much.

She wished Frey was using the voice interface in the other room, secure communications or not. She wanted to know what he was doing.

There was a full-length mirror in the door to the bathroom. She appraised the look for verisimilitude. She had to admit that little else in the closet would match the way her hair got tousled. With the jacket, the tangled wind-dried look seemed intentional. She ran her fingers through her hair as she tested the jacket for mobility. The jacket wasn't a perfect fit, but it didn't catch her arms. That was good. Some clothes looked like they fit her until she tried to flex her arms and wound up splitting the seams on the arms or the back. She zipped the jacket up and had to stop halfway up her chest. She had small breasts, but they were on well-developed pectorals.

While the jacket hid the physique of her upper body, the form-fitting jumpsuit still showed her legs. She decided they weren't that noticeable. The legs of a marathon runner, but not abnormal.

She looked like a street punk or an art student.

She reached under the jacket and zipped open a specially tailored pocket in her jumpsuit, under her left arm. It became a holster. She slipped the Mishkov into it, and she slid the barrel extension into a long pocket on her right leg.

In the mirror, the jacket was tight enough on her upper body to show the bulge. She unzipped the leather to the waist, until the gun disappeared. Magazines for the Mishkov went into other pockets. The only other things she took from the backpack were a selection of false IDs, a roll of twenties, and the black ramcard she'd looted from the canine.

When she put the twenties in one of the jacket's pockets, she found a pearl-handled switchblade. She shrugged and put the money in another pocket.

She took off the shades and looked into her own eyes. Golden-yellow eyes glowed green through a slitted pupil as they looked back.

What was going on here?

She wasn't engaged in any sensitive work for the Agency. She wasn't working on anything remotely dangerous. Her job was cooking projections on the geopolitical situation and forming contingency plans. Her last "fire" assignment had been six years ago in Cleveland.

The four aliens had been sucked into the black section of the U.S. government, and the effects of that had worked themselves out a long time ago, hadn't they?

That had been the last time she'd heard Frey's voice manning the Aerie . . .

Frey walked into the bedroom behind her. She replaced the sunglasses.

"Good job," Frey told her.

"What now?"

"In five minutes, six-fifteen, we'll start walking down East 60th. Between here and the Queensboro Bridge, a remote cab will pull up next to us. We get in, stay down. That's it."

Five minutes was pretty quick reaction time for the Agency. She could hear Colonel Abdel telling her to trust her instincts, and her instincts were telling her that things were rotten.

What could she do about it?

She walked back into the living room. Frey didn't follow her immediately. She glanced back and saw he had straightened out the closet of women's clothes she'd rummaged through. Frey's back was turned and he was picking up the sneakers she had abandoned. She expected him to return them, but, instead, he placed them neatly next to a pair of red stiletto high heels in the closet.

He turned and caught her looking. There was an embarrassed half-smile under his mustache. "Some people collect coins." He shrugged and stood up.

"Your shoes are a more than fair trade for Shelly's jacket."

She wondered exactly how Frey figured that. She also wondered who Shelly was. Frey closed the closet and walked toward the door where she still stood watching him.

Instinct was telling her that the situation was wrong, but instinct was also telling her that Frey hadn't turned. Instinct also told her that, once this was over, Frey *was* going to make a pass at her.

She could sense it building in the man. A civilized and very earnest lust that didn't seem to belong to somebody who was about to toss her to the wolves.

But he was still a part of what was going on, and he was hiding something.

Just before they left, he asked, "When was the last time you talked to your superior?"

"You mean the Aerie?"

"No, that's the field office. I mean Hofstadter, the man you report to now."

How the hell did Frey know that? "The week before my vacation."

"In person?"

"Yes."

"Did he seem . . ." Frey seemed to search for the word. "Worried? Preoccupied?"

She thought back, but the only image she came back with was the picture of Hofstadter smiling to himself as he told her about her upcoming vacation. The plump German economist telling her how much she'd earned this, while all the time he seemed to be laughing at some private joke. She told Frey.

Frey's reaction was another subvocalization. "I should never've gone on vacation."

It had been five minutes, and Frey led her out of the apartment. He called to the elevator, "Down."

She had to confront him. She backed away from him, confident she could draw her gun faster if shit happened.

"Doesn't you being here, within a few blocks of me, strain coincidence?"

Frey seemed unconcerned. He remained facing the elevator door, tapping his foot. "The Agency tries to spread their agents around, but I'm on vacation. If I were on duty, I wouldn't be anywhere around—"

"*I'm* on vacation." Evi backed a little farther down the hall. There was an emergency exit to her immediate right, next to the bank of elevators.

Frey stopped talking.

"They hit me in my new penthouse—"

Frey turned to face her. "I'll clear this up when we get to the safe house."

Evi began to reach for the door.

Frey took a step toward her. "I need your help—"

The elevator doors opened, releasing the overpowering smell of human blood.

Frey turned toward the elevator and said, "Oh, shit!"

Evi dived at the door to the stairs; screaming at Frey to run. Not because of the smell of blood, but because the lone occupant of the elevator wore a familiar face.

Somehow the peeper had survived.

Chapter 4

Evi was on overdrive, rolling out into the stairwell to the sound of gunfire. She was still figuring out what she had seen.

The peeper had been in the elevator, wearing a blood-soaked trenchcoat. As the elevator doors opened, he had swung a Vindhya 10-Auto out from under his coat.

The Vind Auto was Indian make, a ten millimeter submachine gun. It could empty a fifty-round clip in under two seconds. No one made a silencer for it.

She never saw Frey move. He was a long time removed from the field. He had long ago been promoted to command and control. High enough up in the Agency to be far removed from the danger. His reaction was too slow, much too slow.

The fire door closed behind her, muffling the jackhammer spray of the Vind. She concentrated on running as fast as she could while pulling the Mishkov out.

She started going down, but she could hear boots on the concrete steps below her. She could smell at least one canine.

Damn it.

She started running up the stairs.

She stayed close to the wall and made five floors before she heard the peeper explode into the stairwell, yelling in Arabic. The canine was running after her. That was bad. The Afghani dogs were fast, faster than most other moreaus, as fast as Evi. She'd have trouble outdistancing one even without the bruised muscle on her calf.

She could see the shadow of the canine four floors down.

Ten more floors and she looked again. The canine's shadow was three floors away. The dog was gaining.

How the hell did they find her?

Frey turning didn't make sense. If he was working for the black bats, his own team just blew him away.

Only the canine was following her now. She couldn't hear the peeper, and she should have been able to smell him, covered in blood as he was. The peeper must be trying to get back on the elevator, to get above her and cut off her escape. Her options were rapidly diminishing. The doors out of the stairwell weren't offering much, the halls had no cover, no doors that opened into anything but dead ends. There was a good chance that the canine would catch up.

The peeper was trying to be quiet, but she heard the pneumatic hiss of a door on the thirtieth floor. The canine was closing on her; it was only two floors away by the sound and the smell, and she had no time to stop and think.

She could hear the peeper start down the stairwell.

She rounded a landing on the twenty-eighth floor and faced the peeper. From his expression, he didn't expect her to be this high up in the building yet. The echo of her Mishkov set the iron handrail resonating. She had been aiming at the peeper's head. She didn't want him getting up again.

She had to be satisfied with hitting him in the neck, under the adam's apple.

She was already passing the peeper before he fully realized he'd been shot. He was slumping against the wall, clutching his throat. As she passed him, she hooked her left hand under an armpit and pushed him down the stairs. She hoped to give the canine some second thoughts.

On the fortieth floor, the stairwell terminated in a solid red fire door.

She hoped they didn't have people on the roof.

She slammed through the door, setting off the fire alarms. She was getting sick of the sound of sirens.

She emerged on a flagstone terrace overlooking Central Park. She could hear the canine behind her, only a couple of floors away. The roof was flat with no cover for fifteen meters in any direction. Empty pool, tennis court, penthouse on the other end of the roof that she couldn't make before the canine drew a bead on her.

"Shit." The curse came out in an uncharacteristic puff of fog. She was pushing the edge of her endurance. The canine was going to have to be slowed, somehow.

Her left hand shot into her backpack and withdrew another grenade. She pulled the pin and tossed it down the stairs. She wished she had another frag grenade. In her situation it was common to wish for everything from a minigun to tactical air support. For now, tear gas would have to do.

She slammed the fire door shut while the grenade was still in the air. What now? The dog was still just going to stumble up to the other side of the door. It was only a matter of seconds.

Evi pulled the barrel extension for the Mishkov out of its thigh holster and did her best to wedge it between the door and the jamb. It didn't want to go. She forced it and heard the screech of bending metal.

Then she ran like hell toward the penthouse.

She had only gotten three meters before she heard pounding on the other side of the door, but the door stayed shut. If she was lucky it would give her enough time to get into the house and behind something.

She rounded the end of the empty swimming pool and saw someone moving behind the French doors of the penthouse. He was in his mid-thirties, wearing an expensive-looking robe. He had the door halfway open by the time he noticed her running at him.

She reached the door and dived through the gap, tackling him. At the same time, there was the sound of tearing metal back by the fire door. Evi felt microscopic wisps of tear gas rip at her sinuses.

She had her arms wrapped around the civilian as the back of his legs hit a low-slung couch. They both tumbled over it and into a sunken living room that was the twin of Frey's. The canine opened fire as they hit the ground. The windows ripped apart behind them, and the couch started shaking from multiple impacts. She could tell the shots were going wild. Even with only a few seconds of exposure to the gas, the dog would be in sad shape.

She was thankful that the canine mercs had the habit of spraying their weapons. She waited until the dog swept his fire past the couch. When she heard windows tearing way off to her left, she whipped off her sunglasses, popped up, and braced the Mishkov on the back of the couch.

The tear gas was invisible to ultraviolet.

She took a second to aim.

The Mishkov barked once. The canine's head jerked up and to the left, as if someone had just cracked its neck like a whip. The dog fell backward, its Mitsubishi continuing to fire uselessly. The dog's body followed the motion of its neck, turning to the left and falling into a heap. Its right leg jerked, once.

The Mitsubishi stopped firing.

Evi waited for another target, but for now it seemed that the dog was it.

A sudden breeze carried away the tear gas. It brought with it the sounds of sirens and the smell of the East River. The sky to the east was beginning to lighten with the coming dawn. The light did nothing to lift the chill in the air.

It was twenty after six.

Underneath her a voice spoke in a very restrained monotone. "What do you want?"

She looked down at the civilian and revised her original age estimate. He was a well-preserved forty, maybe forty-five. His hair was colored, but not his mustache, and he kept himself in shape. She figured him as a veep for some corporation or other. A fairly important one, she thought. She could read the guy's expression and tell that he'd been in at least one exec terrorism-hostage workshop. He was following the numbers on how not to get yourself killed. She admired the guy's self-control. She could smell that he was on the verge of a panic attack.

She replaced her sunglasses and got off. She kept the Mishkov aimed at him as she backed away. "Get up."

He slowly got to his feet. The hostage training showed. No sudden moves, and he kept his hands in sight without being told. He didn't even move to close the front of his robe. Evi gave him high marks. In some situations, modesty could get you killed.

"Now what?" The same monotone, but she heard the fear resonate in the man's voice. She was pretty sure this guy expected to die.

"Do you have an aircar parked up here?" If he was really a veep, it was a reasonable expectation.

He nodded. The air was cold from the broken windows, but he was sweating.

"Company car or private?"

"Private . . . a Ford Peregrine."

The sirens were becoming louder. She wanted to go over the canine's body, but there wasn't going to be enough time to find out anything new. The sooner she got out of here the better. "Well, I am afraid that I am going to have to trouble you for a lift."

The Ford was a luxury sedan. Any aircar is a luxury item by definition. It had oversized leather seats, vat-grown wood paneling, and a nearly soundproof cab. Evi sat in the rear seat, concentrating on covering the veep with the Mishkov. The Peregrine slid into the noncommercial air corridor without any squawks over the vehicle comm, so she assumed that her veep hostage hadn't done anything stupid.

Once they hit two-hundred klicks per, shooting over Manhattan, he finally spoke. "Where are we going?"

"You have an office and the codes to land there, correct?"

He nodded. "Security will call the police. I can't prevent that."

The veep seemed to be calming down. That was good. She would prefer to avoid civilian casualties. "Just land. The rest is my problem."

The Peregrine slowed and started a slow turn toward Brooklyn. For the first time some emotion showed in his voice. "Do you know who I *am?*"

Evi shook her head. "You're someone who needs to take a humility pill."

The Ford slowed and started descending toward the blue chrome obelisk of the Nyogi tower just as a sliver of molten orange sunlight started slicing across the eastern horizon. The aircar slid in on a preprogrammed approach and landed three levels down on the topside parking garage. No welcoming committee, and practically no cars either.

"Don't kill the engine, just open the canopy and get out."

He got out and started shivering immediately as the wind whipped his robe around. He was four hundred meters up in the open air with nothing but a silk bathrobe. She felt a little sympathy, but not much. In about ten minutes, his problems would be over. Evi had a feeling that things were just starting for her.

"Open the hood."

"But the engine—"

"Open it." He might be speaking more freely, but he remembered who had the gun. Once the hood was open, she motioned him away from the car and got out of the back seat. Her bruised leg was thankful, even though she had only spent ten minutes in the back.

She moved around to the front. With the hood up, she had to raise her voice to be heard over the flywheel. "Don't move."

He didn't.

She looked next to the flywheel housing. There was no mistaking the bright orange plastic that housed the transponder and the flight recorder. She turned the Mishkov around in her hand. Then she slammed the butt of the gun on one corner of the sealed plastic box. The shock of the impact started a throbbing in her right shoulder. She could hear a slight pop over the whine of the flywheel.

Out of the corner of her eye, she could see the veep wince.

She leaned over and saw a stress fracture halfway around the heat seal of the lid.

She braced herself and brought the butt of the Mishkov down on the opposite corner.

There was a much louder pop, and the slight hiss of pressure equalizing.

She holstered the Mishkov and pried off the lid of the housing. Once it was removed, she was greeted with a black and fluorescent-yellow warning label that announced that unauthorized tampering was a felony. The label adorned the lid of a brushed-gray metal box. Four bolts held the lid on. Each was sealed with a thin coat of clear plastic.

Evi looked at her gloves and wished she had a wrench.

She gave the veep a cautioning look as she grabbed a bolt in either hand and turned. The plastic seal made an audible tearing sound, even over the flywheel. It took her nearly three minutes to loosen all four. Under the lid there were two panels. Red for the transponder, green for the flight recorder.

Her gloves were shredded, so she took them off. Then she reached in and pulled the handle on the red panel. It slid out easily, along with the attached circuit board. The engine died immediately.

She slammed the transponder unit on the concrete of a neighboring parking space. The board shattered with the slight smell of ceramic dust. She followed with the flight recorder. Electronic shrapnel went everywhere. She picked a small wire out of the wasted electronics.

When she reached in and jumped the socket for the transponder, there was an obliging spark and the engine resumed operation.

She turned around to face the veep. "Go."

He backed away slowly. He seemed unsure if he was getting away that easily.

"Go, call the cops before someone else calls you."

He could take a hint. He made for the elevators.

She slammed the hood shut and jumped into the cockpit. Five minutes seemed an inordinate amount of time to spend hot-wiring a car. But at least now, without a transponder, someone would have trouble tracing her movements.

Evi lowered the canopy and engaged the fans. The Ford obliged and slid out into the onrushing sunrise.

Manhattan unfolded beneath her and she dropped down between the skyscrapers. Illegally low, but not low enough to draw attention. She was safe, for a moment.

However, without a transponder, if she hit either river, NYC Air Traffic Control radar would tag her like a signal flare. She didn't want to mix it up with the NYPD. She was committing a dozen felonies by being airborne in this thing.

A cloudy-white dawn light was catching the tops of the sky-scrapers around her.

She couldn't believe what had happened to her. It still made no sense. A sniper *and* the merc team?

Wait a minute . . .

The realization struck her so forcefully that she shot by the U.N. Building and had to pull a tight turn to avoid shooting over the East River.

The mercs didn't want her dead. They were trying to take her alive. They went in when she was most vulnerable, and the overkill made sense if they were aiming to take her without a fight. None of the dogs fired at her, except in self-defense.

The guy with the doberman paused to talk when he should have shot her. And what he said, asking if she would go quietly, had more than one interpretation.

Abdel reminded her that the sniper *was* trying to kill her.

She turned left around one of the cranes disassembling the Chrysler Building. Scaffolding shot by underneath her as she flew through where the eightieth floor used to be.

Did the sniper necessarily have anything to do with the mercs?

Two separate hits, simultaneously, was as bizarre a coincidence as Frey coming out of nowhere to save her. Unless they were some-how related.

"What if the mercs wanted to take me alive, and, for some reason, the people running the sniper didn't want that to happen?" she asked as she pulled a leisurely loop over Union Square.

That would make sense if the sniper's timing was dictated by the mercs' operation. She had just returned from vacation, and this had been her first vulnerable moment.

That still didn't explain Frey.

Enough looping around the city. No one was following her, and the longer she stayed in the car the more likely a cop would tag her. She descended toward a parking garage near Times Square.

She'd cook the autopilot and send the car out over the ocean. Then she'd go to ground somewhere and call in to the Agency herself.

Chapter 5

It was bad. Evi was only sixteen, and she had never felt so alone.
She was on the wrong side of the front, and somehow she had
lost her team. She hugged a crag of desert rock, and less than fifty
meters away she could see an endless column of moving armor. According to the briefing, it wasn't supposed to be there. She and the
rest of her team were supposed to take out a Jordanian observation
post, preparatory to an air strike on a few small units of infantry.

There wasn't supposed to be any Axis armor anywhere near this
position. It was supposed to be massed up north, in Lebanon.

Worse, the armor was moving. The sound of the moving tanks
merged in a single deep bass note. Evi's crag resonated, and she felt
the sound deep in her chest.

She hoped the rest of her strike team got a chance to use the uplink. Somehow intelligence had managed to misplace at least two
divisions of Arab armor.

The armor stopped.

An infinity of sand sucked up the noise from the column. The
only sound that carried to her was a radio from somewhere. It
broadcast someone counting down in Arabic. For some reason, she
felt an urge to look up into the moonless night sky.

A huge black glider flew in low, soundless, and incredibly fast.
It was only in sight for a second or two, but she could tell, from the
sloped lines of the thing, it was a stealth aircraft.

The count was on one hundred.

She told herself that air defense was going to get the damned
thing.

Silently, the infantry that was accompanying the armored division took cover down on the ground or behind the tanks. The tanks themselves began to button up.

The glider was pointed at Tel Aviv, so of course air defense was going to get it. No Arab aircraft, all through the war, ever got that far into Israel.

The count was on fifty.

Evi had a very bad feeling.

Twenty.

She resisted the urge to look back to where the glider had gone.

Ten.

She felt warmth on her cheeks. She whispered to herself. "Please."

One.

There was a blinding flash of white light from the west, behind her.

She jerked awake.

She wiped off her cheek and looked around the darkened theater. Little had changed but the movie.

It was still the same overheated musk-filled dark. The atmosphere made her feel sticky. She could smell three different species and counted seven other people in the seats. Only one of them, a ragged-looking moreau rat whose fur was coming off in patches, had been there when she'd ducked in the place.

A large and slightly blurred holo screen was showing an impossibly endowed canine moreau who was loudly and sloppily sodomizing a hefty human woman who was similarly endowed in corresponding areas. There was much rustling of fur and rippling of naked flesh.

Not all the moaning was coming from the screen, and the musty smell of fresh semen certainly didn't come from the dog.

She squinted at the screen. She could tell from the short brown coat that the dog performing up there was probably Pakistani. The way his ear was flapping, she could almost make out the tattoo that would place the dog's unit.

What the hell was she doing?

She closed her eyes and rubbed her forehead. Who cared what unit a porn actor used to belong to?

She wished she could have risked flying the Peregrine off of the island. But by now the aircar had topped out at its maximum ceiling and followed Seventh Avenue out past the Statue of Liberty.

Where it should have found its rest, safe under the waves of the Atlantic.

She'd been in the porn palace for at least two hours before she had fallen asleep. She'd been waiting for the black hats, but the only thing that had caught up with her was fatigue.

That meant the NYPD, the black hats, and anyone else involved were still sorting through the mess and trying to figure out what had happened. Just like her.

She massaged her leg and winced. Her calf was beginning to swell, and she felt as if she had just run a marathon. It seemed as if someone had used a belt sander on parts of her body.

She owed her life right now more to luck than to her own skill, and if she didn't figure out what was going on, she would end up dead.

A human male was sitting two rows in front of her. He was grunting, and his seat was banging rhythmically. That was where most of the fresh musk was coming from. Wet sounds came from in front of him, out of Evi's line of sight.

She tried to tune the guy out as she thought.

Assume two teams, the sniper's team and the peeper's team. The peeper's team might only want to capture her. They could afford to hire those Afghani dogs as their front line. The Mitsubisbis and the cyborg doberman showed they had access to old Japanese technology. The peeper had been speaking Japanese to someone. From the looks of things, to the guy with the doberman.

The cyborg doberman worried her. All the neural interface technologies were supposed to have been lost or destroyed by the Jap megacorps when the Chinese nuked Tokyo. That was twenty-some years ago.

The sniper's team wanted her dead, period. The sniper's team would have set the bomb in her Porsche.

That didn't explain Frey. He showed up out of nowhere. He was living too damn close to her own address. He was too unconcerned about the coincidences.

Frey had known something.

Frey had obviously had some contact with David Price. "Price was right," Frey had mumbled to himself. Price was a member of the domestic-crisis think tank she worked for. He was the one member who had deigned to meet with her socially, despite the fact that she wasn't human.

Price was a political scientist. He specialized in conspiracy theories.

And Frey was worried about Hofstadter, her and Price's boss. A German economist, of all things.

She couldn't shake the feeling that Frey knew what had happened to her. He had been running flat out to the scene. What really bothered Evi was the fact that he seemed to know what was going on, and he was the *only* one running toward Evi's building. He should have called in some Agency support before he dived in.

"Is the Agency involved?"

It came out in a whisper only she could hear over the grunts from the screen.

That was a frightening thought.

There was only one way to find out. She had to call in.

She put on her sunglasses, gathered the pack up from under her seat, and walked out of the theater and into the lobby.

The manager was sitting behind the concession stand. Huge and buddhalike, he watched her with jaded eyes. Then he bent to return his attention to the card reader in his hands.

The atmosphere under the yellow lighting was as moist and sleazy as that in the theater. A public comm squatted next to a magazine rack that held packs of garishly labeled ramcards. A sign above the rack read "NH/IS." She noticed titles like "Animal Lovers," "Lapdogs," "Morey Love," and the creative "Sex, Sex, Sex." She slipped into the half-closet that housed the comm. From the smell, the place wasn't just used for outgoing calls.

Someone had drawn a rather anatomically detailed erect penis on the screen of the comm. She didn't figure the Agency would care. She slipped in one of her false bank cards and called the emergency number.

The screen stayed blank after she gave the number. It didn't even show snow or a test pattern. Even with the dead screen, she could hear the soft electronic sounds of a connection being made.

"Aerie," a voice announced. One she didn't recognize. That wasn't suspicious in itself. The Agency rotated controllers, often without notice. It had been six years since she'd contacted the field office. Of course she'd be unfamiliar with anyone who manned Aerie nowadays.

She started with her code designation, "Bald Eagle—"

"You're on a proprietary comm channel. Where did you get this number?"

What? "This is Bald Eagle—"

"There is no Bald Eagle."

Oh, shit.

The transmission was filtered, but she heard a voice in the background. "I DL'd her data image. Cut the comm before the channel is compromised. We don't want any sampling of our encryp—"

There was a blue phosphor wink as the comm was cut.

The Aerie didn't know she was an operative. She *couldn't* come in.

"What the fuck is going on?"

For once, she was at a loss for what to do.

She looked out from the public comm booth and into the lobby of the theater. It was suddenly a totally alien environment. The artificial yellow light reflected off the pictures on the racks of ramcards. Contorted bodies took on the aspect of hieroglyphics. Transparent cases held devices of undecipherable purpose and origin. Evi stared at the leather-clad man perusing the "Bi,TV" rack of ramcards. He had slick leather boots that came to mid-thigh, a studded leather vest over a bare chest, a ring through one nipple, and a bulging codpiece. He resembled an inhabitant of another planet.

"Get a grip Evi." She echoed Abdel's mental voice.

What was she going to do?

Price, she thought. Frey had mentioned his name, and Price knew her. She knew his address, she could call him. Would he be home? It was New Year's Eve, of course he'd be home.

Evi called Price.

The message came back that Price's home comm was not accepting any incoming traffic.

She slammed her fist into the side of the comm in frustration. The buddha manning the desk looked up from his card reader.

She called the think tank, Hofstadter's private line. The office comm would forward the call to Hofstadter, wherever he was. She was leap frogging over proper procedure, but Aerie was supposed to handle things like this. If Aerie didn't acknowledge her—

Hofstadter was in his office. Behind him was a man she didn't recognize. "Isham, what're you doing in Times Square?"

The way he said it made her suspicious. "I'm safe, but all hell's breaking loose—"

"I know, I know. Have you called in yet?"

"Yes, but the—"

Hofstadter was reddening. "Damn, damn, *damn*!"

The man behind Hofstadter leaned over and whispered into his ear. "Gabe's last report puts him ten minutes from target's position—" She wasn't supposed to hear it, but humans had a tendency to underestimate her capabilities.

Hofstadter pushed him back roughly, "Shut up, Davidson—Isham, get over here, to the think tank. We need to debrief you."

She was backing away from the comm. *Hofstadter?* Frey had said "Gabe, you bastard," when she'd mentioned the sniper. Gabe was the sniper, and her boss and this man Davidson were running him.

"Isham" Hofstadter was saying as she backed out of the booth.

As she headed to the theater doors, she could still hear him talking. "Davidson, you idiot, the frank heard you."

Hearing Hofstadter call her a frank finally made the panic clamp on. She backed up to the doors feeling a hot iron band grip her sternum. It felt as if the world were collapsing in on her.

She could hear Hofstadter cut the connection.

She leaned against the black-painted lobby doors and went through the relaxation exercises that Abdel had taught her. She breathed deeply and closed her eyes.

Behind her she could hear the city noise over the moaning in the theater. The door rattled with the traffic on Seventh, the workers readying things for New Year's, the sirens . . .

Sirens?

Evi opened her eyes.

Sirens were *the* ubiquitous city noise in New York, but these were getting louder, closer, and there were a lot of them. It could be anything.

But in her line of work, paranoia wasn't only an occupational hazard.

It was a survival trait.

She opened the door and looked outside. The sun was a cold white spotlight that sucked the edges off the people on the street. The rows of porn palaces seemed to go on forever with their yellow signs and ranks of almost explicit holo displays that kept showing the same five frames, over and over.

And shooting down Seventh toward her theater were three NYPD aircars in tight formation, flashers and sirens going.

She slammed the black-painted door shut. The sirens kept getting louder. It wasn't just the three cars either. She could pick out at least four more by the sound.

Gabe was supposed to be ten minutes away—

No, this wasn't the sniper.

Could the NYPD be after her, too? She didn't intend to stick around and find out.

However, Seventh was out.

Looking for an exit, Evi's gaze passed glass cabinets of dildos, vibrators, and devices less comprehensible, as well as the endless racks of ramcards.

The manager was still watching her. The volume was peaking on the sirens, and the crowd noise was intensifying outside.

She was rapidly being cornered. She had two choices: go back into the theater or go up the stairs to the restrooms, balcony, and, presumably, an old projection booth.

The leather queen was staring at her, too.

She ran up, away from the stares. She was hoping the restroom had a window. She rounded the landing at the head of the stairs and pushed through the first door she came to.

The smell was overpowering. Five flavors of human and non-human excretion. She had to sidestep a drying pool of vomit on the rust-stained hexagonal tile. However, at the end of the short line of stalls, there was a small black-painted rectangular window. She made for it.

Outside she could hear the whine of feedback from someone opening the channel on a PA system.

She raised one foot and set it on a radiator that shed rust and flakes of white paint. Her nose passed in front of a piece of graffiti asking for volunteers to ride the hershey highway.

Outside she could hear a too-amplified voice ". . . TESTING, ONE, TWO—" It degenerated into more feedback.

With her head even with the small window she scratched some of the black paint away from a corner with her thumbnail. Taking off her sunglasses, she put an eye to the hole in the paint.

Outside, the PA system squawked, "Attention. You have five minutes to release your hostages. Throw out your weapons and come out with your hands in plain view."

She saw another window in a brick wall. It was about three meters away. She looked down, and there was already a group of cops swarming the alley below.

That was damned quick for New York. What the hell was going on?

And what was that bit about hostages?

All she knew was that one of her calls must have triggered the cops. But this response time was unheard of for the NYPD.

Unless all those squads were already there, primed and waiting for a call.

She sat down on the radiator in frustration. For the first time she noticed the row of urinals. She'd stormed the men's room.

She had five minutes to decide what to do.

The patch-balding rat ran into the restroom carrying a large bag of something. He slid in the vomit, almost fell, and ducked into a stall, all without noticing Evi.

Over and over he was saying, "Damn, damn, damn pink cops . . ."

There was a rustling sound, and then the rat started flushing.

There was ringing feedback from the police PA system. "You have four minutes, come out with your hands in sight."

If her time sense was right, the cops had just cheated her out of twenty seconds. Must have fast watches.

She took the silenced Mitsubishi out of the backpack and prayed that she wouldn't have to use it on a cop. The rat came out of the stall without his package. He saw her and threw himself on the ground, groveling.

"Don't shoot, harmless me, do nothing, don't shoot." The rat kept babbling, facedown on the filthy floor. Evi passed him and smelled the strongest concentration of flush she had been near since she'd been in Cleveland. The hallucinogen, flush, had the unmistakable smell of spoiled cherries.

As she slipped out of the bathroom, leaving the rat prostrate, she thought that it was an appropriate smell for the john in a porn palace.

Her silent laugh hit her involuntarily.

Chapter 6

Okay, Evi, the good news is that real cops don't shoot human-looking people without warning."

She covered the hallway with the Mitsubishi. No one in sight. The hallway led straight through the building, with a stairway at either end. It was bathed in red half-light that nearly hid the cracked plaster. The speckled-red carpet was worn through in places to the black rubber underside. Five doors, all on her right, toward the theater. The door at the other end of the hallway had to be the women's room. The door in the center, the old projection booth. The doors flanking it must lead to the balcony.

"The bad news is, they've warned you."

She made her way to one of the balcony doors and pushed through.

She made her way down the aisle and asked herself, again, *now what*? She had a slight edge in the dark, but she wasn't trying to hold her position, she was trying to retreat.

Below her, chaos was brewing.

On the screen the Pakistani dog was spurting toward the audience, helped along by the tongues of his human partner and a female vulpine. The spectators down there weren't paying attention. They seemed to have just realized that the building was surrounded by cops.

Two humans were fumbling toward the lobby in the dark. The guy who'd been sitting in front of Evi earlier was busy trying to get his pants on. Getting up from the floor next to him was a morey fox who bore a passing resemblance to the vulpine porn actress who was now licking the semen off the dog's fur. Two human women were running down the aisle toward the emergency exits.

Of all of them, the vulpine seemed the calmest. She was dressed like a streetwalker, and Evi supposed she'd been through raids before.

All of a sudden, Evi heard a gunshot.

Who the hell was shooting? That shot was going to bring the cops down on the theater faster than the actresses were going down in the movie here.

Over the PA system, as if in response to her thought, she heard, "FIRE!"

She heard the breaking of glass from the direction of the lobby and above her.

Below, the leather queen she had seen in the lobby ran into the theater. He was waving a gun, a matte-black ten-millimeter H&K Valkyrie. What she saw of his expression made her guess he was a regular customer of the rat back in the men's room. He was screaming, "Fascist pigs! You'll never take me back!"

He fired the gun again, at the screen.

The Pakistani dog had the most explosive orgasm in cinematic history. For a split second, the image distorted, turning upside-down and backward. Then the scene flipped inside out around the bullet hole. An arc of electricity shot out from the screen and hit a chair in the front row. The colors separated, and the screen exploded.

Evi dived to the ground too late to avoid being hit in the shoulder by a flying piece of mirror.

She slowly got back up, fully intending to shoot the nut with the Valkyrie. Unfortunately, the leather queen was nowhere to be seen. She could hear him, off somewhere else in the building, threatening to bugger any cop that came within ten feet of him.

Great.

Without the holo movie, her eyes took a moment to adjust to the dark.

By then, the fox was bolting away from the smoking wall where the screen had been, and the guy with the pants was struggling to get up off the ground. The other humans had made it out already.

Outside again, she heard "FIRE!"

She heard more breaking glass.

She began to feel the telltale sting of tear gas in her nose and eyes. Her left shoulder felt warm. She looked and saw a sliver of

silver metal the length of her finger sticking out of the leather. She
gritted her teeth and pulled it out of her shoulder.

The tear gas was getting worse. It was only a matter of seconds
before the police stormed the building. She had no desire to fight it
out with a well-trained SWAT team. At the moment she felt as
though she'd have problems with a fifteen-year-old kid.

She rummaged in her pack. She had been equipped with a tear-
gas grenade, and she had a mask to go with it. One of the eyepieces
on the compact, black gas mask had cracked with all her running
around, but the seal still looked tight. Evi took off her sunglasses
and put it on.

She had one grenade left, a smoker. It gave off gas that was
opaque to UV and IR. Unlike the tear gas, she wouldn't be able to
see through it. Neither would the cops if they were equipped with
vision enhancement systems. If she dropped it, she might be able to
slip somewhere unseen.

But where could she go?

The guy with the pants stumbled out an emergency exit. She
could barely hear a cop outside order him to hit the ground with his
hands in view.

She looked around the theater. The holo screen was a smoking
hole in the wall smelling of charred insulation, gunpowder, and
mercury. The walls were covered by heavy red velvet drapes. Tear
gas was beginning to seep down from the gaps in a suspended ceiling.

The ceiling.

Evi dropped the grenade into the theater below and grabbed a
handful of red velvet. There was a sharp pain from her wounded
shoulder as she pulled herself up the wall. She tried to ignore it.

As she climbed, the theater filled with smoke. The dead-white
smoke from her grenade hung heavy to the ground, building up like
a fog bank. At the same time, the semitranslucent tear gas billowed
in from the lobby and down from the ceiling. Soon she was enveloped in it.

The mask prevented the gas from becoming disabling, but it still
felt like hell. It caused godawful itching all over her skin, especially
her crotch. It drove daggers into the open wound in her shoulder,
and her view out the cracked eyepiece was blurred and watery.

The white smoke from her grenade caught up to her and
wrapped her in a gray fog. The smoke sucked up sound, but she
could hear the muffled noise of the cops pouring into the lobby.

Her head bumped something. She looked up and saw a fiberglass acoustical tile, painted black. She held tightly to the drape with one hand as she pushed up on the tile. It gave, with a shower of black grime and a billow of tear gas. A fresh dagger twisted into her shoulder.

She pulled herself into the hole and pushed the tile back after her. It was a good thing she didn't weigh much. The skeletal armature she rested her hands and knees upon was producing some ominous groans. For a while, she didn't dare move. She just stayed still and hurt.

How long?

She could hear the cops storm in. They came in from all corners, the lobby, the fire exits, the balcony. She could tell when they hit her smoke; their movements became cautious. She could hear them talk, but between the smoke, the tile, and the mask, it was hard to make out more than a few sentences here and there.

"—ver the exits. Wait for the sm—"

"—ed and extremely dangerous—"

About half a minute, "—Bureau in five—"

The FBI? Something real big had been twigged onto her. She did a few more breathing exercises.

Where was the nut with the Valkyrie? She hadn't heard any more gunshots.

The gas was dissipating, making it easier to breathe. A lot of the itching had stopped, but her left eye was nearly swollen shut.

"—clearing some—"

"—no sign of sus—"

The voices were becoming louder. They were on the balcony directly underneath her. The tear gas was letting up, and so, by now, was her smoke. Fortunately, she had calmed down enough that her metabolism would be cutting down on her heat signature. IR enhancers wouldn't pick her up.

Evi started looking for an escape route.

"—back. Upper floors have cleared." Pause, then, "None of the terrorists seen leaving the building."

Terrorists?

"Yes, sir," the same voice responded to something she couldn't hear. "This is for *everyone*, hold your positions and wait for the Fed."

There was grumbling from at least five sources down there.

"*Orders*, damn it!" The cop didn't sound pleased. How long? Four minutes? Three?

How do you get out of a building ringed by police, in broad daylight?

Forget the building. Where could she go from here?

A light shower of plaster dust rained down on her head, accompanied by a creaking floorboard. Evi looked up at the original ceiling of the theater. There was a good reason for the suspended ceiling. The old plaster arches above her were, for the most part, crumbled and fallen away. She was looking at a study in dry rot and faulty wiring.

What was left in her pack?

Not much. Some bugging and surveillance devices, a tool kit, the peeper's Long-Eighties, a spare barrel for the Mishkov, a medkit and airhypo with a few dozen illegal drugs, and a military stun rod.

She pulled out the stun rod. She had carried one ever since that weird business in Cleveland, the business with the aliens. The rod measured a half-meter long, was dead black, and doubled as a billy club. It delivered a charge that would turn a hundred kilos of muscle to jelly for about fifteen seconds. She pressed the test button and a green LED winked at her.

The floorboard creaked, and more plaster filtered down.

This could work.

If you're totally silent, if he's not in radio contact with anyone, if you're right and no one else is up there right now . . .

Abdel, she asked her mental voice, *you got any better ideas?*

Abdel didn't.

She shouldered her pack and slowly, very slowly, raised herself into a squatting position under the creaking floorboards. She made sure to brace each foot next to one of the wires that supported the framework of the suspended ceiling. The last thing she wanted to do was try this only to end up pushing herself through in the wrong direction.

She wished she had a pair of morey ears. Her hearing was good, but the engineers could only go so far and have the ears remain human-looking. Eyes were easier to hide.

She was relying only on her hearing to place the target, and that was very iffy. It was her one chance, and it was a slim one. She braced herself, grabbing an exposed beam with her left hand. Her fingers sank into the rotting stud that ran under the floor above her. She waited for the floorboard to creak again.

It creaked.

She brought the rod up with her right arm, putting everything she had into the swing. The rounded end of the rod hit the center of a floorboard. The board gave with an anemic crack that still ignited a shivering wave of pain all the way down her arm. The rod shredded some carpeting and kept going upward. For an agonizing half-second she feared that she had misjudged and wasn't going to hit a damn thing.

The rod hit something and there was the telltale buzz of a discharge. She caught a whiff of charred fabric as something very solid thumped to the floor above her. More plaster rained down.

She wanted to wait to hear if there would be a reaction from other cops, but she didn't have the time. She pushed two more floorboards up. They cracked much too loudly for her taste. She scrambled through the hole and the torn carpeting, wrenching her abused shoulder again. She bit her lip hard enough to taste blood.

She found herself in a dimly lit interior hallway. Sprawled on the cheap gray carpeting was a cop done up in riot gear; vest, gas mask, boots. The rod had hit the cop halfway up his inner thigh. The point was marked by a circular burn and a halfway-melted patch on his trousers. Evi withdrew the airhypo from her backpack as the cop showed signs of coming around.

The hypo was a high-pressure model that could shoot right through thin fabrics, which was good. Evi had no time to roll up a sleeve. The cop looked close to sitting up when Evi put the hypo against the stun mark and tranked the cop to high heaven.

No commotion, no pursuit . . .

No partners?

Shut up Abdel, it worked, didn't it?

Evi pulled the gas mask off the cop.

The cop was a short-haired oriental woman. Even better, the cop was about Evi's size. There wasn't time for a complete makeover, but Evi could manage the pants and flak jacket over what she was wearing. With the cop's gas mask she could pass at a distance. She hoped that would be all she would need.

She was rushing for dear life, pulling the stuff on, but she couldn't avoid seeing the giant orange "FBI" on the back of the flak jacket.

The cops downstairs were still waiting for the Bureau. What was an agent doing here?

What was an agent doing up here, alone and with no backup? She had a bad feeling about that. The agent was oriental, female, about her size . . .

Evi pulled up one of the agent's eyelids. The agent had been wearing contacts, and one had slid aside. A deep, almost iridescent, blue iris was beneath the brown contact, and there was no mistaking the reflective green retina. Evi could tell that the pupil was slitted, even when fully dilated.

Evi had always known that the Jordanian project's technology was bought from the Japanese prior to the war. However, she had never expected to meet one of her oriental sisters. The pool of her species was so small that the agent was almost certainly a blood relative.

It was just as certain that the agent was there to make sure Evi was taken out. Evi didn't know if she belonged with the peeper or the sniper, but it didn't really matter right now.

She grabbed the agent's ID. It read "A. Sukiota, Special Agent, FBI."

" 'On loan,' I bet," Evi whispered.

Evi'd been " 'on loan' " to the FBI before. There was a good chance that Sukiota belonged to the Agency.

She recalculated the dosage on the hypo and tranked Sukiota enough to keep her out of the picture for the next six hours. Then she lowered her through the hole in the floor, carefully so the cops below wouldn't hear.

The sounds of more sirens came from outside. Must be the real FBI agents. Evi counted on a little interagency jurisdictional chaos to distract the players. Because, right now, there was no avoiding a blatant walk in the open.

She made it to the stairs, turned a corner, and almost bumped into a cop in full gear. Their gazes locked. She hoped that the jacket with the ID clipped to it would be enough. She also hoped that the cop didn't know Sukiota . . .

Oh shit, her eyes! The cop was staring directly into her eyes. She'd forgotten about her sunglasses, and she didn't have contacts like Sukiota.

However, the cop was just staring. He didn't call out on his radio, he didn't ready his weapon, he just stared.

Evi felt a wave of deja vu crash over her. She had played FBI for the Agency before, and while in that situation it was procedure to follow the forms and pretend you were human, almost always the people you were working with figured it out. If Sukiota had been working with the NYPD for any length of time, there must already be rumors she was a frank.

It probably had yet to pass the cop's mind that he wasn't looking at Sukiota.

Evi hoped her mask muffled her voice enough. "Problem, officer?"

"No, none." He said too quickly and broke eye contact. He avoided looking at her now, keeping his eyes down toward the corridor he was watching. Better and better. Evi headed down the stairs.

Three flights she went down. She passed two more cops guarding the exits. She pretended to belong here and clamped down on the panic that was brewing inside her. The cops nodded as she passed, and she was thankful that no words were exchanged.

The stairway ended in a doorway under the marquee, to the left of the lobby exits. She looked outside and saw at least a dozen black-and-whites screwing the traffic up and down Seventh. She could pick out six snipers stationed across the street and wondered if one of them was Gabe. A half-dozen Dodge Haviers with flashers out were pulling up behind the NYPD, in some cases pulling onto the sidewalk to do so. Civilians were poking their heads out of windows, climbing onto parked cars, crowding traffic cops who were trying to keep the spectators at a reasonable distance.

Three aircars from the major NY vid news channels were hovering over Times Square, screwing the air traffic as much as the cops were screwing the ground traffic. All eyes were on the entrance of the theater, and she'd be walking out, center stage. She didn't have much time to decide what to do next. Sukiota bought her some time and protective coloring, but she might only have a few minutes before someone found Sukiota.

She went through the pockets of Sukiota's clothes, searching for inspiration. She came up with a small remote control with the GM logo on it. A host of buttons sat above an oval thumbpad. Where was the car?

Wait a minute.

She examined the control more closely. It belonged to a GM Maduro. A sports car like that was hard to miss, and no Maduro was parked outside.

She placed her thumb on the pad. If the car was anywhere around, the alarm should start going off. No alarm sounded. She suspected that this remote belonged to a metallic-blue Maduro that was now smoldering wreckage in a parking garage on the upper east side. Her hand clenched around the small remote control and she could hear plastic cracking as her knuckles whitened.

Somewhere, someone screamed.

She looked out at the commotion ringing the front of the theater.

A knot of plainclothes NYPD was arguing with a similar knot from the FBI. They were standing, partially covered from the front of the theater by a SWAT van. They were all turning to look up, toward the marquee.

A cop to the rear, manning the police line keeping the civilians back, turned in response. The poor guy was nearly swamped by the crowd he was holding back. He was holding back a ten-foot line of potential riot all by himself.

She could hear the leather queen. He was the one screaming.

The snipers started to open fire on the marquee, and all hell broke loose.

The lone cop who was swamped at the thinnest part of the police line took a running step, and his chest blossomed in a spray of blood. Evi couldn't tell if it was the queen with the Valkyrie or a stray shot from the cops who were now firing unreservedly at the marquee.

The civilians moved. They were panicking. The cop who'd been shot fell over the curb, and suddenly a hundred civilians found themselves unconstrained. They wanted to go back, but there were too many of their fellows crowding behind them. They had only one direction to run.

The police line evaporated. Blue uniforms were swamped.

The leather queen either jumped or fell into the crowd.

Now or never.

Evi slipped out the door and ran for the riot and waded into the sea of leather, business suits, hard hats and fur, all the time feeling a sniper's cross hairs focused on her back.

Chapter 7

She ditched the FBI flak jacket somewhere in the midst of the crowd of civilians, and the gas mask ended up in a waste kiosk on 42nd Street. Evi didn't bother to retrieve the dollar or so the kiosk credited her.

The crowd returned to normal intensity by the time she reached Bryant Park. She turned off Broadway and eventually came to rest under the one remaining lucite-enclosed lion by the steps to the library. The weak noon glow from the white sky was dimming, and a few flakes were filtering down.

As she looked at the sky, three police aircars escorted a helicopter, going north, headed for the commotion up by Times Square.

She sucked in gasps of air, trying to relax, to think.

The only thing she could think about was how much her leg and her shoulder hurt.

Every instinct was calling out for backup. She needed to come in out of the cold. But there was no longer an "in" to go to. A large part of Evi's carefully structured universe had fallen into a black abyss, and suddenly *everywhere* was hostile territory. It was the Axis invasion all over. She was sixteen again, cut off, abandoned.

She noted the way a few passing civilians eyed her and realized that she had better get inside somewhere and clean up. Evi looked up at the library and wondered if, like the Mishkov, the Mitsubishi in her bag was designed not to set off metal detectors.

She decided not to risk it. The Mitsubishi SG found its resting place in a storm sewer running under Fifth.

Ten minutes in the library's public washroom helped her looks, if not how she felt. Evi stuck her head in a sink and let cold water run over the back of her head and the left side of her face. She had no idea how much her left eye had been hurting from the gas until she flushed it out. It was a relief just to rest her cheek against the cold porcelain. For a few minutes she didn't care if anyone tried to jump her.

No one did. The only people who passed through the bathroom were a pair of bouncing blonde teenagers who babbled around her, apparently doing their best to ignore the leather-clad woman with her head in the sink.

When the girls left, she raised her head and looked at herself in the mirror. Her left eye was bloodshot and puffy, and a circular patch of red irritation marked where her gas mask had pressed into the flesh.

With her eyes squeezed partway shut, she could see her Asian heritage.

She bore a very close resemblance to Sukiota. So much so that the Semitic cast to her features seemed to be briefly overshadowed.

It was unsettling, even if they *were* sisters. They were closer than any blood relatives outside identical twins. Evi knew of at least two living women of the same heritage with whom she shared a DNA signature.

The heritage was Hiasbu Biological. Specifically, "General Purpose Human Embryo—Lot 23." The last commercial strain prewar Japan ever produced.

She removed the leather jacket and partially unzipped the monofil jumpsuit. Her shoulder had bled enough to make pulling the jumpsuit away painful. She grimaced as she pulled down the collar, revealing the wound behind her left shoulder. She saw in the mirror that the puncture was small and shallow. Splashing some water over it cleaned the blood and revealed a dark purple bruise that was spreading down her back. Looking at the bruise reminded her how much her leg was aching.

She dressed the wound with an antibiotic patch from her medkit. Good thing the damage was minor. She wouldn't be able to fix a bullet wound in here.

She didn't even want to think about getting a major injury in the field.

She zipped herself up, replaced the jacket, and put on her shades.

Now she looked more the street kid than the art student.

She walked out into the hall, limping, soft leather boots squeaking on the new marble. Muffled construction sounds were emerging from behind white plastic panels on the wall opposite the bathroom. It had been nearly six years since the Bronx Bensheim clinic was firebombed, and here they were, still repairing the damage from the moreau retaliation.

'53 had been a bad year all around.

She smiled to herself. If it hadn't been for her work in Cleveland, it could have been a lot worse.

But her leg hurt, and she wanted to sit down.

She found a comm booth in sight of the front door and slipped inside. It was much nicer than the comm at the theater. It still had the new factory smell about it. The booth was soundproofed behind its tinted glass and provided a contoured bucket seat. The lighting was low, and the plastic was a soft charcoal gray, not the more common glare-white.

Just sitting down made her feel a lot better.

The booth gave her a much needed sense of privacy, despite her paranoid thought that someone at the Agency might be using the Langley mainframes to leach the comm signals from Manhattan for her image. That kind of extravagance would be unlikely. The cost would be hard to explain down in Washington, even with a black budget. Besides, this comm's primary use was to access the library database. She doubted her picture would be out on the net unless she tried to access an outside line.

The comm began flashing a green message at her. It wanted her to insert her card and choose a function. Damn, it wouldn't let her sit there and think. She picked out one of her false ID cards from her pack. The one she'd gotten herself, without Agency intervention. Eve Herman's existence was shakier than the personae created by the Agency, but Eve didn't exist in any file on any member of the intelligence community, foreign or domestic.

Eve logged onto the library database and began an interminable search on the incredibly large subject of "Japan" while Evi leaned back and thought about why she had become such a prize target.

The Agency had turned on her. Frightening, but not unheard of. It wasn't spoken of in the open, but the stories did circulate. The Agency decided someone was a liability, and something happened to them. They stepped onto a transport that never landed at its destination, or they had an appointment with a superior and never returned. Somehow, their mail gets forwarded to some anonymous post office databank, their furniture gets moved to some small dead town in northern Nevada, their cover identities quit their jobs because of vaguely defined "family problems," and their lives dry up and are forgotten.

The past seven hours didn't fit the Agency's M.O. for "retirement." That was despite the fact that her boss, Hofstadter, was the hand behind the sniper. The Agency wouldn't bother assassinating agents in the field when they could simply be ordered to attend their own execution.

Unless there was a time factor and they had to do it now, this instant.

The mercs must have forced their hand. If she was right and the sniper was there to prevent the mercs from taking her alive, it would almost make sense. A sniper was much more the Agency's style. They didn't want her taken and would kill her to prevent it. That sounded like Agency thinking.

That didn't explain why she couldn't call in.

It also didn't explain Frey. Frey was supposed to take her in, but Aerie didn't acknowledge her existence anymore.

Whoever Frey talked to, it wasn't Aerie.

The screen was flashing at her. The comm had stopped its search at half a million items. It wanted more qualifiers. Eve told it to drop any references prior to 2053.

The Aerie didn't recognize her code. That meant someone had nuked her Agency file.

Why bother?

There was something else going on here.

Then there was A. Sukiota. Sukiota was definitely an Agency creature. Sukiota had been on her heels twice already—once in the theater, once during the chaos in Evi's building, presuming that it was Sukiota's Maduro that Evi had blown up. Sukiota was working with the NYPD, if not running the show.

Both Sukiota and the cops were after her. Evi could understand the cops, but why Sukiota? The Agency already had one sniper after her, Gabe. Were Sukiota and Gabe the same person?

The comm flashed at her.

There were a hundred thousand references to Japan post-53. For the first time she really looked at the search she was running. She had thought she was just throwing the comm into a random search to let her think. Now her choice seemed less than random.

Japan.

The peeper was speaking Japanese to somebody, probably the man with the doberman. The Afghani mercs were armed with Mitsubishis. Evi had blown away a dog, a generic un-engineered doberman that had hardwired bio-interfaces.

What did Japan, old Japan, have to do with her? She was only ten years old when Tokyo was nuked and the Chinese overran the island. But, if anything, the Japan that was touching her now was the prewar Japan, the techno-colossus that had been gone for more than two decades, not the modern little client state that no one ever heard about anymore.

Her job barely touched that part of the world. At the think tank, that was more Dave Price's area. His doctoral thesis was on the U.S. nonintervention in the Pan-Asian war. It was definitely Hofstadter's area. His main area of study was Pacific Rim economics.

In the dozen years she'd worked for the Agency, she'd had only one operation where Japan was even a small part . . .

2053, Cleveland. Neutralizing Hassan Sabah.

Her last "fire" mission.

The last time she'd heard Frey manning the Aerie.

And Hassan Sabah was an Afghani canine assassin, just like the mercs that had overrun her building.

Could all that be a coincidence?

"Hell, no."

She keyed the search to concentrate on Japanese Nationalist activity. That had been Hassan's last known affiliation before he smuggled himself into the States. Evi had tracked Hassan to Cleveland during the steaming August of '53 and had opened a can of worms that had led to the indictment of twenty-three congressmen and the resignation of fifty more.

As far as she knew, that can of worms had nothing to do with Japan. In fact, it originated about as far from Japan as you could get. A few light-years at least.

As far as she knew.

There was a knock at the door to the booth, and it was all Evi could do to keep from drawing her gun. She looked and saw a young sandy-haired man leaning over and smiling through the tinted window. His name tag said his name was Paul. She opened the booth.

"Yes?"

"Sorry, miss, but because of the holiday the library is closing early."

She looked behind him, at a large digital clock hanging over the main doors. The clock was part of the reconstruction and looked a century out of place in the building. The time was 2:53.

"Thanks for the warning."

"No problem. There's an announcement over the PA, but you can't hear it in these things."

The guy still hovered there, smiling. She allowed herself to smile back.

She had the comm download all the Japanese info onto a ramcard while Paul watched. "You know, I wrote my thesis on the Chinese occupation."

She stepped out of the booth and stretched. She tried not to wince at the pain it triggered in her calf and shoulder. "Very interesting, but it's not polite to read over people's shoulders."

Paul gave a lopsided shrug and broadened his grin slightly. She could smell a little lust and some well-hidden nervousness about the guy. "Ask me something."

"What?"

"Ask me about whatever you're searching for," Paul hooked a thumb back at the comm booth.

This was getting a little annoying. "I'm not even sure what I'm looking for."

"Then ask me something at random, and I'll leave you alone."

Why not? "Tell me about Japanese Nationalist activity in '53."

Paul rubbed his chin. "Busy year, but then you probably knew that. Five—no, six—high-level political assassinations. Started with Yang Peng, assistant political director in Yokohama. The NLF hired a professional assassin, took an antitank rocket to his limo." *That had been Hassan's work,* Evi thought. "That was in March. A ground-to-air missile shot down an Air-bus ballistic shuttle on take-off. That killed the Chinese foreign minister and about a hundred tourists. That was in Shanghai in May. The director of the State Office of Science and Technology along with a few dozen Chinese scientists and engineers were killed by a suicide car bomb during a Tokyo excavation—"

Scientists and engineers? "What were they doing?"

Paul smiled. He seemed happy that he had finally piqued her interest. "The Chinese government never made an official statement, but their State Office is mostly known for rooting through whatever was left of the Japanese technological base for their discoveries. I did some research at the time, and the location of the explosion is around where the Japanese space agency warehoused some of their prototypes—"

"Thank you." Yes, it was much more than a coincidence. She turned to go.

"You're welcome." She didn't hear Paul follow her, and for that she was grateful.

"Hope to see you again."

She reached the door, sighed, and turned around. "No, you don't." She slipped outside, not waiting for Paul to respond.

She walked back out on the street, wading through the press of people. She knew the pieces fit together, but she didn't know how. What was clear, however, was that her involvement in breaking up that cell in 2053 was the reason behind what was happening to her. She didn't know exactly why, but there were too many parallels between now and five years ago.

Everyone was after her because of the aliens.

She pushed through the crowd, uncaring. She forced her way past a growling moreau jaguar. She ignored him. She was barely aware of where she was going, until a chain-link fence adorned with warning signs stopped her.

She looked up and found herself facing the scaffolding enveloping the truncated tower of the Chrysler Building. The demolition of the tower had halted for the holiday, and she'd been stopped by the fence that crossed 42nd. The Chrysler Building was the only thing standing in a city block of plowed rubble.

It looked like as good a place as any to go to ground.

She scanned the crowd around her on this side of the fence. Scurrying civilians were doing their best to ignore her, the homeless moreaus huddled in the doorways and into each other. New Yorkers all, and not a cop among them. She might as well have been alone.

She grabbed a handful of fence and hauled herself up to the top. The barbed wire was only a deterrent. It wouldn't stop anyone who took a little care in climbing over it. Once she was over the wire, she vaulted into the construction site. None of the civilians commented or looked in her direction.

She limped toward the surreal monument of the Chrysler Building over a small mountain of broken concrete and powdered stone. The land was cleared for half a block in every direction, as if the city had drawn back in rejection of one of its oldest skyscrapers.

She made it to the base of the building, weaving through a dark jungle of scaffolding to reach the doorway. She didn't go inside. She just sat down in the entranceway, giving a casual glance at the graffiti that covered the exterior for three stories.

"Off the pink," read one sentiment. It was a morey phrase. "Pink" was morey slang for human.

It reminded her of Cleveland, and the aliens.

Evi had handed the aliens to DC and Langley.

It still frightened her. No one in the community had seemed to have had any official knowledge of the cell that had been based in Cleveland. She had stumbled on it while tailing Hassan.

The mission had started out as a simple game of "bag the terrorist." But the people Hassan killed in Cleveland hadn't been killed for political reasons. They'd been killed because they'd known about the aliens. Hassan had eliminated dozens of people to cover up the existence of a conspiracy buying influence in Washington.

She remembered sitting in her Porsche, waiting outside a darkened office building, headquarters to Midwest Lapidary Imports, fuming at the Aerie. Even then, before she realized the origin of the conspiracy, the scope of what she'd uncovered boggled . . .

A cell controlled by some foreign agency operated behind this corporate front and bought billions of dollars worth of influence in Washington.

Congress, the Judiciary, the White House, nothing had been immune.

There were eight thousand employees working for Midwest Lapidary who only existed as bits in some databank. At that point the latest info was that the data trails led back to Langley. As if the CIA could finance something like that. It had been just another fictional artifact engineered by the people in charge of Midwest Lapidary.

If they were people.

Even then, she wasn't sure if they *were* people. She had seen the corpse of one of the creatures that ran Midwest Lapidary. The being had been called a frank, but it was no frank she had ever heard of. She had an encyclopedic knowledge of human-engineered species, and the corpse of John Smith found no home there. The corpse she had seen had been 300 kilos of white hairless blubber that had been only roughly molded into the shape of a man.

And the corpse had melted.

Nothing she had ever heard of did that.

Smith had been killed by a stun rod, so her team had been so equipped. However, she wanted to try and get these things alive. She had a lot of questions. For that reason, the team also had trank guns.

But God knew what a trank would do to a design so exotic.

And the Aerie had just told her to pack it in.

She had a specimen jar on the dashboard. Inside swirled a milky-white liquid, somewhat more viscous than water. A smell of bile and ammonia hung about it. The rest of Smith's "remains" had been at a lab being analyzed.

Hassan had bombed the lab where the specimens had been stored. It was a total loss. All that was left of Smith was the few ounces of liquid sitting on Evi's dash.

But since Hassan was dead now, Aerie seemed unconcerned. Hassan had been the mission.

She had found that a foreign government was in at least partial control of nearly a hundred Congressmen, and the Agency was happy to pack it in now because a local private investigator threw Hassan off the top of a parking garage.

In fact, her new orders were to track down that damned PI. Nohar Rajasthan, a 300-kilo, two-and-a-half meter tall moreau tiger. A descendant of computer-evolved Indian special forces, all fur, teeth, claws, and muscle. If he had any formal combat training, he'd be scary.

As far as she was concerned, that was pointless.

Nohar just had the bad luck to be investigating Hassan as well. He had uncovered the same mess she had. She had thought he was safely under wraps at the hospital. It wasn't the tiger's fault Hassan bombed the place.

Apparently, after the explosion, there was a battle royal between Nohar and Hassan, after which Nohar disappeared. The Agency was still operating under the assumption that Nohar had links to radical moreau organizations.

She was still fuming at the Agency when the comm buzzed her. "Agent Isham here."

"Isham? This is Agent Conrad. We found one of the people you've been looking for. Alive and well."

"Who?"

"Ms. Stephanie Weir, from the Binder Senate campaign—" Weir was the one executive officer of Binder's staff that Hassan hadn't killed.

As far as Evi knew, Nohar was the last person to have contact with her.

There was a muffled cursing and a female voice. "—give me that. Agent Isham?"

"Ms. Weir?"

"Nohar said that the MLI office building is a front, that they're at NuFood—"

"What?"

"—he said they're based on dextro amino acids. He's gone there."

Sitting at the base of the Chrysler Building, Evi remembered that moment clearly. The moment when she knew. She had pulled out on to the street by the time Weir had reached the word "gone." At the time, she thought the ideas running through her head were insane.

But it had made sense.

All those billions had been spent in a largely successful effort to erode the technical base of the United States. Especially in defense and space. The phony corporation of Midwest Lapidary was backing dozens of senators that would scuttle NASA's deep-space probe project once it came to a vote that session.

And John Smith didn't match any gene engineering project that Evi had ever heard of.

And Weir had just said Nohar Rajasthan believed they were based on a mirror-image biology.

"Agent Isham? What's that *mean?*" Weir had asked.

Nearly everything alive on earth was based on levo amino acids. A creature based on a dextro amino acid biology wouldn't be able to metabolize any food on the planet. Except the exotic dietary foodstuffs that NuFood produced. For the first time, Evi had realized that these were things that hadn't been born on this world.

Evi's response had been, "You don't want to know."

Six years later, she still shivered at that realization. She was more frightened of the idea of otherworldly beings manipulating the government than she could ever be of the Agency.

And, since the library, she had realized there'd be other cells. The aliens, wherever they came from, were interested in preventing anything from Earth interfering with "their" worlds. However, the Untied States hadn't been the only nation planning interstellar probes.

Prewar Japan had been much farther along. So had prewar India.

There *had* to be cells in Asia. If the Nippon Liberation Front bombed a Tokyo excavation of space-probe prototypes, it was a good bet that they were backed by the aliens.

There were two players she was running from.

The sniper was Agency material.

Could it be the NLF that was behind the others? They employed Afghanis and had access to old Jap technology, and they had a possible link, though circumstantial, to the aliens.

But why her, and why now? It wasn't as if she were the only one who . . .

Evi realized that Nohar was the only non-Agency person who knew about the aliens.

Chapter 8

The last time Evi had seen Nohar, he had been in a hospital bed. She had dug him, and the four aliens, out from under a warren under NuFood. He had been in sad shape, and the Agency more or less forgot about him. She'd never emphasized Nohar's role in the whole mess.

When she felt safe, and the night had wrapped around the city, she left the wreckage of the Chrysler Building and walked to a public comm. It took Eve Herman nearly ninety minutes and two hundred dollars to find Nohar Rajasthan again.

All the time Evi was thinking of aliens.

Her thoughts kept returning to the aliens' lair under the NuFood complex. Organic shaped tunnels of polished concrete that had smelled of sulfur, burning methane, and aliens. The aliens emitted an evil bile-ammonia odor that she would never forget. The four creatures she'd captured made her think of white polyethylene bags of raw sewage.

She finally found Nohar at some New Year's Eve party in Hollywood. On the other coast it was seven o'clock. If anyone was interested in Nohar, they hadn't done anything about it yet.

What she hadn't anticipated was how difficult getting to talk to the tiger would be, even when she found out where he was. It had been a long time since she had dealt with the real world.

The blonde who answered the comm was stoned out of her mind, and it took Evi nearly fifteen minutes to explain to her that the call wasn't for her. At which point the comm was abandoned, leaving Evi with an oblique view of somebody's expensive chrome living room filled with nearly equal numbers of moreaus and humans.

She had nothing better to do, so she waited for somebody else to answer her call while she looked out at Third Avenue expecting the city to collapse in on her.

Both snow and traffic were getting worse.

Occasionally she shouted to get the attention of somebody moving close to the comm. Eventually, that worked. A pudgy lepine moreau noticed her yelling at the comm. Third generation, she thought. A Peruvian rabbit, probably a mixture of a half-dozen strains. But he didn't look stoned.

"Hello?"

Finally. "I need to talk to Nohar Rajasthan."

The rabbit cocked one drooping ear toward the comm. *"What?"*

Between the traffic on her end and the party on the other, she had to shout. "Nohar Rajasthan, I need to talk to Nohar *Rajasthan!*"

The rabbit nodded. "Rajasthan, right."

The light at the end of one tunnel at least.

She watched the rabbit melt into the party, and waited for Nohar to show up.

She didn't expect the black-haired woman who ended up sitting in front of the comm a few minutes later.

"Stephanie Weir?"

The woman grimaced and read Evi's alias off the screen. "I know they don't recognize it in New York," Stephanie shouted over the party, "but the name is *Rajasthan*, Ms. Herman."

Evi should have noticed the ring on her finger. "I wanted to talk to your husband."

Stephanie smiled. "That was good. I didn't even notice a wince when you said that."

Evi sighed. "Can you get him for me?" She decided that Stephanie was one of those women who became excessively catty when she'd had a few drinks.

"No."

Abdel, what do I do when I can't throttle her? "It happens to be an emergency."

Stephanie nodded. "Matter of life and death, do or die, now or never—You'd be surprised how common that is, Eve. They're *all* emergencies. But it's New Year's. You're going to have to wait until Thursday."

There was a broad smile on Stephanie's face. She was obviously enjoying what she was putting her through.

"It can't wait—"

"Then I'd say another detective is in order."

"Mrs. Rajasthan, there's a good chance that someone is going to try and kill your husband if you don't shut up and listen to me."

Stephanie lost the smile. "You look—"

Evi wanted to punch in the screen. "You look! Tell Nohar his life is in danger—" Evi whipped off her sunglasses. *"Get him!"*

Stephanie looked as if she was about to make another comment. Instead she just stared at the comm, color draining out of her face.

Nohar had told her. Probably a long time ago, but Nohar had told her. Evi could read it in her face. She had never met Stephanie face-to-face, but she had made an impression on Nohar. Any description he gave would have included her eyes.

Stephanie backed away from the comm. "Damn," she whispered as she pushed back into the crowd.

Now she was getting somewhere.

It took less than a minute for Nohar to get to the comm. The tiger was an impressive figure even on the comm's small screen. The party was blocked by a wall of yellow and black fur, all shoulders and face. Nohar had wrinkled his muzzle in a grimace and was emitting a low growl. She noted a few gray hairs around his broad nose.

"You." Nohar made it sound like an accusation. It probably was.

She could understand how he felt, but the attitude still annoyed her. "Six years ago, I promised my goodwill if you helped me out. I'm paying you back."

"Point is?" Nohar was not one for a lengthy monologue.

"Point is, the company I work for is trying to assassinate me."

There was a subtle transformation in Nohar's face. If she weren't an expert in reading moreau expressions she might not have noticed that Nohar had stopped displaying his teeth. The way his feline cheek was twisted, it would still be called a grimace. "What happened?"

"There's a good chance I've been targeted because of what happened in Cleveland. Because of the 'franks' who ran Midwest Lapidary."

"Shit." Nohar let out a long breath. "That means—"

"Only maybe."

She could hear Nohar's claws rake the chair he was sitting on, even over the noise of the party. "What do I do?"

"Disappear. Go on a real vacation, pay cash, don't tell anyone where you go, leave the country for a while."

Nohar shook his head. "Asking a lot."

"I'm not *asking* anything. What you and your wife do is up to you."

"When will things be safe?"

"I don't know."

"You're not making things easy."

"I didn't have to call."

Nohar let out a low rumbling sigh. "I owe you one."

"You did my job for me back in Cleveland. Consider it even."

"Not quite. You're one up on me. Let me give you something." Nohar typed on his comm's keyboard and text began to appear on her screen. It was an address. Evi knew enough about New York to know that it was deep in the Bronx, Moreytown. Nohar also typed "G1:26."

Nohar gave Evi a close-lipped smile. "You might be able to use that."

Nohar cut the connection.

What the hell was "G1:26" supposed to mean? Numbers separated by a colon. Greenwich mean time?

Evi used the memo function to record the note on Eve's card. She'd ponder it later. Nohar obviously assumed she'd know.

She left the booth and started walking down Third, away from the Chrysler Building, away from Central Park, away, she hoped, from the more intense searches for her.

She kept walking south, hiding herself in the eternal press of New Yorkers. It was getting close to nine, and traffic was grinding to a stop. Half the cars she passed had out-of-state plates. Aircars buzzed above, their red landing lights like embers caught in an updraft.

She kept walking, at random for the most part, keeping close to the buildings. She kept one eye open for the police. There, again, the holiday was working in her favor. The NYPD was understaffed to begin with. New Year's in Manhattan overloaded them by an order of magnitude.

Why her and not Nohar?

She kept mulling over that question.

She was pretty sure, despite her warnings, that if the people who were after her were after him, they'd have gotten to him long before she'd called. For some reason, she was more valuable.

The only difference she could think of was the fact that she worked for the Agency, and Nohar was a civilian. The peeper's team, the NLF, seemed to want her alive. And it seemed that the

Agency was willing to kill her to prevent it. That extreme reaction by the Agency would make sense if it was something about the Agency itself the NLF was after.

She shook her head. If that was so, then where did the aliens fit in? They had to be involved, there were too many links.

And it still didn't explain why the Aerie emergency number didn't acknowledge her existence. If the Agency was trying to keep her out of the hands of the NLF, it was *stupid* to prevent her from coming in.

And who the hell was Frey talking to when he pretended to talk to the Aerie?

He was Agency, why didn't he shoot her?

She walked south down the axis of Manhattan, her mind traveling in circles over the same set of facts. She managed to avoid crossing paths with any cops.

It was a few blocks south of Canal Street, right in front of the marble pagoda of the Chinatown Memorial, that she heard an aircar do a low flyby and realized that fatigue had made her careless.

She backed to the memorial and leaned against a brass plaque listing the dead from the '42 riots. She was confronted on one side by post-riot buildings. Sleek security condominiums, shades drawn against the empty street. Behind her was the monument to the riot and five square blocks of inadequately lit park that had once been a business district.

The crowd had thinned a little, and the street here was mostly empty of traffic.

The aircar had buzzed by, and she suddenly realized that one of her engineered survival traits could be a severe liability. Her body's metabolism had a very low thermal profile. It was supposed to help her hide from infrared imaging. However, that unusual heat signature would single her out of a crowd of normal humans . . .

The protection the crowd was offering her was illusory.

She stood out like a beacon.

She should have realized how tired she was. She must have been asleep on her feet to walk into a scene this perfect for an ambush. Abdel volunteered that she should have chosen a spot and gone to ground until she figured out what to do.

But she was still here and hadn't been blindsided yet. She rubbed her aching shoulder and noticed that her hand was shaking slightly.

The snow was painting a thin cover on the ground, and she was beginning to feel the chill in the air.

While she was still in the midst of deciding where to go from here, she heard a car coming down Center Street. She didn't want to take any chances. She faded into the shadow of the pillar bearing the memorial plaque and put her hand on the butt of the Mishkov.

The people walking back and forth down the streets ignored her.

The car, a white late-model Jaguar, jerked to a stop, double-parking almost directly in front of her, pointed the wrong way. She was so tense that she nearly shot the driver before she heard the voices. The voices from inside the car were a relief. They all sounded drunk. The car held a man and two women.

None of them sounded like a threat.

One of the women wobbled out of the passenger side door carrying what appeared to be a magnum of champagne.

Evi was about to holster her weapon when she realized she was hearing another engine, above her. The aircar was back in the vicinity. She looked up and didn't see any lights. Legit air-traffic *never* cut the lights.

The civilians across the street were arguing.

"I told you we'd make it," the man was telling the one bearing the champagne as he followed her out of the passenger door.

"Sure, and we only have, like, a half hour to go."

The woman still in the car was the driver; she sounded the most sober. "You wanted to go to Desmond's party first."

"We should have stayed at Desmond's. A fucking waste spending two hours in the car on New Year—"

"Girls, girls—" The guy was trying to calm things down. Meanwhile, Evi tried to spot the aircar. She would have been able to see if it weren't for the streetlights. The bright mercury lamps were washing out her ability to see any infrared beyond a few meters. However, from the sound of it, the aircar was hovering.

She was in trouble.

A tiny, glowing infrared dot sprouted too close to her head and Evi ran. A bullet struck the pillar behind her. A chunk of marble shrapnel whizzed by her ear. The gun was silenced. She never heard it fire.

People cursed her as she slammed through the crowd.

Things were going too fast, and she still had no real idea where the aircar was.

She ran at the Jaguar. The trio hadn't noticed the shot or Evi running at them. The guy was leaning in the driver's side door and trying to coax the remaining woman out. "Come on, Kris, we'll miss Diane's party."

Evi bolted across the street and felt more than heard the next shot hit the ground behind her left foot.

"Not until Red apologizes."

Evi was halfway across the street and the infrared dot leapt ahead of her. She dodged as a bullet plowed out a small crater in the street.

"Come on, Sam, let's leave her—huh?"

The one with the bottle had noticed Evi running full tilt across the street, gun down. She shoved her out of the way and dived into the open passenger door.

"Get out!" Evi yelled. She was pointing the gun at the driver, but only got a blank look in response.

"No, not my dad's car."

"Lady, this is a real gun."

"You're not steal—" A bullet punched through the roof of the Jaguar and split the armrest on the passenger door. That was too close. The driver let out a squeak and floored the Jaguar.

The man barely had time to dive for the safety of the sidewalk.

The woman, who looked barely nineteen, was looking at her. *"They're shooting!"*

Another shot ripped through the rear window, shattering it. There was a shuddering scrape as the Jaguar bucked forward and sideswiped a parked BMW, slamming shut the driver's door.

"Fuck, somebody's shooting at us—"

They were in the wrong lane.

"Get in the right lane, lady!" Evi shouted as she struggled to sit upright in the passenger seat and get the seatbelt on. Then she began to reach out and close the passenger door.

"Name's Kris," said the driver as she swerved way over the center of the road, rocking Evi too far out the open door. Evi had a brief, terrifying, view of speeding asphalt as another gunshot shattered the passenger window. Kris was still talking, eyes locked on the road now, "My dad's going to kill me."

The Jaguar kept swerving to the right until it bumped up on the curb. Evi was thrown back into the car as a fire hydrant rendered the passenger door irrelevant. The door was torn away with Evi's head barely inside the car.

The windshield in front of them shattered as another shot tore through the length of the car. Kris screamed. Snow began slicing in through the window, burning Evi's cheeks. She didn't want to look at the speedometer.

"We're going to die," Kris was saying now, "it's New Year's Eve and we're going to die—"

"We're not going to die—"

Kris somehow managed to slam the Jaguar through an invisible gap in the traffic on Broadway, scraping at least four cars on the way through the intersection. A bullet hit the hood of the Jaguar, and the engine began to make ominous grinding noises.

"Get under some cover. They're in an aircar."

"Who the hell are *you?"*

"Look at the road!"

Kris snapped her head around. The Jaguar had drifted into the wrong lane again. A van was headed right toward them, horn blaring.

Kris pulled a cornering move that shouldn't have been possible. From inside the car it felt like the ninety-degree turn the car did had a point on the corner. The van scraped by the rear of the Jaguar, and Evi heard its windshield shatter as the sniper let loose another shot.

The Jaguar streaked through an alley, plowing boxes and garbage in front of it. Evi maneuvered around in the seat to look out the rear window. She could finally make out the aircar through the snow. It was a faint shadow lurking in the crack of sky between the buildings.

Evi braced the Mishkov on the back of her seat and aimed. The shot was as difficult as it could be, hitting a barely visible high-speed moving target from a moving platform. She gave herself one chance in ten.

She fired the Mishkov and Kris screamed. The sound was a deafening explosion in the enclosed space, even over the roar of the wind through the broken windows.

The aircar looked undisturbed.

Evi took another bead on the flyer as a bullet plowed into the trunk, about a foot away from her. Before Evi fired, the Jaguar pulled a shuddering left turn back into the open to the blare of a dozen horns.

The aircar could be anywhere now. Evi had lost it in the glare of the streetlights. The Jaguar passed a restaurant window, which shattered as another shot missed them.

Evi looked ahead of the car. The Jaguar shot through a crosswalk, clipping the front of a cab, and Evi got a look at a street sign—

How the hell did they get north on Hudson? There must have

been a turn or two Evi had missed. However, that explained the traffic. Their car was shooting by dozens of vehicles.

"Get off of Hudson!"

Kris took a hard left across another crosswalk, crashing through a sign directing people to the Holland Tunnel. A bullet shattered what was left of the driver's side window. Kris was screaming to be heard over the wind. "Damn it! Who *are* you?"

Kris was crying. Her tears were diagonal streaks in the wind.

She jumped another curb and sideswiped another cab getting onto Canal Street. They were heading straight for the Hudson.

Evi kept watch behind them, looking for the aircar. It was still lost in the glare of the streetlights. She thought she saw a muzzle flash, but since the gun was silenced and nothing hit their vehicle that time, she couldn't be sure. "Kris, I'm sorry—"

"You're sorry?"

"I should have pushed you out of the car."

"I'm soooo happy." Another shot plowed into the hood of the car, and the engine's grinding became an ominous rumble.

Up ahead Evi saw a giant orange detour sign. Kris ignored it.

They passed another sign, unlit, which read, "New West Side Expressway, Southbound." Under it was another sign, blackened with old grime, "CLOSED." They hit an entrance ramp and slammed through a rusty chain-link fence.

The road immediately began to shake the car's suspension apart. The rattling under the car's hood took on an urgent tone.

They passed a third sign, "NY Urban Infrastructure Renewal Project. New West Side Expressway opens May 2048. Your tax dollars at work." The old sign sprouted a bullet hole as she read it.

The Jaguar bumped through a gigantic chuckhole as they passed a last sign, "Expressway condemned. No Trespassing. Enter at own risk."

Now we're going to die, she thought.

Abdel gave her a mental slap for getting fatalistic in combat. *Think that way and you* will *die.*

She tried to ignore it when Kris pulled a shaky U-turn to avoid a hole that crossed all four lanes and fell straight through to the ground, twenty meters or so. Instead, she tried to get another bead on the aircar. Fortunately, on the abandoned expressway there were no active streetlights and Evi could pick out a flying shadow banking low over the Hudson to follow them. There was a point, at the end of Kris' turn, when the aircar seemed to hover for a split-second, almost stationary.

Evi aimed at the brightest infrared source and fired.

Kris screamed, "Shit," at the sound of the gunshot and the Jaguar swerved and sideswiped a guardrail, knocking a chunk into the darkness. But Evi thought she saw the flying shadow sprout a spark near its mid-section. She'd hit it . . .

Unfortunately, the aircar showed no signs of slowing down or stopping.

Smoke began to emerge from the Jaguar's hood, carrying the taint of ozone and burning insulation. Red lights began to blink on the dash. The inductor was overheating, the superconductor was losing charge, and the rattle was turning into a scraping whine.

Kris was pumping the gas, and they were still losing speed.

Evi looked up ahead, and they were aiming right for a thirty-meter gap in the expressway.

The sniper in the aircar fired again, and this time Evi heard the shot. It wasn't the gun she heard. It was the right front tire of the Jaguar blowing out and shredding.

"Hang on!" Kris yelled over the screech of the brakes.

Evi could tell when they hit the hole in the road, because the screech of the brakes stopped and the bottom fell out of her stomach.

The Jaguar spent a full second in free-fall, its nose arcing downward. It seemed to Evi that the second washed the night clear of sound. The Jaguar tumbled and she saw, briefly, the crumbling concrete support pillars rush by the front of the car. Then she was looking straight at a pile of rubble that sloped up under the condemned expressway.

There was a bone-jarring crunch, and then all she could see was an airbag. She'd been turning to face forward under the seatbelt. The shoulder belt dug into her left shoulder, and she felt a burning wrench. The car had stopped moving, and for a moment it felt as if the car were going to stay here, vertical, nose-end into the ground. Then, as the airbag began to deflate, she felt the car tip backward.

The Jaguar slammed its wheels into the rubble. She heard the inductor explode under the car, releasing the smell of melting ceramics and burning insulation. She wrestled the airbag out of her face as the Jaguar slid down the grade.

The hole was receding above them as the car slid backwards and stopped.

"Kris?"

Evi looked to her left when no answer came. Kris was leaning back in the driver's seat, eyes wide open. A trickle of blood was running from her mouth, and her head was leaning much too far to the right.

"Shit, no," Evi whispered.

There was no airbag draped over Kris' lap. The cover that housed it had popped off the steering wheel, and perfectly centered on the cover was a bullet hole. The bag had never inflated.

"*No!* She's a damn civilian."

She popped her seatbelt and felt for a pulse in Kris' neck. "Please, I don't want to be responsible for this. Everything else, but not this, too."

As the plastic fenders on the rear of the Jaguar started burning from the heat of the melted inductor, she placed her right fist between Kris' breasts and began pumping. She ignored the shivers of agony that it drove into her shoulder. Five pumps, then she pinched Kris' nose shut and breathed into her mouth. It was like blowing into a hot water bottle, tasted of blood.

No pulse.

Five more, breathe.

No pulse, no reaction.

Five more, breathe.

Nothing.

"Don't die!"

Five more, breathe.

She heard an engine above her.

"Damn it! Not now!" She was shouting now, it felt like someone was driving a hot poker into her guts. Damn them, whoever they were. Didn't they care who got in the way? She bent over and pulled the Mishkov out of the footwell, where she had dropped it.

Evi could see the aircar clearly now. It was silhouetted through the hole, against the night sky. She clutched her injured arm to her chest and braced the Mishkov against the dashboard and aimed at one of the forward fans.

"*BASTARDS!*" Evi fired.

There was a grinding whine from above her. A shower of sparks erupted from the front of the aircar as a blade from one of the forward fans sheared through its housing. The aircar's nose dipped and its tail began rising. The car became terminally unbalanced. It fell out of the sky, the fans giving it a lateral acceleration toward the river. The nose of the aircar skipped along the side of the slope of rubble and caught on a chunk of concrete. The car flipped on its back, fans still going, and started rolling. It rolled past the Jaguar and plowed into a concrete retaining wall.

Evi lowered the Mishkov and started shaking, watching the air-car.

The aircar's power plant exploded in a flower of sparks, orange flame, and toxic smoke.

The smell of burning plastic finally got bad enough to make her turn around. The Jaguar's trunk was burning now. She unhooked Kris' seatbelt and, gingerly, dragged her away from the car. Once Kris was clear of the wreck, she tried CPR again, not caring if a survivor from the aircar decided to shoot her, or about the agony in her shoulder, or if Kris' blood could be tainted . . .

And she knew it was hopeless five minutes before she stopped.

For a while, she just looked at Kris. Kris had been blonde, attractive, nineteen.

"Damn it, what else could I do?" She asked no one in particular. *You can't get soft-hearted in your line of work.*

"Maybe I'm in the wrong line of work, Abdel," Evi whispered. *You were drafted, too.*

There was a distant sound of popping, and at first she thought it was gunfire. Then car horns began sounding, along with foghorns from the river, and she realized that the popping was the sound of fireworks.

She reached down and closed Kris' eyes.

"Happy New Year."

Chapter 9

It hurt to holster her gun, so Evi put it into her pack as she gathered all her spilled equipment. Then she hung the backpack over her right shoulder. She limped up to the remains of the aircar, but within ten meters she could tell that examination was hopeless. The power plant had only smoldered briefly after the explosion, but the cab was crushed against the concrete retaining wall. The only way she'd get to examine her assailants would be to move the whole wreck.

She had been here too long. The aircar would have had to have been in radio contact with someone. Someone who would be on their way now. Even if, for some reason, there wasn't any backup for the aircar, there would eventually be cops, ambulances and firemen to take care of the crash.

She stepped on something and heard cracking plastic.

She looked down and saw her sunglasses. They must have flown off during the Jaguar's descent. She picked them up with her good arm. Most of the lenses stayed on the ground.

There just went most of her protective coloration.

She spared Kris a last look and then limped through a gap in the eastern retaining wall, opposite the aircar. She limped away from the graffiti-emblazoned wall, left arm clutched to her stomach, realizing just how little time she had left. She was hearing sirens, and with the sirens would come more unmarked aircars.

She stumbled through an intersection and saw she had crashed into Greenwich Village.

She pushed through an obliviously drunk crowd of mixed moreaus and humans and nearly passed out when one of them brushed her shoulder. She fell into a doorway after that, breathing heavily and sweating.

Her shoulder had dislocated, and she had to do something to fix it.

The medkit in her bag had some painkiller, but the airhypo had broken in the crash. She tossed the hypo to the ground in disgust. "Just gets worse and worse . . ."

She saw a police aircar fly over her, flashers going. She fell back further into the darkness the doorway provided. She backed until she was stopped by the door itself, a metal security job with bullet-proof glass. She tried the latch with her right hand. It was locked.

A very bad idea crossed her mind. She didn't want to do this herself, but she had to do something about her shoulder.

The handle on the door seemed to be high enough off the ground.

The hall beyond the bullet-proof glass was dimly lit. She didn't see anyone in the building. She hoped it would stay that way. It would be very bad for someone to try the door while she did what she was considering.

She put her back flat to the door and unbent her left arm. It felt as though someone had spiked her shoulder with ground glass. She took deep breaths as she locked her elbow. She had to breathe through her nose because her jaw was clenched shut.

With her arm straight at her side, she unlatched the strap from her pack and wrapped it around the door's latch and her left hand.

She wiped the sweat from her forehead and whispered to another passing police car, "So much for the preliminaries . . ."

She took a deep breath, gritted her teeth, and started bending her knees.

The pain was a white-hot shuddering rush that originated somewhere in her left shoulder socket, raced down her back, and pulsed through her head to spike between her eyes. As she continued to lower her torso and rotate her arm up and back, the fire in her shoulder planted a hot coal in her guts that shriveled her stomach into a small vibrating ember. Somehow she managed to keep her elbow locked as the pain whited out her vision with dancing sparks . . .

There was a grinding pop in her left shoulder and Evi threw up.

She stayed there, on her knees in the snow, for a few seconds as the world returned to normal. Her left shoulder still hurt like hell, but it was an endurable hurt. She slowly untangled her left hand from the door latch and staggered to her feet.

She stood there a moment, slowly bending her left elbow, rocking the arm fractionally back and forth and wincing. Her shoulder seemed to have regained some semblance of mobility. Her engineered metabolism was supposed to take damage like that well.

She didn't want to see it take something badly.

At least it wasn't broken.

No more police cars screamed by. It'd be safe on the street for a moment or two. But she needed to get inside, preferably within the next five minutes.

A pair of people passed close by her door: a black human and a drunk fox. The man had his arm around the fox and was doing his best to keep his moreau friend from weaving. Even in the beginning of a snowstorm, the fox was wearing as little clothing as he could get away with legally. The human was wearing a shredded denim jacket that was covered by hand-lettered slogans: "Fuck the PTB," "Blow the foundations," "Support your local police—from a rope."

She wouldn't be surprised if the guy had the seminal "Off the Pink" on the jacket somewhere, even if he was human.

What caught Evi's attention was the shades the human wore.

Why not? He certainly wasn't Agency material.

Evi stepped out of the doorway, in front of the pair. The two stopped short. Other groups of humans and moreaus began passing around them. She made sure the streetlight was behind her, so her eyes were in shadow.

From the expression on the human, she must have looked like hell.

"How much for the sunglasses?"

"What?" said the human.

The fox reached up and grabbed the glasses, "She wants your shades—" The fox turned and addressed Evi in a slurred brogue, "Fifty he wants, lass, for this prim—premi—quality eyewear."

"Damn it, Ross. Give those back." The human reached for the shades, but the fox had longer arms.

The fox shook his head. "Quiet, Ross is negotiating."

During the exchange, Evi had the opportunity to liberate three twenties from the roll in her pocket. "I'll give you sixty."

The pair turned to face her. The fox lowered his arm and made as if to chew the end of the glasses in thought. "Now, Ross will have to think about—"

The human grabbed the sunglasses and yanked them away from the fox. "They're my glasses, you Irish furball." He looked at Evi, still disbelieving. "You serious?"

She flashed the three twenties.

The guy tossed her the sunglasses and the fox took the money. Then they rushed around her as if they were afraid she'd change her mind. As they receded she could hear the guy say, "Give me the money, they're my glasses."

"Ross should get some. He did all the haggling."

She put on the sunglasses. These were much darker than her own, not only did they cut out the UV and a lot of the human-visible spectrum, but they chopped out the IR as well. She'd have to make do.

As much as the contacts irritated her, she wished she had them right now.

Another mix of drunk and half-drunk moreaus and humans passed by. They came from a bar two doors down. She guarded her shoulder as the patrons passed. The humans were four males, heavy on the jewelry, leather jackets with more anti-authoritarian slogans. Evi read a button on one that said, "The only thing of value to pass through a politician's mind is a bullet." The moreaus consisted of two female rabbits, a male rat, and another male fox. Like the previous fox, these wore as little as possible. The moreau females even went topless. But then, moreaus didn't have prominent breasts.

From the look of it, she could get by as a patron without too many weird looks. From her reflection in the glass, she didn't look much worse than the positively trashed fox, whom the rat was trying hard to keep vertical.

She pushed through the door with her right shoulder and found herself in the middle of the highest concentration of moreaus in any one place that she'd ever seen on Manhattan. The place was dimly lit and caught in the middle of a New Year's celebration. There was no shortage of the traditional noisemakers and funny hats. In one booth, a collection of humans and morey rabbits, all female, were being led by a white female tiger in a rendition of "Auld Lang Syne."

The mirror behind the bar was also a holo screen that was currently displaying the typical scene of Times Square. She could barely hear the broadcast over the noise from the bar. She led with her right shoulder as she pushed through the crowd of leather and fur. No one seemed to pay any attention to her.

Good, Evi very much wanted to disappear right now.

She decided she needed a drink to blend in with the crowd around her. With that in mind, she slipped through to the bar. Wincing every time a patron brushed her wounded shoulder.

She squeezed into a small gap between two occupied barstools. To her left was a rat sitting in front of a half-dozen glasses. He was wearing the conical paper hat on the end of his triangular muzzle. Someone was finding it funny. To her right sat a female lepus, drinking something red with an umbrella in it.

The bartender, another female white tiger, walked up to Evi. "You're in time for the last of the champagne—"

Champagne was the last thing Evi wanted. "Something strong, please."

"There's strong and there's strong. I mean we have Ever-clear—"

"I'll take it."

The tiger cocked a blue eye at her. "Anything to go with that?"

"No."

The tiger shrugged. As she turned to fix the drink, Evi noticed a shaved patch under her right ear. On the skin underneath was a white floral tattoo, a very intricate, and somewhat erotic, design.

Evi, not believing in coincidence, turned toward the booth of female revelers. The white tiger leading the singing had a similar patch under her ear.

"I know what you're thinking," the bartender addressed her as she put down the drink.

Evi fumbled in the pocket of her jacket to peel a twenty off the roll of cash she had. "What am I thinking?"

"Is she a friend or a relative?"

The thought had crossed her mind.

The bartender leaned forward and said in a husky voice that reminded Evi of Nohar, "She's a friend. *My* friend."

Right. She finally managed to liberate a twenty and placed it on the bar. "Keep the change." She picked up her drink and moved to the rear, back in the shadows. Near the door to the bathrooms.

There was nowhere to sit down, so she stood in a corner where she had a good view of the door, through the crowd. That's when she allowed herself to start shaking.

She felt like she was on the verge of a physical and emotional collapse.

She looked down at the drink in her hand; the surface was rippling. Abdel told her that it wasn't a good idea. She should be concentrating on getting out—

Fuck it. Thinking what Abdel would tell her in this situation didn't do a damn bit of good.

She was a professional, she told herself, a soldier, and at one time she had been a trained assassin. People had always died around her, and for a good part of her professional career her life had been in danger. She had been in worse before, and she had come through without having a nervous breakdown.

She had managed to escape from Palestine when any connection to the former Israeli government was an instant death sentence. She had nearly starved before she had gotten to Cyprus.

She had gotten through that.

But what she had just gone through, having a totally innocent person die because of her . . .

Evi wanted to chuck it all right there.

She put away half her drink in one fluid motion. It burned going down, but the pain in her shoulder began to fade.

A female voice addressed her. "You look like you need to sit."

Evi had been keeping her gaze locked on the door to the bar. She hadn't expected anyone to talk to her. She turned and looked at the owner of the voice.

Sitting next to Evi, in a small two-person booth, was a pale redhead. Her hair spilled halfway down her back. She was wearing a metallic-red blouse and tight jeans that showed off a pair of well-sculpted legs. As if her figure weren't arresting enough, she'd chosen to wear black lipstick that altered the appearance of her skin from pale to cadaverous. Her nails matched; they were painted gloss-black and sharpened to points.

The woman was wearing sunglasses, too. Black one-piece things that hid not only her eyes but half her face as well. For a brief surreal moment, Evi thought she was being addressed by a fellow frank. That thought—Evi wasn't sure if it had been hope or fear—was put to rest when she turned her full attention to the booth. The smell of the woman was definitely human.

She considered ignoring her, or moving away. But she didn't want to be conspicuously solitary. Also, she did need to sit down, and it looked like the seat this woman was offering was the only vacancy in the place. Evi moved into the booth opposite the redhead.

Evi looked around at the standing-room-only crowd. "How come you rate a table to yourself?"

The redhead chuckled. "Is that what this is? Thought it was a comm booth they never finished."

She sipped from her own glass. "Leo, the guy whose seat you're taking, just had an urgent call of nature."

"What if he wants it back?"

The redhead shrugged. "I've had enough of his moreau separatist bullshit."

"Well, thanks for the seat."

"You look like you need a friend."

Evi gave her host a sad, silent chuckle. "Suppose I do."

"You want to talk about it?"

"Not a good idea."

"Sometimes it helps."

Evi felt an urge to tell her to go to hell. Instead, she realized that there was genuine concern in the redhead's voice.

"I've lost my job, my home, and I've been through some thoroughly rotten experiences today." What was she doing, talking to a stranger like this? It went against all her training . . .

To hell with her training.

"Christ—" Her host said as Evi's appearance seemed to sink in. The redhead removed her own sunglasses, revealing a pair of green, very human eyes. "Are you hurt?"

She realized that the redhead had just noticed her shoulder and probably some marks on her face. "Someone tried to kill me."

Shut up, Evi. She looked in her glass and realized her drink was gone. She had to keep a tighter rein on what she was saying. Why the hell was she spouting off like this? She didn't want to believe that it was because this woman seemed to be the only person who seemed to give a shit.

Damn, was she about to get another innocent person involved?

"Have you called the cops?" The redhead started to get up.

"No cops."

"You can't let someone get away with—" The redhead was standing up now and sounded angry. Evi grabbed her wrist with her good arm and pulled her back down. The redhead hit the seat with a thud and a surprised squeak.

Evi looked into those green eyes, which were growing wider, and addressed her in a harsh whisper. "*No cops. I said tried.* They didn't get away with anything. They didn't get *away*, period."

She realized that she was squeezing much too hard. She let go and saw her hand was shaking. "Sorry—"

"Name's Diana." The redhead began rubbing the wrist Evi had grabbed. "Don't apologize. Your business, but I get sick whenever someone gets assaulted, mugged, *raped*, and doesn't even try to put the bastards away. You should call—"

"Diana, the police would probably shoot me."

Diana just stared at her. She seemed to be taking her in for the first time.

The bartender, who had noticed the commotion, pushed through to the booth. "Is there a problem?"

The tiger was addressing Diana.

Diana shook her head without taking her eyes off of Evi.

"Are you sure?" The tiger gave Evi a nasty look.

"Yeah, Kijna." Diana's voice sounded far away. Then she cleared her throat, looked at the tiger, and her voice regained its confidence. "We're fine, thanks."

The bartender left, but kept looking back, through the crowd, at Evi.

Diana sounded apologetic. "Too nosy. Sorry."

"Maybe I should go."

"Do you want to?"

"I should."

Diana shrugged. "If you don't mind, stay."

Evi remembered Kijna and her "friend." "Are you trying to pick me up?"

"Would you mind terribly if I was?"

"I just ducked in here to get off the street."

Diana responded with a funny little half-smile. "Doesn't answer my question."

Evi felt the sad little chuckle return. "You never answered mine."

"Touché."

Diana found a touch-sensitive spot on the table, and a keypad and screen lit up under the fake wood surface. "You want anything more to drink— What *is* your name?"

"Ev—Eve." Damn. Evi cursed herself, she was slipping over her alias.

"Eve?"

"Eve." Evi nodded. Diana was still waiting to hear if she had an order.

She shouldn't, but her shoulder had stopped hurting, the shakes had gone away, and she no longer felt on the verge of a panic attack.

"Order me whatever you're having."

Diana typed in an order. "You have a nice accent."

"Thanks." Evi listened to herself and realized that her accent was returning with the liquor.

"I've heard it before, but I can't remember—"

"It's Israeli."

"Palestinian?"

"No." Evi felt an irrational wave of irritation. *"Israeli."* The drinks came, and she used the opportunity to change the subject. "What on earth prompted you to invite over someone in my condition?"

Diana took one mug of thick beer and sipped. "My friends say I have an attraction to strays."

Evi laughed at that, a real laugh this time, though inaudible. "I'm about as stray as you get."

All the shit that had happened today seemed far away for once. Though she knew Abdel would throw a fit at her right now for drinking and leading on the local lesbians.

Diana must have noticed a change in her expression. "What's the matter?"

"A little voice telling me to have second thoughts."

"About what?"

"The way I'm reacting to the disaster my life has become." Evi drained her mug. She didn't bother tasting the beer. "Also says I'm leading you on." This time Evi typed on the control panel. She ordered something at random.

Diana grinned. "How so?"

"I drive on the right side of the road and have no inclination to jump the median." Though the odd thought did have some appeal. Especially when she thought of how most men reacted to her genetic heritage.

Diana took a second to catch Evi's slightly inebriated metaphor. "You should try it some time. Dodging oncoming traffic can be quite a rush."

They both broke into laughter at that one. Evi couldn't help thinking of the last half-hour of her life, and she was laughing and crying at the same time.

Maybe she'd brought all this on herself, deserved it even. For a long time she'd been nothing more than a glorified assassin. She had a dirty job.

Evi was thankful that her sobs were as silent as her laughter.

Someone came and placed a shot glass in front of Evi.

After a few minutes of silence, Diana said, "To answer your old question. Initially, I called you over because you looked like you needed help, not to pick you up."

Evi watched Diana drink a liberal portion of her beer and asked, "Initially?"

"Well . . ." Diana waited until Evi had started drinking. "You *would* make a very attractive dyke."

The comment almost had the, apparently intentional, effect of putting the drink through Evi's nose. The back of her sinuses burned and her eyes watered. Apparently she'd ordered a shot of tequila. She coughed a few times and managed to choke out, "I'm flattered." It felt strange hearing that from another woman.

"If you don't have a place tonight, you can crash at mine."

Evi stopped in the middle of wiping her nose with a napkin.

"It's not *that*. But I do have this thing for taking in strays."

"I appreciate the offer," Evi thought of Kris, "but you shouldn't get involved."

Diana looked down and shook her head. "I shouldn't have. I know what it looks—"

Evi put her hand on Diana's arm. "Shhh."

"But—"

"Shhh, Diana. Don't apologize. You don't understand." Evi leaned forward. "People will be looking for . . ."

Evi trailed off because there was a commotion behind her in the bar. She turned, briefly, to see what it was.

Two NYPD uniforms had just walked into the bar.

Evi turned away to hide her face. "Shit," she whispered.

"Eve, maybe I do understand—"

"Shhh," Evi silenced her.

Evi listened to Kijna confront the cops. Kijna seemed very protective of her clientele. The cops said they were looking for a hit-and-run suspect.

"Diana, is there a window in the bathroom?"

"Yes, but, Eve—" Diana started to move, but Evi kept an iron grip on her arm.

"No, don't. They haven't noticed me yet and I'm only going to have a moment while Kijna distracts them. What's behind the bar?"

"Trash, and alley, fire escapes, but—"

"Thanks. I appreciate the offer, but, Diana, you never saw me." Diana nodded.

Evi tried to hug the shadows as she slipped into the alcove that led to the bathrooms. The two cops didn't appear to see her before she had backed into the john.

The woman's room this time.

There was a small rectangular window snug up against an upper corner of the far wall. It looked as if Evi could wiggle through it, but just the idea of doing it reawakened sympathetic pain in her shoulder. The window was above one of the two stalls. Fortunately, it wasn't above the one that was in use at the moment.

Evi locked herself into the unoccupied stall and stood on the seat of the toilet so she could reach the window. It was double-paned fogged polymer, clean but painted shut. She took a few seconds to figure out exactly how the thing was originally intended to open.

The curly-haired brunette sitting in the neighboring stall was resting her head against the tile wall and staring up at Evi. For no particular reason, Evi smiled and nodded at the brunette. The brunette responded with a confused wave.

Too much to drink. Her judgment was screwed.

She found the partially hidden handle sunk flush in the top frame of the window. She slipped her right hand into it and pulled.

The paint cracked and the window tilted outward in a shower of flakes. She kept pulling a little too long. The strut that held the open window in place was old and had been unused for a long time. It folded out, then, after a protesting creak, sheared the bolt that held it to the wall. The whole window tumbled out. It was all she could do to keep a grip on the unwieldy thing and ease it to the ground without a massive crash.

There wasn't going to be a question over where she went.

A cold wind blew a shower of flakes into the bathroom. Evi chinned herself up to the sill with her good arm. The brunette gave her another weak wave goodbye.

Evi tumbled through the opening and her feet landed too far apart on a trash bin below the window. She stumbled once, slipped, and fell on her ass in the snow-covered alley.

Definitely too much to drink.

Abdel, where are you?

"Face it. He's just an excuse to talk to yourself."

She stood up and looked around. She was in a long straight alley, with a T-intersection at each end. She needed to avoid the street that the bar was on; the NYPD and less savory characters would be watching it. She also needed to get away from here as soon as possible. Once the two cops reached the bathroom, they'd see the window and put two and two together.

She made for the left end of the alley, running. She nearly slipped and fell on her ass again, twice, but the cold air and the adrenaline seemed to be washing out the alcohol.

As soon as she reached the intersection, she was spotlighted by a pair of headlights turning into the alley from the street. As if to drive the point home, as soon as the vehicle completed its turn, the engine revved and started rocketing toward her.

Evi ran back into the alley behind the bar. What the hell was she going to do? She couldn't outrun the damn thing. With her limping gait right now, there were few *humans* she could outrun.

She began to fumble in her pack for the Mishkov, spilling the medkit.

The car was getting louder as Evi passed a trash bin and took cover behind it. Her breath was steaming and beginning to fog her sunglasses.

Evi braced the Mishkov on top of the trash bin one-handed and fired as soon as the car screeched to a stop at the intersection. The Mishkov clicked on an empty chamber. She had forgotten to reload it.

From the cherry-red Ford Estival, Evi heard a familiar voice yell, "Hey, Eve!"

Evi looked at her gun, and where it was aimed, and shuddered.

Chapter 10

The press of traffic made the Estival's progress agonizingly slow. But nobody stopped the car.

Evi's view sucked. She was wedged in the footwell of the rear seat. Anyone observing Diana's Ford would only see the driver, but Evi couldn't see anything but an oblique cross section of Manhattan's skyline.

"Do you have any idea what kind of danger you're in?"

"Some." Diana eased the car out of what seemed to be the mainstream of New York's gridlock. "I counted at least five unmarked cop cars up and down Bank Street."

"Why the hell did you—" Evi kept thinking of Kris. "I could get you killed."

"What's the diff between a cop shooting you in the middle of a pro-morey demonstration and getting blown away helping a quote-terrorist-unquote."

Evi shook her head. She had trouble following Diana and couldn't decide whether or not it was the alcohol. "What are you talking about?"

"I know who you are. Anyone who gives the PTB the shits like you did is okay in my book."

"Powers that be," Evi whispered to herself. "You know who I am?" Evi asked, "Then who am I?" She wasn't too sure any more.

Diana chuckled. "You're a radical pro-morey terrorist. Responsible for an attack on an Upper East Side condominium that caused at least three million in damages, not to mention a few dead cops."

Evi felt the bottom fall out of her stomach.

"All bullshit, of course, but I'm intrigued by a girl who is in the middle of that much trouble."

"That's sick."

"I never said I wasn't neurotic."

"Is that what's going out over the news?"

Evi studied the side of Diana's face. When Diana nodded, her right earlobe became briefly visible. She wore as an earring a small silver anarchy symbol. Before today Evi would have found such disenchantment with the government hard to relate to.

"You've made the top story on every news channel. Largest manhunt," Diana repressed a laugh and it came out a snort, "in the city's history. Though so far you're an 'unidentified female.' "

This was getting too bizarre, even for the events of the last twenty-four hours. "So naturally, when you realized who I was and that the cops were after me, you decided to pick me up."

"Just funny that way, I guess."

"You're nuts." Evi wondered if she should be looking to jump from the car.

"What, are you complaining because I'm helping you?"

"Yes, too many people have been hurt—"

"Are you going to tell me that the moreau underground is suddenly working with Afghanis?"

"What?" The Afghani canines were mercenaries who cared nothing for politics. They usually worked for humans; the pay was better. "No, but—"

"You going to tell me that the morey underground had suddenly changed tactics and is going after civilian targets?"

"No," Evi said. The main thrust of moreau violence, as little as there was in the past few years, had been "military" targets— communications, power, police. She fell silent.

The Hassan case in Cleveland echoed through Evi's mind. Then, as now, there had been the attempt to pass off the Afghani mercenary activity as part of the radical moreau movement. Evi could see the same people using the same phrases now as they did six years ago. A group of people high up in the Agency didn't want anyone following the canines to their source.

Diane was continuing to talk. "So, are you going to tell me that you really are a terrorist and evil incarnate?"

Evi stared at Diana and tried to make sense out of her benefactor. "I have the feeling if I told you I was the Antichrist, you'd just get excited."

Diana shrugged. "Going to bite the hand that feeds you?"

"That isn't the point."

"What is?"

"The point is that someone could kill you if you hang around me." Evi surprised herself with the force of her protest. Did she really want to have the only person to help her abandon her?

Evi knew that she desperately did not want Diana to end up like Kris.

Diana was silent for a moment before she spoke. "If my name's on a cop's bullet, it was put there back in the forties."

The Estival drove on in silence. It hit a bump, turned down a side street, and stopped. "Speaking of names, is Eve your real name?"

"Huh?"

"You don't look like an Eve."

Evi sat up and winced, she was feeling her shoulder again. Once she was upright, she could see where the Estival had parked. Diana had maneuvered the car into a bare alley between the back end of a line of refurbished brownstones and the blank cinderblock of an old warehouse.

"It's Evi. Evi Isham." Evi picked up her pack and opened the door. "Diana, thanks for the help. But I can't risk you—"

Diana reached over the seat and put a hand on Evi's good shoulder. "Wait."

Evi stopped and looked at Diana. The alcohol was mostly gone now, a benefit of an engineered metabolism. With the haze gone, she could feel some of her judgment returning. She tried to cultivate some of her normal suspicion as she listened.

Diana squeezed Evi's shoulder. "If the cops were going to land on us, they would've already. You aren't going to drag me down unless you want to."

Evi ducked out from under Diana's hand and stepped out of the car.

Diana continued to talk. "I used to have close ties to the nonhuman movement, a long time ago. I know you aren't a part of it. A human as high profile as the news is making you out to be, I'd know—everyone in the Village'd know."

Evi turned around to face Diana. Diana scooted across the front seat and stepped out of the passenger door in front of Evi. "The people in that bar have no love for the cops. Your shadows've been sent off in a dozen different directions. You're safe. I'm safe."

The world was eerily silent, wrapped in the blowing snow. The way the sounds were sucked into the night reminded Evi of the Jordanian desert. Evi felt alone, and she felt that Diana was taking advantage of that feeling. It was a twisted feeling. If anyone was being exploited, it was Diana.

Diana was trying to force Evi to use her.

"Damn it." This was pissing Evi off. She turned on Diana and yelled, *"Why do you want to help me?"*

"You want to know why?"

Evi tossed her pack to the ground and spread her arms wide, ignoring pain in her shoulder. "Yes, I want to know *why*. Why someone would choose to get involved in this shit. This *isn't* your fight!"

Diana shrugged. "In the bar, I saw how you looked. I've seen it before—" Diana looked up into her eyes so deeply that Evi raised her hand to make sure the sunglasses were still there. "Ten years ago. Smuggling nonhuman refugees into the country. Saw a lot of people with that look."

Evi lowered her arms. "What look?"

"Despair, loss, lots of fatigue. The look of someone who's lost everything. Someone who's been running too long—Close?"

Evi could feel her shoulders slumping. She still tried to cultivate her instinct for suspicion, tried to see Diana as a potential foe. But even Abdel was remaining mute on the subject.

"Damn."

"Close to calling it quits, weren't you?"

"You've made your point," Evi whispered. She wasn't going to get out of this without trusting someone. She sighed. "God. I need a rest."

Diana closed the car door, picked up Evi's pack and shouldered it. "The offer's still open, to crash at my place." As an afterthought, she added, "I have a couch."

"Where?"

Diana hooked her thumb at the warehouse and started toward it. Evi followed.

The entrance to Diane's apartment was a decrepit freight elevator that could fit the Estival inside it, but no way could have lifted it. They shuddered up four floors, past converted studio apartments, to the sound of an overtaxed electric motor. Evi smelled grease, rust, and static electricity, and as the haze of alcohol continued to lift, she could smell Diana. Jasmine touched by a hint of sweat and beer. And . . .

The elevator chunked into place and the smell of incense wafted in, overpowering any subtler odor.

Diana opened the gate on an impressive studio apartment. A

small kitchenette to their right, a wall of glass block to their left, and, in between, a low entrance hall that opened out into a vast open space. They faced a vast sweep of windows that looked out over the Hudson River.

When they walked out into the room, grudging lights came on, erasing the skyline of Jersey City out the window.

"My place."

"I'm impressed. I didn't think there were places like this left on Manhattan."

Evi walked toward the couch that formed the centerpiece of the room. It faced an old comm that squatted in front of the windows. She rotated, slowly, until she was facing Diana and the elevator. Above the elevator was a loft draped with curtains.

She stood there a moment taking it in.

After an uncomfortable moment Diana shook her head. "I'm being a poor host. Do you want something to eat? Drink?"

Evi ran her hand through her hair and winced when it caught in the tangled mess. "Thanks, but I'd like to clean up first."

Diana stopped in mid-step toward the kitchen and turned toward the glass block. "Yes, of course. The bathroom's over here."

The bathroom was cavernous. The shower could have easily accommodated a half-dozen people. "Leave your clothes by the door, and I'll try to find something clean for you to wear." Diana put Evi's pack down between the john and the bidet. Diana fidgeted a moment or two before she left.

The bathroom was nearly eight meters on a side by five high. Half the walls were tile, half glass block. One wall was faced with mirrored tile; the upper half of the opposite wall was eaten by ranks of windows. The view out the windows consisted of glowing swirls of white flakes against a totally black background.

Evi shucked the jacket.

"I shouldn't be here," she whispered. The sound bounced off a dozen walls and the corrugated steel ceiling before it laid itself to rest.

She emptied the pockets of the jumpsuit, including the clips for the Mishkov, back into her pack. Then, slowly, she unzipped the jumpsuit.

She kicked the boots and the jumpsuit back by the door and walked to the shower, not looking in the mirror.

She'd forgotten how good a long, hot shower could feel. She stood under the stream of water for nearly five minutes before she realized she still had on her sunglasses.

She put them in the soapdish.

Once out of the shower, she looked in the mirror. She expected to look worse than she did, after what she had been through. Again, the benefits of an engineered metabolism.

The bruise on her calf had faded to a dull yellow, while her tear-gas irritated eye was more-or-less normal looking. The shoulder, however, was an ugly sight. The shrapnel wound had closed up, but from the wrenching injury in the car crash, the entire area had turned a dark purple.

Evi tried each axis of movement in her left shoulder and each sent a shuddering wave of pain.

"This could be a problem," she told her reflection. Even with her metabolism, it could be three days before she could even think about using that arm.

She opened her pack. Most of her medkit had fallen out, but the bottom of the bag was littered with items that had spilled out of the kit. The mess was mostly drug cartridges that were useless without the hypo, but she thanked the gods that one of the items that stayed was the heat-activated polymer support bandage.

She strapped up her injured shoulder. Her body heat was supposed to fuse the white bandage into a single tight piece. Her metabolism wouldn't cooperate on that score, but Diana's dryer did just as well.

With the bandage in place she could use the arm, a little. Very little.

Diana had done as promised and left her some clean clothes in place of the jumpsuit and leather. She had been thoughtful enough to leave a number of things to choose from. After trying on a few items, it was clear that Diana had no clothes to fit Evi's relatively compact scale.

She finally settled on a red kimono that would be a racy number on Diana's six-foot tall, robust frame. On Evi it was a modest robe that came down past her knees and covered her rather completely.

Sunglasses . . .

She looked at her reflection in the mirror and at her eyes. The pupils were narrowed in the light. She wished she had contacts.

She put the sunglasses back on. She would rather explain away that than try to deal with the reaction her eyes might cause. She kept remembering Chuck Dwyer's face. "You're a frank." Like she was a piece of diseased meat.

"So, I'm a frank," she told her reflection. "No need to bother her with that fact."

She picked up her pack and the extra clothes and left the bathroom.

"If she asks, it's because I have sensitive eyes."

Diana never asked.

In the kitchenette, she served her tea and some Chinese dish with pork and tofu. Evi ate ravenously while Diana seemed to abort her own attempts at conversation.

She was fully prepared to answer most of the questions Diana should have been asking. But she wasn't asked. After a few false starts, they ate in relative silence. Evi could smell a host of confused jasmine-flavored emotions floating off of Diana. She didn't press.

Eventually, Diana led her to the couch in the middle of the studio's main room. Diana left her there in the dark. Evi took off her sunglasses, wrapped herself in a blanket, and fell asleep instantly.

Chapter 11

Something brushed her hair and Evi snapped awake. Her hand had struck out before she was fully aware of what was going on.

According to her time sense, she'd been sleeping for four hours.

Diana was perched on the end of a coffee table, backlit by a streetlamp shining through the growing snowstorm. Evi had reflexively grabbed her wrist. Diana's fingers were barely touching her hair.

"Sorry. I didn't mean to wake you." Evi could see Diana's flush as a slight infrared pattern in her face. The combination of blush, red hair, and reflected light from Evi's borrowed kimono gave Diana a rose glow, as if an internal fire illuminated her.

The black lipstick was gone.

Evi slowly released Diana's wrist. "Old reflex. I didn't hurt you, did I?"

"No," Diana said. She was looking down at her lap and had let her arm fall to her side. All she wore was an oversized satin pajama top.

Evi sat up and looked at Diana, who had perched herself on the edge of the table, long legs crossed under her. The pose showed off her calves. More rounded and shapely than Evi's legs. Something to be said for more than four percent body fat.

Evi realized that the silence was stretching out to an uncomfortable length. "Is something the matter?"

Diana looked up and shook her head, rippling her hair. "I don't know."

That was another thing Evi envied. Long hair was a liability in her line of work.

Her former line of work.

Diana was staring into her eyes.

No!

Evi's hand shot out toward the coffee table and grabbed her sunglasses.

"Evi?" There was a quavering note in Diana's voice.

Damn, damn, damn! The eyes, why did it have to be the eyes? No one was ever going to be able to relate to her normally because of the damn eyes. Evi put on the sunglasses in a vain hope that Diana hadn't seen them.

She was still putting them on when she felt Diana's hand on her own.

"Your eyes—"

Go on, say it. I'm not human. I'm a goddamn frankenstein—say it.

Diana slowly pulled her hand down, along with the sunglasses. She didn't bother resisting the pull. Diana kept staring into her eyes.

Evi wanted to scream.

"Why do you hide them?" Diana's voice was barely a whisper. "They're beautiful."

She stared for a fraction of a second, leaning forward. Then, with a gasp and a violent shake of her head, Diana turned around and fled to the window. Evi was left sitting on the couch, confused, sunglasses halfway to her face.

Did she hear right? All of a sudden she felt very warm.

Diana was standing in front of the windows, arms clutched around herself, staring out at the snow. The white top she was wearing took on a glow from the streetlight. No fires raged now. She looked like an ice sculpture.

Diana's shoulders were shaking.

Evi put down the sunglasses and walked up to the window. Diana was softly crying, leaning her forehead against the glass. Evi put a hand on her shoulder, forgetting that Diana knew she wasn't human. "What's wrong?"

"I shouldn't be doing this."

"Doing what?"

Diana gave her a look telling her she should be perfectly aware of "what."

She supposed she was. "I really don't mind."

Diana turned around and sat on the floor, back to the window. "*I* do. You said you didn't have any intention of 'crossing the median.' "

She had, hadn't she? Even so, there was no denying the way her pulse was accelerating. It could be despair, fatigue, or the fact she needed someone, anyone . . .

But explaining it didn't make it go away.

Evi shrugged, hurting her shoulder. "There's nothing wrong with trying to change my mind."

"You have no idea." Diana was shaking her head. Moisture on her cheeks threw back frozen glints from the streetlight outside. "I knew this guy once. The sleaze took pride in seducing and 'initiating' poor, naive, young college kids. He *bragged* about the kind of damage he did."

"I'm not a poor, naive, young college kid."

"One of those kids couldn't live with it. He shot himself." Diana shook her head. "I'm never going to be like that man. That evil bastard."

"You're not—"

"You can't. If someone isn't prepared. Not sure." Diana stopped talking and just started shaking her head.

Evi stroked Diana's hair with her good hand. It was fine, silky, similar to how Evi imagined that satin pajama top might feel. "I know."

They stayed like that for a while. Then Diana said in a low voice, "I don't want to hurt you."

Evi liked the feel of Diana's hair. It had been too long since she'd been close to anyone. It felt good simply to touch another person.

"Diana, what did you say about my eyes?"

"What?"

Evi slid her hand to Diana's shoulder and knelt in front of her. "Tell me about my eyes."

Diana sniffed. "I've never seen anything like them. They, they glow—"

Evi leaned forward and stroked Diana's cheek, silencing her. "I'm not going to be hurt."

Evi placed her lips over Diana's partially open mouth.

She felt the blood rush to Diana's face as well as her own. Evi's metabolism forgot it was supposed to have a low thermal profile. Diana's sharp intake of breath sucked the air out of Evi's mouth, pulling her tongue after it. Evi tasted the remnants of Diana's toothpaste and a slight cherry flavor from some lip balm.

Over everything was the rich, warm scent of jasmine.

The ice sculpture melted.

It was a warm, wet, hungry kiss, and Diana seemed to lie back in a state of shock throughout the experience.

After half a minute Evi drew back, smiling so widely her cheeks ached. Diana just stared at her with a red-eyed expression of disbelief. "I thought you weren't a lesbian."

A small part of Evi's brain was just as disbelieving. What was she doing?

"I'm not." Evi kissed her again, before Diana could object. This time she embraced Diana with her good arm and rolled. Diana wasn't fighting, so she ended up pinned under her.

Evi's combat training was useful for things other than infighting.

Once Diana's lips were unrestrained, she managed to sputter, "But—"

"Objecting?" Evi unhooked Diana's neck and got to her knees, straddling Diana's hips. Not entirely by accident, the kimono fell open.

"No." To emphasize the point, Diana sat up herself and hugged Evi, giving her own gentle kiss. Diana was uncertain, probing, as if still not quite sure she was welcome.

During the lingering embrace, Evi's skin was caressed by Diana's satin top. Every brush ignited a flash of warmth that sank down to the core of her body. Evi wasn't satisfied with the tentative contact and wrapped her good arm and both legs around Diana, pulling her toward her.

Diana's breasts pressed against her, and Evi could feel Diana's nipples harden against her own skin. The satin separating them had become a sheet of silken fire.

They came up for air, and Evi could feel Diana's hands behind her, finding the collar of the kimono. Diana nipped at Evi's earlobe and whispered, "Why?"

While Diana fumbled off the left side of the kimono, being careful of Evi's shoulder, Evi's right hand slipped under the pajama top. She was asking herself the same question. "I'll give you a list."

Diana helped Evi lift her top over her head. Diana's pale skin glowed from both the reflected streetlight and its own internal heat. Evi kissed her cheek. "I'm lonely. I need you. Badly."

Evi kissed the hollow between Diana's collarbone and the nape of her neck while gradually easing them both back to the ground. She lifted her head and traced Diana's jawline with her right hand.

"You helped me . . ."

They were lying side by side now, skin touching. Diana was beginning to breathe heavily. Evi slid down and kissed Diana's left breast, lingering, sliding her tongue around the nipple while her right hand gently brushed its twin.

Diana arched her back and Evi rolled on top of her. Evi glided down further on a slide of Diana's perspiration. She kissed Diana's navel, sliding her mouth around her abdomen. Evi could smell that Diana was becoming very wet. She looked up. "Most important . . ."

Evi slid down the rest of the way.

"You liked my eyes."

Evi lowered her head between Diana's legs and began to kiss Diana under the silky red hair she found there.

The conversation died after that.

They remained locked together for the better part of two hours. Somehow they managed to avoid breaking anything or popping Evi's shoulder out of its socket.

It was hard to place exactly when the lovemaking evolved into a simple embrace. But that's what it was when the sun began to rise. Evi rested her head on Diana's shoulder as they sat on the floor in front of the couch, wrapped in Evi's blanket. The table had been pushed aside, and Evi was looking past the comm, out the window.

Sunlight was just catching the tops of the buildings across the river. The snow had stopped, leaving the sky a crystalline blue. Somehow, the world looked worth living in again.

Evi felt Diana's hand brushing her hair. "Awake?"

"Yes."

"How do you feel?"

How did she feel? Damn confused, really. Not that she hadn't wanted to. What was strange was that she wanted to in the first place. It was unnerving to realize that she couldn't predict her own behavior.

She did have to admit that sex with Diana had been more gratifying than the sex Evi had had with any number of men. Evi didn't know if that was because she really was a lesbian or because she never gave a shit about the men she'd slept with.

Maybe it was because Diana was the first lover she'd had without the benefit of those damn contact lenses. All the others had been Chuck Dwyers waiting to happen.

"Better," Evi finally told her. And she did feel better. She had needed someone for a long time, since long before all this started.

There was a long pause before Diana went on. "Tell me something about yourself."

Evi closed her eyes. "A lot of it you wouldn't like . . ."

"Do you have a family?"

"No."

"No one?"

Evi thought back to Israel. "I had a family of sorts. About four dozen sisters, one father."

Diana stroked her hair. "I'm an only child. That many sisters sounds like quite a family."

Evi let out with her silent laugh. "We were Japanese-engineered humans, batched in a Jordanian experimental facility, and we were all captured by a Mossad commando raid. I was raised in something between a boarding school and boot camp."

"You said you had a father?"

"Colonel Chaim Abdel. He ran the place where I was raised."

"What happened to them?"

Evi shrugged. "War broke out. We lost."

"That was a long time ago. How old were you?"

"When they nuked Tel Aviv, sixteen."

Diana didn't respond for a long time. After a while she said, "I hoped it would be a long time before I heard stories like that again."

"What do you mean?"

"Oh, back in the forties I helped a lot of moreaus into the country. Especially after the riots when the borders were closed."

It was surreal, listening to that. For a long time after Evi made it into the country and was more-or-less forced into the Agency, her job had been busting people like Diana. Talk about strange bedfellows.

"When did you come to the States?" Diana asked.

"Forty-five."

"How'd you manage that? The INS is still uptight about engineered humans."

Evi thought about the round-faced State Department official at her debriefing. He had said that no franks were being let into the country. It was the first time Evi had heard that word. However, if she agreed to work for the government, perhaps he could work something out.

"I had to make a few concessions," Evi said.

"I'll bet."

Evi felt dishonest. She should be telling Diana the whole story, but Evi was suddenly afraid of losing her. How exactly could she tell this woman that she had spent the last twelve years working for the government?

She was also still very tired.

Evi sighed. "I still need to finish that good night's sleep you interrupted."

"Oh." Diana got to her feet and gathered up her top. "Good night—morning."

Diana began walking to the stairs that led to the loft and Evi cleared her throat.

Diana turned around. "What?"

Evi stood, holding the kimono in her good hand. "After all that, I sleep on the couch?"

On noon of New Year's Day, Evi woke up. She got out of bed carefully, to avoid waking Diana, and went down to the kitchen.

After she'd heated some leftover tofu, she took the ramcard from the library out of her backpack and slipped it into the reader for the comm. The comm took a second to warm up. She dug around and found the remote. It had been kicked under the couch sometime during the night.

A commercial station came on the screen, Nonhuman League Football. The game was halted for an injury and she briefly heard something about a twenty-yard penalty for illegal use of claws.

Evi found the database function on the remote and called up the information on her ramcard.

The N.Y. Public Library logo replaced some unnecessary roughness on the first down.

"Japan," she said to herself, wishing Diana had some more complex functions on her comm.

She spent a few hours going over what she already knew. Assassinations, car bombs, downed airplanes. Sometimes, however, a detail or two could catch her attention.

For instance, at least half of the assassinations the Nippon Liberation Front claimed responsibility for were in some way involved with the Office of Science and Technology. The NLF hit hardliners, but a few of their targets were distressingly liberal. Some victims had actually been reformers who wanted to grant some limited independence to occupied Japan.

The NLF also had little tolerance for rival organizations. They were particularly gruesome to anyone who purported to speak for the Japanese people.

From Evi's point of view, she was looking at an organization that, despite its rhetoric, had a vested interest in the status quo.

That didn't mean anything in itself. Any organization was vulnerable to bureaucratic inertia and power games. Even terrorists, especially terrorists, could get so caught up in dogma that they lost sight of their original goals.

However, while the NLF's strikes were doing nothing for the liberation of Japan, they were very efficient in slowing technological development throughout the entire Pacific Rim. Especially in areas where Japan had excelled. In fact, she thought that it wouldn't be far-fetched to presume that the NLF was responsible, in large part, for the Asian scientific community becoming insular and paranoid.

As effective as the aliens' pet congressmen were in passing counterproductive legislation.

That brought her mind back to a line of thinking she'd been on earlier but hadn't followed to its ultimate conclusion.

The U.S. hadn't been the only country capable of interstellar probes. Before the Pan-Asian war, both India and Japan had been far ahead in their space programs.

Before the war.

That war was one of the ugliest chapters in world history. Close to a hundred million human dead. No one knew how many nonhuman. Two decades of fighting. And all the wrong countries won.

Could that have been caused by—

"No."

She didn't want to think about it. Past was past. What she needed now was some line on the NLF that could tell her if it was the Nippon Liberation Front after her, and if so, give her some idea why.

Money.

Finances always struck near the heart of the matter. It was the money trail that finally brought down that cell in Cleveland. If she found who put money in the NLF, she might be able to sharpen her focus. She needed specifics, not broad generalities.

Specifics . . .

She manipulated the control while she heard Diana awaken in the background. Text flew by as she listened to Diana shower, dress, and fix a pot of coffee.

The coffee smell closed on her, and she felt Diana sit down by her.

"Morning."

"Three-thirty in the afternoon, really," Evi responded.

"Picky, picky. I notice you left off the sunglasses."

Evi automatically put her right hand to her face, nearly bashing the remote control into her nose. The database stopped scrolling.

"What's on the comm?"

Evi set down the remote and looked at Diana. Diana was wearing an oversized sweater that hung on her very well. "Trying to find out who those Afghani mercenaries were working for."

Diana sipped her coffee and asked, "They work for Nyogi Enterprises?"

"Huh?" Evi looked at the comm. It had stopped on a U.S. Newsfax article about a ten-grand-a-plate dinner held by the board of Nyogi Enterprises. The text with the picture insinuated that the Japanese relief effort the dinner was raising money for was really the NLF in a very thin disguise. The article itself was rather low on facts and high on innuendo.

But as far as Evi was concerned, the picture was damning. Sitting at one of those ten-thousand-dollar plates was a face that Evi would never forget.

The peeper.

Chapter 12

"Nyogi Enterprises," Evi read, "Established in 2040 by refugee Japanese industrialists and financiers. Corporate headquarters, New York City. Major factory supplier to Latin American consumer electronics companies. Major stock holdings, they say zip. Major stockholders, they say zip. Assets, not specific, but they're compared to General Motors . . ."

Vague, vague, vague. Evi wanted to hit the comm. She thought of calling what's-his-name at the library, the one with the thesis. Except she didn't need to know about Nyogi Ent or its shadowy board of directors. What she needed to know was who the peeper was.

At least Evi had convinced the comm to crop and print out a copy of the peeper's face. "Are you sure that your comm can't be configured for a graphic search?"

"You've got to be kidding. That thing?" Diana started to laugh. Then she choked it off and drew her knees up under her sweater. "Sorry, I'm not being very helpful, am I?"

"If it weren't for you, I wouldn't have a picture of the bastard." *Or be here at this cheap hunk of annoying electronics.*

She ejected the library's ramcard and the comm's screen returned to football.

She looked at the picture she had of the peeper and realized that she still had the Long-Eighties. There was still a ramcard in the peeper's binoculars. He might have recorded something useful.

Evi zipped open her backpack and pulled out the Long-Eighties. They were a sensitive collection of British electronics and they'd been trashed. The video lens was cracked, and the LCD eyepieces showed kaleidoscopic patterns of green snow laced with dead-black nothing. Evi had to pry off the housing to remove the ramcard.

"At least he was recording."

The ramcard went in as a vulpine place-kicker for the San Francisco Earthquakes made the extra point.

She played the card at high-speed, backward. The video started with a blank screen imprinted with a timer and yesterday's date. The time counter started speeding backward as she raced over the all-too-familiar scene of her jumping around in the nude. Evi heard Diana stop breathing and turned to look at her. Diana was perched, leaning forward, on the edge of the couch. Evi watched Diana, who was absorbed in the video, until Diana waved frantically at the screen. "Stop, what was that?"

What was what? Evi started the comm playing forward again. The binocs were focused on a grainy green image of herself, on the balcony, doing her leg presses. Then she moved and vaulted on to the roof. There was a clear shot of a bullet impacting the headrest of the weight machine.

The binoculars didn't follow her.

Their view whipped around for a badly-angled shot of the neighboring condominium. The peeper focused in on the open window in time to see a definite muzzle flash. Briefly, she though she saw a face, and then the peeper whipped the binoculars back on her.

She backed up the video, frame by frame, until she caught the scene that gave a partial view of the sniper's face. She got a printout of that as well.

It wasn't Sukiota.

"Know him?" Diana asked.

Evi shook her head. "I think his name is Gabe."

"A cop?"

"I sincerely doubt it."

She started the reverse playback again.

Evi watched herself back into the apartment early yesterday morning, and then there was an abrupt jump cut to, according to the date on the record, a week earlier.

It was a daytime shot, in color, and Evi recognized the scene.

The peeper was looking through a window into Frey's apartment. Frey was there, with two people Evi recognized from her office. One was her fellow think tanker, David Price. The other was her immediate superior, Erin Hofstadter. The man she had reported to for the last six years.

Three others were in the apartment. One she didn't recognize. One she couldn't see clearly.

The last was the sniper.

"What the fuck is going on?" She froze the scene on the sextet so she could compare faces. The view she had printed of the sniper was fuzzy. There was a slight possibility that she was wrong. She doubted it.

She reviewed the card; there was all of five minutes of Frey's apartment on it. The scene was bracketed by Frey opening the window at the beginning and a jump cut at the end.

She sighed and played the five minutes she had, running the video back and forth and trying to read lips. Frey opened the window and looked out. ". . . ains, do we bring her in?"

Frey was standing in front of Hofstadter, keeping Evi from seeing his response.

One of the unknowns, an old professor type, spoke to Hofstadter. He was in profile, and she could only make the words "stupid idea" and "a vacation." Then the prof put his face in his hands and shook his head.

Price was facing the window and was only partially obscured by Frey. He spoke across Hofstadter, at the prof. "Doc, stick to—" Price leaned forward and she lost the next few words. When his mouth was visible again, she made out the word "xenobiology." She rewound the video three times to get that word right.

Frey waved them down. He was still looking out the window. "Cool it. We can't afford internal bickering."

One of the ones she didn't know, one dressed in an impeccable black suit, spoke up. She could barely see him from around the window frame. He waved his hands, but his lips were only in view for the phrase "I warned."

Price turned a pleading look at the sky and said a whole sentence she could make out. "You and your fucking tachyons."

"Shut up Pr . . ." Frey turned around and delivered an inaudible tirade. Then he sat down, facing the five others across his black lacquer holo-table.

"Agreed," Hofstadter responded to something Frey had said. Now that Frey was sitting, Hofstadter and Price were the easiest people to interpret. "But I am still against it."

The suit said something with a dismissing wave of his hand. Evi wished he'd lean forward so she could see his face. The glimpses she was getting of his profile were tantalizingly familiar.

The suit's speech, whatever it was, initiated a shouting match that started everyone talking over everyone else. Then the suit leaned into the frame to emphasize something.

She froze the frame and looked at him. She had seen his face before; he had been the man standing behind Hofstadter when she had called from the theater.

There they were, she realized, the majority of the people after her. This guy in the suit, Evi remembered Hofstadter calling him Davidson, Hofstadter himself, and the sniper, Gabe.

If Frey was sitting there, in the middle of it, why didn't he do Gabe's job and blow her away when he had the chance?

She looked at Gabe, standing in the background of the frozen scene. The sniper stood by the door and apparently contributed nothing to the conversation.

She rewound the shouting match and watched each face separately.

The suit leaned in to say, "—against bringing a non-human into the community."

Price was responding. "—in on the beginning, Davidson—"

Hofstadter was saying, "—late date would be counterproductive—"

The prof was saying something out of Evi's view.

Gabe remained close-mouthed.

Frey shouted them down, though Evi couldn't see what he said. He started pointing around the circle.

He pointed at the suit, Davidson. She couldn't see him, he'd leaned back out of the frame.

He pointed at Price. "Yes."

Hofstadter. "No."

Evi couldn't see the prof's response.

Gabe. "I abstain."

Frey nodded and the video jumped to a night-enhanced picture of Evi leaving her apartment.

"That's it," she said and ejected the ramcard.

"What was that?"

She looked at the unlabeled ramcard, "I wish I knew, exactly." The card caught the light, which rippled rainbows across its surface. "I also wish you had a better comm."

Evi fished out the last ramcard she had, the one she'd found on the Afghani mercenary in the elevator shaft. It was dead black, with what appeared to be a serial number across the top of the card. It could be anything.

She slipped it into the card reader.

All the memo function would read off it was the message, "Property of Nyogi Enterprises. Authorized use only. Unauthorized use subject to prosecution, ten years imprisonment, and minimum fines of $500,000." Everything else on the card was encrypted and copy protected.

"I'll be damned. It's a card-key."

Evi looked over her shoulder at Diana. "You're right. The dogs work for Nyogi."

Diana got up and stood behind the couch, putting her arms around Evi's neck. Evi pressed the eject button on the remote, and football returned. She pressed the mute button.

She cocked her head back to look at Diana. "What?"

Diana kissed her on the forehead. "I'm just wondering what you're going to do now."

Evi closed her eyes and rested her head against Diana's chest. "I'm not sure. I want to rest and heal up, but there are still people after me."

"Nyogi?"

She nodded.

"They've treated you rudely."

Almost as rudely as the Agency. "They started the whole mess I'm involved in."

Diana's hand brushed against her right breast, and Evi reached up and held it there. She was warm again, and she realized that a repeat of last night could happen very easily. As far as Diana was concerned, she was a lesbian.

"What are you going to do?" Diana asked again. "I might be able to unearth my old contacts from the forties. The moreaus might be sympathetic—"

Evi shook her head. "I need to find out why this is happening before I go running off to the Bronx."

"Are you just going to walk up to a Nyogi exec and ask him?"

Evi opened her eyes and looked up at Diana. The veep she had liberated the aircar from had landed in a privileged space in the Nyogi tower. He had to be high up in the corporation. "Why not?"

She kissed Diana for giving her the idea. When Diana raised her head, Evi spit out some red hair and told her, "I can be very persuasive."

*   *   *

A half-hour on a public comm gave her the veep's name, Richard Seger. She had called his apartment——no way was she getting near that condo again——and been forwarded to Nyogi. She hung up before the call made it all the way through to the veep's office. It had confirmed what she wanted to know: Seger was working this New Year's Day.

At least he was in the Nyogi building.

Evi walked back to Diana's Estival. Diana lowered the window as she approached. "Are you *sure* you want me to leave?"

Evi nodded. "You shouldn't be near me when this goes down. No one can trace me to you. Let's keep it that way."

"The way you're dressed, I'm glad." Diana smiled as she said it. She was the one who had found the androgynous exec suit on such short notice. Diana had borrowed it from one of the warehouse's tenants. Male or female, Evi didn't know. The suit fit loosely, but it let Evi look like a junior corp type, and it hid the Mishkov.

Diana reached into the pocket of her jeans and pulled something out. "Here, before I forget." She handed Evi a pearl-handled switchblade. "It fell out of your jacket."

"Thanks." Evi slipped it into the top of the leather fringed boots she still wore. Then she leaned forward and kissed Diana good-bye. "You'll hear from me."

"I expect to," Diana responded as she drove away.

So I'm a lesbian, Evi thought.

She put on her sunglasses and walked back to the limo she'd rented. She had wanted a less conspicuous vehicle, but the limo company was the only place open today that would take cash. She had rented the thing for only six hours, and her roll of twenties had been reduced to a small wad.

It was closing on six o'clock, and she was parked across Eighth from the entrance to the Nyogi parking garage. She could see the Empire State Building, down 33rd. After its recent refurb it outshone the glass and metal obelisks that swamped it. Unlike the Chrysler Building, people had spent money to fix up the old skyscraper. Steam belched from a chuckhole a car-length from her limo and Evi had the cynical thought that the Empire State Building was the only thing people spent money to fix up in this town.

She passed the time by popping the cover off the dash and disabling the collision-avoidance systems on the limo.

The sky darkened from a crystalline blue to a dark purple. She kept watch on the exit from the garage, as well as on the passing traffic. For more than an hour, nothing left the garage, and the cars that passed her were, for the most part, taxis.

By seven-thirty the sky was dead-black beyond the streetlights. According to the dash clock, and Evi's time sense, it was exactly seven-thirty when a car pulled out of the Nyogi parking garage. In the back, she could see her friend from the penthouse. She'd been right about him not being able to replace that Peregrine so fast.

Driving the Chrysler Mirador was a huge Japanese. Evi supposed that the chauffer doubled as a bodyguard. She let the sedan get a few car-lengths ahead of her on Eighth before she pulled the limo into the traffic behind it.

As they drove past the mid-forties, she passed the Mirador. She made sure she pulled in directly in front of the veep's sedan. She slowed the car under the speed limit as they came to the red light at 56th. The light changed to green as she approached, so she accelerated.

As soon as the Mirador picked up speed to follow her, she slammed on the brakes in the limo.

The chauffer and the Mirador's computer tried to keep from rear-ending her, but the snow and the distance between them made sure there was a satisfying if undramatic crunch. Both cars slid to a stop midway into the intersection, and every taxi in New York City used it as an excuse to lean on the horn.

Evi smiled to herself, cut the engine to her limo, and got out of the car.

"What've I done?" She put on her most innocent tone.

The driver getting out of the Mirador looked unsympathetic. The huge Asian was round, solid, easily 200 kilos and two meters. She couldn't help but think of videos she'd seen of old sumo wrestlers. She smelled the taint of the modified testosterone in the driver's veins. He had a bald scalp and a deep shadow on his chin that she knew no amount of shaving would eliminate.

He was a frank. She knew what brand, too. He was one of Hiashu's early combat models. The first one they started playing glandular games with. They weren't known for their intelligence.

"Lady, what the fuck did you think—"

She walked up to him, shaking her head. "Look, I'm really sorry about this. It's my fault." She put her good hand on his shoulder. "I'll pay for the damages. Do we have to get the cops involved?"

She brushed his cheek, and she could smell a wave of overpowering lust sweating off the man. He couldn't control it, not after what the Hiashu engineers had done to his gonads.

He looked indecisive.

She slammed her knee up between the man's legs.

His eyes widened and he gasped. His arms began to move into a defensive posture, too late . . .

She kneed him again, and his eyes rolled back into his head. With her right hand she gave him a shove that guided his collapse. The man lost consciousness as he fell on his side in the snow next to the limo.

Oversized glands made a convenient target.

The Mirador's engine was still going, and Evi walked to the still-open driver's door and got behind the wheel. She backed away from the limo and turned onto 56th.

That went smoothly.

She glanced back at the veep, who was still looking back at the limo. He turned around to face her with a look of stunned disbelief. She smiled at him. "I won't ask if you remember me."

Evi headed for the Queensboro Bridge.

Chapter 13

The lower level of the bridge was undergoing repairs. The work had stopped for the holiday. Evi drove the Mirador through a few sawhorses and past a few detour signs to get on the lower thoroughfare, where she could have some privacy.

She drove past city vehicles, dumptrucks, and silent construction equipment. She slowed as she went on, and the Mirador started vibrating as she hit the old concrete. To her right, the guardrail abruptly disappeared. She shut down the car, leaving it in gear.

The only sounds were now the wind and the rumble of traffic driving by above them.

She drew the Mishkov and pointed it at the veep. "Get out."

"But—"

"If you're cooperative, we can get through this without any bloodshed."

The veep spread his hands and let himself out of the back of the car. Evi followed, keeping the gun trained on him. With her left hand she reached into her pocket for a pair of handcuffs she'd liberated from Diana's bedstand. It hurt her shoulder, but she wasn't about to lower the gun.

She tossed the cuffs to the veep. "Cuff yourself to that." She waved the gun at the scaffolding at the near edge of the hole in the side of the bridge.

The veep looked at the velvet-lined cuffs and arched an eyebrow.

"You're right," Evi said when he didn't move immediately. "Maybe I should just shoot you."

He moved, cuffing himself to the scaffolding. "What—"

Evi put the gun away and walked to the edge of the bridge where the guardwall should have been. She looked down over the East River. Then she walked over to the Mirador and picked up a loose steel reinforcing rod.

"What," he repeated, "are you doing?"

"I'll get to you in a moment," Evi said as she slammed the windshield with the rod. She hit it a few times to clear out most of the glass. She did the same to the rear window.

She dropped the iron rod and turned to the veep. "Don't want any trapped air keeping this thing afloat."

She reached through the driver's window and turned the wheel toward the hole in the side of the bridge.

"You're not . . ." he said.

She pushed the Mirador toward the edge, until the front wheels left the pavement and hung over empty space. She looked down again; still no boat traffic.

She got behind the car and kicked it in the ass. There was a short scrape, and the rear end bounced a little. She kicked it again, and there was a longer scrape. The rear end bounced some more. This time the rear wheels came a centimeter off the ground.

She stood there and looked at the precariously balanced sedan. Then she looked at the veep, hooked her right hand under the bumper, and lifted. She rocked the car up to the point where the rear wheels were a meter off the ground, and gravity took over.

There was a sickening scrape as the chassis slid against the edge of the bridge. Then the rear wheels hit the edge and they rolled, silently pushing the car off.

A few seconds passed before she heard a splash.

Then she walked up to the veep, smiling.

He was staring at the river. "Someone saw that. They'll call the police."

"No lights on the car, no lights under here, and if someone did see, police response time in this city is fifteen minutes, minimum. Long enough." She stopped a half-meter from the veep. "Now, will the cops find you cuffed to the scaffold?" She jerked her head in the direction of the river. "Or when they dredge the river for that car?"

"What do you want?" The veep hugged the scaffold and kept looking down at the river. The Mirador was drifting by, and sinking as it did so.

"In the aircar you asked, 'Do you know who I am?' I decided to find out, Mr. Seger."

"All I do is acquire real estate for Nyogi Enterprises."

"Like the building you live in?"

"Yes."

"Like other condos up and down Fifth?"

"Yes."

"Like condos that got plastered with dead Afghani dogs?"

Seger choked. "Yes, yes, damnit."

Nyogi owned her building. Nyogi had owned Frey's building. This had been going on for a while. She was on the right track. Evi ran her hand across Seger's face. He had a day's growth of beard, and it looked like he'd slept in his thousand-dollar suit. He had lost all vestiges of his hostage training. She ran her fingers through his hair and balled her hand into a fist. She yanked his head back. "Why is Nyogi after me?"

"I don't know."

She leaned next to Seger's ear. The smell of his sweat overpowered the East River. "You've spent over a grand on hair replacement. Don't risk that investment by lying to me."

Seger tried to shake his head. "I don't."

Evi let his hair go and pulled out the Mishkov. She placed the barrel on his temple. "Who instructed you to buy those properties?"

Seger swallowed and stayed silent.

She raised the Mishkov and whipped it across Seger's face. "I'm not playing games here!" Blood trickled down from a cut she'd opened in the veep's cheek.

"Okay . . ."

"Good. Now—" Evi ran the barrel of the Mishkov down Seger's cheek, under his chin, and used it to turn his head to face him. "Who told you to acquire those properties?"

Seger swallowed again. He was drenched with sweat. He was even more scared than he'd been when she stole his aircar. Seger sputtered, "Hitaki, Hioko Hitaki."

"Nice Jap name. Works for Nyogi?"

Seger took too long to answer again.

"That should've been easy, a simple yes or no question."

"Are you trying to get me killed?"

"That's a stupid question to ask with a gun in your face. You're stalling."

Seger nodded violently. "Yes, yes. damnit. He works for Nyogi. He's Special Operations—"

That was a familiar euphemism.

"He also works for other people, doesn't he?"

Seger nodded, weakly.

"Japanese Nationalists?"

Seger froze, looking down. She jabbed the barrel of the gun into the flesh under his jaw, forcing his head up.

"Yes or no?"

"If I told you—"

She smiled. "That's enough of an answer. I know who to thank for the Afghanis who tried to kill me. Now we come to the million-dollar question—"

Evi leaned in until they were barely a centimeter apart. "Why?"

"I just handle the real estate. They don't tell—"

"I'm going to ask you again. Why? If you say you don't know, I'm going to put a bullet through your head and toss you into the East River."

Seger sucked in a breath and started shaking. Evi could hear him subvocalize, "Where the hell are they?"

"Where the hell is who?"

Seger looked her in the face. He was on the verge of panic. "No one—"

That's why he was stalling. Evi backed away from Seger, pointing the gun at him. "Where is it?"

"What are you talking about?"

"The tracking device, where is it?"

The color drained from Seger's face. "They made me eat it."

She kept backing away. "I should blow you the fuck away—"

"Damn it, you think I wanted this? Do you know what those creatures are like? I was treated like an *animal*—"

"*WHY?*" Evi yelled at him. Her gun was shaking.

"They want their people back—" He was interrupted by the sound of an approaching aircar. He looked out over the river. Evi could see the sleek black wedge of a Chrysler Wyvern.

Seger started waving his free hand and shouting. "Here, over here!"

She could see what was about to happen. She got on the ground behind a city truck and yelled, "Seger, get down!"

Machine gun fire strafed the lower level of the Queensboro bridge. She looked out from under the truck and saw Seger jerk backward and lose his footing. He ended up dangling from one velvet-cuffed arm.

A bullet came too close, blowing out the truck's tire opposite her.

Damn.

She wedged herself between the truck and the concrete median, her back to a rear tire. She was pinned where she was. She could hear the Wyvern hovering on the other side of the truck. Was the driver going to try to slide into the hole in the wall?

Damn it, he was. She could hear the whine of the fans change in character as the Wyvern made its approach. She could smell the electricity off its inductor. Then a breeze started blowing around her as the aircar began to dust the concrete.

Evi swallowed and checked the Mishkov.

She had six shots and the switchblade in her boot. She wondered if it would be enough. She doubted it. The hit on her condo had been a costly mistake, a mistake that people like the NLF rarely made twice.

She could smell the canines now, more than three of them.

She had two choices, sit or bolt.

If she bolted, they'd shoot at her. She didn't like that idea. So far she'd avoided getting a bullet in her. She'd like to keep it that way.

Perhaps now was the time to test the hypothesis that they wanted her alive.

Someone hit the underside of the Queensboro bridge with a spotlight. What had been the sound of a slow advance behind her became running and scrambling. The night was sliced open by sirens and the sound of helicopters.

An overamplified voice over a PA system ordered, "Step away from the aircar."

There was the sound of machine-gun fire from behind her, the distant sound of shattering glass, and the spotlight went out. She heard the Wyvern rev up.

The cops opened fire.

She pulled herself into a little ball. Concrete chips flew by her. Bullets ricocheted off the truck she hid behind, carrying the smell of sparking metal. Two more tires blew out.

There was a loud pop and the smell of molten ceramics as a bullet clipped an active inductor. It had to be the Wyvern. She heard the fans die, and the gunfire ceased in time for her to hear the Wyvern splash home.

Another spotlight lit up the lower level, and she could hear cars approaching from both directions. Red and blue began to cut into the white of the spotlight. Short of dashing for the edge of the bridge and diving into the East River, there was nowhere she could go. The Wyvern might have had her pinned, but the cops had her surrounded.

It had been only ten minutes since she ditched the Mirador. She had been overly pessimistic about NYPD response time.

She put the Mishkov on the ground next to her, and when a NYPD uniform ducked around the truck, gun drawn, she spread her hands wide. "I surrender."

The cops pulled her out into the open. Black-and-whites were everywhere. Way too many for deep-sixing a car. Like the cops that had surrounded the theater on Times Square, these boys had come out of nowhere. It was as if there were a whole division of NYPD cops primed and ready to . . .

To what?

The cop bent her over the hood of a new Chevy Caldera cop car. He patted her down and emptied her pockets. Three cops stood by with ready weapons. The cop liberated her wallet, her backpack, and several magazines for the Mishkov.

The cop car was too damn new. The cops also had a pair of helicopters. One swept the East River with a spotlight while the other just hovered with its light trained on the bridge. The cops themselves were too well equipped.

They were also too white.

By the time the cop took her sunglasses and started ushering her to a windowless van, Evi realized that there were only two blacks in a group of nearly thirty NYPD officers, and there were no Hispanics, or Asians . . .

She was roughly cuffed to a bar inside the van as she realized she was looking at a well-camouflaged Agency operation.

They let her stew for two hours after the van stopped moving. There wasn't any light, and there was nothing to do but sit and try not to think about the way the cuffs hurt her shoulder.

Why am I still alive, Abdel?

Obviously, came the reply, *we're guilty of faulty reasoning at some point. The Agency wants something beyond your demise.*

The Agency proper didn't want to ice her. Hofstadter was acting on his own initiative with the sniper. That would explain why Frey was helping her rather than trying to kill her.

It didn't explain why the Aerie wouldn't acknowledge her existence.

It also didn't explain what the peeper had recorded on his binoculars.

It was after ten when the door on the transport opened. She was as far from the door as the chain on the cuffs would allow. The rear of the van whooshed aside and the first thing that hit her was the smell. The New York subway system was the only place where she had ever come across that particular flavor combining the odors of fermenting urine, century old grease, stagnant water, overheated transformers, and dead air.

Somewhere, a train passed by. The noise rattled the walls of the van and made Evi's teeth ache.

The open door faced an anachronism. Amidst the cracked dirty tile, blackened girders, and crumbling concrete were scattered brand-new comms, electronic surveillance equipment, and dozens of people in NYPD uniforms.

The small command center had taken over an old subway platform, and Evi couldn't see more than ten meters past it because the entire area was lit by extremely bright temporary lamps that hung from a ceiling that was invisible beyond them.

Most of the "cops" swarmed around the equipment and ignored Evi and her van; three didn't.

Two were leveling automatic weapons at the van. They were Agency. The NYPD didn't issue Uzis to patrol officers. As if to drive the point home, the third was Sukiota.

Sukiota climbed into the back of the van. The door remained open, and guns remained leveled at Evi as Sukiota walked in front of her. Sukiota balled her hand into a fist and slammed it into Evi's stomach. It was so fast that Evi had no time to prepare for the impact. She doubled over and started retching.

When she was done spilling pork and bean curd over the floor of the van, Sukiota grabbed her by the chin and lifted her head to face her. "For my car, Isham, and the theater."

A gob of half-digested tofu dribbled out of Evi's mouth. "Sorry," she managed to choke out.

Sukiota slammed her knee into Evi's solar plexus. The pain spasmed every muscle in Evi's body. She shook with dry heaves, and she prayed that she wasn't suffering any internal injuries.

"Want to know why you're alive?"

All Evi could manage was a hoarse monosyllable.

"You're alive because you are screwing with my mission." Sukiota grabbed Evi's bad shoulder and violently pulled her upright. A dagger of fire raced down the length of Evi's arm. *"And I want to know why!"*

She looked at Sukiota, and she began to realize that something else was going on here. Something she hadn't known, or guessed at.

Sukiota released Evi's shoulder and sat down across from her. "Do we have an understanding?"

Evi nodded. She understood. She knew the type of agent Sukiota was.

Another train passed nearby, the lights outside dimmed briefly, and dust filtered in through the open door to the van.

"Who do you work for, Isham?"

She couldn't stop her silent laugh, even if she was risking being hit again. "Same people you do."

Sukiota hit her with a backhand slap that was more irritating than painful. "Bullshit. I thought of that, when you called the Aerie. You aren't on the database."

"Then I got erased."

"Convenient. You were carrying a ramcard of surveillance footage. Who are the principals in the apartment?"

Evi told her. If Sukiota was on the ball, she knew already.

Sukiota nodded at the names she knew. "Good. Now I'd like you to explain to me how seven *dead* people are screwing with my mission."

"What?" Dead?

Sukiota leaned forward. "Ezra Frey died in an explosion on an Agency mission in Cleveland in August '53. Erin Hofstadter has been missing ever since a State Department fact-finding mission into occupied Japan in December '53. David Price drove his car into Chesapeake Bay in September '53. Davidson, his first name is—was—Leo, burned in his house in San Francisco May 23rd, 2055. The professor-type's name is Scott Fitzgerald, and he was supposed to have fallen from a radio telescope and broken his neck in '53 . . ."

Sukiota paused, apparently to gauge Evi's reaction. Evi knew she must have looked as shocked as she felt. "I suppose you *didn't* know you were looking at a recording of a room full of corpses? Two more are on the walking dead list, Isham. The guy you called 'Gabe' had the code designation 'Gabriel,' a freelance assassin. He was reported neutralized in '54—"

"You said two." Sukiota had gone through the whole room.

Sukiota smiled and pulled a ramcard out of her pocket and looked at it as if she could read it with the naked eye. "You mean you don't know? Someone invested a lot of time and energy to falsify dozens of secure databanks on your behalf—"

"What the hell—"

Sukiota grabbed her by the neck, choking off her statement, and held the edge of the ramcard a few millimeters from her eye. Evi watched a rainbow shimmer shoot across the edge of the card.

Stikiota shook the card. "Don't play dumb, Isham. The Aerie doesn't respond to dead agents. And you *died*, Isham. In December 2053, a few days after Hofstadter disappeared—"

Evi's eye was beginning to water. She couldn't take her gaze off the edge of the ramcard. "I was transferred," Evi whispered.

"Where."

"We call it the Domestic Crisis Think Tank."

Sukiota loosened her grip. "All these corpses work there?"

"I don't know." Sukiota tightened and Evi speeded up. "Dave Price and Hofstadter I'm sure, Davidson maybe. The others I never heard of before yesterday."

"Who runs the place, and where is it?"

"Hofstadter runs my department. It's all in a building off Columbia. Broadway. 109th."

Sukiota leaned back, rolling the ramcard in her fingers. "That's good. See how simple it is. You answer my questions and bad things don't happen. Now you are going to tell me what happened in your condo."

Chapter 14

Sukiota questioned her for three hours. The only thing Evi tried to hide was her evening with Diana. Thankfully, Sukiota didn't seem to care much where Evi spent her night. What Sukiota wanted were details, details about the Afghanis and the NLF, and details about the Domestic Crisis Think Tank . . .

Sukiota never once asked about the aliens.

Evi had mentioned the aliens, when Sukiota had questioned her about the scenarios she'd been cooking for Hofstadter. Evi'd responded with the studies she'd written up on a hypothetical invasion.

Sukiota's only reaction had been a condescending smirk. She'd been much more interested in Evi's studies of hypothetical moreau violence.

When Sukiota finished the questions that interested her, she uncuffed Evi and, escorted by five Uzi-toting pseudo-cops, led her back on the abandoned subway platform and tossed her in a holding cell.

The cell was as makeshift as the rest of their headquarters. It used to be a public john. The place had been stripped to the walls. Dead pipes jutted out of the walls. The musty urine smell had stayed, as if it were baked into the yellowing tile, under the cracked glaze. Spray-painted graffiti wrapped around the walls, mostly gang names. The name "Pendragon" seemed to predominate. That and the 130th Street something-or-other. They cuffed her to a pipe in the wall near the floor.

One lit fluorescent tube dangled from the ceiling by a pair of frayed wires. It rattled and blacked out every time a train passed close by.

A pipe near the door dripped irregularly. The echo was irritating enough that Evi thought they had purposely chained her out of reach of the drip as a low-grade torture.

At least she'd learned something about what was going on, although it was depressing to learn that someone had already written her obituary back in 2053.

It was clear that the Domestic Crisis Think Tank had stepped beyond the Agency's purview. Not only that, Sukiota showed no knowledge of the aliens. At the think tank, the aliens were taken as a given. A top secret given, but a given. It looked as though everything that Evi had uncovered in Cleveland had never gotten beyond Frey, who'd been fielding the operation.

Instead of booting the aliens upstairs, Frey must have bottled up everyone involved and siphoned off funds for his own operation. For six years she had been working for some private conspiracy.

A private conspiracy that wanted her dead.

Hofstadter was behind the sniper.

Frey had been surprised at what was going on. Frey had been running toward her building. Frey had asked her about Hofstadter's state of mind. And Frey had mentioned that he had been on vacation himself. The last thing he had ever said was that *he* needed *her* help.

Frey set up the conspiracy that ran the think tank. He had to be the person behind it. He was the only one in a position to bottle up knowledge of the aliens. And the timing of most of the "deaths" had been shortly after the Cleveland mission.

He might have set up the conspiracy, but it looked as if he had lost control of it. Hofstadter had taken over. That would explain Frey's behavior . . .

She remembered something Frey had said. "Price was right."

If Hofstadter, Davidson, and Gabriel were the forces arrayed against her, perhaps Frey and Price were allies. Frey was dead, but Price might still be out there. He was locking out calls to his comm, but Dave could still be sitting in his house in Jackson Heights.

Queens, Evi thought.

Frey was going to take her to a "safehouse" in Queens.

Evi let out with her silent laugh. Price *was* an ally, if he was still out there. She looked around the pit she found herself in. How the hell was she going to contact Price?

She had to get out of here. She didn't trust the Agency, especially after finding out that for six years she'd been a de facto traitor. She didn't picture Sukiota allowing her to outlive her usefulness. She might have already passed that point.

She looked at the pipe she was chained to. If she could get free of it, she might have a chance to get out of here. They hadn't found the switchblade in her boot.

A switchblade against Uzis?

Shut up, Abdel.

One cuff was around her right wrist, thankfully her good arm; the other was cuffed around the base of a pipe extending out of the wall. The pipe terminated in a lip that held a large connector that would have attached to some part of a john. The piece was rusted and fused into a single object.

If she could loosen the connector, she could slide off the handcuffs.

The catch was, she had to do it lefthanded.

Evi gritted her teeth and grabbed the connector with her left hand. Just bending her arm to reach it shot a lance of pain through her shoulder.

"This isn't going to be fun," she whispered to herself.

She sucked in a deep breath and twisted the end of the connector as hard as she could. It felt as if she were trying to twist her shoulder out of her socket. She kept pushing, trying to ignore the grinding she felt in her shoulder. The rough, rusty surface of the connector bit into her fingers, and her grip began to slide on her own blood.

She heard a snap, and her hand slipped off the pipe. She fell to the floor and, for a few seconds, thought that the snap had been the bone in her shoulder. But as the pain receded and her breathing returned to normal, she realized that the noise had come from the pipe.

The connector had remained fused to the pipe, but the pipe itself now rotated freely. She pulled on the end of it, and it slid out from the wall. The end that came out from the wall was threaded and polished smooth. The handcuffs slid easily over it.

So far so good.

She wiped her left hand on the exec trousers, leaving a dark stain. Then she pulled the switchblade out of her boot.

If Sukiota stayed true to form, she'd leave the guards by the door when she came. And she'd come in unarmed. Coming in unarmed would have a point when you didn't want the prisoner to steal a weapon. However, it gave the prisoner an advantage if she was already armed.

Evi slid the pipe back into place and folded her body over it and her right arm so they wouldn't see her hand was free. She waited.

It was five-thirty in the morning when Sukiota opened the door and walked into the cell. Two of the pseudo-cops stood outside with their Uzis pointed into the room.

The cops were human; their reaction time wouldn't be quick enough. At least she hoped so.

Sukiota walked into the middle of the room. "We're going to have another little talk."

"You bet we are," Evi responded in as insolent a tone as she could muster.

"You—" Sukiota stepped toward Evi, hand raised.

Evi leapt. She tackled Sukiota to the far wall, slamming her good shoulder up under Sukiota's chin. Sukiota's head thudded against the tile. Evi kept close to her, hoping that the guards out the door would hesitate out of fear of hitting their superior.

They didn't fire, and by the time Sukiota had recovered from the head blow, Evi was pressing the knife against her jugular.

For a second, everything stopped moving. One of the cops, one of the token blacks, had stepped into the room. He froze, machine gun leveled at Evi and Sukiota. Beyond the door, out on the subway platform, the pseudo-cops who were manning equipment at the impromptu command center stopped their activity as they turned to watch what was going on behind them. Even the dust from the last train passing seemed to hang in the air, frozen in the lights.

"Drop the guns!" Evi yelled at the guards, keeping her gaze locked on Sukiota.

The vein bulged from the pressure of the knife. A little more pressure, or a quick slash to the left or right, and even an engineered metabolism wouldn't keep Sukiota from bleeding to death.

"*NOW!*"

Two guns clattered to the ground. Evi moved around, to Sukiota's right, so she could keep an eye on the gunmen and her hostage.

"This is a dumb move, Isham."

"Don't make any sudden moves. I'm as quick as you are, and younger."

"Enjoy it. You won't get any older."

The two cops, black and white, were staring at Evi, guns at their feet. "You out there, kick that weapon away."

The one outside the room did as she told him.

"And you," she said to the one in the room with them, "kick that gun over here."

The gun slid across the tile to clatter to Sukiota's feet. Sukiota's eyes glanced down briefly and Evi pressed the knife harder. "Your throat'd open up before you were halfway there." Evi put her foot on the butt of the gun. "Not worth it."

She addressed the black cop, "Get out of here."

He backpedaled out of the room, leaving Evi and Sukiota alone to face each other. Sukiota smiled. "Now what?" She asked.

Evi was becoming aware of the pulse in her neck. There was a coppery taste in her mouth. *Calm*, she told herself, *you have a hostage*. She looked deep into her adversary's eyes and came to a realization. "You *enjoy* this shit."

Sukiota smiled wider.

"Get on the ground, face down, slowly."

Sukiota slid slowly down. Evi kept her knife pressed into Sukiota's neck. A small trail of blood had leaked down the edge to form a small bead on the web between Evi's thumb and forefinger.

She put her knee in the small of Sukiota's back and glanced at the scene out the door. Everyone was facing the cell. A few were trying to ease out of her field of vision.

"All of you, down on the fucking ground, now!"

To the last one, they hit the dirt. They knew when it was not a good idea to play games.

Sukiota was wearing a familiar-looking black jumpsuit. Evi reached down under Sukiota with her left hand, which hurt like hell, and unzipped the top about halfway.

Sukiota was maintaining a level tone of voice. "Are you going to use me as a hostage or rape me?"

Sukiota was trying to rattle her, have her make a mistake. Evi almost slugged Sukiota the way she'd been slugged. In Evi's awkward position that move would have been disastrous.

"Put your hands flat at your side."

Sukiota did so, and Evi retrieved her left hand and pulled Sukiota's collar down to her mid-back, restraining her arms. Only after she had Sukiota somewhat immobilized, did Evi reach over for the gun.

It wasn't a real Israeli Uzi. It was an Italian knock-off. It still carried uncomfortable echoes.

She held the barrel of the gun between Sukiota's naked shoulder blades with her left hand as she slowly withdrew the switchblade and pocketed it. Then she switched the gun to her good hand. "You're going to get me out of here."

She backed off of Sukiota, holding the Uzi with her right hand and the collar of Sukiota's jumpsuit with her left. "Get up."

She did so, stripped to the waist. "You can't—"

"Can the speech. Where's my bag?"

"Over there." Sukiota gestured with her head. Evi saw her backpack sitting on a table next to one of the portable comms out on the platform. "You," she yelled at the cop laying in front of the door. "I want you to get up and slowly walk to that backpack. Bring it here."

The cop looked up at them and Sukiota said in a disgusted tone, "Do as she says."

"Finally being cooperative?" Evi asked.

"It's not like you're going to get away."

"Just keep thinking that." The cop returned with the backpack, tossed it into the room, and returned to his spot on the ground without being told. Evi briefly let go of Sukiota to retrieve her backpack. She made sure the gun was a constant pressure between Sukiota's shoulder blades.

"Even if you get out of here," Sukiota said. "I'll be able to find you."

Evi shouldered the pack with a wince. "You know the drill. We're going to move slow, and by the numbers." She grabbed Sukiota's collar again. "Now, walk out. Toward the van."

It was nervewracking, the slow advance toward the police van. The darkness beyond the lights seemed perfect to hide a sniper, and every eye was locked on her, looking for an opening. All they needed was one person with a gun that wanted her dead more than they wanted Sukiota alive.

Somewhere down the length of the abandoned subway tunnel was the echo of dripping water. Closer was the occasional electronic beep from the equipment. One of the comms began to ring for attention, an incoming call. One of the agents looked at the offending comm but didn't move toward it.

"This is a communications hub," Sukiota told her. "You've cut it out of the loop. How many people do you think are converging on us right now?"

Sukiota was right, too right. This HQ might be makeshift, but there were enough agents, computers, and secret encryption and surveillance equipment here to make any compromising event here a national security risk. A priority risk. Red lights would be flashing in DC right now, and the Feds would be mobilizing everything in the immediate area from the FBI to the Coast Guard.

That triggered another thought, one that was even scarier.

Am I being set up? Evi thought. This seemed to be going much too smoothly.

Evi backed against the side of the police van. The handcuffs chained to her wrist was rattling. She calmed her shaking hand.

"Get in the van."

"It's locked."

Evi didn't like the thought that Sukiota was keeping her cool better than she was. Evi looked at one of the agents hugging the ground nearby. He was the other black guy.

"You, lose the gunbelt."

He looked up at her and fumbled it off. Evi was getting nervous. She'd almost feel better if one of these Agency people dove for a gun. They were being too acquiescent.

But even if it was a setup, what could she do other than what she was doing?

"Come over here and punch in the combination for this vehicle."

She watched him unlock the van door and then had him resume his position on the ground. Evi ushered Sukiota into the passenger seat, fastening Sukiota's seatbelt with her left hand. Between the re-straining of the jumpsuit bunched around Sukiota's forearms, and the seatbelt itself, Sukiota was immobilized.

"Where are we?" Evi asked. The view out the front windshield showed more of the subway platform, which ended about ten me-ters in front of the van. To the right, the platform dropped off to the subway tracks. To the left there was a blank tile wall broken only by a large garage door hanging open next to the nose of the van. That was the only route from which the van could have come.

Beyond the door was darkness.

"There's only one exit."

Evi sighed. "I could, out of view of all the people out there, qui-etly slit your femoral artery and try and bluff my way through using your corpse as a hostage."

You're letting her get to you, Abdel said, *that's what she wants.*

Yes, but someone still ought to bury her.

"We're under East 130th Street."

Evi started the van.

"The hole opens into the parking garage under the new Harlem precinct station." Sukiota wore an evil smile.

Damn. That meant cops, sharpshooters, all waiting for the Feds to show up. That blew her only escape route. No wonder Sukiota was smiling.

Could that be why the Agency people weren't acting? Did they want her to run that police blockade? Was it because they didn't expect her to break through it—?

Or because they thought she could?

Being shot while trying to escape was a venerable method of disappearing troublesome prisoners. That could be it.

Or they could want her to escape.

Evi decided she was getting too paranoid even for the situation at hand. All she knew for sure was that she didn't want to use that garage door as her escape route.

Evi shifted the van into gear, hit the headlights, and gunned the engine. Out of the corner of her eye, she could see Sukiota lose the smile. "What?"

Evi didn't head for the door. She aimed right off the edge of the platform, turning the wheel to shoot the van out on to the tracks themselves. The bone-jarring thud of the impact reawakened the pain in her gut where Sukiota had punched her.

Gunfire sounded from behind her, but none of the shots seemed to hit the van.

While the van was making the abrupt transition from platform to tracks, Evi had a brief fear that there wasn't enough clearance under the van for the rails. After the one big jar, the rail began sliding under the van inside the left tire. Even so, it wasn't a smooth ride. The rotting ties were busy trying to shake the right side of the van apart.

They shot down the tunnel, leaving the platform behind them. The van's headlights cut a hole in the darkness ahead. Concrete walls shot by on the left, while on the right, black grime-coated girders flew by.

The top of the rail that the van was straddling was dark with rust. Evi considered that a good sign.

The speedometer was creeping toward 100 kilometers an hour.

"You're crazy."

She smiled at Sukiota's reaction. "In the last forty-eight hours I think I've earned the privilege."

"You're only delaying the inevitable. Someone *will* catch up with you."

"Think I don't know that? I tried to come in, and I got *you* for my trouble."

"You're not helping yourself—"

Evi felt her pulse race as the scream of a train passed by them. Very close, in a neighboring tunnel. The entire van shook in response, and she had to struggle with the steering to keep the vibrating wheels on course. When she could hear again, she told Sukiota, "I cooperate with you, and I'd disappear. As far as the Feds are concerned, I'm either a rabid terrorist or a great big embarrassment."

"Or a traitor."

A bright light caught the windshield and began to close on them. White washed the front of the van. Evi hit the brakes, for all the good it would do, as the sound of the oncoming train threatened to shake the van apart.

A wall of moving graffiti shot by the van on the track to their right.

She caught her breath, then turned to Sukiota. Sukiota hadn't moved and was looking at Evi in much the same way Chuck Dwyer had.

"You—" She sucked in another breath and looked at Sukiota. "No. Explaining it wouldn't do any good." She swung the Uzi up to Sukiota's jawline. "But cut the 'traitor' shit. I've never turned on anyone."

Sukiota remained silent.

Evi felt her hand tighten on the trigger. "Whatever was going on, it was Frey's operation—"

"You were recruited by a rogue element of the Executive sometime in '53, and when things went bad and they tried to eliminate you, you tried to run back into the fold of the Agency."

There was nothing she could do. As far as the government was concerned, she was fucked. Ignorance never cuts very well as a defense. Frey and the others had separated from the Agency and had followed their own secret agenda.

Why did they drag her along without telling her the full story?

She pressed the gun harder beneath Sukiota's jaw. "Do you *know* what happened in Cleveland in August of '53?"

"The Agency terrorist division attempted to apprehend a canine terrorist named Hassan Sabah."

"Who'd he work for?"

"The CIA. They were trying to cover up an operation to funnel money to political candidates."

"The CIA?"

Evi couldn't believe it. The aliens had gotten away with it. The secret masters, the ones who had controlled the money, had manufactured the CIA story out of whole cloth. The agents in Langley were no more in control than the congressmen who were indicted.

"That was a plant for public consumption. The CIA was just a scapegoat. Who was Hassan *really* working for?"

Sukiota stared at her.

"You think it was a coincidence that Hassan's last known affiliation was with the NLF? The same people the Afghanis you're tailing are working for?"

Evi reached into Sukiota's pockets. She found a wallet, the keys to the handcuff she was wearing, and the white ramcard that Sukiota had been waving in her face earlier.

Sukiota stayed silent.

Why didn't Frey and the others bring her all the way in? Why the hell did they let her be blindsided by all this?

Anger was beginning to twist in her gut. "Let me draw you a picture, sister. I look at you and I see myself back in '53. You're about to tackle something that's a hell of a lot bigger than you are. You're going to get too close to what's at the core of Nyogi and the NLF. You get too close to Frey's little sideline, and everything you thought you worked for is going to go south on you—"

She unlocked the passenger door, popped Sukiota's seatbelt, and prodded her with the Uzi. "Get out."

Sukiota zipped her jumpsuit back up and stepped out of the van. "You aren't going to escape, none of you."

"And you are?"

Evi floored the van, letting inertia slam the passenger door closed.

No more trains passed by her, and the tracks eventually disappeared, leaving a subterranean highway of algae-slick ties and black gravel. She pushed the van beyond any safe speed because she wanted to beat any attempt to cut her off.

As she shot through the bowels of Manhattan, she tried to understand the events that had swept her up.

The first players, the peeper and the Afghanis, were part and parcel of Nyogi Enterprises. Specifically, the subsidiary of Nyogi popularly referred to as the NLF. From what Seger, the veep, said before he was ventilated by the Afghanis, an alien cell was running Nyogi. "You don't know what those creatures are like."

"Yes, I do," she whispered.

The second players were Frey and company. Frey had covered up the situation in Cleveland. Instead of reporting MLI and the aliens to the Agency, they had let the phony money trail to the CIA stand. And someone had appropriated the aliens and MLI's assets for their own use.

Those assets exceeded eighty billion dollars.

For the past five years, Evi had been working for an Agency within the Agency. A totally self-contained organization, answerable to no one. The think tank she, Price, and Hofstadter worked for was totally outside the community. She'd known about the aliens, so the conspiracy had to keep her in its own fold . . .

But they had never brought her all the way in.

Evi was beginning to realize why—

It was because she wasn't human.

Hofstadter called her a frank and was trying to kill her. At least she knew why now. She could finger too damn many of the conspirators. Everyone at the think tank, Hofstadter, everyone who had some knowledge of the aliens back in 2053.

Evi growled and floored the van, intentionally slamming the side of the vehicle against the concrete walls.

She'd been duped. For six fucking years she'd been duped. And they didn't let her in, not for security, not because she was a risk, *but because she wasn't human.*

"BASTARDS!" A bright blue spark flashed across the passenger window as she scraped the front fender across the concrete on the inside of her turn. "All of you. Fucking bastards!"

The tunnel dipped down and, up ahead, the headlights were reflected back at her. She was going one-twenty, and the brakes didn't stop her in time. The nose of the van plowed through a scum of ice, throwing sheets of gray water up and out. Evi heard a buzzing zap and the cab filled with the smell of a blown-out transformer. The headlights and the indicators on the dash died.

The inductor had shorted out.

The van coasted to a stop in almost complete darkness. Even after her engineered eyes adjusted, the world was a dark-gray monochrome shadow that ended about ten meters ahead of her.

She sat in the driver's seat, stunned, as icy water began to collect in the footwell. "You're all hypocritical, manipulative bastards."

Evi, a mental voice began to say.

"Even you, Abdel."

I raised you, Evi.

"Even you." She could feel burning on her cheeks. "What the hell was I, ever, but somebody's intelligence asset?"

But—

"YOU AREN'T MY FATHER!" It echoed into the darkness, faded into nothing.

She slammed her fists into the dash, ignoring the pain in her left shoulder. "They said human experiments were atrocities. What were you going to do when you swept through that Jordanian facility? Kill us all?" She shook her head. "No, you couldn't do that. What a waste it would have been. You took us and trained us to be *your* atrocities."

She rested her head against the steering wheel. "Go away, Abdel. It's my life, and I don't want you any more."

Abdel didn't respond.

She was so damn tired. Tired of being a pawn. Tired of being controlled. Tired of relying on a system that pulled the carpet out from under her. Tired of a world that didn't give a shit about her.

The water was up to her mid-calf, and her feet were falling asleep.

Great, all she needed was a case of hypothermia.

She rolled down the window and looked around the tunnel. Halfway up the right side of the tunnel was a rusty catwalk. At least she could get somewhere without wading. That only left the question, forward or back?

There was no way she was going back.

Dawn broke as she kicked away the garbage holding shut the door on an abandoned subway station. The first sight to greet her upon clearing the top of the concrete stairs was a blown holo-billboard, the mirrored surface marred by the painted legend, "OFF THE PINK!"

Evi knew where she was now. The northern tip of Manhattan, past the barriers. The retrofitted slums of Washington Heights crowded around her, trying to buckle the crumbling streets. A few blocks away from her she could smell the Harlem River. Beyond it was the blasted shell of the Bronx.

The Bronx. The war zone. Moreytown.

Some *moreaus* wouldn't step into the Bronx. She set down her backpack, unlocked the handcuffs still attached to her right wrist, and tossed the cuffs in the bag. Then she reshouldered her bag and headed toward the Bronx.

Chapter 15

Evi walked across the crumbling bridge, weaving through the stray burnt-out cars, and left the human world. She passed under a rust-shot green sign reading, "I-95, Cross-Bronx Expressway." Under it was an ancient grime-coated detour sign saying the expressway was closed for repairs. More of the NY Urban Infrastructure Renewal Project. It was supposed to open the summer of 2045. Someone had spraypainted "abandon all hope" over "your tax dollars at work."

The first thing to hit her as she set foot in the Bronx was the smell. Even a fresh layer of gray snow, which muted odor as much as it did sound, could not hide the smell of animal musk. She was enveloped by the overlapping melange of the three million moreaus who owned the Bronx.

She stepped off the end of a crumbling off ramp.

The view down the street belonged to another continent. Even at this early hour, the street was lined by hawkers at makeshift stalls. A Peruvian rabbit sold gold jewelry out of a white plastic shipping crate. Three leather-clad rats chittering lightning Spanish were selling electronics using a burnt-out Chevy Caldera as a base of operations. Behind a rank of orange cones and old traffic sawhorses, a blind Pakistani canine with only one arm was being helped by a young female vulpine, running skewered meat over a coal pit in the asphalt . . .

People were everywhere, the highest concentration of moreaus in the world. In any direction she looked there was an undulating ocean of fur. Short dirty white for most of the Latin rodents, rabbits,

and rats. Spotted brown for some rabbits and dead black for some
rats. Red to spotlight the British vulpines. Gray, brown, and black
for the Middle Eastern and Southeast Asian canines. Brownish
black for the slow-moving ursoid mountains and the subliminal
flashes of otters and ferrets. Yellow and black for the big cats . . .

She waded into the sea of nonhumans, not bothering to hide the
Uzi. The crowd parted around her as the population turned to stare.
A barely audible growl followed her like the sound of crashing surf.
She got a half-block before she met a portion of the crowd that
didn't break before her.

Upon seeing the creature, her first impulse was to file it in her
knowledge of moreau strains. He was Russian, ursoid combat
strain, Vyshniy '33, first generation.

The bear was a wall of fur reaching up for nearly four meters.
The individual muscles that snaked through his forearm were the
size of Evi's thigh. Dozens of scars picked through the bear's
brown fur; most looked like bullet holes. A diagonal slash originated under one eye and snaked across his muzzle, revealing a slice
of raw pink across his nose. The only thing the bear wore was a pair
of khaki shorts.

It snarled at her. "Pink."

She leveled the Uzi at the bear. Around her she could hear
weapons clearing holsters, guns being cocked. The bear raised his
hand and she knew a solid contact from that arm would break her
neck.

She tensed to duck and roll to the side. "*Look at me!* I'm no
more human than you are."

The bear's brows knit as it stared at her. It took a few seconds
for him to lock eyes, a few more to realize what the eyes meant. His
arm remained raised. "You're a frank?"

Those words seemed to ignite something in the crowd. What
had been a frozen tableau around the periphery of Evi's vision
melted back into motion. Motion *away* from her and the bear. What
had been something of universal concern now seemed to be a personal matter between the two of them.

The bear was still looking for an excuse. "Not pink, but you
can't talk like that to—"

She saw a quiver of motion along the bear's forearm. "Don't."
She shook the Uzi for emphasis.

"But—"

"Your backup's gone."

The bear lowered his arm and grumbled, "Thought you were fucking human."

Evi sighed. "Done?"

The bear gave an all-too-human shrug and limped away. For the first time she noticed that the bear's left foot was a makeshift prosthetic.

She continued down the street, keeping an eye out for other potential conflicts. For the first time she saw her nearly human form as a handicap. Everyone eyed her with suspicion, some with outright contempt, but no one else opted for a direct confrontation. With the exception of some yelled obscenities, growls, and one thrown brick that missed her, she passed through unmolested.

But this deep in the Bronx, the only thing that *would* molest her would be the locals. Humans, cops or Feds, wouldn't come down here. The only people she'd have to worry about would be Nyogi's. And then only if they sent the Afghanis down after her. However, there was a good chance that no one knew where she was.

Not an aircar in sight. Not too surprising, since the FAA restricted the airspace above Moreytown. Allegedly because it was too dangerous, but Evi knew better. Both local and federal policy since '42 was to restrict physical access to concentrations of moreau population.

She needed to find a comm. She wove through main streets between modular mass-produced housing, burnt-out ruins, and old unfinished housing projects, looking. It soon became obvious that there was not going to be any operational public comms out on the street. The few kiosks she passed, whether they'd originally been a comm, a bank machine, a trash depository, or a city directory, had all been gutted long ago.

She walked deeper into the nonhuman city as the sun rose. The night was catching up with her. Evi had a headache that was telling her she had gotten too little sleep, and her left shoulder was a deep ache that flashed into full-blown agony whenever she tried to move her arm. She knew that all the movement last night had canceled any healing her arm had done the previous day and had probably made things worse.

She needed a place to rest.

She walked for two miles. She paralleled the valley of the dead I-95, passing abandoned earth movers and bulldozers that'd been stripped to orange metal skeletons. At eight in the morning, Evi passed an ancient brick structure that hadn't burned. It was wedged between a lot humped with soot-scarred concrete and the girder skeleton of what had, long ago, been an attempt at low-cost housing. The framework stork of the crane still hovered over the project, leaning at an ominous angle over the brick building.

The building's windows hid behind rolling steel doors. The way the graffiti wrapped around, ignoring the division between steel and brick, showed that the front windows had not been opened in a long time. What had stopped Evi, though, was the sign above the open door, "ROOMS."

"ROOMS" was lit in flickering neon that, against all odds, remained intact. The front door gaped open at her, held in place by a granite lion that stood rampant about a meter high. Mortar still clung to the lion's feet, a legacy from whatever facade he'd escaped from.

She needed a place to hole up. "ROOMS" was the best she could expect from this town. She walked in, hoping that the crane gantry would remain upright for one more day.

The lobby was sweltering, and the open door did nothing to help more than a meter into the building. The air was humid from the rust-laden steam heating system.

Behind the desk sat an old brown rabbit, obese, nose running, ears drooping. The lepus' rheumy eyes locked with Evi's for about a half-second of shock. She saw the rabbit's hand moving to something concealed behind the desk. The hand stopped moving when he looked into her eyes.

The rabbit cleared his throat. "Help you?"

She walked up to the desk. "I need a room with a working comm."

"Yeah." The rabbit coughed a few times. "Outside line?"

She nodded.

The rabbit turned and began tapping at an old manual keyboard behind him. She leaned forward to see what the rabbit had been reaching for. In a holster behind the desk was a cheap Chinese revolver, a PR-14. Evi didn't even want to think about fourteen-millimeter rounds. Those things were cheap for a reason. There were a lot of them, and they were just as likely to do damage to the wielder as to the target. The only people who could fire those things accurately were the Chinese ursines.

She thought it was a stupid weapon for a rabbit. That was until she noticed a bracket sunk into the desk. A bracket with a universal joint mount on it that could provide a fairly braced firing platform for the gun.

She turned and looked behind her and saw at least one very large hole in the wall by the door.

"Room 615." The rabbit paused for a coughing fit.

"How much?"

"Twenty an hour, hundred a day, half that if you got cash." The rabbit pulled a gray rag out from under the desk and blew his nose. "I don't haggle."

She reached into her pack and hoped that the Agency had left her wallet and cash in the leather. They had. She fumbled in her jacket and liberated her wallet. What remained of the roll of twenties, after the limo rental, was exactly a hundred in cash in her wallet. There was her phony ID in the wallet, but Eve's identity was compromised now.

"I want twenty-four hours and the balance credited to the comm's account." She handed the rabbit five twenties.

The cash disappeared under a balding hand. The rabbit nodded and handed her a green ramcard with the room number branded into it. "Checkout's at noon." The rabbit glanced at the Uzi. "Any shooting'll bring the wrath of God on you."

She nodded and took the cardkey.

The stairs were littered with garbage, plaster, and unconscious moreaus. Room 615 was on the sixth floor, overlooking the abandoned construction next door. The thick metal door opened on a square room, four meters on a side. The disease-green paint seemed to be the only thing holding the plaster to the walls. Black-specked yellow curtains turned the frozen white sunlight the color of urine. The color matched the room's smell. The sheets on the bed were laced with fur from the previous occupant, as was the claw-marked recliner.

Evi shut the door behind her and turned on the overhead light. The circular fluorescent pinged a few times before it lit with a nervous, vibrating blue glow. Evi pulled the recliner around in front of the comm.

The comm was anchored in a black textured plastic case. The case bore scars from cigarettes and knives but remained firmly bolted to the wall opposite the foot of the bed. She sat down in front of it and turned it on.

As it warmed up, Evi was treated to moans and heavy breathing provided by the hotel's piped-in broadcast. When the black and white low-res display focused, Evi saw a familiar-looking Pakistani canine. It might not be the same movie that had been playing on Times Square, but it certainly was the same actor. Small world.

The first thing Evi did was get on an outside line and call Diana. Diana answered the comm call immediately. *"You're where?"*

"The address is right."

Diana shook her head. "You're in the middle of the Bronx? Are you all right?"

"Yes and yes."

"Mind telling me what happened?"

"Brush with the cops and the Feds. Moreytown seemed a good place to disappear for a little while."

Diana was quiet for a while, seeming to weigh what she was going to say next. "Are you going to come back?"

"There's a lot . . ." A lot she had to do, a lot she had to think about, a lot she had to come to terms with. "I don't know."

There was no mistaking the disappointment that crossed Diana's face. "I appreciate the call. Do you insist on continuing to go it alone?"

Diana had a point. Evi might be able to survive on her own, but if she ever intended to *do* anything about the forces arrayed against her, she needed help. Price might be an option, if she could get to him. However, if she was right and Hofstadter had taken over control of the operation, Price might be as much a solo act as she was at the moment. "You still think the moreau underground might be willing to help me?"

"You're fighting the same forces the movement's been fighting for the past fifteen years."

By doing things like bombing the New York Public Library? She couldn't help picturing them as nothing more than a group of rabid terrorists. Then again, that's what she was supposed to be right now, wasn't it? "Can you tell me who to contact out here?"

Diana looked a little pained. "I haven't been close to the movement for a long time—"

Evi suddenly remembered the address Nohar had given her. It was down here in the Bronx. Maybe Nohar had had the same thoughts about the moreau underground that Diana had. And what *did* "G1:26" mean?

She typed it in on the battered keyboard and asked. "You know what that means?"

"7:26 Eastern Standard—"

"Other than that."

Diana stared at the screen and shrugged. "Hmm." After a few minutes of silence she started mumbling. ". . . after our likeness—"

"What's that?"

"Benefits of a Catholic education. Every time I see numbers separated by a colon, I think chapter and verse."

"You were quoting?"

"Genesis 1:26." Diana's voice took on a pontifical tone. "*And God said, let us make man in our image, after our likeness: and let them have dominion over the fish of the sea, and over the fowl of the air, and over the cattle, and over all the earth, and over every creeping thing that creepeth upon the earth.*"

Evi sat back on the recliner and started laughing, inaudibly. That was one hell of a password for the moreau underground.

"Does that help?" Diana asked.

Evi shook her head. "I think so, thanks."

"You're welcome."

"I guess that's it."

"Good luck." Diana added, "and you really look much better without the sunglasses."

Diana cut the connection.

Evi sighed and emptied her pack. Her jumpsuit was there, clean now, as well as her leather. Most of the equipment she had started out with was trash. The magazines and extra barrel for the Mishkov were useless without the gun. All that was left was her stun rod.

She pressed the test key and a green LED winked at her.

She stripped out of the trashed exec suit and stretched. She considered sitting down, but she looked at the fur on the seat of the recliner and put the jumpsuit on first.

Since she had the comm, she tried calling David Price again. He was still locking out incoming calls. His comm was probably programmed to respond to secure transmissions from Frey's comm.

That did her a lot of good.

She sighed and ruffled through Sukiota's wallet. Not much of anything there beyond the standard ID, a few cardkeys, one with the NYPD logo. The only thing remotely interesting she'd gotten off of Sukiota was the blank white card.

"What's this?" she asked herself.

Evi plopped it into the comm's card reader. She had to hit it a few times to get it going.

The screen fuzzed in on the National Security Agency logo. After a few seconds the screen started flashing all sorts of top-secret and restricted warnings at her. She tapped on the keyboard and the database program asked for her security clearance or the card's info would be wiped.

She debated a moment on whether she should risk her old passwords or pop the card and wait until she found a real hacker. The key word was "wait." She did not feel like she had loads of time.

Besides, clearance passwords for these files were based on security level, not individual agents. It shouldn't care if the Agency thought she was dead.

She typed a ten character alphanumeric.

The screen blanked.

There was a nervous few seconds as she listened to the laser head knocking around inside the cardreader. The green indicator on the front of the case flashed a few times.

Then the knocking from the reader ceased and the screen ran up a menu. Apparently her access codes were still good.

It was a database card, similar to the library's. Only, instead of just the raw data, this one had its own shell program. And from a brief glance at the menu, the data on this card was a lot more specific and to the point. Sukiota must have DL'd the info from Langley as soon as she'd gotten a look at the peeper's surveillance footage.

Each file was ID'd by an NSA picture. She knew the picture for Ezra Frey, David Price, Erin Hofstadter, Dr. Scott Fitzgerald, Dr. Leo Davidson. A picture of the sniper was identified with the one word in quotes, "Gabriel."

Last was a file on her. Her picture was a human-looking one where she was wearing her contacts. The human eyes made the picture look slightly wrong.

She spent a few hours perusing what the Agency's computers said about the conspirators.

Ezra Frey graduated from the USMC to Defense Intel during the hottest part of the Pan-Asian war. Advocated the unpopular position that the U.S. should intervene to defend Japan and the Subcontinent. Frey was saying that in '26, when it looked like things were going well for the Indo-Pacific affiance. A year later, New Delhi was nuked and nine bloody years followed before Tokyo suffered the same fate. In '35 he moved to the Agency, and began making the same noises about the Islamic Axis and Israel. The U.S. remained noninterventionist, and in six years Tel Aviv was blasted into a shallow coastal lake.

Erin Hofstadter had been born in the EEC, a European army brat. Oxford was the least of the schools from which he had a doctorate. He was an Agency advisor throughout his two-decade stint in the State Department. According to the file he'd been missing ever since a fact-finding mission to occupied Japan in late '53. It was presumed that he had been taken hostage by nationalistic factions attached to the NLF even though no credit was ever taken or demands made.

David Price was Pol-Sci, specialist in conspiracy theories. Sent up a few memos that suggested that some unknown agency was manipulating the U.S. government into self-destructive activities. He listed a dozen specific examples, including the U.S. nonparticipation in the Pan-Asian war, the antitechnology legislation by the Congress, up to the mothballing of the NASA deep-space probes when a launch would be cheaper than maintenance.

Dr. Scott Fitzgerald was a xenobiologist. He worked for NASA on the development of sensors on the deep-probe projects, and he had been chief of NASA's orbital ear project. That project had, Fitzgerald alleged, found evidence of intelligent signals of nonterrestrial origin. This was before Congress axed the ear and mothballed the deep-probe project in the space of four years in the early '40s.

Leo Davidson had degrees in computer science, engineering, and physics. He ran a particle collider in the Midwest, looking for tachyons, until the funding was cut and the collider was shut down. For various West Coast companies he tried to redevelop hard-wired biointerfaces, build control systems for fusion-drive rockets, did theoretical work in nano-computers, along with a dozen other cutting-edge disciplines. Each one, close to midstream, ran into Congressional legislation that either stalled or killed the project, generally in the name of public safety.

"Gabriel" was a freelancer. He had worked for nationalists in the EEC, *and* the government of the EEC. He worked for a half-dozen North African countries, where he participated in three successive coups in Ethiopia alone. In South America, he worked for a number of Latin-based megacorps, removing political obstacles in Brazil, Colombia, and Peru. Hitman, assassin, demolition expert, sold himself to the highest bidder. The moral equivalent of the Afghani canines.

All of them were supposed to be dead.

Evi could see how a core of this conspiracy could have formed. Most of these men had been affected badly by the alien intervention. Frey and Price had seen an invisible hand at work in Asia, and Davidson and Fitzgerald were scientists whose research was being interfered with.

Hofstadter seemed to have no such personal stake, and Gabriel was simply a hired gun. A gun probably brought in by Hofstadter.

Hofstadter was, born and bred, a creature of the intelligence community.

Hofstadter had taken over Frey's operation and was trying to clean house by putting a bullet in her.

Nyogi Enterprises was after her. Nyogi's interest was in the cadre of rogue Agency operatives. Nyogi had both her and Frey under surveillance; they'd even purchased the buildings they resided in. The veep had said it: "They want their people back."

She was sure that Nyogi's involvement with the NLF was only the tip of the iceberg as far as political machinations were involved. She had seen it before. The aliens insulated themselves within corporate fronts and used them as funnels to distribute massive assets to further their agenda. The agenda, broadly defined, being the technological stagnation of the planet. Nyogi Enterprises fit the profile. The creatures running Nyogi knew about Frey's operation and wanted the four aliens that Evi had captured in Cleveland.

When she'd found that cell of aliens running Midwest Lapidary, she had initiated Frey's conspiracy. Whatever the exact details were, a group of Agency operatives had falsified records and diverted resources to keep the aliens secret from the government. From all appearances, the conspirators still had the four aliens Evi captured, and somehow the conspiracy was exploiting them.

She sighed and turned off the comm. She was feeling the weight of events bear down on her. It seemed that every reflection brought to light a new set of players with their own agenda.

She yawned and realized how tired she was. For all the fur shed upon it, the bed looked pretty good at this point.

Chapter 16

She woke to the sound of the door breaking open. She grabbed the Uzi and rolled off the edge of the bed opposite the door, sending a shiver of agony down her left arm. Before she could orient herself and bring the Uzi to cover the door, machine gun fire swept the wall above her. Green-painted plaster flew everywhere, yellow plastic drapes shredded, and the window exploded.

"Toss the gun." The voice had a Bronx accent, feline pronunciation. To drive the point home, whoever-it-was started pumping shots into the bed.

Evi decided that she wasn't in a position to argue, and tossed the Uzi over the bed. The gunfire ceased.

"Get up."

She did so, raising her hands.

In the doorway was a jaguar. Black-spotted, two meters tall, and holding a vintage AK-47. The jaguar was female and wore a black beret, khaki shorts, and a black kevlar vest with a corporal's insignia on the collar. Behind the cat, in the hall, was a collection of at least a half-dozen armed rodents, similarly clad.

"Your chance to say something," said the cat. "Make it good."

Welcome to the morey underground, Evi thought. What the fuck did they expect her to say? She stood there facing them, hands raised, trying to second-guess the cat with the gun.

It was worth a try. "*And God said, Let us make man in our image.*"

The jaguar nodded and didn't shoot her.

She'd assumed that Nohar was giving her a line on these people, that the cryptic "G1:26" he typed was some sort of password, and that Diana had interpreted its meaning correctly. That was two more assumptions than she wanted to make in a situation like this.

The jaguar backed out of the room, keeping her covered with the rifle. "The General wants a word with you."

At least she seemed to have made the right assumptions. Appropriate password. Moreaus had a well-developed sense of irony.

The squad of moreaus ushered her out of the building, one rat with her backpack, one rat with the Uzi. There was one point on the stairs where she could have dived out a second-story window and made a break for it. However, she had intended to contact these people. And "the General" seemed to reciprocate the feeling.

Besides, she didn't want to be stuck alone in the Bronx with only a switchblade.

The manager was nowhere to be seen as they hustled her through the sweltering lobby. Three rabbits in black kevlar preceded her out the door and to a waiting vehicle.

Evi stopped and stared at what they had parked outside of "ROOMS." She didn't start moving again until the jaguar prodded her with the rifle.

Where the hell did they get a French APC?

It was trapezoidal, splashed with black, gray and shallow-brown urban camouflage, and squatted on three axles whose tires were Evi's height. The armored personnel carrier had been through a number of refits, so Evi couldn't tell which of five models it could have been. Extra plates had been welded to the exterior. The major modification was a semicircular ring of plates sitting on top of the thing, encircling a machine-gun mount bearing an M-60.

Things like this shouldn't have been in the Bronx. It represented a big change from when she worked in the anti-terrorist wing of the Agency, and it threw a wrench into most of the scenarios she'd worked on for the Domestic Crisis Think Tank.

It did explain how they expected to get around on these rotten roads.

They squeezed her in the back with the rodents; the jaguar drove. The ride seemed to be an exercise in proving the maximum velocity of the APC. Evi swore that the jaguar aimed at every bad spot of road that they passed, and at one point the APC lurched over a huge bump that could have only been a car.

After a while, they slowed and she began to hear noise outside. She could hear gunfire, occasional animal yells, one explosion. The

APC stopped, and the jaguar radioed something ahead in Portuguese, a language Evi didn't know.

After a few more fits and starts, the APC finally stopped and began powering down. The jaguar looked down into the passenger space. "Fernando, Gonzales, you come with me. The rest of you report back to the dorms."

Dorms?

The rear of the APC opened and the jaguar walked by, pulling Evi along by the right elbow. "We're going to the greenhouse. Don't bolt. We aren't enemies—yet."

Evi nodded, thinking of how much emphasis the cat had put on the word "yet."

The quartet moved out. The jaguar and two rats hustled her along unceremoniously. Evi began to realize the scope of what the APC implied. They walked out of a parking garage that was full of all manner of armored vehicles designed for urban combat. There were more French APCs on the mid-level of the garage, and the armor got heavier as they descended, until, on the ground level, she saw two T-101 Russian tanks flanking a Pakistani self-propelled artillery piece. A chunk of the second level of the garage had been knocked out to fit them in.

If these folks were careful, a satellite wouldn't have a clue.

They passed sentries that guarded the entrance to Fordham University. Unlike the Bronx she'd seen up to now, all the rubble had been cleared from the grounds. She saw bulldozers on the edge of the property, parked on a massive wall of rubble that now formed a wall around the campus. Once they walked onto the campus, she saw the rear end of two machine-gun nests embedded in the inside of the wall.

They rounded a corner and, through an opening in the wall, she could see the gray-painted walls of Fordham Hospital and makeshift landing pads that held a quartet of helicopters and dozens of aircars.

She was walking through a fully operational paramilitary base that sat only three-and-a-half miles from Manhattan. If these folks wanted to, they could simply unpark that Pakistani artillery piece and lob shells from Yonkers to Battery Park. Where the Hell were the Feds? The government should have landed on this long before it had gotten this big.

They passed a group of more sentries and a rubble-bordered freeway and walked into snow-covered parkland. As they walked, Evi realized that the snow hadn't covered the terrain naturally. The surface of the snow was artificially smooth, and the snow itself was dirty-brown.

They had buried huge ruts in the grass under the snow, hiding the vehicle tracks from the Fed's spy satellites. These people were good. Then again, why shouldn't they be? The vast majority of moreaus were designed for military use, and most of the immigrant moreys in the States were veterans.

They passed a sign directing them to the Enid A. Haupt Conservatory. Most of the sporadic gunfire was coming from the south.

As they wove through the artificial forest of exotic trees, she kept thinking they were less than four miles from New York. It reminded her too much of Israel. One major difference: the Israeli defenders knew the Axis was there.

She wondered if these moreaus had any missiles.

The lines of the conservatory building were wrapped in overgrown vines and bushes. From the outside the place looked long-abandoned. Inside was different. The original plants and decoration had been cleaned out, walls taken down, and the floor now looked like the situation room at the Pentagon. Under diffuse white light from a snow-covered glass ceiling, there were moreaus of every stripe operating computers, radar screens, and communication consoles. The air was filled with electronic whines and beeps. Maps of New York and the United States faced each other from opposite ends of the chamber.

The rabbits stopped at the door, and the jaguar ushered her around the periphery of the situation room. They stopped at a massive oak door, and the jaguar waved her to go ahead. Evi's escort had long ago shouldered her weapon.

She looked at the jaguar, then back at the situation room behind her, and realized that she'd *better* ally herself with the moreaus. If anyone even suspected that her allegiance was still anywhere near the Agency, she was dead after seeing all this.

She opened the door and walked in.

It was a small windowless office. Behind a chipped-green metal desk sat the biggest ursine that she had ever seen.

She—the bear was female—sat on the floor and still looked down at Evi from a height of two-and-a-half meters. Her fur was a dead black, with the light picking out highlights from muscles that snaked like steel belting. She wore a shoulder holster with a Chinese fourteen-millimeter automatic. The gun hung under a stump. Her right arm ended twelve centimeters from the shoulder in a mass of twisted red scar-tissue. Other than the holster, the only thing she wore was a black beret on her head with a single star as insignia.

With her one hand, she waved Evi toward the only chair in the room. "Welcome, Miss Isham." The bear's voice sounded like a lawnmower laced with molasses.

Evi sat. "You have the advantage."

The bear snuffed, apparently in good humor. "General Wu Sein at your service. Welcome to the Bronx Zoo."

"I thought we were in the Botanical Gardens."

General Wu snuffed again. "I refer to our entire complex. My people call it the Zoo."

"Oh."

"You display an unexpected amount of surprise for someone who is supposed to be working for us." General Wu opened a desk drawer and pulled out a teapot and a pair of cups. "Care for some tea?"

Evi shook her head. "You *know* the news stories are plants."

"Indeed." The general flipped the switch on the ceramic teapot, and it began to glow a little in the infrared. "But such fictions are destined to bring us together— Are you sure no tea? The humans left some very good herbs here when they abandoned the Gardens."

"No, thank you."

The general shrugged and began an elaborate one-handed preparation of her tea. They sat in silence for a while before the general spoke again. "You have questions that you do not ask."

"I didn't think I was in a position to ask anything."

"One is always in a position to ask questions." The general poured her tea. "It is just a matter of not forcing the answers."

"Then tell me what's going on here."

The general sipped. "I think you've perceived that already. An army is being trained and equipped here."

"In secret."

"Of course. If this was known, they would try and prevent us."

"Why?"

The general leaned back against the wall and finished her tea. "Why is a very complex question. Shall I be simplistic?"

"Justify it however you want."

"Simplistically, then. A few years ago a group of leaders in the moreau community, including myself, decided we should have the capability of defending ourselves."

"Defending . . ."

"Broaden your perceptions. You are too used to seeing any

moreau with a gun as a terrorist." The general poured another cup of tea. "If our goal was a political statement . . . You've seen what kind of 'terror' we could utilize."

The general lifted the cup and blew the steam away from the top. "Since half the anti-moreau congressmen were indicted in that CIA scandal six years ago, things have been improving. So we sit, and wait, and hope we're not necessary."

"What would make you necessary?"

She sipped the tea. "Anything we perceive as an attack." The general put down her cup and scratched her stump. "Now. I ask questions."

For nearly an hour, that's what General Wu did. She was polite, meandering, conversational, and as thorough as any Agency debriefing. Halfway through, Evi began to realize that the general had prior knowledge of quite a lot of her story. And, while Evi was intentionally vague about the nature of the aliens because she was unsure how the general would react, the general seemed to know what she was avoiding.

Over the eighth cup of tea, the general asked, "Now, are you certain that these 'creatures' are in control of Nyogi Enterprises?"

"As sure as I can be without any direct evidence."

"You present me with a dilemma."

"How?"

"These beings, you say, bought congressmen. They wish to stagnate technological progress, correct?"

"Yes."

"There's an unfortunate side effect for moreaus. These men they buy get elected on anti-moreau platforms. They hire creatures like the Afghanis, for the humans to point to and say how bad the moreaus are. They're our enemies more surely than any human."

Evi nodded.

"You wonder why this is a dilemma?"

"Yes."

The general snorted. "You never asked who financed my Zoo."

It took a few seconds for that to sink in. "You're financed by Nyogi?"

"If what you say is true, it explains a few things. I told you 'why' was a complex question. All my people have a different reason for working with me. Some are more—hmm—direct than myself."

"You have people split off and go solo on you?"

"Too many, recently. And our financiers have been implying that funds might cease if some 'results' weren't forthcoming."

The general finished her last cup of tea.

"Why're you telling me this?"

"Because I have little choice."

"As far as I'm concerned, you have the advantage here."

"This doesn't just concern you. It concerns a few million more-aus who might suffer a human pogrom if our armed forces become a pawn of these creatures' political aims. You're going to help prevent that."

"How?"

"You are going to do for us what Nyogi wants you to do for them. You are going to help us locate and capture the four aliens you found in Cleveland."

Evi's surprise must have shown.

"Oh, you never did mention the word 'alien' did you? Or 'extraterrestrial.' "

"No, I didn't."

"Wise, I suppose. If I didn't have corroborating information, or people vouching for you, I might have problems believing your story."

"Corroborating information?"

The general nodded as she put away her tea service. Then she hit a button on her comm. Outside, Evi heard an electronic buzzer. "Miss Isham, we'll have a lot to talk about later, but now I have a meeting to attend. So I am going to leave you in the hands of an old friend of yours."

Evi turned her head as the door opened. Into the room walked a 260-centimeter tall, 300-kilo tiger named Nohar Rajasthan.

Chapter 17

Nohar took her to the Zoo's "guest house," an old frat building. The bricks next to the trio of Greek letters had been knocked out to make room for an anti-aircraft battery. He led her through a recycled-plywood door and to the half of the building that didn't serve as an ammo dump. The smell of machine oil and gunpowder hung heavy in the cold air.

She ended up in a small room with a sagging bed and cracked plaster wall. The window overlooked the rubble wall surrounding the campus, and the only warmth in the room was from a small electric heater.

She sat in the bed, and Nohar showed no sign of leaving.

"Babysitter?"

Nohar nodded.

Evi took stock of the changes six years had wrought in the tiger. The one thing that hit her was that the colors in his coat had faded, and the lines between black and yellow had lost their sharpness. Age, or maybe the effect of the California sun. His tail moved a little more nervously. There were one or two more scars on his back where the hair was growing back white. His expression had evolved. The white fur under his rounded chin was longer. The wrinkled grooves, growl-lines, above his broad nose were deeper. And he wore a round gold band in his ear.

That was the first time that Evi, moreau expert or not, realized that engineered feline hands were not well designed for jewelry.

Nohar appropriated an overstuffed recliner that wasn't made for someone of his size. She heard protesting creaks and the twang of a spring giving way. He remained silent, staring out at the rubble wall.

"What are you doing here?"

Nohar sighed, a sound that began as an intake of breath and deepened to a deep bass rumble that sounded like a hostile purr. "Sitting on you so the Grand Dame Ursine doesn't lose an intelligence asset."

She leaned back on the bed, still tired. The ceiling above her was innocent of plaster, and holes had been knocked in the slats to reveal pipes and junction boxes beyond.

"When did you become political?"

"Still trying to link me to moreau terrorism?"

She turned her head to look at the tiger. He was still looking out the window. His right hand was clawing the upholstery on the chair. She was sorry for the fact that she hadn't spent enough time with moreaus to pick up on *their* scent cues. She could read humans like a book, but tigers . . .

Nohar was broadcasting powerful waves of something.

"Sounds like you don't want to be here."

He snarled. "You think I *like* all this?"

She forgot her potential nap and propped herself up on her right elbow to look at him. There was a momentary twinge from her left shoulder when she moved. It quickly faded. She hoped that the much-lauded healing powers of the Hiashu-enhanced human projects were finally at work on her shoulder.

"Want to elaborate?"

He turned toward her. "Wu and company are going to screw us over again."

Evi's puzzlement must have shown.

"I'm a moreau, I should approve?" Nohar shook his head. "Violence breeds more of the same. This is a disaster waiting to happen."

"Wu portrayed this operation as defensive." She wondered how she had gotten into the position of defending what, by most of the definitions she had been using during her professional life, was a terrorist operation. She was astounded by how little loyalty she found in her heart for either the organization or the ideals she had worked for for the past sixteen years. All this time had she been just as much a mercenary as those Afghanis?

"What happens when the government gets wind of this?" Nohar asked.

"They'll . . ." That was a bad thought. There was no question about the military trying to shut this place down. That would definitely fit Wu's definition of a direct attack.

Nohar nodded, as if he heard the rest of her thought.

She could see a national wave of violence in the moreau community, igniting a backlash that could wipe out all the progress moreaus had made toward first-class citizenship. The anti-moreau forces could use that kind of conflagration to finally repeal the moreau amendment. She could see the pogrom that Wu feared.

"I was right," she said. "You *don't* belong here."

Nohar chuckled. If she didn't know moreaus, and this moreau in particular, she would have found the sound threatening. He had an unnerving tendency to show his teeth when he laughed, and his canines were the size of her thumb. "As if I had a choice. It's your fault."

"What do you mean by that?"

"My life may be in danger, the alien business may be rearing its ugly head—where else do you think a morey would go to ground?"

"What about your wife?"

"Safe." From the way he said it, she knew not to ask any further about his spouse.

"How long have you known these people?"

"Four years. From the Los Angeles chapter."

"This is national?"

Nohar chuckled again. "*Look* at this place."

She slowly dropped back to stare at the ceiling and began to reassess her world view. "Why'd you vouch for me? I worked for the Feds."

"You aren't human."

"Meaning?"

"When the shit hits the fan, species transcends politics."

She closed her eyes and tried to sleep.

General Wu finally sent for them, well after nightfall. They were fetched by the same jaguar that had snatched Evi from "ROOMS." She was no longer armed with the AK-47. Evi's standing in this community was on an upswing.

Instead of the conservatory, the jaguar led them across an unlit campus to a blacked-out building. Inside, the place was well lit. It was the windows that had been painted black. The jaguar brought them through a set of doors flanked by lepine guards in black berets and into an auditorium out of another century. General Wu stood at a podium that barely came past her waist. Behind her was a rank of green blackboards set in dark-varnished wood frames. In the audience was a collection of five moreaus. With their arrival, seven moreaus, one frank.

"Welcome," Wu addressed them. She gestured them down to the front with her stump. "My intelligence team has informed me that if we have any time to do what I plan, it is running out."

Evi walked down to the front and sat next to a lean lepus who was missing an ear. Nohar stood; the human desks weren't made for people his size. The jaguar barely fit herself into the seat next to Evi.

Wu continued, directing her comments at Evi. "The NLF team from Nyogi Enterprises must have had you under surveillance for some time. Following your personal contacts, and using you as a stalking horse to uncover the identities of your employers and coworkers. Would this conflict with any of your observations?"

"That makes sense except—"

"Why kidnap you?"

Evi nodded.

Wu tapped at a keyboard hidden by the podium. "We're assuming there was some recent triggering event that made Nyogi desperate. They intend to gain quickly now by force the information they hoped to gain slowly by stealth."

"The location of the aliens . . ." Evi whispered.

The room became very quiet. The only noises were moreys breathing and shifting their weight and the buzzing of the uncertain fluorescents. The pause lengthened uncomfortably until Evi said, "I don't know that."

That wasn't a comfortable admission. Not only because there were eight pairs of eyes looking at her for the answer, a few with blatant hostility, but because it was something she *should* know.

Nohar spoke. "Nyogi assumes that you do."

She turned to the tiger. "I *should*. I was the one who bottled up the aliens in the first place. They assumed I was an insider."

"A human," Nohar said, "would have been."

She shook her head. "Species before politics."

General Wu slapped the side of the podium, drawing the audience's attention back to her. "We need to reach those four aliens before Nyogi does. The window in which we have to act as rapidly closing. Isham and the Feds have set back their operational capability, but it is doubtful that it would take longer than forty-eight hours for a corporation with the resources of Nyogi to assemble another team to go after a secondary target. Someone else who knows where the aliens are.

"Isham, if you do not have that information, you must lead us to someone who has."

Evi looked at the moreaus surrounding her. Nohar was carefully cultivating an expressionless demeanor, though he was habitually making clawing motions with his right hand. The jaguar corporal sitting next to her was staring at her, teeth barred in a expression of silent hostility. The general stood directly in front of her, like a giant wooden totem. The one-eared rabbit to her right looked at her, nose twitching as if in curiosity. The four rats beyond showed mixtures of apprehension and hostility.

It hit her all at once, exactly how far she had removed herself from everything she had known, worked for, believed . . .

"Wait a minute." Evi stood up. "Information is one thing—"

She could feel the weight of the moreau's attention. Not only the ones in this room, not just the complex, but the weight of the surrounding community of three million . . .

"What, exactly, do you object to?" Wu asked.

What, exactly? It wasn't like she hadn't shifted allegiances before. If anything, the goals and principles Wu was offering were clearer than the ones the Agency offered.

"What I object to is a strong feeling of deja vu."

"Meaning?"

"I crossed the Atlantic in '45, before a frank had *any* civil rights in this country. The Feds said, 'Of course you'll work for us.' In a dozen years I managed to convince myself I was working on the side of right and justice, only to have the rug pulled out from under me."

"Isham," Nohar said. She turned to face the tiger, who was the only face in the room that held any sympathy. "You're too used to taking orders. You can work with someone without working *for* them."

General Wu spoke. "We aren't asking you to adopt our politics or join our organization. We're asking only that you aid us in achieving something of mutual, if not universal, benefit: Namely, capturing and publicizing these aliens."

Evi looked up at the general. Nohar was right. The one specific thing that bothered her was the prospect of owing her allegiance to another political entity that would use her as a pawn and sacrifice her without a second thought. She had played that game all her life.

It was time she owed allegiance to herself.

"I'll help you." She sat down and crossed her legs. "With two conditions—"

The jaguar spoke. "You're in no position—"

"Corporal Gurgueia," Wu interrupted. "Miss Isham has been quite cooperative. We'd do well to hear her out."

Evi waited for other outbursts from the crowd. Other than glowering stares from a pair of the rats, there were no overt objections.

"As I said, two conditions. First, this isn't to be a brute force operation. No explosives, and if there's gunfire, that means someone screwed up." She stared directly at the jaguar as she said that.

Wu nodded and the jaguar emitted a quiet growl.

"Second, *I'm* in charge of the operation."

The entire room started talking at once. Except for Nohar, who looked as though he expected her to say that, and Wu, who looked like she was above shouting down the audience.

Despite the dozen objections flying around her, Evi smiled. Yes, she did have little choice but to participate in this escapade. However, the general had little choice but to let her participate on her own terms. General Wu had said herself that the window of opportunity was rapidly closing.

It took nearly five minutes before the moreaus quieted down enough to let the general speak.

"Respectfully, General, you aren't going to seriously consider this, are you?" asked Corporal Gurgueia, the jaguar.

"I'm doing more than that. I am doing just as Isham suggests. We need a specialist in covert activity, not urban warfare. We have too little time to debate command structure." General Wu swept her gaze across the room. "Is there anyone who feels that they'll be unable to operate under these conditions?"

No one spoke.

"Good. Our first order of business is to locate and make contact with someone who has the information we need. Isham?"

"If no one's gotten to David Price . . ."

David Price was the only member of the Domestic Crisis Think Tank whose outside life Evi knew anything about. He'd been the only member of the think tank with whom she'd had more than a strictly professional relationship. He was perhaps the one friend she had in there.

He had a cover identity, David King, who lived in a modular tract house in Jackson Heights. She knew the house; David had once taken her there.

Now, as she flew a matte-black GM Kestrel toward the East River, she wondered about that. He had been a part of Frey's conspiracy all along and had allowed her to be duped. Evi doubted that she had ever had any friends who weren't friends of convenience.

Except, perhaps, for Diana.

The Kestrel was a big aircar, even bigger with most of the interior seats stripped out of it. Even so, they could fit only four members of the team in it. She drove, the one-eared rabbit named Huaras sat next to her, and in the back sat Nohar and Corporal Gurgueia. The extra weight made the Kestrel handle like a wet brick.

It was exactly five after midnight when she hit the shore of the Bronx. As soon as she left shore, she raised the aircar to legal heights and switched on the lights and the transponder. Instantly, it seemed, the comm came alive with frantic instructions from La Guardia Air Traffic Control. No one commented on the aircar's sudden appearance. They wanted them to get into another air corridor, they were too close to Rikers.

She banked away from Rikers Island, and a subsonic rumble rattled the windows as a ballistic shuttle started rising on a steep ascent from the Rikers Island launch facility. The shuttle passed so close that she could see individual heat tiles on its underside.

She did a long banking right turn around La Guardia, over Flushing and Shea Stadium, and as the Manhattan skyline rotated into view in front of them, Jackson Heights slid by below. She cut the lights and began the descent.

The Kestrel put down on a shabby excuse for a back yard, raising a cloud of fresh snow. It sat in a brief blizzard of its own making. The gull-wing doors on the Kestrel flew open, shedding snow, and the moreaus stepped out. The rabbit covered the rear of the house with his machine pistol, Gurgueia tried to cover everything else with her AK-47. Nohar stood out of the way of the guns and waited for Evi.

Evi stepped out of the Kestrel, pulling on a new pair of gloves and taking the medkit and the gun Wu had provided her. The gun was a fairly straightforward Smith and Wesson ten-millimeter automatic. Her wounded shoulder was doped up on painkiller, so she could holster it without wincing.

"Gurgueia, you go cover the front. Huaras, take the rear. Me and Nohar are going in."

Gurgueia seemed to bristle a bit at taking orders from Evi, but she did as she was told. Huaras wordlessly took cover by the Kestrel. Evi ran to the back door. She spared a glance at the driveway. Price's car, an old Chevy Caldera that would have looked like a police car if it weren't for the lime-green paint job, was parked in the open garage, plugged into the vehicle feed. The snowcover on the driveway was unblemished by tire tracks or footprints. Even from where Evi was, she could see the blinking green light on the Caldera's dash that was registering a full charge on the inductors. The car'd been parked for a while.

She got up on one side of the back door, Nohar on the other. Using the doorframe for cover, she tried the lock. The magnetic keypad didn't want to open. She briefly wished for the electronic gear that'd been trashed in her pack.

It wasn't a security building, though. She saw no trace of an alarm system.

She glanced at Nohar to make sure he was covering her and grabbed the keypad-cardkey unit with both hands and yanked it off the side of the house. It came reluctantly, with a rasping noise. It hung on to the doorframe with twenty-centimeter-long bolts that pulled a chunk of wood the size of Evi's hand along with them. It took all of five seconds for her to find the right wire, strip it, and short out the magnetic lock.

A blue spark, the slight smell of melting insulation, and the door drifted open.

She led the way into the darkened house, gun drawn.

The kitchen was a mess. At first she thought that someone had beaten them to Price. Dishes were everywhere, lending the taint of spoiling food to everything in the room. The refrigerator hung open a crack, causing a dagger of light to slice diagonally across the room. She shut the refrigerator with her foot, to allow her eyes to adjust fully to the dark.

After a second of scanning the room, she realized that this was all Price's work. The pots left moldering on the stove, the coffee grounds overflowing the trash basket, the pile of slimy debris that overflowed the trash disposal—the room smelled like a compost heap, but there was no sign of a struggle, just lousy housekeeping.

When she was here before, she hadn't thought Price had been such a slob.

Something was definitely wrong here.

She stalked through the dining room, and the picture didn't change much. On the table sat pyramids of fast-food containers, old beer bulbs, pizza boxes that had been sitting around long enough to begin biodegrading. All the shades were drawn. The only source of light was from a streetlight streaming in the open door behind her.

In the living room sat Price's comm, surrounded by an audience of beer bulbs and news faxes.

On a coffee table between the couch and the comm was sitting a box of ten-millimeter ammunition. The box had ripped open, and bullets had rolled out over the table and the floor. The remains of two more boxes were on the floor. Evi kicked one, for shotgun shells.

She looked at Nohar and whispered, "If a gun goes off—"

"—somebody screwed up," Nohar finished for her.

She started up the stairs. The stairway was strewn with empty food boxes, dirty clothing, and beer bulbs. She also noticed a few bottles of harder stuff. Drunks with guns had to be one of the top items on Evi's list of unpretty pictures.

At the head of the stairs were six doors. Only one, the bathroom, hung open. From the bathroom came the sound of water dripping and an endlessly filling toilet tank. The entire second floor was permeated with the smell of cat shit. As she edged toward the bathroom, where the smell was concentrated, she saw the culprit nestled next to one of the closed doors.

If she remembered correctly, Price had at least four cats. This one's name was Lao-Tze.

The overstuffed black cat looked up at the two intruders. He addressed Evi with a questioning. "Mwrowr?" As soon as he saw Nohar, he arched his back and started hissing, backing toward the bathroom.

She looked into a bathroom and was greeted by the miasma of an overflowing litter box. The cats had long since abandoned the box and had moved on to towels, the rug, stray pieces of Price's underwear.

As Lao-Tze backed away from Nohar, Evi silently thanked him for identifying the bedroom where Price was holed up.

Once Lao-Tze had vacated the doorway, Evi waved Nohar toward it with her gun. She stationed herself by the opening side and listened. There were a number of cats in there, and someone breathing.

She faced Nohar and started mouthing a countdown.

"Three . . . Two . . . One . . ."

Evi threw open the door and dived into the room, rolling and taking cover behind an overstuffed recliner. A displaced Siamese hissed at her. She braced the gun in both hands, aiming over the arm of the chair.

Price lay on the bed, fully clothed, oblivious.

It took a few seconds for her to realize he was alive. But he *was* breathing, and he was radiating faintly in the infrared. He was sleeping off what looked and smelled like a substantial drunk. There were more beer bulbs scattered around this room than the rest of the house. Lying at the foot of the bed was a Vind 10 Auto that had been improperly broken down. Curled up next to the barrel was a black-and-gray tabby. She had remembered Price calling that one Meow-Tse-Tung.

What worried Evi was the fact that Price had a sawed-off double-barreled shotgun clutched to his chest. His finger was resting on the trigger. It wasn't pointing at anything, but if Price was startled out of unconsciousness, he could blow a hole in the wall by accident. Evi would like to avoid the police involvement a gunshot would bring.

She waved Nohar into the room to cover her. She holstered the gun and opened the medkit on her belt. She pulled out the airhypo and slipped in a trank cartridge.

Damn. She almost cursed out loud. She couldn't risk the trank on someone who smelled like a brewery. The drug might put Price into a coma, the state he was in.

She put the trank away and started creeping up on the bed. Easy, she told herself, the shotgun wasn't even pointed at her. She just had to get the weapon away from the drunk before he became aware of his surroundings. Easy.

She was only a half step away from Price, when she found cat number four. The cat had been under the bed with only its tail sticking out. She'd been so intent on watching Price for any reaction, she hadn't kept a good eye on her footing. Her boot came down on the cat's tail accompanied by the loudest and most grating screech she had ever heard.

Price's eyes shot open and Evi dived for the gun. She did the only thing she could think of: she slammed the edge of her right hand in front of the shotgun's hammers as they cocked.

She lay on top of Price, and two nails of pain were driven into her hand as the hammers pierced her glove, and then skin.

But the shotgun remained silent.

A huge furry arm extended over Evi's shoulder and pointed a grotesquely oversized automatic at Price's forehead.

"Don't," said Nohar.

Price froze and Evi gently removed herself and the shotgun. She unhooked the shotgun's grip on her hand, gratified to find that her hand retained its mobility. Even if clenching it into a fist now felt as though she were trying to rip the side of it open.

"Damn it!" She said in a harsh whisper. She broke open the shotgun and dumped the shells on the floor. Then she really broke it by bending the barrel much farther back than it was supposed to go. There was a quiet snap as a connector gave way, and the gun fell to the ground in two distinct pieces.

Price's eyes kept darting from her to Nohar, then back again.

"Cover him," she told Nohar, "I'm going to check the rest of the house."

Nohar nodded as a yellow tabby crawled out from under the bed and began to weave between Nohar's legs.

Of the four remaining doors, three were empty bedrooms. The last was a linen closet.

Evi was closing the door to the closet when she heard three distinct gunshots in rapid succession. She darted into Price's room, but the tableau remained unchanged. Nohar looked as surprised as Price did.

Someone outside had screwed up.

Chapter 18

"Grab him," she told Nohar. "Get him back to the car."

Nohar picked up Price and draped him across his shoulder. Price still seemed too stunned to say anything.

More gunshots, definitely from outside this time. Corporal Gurgueia was trigger-happy. The shades rippled and shredded as a few shots tore into the bedroom window. Evi ducked on the ground with the cats.

A spotlight swept by the window washing it with a white glare and black abstract shadows. She edged up to the window so she could get a good look at the front of the house.

Another Chevy Caldera had slid to a stop diagonally across the street in front of the house. This one *was* a cop car, flashers going, spotlight sweeping for Gurgueia, two cops huddled behind it.

Evi ducked as the spotlight swept by again.

She hit her throat-mike. *"Gurgueia!"*

"Corporal—" Gurgueia paused to lay down more fire. "Gurgueia here."

"Cease fire, back to the car."

"But—"

"Now! I'll cover you."

"Acknowledged."

The cops would stay cautious for a half-minute or so once the firing stopped. Evi peeked over the ledge of the window; neither of the cops looked injured. If they were smart, they'd stay back behind the cop car until reinforcements arrived.

She wanted to give them something to take up most of their attention.

She braced her automatic, two-handed, on the sill, aiming out the busted window. There was a feeling of pressure from under the bandage on her left shoulder. That was her shoulder's way of telling her that if it weren't for the painkiller, she'd be blacking out from the pain.

She didn't aim at the cops but at a small area between the trunk and the back seat.

The cops looked as though they were about to become adventurous, so she emptied the magazine. Nine shots, and at least one hit a charged inductor. She could smell it from here. Smoke began to pour from the remains of the trunk, and the spotlight began to flicker erratically.

She ran for the back door.

Everyone had backed toward the aircar. Nohar was already inside, his arms wrapped around Price. Evi was starting to hear distant sirens.

She dived into the Kestrel, followed by Huaras and Gurgueia. "What the fuck happened?"

They'd left the engine going, so all she had to do was engage the fans. The fans started with a high-pitched whine, and snow began flying around them, caught in the downwash of air.

Gurgueia spoke. "They slowed down and started sweeping that spotlight—"

Evi shook her head and took a few deep breaths as she made sure that the lights and the transponder were off. "So you opened fire."

"I think—" A perceptible growl evolved in Gurgueia's throat. Evi looked at the jaguar, and, eyes locked on her, maxed the acceleration of the Kestrel straight up.

"Never engage without clearing with your commands." Their eyes were locked on each other. The Kestrel kept rocketing upward.

Gurgueia broke eye contact. "You're right, of course, Commander."

Evi turned to look where she was going. The Kestrel was about to hit its maximum ceiling, and they seemed to have made it out of the area without a cop tail. She pulled a long turn and decided not to bother with the transponder.

Behind her, Price asked in a weak voice, "What's going on?"

"Dave, just shut up for now, okay?" She looked back at Price and couldn't help thinking of Chuck Dwyer, and how Chuck had looked at her when he saw her real eyes. It wasn't a rational connection to make. For one thing, Price had always known she wasn't human. For another, Price wasn't even looking at her. He was squeezed in the back with Gurgueia and Nohar and seemed to be dividing his attention between the two big cats.

Huaras spoke up in a heavily accented English, "Where we put down the car?"

Good point. It was not a good idea to put down anywhere near the base. Even without a transponder, Air Traffic Control would have a radar fix on them and would see where they landed. The cops by Price's house would have called them in. It wouldn't take a genius to put two and two together.

Evi could almost feel Sukiota breathing down her neck.

The Kestrel passed by La Guardia, and the comm lit up like Times Square on New Year's with incoming calls. The Kestrel's onboard computer was picking up two aircraft tailing her. One had an NYPD transponder. The other didn't have a transponder at all. So much for not having a cop tail.

"The question, Huaras, is do we put down at all."

She wished she were at the controls of that veep's Peregrine. At least that thing could maneuver. "What do . . ." Price began to say as Evi pointed the nose down at the East River. Altitude screamed by them as the Kestrel accelerated faster than the fans were ever designed to do.

"Nohar, look out the back. On the scope I have an unlabeled aircraft at a hundred meters and closing. Seven o'clock." She had to shout over the scream of rushing air.

Her knuckles were whitening on the wheel, and the plastic was splitting under her fingers. Pressure was building in her left shoulder. The Kestrel was flying down so fast that the snow around them was falling up. Below, Evi could see the landing lights at Rikers flying up to meet them.

"Helicopter, I think." Nohar yelled back.

"Make?"

"You kidding?"

When she could read the logo on the wing of a parked ballistic, Evi flattened out the descent, slamming the forward fans on full. A brick slammed into her stomach, and an invisible giant dug his thumbs into her eyes. She'd just lost a thousand meters in under ten seconds, and once she pulled that high-G turn, Rikers rocketed away behind the Kestrel. She flew the aircar down the East River, barely thirty meters above the waves and going over five hundred klicks an hour.

Both blips on the radar passed above Rikers, and fell way behind them. She hoped she'd slipped beneath their radar.

She slowed the Kestrel and banked to the left. It took a while to find the Bronx. She had overshot and had flown a few kilometers into Long Island Sound. No one talked. She flew low along the Cross-Bronx Expressway from the wrong end and eventually put the Kestrel down on a familiar stretch of pavement in front of a place called "ROOMS."

"F—Finally," Price stammered. He was shaking, and he'd lost most of his color, if he had any to begin with. It was the first time Evi had spared more than a moment to look at him. Price's hair was tangled in knots, he had at least three days of beard, his shirt was wrinkled and sweat-stained, and he was wearing one shoe.

Evi popped the doors and stepped out. She reached in and grabbed Price, who seemed more than a little unsteady. He stumbled out of the car, leaning away from the two big cats who followed him.

Evi held Price up by the upper arm. "Good a place for an impromptu questioning as any. Huaras, take the car back and give the team our location. By the time you get back, we should have what we need."

Huaras lifted off, dusting them with snow.

Price had the confused look of a dog who didn't know why its owner was kicking it. Evi shook him. "Are you with us, Price?"

"Wha? Evi?"

She grunted in disgust and handed him to Nohar. "Hold him."

Evi reached down and grabbed a handful of snow, the chill dulling the throbs of her injured hand. She looked at Price, who still seemed to be looking through an inebriated fog.

"Are you with us?"

"What?" Price said too slowly.

Evi slapped the handful of snow across Price's face. "Earth to David Price, you awake?"

Price sputtered, blinking his eyes. Gray slush dripped down his face, and his eyes seemed a little wider.

Evi picked up another handful of snow. "With us yet?"

"Stop it—" Price began, and got another face full of snow. He spat out a mouthful of slush and said, "Stop. I'm awake." He put a hand unsteadily to his forehead. "*Christ*, am I awake"

Evi felt little sympathy. She led the trio into the sweltering lobby of "ROOMS." With Nohar and Gurgueia behind her, it didn't take much to remind the rabbit proprietor that she still had a paid room upstairs.

They got to the room, which still smelled slightly of gunfire, and deposited Price on the bed. Evi turned the chair around to face him while the two cats guarded the door.

"You have a lot of explaining to do."

David Price backed up until his back was to the scratched-varnish headboard. His face was wet and streaked with dirt. "W-what's going on?"

"For one thing, I've been played the fool for half a decade."

Price ran a shaking hand through his tangled hair. "Evi, wha— what're you talking about?"

Evi leaned forward. Price wouldn't meet her gaze. "Dave, you're an academic, not an operative. Without a script you're a terrible liar. What was I involved in?"

"Ask him about—" Gurgueia started to say.

"Nohar, would you shut her up?"

The tiger put one hand on the jaguar's shoulder. "I think we should leave them alone." He ducked out the door with Gurgueia before she had time to object.

Evi turned back to Price. "So, Dave?"

"You have to understand." He cradled his head in his hands and Evi supposed that he was having one hell of a hangover. She hoped he wouldn't lose his lunch—though he didn't look like he had anything solid to lose. He was quiet long enough for Evi to consider getting more snow. Eventually, he said, "I was against keeping you in the dark."

"How'd you feel about sending this Gabriel character to blow holes in me?"

Price looked up, rubbing his forehead. "You know that? Y-you must know how crazy it got. Davidson proved his hy-hy-hypothesis—"

"No, I don't." Evi drew her automatic from its shoulder holster and rested it on her knee. "And you are going to explain it, step by step, until I do."

"Don't need the gun." Price shook his head and rubbed his eyes. He looked a little more coherent, but that didn't say much. "I'm out in the cold too." He smiled weakly. "Do I look like someone in the loop? I've been waiting for Gabe to show for *me*—"

"Start at the beginning."

Price took a deep breath, glanced at the gun, and told her.

The aliens had never gotten past the Aerie back in that August of '53. Frey had been the one running the show, and he saw implications that went far beyond what Midwest Lapidary's corporate front was doing. He saw the petty influence buying in Cleveland mirrored on a much larger scale. He saw, couldn't prove but saw nonetheless, the alien hand in the American nonintervention policy in the Pan-Asian war. Beyond that, he saw their hand in the war itself.

And he saw no way he could trust his own government.

"You see that, don't you? Those four aliens controlled over a hundred congressmen—"

"They were indicted." Evi stood up and walked over to the window. Snow was blowing in, the glass hadn't been replaced. "Most of them anyway."

"That mattered? These creatures want political chaos. *You only found four.*"

Frey had bottled up the aliens, and with a little electronic legerdemain he had written himself and his people out of existence. Then he began to recruit people. People the alien's activities had adversely affected, people with skills he could use, people who would be sympathetic to him.

Like Scott Fitzgerald, whose orbital ear had picked up on the existence of the aliens and was quickly thereafter quashed by Congress.

Like David Price, whose conspiracy theories no one took seriously.

Like Erin Hofstadter?

"Frey was nutty about Asia. H-Hofstadter was an Asia expert." Price paused to take a few deep breaths and massage his forehead. "Asia expert and the most fascist bastard—" Price dosed his eyes and muttered, "Oh, Christ," a few times, and Evi had to prod his foot with the gun to get him to continue.

"His fault that Gabriel and Davidson got on board."

"What's the matter with Davidson?"

Price shook his head. "Two years in, waist-deep in tech crap. Hofstadter gets Davidson. Worst kind . . ."

"You'd call Davidson a fascist?"

"Leo Davidson in a lab coat and the rest of us, white mice."

According to Price, it all started out as a private enterprise to pump the captive aliens for information and develop contingency plans to guard against further alien interference. The Domestic Cri-

sis Think Tank was legitimate. It just worked for Frey instead of the
Agency.

"You *would* have been brought in if it weren't for H-Hofstadter.
He's pathological about nonhumans."

"And you couldn't let me go because I knew about the aliens."
She stepped up to the bed and placed the barrel of the automatic
under Price's chin. She pushed up so he was finally looking her in
the eye. "So why wait so long before you start shooting at me?"

"It isn't me." His breath fogged the barrel of the automatic.

She was being unfair, she knew. Still, she was so damn angry.
Price might be a potential ally now, but for six years he had strung
her along like everyone else.

Price stared at Evi. Straight into her eyes as the odor of fear
sliced through the crystal January air. "Frey was losing control a
month after Hofstadter came on board."

Hofstadter had quite a different view of the aliens. Where Frey
saw the aliens as a threat, the German economist saw the threat
as the governments that could be so easily exploited. Hofstadter
was interested in *correcting* such vulnerability by building a post-
democratic government on the ruins of the old. A human-only government. Leo Davidson was equally anti-democratic. He saw
politics as an engineering problem.

Price sucked in a breath. "Then, a few weeks ago, all hell broke
loose."

"Explain."

According to Price, the probe launch that the aliens went to such
effort to prevent had gone forward with the captured alien finances
and Dr. Fitzgerald's help. Frey called them the first recon units into
the enemy camp. That was five and a half years ago. Which meant
that the first probe was just entering the neighborhood of Alpha
Centauri. According to Leo Davidson, if the aliens were out there,
with an eye locked on Earth, they would have started detecting the
radiation on the probe's main engine within the past month.

"Davidson was right," Price said. "They have."

She pressed the gun into the flesh of Price's neck. "Don't play
me for a fool, there's no way anyone could know that. Alpha Centauri is over four and a half light-years—"

"Tachyons." Price croaked.

She lessened the pressure on Price's neck. "D-Davidson said the
aliens had the ability to have a t-tachyon communicator. One-way,
massive planet-based particle accelerator to transmit. But the receiver could be compact—"

She lowered the gun. *"That's* why everything is happening *now."*

Price was stammering on, breathlessly. "The project went defensive when Davidson whipped out his tachyon receiver. Untranslatable signals from Alpha Centauri. Whatever aliens were out there to receive—"

"Would know that those four aliens didn't liquidate themselves when they were supposed to." Evi holstered the gun. "So, why were you locked in your bedroom with a shotgun?"

"I'm an academic, not an operative. I could see the operation shifting under Hofstadter's control. That tach receiver came out of nowhere, at least a million in R&D money out of nowhere. I warned Frey, but he didn't believe me, so I went to ground and waited for a knock on the door. Frey didn't believe, not until it was too late—"

"What convinced him?"

"You did."

In the distance, out the broken window, she began to hear sounds of traffic. An aircar, maybe an APC as well. Huaras was coming back with the rest of the team.

"Now the big question. Where is the project keeping the aliens?"

Chapter 19

Someone, thought Evi, someone in Frey's band of conspirators had an appreciation for irony. Only someone with a diabolical sense of humor would have stashed the aliens in the old UABT complex. United American Bio-Technologies was the reason moreaus had any rights in the States. It was also why there was a domestic ban on macro-genetic engineering.

UABT *started* by working on human genetics, but when the UN passed its ruling, UABT dutifully switched to nonhuman genetics.

The interference in UABT's production didn't stop there. Atrocities committed in Asia caused a legislative backlash in the U.S. that led to the most schizophrenic decision in constitutional history, an amendment that banned domestic genetic engineering on a macroscopic scale while granting the intelligent products of nonhuman experimentation the protection of the Bill of Rights. UABT dutifully switched to algae and bacteria.

That wasn't as profitable as the Asian market for military hardware.

When UABT was indicted for the continued production of engineered animals and, worse, engineered humans, the government shut the operation down, and all of UABT's assets fell down a bureaucratic black hole.

One of those assets was a large block of medical real estate parked midway between the UN Building and the Queensboro bridge. Somehow, that block of buildings had fallen under the Agency's purview, and from there it was co-opted by Frey and company.

It was within walking distance of Frey's condo. The aliens were hidden under everybody's nose: Nyogi's, the Agency's, and hers.

At three-thirty in the morning Evi's gray Dodge Electroline van hit Manhattan.

The bridges across the Harlem River looked like hell with abandoned cars and the concrete NYPD traffic barriers. Some of that was camouflage. As Evi wove the van across the 138th Street Bridge, she saw that at least half the cars, despite the burnt-out appearance, weren't abandoned. A half-dozen times Huaras got out of her lead van and walked to a burnt-out corpse of a car, and slipped into the remains of its driver's seat. The engine started, and Huaras would open a gap in the wreckage wide enough for Evi's convoy of three vans to pass by, single file.

The last barrier was one of the concrete NYPD roadblocks. A large chunk of one block was taken out by a cab from a cargo hauler. The wreckage neatly filled the gap between two of the concrete barriers. It didn't look like the truck's cab could be moved, even with the help of a skyhook. However, Huaras climbed into the charred cab, and the truck obediently started backing away, scraping on its rims, revealing a gap between the NYPD barriers large enough for an APC. The civilian vans passed through without any trouble.

Huaras got into Evi's van, and van number three split off to head toward a satellite uplink somewhere in Greenwich Village. That left Evi with her van, Huaras, Nohar, and Dave Price, and the second van with Gurgueia and a rat with a vid unit.

If Price could still work the security at the UABT complex, they wouldn't need to fire a shot, and the country would receive a big wake-up call.

The two vans shot through a light snowfall down a lightly trafficked Park Avenue. New York City never slept, but between the hours of three-thirty and four-thirty, it rested a little.

The glass-metal canyon of Manhattan got deeper as they traveled south. The blue-lit spire of Nyogi towered over the smaller skyscrapers, dwarfing them by an order of magnitude.

When Evi hit 56th, she turned away from the sight. It made her nervous.

They closed on the UABT complex, a scattering of onyx dominoes, flat to the ground and stacked at random. Half a block away, she could tell something was wrong. She got on the comm.

"Gurgueia."

"Gurgueia here." There was a pause. "Commander."

"Have Fernando hit the IR enhancer on his gadget, look at the buildings."

Evi slowed her van to a stop, half a block away from the complex as she waited for a response. Over the comm she could hear the two moreys in the tail van confer in Spanish.

"Fernando says there's a hot spot in the building to the right of the parking lot—" Gurgueia was interrupted by more chittering Spanish from the rat. "It's a fire, something's burning in there."

"The cars in the lot?"

More Spanish.

"Half-dozen. A van and a truck with the engine going—" The rat cursed in Spanish. Gurgueia continued. "Fernando sees at least two canine moreaus. Afghanis. Japanese firearms, silenced."

Evi slammed her fist into the dash.

Nyogi had beat them. What the hell could they do now?

What else was there to do?

"Gurgueia."

"Yes?"

"You're going to fall back. Watch the buildings. If they come out with the aliens, follow them. But don't engage them, understand? No heroics."

"Understood."

Evi cut the comm circuit.

"And we do?" asked Huaras.

"We go in." She looked back at her passengers. "Except you, Price."

She gave Price control of the base comm unit and led Nohar and Huaras toward the complex.

On the way, Nohar whispered, "You trust him?"

Without turning her head, she responded. "I don't trust *you*."

One thing Nyogi's canines did, they made it a lot easier for Evi and her two companions to break through security. The fence surrounding the property was dead, and the front gate hung open, unguarded. Unfortunately, the front gate led directly to the parking lot and a pair of Afghani moreaus.

Evi, Huaras, and Nohar made it to the front gate without attracting the attention of the two canines, who were more intent on the buildings. Evi's team hid behind an illegally parked limo that sat near the entrance to the UABT complex.

"Price," Evi whispered over her throat-mike, "is there a way into the complex out of sight of the parking lot?"

"Not without blowing in a window," Price's voice chirped over her earpiece.

"What about the roof?"

"Still have to break in."

Huaras shook his head. "No time but to go in front," he whispered. The one-eared rabbit drew a long knife from a sheath he wore on his back, made a quick slicing motion toward the parking lot, and resheathed it in one fluid motion.

"Gurgueia," Evi whispered over her mike, "does Fernando still see only two canines?"

"Still only two." She wondered if the growl she heard in the jaguar's voice was just interference.

She wished that she'd brought a sniper weapon. The closest they had was the AK-47 hanging off of her shoulder. It would cover the distance, but it would tell everyone they were here. She looked down at Huaras, "Go."

Huaras slipped away, moving downwind of the canines. The brown rabbit seemed to vanish into the landscaping. Despite the fact the weapon wasn't silenced, Evi braced her AK-47 on the hood of the illegal limo and aimed at the parking lot, waiting for Huaras and hoping she wouldn't have to fire.

She could see the two canines. One stood in front of a cargo hauler, watching the front doors of the largest building in the complex. The other paced in front of the rear doors of the trailer, letting his Mitsubishi point at the ground. She could probably disable both of them with one sweep across the length of the vehicle, if she had to.

"How do you feel about humans?" The rumbling whisper from Nohar was unexpected. She forced herself to keep sighting down the gun. She had no idea where Huaras was.

"What kind of question is that?"

"Hate would be easy . . ."

"So?" *Huaras, where are you?*

"Do you?"

Did she?

"I'll get back to you on that"

"I'm not the one who needs to know."

She only got a brief moment to reflect on that. She saw Huaras slip from behind a parked sedan and slip under the cargo hauler. She didn't see any reaction from the canines. She strained, focusing on the cargo hauler. Huaras was sliding on his stomach toward the rear of the trailer.

The canine paced past Huaras, and the rabbit slid out from under the trailer. The Afghani started turning and Huaras jumped. The rabbit's left arm snaked around the dog's muzzle, and the knife seemed to slide out of nowhere, even as the two fell to the asphalt.

Evi moved the AK-47 to cover the forward canine. He knew something was wrong behind the truck. He walked along the side of the trailer, toward his fallen comrade. Huaras came out of nowhere. He fell on the dog from the top of the truck. The dog looked up just in time for the knife to slash his neck.

"Score two for the good guys," Evi whispered.

"Believe that?" Nohar asked.

"No." She activated her mike. "Gurgueia, any more activity going on by the truck?"

"Fernando says that if there's anything going on, it's in the buildings."

"Okay," Evi told Nohar, "we go in."

The two of them ran up to the parking lot. Huaras had stripped the canines of their silenced Mitsubishis and as Evi made it to the trailer, Huaras tossed her one. Evi passed the AK-47 to Nohar. "Could hide bodies," Huaras said, "But dogs, they know, smell them—"

Evi nodded; she had smelled the blood from the dogs as she'd run up. She gave her attention to the van that was parked next to the cargo hauler. The van could hold ten dogs. The truck . . . "Nohar, open the back of the truck."

He reached up and operated the door. When the hydraulic door slid aside, a blast of heat drifted out in a cloud of steam. With it floated the odor of sulfur.

Evi backed up until she could see in the trailer. Inside, it looked like a cave. A stonelike substance crusted the walls, rounding the corners of the interior of the trailer. Greenish-red lights were set in the far corners, casting an evil glow. It smelled of sulfur and ammonia.

"Deluxe accommodations," Nohar said.

Evi couldn't help but wonder how many other unmarked cargo haulers were crisscrossing the country with this kind of cargo. Fortunately, that meant that they didn't use the trailer to ship in the troops. Only enough canines to fill the one van.

"That's what I needed," Evi said, "We have ten to twelve dogs in there, probably in teams of four—"

One of the onyx domino buildings, the one where Fernando had put the fire, erupted in a ball of yellow flame that rolled out the windows and shot upward. As she turned toward it, the shockwave hit her with a blast of heat that threw her against the side of the trailer. As she watched, a secondary explosion shook the parking lot and shattered windows throughout the complex.

"Price!" she screamed over her throat-mike, abandoning any attempt at stealth.

"Yes, I see—That's the computer and administration complex. The creatures are in the *main* building." Price added, weakly, "Shit."

"I hate explosives," Evi whispered.

Nohar and Huaras picked themselves up off the ground. Nohar looked at the burning administration building. "Afghanis don't share the sentiment."

"Main building." Evi waved her Mitsubishi at the doors. She clicked it on full auto and started running.

The doors to the main building were glass, and riddled with bullet holes. She closed on them and could smell human and canine blood. In the hall beyond the door fluorescents flickered erratically. She saw two security guards draped over the desk in the reception area. She kept low; nothing offered her cover from the lobby.

She stayed in a crouch, next to the doors, looking into the lobby through a hole where a picture window used to be. Wind rattled the remains of a set of black lacquer venetian blinds. She swept her gaze past the overturned chairs, over glass-covered carpeting, past the massive concrete planter that was the centerpiece of the room, past the desk with the dead security guards . . .

Out of the corner of her eye she saw some movement.

Evi dived through the window, seeking cover behind the concrete planter. She hit ground on top of a pile of black lacquer slats as bullets tore through plastic foliage. Before she could get oriented, the firing ceased, punctuated by a solid thump and the rustling of fake foliage. The smell of fresh canine blood filled the air.

She cautiously got up and looked around.

Laying face-first in a fake palm was an Afghani merc missing most of the back of his skull. Walking into the building behind him, was Huaras clutching the other commandeered Mitsubishi.

She looked at the one-eared rabbit and asked, "Where'd he come from?"

Huaras gestured at the rank of elevators lining the wall to the right of the lobby. "Got here, just. Think maybe he check on why other two dogs no longer talk on radio. No?"

"Think he got word to the other dogs?"

"No way we know. Think not."

Nohar followed Huaras into the lobby. "Where from here?"

Evi walked over to the desk. "We stay here for a few minutes. Cover the elevators, both of you."

On the desk were two dead security guards. She rolled the bodies off the desk as she moved behind it. The guards never even had time to draw their weapons.

"Price," she asked over her mike. "Where're the aliens being kept?"

"Sublevel three."

She looked over the vid displays set into the desk. Many showed snow. She kept hitting keys, changing cameras, until she got a picture showing Afghanis on it. "Sublevel three," the camera said, "maint corridor five."

It was a war. The camera was aimed down the length of a concrete corridor, toward a steel vaultlike door. Trapped in front of the door were easily a dozen humans, security guards and scientists, wielding handguns. The humans were using crates and overturned lab carts as cover. Three of them were on the ground and looked dead.

Pinning the defenders down were six or seven Afghani canines. The dogs had ripped a fire door from somewhere and were bracing against it as they swept wave after wave of machine-gun fire past the humans.

As she watched, a human wearing a lab coat jerked backward and sprayed blood on the vault door from a wound that sprouted in his chest.

"Price, I'm looking at a camera pointed down maintenance corridor five straight at an airlock-looking door."

"That's them," came the response over her earpiece. "Fitzgerald wanted them in their own environment, 2.25 atmosphere—"

"All I want is another way in, Price."

"Blocked?"

"Yes, damn it, it's blocked!"

"Let me think—"

"We don't have time—"

"Isham," Nohar yelled back at her. "One of the elevators is moving!"

"If it's a dog, shoot it." She looked at that end of the lobby as Nohar and Huaras leaned up against the wall on either side of the moving elevator. The elevator was coming from the sublevels. "Price," she yelled.

"I don't have the floorplan memorized. Give me a minute."

Evi looked up and the elevator was on sublevel two. She looked down at the monitor and saw that another human had fallen, as well as one canine. She began switching cameras at random, looking for another way down there.

"The methane jet." Price said over the radio.

"What?"

"There's this massive flame-jet set up in the center of the alien habitat. All the works for it are a level below—"

"How do we get there?"

"Same as the air lock you're looking at, but a floor below."

She punched up a camera and looked at a view labeled. "Sublevel four, maint corridor five." It was the twin of the one where the battle raged, but empty of people, canine or human. If they could get there before the Afghanis plowed through the humans—

The elevator dinged.

She ducked behind the desk and covered the doors with her Mitsubishi. The elevator doors slid open reluctantly. Nohar and Huaras were leveling their weapons when Evi could see inside the elevator.

It wasn't carrying a dog.

Erin Hofstadter bolted out of the elevator. Huaras and Nohar both hesitated as the round German economist ran past them. He didn't seem to see either of them as he headed straight for the doors.

Evi leveled the Mitsubishi and yelled. *"FREEZE!"*

She could feel her finger tighten on the trigger even as Hofstadter stopped moving. It took a great effort of self-control not to shoot her old boss.

Hofstadter turned around, "Isham?"

"Grab him, Nohar."

Hofstadter started to back away from the advancing tiger. "What the hell is this, Isham?"

She couldn't help grinning. "It's poetic justice."

"You work for the Feds." He was turning red. From exertion or anger, Evi couldn't tell. "What're you doing with a gang of moreau terror—"

Nohar put a massive tawny hand on Hofstadter's shoulder. The economist gasped when it happened. It looked as if he tried to shrink away from the contact, but the tiger kept a solid grip on him.

Evi walked around the desk. Fear, that was the overriding smell that floated off her old boss. He was sweating, and the white shirt he wore was drenched. From him, she could smell traces of bile and ammonia. With all the anger that was swelling in her, all she could think to say was, "Any nonhuman with a gun is a terrorist to you."

The fear got worse, and Hofstadter's face was purpling, "You've turned."

She took her right hand off of her weapon and slapped him across the face as hard as she could. His soft flesh crushed under her hand, and he was thrown against the tiger, spitting blood.

"How dare you!" She yelled at him. "You turned against your government, and then you turned against your own conspiracy."

Hofstadter was on his knees, sputtering. The left side of his face was discolored and swelling and it looked as though he might have a broken cheekbone. She could smell urine. Hofstadter spat up blood. "So you're—" he gasped and clutched his chest. "Kill me, too?"

"I should—" She leaned in and realized that Hofstadter did not look good.

"Time, it is short, yes?" Huaras said from behind her.

No time for personal business. "Hofstadter, look at me."

He turned. His eyes were bloodshot, and he had trouble breathing. He still clutched his chest.

"Are the aliens still in the habitat, Hofstadter?"

He started laughing. It started as a giggle and moved up the scale to a desperate grasping wheeze.

Then he started choking, doubling over as he clutched his chest. He collapsed at Nohar's feet. Evi dropped her gun and turned him over. Hofstadter stared up at her with an expression somewhere between a smile and a pained grimace. He sucked in a shuddering breath and whispered, "Ten minutes and no aliens."

Evi stopped as she was unbuttoning his collar. "There's a methane—"

"Yes." Hofstadter wheezed and closed his eyes.

Evi looked up at Nohar. "I hate explosives."

Chapter 20

Not good, we leave, yes?" asked Huaras.

"Damn," Evi said. "Drag him out of here. Wait back at the vans."

They picked up Hofstadter, who had lost consciousness. As they left, Nohar looked back over his shoulder. "Isham?"

"Move!" she yelled back at them. She headed for the elevators.

Hofstadter said they had ten minutes. She was confident she could disarm any explosive that Hofstadter could have rigged. The problem was getting there and finding it.

"Price," she called over the mike as she waited for an elevator to reach her. "Give me the access codes for the sublevels."

Price gave her two sets of six numbers, one for the elevator and one for the air lock on sublevel four. "I don't know if they'll work. They're my codes and I—"

"They'd better work, Price."

An elevator dinged into place. The door slid aside, stopped as the lights in the lobby flickered, and resumed opening the rest of the way. "Price, before I drop out of radio contact, where would you hide a bomb around that methane jet?"

"What?"

The doors started closing.

"Never mind," she said as she slipped inside the elevator. The voice of the elevator was repeating the phrase, ". . . stairs in case of fire. Elevators should only be used by emergency personnel . . ."

The voice pickup was dead, so she keyed in her destination

manually, along with the six-digit security code. The elevator descended.

She passed the third sublevel and the lights flickered again and went out. Emergency lights came on. Apparently the fire in the administration building, probably Hofstadter's work, had finally nuked the power grid for the complex.

If Hofstadter had been right, she had all of eight minutes left.

She wedged her fingers between the doors to the elevator and pushed them apart. Her left shoulder felt it, even under the anesthetic. With the door open, she could hear gunfire on the third sublevel. The lower halves of the elevator doors leading to that sublevel were riddled with bullet holes.

She kneeled and tried to separate what she could see of the doors for the fourth sublevel. They came apart reluctantly. The ceiling of the fourth sublevel only cleared the floor of her elevator by a meter. She rolled out.

Emergency lights cast a stark white light on the bare concrete corridor. To her right the corridor shot a straight twenty meters to an airlock door. Above the airlock a red light was flashing some kind of warning.

She looked to the left. Ten meters away she saw a canine coming out of the door to the fire stairs.

Evi rolled back to take cover in the shaft. She grabbed one of the elevator doors and swung inside. The bottom of the elevator brushed her hair. She didn't hear any shooting. The dog might not have seen her.

She hugged the wall of the shaft, one hand holding on to the door for dear life, her left hand clutching the Mitsubishi. Her feet were half-hanging off of the girder that ran across the shaft, level with the corridor's floor. She looked down the shaft behind her and saw three more sublevels before it ended in a flat slab of concrete.

She was breathing hard and beginning to sweat. Her pulse throbbed in her neck, and the copper taste of panic soured her mouth.

This dog could be point for a recon team, looking for another way in to the aliens. There could be as many as five of them if her original estimate was correct.

The smell began to drift toward her. She could distinguish two separate canines before she heard the fire door swing shut.

Six minutes left.

She could hear a dog talking on the radio, in Arabic. ". . . similar air lock design, no defenders. We're going to—"

Her eavesdropping was interrupted by the abrupt return of power. The elevator began to descend.

She began crouching as she lost clearance. Her footing began to slip.

With a meter and a half left, she bolted. She leaped back into the corridor, turning to swing the Mitsubishi with her bad arm. She sprayed the corridor and prayed that she hit something.

The silenced Mitsubishi made a sound like someone jackhammering mud. Both dogs were taken by surprise. She managed to get one in the abdomen. Then she landed on her ass, and as she slid on the concrete floor, her remaining shots bit the ground at the other's feet. One canine folded, collapsing in a heap, while the other took cover behind a large pipe that ran floor to ceiling. That one crouched and snapped off a burst.

She still slid across the floor. As the dog shot at her, she felt something like a sledgehammer hit her left arm. The impact tore the gun from her hand and rolled her over. She came to rest by the wall opposite the elevator in a slick of her own blood.

The elevator dinged and its doors closed.

The wound was a burning pressure in her bicep. Most of it hid under the effects of the painkillers that already doped her arm. But she knew it was a bad hit, because she couldn't move her arm anymore.

The canine was getting out from behind the pipe he was using for cover. He pointed the Mitsubishi at her as he crept over to his partner. She supposed she looked dead.

He turned to look at his downed comrade.

Evi used that break in the dog's attention to draw the Smith and Wesson from her shoulder holster and pump three shots. Two hit the canine in the face. The dog hit the ground before the cannon shot echoes died.

Five minutes.

She didn't have time to look at her arm. She got to her feet and ran for the airlock door. She had to holster her automatic to operate the keypad. "The code better work, Price." Price didn't hear her; the few tons of concrete above her had killed her radio.

After she entered the code, it took the computer an inordinate time to respond. After a short eternity, the door slid aside, revealing a square chamber beyond, with a smaller door on the opposite wall. Red lights flashed at her from the corners of the air lock. She stepped inside and the door started sliding shut.

It stopped when the power died again.

"Shit," she whispered.

Next to the opposite door was a glass-covered recess. Beyond the glass was a red lever. The writing on the glass said "emergency release." She punched in the glass and pulled the lever.

The door cracked open, filling the air with a high-pitched whistling. Wind razored by her, trying to scour her skin with wind-blown sand. She had to hang on to the lever to remain upright as the door continued to slide away. She closed her eyes and turned away.

The air that blew by her, trying to force her down, was hot and moist. It would have been saunalike if not for the smells that seared her nose. Bile, ammonia, sulfur, brimstone, lava. Molten smells, diseased smells.

She hung on to that lever for thirty seconds as the pressure equalized between the two environments. When she could face into the chamber beyond, she had only three minutes to find Hofstadter's bomb.

The chamber beyond the air lock was cylindrical. The ceiling sloped upward into an irregular concrete cone. At the apex of the cone was a roughly circular hole about two meters in diameter, beyond which shone red-green light. A massive network of pipes snaked upward in the center of the room, terminating in a flared nozzle that stopped about a meter short of the hole in the top of the cone. The methane jet.

No fire shot out the top of the nozzle though. Instead, Evi heard a steady low hiss. The wind from the pressure equalizing must have blown it out. The nozzle was now pumping methane into the room.

Where did he stick it?

When she didn't see it immediately, she had a fear that Hofstadter had planted it on the floor below, where the pipes seemed to originate. She told herself that if she didn't find it in sixty seconds, she'd run and take cover in the stairwell.

When she circled the base of the pipes, she saw it. A small brick of plastic explosive and a small electronic timer/detonator. The timer said that Hofstadter had overestimated the amount of time they had.

The display had already rolled over to under a minute. She had forty-eight seconds to turn the thing off. She ran up to the pipe and instantly realized that Hofstadter was taller than she was. The bomb was out of her reach.

She could see it clearly, nestled between a thin pipe that seemed to be part of the ignition system and one of the big gas pipes. She grabbed the smaller pipe and pulled herself up to within reach.

It was a standard timing element. An idiot-proof detonator mass-produced for the defense department. Nothing exotic, but she had expected as much from Hofstadter. If Hofstadter had been an operative and not an economist, she wouldn't be down here risking this.

The trigger didn't even have a motion sensor. The extent of its booby-trapping capability was the ability to send a triggering spark into the explosive block if the wires were pulled out prematurely.

The little timer window rolled over into the thirties.

She tried to find footing, but her feet kept slipping on the base of the pipes. Damn it, all she had to do was hit the reset button on the thing. It wasn't brain surgery. All she needed was to get her hand free.

The timer hit twenty-nine.

She looked down at her wounded left arm. The jumpsuit was wet with her blood from the shoulder down. She tried to move it.

The painkillers lost their effectiveness. Not only her shoulder burned, but there was a white-hot poker twisting in her bicep. Sweat stung her eyes, but she saw her arm move. She raised her shaking arm as lightning flashes of pain shot up her arm to settle into her gut. Every pulse of her heart ground a branding iron into her upper arm.

It seemed to take much longer than twenty seconds to raise her arm to the bomb. However, when her hand reached it, the timer still had nine seconds to go.

She blinked the sweat from her eyes and saw that Hofstadter had broken off the reset button.

"You BASTARD!"

Six seconds. Evi wrapped her hand around the detonator and hoped that Hofstadter's primitive method of protecting his device meant that he wasn't technically adept.

Five seconds. She knew she was going to die. She could taste it in her mouth, feel it breathing on the back of her neck.

Four seconds. "If this doesn't work, at least I'm the one who did it."

Evi ripped the detonator from the block of explosive. When she did so, her grip slipped and she fell backward. Even as she was in the air, she knew that it had worked.

To booby-trap the detonator the operator had to crack the case and wire a jumper inside. Hofstadter didn't have the time or the technical inclination to attempt that.

The detonator beeped at her as she hit the ground and blacked out.

*   *   *

The first thing she became aware of was the pain. It felt as if someone were squeezing her arm, and every squeeze sent a wave of fire across her shoulder.

It took a second to realize that someone *was* squeezing her arm. Her eyes shot open. The first thing she saw was the peeper. She tried to reach for her automatic. Her right arm didn't move.

There were three canines on her. One held down her right arm, one her legs, and one seemed to be doing first aid on her wounded arm. The peeper was leaning against the piping, holding the detonator.

"Evi Isham," he said. "Finally."

She looked with alarm at the dog who was tending her arm.

"Don't worry, Sharif is an excellent combat medic."

The dog jabbed something into the wound. Fire exploded inside her arm, burning out the inside of her skull. Her back arched, and when the pain receded, she could feel the ache of stressed muscles from her neck all the way down her spine.

The peeper gave her a lopsided smile. "I thought you'd like to experience the full effect of that wound." The peeper pulled the collar of his khaki shirt away to reveal a puckered red scar in his neck, under the Adam's apple. "Like I did."

The world had finally fallen in on her.

"Ironic," the peeper said as he hefted the detonator. "You probably saved my life. I doubt the Race's little beasties could patch me up after an explosion. It's one of the ways you kill *them*."

Sharif silently ripped what felt like a meter of barbed wire out of her arm. She turned to look at him tossing aside a few dozen strands of carbon fiber from her jumpsuit.

"What are you going to do with me?" She asked. She was ashamed of how weak her voice sounded.

"If it was up to me," he said, looking down at her and his smile disappearing, "I'd cut out your eyes and toss you naked into the Bronx."

Sharif finally finished his job. Evi felt the pressure of an airhypo injecting something into her arm. Then Sharif wrapped her arm in a dressing.

The peeper went on. "Unfortunately, for both of us, the Race has an interest in you, beyond the retrieval of their—" He hesitated and said the last word with distaste, "people."

Sharif backed off of her arm and the peeper told her, "Get up."

The canines retreated, letting her stand. The world felt oddly disjointed, as if she were watching events from a distance. She wondered if it was an effect of the pain, or hitting her head, or what they'd doped her with. They'd shot her up with something, and it wasn't painkiller. The fire in her arm was a razor-sharp sensation, while the rest of the world seemed fuzzy and indistinct.

"Who are you?" The words came out in slow motion, as if they had to fight her tongue to get out. "NLF?"

"Move first. We've outstayed our welcome."

He prodded her and she started walking. She knew enough to realize she was drugged. She walked through air that felt like molasses, and she couldn't bring herself to resist the peeper's commands.

The three dogs escorted her out the air lock and down the corridor, the peeper in the lead. The power had died, and they walked under the periodic spotlights of the emergency lights. The peeper kept talking, his voice a small rattle in a gray-cotton silence. "Dimitri's what *they* call me. NLF was Hioko's little boondoggle, before his brain had an argument with a bullet . . ."

When they reached the fire stairs, she had a brief fear that she had forgotten how to climb them. She stopped short, confused, as the peeper's, Dimitri's, voice faded in her awareness. Someone pushed her from behind and she had to struggle to move. It took an inordinate amount of concentration, and Dimitri's voice kept fading in and out of her awareness.

". . . never trusted the Race, smart move though it killed him . . ."

". . . don't kill you is because what the Race'll do instead . . ."

". . . need folks like you. What they give is almost worth it . . ."

Somehow she made it to the ground level. She was briefly curious about how long she'd been in the bowels of the UABT complex, but her time sense had left her. All she knew was that it was still dark outside, and the cargo hauler was gone.

Where was her backup? Gurgueia, Huaras, Nohar, and Fernando with his video camera who was supposed to document the aliens and the conspiracy. She remembered that she'd told the jaguar to follow wherever the aliens went; she must be following the truck.

The administration building still burned. The roar of the fires seemed to heighten in volume in time to her pulse. For some reason she couldn't focus on the fire; her eyes kept darting after random motions, following smoke around in circles.

Someone prodded her, and she realized she had stopped moving.

Dimitri's voice faded into her awareness. ". . . not get distracted. Once you're in the van, your attention can wander all you want."

She nodded. It made a lot of sense at the time.

Once she settled into the seat in the van, she allowed her gaze to drift again. It took too much effort to focus her attention on any one thing. She cradled her arm and looked out the windshield. Dimitri talked on in the background, but she couldn't keep a grip on what he said. As she faced the windshield, the van shook. That was briefly of interest, since no one had started the engine.

Glass fell from the windows of the main building, looking like black ice. Blue-green fire rolled out from the lobby, upward. It struck Evi that something had ignited all the methane that had been pumping out of that jet. She turned her head to the rear window, where, in the distance, she saw red and blue flashing lights. Police, she thought. NYPD or Agency impersonators? She didn't know, or care.

Dimitri climbed over her and into the driver's seat. She followed him with her eyes and her gaze rested on the back of his neck as he turned on the van and slammed on the accelerator.

As the van rocketed forward, she recorded a brief amazement at the fresh red scar under the edge of his close-cropped hair. It was obviously the exit wound from the bullet she'd placed in his neck less than seventy-two hours ago. Nothing healed that fast.

The van hit a bump and her head rolled aside. There were four Afghanis in back here with her. She wondered what these shaggy dogs thought about her. She was responsible for the death of a lot of their fellows. This breed of moreau was the least "human." The Afghani dogs were pack oriented and had little concept of individuality. They were so well engineered for combat that they couldn't adapt to any other environment. No room in their psyches for personal vendettas. They took orders, killed people, and usually died violently.

As the van shot through the gate and a space that used to hold a parked limousine, she closed her eyes and wondered if she should try to force her thinking into a more coherent pattern.

Chapter 21

The ride in the van was a long sequence of disjointed imagery. Evi tried to force her mind on one track of thinking. The effort had the edge of desperation, and she embraced it. The feeling of desperation helped to fight the sense of apathy that enveloped her like quicksand.

If she closed her eyes and concentrated, to the exclusion of the outside world, she could think straight.

The first coherent thought she had was that there was no way she could escape this situation while she was drugged. But the fact that she could force herself to think coherently meant the effects of the drug were waning. Her metabolism tended to race such things through her body. If she got lucky, Dimitri wouldn't know that.

One consolation about her capture. It looked as if they assumed she was still working solo, or with Frey's people. They didn't seem to be aware of the moreaus; that was good. If Gurgueia followed her orders, they would track the cargo van to its destination. With Fernando, they'd complete some of the mission, getting some record of the aliens' existence on video.

Only surveillance footage of aliens being transported from point A to point B wouldn't be as effective as their original idea of broadcasting straight from the alien habitat itself. However, it might still shake something loose.

Unfortunately, for her that was all moot now. She had hoped the plan would nullify the reasons everyone wanted her, dead or otherwise. With a public broadcast, Hofstadter couldn't keep his secrets by killing her, the Agency couldn't save itself embarrassment by disappearing her, and, if they'd done it right, Nyogi would have other problems than kidnapping her.

Now, it seemed, Nyogi wanted something from her, beyond getting their people back. From what she remembered of Dimitri's speech, whatever that was, it wasn't pleasant.

The van came to a stop and she opened her eyes. The world became disjointed again, but it was easier for her to concentrate. The van had parked in a huge elevator, easily the size of Diana's entire loft. There was the whir of distant motors, and the ceiling was receding above her. She found herself focusing on a concrete beam in the ceiling above that must have had a cross section larger than the van's.

She forced her gaze down, into the van. The only residents were herself and Dimitri. Dimitri was covering her with an unsilenced Mitsubishi.

Where were the Afghanis?

Dimitri seemed to notice her looking. "The canines aren't allowed where you're going. Few creatures are, other than the Race themselves."

"Race?" She managed to slur.

"What *they* call themselves."

She found that, with a considerable effort, she could keep her gaze locked on the peeper. "Why," she forced herself to say, "you work for . . ." It took too much effort, she let the question trail off.

"Why'd a human turn on his whole planet?" Dimitri smiled. "Why'd a nonhuman work for a bunch of humans?"

That sliced through the fog. "I never had a choice." Her voice actually sounded coherent that time.

"We all have choices, Isham," Diniitri said. "Sometimes we make the wrong ones to save our asses."

The elevator came to a halt, and Dimitri pressed a button on the dash that opened the rear door.

It wasn't until the door opened that she realized that the air conditioning in the van had been going full blast. Heat slammed into the van in a wet, rancid blast. She turned to look out the rear doors and saw a massive room beyond. The room was a warehouse. She could see crates, robot forklifts, and cargo haulers in a massive loading dock, everything in the room disturbingly normal.

The normalcy was disturbing because the construction of the room itself was alien. The entire warehouse area was a squashed sphere, ovoid in cross section. The ovoid was maybe a hundred meters in diameter and easily twenty meters tall at its highest point.

Cones projected from the walls at regular intervals, shooting blue-green jets of fire that added to the ranks of red lights that were sunk into smooth depressions in the ceiling.

This dwarfed anything she'd seen in Cleveland.

A small robot golf cart rolled up to the back of the van. Dimitri gestured with the gun. "Get in the cart."

Dimitri stood back in the air-conditioned van and watched her from behind his submachine gun. The heat started her sweating and made her dizzy. By the time she had dragged herself to the cart, she wanted to pass out.

It had to be forty degrees down here, she thought. It felt as if she were buried under a burning compost heap.

She closed her eyes when she collapsed in the back of the cart. She could hear Dimitri walk up to her. This was the time to make a break for it, she thought. She opened her eyes and saw Dimitri standing in front of the cart as it started moving. He faced her, never lowering the barrel of the gun. She tried to sit up, and the wave of disorientation she felt when her head moved told her that at the speed she was operating, Dimitri would put three shots in her chest before she got halfway to her feet.

The cart rolled through the cavernous warehouse. The lack of right angles or straight lines in the room made it hard for her to judge distance. Holes collected in the walls in irregular groups of eight. She couldn't tell if the openings were small and close by or huge and impossibly far.

They passed through one of the holes long before she expected to. Suddenly she was slipping through a nearly cylindrical concrete tube that was of a much more manageable scale. It could have been a storm sewer if it weren't for the red lights sunk into the ceiling in organically smooth pits. The concrete walls were polished to a sheen that reflected light like wet marble.

They traveled through miles of sameness. The concrete tubes had branches that resembled the inside of a stone giant's circulatory system, and the ovoid openings that broke into the sides of the tube resembled ulcers. Most of the doors showed only darkness beyond, but behind at least one she saw a pulsing white amoebic form.

The farther they went, the hotter it became.

The cart pulled to a stop when the tube emptied into another squashed spheroid. This room was much smaller than the warehouse, twenty meters across. It was big enough for the cart to pull in and circle halfway around the perimeter, around a hole in the center of the floor.

She noticed eight corridors that slipped out of the room at regular intervals in the walls. Still in a drugged fog, she couldn't pick the one the cart had come from.

"End of the line," Dimitri said. "Everybody out."

As he spoke, there was a sucking sound, and a blast of cool air came from the center of the room. She looked in that direction and saw a metal lid opening in the room's central pit. It reminded her of a trapdoor spider. Light came from underneath it, a more reasonable white light.

"That's where you're going."

She looked at him. He was sweating profusely. It might be possible . . .

She stood, and the wave of vertigo made her reconsider. She climbed out of the cart, trying to be careful of her footing, and slowly walked across the too smooth floor toward the blessedly cool pit.

When she reached the edge, she looked down. It was a steeply angled tube that quickly slipped out of her sight. It was clear she was intended to slide down it.

Dimitri waved his gun. "Go."

She quietly told herself that, if Dimitri and company wanted her dead, they would have killed her long before now. Then she stepped into the hole, protecting her arm with her body.

Her slide down the chute was much faster than she'd expected. The vertigo returned with a vengeance, heightened by the fact that the tube was smooth and uniformly white, giving her eyes no landmarks to lock on.

The dizziness was so intense that she didn't realize she'd passed out.

Evi opened her eyes and found herself looking at a bearded man in his early fifties. She recognized him from the surveillance footage from the peeper's, Dimitri's, Long-Eighties. He was the professor type, Fitzgerald, the xenobiologist.

"Are you all right?" he asked.

The quickness with which she grabbed his lapel told her she'd been out long enough for the drug to work its way out of her system. *"All right?"* she yelled at him. *"What do you think?* After you, and Frey, and everyone else screwed me over." She pushed him away, hard, and sat up. No waves of vertigo hit her this time; for that she was grateful.

She got off the bunk she had come to on, and looked around.

Fitzgerald backed toward a regular *flat* wall. Two bunk beds sat opposite each other in the rectangular room, and the lighting came from recessed fluorescent tubes. An air conditioner thrummed low in the background, and cool breezes flowed from vents high in the walls.

She stood in a room normal-looking enough for her to briefly think that her travel through that alien environment had been a drug-induced hallucination. It hadn't been. She could still smell the taint of sulfur and burning methane that filtered through the overworked air conditioner.

If she had any other doubt, the fact that the only entrance to the room was a circular hole on the far wall between the bunks showed that what she'd seen was more than a hallucination. The drug might have played with her sense of scale, but what she had seen of the alien habitat must've covered several acres at least.

Fitzgerald took a tentative step forward. "Miss Isham?"

"WHAT?" She advanced on him, feeling three days worth of adrenaline course through her blood. "What, by the name of all that's holy, what could you possibly have to say to me?"

Fitzgerald sputtered, "But—"

"Are you going to tell me how sorry you are? You folks didn't *mean* to keep me in the dark. You didn't *mean* to make me a traitor!" She pushed him to the wall with her good hand. "Or are you going to apologize for being the one to hand your own conspiracy back to the damn aliens. You were the one, weren't you?"

"I—"

"How about Gabriel? How did you feel about him trying to blow me away?"

"He's dead." Fitzgerald said in a hoarse whisper.

"What?" She realized that she had wrapped her right hand around the professor's throat. It dawned on her that she could have killed the man. She backed away and began deep-breathing exercises. "Who's dead?"

"Everyone," Fitzgerald croaked. "Gabriel, Davidson, Frey. Hofstadter tried to blame it all on you—"

She thought back over what had happened to her.

"How did Davidson and Gabriel die?"

"Their car crashed on the Southeast side of Manhattan."

The aircar, she thought, the one that had chased her into Greenwich Village. "I'm sorry I jumped on you."

He shook his head. "Did you kill Frey?"

"No!" She could still smell Frey's blood, still feel the panic

she'd felt then, when she first began to realize the scope of what had happened.

"Gabe and Davidson—"

"Were trying to kill me."

"You have to understand." Fitzgerald wrung his hands. "This was never supposed to become violent. It was research—"

She snorted.

"—first contact with an alien species. Do you have any idea what that means?"

Evi sat down. "I have a pretty damn good idea." The air-conditioning vents were too small, the tube was an impossible climb, and the walls were solid concrete. She was stuck here with the professor.

"It was my life," he went on. "Can't you realize—"

"Your *profession*," she snapped. "*My* fucking life."

Fitzgerald lapsed into silence.

The quiet got on her nerves. "So, in six years of research, did you find out *anything* useful?"

He walked over and sat down on the bunk across from her. "What do you want to know about them?"

"Everything."

Fitzgerald obliged her.

The Race had developed on a nearby world, a massive, hot, tectonically active ball of rock circling a dim reddish sun. They had populated a number of planets, between six and a dozen of them, including a planet orbiting Alpha Centauri A. They were very aware of Earth and the creatures populating it.

They needed the resources of the planets they'd colonized, and Earth was a potential rival. Once Earth reached out of its solar system, there'd be a costly war for territory on those new planets.

As Earth turned on, into another millennium, the Race had a political dilemma. How to prevent a seemingly inevitable conflict. The decision, after a long-distance study of Earth's culture, was a covert operation. The aliens on Earth would prevent any force on the planet from gaining the technical expertise or the inclination for interstellar travel for as long as possible.

"It's interesting," Fitzgerald said, "to see how mankind isn't the only species capable of hypocrisy and self-delusion."

Evi ignored the subtle racism implied by the word "mankind." Fitzgerald probably hadn't even noticed it.

"You see," he continued, "the Race has a long history, as bloody as any human account. They now have a culture that prides itself on the 'honor of nonconfrontation.' Direct violence is anathema to them."

"What do you mean?"

"I think of it as 'the hand on the knife' syndrome. The Race's culture puts the highest taboo, not on the knife going in the back, but on any honorable person having his hand upon it."

"I find it hard to believe that these things are nonviolent."

"That's the irony. *They* believe they're nonviolent. Ever since they landed on this planet their *modus operandi*, if you will, has been to employ politically active 'locals' who are instructed to carry out their agenda. It doesn't matter if the 'local' is a member of parliament, a military commander, or a terrorist. If a few people die as the 'locals' are carrying out the alien's agenda, the Race feels no responsibility."

Fitzgerald leaned forward and smiled. "In fact, if people get killed, the Race simply considers it an example of our own moral degeneracy and a justification of their mission here."

She thought the whole thing was twisted enough to be human.

Then Fitzgerald went into a catalog of what events could be traced to the Race's interference, and what started out being ironic and twisted became truly frightening.

Fitzgerald said that it was almost certain that the Iranian terrorists that slaughtered the Saudi royal family in '19 were backed financially by the Race. That had been the sparking incident that led to the Third Gulf War and the formation of the Islamic Axis. The fundamentalist Axis made sure that the only real technical progress the region made was in the area of warfare. Embryonic space programs in Saudi Arabia, Egypt, and Pakistan all died on the vine.

Funds from the Race led to the rise of a rabid anti-Islam regime in India and a fascist technocracy in Japan. The rise of tensions between India and the Islamic Axis, and Japan and Socialist China broke in 2024, when the first shots in the Pan-Asian war were fired. In '27, New Delhi was nuked. In '35, Tokyo followed suit.

It took only a few years for the Islamic Axis to finally turn its attention to liberating Palestine. In '41, Tel Aviv was nuked.

By the time Fitzgerald reached Tel Aviv, Evi was shaking. Forget the war itself. Forget a trail of blood that ran across two decades. Forget everything but those three cities. New Delhi, Tokyo, Tel Aviv . . .

Those three names represented the only grave markers for nine million people.

"It seems that the Pan-Asian war was so successful in keeping us earthbound that the Race is trying to foment a civil war here in the States. The Asian war left the U.S. with the only viable space program looking beyond the solar system."

She raised her head. Images of what she had seen when she passed through Tel Aviv were still fresh in her memory. She had to pull herself out of that private horror to pay attention to what Fitzgerald was saying now.

"With one hand," he was saying, "they try to get anti-technological, anti-moreau politicians elected. You uncovered one of those operations."

"With the other?"

"With the other, they finance radical moreau groups. One group plays against the other, and the resulting explosion keeps people too busy to look beyond the local gravity well."

She thought of General Wu and her military hardware. It looked like it was getting damn close to an explosion. She could only imagine what would happen if command weren't in the hand of that cautious, serene bear but rather in the hands of a hothead like Corporal Gurgueia.

She thought of the probe that was, "even now," Price had said, entering the neighborhood of Alpha Centauri. The whole reason the Race was here was to prevent that. That had been what triggered the shit hitting the fan.

However, it wasn't just her. It was a national shit, and the fan was the size of a continent.

She looked at the scientist, who had seemed to shrink even as he conducted his animated discussion about the Race. She leaned toward Fitzgerald. "Did you think of the reaction you'd provoke if you launched those probes?"

"What?"

"The reason all this happened is because of those probes. It isn't just us, or Frey's little group. You've given the Race—" She snorted at the pretentious name. "—incentive to push even harder to drive this country over the edge."

"No one anticipated that they had faster-than-light communications—"

"Except Davidson. And all that means is you would have had, what, another four years or so before the aliens here got word of the launch?"

"By then we would have—"

"What? Gone public? I doubt it. Know the Race better? I think you had what you needed to know six years ago."

"You don't understand—"

"I understand that for six years you sat on this. You studied it, got involved in your own political rivalries, and became enamored of your own discoveries." She stood up and jabbed her finger into his chest. "And none of you did anything about it."

"Frey wanted—"

"Frey was too damn paranoid. He couldn't trust anything that wasn't under his own control. He was so afraid of betrayal that it became a self-fulfilling prophecy."

"The Race had bribed so many—"

"If you had gotten word to enough people in enough departments, they couldn't have suppressed it. They *aren't* omnipotent, they *aren't* all-knowing—"

There was a hiss from behind her and foul air drifted in from the opening that led to the chute. A cable descended from the hole. She heard Dimitri's voice echo above. "Time for your audience."

There was a handle on the end of the cable.

She turned back to Fitzgerald. "Did you force yourself to believe you were doing the right thing, or did you simply ignore the question?"

She picked up the handle, and the cable drew her up the chute before she heard him respond.

Chapter 22

"Sorry to keep you waiting," Dimitri said as the cable pulled Evi through the trapdoor. The cable was dangling through a hole in the ceiling and seemed to operate under remote control. During the ascent, she had thought of swinging up when she cleared the hole, and throttling Dimitri with her legs, much as she had the first dog she'd killed.

Her friend the peeper must have anticipated her thought. He stood well out of reach and covered her with the Mitsubishi.

The cable stopped and she swung herself to the side and stood. "Now what?"

Dimitri tossed her a pair of handcuffs, "Put those on."

She managed to catch them with her right hand. She looked at her left arm and winced at the thought of cuffing that wrist.

Her left hand was clutching her stomach inside the remains of her leather jacket. The heat was getting to her. She was sweating profusely, and she realized that one of the reasons she'd been about to pass out on the first run through was she'd been too drugged to think of shucking the leather.

She peeled off the ruined jacket and got a good look at her arm.

The dog had given her a decent field dressing. But under the shreds of her jumpsuit, the bandage was ripe with her blood. The heat was making it itch.

"Hurry up, Isham. Important people are waiting." Dimitri said "people" like some humans said "moreau," or "frank."

She fumbled with the cuffs, trying to get them around her left wrist without moving that arm. Even with the effort, she had to grit her teeth and endure fiery daggers cutting deep into her shoulder.

When she had the cuffs around her wrists, she gasped. She'd been holding her breath. She looked up from her work to see that Dimitri had used the time to fetch Fitzgerald and have him cuffed.

"Into the cart." He waved them ahead of him, always keeping the gun on Evi.

She watched him as closely as he watched her, and she never saw an opening. Fitzgerald climbed into the back of the golf cart, and when she followed she tried to do it without using her arms. Humidity had condensed on the runner of the cart and she slipped, slamming her left shoulder into the cart.

Pain washed out her vision as a white nova exploded in her arm.

She was on her knees next to the cart, and Dimitri was laughing. She turned to look at him, the smoldering pain turning to rage. She looked at him. He made no move toward her, and the gun never wavered.

He stopped laughing. "Get in the cart."

The heat and the pain made an anger that had been three days festering erupt into a full-blown rage.

She was going to kill this man. She no longer cared about anything but bringing the house down on the people, the things, *the Race*, responsible for the last three days, responsible for the betrayal of the last six years, responsible for the destruction of her homeland. And she would start with Dimitri.

She stared into his eyes. The gun didn't move. She was too far away. She was quicker than he was, but she wasn't quicker than a bullet.

Slowly she stood, nodded at him, and carefully climbed into the back of the cart. There would be a moment when that gun would lower, and then she would move.

"Don't worry about that arm," Dimitri said. "In a few minutes it's either going to be good as new, or else it isn't going to matter."

The cart started rolling through a new set of tunnels, larger ones that grew even larger as they moved away from the cell. Other tunnels emptied into the main one until the tube they were traveling through became ten meters in diameter.

The stench of bile and ammonia, not to mention burning methane, became much, much worse.

The tunnel didn't end so much as have the walls roll back into another ovoid chamber.

The chamber they drove into was another squashed sphere,

thirty meters across. In the center was a two-meter tall, polished-concrete cone that belched a jet of methane flame.

The chamber was taller in proportion than most of the rooms Evi had seen down here, and the reason was obvious. A spiraling two-meter wide ramp snaked around the edges of the chamber three times.

The room was a small auditorium, and the ramp provided seating for the audience.

And the audience was the Race.

The aliens.

There were over a hundred white pulsing forms sprawled on the gradual slope of that spiral ramp. The mass of them exuded a bile-ammonia smell that made it hard for her to breathe. No two of the Race held exactly the same shape: some were conical, some spheroidal, some cylindrical. Most had erupted white tentacles the length of a human arm, in some cases three or four of them, and waved them at the cart that was trundling in the only entrance. They all undulated to a pulsing rhythm she couldn't hear.

The cart pulled to a stop just inside the chamber.

"Get out," said Dimitri. "You're about to be honored."

The gun was still locked on her, so she did as she was told. Fitzgerald followed her, a look of awe on his face.

The three of them seemed to be surrounded by acres of white featureless flesh. A leprous wall of pulsing wax that made soft bubbling sounds that echoed throughout the chamber.

Polyethylene bags of raw sewage, she thought. They smelled like they'd been scraped off the floor of the john in that porno theater.

She hated every last one of them.

But Dimitri would not move that gun off of her.

Fitzgerald walked toward the end of the room opposite the one entrance. The ramp terminated near the ceiling there, and at that point of precedence was a Race that had taken a rough humanoid form. It had a soft, blubbery body, four limbs, and a head built around a hole that formed a mouth of sorts.

This one didn't go to the lengths that the ones in Cleveland had gone to. The ones there had worn fake plastic eyes and dentures and had taken to human clothing to rein in cascading flesh. This one did none of that, and there was no way, even with its token humanoid form, that it could be mistaken for an earthly creature.

Evi rounded the cone, following Fitzgerald. Dimitri stayed a good distance behind her, the gun tracking her every move.

"Welcome," said the lead creature. "In the name of the Octal and the Race."

"Some fucking wel—" she started to say. She stopped because she could now see a concave depression in the floor between the cone and the far end of the room. The cone had blocked it before. The depression sank for two meters, and had stopped Fitzgerald's progress toward the lead creature.

Sitting in the center of the pit was a creature that was neither Race nor anything from Earth.

The thing was a pulsing amoebic form, like the Race. It formed a rough spheroid. Unlike the Race, it was a dull red in color. And rippling across its body were hairlike tentacles that resembled red grass waving in the wind.

The smell of rotting meat hung over the pit.

"Show some respect," Dimitri said. "That's about to become your mother."

Evi couldn't repress her shudder.

"Evi Isham," the leader continued in its bubbling monotone. "You show an aptitude that we find useful when you work for us."

She looked up from the pit. "You've got to be kidding."

The creature went on. Either it didn't understand her or it was ignoring her. "We find few natives useful enough for us to offer what we offer you. You are much more effective than the canines we employ. More effective than Dimitri, the last one we offer this."

She was dumbfounded. After what she had gone through, after what these things had done to her and her planet, they were asking her to . . .

"No," she whispered. "I'm not going to work for—"

"You don't have a choice." Dimitri said from behind her.

The creature kept going on, ignoring her, as if it were reciting a memorized script. "You join with us, bond with us, become one of us. Commune with Mother."

"What the *hell*?" She looked into the pit that smelled like rotting meat. The red spheroid undulated on, oblivious.

"Mother," Dimitri whispered at her. "Race have trouble with English." He laughed. It sounded more ironic than anything else. "Wonder why I keep walking? After a bullet through the neck?"

Evi looked over her shoulder at Dimitri. The gun was still locked on her, he was still too far away, and he was smiling. "I didn't kill you because they're going to do to you what they did to me."

She looked back into the pit. The lead creature went on, but she was only listening to Dimitri now.

"Mother lays eggs," he said, his voice low, almost seductive. "Lays them in any living tissue. The microscopic larvae bond to your cells. They'll do just about everything to keep you alive, until they mature, of course."

She was feeling sick to her stomach.

"Up to that point, you're as invulnerable as the Race are. Fire, acid, electricity, that's it. Only two problems."

"What?" she found herself asking, unable to tear her eyes off the creature in the pit. She was focusing on it now, letting it fill her field of vision. She could see that the cilia that waved across its back were actually hair-thin hollow tubes. The tubes were pointed at the end and resembled hypodermic needles. That must be what they were, ovipositors, designed to inject microscopic eggs into a host.

Thousands of those injectors, millions of eggs.

"Problem is," Dimitri said, "you have to eat *their* food, or the little beasties die off and take you with them. The other is, you have to take the Race's suppressant drugs or the larvae mature."

And the Race thought of themselves as nonviolent.

"You'll embrace Mother, Isham." Dimitri said. "Then, if you don't work for the Race, you'll be eaten alive."

Rage, that's what she felt, that and a fear bordering on panic. She was going to be used, again. Used in the worst possible way. She looked at Mother and could only think that she was about to be raped, and she was panicking because she couldn't see how to fight it.

If only she could do something. If it weren't for that damn gun.

"Scott Fitzgerald," she heard the creature say.

It crossed her mind that it was about to go through that whole speech again for the professor.

Not even close.

"You help in locating our four others. For that you are thanked. Your purpose for the Race and the Octal is served. We allow Dimitri to deal with you as he sees fit."

She got a ten minute speech. Fitzgerald got barely ten seconds. She supposed that it was poetic justice. She'd been duped; Fitzgerald, apparently, had sold everyone out.

Fitzgerald backed away from the pit. He opened his mouth but didn't say anything. He began to shake his head violently.

"No!" was what finally came out. "Not after all—" He broke off, choking on his own words. Evi turned toward him and began to realize what must be going through Fitzgerald's head. His life's work had led up to this point, and he'd just been dismissed as so much extra baggage.

He might have *wanted* what the aliens were offering her.

If she could, she'd trade places. Alien larvae or not, she thought she could take Dimitri in a fair fight.

Fitzgerald was backed all the way to the cone. "I will not let you do this to me." Then he surprised the hell out of Evi by jumping Dimitri. The doctor was still in the air as Dimitri turned the Mitsubishi around to empty half a clip into his chest. Fitzgerald jerked and fell face-first onto the smooth concrete floor with a dull wet thud.

The bubbling around the perimeter of the chamber increased in volume.

Evi was primed for action. The second that Dimitri turned the gun away from her and began firing, she jumped. She was much faster than Fitzgerald, faster than Dimitri. She got behind him and lowered her arms over his head, to pull the chain on her handcuffs across his neck.

Dimitri was trained. He saw her arms lowering and in the split-second he had, he raised the Mitsubishi up to his neck. Her arms met the hard resistance of the submachine gun's short barrel, and the impact sent a shuddering flame of agony down her left arm. Dimitri's right elbow slammed into her abdomen, awakening deep bruises left there by Sukiota's interrogation.

She slammed him face-first into the concrete cone. She felt an explosion in her left wrist; the cuffs were becoming burning brands.

Dimitri jerked against her, rotating. He was now turning to face her, and the gun had come loose. She was no longer clamping on the vulnerable portion of his windpipe; her hands were feeling the back of his head.

They were too close together, leaning by the side of the cone. Dimitri was pushing against her with his knee, trying to clear a space to point the gun at her.

She glanced up at the jet of burning methane shooting out the top of the cone. He glanced up there, too.

"No," he said.

Evi clamped her forearms tight on either side of Dimitri's neck, under the jawline, her hands entangled in his hair. The effort of tightening the muscles flamed up her arm and blurred her vision. She wanted to scream or pass out. She let herself scream.

She put everything she had into the lift and the swing, all the rage, all the pain, all the strength she could squeeze out of her genetically engineered muscles. She could almost hear the bicep in her left arm tear as Dimitri's hundred kilos left the ground. As her forearm brushed the lower edge of the methane flame, every nerve in her shoulder was flayed open and ignited as her shoulder redislocated.

When Dimitri's chin caught on the lip of the gas nozzle, she couldn't hear his screams over her own.

She hung on to the back of his neck, arms on either side of the concrete cone, as Dimitri's face was forced into the fire. His arms flailed widely on the other side of the cone, clawing at her arms. He stared at her through the blue-green flame, and she stared into his eyes as his face reddened, blackened, melted . . .

Evi closed her eyes.

Dimitri stopped struggling.

It took her five minutes or longer to disengage herself from the body. She had to slowly pull her arms over Dimitri's head, and that hurt, especially because the insides of both forearms were badly burned. The only reason she didn't burn herself worse when disengaging herself was because, when she pulled on the back of Dimitri's head, it nodded forward and plugged the hole. That put the flame out.

Once she got the handcuff chain over the back of Dimitri's skull, she slid off of the cone and landed on her ass next to Fitzgerald's corpse. Dimitri fell off of the cone in the opposite direction.

The room filled with the sound of hissing, flameless methane.

She sat down, clutching her arms to her stomach, breathing heavily. She wanted to throw up, but her stomach was empty.

She sat there for a long time it seemed, only aware of the pain in both her arms. She forced herself to look up. The Race were still there, unmoving, bubbling, pulsing, unaffected by the little drama that had played out before them.

"You freakish bastards. You just don't give a shit do you?"

The leader, the one at the head of the spiral ramp, spoke in its underwater monotone, "Personal native arguments do not concern the Octal. We appreciate now that you step in and embrace Mother."

Evi got to her feet, clutching her stomach with both arms. Her laugh broke from her in racking silent spasms. "Fuck you."

She backed away from the pit and the hissing gas jet. "You'll have to kill me first." She was grinning, and that scared her. She was losing it, and it was a bad time to lose it.

"The Race does not kill. Lesser species kill."

She had backed to the cart at the entrance. There seemed to be a shuffling movement along the ramp. The bubbling was deepening in intensity and increasing in volume. Both her arms were burning, the wound on her left arm had burst open and she was bleeding all over the place, and she couldn't help laughing. "Bullshit."

"Evi Isham, you embrace Mother for your own good. You are wounded. You die without Mother's aid."

She looked down at her arm. That *was* a hell of a lot of blood. There was a clear trail from her all the way back to the hissing cone. She clamped her right hand over the wound to stop the bleeding.

The bubbling was reaching a crescendo and the leader continued. "We leave you here to decide as we handle infrastructure problems."

One creature, the one nearest the bottom of the spiral ramp, descended toward her, the cart, and the exit.

Evi looked at the creature, then to the cone back in the center of the room. Flameless methane still hissed into the room.

No wonder these things were acting nervous. Fire was one of the things Dimitri said could hurt the Race. This whole room was about to become a bomb.

She turned to look at the robot golf cart. Electricity was another . . .

She raised her foot and kicked the cowling off the rear of the cart. The plastic cracked off, revealing the inductor housing and the lead wires. She bent over it and grabbed an insulated wire in each hand, even though it hurt like hell. She pulled the wires away from the engine, which sat under the cart, and something out of her sight gave.

She fell on her ass with about a meter of wire in each hand. Even though the pain in her arms whited out her vision, she managed to keep the red wire from touching the blue one. She managed to croak out, "Stop moving. I think there's more than enough juice in this to liquefy you."

When she opened her eyes, the creature had stopped short of the end of the ramp. She got to her feet, hands shaking. More blood was streaming down her arm, and now she couldn't put any pressure on it. Her left hand had stopped hurting, even though she thought her wrist was broken. Felt like it had fallen asleep.

Slowly she turned toward the other end of the room. Yes, she had enough play in the wires to cover the end of the ramp from where she stood. If aliens started bailing from the ramp in other parts of the room, they could make it out the other side of the cart, but it didn't look as if they were built for jumping. "Wrong answer," she told the head alien. "Try again."

"You bleed to death without Mother—"

"You have a one-track mind. Get the picture. *I'm taking your worthless asses with me.*"

The room, not just the leader who'd been addressing her, but the entire room, became silent. The bubbling quieted. Tentacles stopped waving. Undulation ceased.

The only sound was the hissing gas from the methane jet.

"This makes no sense. Such an ending when other options—"

"You've been fucking with this planet for so long that you don't understand revenge?" She couldn't believe she was grinning at the thing. She was feeling light-headed and giddy. Her entire left arm was asleep now.

There was a thudding plop and Evi turned around. One of the Race had jumped from the ramp. It wasn't going to be much more of a standoff. They were going to rush the exit now.

The ground shook under her feet. "What?"

She looked back down the tube of the corridor, and she thought she could hear a crash or an explosion back in that direction.

She turned back to the alien that had jumped the ramp. It wasn't moving toward the exit. It had turned grayish and was pulsing quietly.

The leader spoke again. "We reconsider our offer. Put down the wires and we discuss other options."

The leader sounded weak and was turning gray, too. In fact, all the creatures near the top of the chamber were becoming grayish. As she watched, a dull gray pulsing cone with five tentacles collapsed into itself and rolled off the edge of the ramp, hitting the edge below, pushing aside two grayish fellows.

Damn, Evi thought, *this might look like home to these guys, but I bet, back home, their volcanic vents don't go out.*

The room was filling with methane and they were asphyxiating. A wave of dizziness hit her. *I could use some oxygen myself.*

That started a silent laugh that degenerated into a gasping wheeze.

She thought she could smell smoke under the sulfur-ammonia smells now. She wondered if she really heard gunfire in the background or if it was just wishful thinking.

"We give you what you want," said the lead creature. The

pseudo-humanoid form it wore seemed to be melting into a gray slime. "Name a wish, it is yours."

"I want my life back, I want my country back, most of all—" She paused to catch her breath. "I want to see you dead."

"Isham." Where the hell did that voice come from?

"Isham." The voice came again as the alien spokesman slipped off its perch and slammed into the ramp below. She looked around the room and at first saw only collapsing aliens. Then she saw Dimitri's corpse move.

"Oh, shit."

Apparently Dimitri could still hear, because a blackened skull turned toward her. Empty sockets looked for her as Dimitri's hands groped about him. "Kill you." It came out as a moan.

There was no way that this man could still be alive. His face was burnt off. Despite that, he was on his hands and knees groping around.

Dimitri's right hand brushed the Mitsubishi.

Evi looked from the gun to the methane jet to a few dozen gray asphyxiated aliens, dropped the wires, and ran.

She was twenty meters down the hall before the thought struck her that if Mother's larva were bonded to *all* of Dimitri's cells, then she needed total immolation to kill him, not just burning his face. Thirty meters down the tube and she was sure she could hear gunfire ahead of her. Forty meters down the tube and she heard gunfire from behind her.

She felt her feet leave the ground as a pressure wave blew by her. A flaming hand slammed her into the ceiling. Her last coherent thought was how much she hated explosives.

Chapter 23

Evi woke up in a hospital. They kept her drugged and at the fringes of consciousness for days. By the time she was conscious enough to take full stock of her surroundings, she had been there for at least a week.

The place was an Agency hole. Evi could tell. Her room was private, windowless, and—when she managed to get out of bed once—locked. No comm. Her only contact with other people were with the doctors and nurses, none of whom talked to her.

Go from the frying pan to the fire, Evi thought. *Where do you go from the fire?*

No answers.

Someone had to have gotten to her within five minutes of the explosion, or she would've bled to death. From the looks of things, the Agency.

She had started off in bad shape, but they gave her a lot of time to recover. One thing about an Agency hospital, they knew more about her engineered metabolism than any civilian medics—even though they pretended not to know English.

Or Spanish . . .

Or Arabic . . .

Or any other language she came up with.

At least it gave her a chance to think. And those thoughts brought a whole raft of mixed feelings. On the one hand, she'd been willing to give her life to see those aliens go down, and somehow she'd managed to see that happen and live through it. On the other hand, it was the Agency who'd done it, and that was uncomfortably familiar—not to mention that she was a de facto traitor.

She was also their prisoner.

Evi wondered why they even bothered with fixing her up if they were going to just disappear her.

The more she thought about it over her days of recuperation, the more she wondered about the Agency showing up. It was so convenient, even if it had saved her life. Evi had the uncomfortable feeling that she'd been used, *again*.

When the bones had knitted together, and she'd become ambulatory, she had a visitor who confirmed some of her worst suspicions.

Evi was in the midst of a hundred push-ups—she knew if she tried anything medically objectionable, the silent doctors would come in and stop her. She'd long ago determined that even the bathroom was under constant surveillance—when the door opened. Instead of a doctor or nurse, the door let in Sukiota.

She wanted to ask why she was still alive.

Evi stopped her push-ups, stood up with the help of a crutch, and said to Sukiota, "Someone had to have gotten to me within five minutes, or I would have bled to death."

Sukiota shook her head. She was dressed in an anonymous androgynous suit; the only sign of authority was a ramcard clipped to her lapel. "We got to you in less than thirty seconds, if you're counting from that explosion."

Evi shook her head, somewhat gratified to have someone here respond to her. She'd half expected Sukiota to pull the same mute act that the doctors did. "Now what? Am I under arrest? Now that I'm almost healed, am I about to disappear down some Agency hole?"

Sukiota smiled. "Actually, I'm here to thank you."

"What?"

Sukiota's smile was surreal, as if Evi was looking into a distorted mirror. Physically they were so much alike. Evi didn't like the fact that Sukiota's smile looked so much like her own. "You gave my operation a chance to crack Nyogi. I've been trying to get approval to take them down since I started investigating the Afghanis."

Evi shook her head. She didn't like the way Sukiota's talk was drifting. "Last time you were throwing words like 'traitor' at me."

Sukiota's smile never wavered. She took an opaque evidence bag from her pocket and began to toss it from hand to hand. "I suppose so. If it weren't for certain expediencies on my part, the Agency would have considered you part and parcel of that extra-Agency conspiracy. The Domestic Crisis Think Tank you called it. We finished mopping it up weeks ago."

Evi realized that she had been here a long time.

"Everybody?"

"We're checking the records, but I believe we have all but one accounted for. Of the people you fingered, Frey, Gabriel, and Davidson are on slabs, Fitzgerald is so much carbon, Hofstadter was dumped at a critical care unit in upper Manhattan in the late stages of a stroke and is vegetating two floors below us . . ."

"Price?"

"He's the unaccounted one."

Sukiota was still smiling, and it was getting on Evi's nerves. "Did you set me up?"

Sukiota tossed the white evidence bag up, following it with her eyes. "I was pissed with you." She caught the bag and tossed it to her other hand. "But I needed you. You served your purpose."

"That whole scene in the subway—"

Sukiota shrugged and caught the bag.

"You bastards set me up!"

"You didn't do anything that you weren't about to do anyway. I saw a good chance you'd go straight to our target—"

"Damn it," Evi yelled. "You knew about Nyogi all along. You could have stormed the place any time you wanted too."

"You know better than that, Isham. The Feds give the Agency major latitude in domestic covert ops, but Nyogi is a major corporation with major congressional and Executive support. I couldn't get approval to go in."

"But you went in."

"After you."

"What?"

Sukiota laughed. "I told you I carried out certain expediencies on your behalf. Before we let you escape, I resurrected your Agency file."

Evi just stared.

"Different rules apply to hot pursuit, especially when an active duty agent is involved."

"You used me as an excuse?"

Sukiota nodded. "And after we did that, we couldn't very well let you die. That would have been embarrassing."

All of a sudden she had just come full circle. She was right back where she had started, an Agency creature. And, again, as always, she had no choice in the matter.

Evi sighed. It might have been fatigue, but she felt that she had used up all of her anger. Her emotions were one vast plain of resignation. "What about the aliens?" she asked.

"I'd say that's on a need to know basis, but that'd be a fraud. Rest assured, the Feds are sifting through the UABT complex, the buildings at Columbia, and underneath the Nyogi tower. We've captured a number of aliens—" Sukiota seemed uncomfortable with the word—"and enough people and agencies are involved this time that no one is going to bottle this up." Sukiota shook her head. "Everyone from the Biological Regulatory Commission and NASA to Defense Intel and the Department of the Interior . . . The Agency handed the alien problem off to everyone else. We've got other problems."

"Like what?" As if the aliens weren't enough. What the hell could take precedence over that in the Agency's agenda?

"You should know. We had a tracking device on you all that time. RF, audio, limited video . . ."

It began to sink in, exactly what that meant.

The Bronx.

The entire military setup. Evi had waltzed through all of it, handed it all to the Agency.

It must have shown in her expression because Sukiota nodded. "I see you *do* know what I'm talking about. That's why I'm here, really. I resurrected your file, and I have to release you, but I'm retiring you. You're not going to interfere with any future operations."

"I'm not—"

"No, you're not, even though I think you have an inclination otherwise; it would be embarrassing. And since it would be inconvenient to threaten you—" Sukiota tossed the evidence bag at Evi. It sprung open on the foot of the bed.

Evi leaned over on her crutch, grabbed the end of the bag and upended it. Out fell a pair of velvet-lined handcuffs. The same ones she had liberated from Diana's bedstand. They still had a splattering of blood on them from the veep.

"It would be very nice for Diana Murphy if you led a nice quiet life as Eve Herman from now on."

Sukiota left her.

Evi stared at the cuffs.

*   *   *

When Evi hobbled through the threshold of Diana's loft, she was the recipient of a shocked expression, then of some very tall hugs. The reunion was so teary that it took nearly ten minutes before either of them was close to being coherent.

"I thought I'd never see you again," Diana said, wiping her eyes.

"I never thought I'd see anyone again," Evi said. "Can I sit? The leg's still kind of bad."

Diana helped her over to the couch, peppering Evi with questions. How was she? What happened?

Evi shushed her. She hadn't realized how much she had missed Diana until then, how she had worried. She finally told Diana *everything*.

Diana's reaction was unexpected. "Damn, until now I thought the whole thing was some kind of silly hoax."

"What was a hoax?" Evi asked. She hadn't expected to be believed so readily.

"The broadcast—"

"What broadcast?"

"That's right, you've been incommunicado. I recorded it. I'll try and find the ramcard . . ."

Diana moved up and switched on her comm. She sifted through the pile of ramcards as the thing warmed up. Then she inserted the card and fell back next to Evi on the couch.

"I really missed you," Diana whispered.

Evi stroked Diana's hair, for the first time with her left hand, and watched the comm. There, centered in a frame that was obviously shot from a hand-held camera was David Price.

Behind him was a familiar-looking cargo hauler, and lined up by the end of the trailer behind Price, were four blubbery-white aliens. Evi watched as David got very chummy with Corporal Gurgueia. The Jaguar was holding an AK-47.

"They hijacked the damn truck," Evi whispered.

Diana whispered into Evi's ear. "What?" Evi could feel the warmth of her breath.

"They hijacked the damn truck!" Evi shouted, smiling from ear to ear. They had done it. By everything that was holy, they'd completed the objective . . .

She realized that she was being unreasonably happy. Sukiota had told her, almost point blank, that the shit was about to hit the fan.

Even so, Evi couldn't help grinning. It was a small battle, but she had won it.

They had won it.

A battle, but the war was still out there.

Evi hit the mute on the remote sitting on the table in front of her. Then she hugged Diana back. She was free. Sukiota had retired her, and now she owed her allegiance to no one.

Evi looked up into Diana's human eyes and realized that that wasn't quite true. She also realized that she hadn't worn sunglasses or contacts for nearly two weeks.

"Diana."

"Mmm?"

Right now Evi was holding Diana about as close as she could while staying a separate person. She finally had choices. If she wanted, she could divorce herself from everything the Bronx would bring.

"You know," Evi told Diana, "I've become unreasonably close to you in a short time."

"Feeling's mutual."

Evi had choices, but Sukiota had pressed the point home that, if she chose not to remain aloof, she would drag along someone she loved. "I have a decision to make." Evi whispered. "One I can't make without you."

"Later," Diana said, kissing her.

SPECTERS
OF THE
DAWN

Dedicated to three remarkable women:

First—
Jane Butler, my agent, without whose unbounded enthusiasm my career wouldn't exist.

Second—
Sheila Gilbert, my editor, who had the temerity to buy this before it was written, and without whom this book wouldn't exist.

And most important—
Margret Ann, Peg, my mom, without whom I wouldn't exist, who infected me with this creative mania in the first place. (Placing the blame firmly where it belongs. At least I'm not too far gone. I could have been a poet.)

Acknowledgment

Thanks to the Cleveland SF Workshop.

Chapter 1

It was a clean sweep for October—the fourth Monday in a row that Angelica Lorenzo y Lopez wanted to tell her boss to grease his head and go pearl diving for hemorrhoids. Her shift was a half hour into nirvana and they could have flushed the whole place for all she would care. *Ralph's Diner* was dead in the water. Half an hour waiting for Judy to show up to relieve her, and Angel hadn't waited on one effing table.

Her greaseball boss, Sanchez, was sitting in his little yellowing manager's office, peering through his little one-way mirror at his nickel-and-dime empire as if he was too lordly to cover for Judy. Angel thought of giving the finger to the mirror. She admired her self-control for not giving in to the temptation.

Judy was late every effing Monday and Sanchez gave no never mind every time Angel complained. Angel had decided that it must be one of two things—either Judy was going for joyrides in Santa's lap back in the manager's office, or it was because Angel was the only nonhuman who worked in the place.

Probably both.

A restaurant in the Mission District, of all places, and Angel was the only moreau serving tables. And Sanchez wondered why business sucked.

And boy, did business suck.

There were a total of *three,* count them, *three* whole people in the place. One was a regular, one of the street people who came in for coffee every afternoon. He was an old graying rodent with thinning fur and naked spotted-pink hands that shook as he drank his *one*, count it, *one* cup of coffee. In the back sat a small black-and-gray striped feline who was slowly shredding a bacon cheeseburger—a pink's food, but the cat didn't seem to mind. The cat's ribs showed under his fur, and Angel tagged him as a recent immigrant who'd probably never seen real human food.

Those two, and her. A rat, a cat, and a rabbit. For once, at a hundred and twenty centimeters—not counting ears—Angel was the biggest one in the room. *Ralph's* was so empty you could land a ballistic shuttle down the checkerboard linoleum aisle.

From the looks of things she didn't even have a reasonable expectation of getting a tip.

During Angel's third glance at the clock, Judy finally showed.

"About time, pinky," Angel said as Judy ran through the front door, out of the fog.

"Don't harass me today. I've had enough sh—"

Angel hopped down off the stool she'd been sitting on. She could hear Judy trying to quiet her labored breathing, and Angel's nose told her that the moisture on Judy's face was more sweat than condensing fog. Judy had rushed to get here more than forty-five minutes late.

Angel's heart bled. "I might miss the whole first quarter—"

"I'm sorry about your football game."

"Yeah, right." Angel stretched to remove her denim jacket from the coatrack.

"You'd want me to risk my life on those roads—" Judy started.

"Don't do me no favors, pinky." Angel stormed out the door without bothering to clock out.

Angel had little sympathy. The pink wench had a car, while the poor ol' morey rabbit had been doing without wheels since she'd sold her ancient prewar Toyota to cinch the money to move to this burg. Somehow, this poor old lepus pedestrian was always on time—

Except, of course, when some human woman goes and makes her late. Angel sighed as she pushed through the thickening fog on Howard Street. All those moreaus who weren't eating at *Ralph's* were probably at the game or at some bar that had a holo feed from the action. She, unfortunately, was due for the latter. Tickets for Earthquakes games were at a premium that she just couldn't afford.

Her destination was a little bar nestled in the newest part of the coast south of Market Street, *The Rabbit Hole*. Unfortunately, *Ralph's* wasn't on the coast. Angel had thought she'd have the time for a nice leisurely walk—she should have assumed that Judy would be late again and scouted a game cast that was closer by.

It was a rare bar that didn't charge a cover that rivaled the ticket prices. The NFL would have had a monopolistic conniption, but the NonHuman League didn't have much legal clout, and was probably grateful for the exposure.

She didn't have much of a choice if she was going to be in time for the game. She took a deep breath soggy with fog, and started running.

Small Angel was, but she was a genetically engineered rabbit whose great-grandparents had been designed for combat as part of the Peruvian infantry. The musculature on her thighs was half again as broad as her hips, and her feet were as long and as broad as her forearms. A few humans thought lepine moreaus were funny-looking or cute—but with rare exceptions, they were the fastest infantry ever to come out of the gene-labs.

She bolted down Howard at full speed, with barely three meters of visibility, telling herself that it wasn't the smartest thing to do.

Even as she thought it, a band of ratboys emerged in front of her. The fog sucked up sound and smell as well as light, so she had no time to stop when she realized they were there. She was leaping over their heads before they had time to realize she was bearing down on them. She retreated down a steep section of hillside, letting the fog soak up their curses.

She tried to pace herself so she hit the cross streets with the lights. She only had one close call with a remote driven van that freaked when she appeared in front of it. She left the Areoline van with its horn blaring, hazards going, and its collision avoidance program absolutely convinced it had hit something.

She made the trip in less than ten minutes. It was five to six when Angel got to *The Rabbit Hole,* to find it almost as empty as *Ralph's.* One table of moreaus, two feline, two canine, and a fox. That was it.

"Wha?"

The answer was on the holo behind the bar. Angel walked up, mesmerized. On the holo was the president of the United States. He was in the process of blaming the latest run of interspecies rioting on aliens from Alpha Centauri.

"Shit."

Angel climbed on to a seat in front of the bar and watched President Merideth do his schtick. It was a lost cause.

"Shit."

She'd been looking forward to the game all week. Frisco vs. Cleveland, and she wasn't even going to see so much as one down. She twitched her nose and said, "Ain't fair. Bet he'd wait till the end of the game if it was the N-effing-L."

She waved the bartender over. He was a moreau rabbit, but his fur was white as opposed to her spotted tan. She ordered a Corona and lime and closed her eyes. Yeah, she'd just missed a crowd of moreys. The scents of a dozen species still hung in the bar's air along with the perfume of a like number of beers that had christened the bar in the past hour. A rich, empty smell.

Angel chugged the Corona and ordered another.

Another boring weekend loomed on the horizon. Home with Lei, or more likely, alone. Lei always seemed to find things to do with her free time. Things that generally blew more capital than Angel could afford. Sure, Lei was willing to pay Angel's tab for an evening out—

But Angel was never comfortable with that. She'd stay home and probably vegetate in front of the comm watching the latest news reports of the fighting in New York and LA.

Around the fourth Corona the bartender's whiskers sat at a slightly condescending angle. "What can I do for you, Miss?"

"Refill me."

"Don't you think you've had enough?" It irritated Angel to notice that the bartender's voice held no trace of the slight lisp normal for a lepus. Almost sounded human.

"Ain't driving, and the game got zeroed." She pushed her glass at him. "Nothing better to do."

The bartender shrugged and bent over behind the bar.

Angel stepped up on the seat so she could lean over the bar and add, "Find a lime that doesn't taste like a used rubber."

The bartender shoved another Corona at her while, on the holo, Merideth began to invoke the names of the Joint Chiefs and several leading scientists.

Angel snorted and sipped her drink.

Preempted by aliens. Great. Angel was effing sick of aliens. She had hoped the media would have gotten over its alienitis over the course of the summer. Hell, everyone and their brother had been milking the story since January.

Still no end in sight.

So the CIA or the FBI or someone finds a bunch of white blubbery things nesting under the Nyogi tower in Manhattan. Even if the MannSatt news service had done a God-help-us live broadcast from an alien "lair" under the Nyogi tower two months before Bronx artillery zeroed the building. So what? Even if they come from another planet, it's better than letting the Japs run things, right? Look what happened to them.

But it kept coming, aliens, aliens, aliens. It couldn't be escaped even if you killed the comm, because that effing huge white-dome alien habitat they built over the ruins of Alcatraz was the most prominent thing on the Frisco skyline.

So what are we going to do? Go to war with a planet a few light-years away?

Talk about unreal.

Tabloid stuff, but it was tabloid stuff that was getting hard news coverage. After a half century of isolationism, it seemed that the U.S. had found a new evil empire. Leaks from the blessed U.S. government made the aliens look like some sort of interstellar covert action experts that were doing the kind of political destabilization games that the CIA used to excel at—or said it excelled at, anyway.

All supposed to keep anyone from getting off this rock.

"But why," she mumbled. "It's such a *lovely* planet."

Personally, Angel thought Merideth was just grabbing at anything that gave him even a remote hope of reelection. Or, failing that, of leaving office without becoming the most despised president since H. Ros—

Angel felt the hackles rise on the back of her neck, under the collar of her denim jacket. She looked up the bar and saw that the bartender was gone.

She smelled a pink smell.

"One furball left. Seems upset about something . . ." A human voice, behind her.

No, Angel thought to herself, don't turn around. The bartender was right, you've had too much to drink.

Did everyone else just up and leave?

"Wassa matter, something *wrong* with our President?" Another human spoke.

The Rabbit Hole was a morey hangout. Why'd pinks have to walk in and fuck with her? They didn't hassle the other moreys. She would've heard *that*.

She tried to ignore them. Perhaps they'd leave.

"Think he's bein' disrespectful." The first voice. How many were there? Angel should have been able to gain a rough estimate from their smell, but stale lime was flavoring everything.

And, damn it, they couldn't even get her gender right. Just because she didn't have globs of fat on her chest like a human woma—

"Talking to you!" said a third pink with the ugliest bass rumble excuse for a voice that Angel had ever heard. A hand grabbed her shoulder and spun her around on the bar stool. Her drink flew out of her hand, splashing on the legs of the nearest human.

Three young human males. Hispanic, black, and anglo. She was the only morey left in the bar.

The three closed in around her, a wall of jeans, leather, and hairless flesh. Even the heads. They were all shaved totally bald, down to the eyebrows.

The baldness meant one of two things. Either they were some rabid prohumanists who'd taken the morey slang term *pink*—meaning hairlessness—to heart and depilatoried their whole bodies. Or they were Hare Krishnas.

They weren't chanting.

The anglo pink had his hand on her shoulder. He'd been the one she'd doused with Corona. The sleeves of his jacket were torn off, revealing one bicep tattooed with a flaming sword. The glass she'd been drinking from rested by one of his boots. He raised his foot and placed it on top of the glass. A second later there was the gunshot sound of the glass giving way.

He ground the pieces under his boot, smiled, and looked like he was about to enjoy a nice game of trash the rabbit. The black was shaking his shoulder. "Chuck the bunny, Earl. That's not what we're here—"

She told herself that these guys weren't a hard-core gang, or they'd have trashed the bar by now. The adrenaline was pumping, and she could feel the edge on her nerves driving her to do something. She held herself back, but her muscles were vibrating with the effort. She couldn't explode, not when she was drunk, and if she went along, she might get out of this with her hide intact.

Earl wasn't listening to his friend. "Look't he did to my jeans—"

The pronoun did it. "*I'm* a girl, *you shitheads!*"

Angel grabbed the seat of the bar stool, spun around, and planted a back-kick directly between Earl's legs.

That ugly bass voice gasped and was choked off with a breathless squeak. He lost his grip on her shoulder and fell to the ground, clutching his groin. Angel's kick was something of consequence. Especially when she *meant* it.

The bar stool was still spinning, and time rubberbanded, slowing as it stretched.

"Earl, you fuckhead—" Angel heard the black say to the lump on the ground. She was slipping off the stool, into the gap she had made in the wall of humans, even as she heard the whistle of air toward her.

She ducked, but not in time, as something very hard slammed into the right side of her head.

She stumbled away from the bar stool, head thrumming, vision blurred. The fur on that side of her face was suddenly warm and tacky. She backpedaled, paralleling the bar, retreating toward the bathrooms.

The hispanic was twirling a chain in his right hand.

To hell with the non-human gun control laws. She was going to dig her automatic out of the underwear drawer and start carrying it again.

The hispanic swung the chain, but she managed to dodge it.

As she dove, blood got into her eye. Blinded, she ran—and slammed into a wall. The entire right side of her body went numb with the shock of the impact. She didn't start aching until she was assdown on the floor.

The hispanic laughed. Angel didn't feel fear or pain, just a stomach-churning embarrassment. Even after five Coronas she should be able to handle herself better.

The hispanic's laughter stopped so abruptly that she forced her eyes open, despite the blood gumming them shut.

She was on the floor next to the "men's" room. It gave her an oblique view of a black-furred arm sticking out the door. In the hand was an equally black Heckler and Koch 10-millimeter Valkyrie automatic.

Her gaze shifted to the three punks. Earl, the fuckhead anglo, was on the ground in a fetal position. The black was bent over him. The one with the chain was halfway to the door to the bathroom.

A calm voice with an almost liquid Brit accent echoed out of the bathroom. "Please drop the chain."

"We know you. Fucking hairball don't . . ."

"Scare you?" The owner of the arm stepped out of the bathroom. He had to be the handsomest vulpine Angel had ever seen.

"Chico," said the black, "I think Earl's dyin.'"

"Shut up with the names, man." Chico, the one with the chain, was losing his bravado. He tried to face down the vulpine. "If cops catch you—"

The fox laughed. A soft sound, but deep. "They'd approve of you? Please, drop the chain and leave."

"Damn it, Chico, I'm calling an ambulance." The black ran out of the bar. In search of a public comm, Angel thought.

She looked at Earl.

Earl wasn't moving.

She looked at Chico.

"You can't fuck with this—" Chico wasn't moving either.

The fox cocked the automatic. "Please."

The sound of the gunshot was deafening. It was still echoing in Angel's sensitive ears when she heard the sound of metal hitting the ground.

The truncated section of Chico's chain was swinging about three centimeters short of his right hand. The rest of the chain lay on the floor.

"Fine, keep the chain," said the fox. "Just leave."

Chico bolted, nearly tripping over Earl. The fox kept his gun aimed at the doorway for a few seconds before he holstered it.

He wore a green suit that looked good on him—unlike most every other sort of pink-type clothing you could drape on a morey. The green brought out the luster of the red fur on his face and tail. She barely noticed that it was tailored to conceal a shoulder holster.

He held out a black-furred hand to Angel. She realized that she'd been on her ass all along. She grabbed his hand and frantically pulled herself to her feet.

"Please," he objected. "Be careful. Head wounds—"

"Bleed a hell of a lot," Angel snapped. She shook her head. "Sorry, I shouldn't be short with you."

"You can't help the way you were designed." His engineered vulpine mouth managed to form a rather nice smile. And Angel realized that her savior had just taken a cut back at her.

She rolled her eyes and walked over to Earl. The world was looking a lot less shaky. A combination of adrenaline and an engineered metabolism seemed to have cooked off most of the alcohol. She was somewhere between the tag end of a buzz and the start of a splitting migraine.

Earl was curled into a ball. It looked liked she had not only done a number on his balls, but had had a pretty bad influence on his pelvis and a few ribs as well. Earl'd coughed up his share of blood. Fortunately, Angel could still hear him breathing. She shook her head. "I didn't think I hit him that hard."

Yeah, but look at him now—sailed two meters before he landed.

She felt the fox's hand on her shoulder. "Are you going to wait for the ambulance to show up?"

From the way he said it, she knew he didn't intend to stick around. She didn't blame him. It was illegal for a morey to own a firearm, and considering what was happening in the rest of the country, it wouldn't be pleasant to have the cops catch you with one.

"Think his friends really called an ambulance?" she asked.

He shrugged. "There's a comm up on the corner. We can call one from there."

Angel nodded.

Behind them, on the bar's holo, President Merideth finished speaking with a plea to end interspecies violence. The broadcast rejoined the morey football game. Frisco-Cleveland, scoreless in the third quarter.

Angel ignored it.

They saw the ambulance land from across Mission Street. Its lights were barely visible descending through the fog—rotating flashers cutting slices out of the night air. For a few seconds, sirens and the foghorns off the bay fought a muffled battle for attention.

The ambulance led the cops by about twenty seconds. A crowd had gathered out in the front of *The Rabbit Hole,* and Angel and her companion were half a block up the street. The cops didn't pay any mind to them or to any of the two or three dozen moreaus up and down Mission.

The two of them stood in the doorway of an old earthquake-relief building, a whitewashed cinder block cube that was wrapped in a cloak of graffiti, across the street from another relic of the '34 quake, an on-ramp for the old Embarcadero Freeway. The on-ramp rose into the fog, so the abrupt stop it made in midair wasn't visible. The end hung somewhere over Howard Street and anyone who drove on it now would eventually crash into the luxury condos that held sway on the new coast south of Market.

The ambulance took off, sirens blaring. Angel shook her head and winced when she started feeling the cut on her cheek again. She'd managed to wipe most of the blood off with a towel she stole from the bar, but she needed to get home and clean up.

The fox noticed her distress, and he handed her a handkerchief.

She pressed it against the side of her face. "Shit like this ain't supposed to go down here."

"It happens everywhere."

"This is San Francisco. We're supposed to dance hand in hand over golden hills with flowers behind our ears."

A soft laugh came from the fox. "Would you prefer LA? An incident like this down there and police would start a house-to-house—"

"And in New York the National Guard would call in an air strike. I'm still disappointed. I moved here to avoid this shit."

"Where's you come from?"

"Cleveland."

"I'm sorry."

They stood there in silence for a few minutes, watching the phoenix-emblazoned cop cars disappear into the mist, one by one.

"Damn," Angel said. "I don't even know your name."

The fox turned his head toward her and smiled. "We've missed the formal introduction, haven't we? My name's Byron."

Byron held out his hand, still smiling. Most moreaus Angel knew of didn't have much of a repertoire as far as facial expressions went. Angel's own smile amounted to a slight turning at the corners of the mouth, but Byron's muzzle crinkled, his eyes tilted, his cheeks pulled up and his ears turned outward slightly. He smiled with his entire face, and somehow it looked natural, not like a fox aping a human.

Somewhere there was a British gene-tech who was very proud of himself.

The smile was infectious and Angel mirrored it, even though it hurt her cheek. She took his hand. "Angel."

"Angel." He said it slowly, his voice lending her name an exotic tone. The smile grew a touch wider, as if she'd just provided him with the answer to a complicated problem as opposed to just her name.

"Lovely name," he said and Angel thought to herself that an English accent seemed to fit perfectly in a vulpine mouth.

And she'd always thought of her name as casting against type. "Where'd you learn to shoot like that?"

"Section 5, Ulster antiterrorist brigade. God save whatever's left of the monarchy." Byron shrugged. "U.S. citizen for fifteen years, but I can't shake the accent."

"What's wrong with your accent?"

"A vulpine accent is a few steps below Cockney. I'd lose it in a minute if I could."

Angel thought of the bartender who tried so hard to sound human. "Don't. I like it."

Byron shook his head.

"Trust these ears. You have a very sexy voice."

Byron smiled again. They were still holding hands and he brought his other hand up to trace the undamaged side of her face. "I would never argue with an angel."

He lowered his hand and looked down Mission. The cops had all left, and the sky was dark beyond the fuzzy light of the streetlamps. A late October chill rolled off of the water. Angel shivered slightly.

"Apparently," Byron said, "the crisis is over."

Angel nodded and let go of his hand.

"We really should do something about your face—"

"Fine, really."

"I have a first aid kit in my car."

Angel looked up at Byron's face and the look in his eyes made her wonder exactly what he was thinking, and if it was anything close to what she was thinking.

Chapter 2

Angel knew something unusual was going on when Byron walked off toward the bay. Wordlessly, she followed him as they paralleled the water past the new Oakland Bay Bridge and into the forest of condos on the postquake coastline. Occasionally the fog would roll back far enough for Angel to see some of the coast-hugging "reef" out in the bay. Even though it was less obvious here than it was on the coastline between Market and Telegraph Hill, if you looked at the forms sticking out of the water, it was easy to imagine the fifty-sixty meters of wharf and landfill that had slid into the bay during the big one.

There was something perverse in having people pay a good five hundred K to live right on the edge of the destruction in a shiny new luxury condo. If anything, it proved a direct relationship between wealth and stupidity. Angel could only make out the vaguest out-lines of the first story of the building they approached—but from that glimpse Angel decided that the people living there had to be *very* stupid.

Byron led her to a secure parking garage adjacent to the build-ing. His car was parked in one of the reserved parts of the garage. Money to service the parking had to run better than the rent on her apartment. The car fit the place.

Angel finally spoke. "A BMW?"

"A BMW 600e sedan," Byron responded. He pulled a small re-mote out of his pocket. He pressed a few buttons and the trunk popped open.

"I'm impressed." The sloping blue vehicle did everything to

exude money and power short of grabbing her by the scruff of the neck and shaking her. She could be looking at a hundred grand, easy.

Angel finally noticed the cut of Byron's suit. A morey wearing a suit had to have money. But Byron's suit wasn't an altered human three-piece. The damn thing was tailored for a fox. That was nearly as impressive as the car.

Byron rummaged in the trunk and came out with a green case with a red cross on it. He handed it to her. "Let me give you a place to sit." He pressed a few more buttons on the remote and the passenger door opened behind her. The leather bucket seat rotated ninety degrees to face the open door.

Angel stared at it and didn't move.

"It isn't going to bite."

Angel shook her head. "Never seen a car that did that." Sitting, she sank five or six centimeters into the contoured seat. She wished she had furniture this nice at home.

The first aid case rested on her knees. Byron opened it. "First thing, let's clean that off." He withdrew a package of gauze and a bottle. "This may sting a little."

Byron opened the bottle and Angel got a sharp whiff of alcohol. He doused the gauze and rubbed the fur on her cheek. Her eyes watered and her wince must have been noticeable. Byron pulled away the gauze, which was now red with her blood.

Angel looked up at a slightly blurred fox. "What?"

"It looked like I was really hurting—"

"I'm fine."

"You're crying."

"I'm not crying!" she sniffed. "Just dress the thing."

Byron nodded and went back to cleaning off her wound. It hurt like hell. Angel tried to get her mind off of it. "So—" She grimaced as Byron applied fresh gauze. "—what you do for a living?"

He pulled a small razor out of the kit. "Overpaid delivery boy." Byron shaved the hair from around her wound. She felt a slight tug, and one of her whiskers fell in her lap. "Until I was laid off." Byron finished. From the sound, he didn't want to talk about it.

Angel sat, silent, as he finished binding up her face. When he was done, she was scared to look in the sideview mirror. But despite her fears, the dressing only formed a small rectangle on her right cheek.

She touched her cheek lightly. "At least the scars will be symmetrical."

He leaned over to peer into the small mirror. "I'm curious about that other one." He reached over her other shoulder and touched the reflection of her other cheek. On her left cheek was a scar that pulled up one corner of her mouth in a permanent smile.

"Long time ago. You don't want to hear."

"Maybe I do." His finger dropped from the mirror, but his arm remained draped over her shoulder.

Angel sighed. He really didn't want to hear this. "Ten years ago, a sleazy excuse for a ferret tried to rape me."

There was an uncomfortably long silence. Byron finally said, "I'm sorry."

"I told you."

"Perhaps I should take you home."

Did she screw up? Still had his arm around her shoulder—good, Angel thought. Let's just not tell him what *happened* to that ferret.

"I'd appreciate the ride."

Byron let go of her and walked around to the driver's side. "Where am I going?"

"The Mission District," Angel said, rehearsing in her mind how she was going to ask him up to her place. If he was paying any attention, he could probably smell what she was feeling. She certainly could—even over the stale lime from *The Rabbit Hole*—and the lust-smell was making her self-conscious.

Angel's building was near the center of the Mission District, in the heart of a swath of San Francisco's ubiquitous Victorians and pseudo-Victorians. Many of the houses Byron drove by had survived two major quakes—in fact, there were jokes that restoration work had done more damage in this part of the Mission District than any earthquake could.

Despite the historical context, Angel still thought of her place as an architectural assault. A bay window squatted over an entrance that tried to look like a Roman arch. Both were flanked by square towers that were topped by merlons, of all things. The whole thing sat on a brick foundation wrapped in wrought iron that was close enough to the tilted street that it gave the illusion of being canted at a dizzying angle. The street was so cockeyed this far west of 23rd that, while there were six steps to the door on the right, there were only two to the left.

Byron pulled to a stop between a beat-up off-blue Ford Jerboa and a hulking, heavily modified Plymouth Antaeus. He turned his wheels to the curb and said, "Nice place."

Angel glanced up and down 23rd, but he had parked right in front of her house. "You're talking about that house, there?"

Byron shrugged.

No accounting for taste. Give it time, Angel thought, eventually she'd be in love with anachronistic monstrosities like the rest of the city.

But she wasn't going to hold her breath.

"Come in for a drink?" She wished she'd come up with something less cliché-ridden for the time she spent thinking about it.

"My pleasure, Angel." It might have been her imagination, but Byron made her name sound like an endearment.

Angel led him upstairs to her flat, having forgotten totally about her roommate. And, having forgotten about Lei, of course Lei was there in the living room waiting for them.

Angel had barely opened the door before Lei bounced off the couch and said, "Early night. How are you—What the hell happened? Are you all right?"

Angel opened her mouth to say something.

"And who's this?" Lei finished without taking a breath.

Lei was a Vietnamese canine, but Angel had suspicions that she was really an odd-looking ferret with hyped reflexes. Lei was already shaking Byron's hand before Angel had managed to get a word out.

"Lei," Angel finally managed, stepping out of the way so Byron could enter the second-story apartment. "Byron. Byron, Lei." Angel felt a little overwhelmed, being squeezed between a pair of two-meter-tall moreaus.

"Pleased, I'm sure." Byron said with a slightly amused smile plastered on his face.

"Sorry I'm back early," Angel said, "but things came up."

"Really no problem," Lei said, then whipped her head back to face Byron. "I can *imagine*." Angel felt Lei's tail swat her on the ass.

"*Lei—*" Angel began.

"How did the game go?" Lei asked as she stopped pumping Byron's hand.

Angel stood there, for a second not getting Lei's question.

"Angel, the *game*."

"I, uh—" For some reason Angel glanced at Byron. "Don't know."

"After all your—" Lei glanced at Byron herself. "Oh, yeah, things came up, didn't they?"

"Well, yes, you see—"

"Oh, my, look at that time." Lei didn't look anywhere near a clock. She reached past Angel to grab a purse hanging off the back of a chair. "It was nice meeting you, Byron." She pumped his hand again. "But I have to go. Things to see, people to do."

Lei turned and gave Angel a very broad wink before she slipped past Byron and out the door.

"Lei?" Angel sighed as she heard the door downstairs swing closed. "I hate that."

"Interesting person."

Angel closed the door as Byron walked in. She looked over the living room. Great, Lei'd been cleaning again. Byron was going to think she was some anal neat freak. "Make yourself at home." Were clichés the only thing she could come up with? "I'm going to change into something more—" *Don't say comfortable!* "—clean."

"Please, take your time."

Angel walked into her bedroom and ripped off the blood-spattered shirt and looked at herself in the mirror. "You're still a little drunk," she whispered at her reflection as she manhandled her jeans off over her feet. "Got to be it."

She looked around for something to wear. Compared to the spotless living room, her room was a blast crater. Angel started by trying to find something that smelled clean, and ended up shoving a double armful of clothes into the closet.

She had to make an effort to avoid further cleaning. "Calm down, Angel," she whispered.

She looked at her reflection. She could just forgo the clothes. Clothing was a human quirk anyway. It was her place, right?

She grabbed a robe from the closet, a metallic-green thing that she'd bought in Chinatown. She almost walked out without ripping off the price tag. She tossed the tag under the bed.

"I really need a drink."

Angel walked past the living room and rummaged in the fridge. Coke, Budweiser, a lonely bulb of Ki-Rin, a bottle of white wine . . .

She grabbed the wine.

Angel walked out into the living room and Byron was leaning back on the couch, jacket and tie off, watching the comm. Angel walked up next to him and handed him a glass.

"The local game's blacked out, but I found the Denver game."

Angel looked up in time to see the Denver Mavericks' quarterback get destroyed in a sack that involved a fox, two tigers, and a canine. *"Yes!"* Angel said at the sight almost spilling her wine. "You a fan?"

"Was there any other reason to be in that bar?" There was something odd in the way Byron said that. "The service is bloody rotten and I can't say much for the clientele. With one exception, of course." He toasted her with his glass. God, she loved that accent.

Angel killed the light and sat down next to Byron.

Byron continued, "Of course, I started watching *real* football—" The Mavericks were second and five, and Al Shaheid, the canine quarterback, sent an incomplete pass off into nowhere. Byron winced. "Didn't he see that? Rajhadien was wide open."

"What do you mean *real* football?" Third down and Shaheid was backpedaling with the ball. "Sack the bastard!"

"Soccer." Somehow, Shaheid slipped through a gap in the defense and ran for ten and a first down. "Yes!" Byron said with as much enthusiasm as Angel had shown in response to the sack. "But, as far as I know, the States is the only place they let moreaus play anything professionally."

"What's your team?" Angel asked, sliding into a comfortable nook under Byron's left arm.

"Denver—"

"You bastard! I'm tempted to throw you out right now." Byron's tail moved around behind her, and Angel reached down and idly began to stroke it.

Angel felt Byron's sharp nose nuzzle her ear. "I suppose you're Cleveland?" he whispered.

"Are you kidding? The worst team in the league?"

"How about the Warriors?" Byron asked as the Mavericks' opponents got a flag on the play. Someone had used their claws again. Trust the Bronx Warriors to do that at least once a game.

"I don't believe you." Angel slipped a hand into Byron's shirt, stroking the fur on his abdomen. "You're in the town with the best team in the league."

"Last year maybe."

Angel set down her drink and started undoing the buttons on his shirt. "Last year, this year, next year, every year—"

"That's why I'm not an Earthquakes fan." Byron set down his own drink. "They're all so full of themse—" One of the Mavericks' receivers had broken out and was running down the sidelines. "Go, go, go." Byron began quietly chanting, as Angel undid his pants.

Angel glanced back at the comm and saw the touchdown. They put up the score and it was Mavericks, 25 to zip. There were a dozen seconds left on the clock for the first half. The Warriors might as well just pack up and go home. Not that anyone in his right mind would want to go to the Bronx right now. At least not until there was a cease-fire.

Byron reached over and hit the mute button on the remote.

"You were really upset when the game got preempted," Byron said as his hands slipped the tie from her robe.

"I was looking forward to a decent massacre." Angel nipped at one of Byron's triangular ears.

"The president was talking about a massacre." Byron rolled over and stretched on the couch under Angel.

Angel sighed and lowered her face until their noses touched. "Political games. At least with football, there isn't the pretense that it means anything."

"That's rather cold."

"So I'm a cynic." Angel slid back on to Byron's hips and nuzzled his chest.

"A few years ago I would've argued with you."

Angel rested her chin on Byron's chest. Somehow their clothes had ended up as a nest underneath them. The silent comm was the only light in the room.

Byron placed his hand on the back of her head, and began stroking the length of her back. "Let's change the subject."

"You were just telling me how cold I was." Angel found one of his nipples under his chest fur and teethed it.

Byron smiled his incredible smile, and Angel felt his tail wrap around her midsection. "I was mistaken. You're actually very warm."

Angel reached between his legs and said, "So're you."

Lei didn't come back until the following morning, and for that, Angel was very grateful.

Chapter 3

The first Wednesday in November, she ran into Balthazar on her way home. The ancient forty-year-old lion was her downstairs neighbor, and she didn't see him come out very often. But when she made it to the stairs, she heard a whispery growling voice from behind her, "Missy?"

She turned around and saw the old lion, sitting in a wheelchair behind the half-open door to his apartment.

"Yes?" She felt a little uncomfortable as she approached him. She had never really talked to Balthazar before. Her only contact with him had been the sound of his comm drifting through the door.

"Come closer, hearing's shot." He waved her over with a hand that arthritis had twisted into a nearly useless paw. It was an uncomfortable reminder of her own mortality—and how the more the pink gene-techs fiddled with something, the more age would ravage it.

Angel walked up to the door.

Balthazar had been a huge morey. Had he been able to stand, he would have been close to twice her height. His eyes were clouded, his teeth were chipped, but the mane was still regal. Even in decline, the leonine moreau had the bearing of royalty.

Which was why Angel nearly burst out laughing when she saw that the blanket that covered his legs was covered with cartoon characters. She kept a straight face and asked, "Can I help you?" She was still in waitress mode.

She stood in front of the lion, looking up at him even though she was standing and he was seated. He coughed a few times, and asked in a hoarse whisper, "Angel?"

She nodded, trying to avoid staring at the old blanket. Gray rabbits, black ducks, other things too faded for her to make out. The blanket looked almost as old as Balthazar himself.

"You're with that fox who's been in and out for the last week."

"Yes, yes." And she was getting impatient because that fox was probably waiting for her upstairs.

She could see his comm in the living room beyond him. It was playing some sort of animation, a black duck going on about how something was "despicable."

"He left you something."

"What?" Angel found her attention drawn back to the old lion.

"Here." With some difficulty, he pulled out a plain-wrapped package the size of a wallet. There were no markings on it at all. He passed it to her.

Angel hefted the package, feeling a little confused. "Byron left this with you? Why didn't he just give it to me him—"

"Said he had to leave." The lion erupted into another fit of coughing, shaking his head, and rippling his mane.

Angel held the package and was enveloped by a very bad feeling. "Thank you for holding this for me."

"Cost me nothing."

Angel nodded and headed toward the stairs.

"Missy?"

She turned back toward the lion.

"None of my business, but I don't trust him, too smooth."

"You're right. It's none of your business."

Balthazar grunted and began to wheel his chair back into the apartment. Before the door shut completely, Angel thought she could make out a chanting refrain from his comm, "Rabbit season, duck season, rabbit season, duck season . . ."

She had no idea what it meant, but it didn't make her feel any better.

The package was still sitting on the coffee table in front of the comm, unopened, when Lei came home. Lei asked about it, and Angel had the bad sense to tell her.

"Why haven't you looked in it?" Lei asked her, picking up the small plain-wrapped bundle.

"I don't—" Angel retreated into the kitchen. She didn't want to look at the thing. She'd yet to get to the point where she had a lock on what she was afraid of. Instead of thinking about it, she started to fix herself dinner.

Lei didn't leave it alone. When a few minutes passed without an answer from Angel, she followed her into the kitchen.

"Open it," Lei said, brandishing the package. Her brown-furred canine face was twisted somewhere between a growl and an amused smirk.

"Let it rest," Angel said as she tried to get past her and put her bulb of soup in the micro. A thin brown-haired arm blocked her. Playing defense, Lei had the advantage of a much longer reach and about 80 centimeters of height—if you didn't count Angel's ears.

Lei slipped in after the arm. "I won't until you open it up and read the thing."

Angel tried to break through one last time and only got a nose-ful of canine-smelling fur.

Angel tossed the bulb on the kitchen floor in disgust. It bounced once. She had wanted it to burst open. She stormed out of the kitchen and threw herself down on the couch. "Mind your own business."

Lei followed her out to the living room and tossed Byron's package on the table. "I don't understand you. What's your problem? What did Byron do?"

Angel shook her head. "Nothing, I just *know* . . ."

Lei paced in front of the couch, tail swatting the air. "Know *what*? He's handsome. He's charming. He has money." Lei paused and made a sweeping gesture. "He likes you better than he likes me, God knows why. He's—"

"Too good to be true."

"What?" Lei stopped pacing and turn to face her.

Angel looked at the small bundle on the coffee table. "Someone had to wake up."

"Bullshit!"

Angel shrugged. "Par for the course."

Lei sat down and hugged Angel's shoulders. "Don't you see how silly you're acting?"

"It's not silly."

"How long have you two been going out?"

Angel reviewed the dates in her mind to get the passage of time straight—the football game, the Hyatt Memorial, Golden Gate Park, Chinatown. . . .

"Nine days." Only nine? Yes, today was November fifth, only nine.

"And this is the second night you haven't spent together?"

"First. Wednesday we never made it back here."

"So I managed to get one good night's sleep out of that nine days—"

"We're not that loud."

"You're stressing 'cause you aren't going out tonight?"

"Well—"

Lei shook her head and chuckled. She rubbed her knuckles in the space between Angel's ears. "What're you going to do, graft yourself to him? Maybe he just had the urge to go to the john a few times and hold it himself."

Angel sighed. Lei was right. She knew Lei was right. But she couldn't shake the feeling that something was wrong. "So I'm not rational."

"He didn't do anything to bring this on? Did he?"

"No."

"He didn't break any plans you had tonight, right?"

"We haven't planned anything in advance yet. Just seems to happen."

"So what's eating you?"

Angel reached for the package. No, he never said one damn thing that could explain the awful feeling she had in the pit of her stomach. "I don't know."

Maybe it was what Byron didn't say. "He's keeping stuff from me."

"Ah," Lei shifted around so she was sitting on the coffee table and propped her muzzle in her hands. "He's married."

"No!" Angel leaned forward and tried to stare Lei down, but her roommate's expression told her that she wasn't serious. Still, the suggestion made her nervous.

Maybe the problem was that she was so caught up in someone she knew so little about. She'd been so sure she'd dived into this of her own accord. Why did she feel that she had lost control somewhere?

"What, then?" Lei was asking. "Tell me."

Angel sighed. "Everything. Nothing. What does he do for a living?"

"He hasn't told you? Have you *asked* him?"

Only the once, Angel thought to herself and cursed. If only he didn't make her so self-conscious. As if she constantly had to cover for the fact that she was raised on the streets, a well-used rabbit who'd been homeless for half her life.

Angel flopped back on the couch and stared at the ceiling. "Moonlit strolls, romantic dinners, dancing—with my feet, dancing—watching the sun set in the Pacific and watching it rise over the bay, talking, talking, talking . . ." And nothing ever got said, she thought. Nothing but the right things to say.

Lei tapped her on the shoulder and Angel lowered her head to face her. "Well, open the damn thing."

"I'm afraid to." Too soon into this and Angel had an uncomfortable emotional attachment that seemed too fragile.

Too much, too soon.

"Don't be a wuss."

Angel glared at Lei and ripped the wrapping off the package.

At least a dozen ramcards fell out, all emblazoned with a holographic blue and white thunderbolt—the San Francisco Earthquakes logo.

"Holy shit." It was all Angel could manage to say. She stared at the tickets, feeling real silly.

"Your expression is priceless."

"Box seat season tickets, the fifty yard line, where the hell did he get—?"

"I wish I had a camera."

Angel picked up a note that'd fluttered out of the package. In Byron's flowing script it said, "By now, my little angel, you've peeled yourself off the ceiling. There are two sets of tickets, and while I am NOT an Earthquakes fan—no matter how much you threaten me—you *better* take me to the Denver game.

"I want to be with you right now, because there is a very important question I have to ask you. However, I have to deal with some leftover responsibilities first, then I can think about the future.

"Love, your Byron."

Angel let the paper slide through her fingers.

"What?"

" 'Important question—' " Angel said, suddenly unsure of how she felt. "Am I misreading that?"

Lei picked up the note and began reading it.

" 'The future?' " Angel felt her heart accelerate and told herself that she was getting irrationally emotional again.

"Oh, my," Lei said.

Angel got off the couch and walked to the door, paced back, walked to the window. "Is that all you have to say? 'Oh, my?' "

"He could be talking about anything—"

Angel stared out the window. "Damn." Angel rested her forehead against the glass.

Lei walked up behind her. "What's the matter? You look worse off than before."

Angel shook her head. Why couldn't he wait a little while? Why'd he have to force things so damn quickly?

"Angel, you're crying . . ."

"I'm not crying!" In a much quieter voice she said, "I'm not ready for this."

Lei rested a hand on her back. Angel felt herself shake under Lei's hand and realized that she *was* crying. "Damn it. I don't want to lose him—"

"Shh, you aren't going to lose him."

Angel stood there, crying, unconvinced.

Thursday morning, Angel wasn't ready for the breakfast crowd. As her shift drifted toward noon she was so distracted that she confused orders at least once, giving a young tiger a plate of greens and giving a trio of white rabbits the tiger's plate of bleeding hamburger. She could scratch two tips right there.

Sanchez rode her even harder than usual, even coming out of his little shoebox manager's haven to order her to pick up the pace. All the time her mind kept drifting off the orders and on to Byron.

Foxy knew she'd freak if he popped the question unprepared. Of course he did. And she *had* to live in one of the three states that recognized moreau weddings as legit. The only state that recognized interspecies marriage—even the Catholic Church in its latest liberal wave had yet to go that far.

If she still lived in Cleveland, she wouldn't even have to think about it. But then, in Cleveland, she'd have more pressing worries—like stray gunfire.

It was unnerving for her to realize that if she was going to marry anyone, Byron'd be it. Worse, he obviously knew it.

Yeah, right. She was going to marry anyone? Bloody fat chance, as Byron would say.

"Yo, fluffy!" came from part of the rodent brigade of the lunchtime crowd. "Where's my fries?"

Spuds for the spud. Obviously she had to stop whatever she was doing so a fleabitten member of the rat patrol could get his daily allotment of grease. She almost served the ratboy a handful of abuse, but Sanchez had come out of hiding to lord it over his lunchroom kingdom and his look said, *He's a customer—*

Angel returned Sanchez's look with one that said, *Yeah, a rare breed here,* and got the rat's fries from the kitchen.

Byron and her, she thought. It was too soon.

She shook her head. Whatever happened, she'd be asking the same question a week, a month, a year from now. And she was getting older. Balthazar was an uncomfortable reminder of that. She was doing well for her age, but twenty was three years the far side of middle age for a rabbit.

At least with Byron she wouldn't have to worry about kids—unless they wanted to go to a Bensheim clinic and make some.

Angel had a vivid mental image of a litter of rabbits being infected by Byron's seductive Brit accent. It brought a smile wide enough to make the old cut on her cheek ache.

Was she really thinking about this, seriously?

"Where's my ketchup, fluffy?"

Angel looked at the black rodent and wondered if it was some genetic quirk that made all rats assholes. Angel looked at him, street kid, pissed at the world, age pushing double digits. He was making points with his friends here by harassing the help. Rat would probably die of old age before he had to work for a living.

The fries were steaming from the fryer and Angel had an urge to insert them into that shiny pink nose of his. Instead she said, as sweetly as she could muster, "Just a moment." She couldn't bring herself to say "sir." It'd dock her a few points in Sanchez's book, but at this point she didn't give a damn.

She was heading off to get a bottle from another table—the rat had probably stolen the one that was supposed to be on his—when she found herself facing two pinks.

From a decade plus on the streets she ID'd the pinks as pure cop the instant she laid eyes on them. Not just the fact they were pinks in a morey joint. Cop emanated from the shoddy suits like the bald one's cheap cologne. The barely hidden shoulder holsters didn't help. A matched set, and from the way they spaced themselves— out of arm's reach from each other—there wasn't much love lost between the two.

The one on the right was Asian, jet black hair, razor mustache. The other was balding, rumpled, and carried a gut that could have comfortably hidden Angel in its girth.

She was still in waitress mode, so she asked, "Can I help you?"

"We're looking for a Miss Lopez," said the Asian.

The urge to simply bolt for the door and disappear became overwhelming. Why'd Frisco PD want her? She was clean—except for the damn gun in her underwear drawer. Angel began cataloging all the shit leftovers in Cleveland. There was a lot of six-year-old crap nobody had tagged her for yet.

She was thinking of stonewalling when Sanchez bellowed. "Get your butt moving, Lopez."

So much for stonewalling. The balding one pulled out an ID and flashed it at her, too quickly. "Detectives White and Anaka, San Francisco PD. We need to talk to you."

Angel bent around the Asian and grabbed the ketchup squeeze bottle off the table. "What about? I'm working."

She was going to go about her business and get the rat his ketchup. But something about the way the two cops smelled made her hesitate. There was a little too much nervousness hanging in the hair around them.

Instead of delivering the bottle, she stood and waited. The cops' manner was beginning to worry her.

"Miss Lopez," the balding one asked, "do you know a vulpine moreau by the name of Byron Dorset?"

She didn't even feel the bottle slip out of her fingers as she asked them what had happened.

Chapter 3

B yron was dead.

She had known it from the way the cops acted, even before they told her that he'd been killed in some hotel in the Tenderloin. When she went with the two detectives, she said nothing, even as Sanchez asked her what the hell was going on. She was in the cops' unmarked green Plymouth before she could begin to think.

Byron was dead.

She couldn't shake the phrase. It kept running through her mind over and over.

Get a grip, she thought. A cynical part of her brain was telling her how insane this all was.

Why?

Angel's mind locked on that word like a mantra as the cops shot down Market toward the police station. The fat pink, White, tried to be comforting, but his words didn't jell into anything coherent— just another noise, like the engine and the abused suspension. Anaka said nothing.

Why?

Why him? Why now? Why did this have to happen before she knew what she felt?

Maybe the cops were wrong and it wasn't him. To most humans, moreaus all look alike, right? Even cops. Even to some cops who worked the moreau districts—

Angel shivered when she realized that they were going to ask her to identify the body.

Could she handle that?

Damn it, of course, she could handle it. She'd seen corpses before, some of them her friends. She'd led a fucking street gang. She'd seen more death up close than some morey veterans. She was tough, a survivor. . . .

She never should have let someone get that close to her.

The new, supposedly earthquake-proof, police headquarters squatted on the foundation of the old post office. It tried, too hard, to look contemporary with the surviving structures in the cluster of civic buildings across Market. The Plymouth slid into a tunnel that fed into the parking garage. Even in the car Angel could feel the temperature drop and smell the ozone of a few hundred confined vehicles. The lights buzzed, and the echo from that made the scene feel unearthly.

Anaka parked the car near the bottom of the hole. The garage was a concrete tomb. It was dark, hard, and cold. White led her out. Anaka had stepped out of the car to follow them, but White stopped him. "Go check with the coroner—"

"But—" Anaka began to say.

"Meet us back up on three."

Anaka stepped back into the car, slammed the door shut behind him, and pulled away.

White put a hand on Angel's shoulder and maneuvered her toward the elevators. Angel stayed pliant, saying nothing.

They entered the elevator and White flashed his badge at a sensor. "Detective Morris White, third floor."

"Confirmed," the elevator responded

Angel took a few breaths and tried to find her voice. "Where are we going?"

The doors slid open, and White led her to a desk, behind which sat a bored looking uniform.

White acted a little uncomfortable. He addressed the uniform first. "I have an appointment for a vid room."

"Detective White, right?" The uniform held out his hand. White handed over his badge and the cop ran it through a scanner. "The lawyers are waiting for you, 5-A."

"Lawyers?" Angel asked, forcing herself to regain a little touch with reality.

"We want you to ID our suspects." They walked past the desk, and down a long corridor. They passed doors every ten meters or so. One door near the end of the hall hung open. White paused in his walk down the corridor. "Are you up to this?"

"Me? ID the suspects?" Angel spoke slowly. She'd agreed to go with the cops, mostly out of shock. She still didn't trust police, and she was beginning to wonder exactly what was going on here. Who the hell could she identify? She barely knew Byron.

Yeah, said the cynical part of her mind *so why are you so torn up over this?*

I might have married him, she answered herself.

Out of love, replied the cynic, *or because he was the only person to ever show any interest in a well-used lepus that barely scraped herself off of the pavement back home?*

"Let's talk inside," White said, taking her nonanswer as a yes.

White led Angel the rest of the way to room 5-A, and shut the door behind him. The room was a stark white rectangle. The far wall was covered by ranks of vid screens. A long table squatted in front of the screens. Two empty chairs faced the table and the screens beyond. Two chairs at either end of the table were filled.

Both occupants wore conservative dark blue suits. The one on the far right was a redheaded human woman who was idly tapping at a wallet computer. The other one was a moreau ferret. The ferret turned a sinuous gaze on the two of them and shot White a chuckle. "You finished prompting the witness?"

White sighed. "Miss Lopez, let me introduce Mr. Igalez from the public defender's office."

The ferret whipped a nod.

"And Mrs. Gardner, Assistant District Attorney."

Gardener glanced up, and her head moved in a nearly imperceptible acknowledgment.

There was a third person in the room. A uniformed cop sat at a control console next to the door. White didn't introduce him. From the way the seats were arranged, Angel couldn't see him when she sat down.

White sat down next to her. They faced a wall full of test patterns. He pulled a microphone over to her face. "I want you to understand, you're here as a witness, not a suspect. But you do have the right to have your own lawyer present."

Yeah, right, a morey with a lawyer. A morey waitress ex-gang member with a lawyer. She wondered where Igalez came from, and who he was defending.

Angel sighed and asked, "What do you want from me?"

Gardener, the DA, started. "We want to know about the events of October 27, 2059."

After a long pause, Angel finally asked, "Monday?"

It all slipped into place. *The Rabbit Hole.* That's who White's suspects were—

The three punks who'd jumped her!

She'd been feeling numb, in shock, ever since White and Anaka had picked her up. However, she had no idea how truly pissed she'd been until she had something to focus her anger on. Angel bit her lower lip until she tasted blood. She wanted to kick something.

She'd see those skinheads fry.

The questions went on about *The Rabbit Hole,* and the punks who'd attacked her. The DA asked calm, sometimes leading questions, while the Public Defender was hard, angry, trying to rip any hole in her story, and, failing that, trying to cast her in the worst light possible.

The questioning was accompanied by a rapid drumbeat that Angel only realized belatedly was her own foot pounding the ground, hard.

Igalez got to her. Not that he made her admit anything, but having a fellow moreau try to make that fight look like she'd provoked something. . . .

"Are you saying that crushing that man's testicles was not excessive force?" asked the ferret.

"Three bald punks were about to spike me like a football." Her pounding foot doubled its speed against her volition. The table vibrated in time to it and Angel realized that White was staring at her.

"You could see no other way to remove yourself—"

Angel jumped on to the chair, tensed like a spring. She leaned toward him. "You ever been raped, Igalez?" She was amazed how calm her voice sounded.

"Miss Lopez—" White said. He put a restraining arm on her shoulder.

"Have you, Mr. Public Defender?" The pounding was now her own heart, and the smell of the blood from her lip seemed to fog the room. She was riding a razor-thin edge here, and be damned if she wasn't pushing the envelope.

Gene-techs all over the world had designed moreaus for battle, and most designs had some combat mode written into their genes. All Angel really needed was to get pissed enough and she'd go crazy on her own adrenaline.

"No—" From the way the ferret looked, he could smell how far he'd pushed her. The fear he broadcast, and the sound of his own heartbeat fed into Angel's state.

It was like a wind at her back, pushing her to *move*. She'd reached a point where she'd fired every cell of her body to scream *threat*. "A ferret—kinda like you—tried to rape me once. If I'd kicked him in the balls, he might still be alive." She jumped. White didn't expect the move, and she was so hyped that she was across the table and on Igalez before anyone else could act. By a supreme act of will, all she grabbed was his tie. "I let him get too close." Her nose was only a few centimeters from the ferret's. She could hear other people in the room scrambling around the table. Every sense was sharpened on a metabolism her anger had driven to just this side of panic.

She gave Igalez her best smile. "I had to chew through his throat."

Some sense started leaking in, and she began to force it all back. Her body wanted to rebel, but it recognized that she was still in charge, barely. She let go of his tie and he dropped back into the seat. "The scar on my cheek's from a chunk of his cartilage."

She backed off, barely able to admit to herself that what she'd just done had scared her as much as it had Igalez.

White was about to grab her, but she hopped back into her seat without assistance. "Excessive force, my ass."

Had she really been about to do to Igalez . . .

It took a few seconds for everyone to return to their seats. Even the uniform by the door had vacated his post. The color had drained from the Assistant DA's face, and her hand shook her wallet computer slightly. White glared at her, wiping sweat from his balding skull. The uniform's hand hung a little too close to his weapon.

Angel shook. Losing control like that wasn't good. The only person who knew how close things had come was Igalez, the only other morey in the room.

And Igalez looked truly spooked.

"Are you contending," Igalez asked, regaining his composure and spending a few seconds loosening his tie, "your belief at the time was that these humans were going to—"

"Beat me up, rape me, kill me, and bugger me up the ass? In that order? Damn straight," Angel said quietly, trying to hide her own discomfort.

The questioning was subdued from that point on. Dates, facts, times. Igalez didn't go into motivation or justification again. They covered the fight at *The Rabbit Hole* two or three times, and only briefly did they go over the time between then and now. The fact that they didn't ask her much about relatively recent history struck her as odd, but she didn't dwell on it. She was too shaken.

When the questions ended, White said, "Now, what we'd like you to do is identify the three men who attacked you."

White waved back at the uniform and the test patterns dropped from the screens; Angel faced a wall of faces. Over twenty of them slowly rotated in front of her—

"First of all, I told you, they were all bald."

In response, the pictures with hair froze as the computer erased the hair, pixel by pixel. After a half second, she was facing a wall of bald humans. Angel stared, looking for Earl, Chico, and the black dude. Earl was the first one she recognized; he wore a face she'd never forget.

"Freeze number twelve. That's the guy I kicked."

Twelve froze and the Assistant DA said, "We're more interested in the other two—"

"Can we avoid prompting the witness?" The ferret stepped on the DA's speech.

Angel ignored them and studied the black faces on the wall. She didn't know his name, but ten days ago he was standing closer than White was now.

"Six, number six." Six froze, facing them expressionlessly. "That's number two—"

"Are you sure?" asked the ferret.

"What did you say about prompting the witness?" the DA said.

Angel couldn't find Chico on the wall. "Are there any more pictures?"

In response the entire wall changed, and she looked at another army of bald faces. Chico was almost dead-center, staring at her. "Fifteen, that's the fucking bastard, fifteen."

Fifteen froze. The other faces blanked and the other two came back, flanking Chico. "Now we want you to be sure—"

"Those are the bastards who attacked me."

"You chose rather quickly—" the ferret started.

"That's them." She stared down Igalez. "The scum you're defending'd kill you for not being human."

White put his hand on her shoulder. "I think we're done here." White led her out of the room, and Angel was glad to get out of Igalez's presence.

Anaka was waiting by the desk, looking impatient.

*   *   *

She'd been right. They needed her to identify the body. They took her to St. Luke's Veterinary. She sat in the back of the car, numb, silent, while Anaka and White talked about what cops talk about.

They were going to stick her face-to-face with Byron cold on a slab and Angel wasn't sure she wasn't going to lose it. Hell, it felt like she'd lost it already. It was a damn close thing with Igalez.

She was stronger than that, though. She had more control.

Hoped she had more control, anyway.

Stop brooding on it, she told herself. *Soon the whole thing will be over. Over already, really.* Byron was a slab of meat and there was not thing one she could do about it.

Anaka and White argued around her, oblivious.

"I'm telling you," Anaka was saying. "Ellis is hiding something."

"I don't want to deal with your conspiracies today." White sounded more resigned than argumentative.

"Why's she doing the Dorset case? She's not a vulpine expert."

"Who gives a shit, Kobe? Our job's to bust the Knights, remember?"

"And if something's funny about the autopsy—"

"Damn it, Kobe, if we do this right, the skinheads will plead, roll over on their masters, and we'll never have to bring up the body . . ."

Angel was almost tempted to ask if that was so, why they needed to put her through this. She didn't. Who cared what kind of internal politics these cops were going through, she just wanted to get the damn ordeal over with.

The pair argued with each other all the way to the hospital. After a while Angel stopped listening.

The detectives took her to Byron's resting place, the morgue in the basement of St. Luke's Veterinary. The morgue's white tile walls echoed sounds to unnatural lengths. Cheap pine-scented disinfectant didn't quite cover the smell of dead flesh that'd sunk into the walls.

Angel was cold down here.

Byron lay on a stainless-steel table. As soon as Angel saw the body, there wasn't any doubt that it was him. Blood had caked on his fur, but it was the same face. . . .

"I love you, Byron," she whispered for the first and only time. She said it so quietly that she was unsure if she had said it at all.

"Is it him?" Anaka asked for perhaps the third time.

Angel was still trying to find her voice.

She kept thinking how cruel it was. The slash on his neck had cut halfway through his throat and up the side of his face, pulling his cheek into a slack grimace. She was glad for whoever it was that had closed Byron's eyes. If Byron's eyes had been open, she was sure she'd go running off screaming—

After an eternity she managed to drag her gaze from the corpse. She nodded at the cops. She screwed her eyes shut, but it felt like the image of Byron on that table had glued itself to the inside of her eyelids. She felt White's hand on her shoulder. "Let's take you home."

The cops took her back to the Mission District. White drove this time, Anaka next to him, leaving her alone in the back. For most of the ride they sat in silence, which was fine with Angel. She was still trying to deal with it, not just Byron, but her reaction to it—

She should be able to handle this, but she was on the verge of falling apart. *Come on,* she told herself, *you only met him ten days ago.*

They paralleled Market on Harrison, traveling toward the Mission District. As they made the turn south, Anaka finally asked a question.

"Miss Lopez, would you know *why* Bryan Dorset would want to meet with those two?"

"What two?" Angel whispered. She didn't want to deal with more questions.

White sighed.

Victorian architecture began to slide by the car as Anaka tackled Angel's hill. The cockeyed angles of the old homes made Angel's head hurt. She put her face in her hands.

It was wrong.

Not just the offense of someone killing Byron. There was something else that was wrong—

White pulled the car up in front of her place, between the Antaeus and the Jerboa. Angel looked at Anaka before she left the car, "What are you talking about. Meet who?"

"He was killed in a hotel room rented by the Knights of Humanity—" Anaka began. "The information that led us to the body also said that there was a meeting scheduled within a hour of the time of death."

A meeting? Why?

"No." Angel said, backing away from the car. "I don't have a damned idea why he'd want anything to do with those sleazeballs. What information—"

Anaka chuckled. "You don't know? It's—"

"Time you got some rest," White said, and drove the car away.

Angel watched the car leave and smelled something worse than the morgue scent that clung to her fur. . . .

Chapter 5

A ngel didn't bother going back to work, didn't even call
Sanchez. It seemed pointless—

Everything seemed kind of pointless.

She sat on the couch, turned on the comm, and tried to stay
numb. By seven she was watching Sylvia Harper, the senior senator from California, from behind a forest of beer bulbs. It was the
third time they'd put up bites from Harper's speech in the Bronx. It
was about Angel's tenth beer.

Angel thought to herself, not for the first time, that the woman
had guts to be human and anywhere near the Bronx.

"—the twenty-ninth amendment was not a mistake. Some people think that, because of the violence that is tearing at our cities,
the United States should have never opened its arms to you, the
nonhuman.

"These people forget what America represents. The ideals of liberty, equality, freedom—"

La-te-da, Angel thought. She might be some dumb uneducated
bunny—but she knew *some* history. The grand ol' United States always had that effing "liberty" at the expense of someone—morey,
Amerind, or blacks like Sylvia up there.

Angel wondered if Sylvia was grateful that the moreys took the
bottom rung for her.

The station jump-cut to another sound bite.

"When we tolerate slavery, we destroy ourselves. A lesson we
must constantly relearn. Not just the slavery of physical bondage.

It's easy for us to say you cannot own another person, that you cannot *make* another person.

"But what will destroy us is *mental* slavery. The slavery of bigotry. The slavery of discrimination. The slavery of nonhuman ghettos that are allowed to spiral into poverty and despair. The slavery that allows a human being to say that because you are a different species, you have no human rights."

"Human" rights, there's a nice bit of ethnocentrism. Great, Sylvia, and you wanna be president?

Angel took another swig of beer. The room smelled like a yeast culture, but at least she was getting a buzz.

Angel heard Lei come in during the lead-in to the next story.

"Angel . . ." From the sound of Lei's voice, she knew about Byron.

"Shh," Angel responded as she downed the last bulb, the bottle of Ki-Rin. Right after Harper, the news went local. Still leading the local news was the murder of a moreau. Only in San Francisco would Byron's death be a lead story. Human suspects helped make it the lead.

"Angel, I'm so sorry." Lei sat down and put her arm around Angel.

"I knew I was going to lose him." Angel threw her empty beer bulb at the screen. It bounced off.

Lei squeezed her shoulder, and for once remained quiet.

"Laid his throat open. I had to ID his body." The comm prattled on about martial law in LA. Angel closed her eyes on the aerial shots of the fires. "How could he be so careless?"

Lei stayed quiet.

"They're psychos, and they're *pinks*. How'd they get *close* enough to do that?"

Lei rubbed the back of Angel's head between the ears. "You need some rest."

Angel buried her face in her fur. "It's so unfair."

"I know."

"I miss him."

"I know."

Angel had a restless sleep, and upon waking, sat herself in front of the comm again. She called in sick, almost cussing out Sanchez. Then she turned on the news and tried to think clearly.

Byron was still news. Now the vids had planted a camera in front of the seedy hotel on Eddy Street where he'd been killed. The voice-over said a pair of human members of the Knights of Humanity were being held for suspicion in the knifing.

They made her ID *three* suspects, and it hadn't looked like a knife wound to Angel.

Then again, news was fucked more often than not.

Byron's letter was still sitting on the table. Angel picked it up while, on the comm, Father Alvares de Collor, a moreau jaguar, was talking about making Byron's funeral a show of moreau solidarity.

There is a very important question I have to ask you, Angel read, *but I have to deal with some leftover responsibilities first, then I can think about the future.*

"Leftover responsibilities," Angel repeated, aloud. "Some future."

Dawn light began to filter though the bay windows behind the comm. Angel could hear Lei wake up and start her shower.

" 'Unfinished business.' "

What the hell *had* Byron done for a living?

The news switched to an update on the fighting in Los Angeles. Like New York, other than a few fires here and there, things were static. The moreaus had carved themselves out the heart of the city, and local politicians were calling it a civil war. The National Guard had yet to go in, and Angel got the impression of a blast crater ringed by troops pointing their guns into the hole.

The Guard had good reason not to press the standoff. The Moreau Defense League had heavy armor on both coasts. On Manhattan, the blackened wreckage of the Nyogi tower testified to the last Federal push into the Bronx.

LA was supposed to be next on the Sylvia Harper urban violence tour. To Angel, it seemed a pointless gesture. Harper might chair a committee on interspecies violence, but no pink politico was going to calm things down there.

To a lesser extent, violence was occurring in every city with a large concentration of moreaus.

Not here, Angel thought. *San Francisco is different.*

At least it felt different before a bunch of bald pinks jumped her.

What the hell did those cops mean, he was going to *meet* with those punks? And Anaka acted like she should have known where they were getting their infor—

Angel slapped her forehead for a fool. Of course there were only two suspects in Byron's death. Earl must still be in the hospital after what she'd done. In the hospital and being pumped for all he was worth. Earl was the cops' source.

"Damn it, Angel, what are you doing up at this hour?"

"Trouble sleeping."

Lei was half dressed for work, swishing her tail, and tapping a digitigrade foot. She stepped over and picked up the remote for the comm and switched off the news. "Are you going to keep torturing yourself?"

"That's not it. It—"

Lei shook her head and pulled on a blouse.

"Something's wrong about Byron's death."

"Tell the cops. It's their job. Then stop worrying about it." Lei leaned over and turned Angel's head to face her. "Dear, you don't need any *more* reasons to feel bad." Lei rubbed noses and stepped back. "I'll be back right after work to see how you're doing, okay?"

"I'll be fine."

"Sure?"

"Sure." Angel nodded.

She waited until Lei left, then she put her face in her hands and shook. Did it really matter? Byron was gone, and that was that. Even if there was something strange about what was going on, it wouldn't bring him back. Those two pinks were scum anyway. Who cared?

Angel could smell her own blood and realized she was biting her lip.

She cared.

And she was going to drive herself crazy thinking about it. Lei was right, it was the cops' job. She should take her problems up with White or Anaka—If she could figure out what was wrong.

She called the Frisco PD and the reaction of the uniform answering the comm made her grab a robe. It had slipped her mind that she was calling humans and they considered it polite to wear some sort of clothing on a comm call.

Little details like that were slipping by her.

They transferred her call through three or four departments before someone realized that someone might actually want to talk to her—in that respect, Frisco wasn't any different from Cleveland, New York, LA, or anywhere else. . . .

Sun was beginning to leak in through the bay windows and the omnipresent fog by the time she got through to Detective White. The pink didn't seem any less obese. If anything, he seemed even bigger cramped into the screen on the comm.

He was in the middle of eating breakfast out of a mass of Chinese fast-food containers littering the desk between him and his comm. White had just speared a chunk of beef with a chopstick. The sight made Angel feel a little ill.

"Miss Lopez," White said between bites. "What can I do for you?"

Angel sucked in a breath. "You people sure those guys I fingered were the ones who did Byron?"

White was in the middle of swallowing and started coughing. He ended by hacking up a chunk of meat and spitting it into the container he was eating from. *"Jesus Christ."* He dropped the container and pulled a dirty-looking handkerchief to wipe his face. "You're not going back on your testimony—"

"No, but I—"

White was shaking his head. Angel saw something hard begin to surface in his expression. "You *will* press assault on these guys—"

"I will, but—"

White leaned back, and Angel could hear the stressed office chair creak over the comm. "Whew, you scared me, lady."

Angel pulled the green robe around her and sat on the coffee table, scattering empty beer bulbs. "What the hell's going on here?"

"Miss Lopez, we want these guys—*all* of them. Your testimony on the assault is what we got. Without that—" White clasped his forehead and shook his head.

"Damn it, what *have* you got about the murder?"

White leaned forward. "What are you asking, Miss Lopez?"

"How do you know *they* killed him?"

White was silent for a long time. Eventually he said, "They killed him."

"How do you know?"

He rubbed his forehead. "I know that because half a million moreaus in this city believe it's true."

"What?"

White looked really angry. "We have them dead on the assault charges. They're guilty as sin."

"The murder?"

"We have enough to get things past the grand jury."

For the first time, Angel began to realize just how little the cops must have. "The bastards who did this might still be out there, and you—"

"We *have* the bastards who did this." White stared at her. "And if you want to see the guys who were going to 'beat you up, rape you, kill you, and bugger you up the ass' put away, don't do anything to jeopardize our case."

"What case?" Angel asked, and cut the connection.

"Great!" she yelled at the ceiling. Not only did White do nothing to settle her fears, but he as much as said that it didn't matter. The SFPD had their men, job done, let's break out the wine and fucking cheese. If we can't pin murder one on the geeks, we can put them away for a year or two for talking mean to this here rabbit.

Angel walked to the bay window and looked northeast, toward downtown. "The system sucks!" She slammed her fist into the windowframe. "It ain't just when it's against us! It *always* sucks!"

Angel turned her back on the city and slid to the ground. She sat there for a long time, thinking that she might as well've stayed in Cleveland.

Angel didn't realize she had fallen asleep until the comm woke her up by buzzing for her attention.

"Who the hell?" she mumbled, debating about letting the computer answer it. She decided against it. "Got it!" she yelled. The comm heard her and obliged by putting the call through.

"Hello, is there anyone there?" said a slightly familiar voice. She wondered where she'd heard it before.

"I'm coming," Angel said, pulling herself up from in front of the window. While she had slept, full daylight had come to burn off the fog for a while.

She had to limp around the comm because her foot had fallen asleep. For the first time in what seemed like two days—or was it only one—she realized the mess she must have looked. She hadn't cleaned her fur since—

Who the hell was this guy?

Large spotted feline, a Brazilian jaguar. The jaguar's eyes followed her to the front of the comm, golden eyes with tiny pupils. The large cat wore a grave expression, carefully avoiding either a show of teeth or creasing his muzzle. It wasn't until she saw the priest's collar that she realized who it was.

"Father Collor?" It was an easy guess to make. There were only three ordained nonhuman Catholic priests in the States at the moment. Alvarez de Collor was the only feline. Angel felt stupid for missing who it was. She'd seen him on the news just this morning.

"Angelica Lopez?"

Oh, great. "This is about Byron, has to be—"

"You're Miss Lopez?"

"Yes, yes." Angel rested her head against the top of the comm. Let the priest get a great shot of her robe, she didn't care. "What?"

"Miss Lopez, I apologize for breaking in on your grief—"

"Cut to the point, padre."

There was a long pause. "I need your permission to make funeral arrangements for Mr. Dorset."

Silence hung in the air for a long time. Angel pushed herself away from the comm and looked at the feline priest. "What the fuck?"

The priest made a visible effort to ignore the vulgarity. "We need to show a united front to the kind of people who did this—"

"What the fuck?"

"As his fiancée, you're his heir and only next of kin."

"Is this some kind of sick joke?"

"Please, can we discuss this calmly—"

Angel's head was whirring as she began to figure out how the pieces of the priest's little world slid together. "You made a statement to the press."

"Miss Lopez—" He was starting to show signs of distress. His eyes were darting past the comm's screen, as if there were spectators out of Angel's view. This was obviously not going as he'd planned.

"Before you had any—before you even talked to—" Angel realized she was pacing around the coffee table, trailing the robe behind her. She stopped and faced Father Collor. *"You want to turn this into a circus!"*

"That isn't it at all." He was looking to the left and right. Angel was positive now that there were people offscreen, and he was looking at them as if to say, "This isn't my fault."

Angel wanted to kick something. She brought her fist down on an empty beer bulb, and traces of froth splattered over the table, the wall, and the comm. "How'd you get a hold of my comm?" The bill was in Lei's name, Angel wasn't listed in any directories.

"I assure you—"

"Father, go chase another ambulance." Angel cut the connection.

The world seemed to be conspiring to piss her off. Who the hell did that self-righteous feline think he was? Byron wasn't even Catholic—

One of the jaguar's statements began to sink in.

"Fiancée and sole heir?" Angel felt a little dizzy.

She sat down on the couch. How the hell did she suddenly become Byron's fiancée?

The comm rang and Angel answered it, somewhat afraid of what it might be.

The call announced itself as being from Krane, DeGarmo and Associates. Sounded like a bunch of pink lawyers.

That's what it was.

The lean black-haired human who'd called her was Paul De-Garmo, Byron's lawyer and the executor of his will. What the jag priest had said was half-right anyway. She was Byron's single largest bequest.

DeGarmo didn't seem to find this odd at all, even though Angel had only known the fox for nine days.

What the hell was going on here?

She silently took the security codes for Byron's car and his condo. She nodded politely when DeGarmo told her that the body was going to be released on Monday and some sort of burial arranged. He told her a lot of financial details that slipped right by her—estate taxes and such.

All she kept thinking was that she had taken one step into Byron's life and suddenly she was in charge of all that was left of it.

Chapter 6

Angel reread Byron's note for the tenth time since she'd parked the car. The words had begun to blur and lose their meaning—and she was no closer to understanding why Byron might want to meet with those bald psychopaths. It still made no sense.

Angel shoved the letter into her jeans with the Earthquakes tickets. It was no help, and she knew it by heart already.

"What the hell am I doing here?" she asked no one in particular.

She was sitting behind the wheel of Byron's BMW in the parking lot of St. Luke's Veterinary. The engineered-leather bucket seat was jacked up as far as it could go, giving her a view down the sloping blue hood at the moreys coming and going.

It was Saturday afternoon—no work, nothing for her to do but brood on Byron's death. Brooding had brought her here. She was still unsure why. She was unsure of a lot since talking to DeGarmo yesterday.

Everything she was doing felt odd, disjointed—as if someone else was making the decisions and she was just along for the ride. She only felt in touch with her surroundings when a knife edge of emotion slid briefly through the haze. More often than not it was a spasm of grief or self-pity.

But with increasing frequency it was anger. Irrational anger at silly things, like the ease with which she'd retrieved Byron's car from the impound lot. For the first time in her life, cops were being reasonably nice to her, and it felt like she was being bribed—all the cops in San Francisco wanted her to be a nice little rabbit and go along with the program. Most of all, anger at the increasing fraction of her life that was getting public airtime. Father Collor was only the first person to try to make political hay out of Byron's death.

Angel hated politics.

She kept an eye on the Ford Merovia sedan parked across from her BMW. It was the reserved spot for Dr. Pat Ellis, the doctor who'd signed Byron's death certificate. The doctor who Detective Anaka, White's Asian partner, seemed so suspicious of.

Why didn't she just call the doctor?

"What the hell am I doing?" she asked herself again.

The Merovia started, and Angel watched the feed cable automatically withdraw from the curb outlet. Angel saw a woman approaching with a little black remote control in her hand. Must be the doctor.

Ellis was approaching human middle age. Her sun-bleached hair was shot with gray. Her blue eyes were clouded by corrective surgery. She wore a suit whose sharp lines seemed to be working at cross purposes to the plump roundness they contained.

Angel got out of the BMW and moved to intercept Ellis.

Ellis didn't seem to notice her at first. The doctor kept walking to the quietly idling Merovia. Angel had gotten within a few meters before Ellis looked up at her. The doctor's expression showed surprise, and for a second she wielded the remote control at Angel, as if it was a weapon.

Angel stopped, "Dr. Ellis?"

"Y–yes." Ellis responded, looking around the parking lot, as if she expected to be ambushed or something. Angel could smell fear.

"I'd like to talk to you for a few minutes."

Ellis kept looking around the parking lot. "Who are you?"

"Angelica—"

Ellis wasn't looking in her direction. "Yes, I remember, you identified the body."

Angel nodded. "I want to talk about Byron."

"Not here." The doctor opened the door to the Merovia and retreated inside.

"Where, then?"

"Get in," Ellis left the door open for her.

For Angel, things had gone from disorienting to just plain weird. The doctor's paranoia was beginning to rub off on her. Angel slipped into the car, casting a glance over the parking lot at St. Luke's to see if she could find what Dr. Ellis was looking for. Angel didn't find it.

Ellis zigzagged through half of the new city south of Market.

Angel didn't see any sign of the people Ellis must have thought were following her. Every time Angel started to talk, Ellis told her to wait.

Eventually, Ellis parked the car a block east of Franklin Square. "Let's go for a walk around the park." Ellis said, and Angel could tell she was making an effort to sound calm.

"Okay." Angel stepped out of the car and on to the sidewalk. They were surrounded by construction now. The skeletons of new buildings covered the area between Twentieth and the Central Freeway like an iron forest. A combination of earthquake and economic recession made this area one of the last to be rebuilt. It was getting close to seven, and the silence was ominous. Construction had ceased for the day, and the street was empty of cars and people.

Franklin Square itself was getting a facelift—which meant that sidewalks were torn up, piles of dirt covered by black tarpaulins were scattered at random, the park was clogged by construction equipment, and pipes from the old sewer system lay in choked stacks by the entrance.

They began to circle the park, and Angel asked, "What are you afraid of?"

"You wanted to talk about Byron Dorset, so talk about him."

They were walking down a deserted stretch of Sixteenth Street, and Ellis was still looking around as if she was being followed.

"I want to know how he died."

"You saw the corpse. Massive trauma to the neck—"

Angel grabbed the doctor's arm. "You know what I mean. I want to know what sliced him."

Ellis stopped and shook her head.

"News called it a knifing," Angel continued. "What kind of knife tears out that much of someone's neck?"

"It wasn't a knife."

"What, then?"

Ellis looked around again. "I can't be talking to you."

"What was it?" The fear-scent was floating off of Ellis and embracing Angel. It was hard to be that close to someone so wound up and not see eyes peering out of the darkness. What was Ellis afraid of?

The doctor looked torn, and very upset. It was getting hard for Angel to take. She grabbed the doctor by the elbows and shook her. "What killed him?" she shouted.

The fear-smell became sharper, less generalized. Angel could hear the doctor's pulse and breathing accelerate. For a moment, she seemed more afraid of Angel than she was of anything else. "I retrieved feline fur and nail samples from the wound."

Angel let go of Ellis. Suddenly she felt that it wasn't a hill she was standing on, but the crest of a rolling breaker that was dropping out from under her.

"Don't talk to me again." Ellis turned and ran back to her car. So much for a ride back to St. Luke's.

"A morey?" Angel asked herself.

"You're where?" The perennial look of concern crossed Lei's muzzle.

"Frisco General, you know, Potrero—"

"I know where the hospital is. What are you doing *there?*"

"I'm not there, really. I'm in a car across the street." A foghorn sounded from the bay.

"If you're calling to reassure me, you aren't doing it by evading the question. What possessed you to walk down there?"

"I said, I have a car."

"What . . ."

"Look, Lei, I'm fine. I just didn't want you to worry about me not being home."

"Well, I'm worried—"

"I'll explain when I get back." Angel cut the connection before Lei could object.

What *was* possessing her to come here? Did she think the cops would allow her to talk to Earl? Did she think that he'd actually talk to her?

But, damn it, she wanted to know what Earl had given up to the cops. What he'd said that had put two pink Knights away rather than the morey that'd slashed Byron.

And Earl was in stable condition at San Francisco General Hospital, according to the incessant news reports. Of course, the news didn't call him Earl. They called him "a third alleged assailant." Alleged was right, considering that Earl, pink number three, was in the hospital when Byron got sliced open.

Everything about Byron's death was beginning to smell.

As if cued by her thought, she began to smell something odd for Frisco General—moreys. Lots of moreys. She closed on the front of the hospital, and she could see cop cars scattered everywhere, flashers cutting through the humid darkness. An aircar from BaySatt News was hovering over Potrero Avenue, pointing at some disturbance.

Angel slowed her walking and began to listen.

"Chanting?"

A group of a few dozen moreaus, mostly canines and foxes, were holding a sit-down protest in the lobby of the damn hospital. It sounded like they were chanting hymns to the cops.

Angel stopped her approach as police vans started driving up.

Like hell they're going to let a morey in the building now.

Angel had an inspiration.

She avoided the lobby and walked around to the Emergency entrance and the ambulance bays. No moreys here, as Angel had hoped. The protest was aiming for media attention, not at really disrupting the hospital's operation.

What it *did* do was disrupt security.

With all attention on the fracas out front, Angel managed to walk in to the Emergency Room, slip past the nurse's station, and make it to the elevators without being challenged. That was the easy part. Now she had to find Earl and get into his room.

In all the movies she'd seen where this was a problem, the hero always slipped into a lab coat and walked around the hospital unchallenged. Unfortunately, the hero was never a morey.

Before the elevator came, she heard a familiar voice coming up behind her. The voice of detective Kobe Anaka, the Asian cop.

Oh, shit.

She only had a second to think before Anaka and whoever he was talking to—the other voice was much too even and mannered for his partner, White—turned the corner and saw her. She backed away from the elevator, felt a door behind her along the opposite wall, and darted through it just as Anaka and a tall gray-haired human in a white coat came around the corner.

Damn it. She had backed into a closet with no extra room, even for her. She was wedged up against a hard plastic cleaning robot, and she couldn't close the door enough. The door was ajar, with the ten-centimeter gap facing out into the hall, toward Anaka and the doctor. She didn't want to climb up on the robot because the only place to stand seemed to be a touch-sensitive control panel and she'd probably turn the damn thing on by accident.

She was saved from discovery by the elevator. The elevator she'd been waiting for arrived just as Anaka walked into the line of sight with the closet. As if in response to Angel's frantic wish—he and the doctor walked into the elevator with apparently no thought as to why an empty elevator had stopped on this floor.

As soon as the doors of the elevator closed, Angel allowed herself to breathe again. In response, the closet door swung open. She left the closet with the cynical thought that at St. Luke's they had morey janitors rather than these robot things, and the moreys were probably cheaper—

Then it hit her. She needed to find Earl. It couldn't be a coincidence that Anaka was here. The cop had to be here to see Earl.

Angel felt like a fool as she looked at the indicator for the elevator. It was going down—*down?*—and stopped at S-3. They were keeping Earl in the basement?

She wished she had paid attention to what these two had been saying; then she might know whether or not this was a wild goose chase.

Instead of waiting for the elevator, she bolted for the stairs. Inside the echoing concrete stairway, she took the steps half a flight at a time. If she was lucky, she'd reach the subbasement while Anaka and the pink doctor were still in earshot.

The last two flights were blocked by a chain and a sign reading, "authorized personnel only." She only noticed because she almost ran into it.

The door to the third sublevel opened on an empty corridor. Angel didn't see any of the directory holos saying "you are here." Angel guessed the assumption was that, if you were down here, you were supposed to know where you were going. A map wouldn't have been much help anyway, since she didn't know where they were keeping Earl.

Angel listened. The tile on the floor and the walls gave a distorted audio picture, but she was pretty sure she couldn't hear more than half a dozen people roaming the halls. Most of those seemed stationary. After some thought, she could pick out footsteps way down the hall on her right. The subdued voices were difficult to make out, but Angel bet that they were Anaka's and the Doc's.

She followed them.

If she didn't blatantly walk in front of a nurse's station or a security booth, she might be all right. There wasn't much she could do about the cameras that panned the corridor—except hope that the protest out front had captured everybody's attention.

She was following the two away from the biggest concentration of human noise. "Too much like the morgue," she whispered to herself. She was reminded of Byron in the basement of St. Luke's. The too-cold walls, the disinfectant that didn't hide the smell of blood and decomposition.

Eventually, her cautious pace lost her the audio clues to where

Anaka and the Doc had gone—and with the disinfectant everywhere, tracking by scent was useless.

She slowed even further, but kept going.

What now?

She turned a corner and bumped into a gurney.

The top edge hit her at about neck level, and under a sheet, she
felt a cold foot hit her face. She fell backward, and the gurney
rocked forward slightly on locked wheels.

Angel rubbed her face and slowly got to her feet.

"Fuck. It *is* the morgue." She slapped herself on the forehead for
saying that out loud.

She could smell the body on the gurney now—blood, shit, and
death. The corridor beyond ended in a massive pair of double
doors. That was where most of the odor of decomposition was
hanging.

"Wrong number," she said, slightly disgusted with herself. Now
she could either continue this fruitless search for the third punk, or
she could slip out and pretend this never happened.

Never happened was starting to sound good.

Then she heard a familiar voice—Detective Anaka's.

They had been going this way . . .

Through the double doors she couldn't make out exactly what
was being said, but she suddenly wanted to see what was going on.
Especially because Anaka sounded royally pissed.

Angel walked up to the doors, but the windows were much too
high for her to look through. If she opened the door, even a crack,
the people inside would notice her right off. She draped an ear
against the door. Anaka was saying, "What do you mean, accident?"

"An error in the computer. It's rare, but it happens." It was the
pink Doc's voice.

"Do you know what your 'error' does to our case?"

"I'm sorry—"

Angel wanted to see what was going on, but she needed nearly
another meter of height to look through the window. She looked
around her, and her gaze rested on the unattended gurney.

How morbid, she thought, smiling.

She unlocked the wheels and rolled the gurney in front of one of
the doors. Then she climbed up on the corpse. Something slipped
out of her pocket, but she barely noticed when she saw the scene on
the other side of the small window.

She already had suspicions about what she was going to see, but it was still something of a shock.

Anaka was standing in the room beyond, running his fingers through jet-black hair. "How the hell could this—"

Doc, in surgical garb *sans* mask, was seated on a stool in a corner of the room tapping at a small computer terminal. "The computer forgot that he was a flush addict."

"How the hell did the computer 'forget' that?"

Angel stared at the centerpiece of the room.

Earl, the third pink goon, rested, naked, on an operating table under a frosty white light. His eyes were open and staring. His abdomen and waist were a study in browns, reds, and blues—his genitalia purple and swollen. Quite dead.

"Oops," Angel whispered.

"If we knew that, things like this wouldn't happen. Somebody flubbed his file, a random power spike, maybe it never was in his file to begin with. As it is, with his flush-weakened nervous system, the muscle relaxant we gave him pushed him into cardiac arrest."

"You're not making me happy."

Angel decided she was overstaying her welcome. Her reason for being here was on a slab. No sense waiting for someone to pick her up for trespassing.

She climbed off the gurney and headed for the elevators.

If Earl was dead, could they try to hang a murder rap on her? It *was* self-defense, and they'd never even charged her with assault.

But . . .

For the first time, Angel began to worry about her own furry hide.

She made her way to the elevators at a dead run and told the computer "ground floor" three times before it understood her. Ellis' paranoia had slipped in and had taken root. She was convinced that Earl's death was no "accident." It was a rock-solid gut feeling that also told her to get out of the hospital *now*.

The doors opened on the corridor of the Emergency Room, letting in sounds of nonhuman singing and sirens. She turned the corner and started to bolt for the exit.

And ran straight into a pink cop. At least that's what Angel pegged him for when she began backing up. Human, two meters, suit, wearing a nearly invisible white crew cut that made him look like one of the Knights if the light was at the right angle. His skin was pale, nearly translucent.

Under his arm was a bulge that spoke of artillery that was ten-millimeter or better—maybe even a machine pistol. As Angel continued to back up, she saw that the suit was too expensive for a local boy, and decided the guy was Fed.

She could see a throat-mike peeking out from behind the knot in his tie, and the nearly-invisible earpiece.

She had just decided that she was in really big trouble when she realized that the Fedboy's smell was out of sync. Hunting excitement tinged by just a touch of fear. He wasn't even looking at her.

He pushed Angel out of the way and made for the elevators. It gave her a chance to see beyond the Fed's sunglasses. Angel thought she saw red irises.

The encounter had lasted less than a second, and she was not one to question good fortune. She split Frisco General, deciding that sneaking into the human hospital had been an all-around bad move on her part.

Chapter 7

It was close to midnight when Angel made it home. Lei's quiet, regular breathing told her that her roommate was asleep in the darkened living room. Angel found Lei curled into a brown ball on the couch, tail wrapped around her muzzle. The comm was in the middle of a pop-political broadcast with a panel of commentators indulging in verbal mud wrestling.

"—Harper is the only potential presidential candidate who's advocating peace—" one of the ones to the left was saying.

"Appeasement you mean." An off-screen voice stepped on his line.

"Merideth's approval ratings have been in free-fall since the crisis began," he continued, ignoring the interruption. "The Democrats are in the worst position they've been in since the CIA scandal. If her Committee manages to reach some diplomatic sol—"

"You must be kidding, Fred. No one seriously thinks a NOA party candidate can win the presidency—"

Angel walked in front of the comm and heard Lei stirring behind her. After a long yawn Lei said, "Finally came back? What did you think you were doing?"

"I don't know."

On the screen, a balding pink was leaning into the camera frame to berate somebody. "You remember what you said about the Greens, Dave? The country's ready for a candidate like Har—"

Angel shook her head. "Wanted to talk to the punk I put in the hospital."

Lei sat up and stretched, Angel could hear her joints pop. "What could he possibly have to say?"

"—the None-of-the-Abovers are a lot more radical than the Greens," The one woman on the show was saying.

"I don't know," Angel said, "the bastard's dead."

"What?"

"—ideth avoided getting tarred with the same brush that hit the rest of the Democrats during the CIA indictments in '54. He's bounced back from worse numbers—"

"I accidentally walked into the morgue. The guy was laid out colder than—"

"Sure it was the same guy?"

"—had over two years to recover for the '56 election, with a better economy, and this 'alien' business isn't helping him—"

Angel walked around the coffee table and sat down next to Lei. "How many tattooed pinks you think check in there with their dicks looking like overripe eggplant? It's him."

"Didn't see anything about it on the news."

Angel picked the remote off of the table and put her feet up. The argument on the comm was reaching a fever pitch with three or four people shouting at once.

"—Gregg and the Constitutionalists are the Democrats' only real rivals—"

"—believe those 'aliens' were cooked in some gene-lab—"

"—ideth had any sense he'd resign now and give his successor a cha—"

"—NOA never held more than ten seats, and that was fifteen years—"

Angel changed the comm to a sports channel, and hit the mute button. "News is fucked, news's always fucked. The police're probably scared shitless about what news of another death'd do."

"How'd the guy die?"

"Some computer glitch."

Lei shook her head and Angel could hear her tail batting against the couch. "Why keep digging? What's the point?"

Angel was silent for a long time before answering. "If I just sit around, I might have to start *thinking* about this crap, and I'm not ready for that."

"You might have to."

Angel waited for an explanation.

"Half a dozen reporters called while you were out. It's not going to be long before you have to talk to them."

"Why me?" Angel tried to sink into the couch.

"And that priest what's-his-name—"

"Collor called again, great. Any other good news?"

"Well, this lawyer—"

"DeGarmo?"

Lei nodded. "Wants to know about funeral arrangements for Mr. Dorset."

"Byron."

"Huh?"

"Never mind." Angel sighed.

"So, are you going to tell me where you got this car?"

Angel turned to see Lei staring at her, muzzle cradled in her hands.

With Sunday came a stormfront sweeping in from the northwest. When Angel glanced out the window, the steel-wool storm-clouds seemed to be parked in a holding formation across the Golden Gate and over Oakland. The spires of Downtown were still sunlit, carving light holes in the dark horizon. All backed by the bone-white egg-shell that had swallowed Alcatraz.

Daily, hourly even, the city was becoming more surreal.

A chain of lightning flashes began to her right and shot back to the west.

Angel looked back down to Twenty-third. The Dodge Electroline van was still there. "He hasn't moved."

"You're going to let one guy and a van trap you here all day—"

"He's been pointing a vid unit up here."

Lei walked up next to her and waved out the window. "You can't avoid reporters forever. They're like children, the more you deny them something, the harder they go after it."

Angel turned away from the window as the sound of thunder reached them. She didn't want to mention the fact that she thought that the van wasn't a reporter. The van was much too generic—a solid unmarked gray job. And the guy with the vid unit bore an uncomfortable resemblance—down to the reddish eyes—to the Fed-boy she'd run into at Frisco General.

Angel shrugged. "What the fuck? Like you said, it's inevitable."

Angel walked back to her room and opened her underwear drawer.

In the drawer, under a collection of pink-designed clothing she owned and never actually used, was a Beretta 031-S nine-millimeter automatic—a matte-black carbon fiber design that fired caseless ammo. She emptied a few dozen rounds of ammunition out of a sock that had been balled up near the back of the drawer.

Lei's voice came from behind her. "What the hell is that?"

Angel didn't look up. She arranged the various components on the clean area on top of the dresser. "You should know what a gun looks like."

"What are you doing with one?"

"Cleaning and loading the damn thing."

Lei watched for a long time as Angel did her best to undo a few years of neglect. When she began to load it, Angel said, "Don't worry, Lei. I'm not about to take potshots at some vid guy."

"Thinking of getting yourself into trouble, aren't you?"

Angel rummaged in her closet until she came out with a loose blouse that would cover the gun when she shoved it in her jeans. "All I'm thinking about is the possibility that a screw-loose morey who offed Byron might still be out there and might have enough reason to do me—"

Lei looked unconvinced.

"Believe me, I am trying hard to avoid becoming a charter member of the paranoia parade." Angel walked out of her room and back to the bay windows. The stormfront was still stationary, and so was the van. "It ain't easy."

Lei stayed by the door to Angel's room. "What are you going to do?"

"Right now? Visit Byron's condo. Nice low-risk activity that shouldn't attract anyone's attention."

"I'll go with you—"

"You don't have—"

Lei walked up and put a hand on Angel's shoulder. "To keep you from doing anything stupid."

Angel sucked in a breath, about to say something, and thought better of it. She spared a last glance at the pink in the van with the camera and said, "Let's go."

Down the stairs to the front door, Angel added, I wish I knew where they got my address and the comm number."

"It's their job."

As they passed the first-floor apartment, Angel heard the ghost of Balthazar's comm. The explosions and bonging sound effects made everything feel that much more surreal. Angel thought about the old, nearly blind lion sitting alone in his apartment, watching the same cartoons over and over again. For some reason, all the humor had leeched out of the image. Now it seemed nothing if not tragic.

It seemed that even Balthazar wasn't immune to the change sweeping her life—even if it was only her perspective.

Angel opened the door and stepped down to the sidewalk. The Fedboy/cameraman, who had intermittently pointed a vid out the driver's side window on the van, was nowhere to be seen. The van was still parked across the street, and the only noise was the distant thunder—

Angel felt her hand creeping toward her waistband. She restrained herself. She looked up and down the street. A few moreys were gathered at an intersection up the street.

"Angelica Lopez!" came a call from down the street. Angel turned with Lei to see a too-perfect-looking hispanic pink making his way up the hill toward them. Following him was a spotted-white ratboy with a remote vid setup. In an instant, the reporter was upon her. The rat was focusing the camera and Angel had the bad feeling that they were on a live feed, because the hispanic was already turning toward the camera and saying, "Daniel Pasquez, here with a BaySatt news exclusive—"

"Fuck this." Angel made an end run around the camera, stepping over the camera rat's naked pink tail.

The rat panned after her and Angel felt a hand on her shoulder. Angel slowly turned to see Pasquez. "Miss Lopez—"

"Get your hand off of me."

"Miss—"

"I'm not here to boost your ratings. Move the hand or you'll shit your own teeth for a week."

Pasquez gently let go of her shoulder. "If you could please give me a few minutes—"

Angel turned and walked to the BMW. Lei had beat her to it. Apparently the press didn't think she mattered. Behind her she heard Pasquez saying, "Don't you want your view heard?"

Angel gave him the finger without looking back. "What an asshole," she said as she hit the combination on the BMW, letting her and Lei in.

Lei got into the passenger seat. "Do you think spouting off at him was a good idea?"

"I don't give a shit." Angel floored the car and rocketed down the hill, leaving Pasquez and the ratboy running for whatever vehicle they were using. "When I find out who leaked my address—"

"Where exactly are we going?"

"South Beach Towers."

Lei let out a whistle of air from the side of her muzzle.

Angel weaved the BMW past the construction clinging to Sixteenth as she aimed for the coast. Without realizing it, she turned on to Mission and drove toward The Rabbit Hole.

"Jesus Christ." She had to slow down because there were fire engines crowding the street. Traffic had slowed to a crawl. Angel could smell the smoke through the air recyclers before she even saw the rubble where the bar used to be.

"The bastards burned the place down."

"It could be an accident—"

"Bullshit." Angel hit the comm on the dash and started scanning through channels hoping to catch some word on what was happening.

She had to stop because one of the ambulances ahead of her was lifting off. As the ambulance cleared ahead of her, she *saw* what was happening.

The comm latched on a news station. "—of arson. This bar was the scene of the alleged attack police believe—"

The pink Angel saw across Mission was white, slight of build, and wore a leather jacket. She had a flaming sword tattoo and a stupid smile on her face. She was almost hidden from view in an alley across the street from the chaos.

She was totally bald.

Damn it!

Horns blared behind the BMW. Lei said something, but Angel didn't listen. Instead, she popped the door on the car and dived out after the pink.

Angel cleared the twenty meters separating them in five running steps. She was in the air in a ballistic arc aimed at the pink's neck before the woman turned to notice a crazed rabbit pouncing on her.

The pink's eyes went wide, and she started raising her arms.

"Shi—" she began to say.

Then Angel landed on the evil twitch with both feet. The flames across the street roared in her ears and Angel had to shout to hear herself. *"You fucked shitheads!"*

Angel's head throbbed with sirens, the roar of flames, the smell of smoke, air heavy with humidity from the hoses, and the vicious pink face framed by wet, dirty sidewalk—

Pinky tried to push her off, but Angel grabbed both sides of the bald head and put her foot into the pink's throat. Pinky gagged and pushed harder but Angel had her fingers firmly hooked around Pinky's ears. A jagged earring was cutting into Angel's hand.

"You want to burn? You want to fucking burn?" Angel let go of one ear and reached for the Beretta. *"You wanna see Hell?"*

Pinky's eyes opened even wider as she saw the gun. She redoubled her efforts to dislodge Angel, but fighting and trying to breathe at the same time seemed beyond her.

"Angel!" called a voice from behind.

Angel brought the gun out of her pants.

"What are you doing?" The voice was Lei.

Christ, what the hell *was* she doing? Was she going to turn this pink twitch into street-pizza with the cops only a few—

Angel whipped her head around to look back at the fire. Thank God, she thought. Everyone was still intent on the torch *The Rabbit Hole* had become. It and three adjacent buildings.

If she didn't draw any more attention to herself, she wouldn't be up on charges for the gun she was waving around. What the hell had she been thinking?

She took her foot off Pinky's neck, letting her roll away. Pinky made a croaking noise, and there was a slight tug from Angel's left hand.

Angel had kept a grip on the jagged earring.

"Crazy freaked hairball," Pinky managed to croak.

"Let's go, Angel." Lei grabbed Angel's arm.

Angel slipped the gun back into her waistband. "Fuck this shit."

Pinky looked her right in the eye as Lei led her out of the alley. "We know who you are."

"Bullshit."

"Come on, Angel." Lei kept dragging her back to the BMW.

When they reached the BMW, Angel could hear Pinky croaking, "A flaming sword of righteousness—" Then the door closed.

Angel floored the car as fast as she could move, past the bottle-neck.

"What is possessing you, girl? You looked about to kill—"

"I was."

"Are you going to start blitzing out on me? If you are, I'd like to know. You going to jump any human you run into now—"

"She wasn't *any* human."

"Then *who* the *fuck* was she? And why were you tap dancing on her neck?"

Angel turned down Beale, under the old Embarcadero Freeway on-ramp. As the BMW passed under the new Oakland Bay Bridge, she said, "She, or someone like her, set that fire."

"How the fuck do you know that?"

"You saw. She's Knights of Humanity—"

"So-fucking-what? Is it suddenly open season on every freako nutball group out there? That's half this city, Angel. I don't think you have enough bullets."

"Don't you see what's happening?" Angel slammed on the brakes and a green GM Maduro laid on the horn and swerved around them.

"What?"

"They set that fire in retaliation. Someone else is going to retaliate for that, it's going to keep going, someone has to, to . . ." Angel leaned her head against the steering wheel. Why did she feel that she was spinning down into some dark abyss? She told herself that the smell of smoke that was clinging to her fur was making her dizzy.

"Has to what?"

Angel felt her eyes watering. "God. I don't know."

Lei hugged Angel's shoulders. "You've been stressed out. It's understandable. Let's go find that condo you inherited and get you something to drink, all right?"

Angel nodded, and took a deep breath. "Sorry, Lei. I've been losing it lately."

South Beach Towers was at the corner of Stanford and Townsend, right on the coast of the bay. In fact, it sat right on the terminus beyond which the Embarcadero and a few million tons of landfill slipped underwater in the '34 quake. Now that she could see it without the benefit of fog, Angel thought the look of the city might improve immeasurably if the white concrete and black glass neo-Aztec building joined the last half-klick of Townsend under the bay.

Angel parked the BMW in the reserved garage and led Lei up to the building.

The combination that DeGarmo gave her let her into the lobby, and she had to spend a few worthless minutes explaining the situation to the security personnel. The rent-a-cops were nice and professional enough that Angel could pretend that it didn't matter that she wasn't human.

Even so, Angel could smell the tension. The veneer was cracking on these guys.

It took a few minutes to double-check and clear Angel through to the elevators. They gave her a personalized ID card and promised that she was now on the computers and wouldn't be hassled again.

On the elevator ride up, she asked, "Did you see it?"

"What?" Lei asked.

"Those guys. They feel it, too, in the air."

"What's in the air?"

"Violence. We aren't immune here. People are beginning to realize it."

"You're just paranoid."

The doors whooshed open on the fifteenth floor, where Byron had his apartment. "Lei, I think it's only a matter of time before all Hell breaks loose."

"This isn't New York or Los Angeles. I think you're too close to all this. You're losing perspective."

Angel led her down a corridor to apartment 156. She tapped in the combination on the keypad next to the door. "What's so different about San—"

Angel stopped talking as the door swung open on Byron's apartment.

They both stood there, silent, staring through the door.

"Shit." Angel finally said.

"I'll go call the police," Lei said.

Angel nodded, not really listening. She walked into the room, stepping over cushions that had been tossed from the couch and shredded. The coffee table was in three pieces, the glass top shattered. The wall-to-wall pile carpeting had been cut neatly into five-centimeter-wide strips, as had the upholstery on what remained of the furniture.

Angel could smell a faint animal musk hanging in the air. Canine or feline, she couldn't tell. It had taken a while to fade, but she knew it wasn't Byron she was smelling.

Yes, Angel thought, *Lei had to go to the lobby.*

That was the comm there, and there, and there—Angel thought she even saw a piece of it on the balcony.

Angel walked through the rubble to the remains of the wet bar and hoped the folks who trashed the joint had left her that drink.

Chapter 8

They were seated out on the patio, under a blackening sky, and Angel was having a tough time figuring out what else could go wrong.

"Did you notice anything missing?" Anaka asked.

"I told the first cops. It wasn't my condo." Angel refused to sit down or even look at the Asian cop. Anaka was just the latest in a series of uniforms, detectives, and lab guys who were busy tearing the wreckage apart. She'd given a statement to one of the uniforms, and she didn't want to go over it again. "Same damn questions, again? Why not zip off and leave me alone—"

She heard Anaka inhale as if he was about to retort. Instead, he hit her with another question. "When was the last time you were in this apartment?"

"Week ago Wednesday. Answer to that hasn't changed in the last half hour."

"It is possible that the humans we're holding—"

Angel whipped around. "The *hell* I'm supposed to know if a trio of hairless geeks could've managed a little party time here?"

Anaka was rubbing his temples. "Miss Lopez, I wish you'd be more cooperative."

"Why you bothering? You have your suspects. They're going down. Your job's over." Angel walked up to Anaka. With him sitting and her standing, they were eye to eye. Under the smell of the lightning, the cop was shedding stress and tension like old fur.

"Sure," she said with an insincere smile. "The fuckheads did *this* too, make life easy for yourself."

"I'm trying to do my job here. There's more to this—" Anaka looked around and stood up.

"Yeah, like I make a shitload of difference?"

Anaka didn't look like he was paying attention. He was looking back into the apartment, where the police were still sifting through debris. The forensics people were dusting the place and sweeping an UV laser around in their search for biological material and prints—paw and/or finger.

Anaka stepped over to the door and slid it shut. Suddenly Angel was reminded of Dr. Ellis. She remembered the rather tense byplay between the two pink cops. White didn't want to deal with Anaka's "conspiracies." Anaka had suspected—

"Something funny about the autopsy," Angel said.

Anaka whipped around. "What do you know about that?" Suddenly she could see all of Ellis' paranoia mirrored in Anaka.

"Ever find out why Ellis the not-a-vulpine-expert was assigned to cut up the corpse?"

"No." Anaka warily backed away from the doors. "I've been trying to contact Ellis on the substance of the autopsy."

"Did she mention a morey did him?"

"What? How do you know that?"

"Ellis told me when I cornered her yesterday. About to crap her pants, too." She was glad to see somebody *else* look confused. Even though the expression on Anaka's face only lasted a second.

Anaka nodded as if something just made sense to him. "Falsified the autopsy, then she panicked. *That's* why she's disappeared . . ." Angel was about to ask him about what happened to Ellis, but he went on, changing the subject. There was an edge of fear, or paranoia, in Anaka's voice. "This is bigger than you know."

He said it with such conviction that Angel backed up to the railing. Chain-reaction lightning shot across the sky, and for the first time she noticed how fatigued he looked. The rumpled suit he wore was the same one he'd been wearing in the morgue. Might have been the same suit he'd worn to *Ralph's*. "What are you talking about?"

Anaka walked up next to her as the peal of thunder reached them. The wind began to pick up, and the few last remaining shards of sunlight raced south, across the bay.

"The first big quake, it was the fires that almost killed this town." Anaka stared out at the water, towards the dome. His voice became harder and more distant. "In '34, it was money. The quake, martial law, the recession, the civic restructuring . . .This town was

bought and sold like it was a public auction. Cops rented out as
hired thugs, firemen paid protection money—"

"What's your point?"

Anaka turned toward her. "I'm not an enemy."

"You're *part* of that machine."

"No." Anaka shook his head. "For twenty years— A quarter
century since the quake, and things haven't changed."

Another bolt of lightning tore open the sky, and a minute long
roar of thunder followed close on its heels, vibrating the railing
Angel leaned against. A drop of moisture struck her square on the
nose.

Anaka was going on now, like Angel wasn't even there. "The
DA's office is rushing a conviction on the shoddiest evidence I've
seen since the National Guard stopped shooting looters."

Rain began to gently patter the balcony, and the rumblings were
closing the gap on the flashes.

"They say they want to shut down the Knights—" Anaka was
raising his voice now. All she heard of the rest of his sentence was:
"VanDyne Industrial?"

"The ones who rebuilt the Pyramid?" she shouted over the
storm.

"And the cable cars, and half of downtown between Market and
Telegraph Hill. They own this building, and most of the condos
overlooking the bay." The rain finally cascaded upon them in full
force, sheeting across the balcony in rhythmic waves. *"Byron
Dorset worked for them,* and if there's a central cog in the San Francisco 'machine' it's VanDyne."

"Does that have anything to do—"

Anaka shook his head. "I'm working on it. Help me."

He slid the door open and rushed inside, Angel on his heels. In
the apartment, the only thing Angel could smell was her own wet
fur. "What about Detective White?"

"He's a good cop." There could have been an edge of sarcasm
in his voice.

"White doesn't like you, does he?"

Anaka shrugged. "Few people in the department do, I'm used to
it."

She looked at the cops and the forensics guys who were packing
things up. Apparently their job was completed. A balding black
human walked up to them and addressed her. "The place's all yours
now, though I'd suggest you take pictures for the insurance companies before you clean up."

"You're done?" There was a slight hint of disbelief in Anaka's voice. "That was damn quick, Beirce."

The man turned to Anaka as if he'd just now bothered to notice him. He ran a hand through what was left of his hair. "And what're *you* doing here? No meat lying around—you *did* make Homicide, didn't you? Paint's still wet on that suit."

"Since when does it take less than an hour to dust up a crime scene?"

"Fuck you. Just because you wear civvies now don't mean you tell me my business."

"Listen—"

"No, *you* listen. I do what I have to do and get out of the lady rabbit's hair—"

"Fur." Angel said.

"Whatever. So, *Detective* Anaka, I suggest you pack your paranoia and do likewise. And if you need a report, you know where you can file it."

Beirce turned around and left the apartment, leading a platoon of men carrying equipment. The uniforms followed, leaving Anaka and Angel alone in the living room.

"What did you *do* to that guy?"

"Me?" Anaka shook his head. "Nothing." Anaka sighed. "I'm going to go before my partner starts missing me, but we'll need to talk later."

"Sure," Angel said, "for all the good it'll do."

"One thing though." Anaka pulled something out of his pocket. "Would you stop poking around on your own?"

"Huh?" She tried to look innocent.

He handed her a folded up paper that she instantly recognized. It was Byron's letter, wrapped around the Earthquake's season tickets.

"Where?" Angel asked as she reflexively stuck her hand in the pocket of her jeans. She began to remember feeling something drop while she was watching Earl's corpse.

"You dropped them outside the door to the morgue."

She took the tickets and the letter and replaced them in her pocket. "I'm sorry. I don't know why I—"

"Just *don't* any more."

She shook her head and felt stupid. She was way out of her depth and felt like things had flown totally beyond her grasp. She didn't say anything as Anaka let himself out.

*   *   *

The BMW kicked up a sheet of water over the sidewalk as Angel pulled up to her house.

"The van's gone," Lei said.

Angel looked at the spot where the gray Dodge van had been watching their apartment. Nothing. "They probably saw what's-his-name get shit for footage and gave up." It would be comforting to think they'd just been reporters.

"I suppose."

They both got out of the car and ran for the door, splashing across a sidewalk that was becoming a shallow river. The storm was still gaining in intensity. The rapid-fire lightning flashes were now simultaneous with the thunder.

The door was open.

"Shit." Angel pulled the Beretta out of her pants.

"You didn't ditch that thing?" Lei asked.

"Why?"

"There were a dozen cops—"

"I was an innocent victim, why search— Damn it, did you leave the door open?"

Lei looked at the door which had swung inward with a slight touch from Angel. "I don't know. I could've in all that confusion when we left."

A blast of wind slammed the door into the interior hall. Angel covered the hall and the stairs with the gun.

"Who're you going to shoot? Balthazar could've—"

"Almost forty, barely leaves his apartment during weather like this?" Angel stepped into the hall and started edging up the stairs, leading with the gun.

Lei followed, keeping a respectful distance behind her. "Are you going to shoot some overeager reporter?"

"At least make him crap his pants. Close the door."

Lei pushed the door shut with her foot. Angel asked, quietly, "Do you smell anything?"

"Besides us?"

Angel nodded. Lei shook her head no.

Maybe she was wrong and all she could smell was her own wet fur, but Angel could swear she could smell something else. Something else that was alien to this house. Neither canine, lepine, or Balthazar's leonine scent. Not an animal smell at all.

Fake pine?

The door to their apartment was closed. There seemed no sign of any forced entry. Angel backed up and leveled the gun at the doorway. She waved Lei over. "Open it. Then stand back."

"Is this smart?"

"Do it."

Lei stood next to the door and punched in the combination. Then she stepped back and cowered as if she expected some sort of explosion. The door swung open a few centimeters, and Angel stood for nearly ten seconds, waiting.

She could feel her own pulse in her neck, and there was the copper taste of excitement in her mouth. Her breath tried to burn her nose.

She took a deep breath and dove through the door.

Through the door, she swept the gun to cover the living room from the kitchenette, past the bay windows, and then to the hall to the bedrooms. She rolled into the hall between the bedrooms and covered, in turn, her room, the bathroom, and Lei's room. It took all of three seconds to see the apartment was empty.

Angel slumped against the doorframe to the bathroom, hyperventilating, pointing her gun at the floor. Lei took a few tentative steps into the living room. "Safe?"

Angel nodded, panting.

"Would you *please* put the gun away?"

She nodded again, unable to get the breath to talk, and clicked the safety on the Beretta. She went and tucked it back in the underwear drawer. There was a nearby lightning strike that shook the house. The lights flickered.

She stood, leaning against the dresser in her room, catching her breath. The shower started, and she realized how wet and miserable she was. She walked back to the bathroom and sat on the john. "Leave some hot water," Angel told Lei through the fogged-glass partition.

As she waited for the shower, Angel kept telling herself that it wasn't paranoia. There really was something rotten going on here. It was perfectly reasonable, what she just did. Someone—she wished she knew who—could have been waiting for them.

She put her head in her hands. Yeah, but jumping that pink Knight on the street today, that *wasn't* reasonable. A fine line she was treading here, and at the moment she didn't know exactly what side of it she was on. It didn't help matters that city employees were feeding into her paranoia.

Detective Anaka just about flat out said that all the corrupt forces in the city government were conspiring to pin Byron's murders on the two punks. Dr. Ellis said Byron got clawed by a moreau, covered the fact up, and disappeared.

And Byron worked for VanDyne Industrial.

What the hell did that mean?

What could a Brit fox named Byron Dorset be doing for one of the major stockholders in the San Francisco civic machine?

And what was he doing on Eddy Street? Was he really going to meet a bunch of bald schizo pinks in their own apartment? If so, why'd he get whacked by a morey?

Anaka was right, this was all *his* job. She wasn't equipped to do any half-assed investigating. She was just a piece of street trash from Cleveland who barely had enough smarts to keep her hide intact. Just thinking about all of this made her head hurt.

The only person she knew who was equipped to unravel something like this was down in Los Angeles behind a blockade of moreaus and National Guard. Even then, she'd be lucky if Nohar remembered her.

So, was she going to sit on her ass and wait until she talked to Anaka again?

"Yeah, right." Angel said with all the sarcasm she could muster. Okay, skulking into other people's buildings was a bad idea. But she'd be damned if she stopped trying to figure things out. Even if she was a half-assed investigator, she was the only one she could trust.

Besides, she had to straighten out Byron's affairs. If certain questions came up in the process, no one could blame her for asking—right?

The dryer came on for a few minutes and then Lei came out of the shower. "It's all yours."

Angel grunted a monosyllable.

Lei leaned forward and rubbed noses. "I understand, but you *could* try and relax a little bit."

"I'll try," Angel said as she shrugged out of her wet clothes.

Chapter 9

San Francisco awoke to a positively ugly morning. The sky was asphalt black. The wind was trying to shake the windows apart. A hazy fog evolved into rain so heavy that Angel could barely see across the street out her bay window.

As far as Angel was concerned, the weather was the least ugly part of her day. She made the mistake of waking up for work, eating an abbreviated breakfast, and driving down to *Ralph's* to start her shift—all pretending that last week hadn't happened.

She should have known better. In a universe that allowed her to drive up to *Ralph's Diner* in a hundred K worth of BMW, nothing could be normal. As she drove toward the diner, she could see something odd was going on, even through the rain. There was too much traffic hovering around, especially for this early—*Ralph's* never had much of a breakfast crowd—and way too many cars for this weather.

Angel rolled past without stopping. She could read the logo of several news services. She pulled to the curb and played with the expensive comm set into the dash. She punched up the BaySatt news feed, and there was Daniel Pasquez, male hispanic archetype, doing the live feed from *Ralph's*.

"Great."

So much for trying to lead a normal life.

She pulled the BMW over at the crest of a hill. She flipped a few switches on the dash, and the small screen of the BMW's built-in comm activated for outgoing calls.

Having a car with a full comm unit, *that* she could get used to.

She called in sick to *Ralph's*.

The response was typical Sanchez. "Why aren't you here?"

"I'm not coming in."

Sanchez did not looked pleased. "What do you mean, 'not coming in'? Where're you calling from—" Angel could see lights behind Sanchez, they were covering his little manager office. What did Sanchez think he was doing?

"I mean I am not coming in. And where I'm calling from is none of your business."

"Damn it, what do I tell these reporters?"

Angel just stared at the screen. Was this greaseball serious? "What?"

"You're just going to blow this opportunity—"

Damn it. Sanchez *was* serious. All he saw in all this was a chance to get some free advertising. The fact that this was her *life* that was being screwed with didn't seem to occur to him. Either that, or he assumed the sad proposition that his every employee lived and breathed that lickspittle job as much as I'm-the-manager-and-have-no-life did.

"You're right, Sanchez. I shouldn't call in sick."

He looked visibly relieved. "Thank—"

"I quit."

"What!" The look on Sanchez's flabby face was almost worth the months of irritation she'd endured.

"I said I quit. I'm tired of your flabass dimestore greasepit. I'm sick of getting shafted on hours because you're boffing Judy. I'm sick of someone who only serves moreys because humans wouldn't stand him. Go wait on tables yourself—your customers will fucking love you."

To make everything clear, she gave him the finger and hit the mute button. It was wonderful to watch, even without the sound. Sanchez's face went red, and he began shouting at her, spraying the screen. It was nearly ten seconds before he seemed to realize that he was coming down on her in front of reporters.

So much for his free publicity. Angel knew that if the reporters couldn't get hold of her, they'd be perfectly willing to give airtime to her manager throwing a rod.

She killed the comm and turned the car around to go home.

It was an odd feeling. She had never thought she'd miss that job, of all the shit places to work she'd been in, but her sudden unemployment worried her. Another part of her life she'd thought stable had crumbled so rapidly that she was still coming to grips with what she'd done when she got back to her apartment.

The calls started around eight, about the time she got back home.

At nine, reporters were calling every ten minutes.

After a while, the opportunity to bitch the media leeches out was outweighed by the annoyance factor and by 10:30, she just told the comm to lock out all the incoming calls.

Amidst the forest of reporters, a few calls came from moreaus. All of those ended up being representatives of Father Collor and his people. They wanted her to think about nonhuman solidarity. She told them all to fuck off.

One call came from a bald human. He only stayed on screen long enough to say: "We know who you are."

The news off the comm wasn't much better once she got over the novelty of seeing her ex-manager getting it over the public net. There'd been a half-dozen incidents of cross-species violence in the city overnight, primarily concentrated in Chinatown during a power failure. There had only been one minor injury, but property damage was estimated at fifty thousand dollars. The vids panned down a street of broken storefronts, and one taxi that had the windows busted out.

They said that the incidents were probably the result of the suspected arson of *The Rabbit Hole*.

At noon, she killed the comm entirely.

They were going to release Byron's body today. DeGarmo wanted to hear about funeral arrangements, too—

"Ahh, shit."

She didn't want to do this. But it had fallen on her head, and who was she kidding if she said she had something better to do? Better she do this than let it fall to someone who wanted to use it to make some political point.

And she'd be damned if she let that happen.

She turned the comm back on and called DeGarmo.

If she'd wanted to, she probably could have orchestrated the entire procedure over the comm. Somehow, that wouldn't have felt right. She had no desire to see Byron's corpse again, but she didn't think she could let him pass from St. Luke's unaccompanied. DeGarmo offered to supervise things for her. But, in the end, there was no way she could stay at home.

So, at 3:30 she met DeGarmo in the parking lot of St. Luke's Veterinary.

When Angel drove the BMW into the half-flooded parking lot, she saw DeGarmo for the first time in the flesh—a tall human, wearing a black trench coat that shone from the rain sheeting off of it. He hung back in the halo cast from sodium lamps mounted next to the ambulance bays. His hair was a matte-black crew cut that enhanced the thinness of a too-lean face.

Angel got out of the car and made for the shelter of the ambulance bays. It wasn't until she was up next to the lawyer that she realized exactly how tall he was. His waistline was just about eye level on her.

DeGarmo was holding out his hand by the time she reached him. Angel shook it with both of hers.

"I'm pleased to finally meet you in person, Miss Lopez."

"Call me Angel," she told him. "I'm sick of 'Miss Lopez.' Ain't mine, the INS picked it for my grandmother."

DeGarmo gave a noncommittal shrug. "We need to get your authorization to move the body. Then we can go to—" DeGarmo looked at a small palm-held computer. "Cabrillo Acres Funeral Home."

He looked up from the computer. "Can I ask why all the way down in Pacifica?"

"First place I called that handled moreaus."

DeGarmo led her into the building where a group of paramedics were standing around a u-shaped desk. As they approached, Angel asked DeGarmo, "How'd you end up in this? What's your angle?"

"Mr. Dorset retained me to handle this."

"How much did he pay you?"

"Don't worry, none of it is from the current estate."

"So when do *I* have to pay you something?"

"As long as it involves the settling of Mr. Dorset's affairs, you don't."

What kind of estate were they talking about? She'd avoided asking DeGarmo about that because it seemed tacky. She wondered about it all the way through the authorization procedure. Then there was the fact Byron did all this bequeathing to her in the nine days prior to his death.

DeGarmo acted as if that was normal.

Once she'd satisfied the bureaucracy, they rolled out a gurney with the sheeted body on it. It smelled of cold rot and disinfectant. It made Angel cringe inside. There was a ground ambulance waiting for the drive to Pacifica. Angel and DeGarmo flanked the body as the medics rolled it toward the waiting meat wagon.

"You can ride down with me," DeGarmo offered.

Angel shook her head. "I'll go with him." She patted one of Byron's sheeted hands—

"Hold it," she said.

"What?" DeGarmo and two medics said simultaneously.

Angel took in a deep breath. She smelled wet fur, blood, disinfectant—and something smelled wrong about the body. And there was something radically wrong with the shape of the hand under the sheet.

"Lift the sheet."

"Do you really want to do that?" asked the medic pushing the gurney. She was a hispanic woman, and her young human face had a look of concern on it. "I don't think you—"

"I need to see him." There was a terrible sinking feeling in Angel's gut. "Lift the sheet, now."

The four of them stood at the points of the compass around the body, blocking the door to the ambulance bay. The hispanic medic gave a questioning look to her partner, who shrugged. She shook her head, as if she thought it was a really bad idea, and lifted the sheet.

"What the hell kind of fuckup is this!" Angel screamed at the medic, before she'd even taken her hand off of the sheet.

It wasn't Byron. It wasn't even a fox.

Laying under the sheet was the body of a brown-furred canine who looked like he had taken a shotgun blast to the neck.

"Who the fuck is this?" Angel yelled.

The hispanic woman covered the body again and reached out for her. "Please, it's just some sort of mixup. I'm sure we'll be able to—"

The other medic practically ran back to the desk and picked up a receiver and began talking rapidly to someone.

Angel shrugged away from the woman. "Damn straight it's a mixup. Jesus-mother-humping-tap-dancing-Christ, *you lost him.*" Angel backed up and turned to the lawyer. "Can you *sue* these shitheads?"

At the sound of that, the nurse running the station got on another receiver and began talking to someone. The medic pulled the gurney and the unidentified corpse back into the hospital.

DeGarmo tried to calm her. "I'm sure this will be resolved in a few minutes."

"I don't like this shit," she said. "Too many people are *fucking* with me! Byron's been on the comm more times than the president and they *lost him*. What're they running here? *What?* Just because he's a morey means he's fucking interchangeable?"

They stuck her and DeGarmo in an empty waiting room and it took half an hour for the hospitals' chief administrator to come down and "explain" what had happened.

The guy was a pink, of course, middle-aged, white, fat, bald, and sweating enough to look like he'd just come from the rain. She could smell the stress and fear off of the guy from ten meters away. The man's emotions were as subtle as a toxic waste dump. He had a salt-and-pepper mustache that seemed to grow whiter as he talked to them.

"It seems, Miss Lopez, that there was a computer error."

"What the fuck happened to—" DeGarmo put a hand on her shoulder to restrain her outburst.

She knew it was bad, whatever it was, otherwise they wouldn't have sent the boss down here. And Dr. Varberg—that's what it said on his ID tag—wouldn't look like he was about to crap his pants.

"Byron Dorset's ID number was transposed with that of another patient, a John Doe gunshot victim. That's why you picked up the wrong body."

Angel sucked in a breath and kept her voice level. "Okay, so what happened to Byron?"

The room was very quiet. Somewhere out in the hospital a public address system spouted something incomprehensible. It took a long while for the answer to come.

"John Doe's body was scheduled—" Varberg paused and rubbed his forehead with a pudgy hand.

"What happened to the body?" Angel said, getting up from her seat and trying hard to keep an even edge to her voice.

"It was cremated at 9:30 this morning," Varberg said quietly.

The scene froze, DeGarmo seated to Angel's right, Varberg standing in front of her. The air seemed to hang dead around her, making it hard to breathe. She tried to say something, but it only came out as a squeak.

"Miss—"

She shook her head violently and slammed her foot back into the chrome-vinyl chair she'd spent the last half hour sitting in. The chair buckled and bounced halfway up the wall behind it, tearing out a chunk of drywall, Varberg backed away, cowering, as if he expected to be next.

Angel took a few deep breaths, and looked back at DeGarmo.

He had vacated his seat and was staring at the wreckage of Angel's chair.

She found her voice. "I've got money, right?"

DeGarmo looked at her and did a good job of regaining his composure. "Yes, I've filed the appropriate tax f—"

"Good. I'm retaining you to talk to this asshole." She pointed at Varberg. "Get what's left of Byron. File complaints, charges, whatever it is you do. Make his life hell." Angel walked to the door and yanked it open. "I've got a few calls to make."

She left to the sound of DeGarmo saying, "Does the hospital have an attorney I can talk to?" Then the door slammed shut.

She pushed her way to a public comm in the emergency room. She'd finally had enough bullshit.

It took her nearly ten minutes to get her call through the various extensions at BaySatt news, but she finally found herself facing a too-perfect hispanic face.

With a demonic grin that reawakened the pain in her cheek she asked, "So, Mr. Pasquez, you want a fucking-A exclusive?"

For close to an hour, Angel vented her spleen at St. Luke's, the cops who cared for little but busting the Knights, the reporters who were trying to make her life hell, the cops, the Knights themselves, the cops, Father Collor, the cops. . . .

She lost count of how many people she'd piss off if this aired, but for a while it made her feel better.

When 8:30 rolled around, Angel said, *"Five million?"*

She and DeGarmo were sitting in a rear booth of *Ralph's*, not because Angel was nostalgic, but because it was the closest place to St. Luke's she could think of—only a few blocks south.

The press was gone, and the place was occupied by a scattering of soaked moreys huddling in from the rain. DeGarmo was the only human other than Judy. Judy seemed unaware of this morning's events, and Sanchez was nowhere to be seen.

Lucky on all points.

A few rats in one corner turned to look at her when she shouted. Angel thought she recognized the black one.

DeGarmo nodded. "After estate taxes the net assets that Dorset left you is about a hundred fifty thousand short of five million." He sipped his coffee impassively, as if he handed news like this to people all the time.

Angel sat, staring at the lawyer. She should be—she didn't know what she should be feeling. A cynical part of her mind kept saying she should be shitting a gold brick and bouncing off the ceiling. She'd just struck the lottery, her ship had come in, she was set for life. . . .

The problem was, the news had finally knocked out whatever feeling of stability she had left in her life. If things could change so damn quickly, *nothing* was certain.

She must've been staring quite a while because DeGarmo lowered his coffee. "Are you all right?"

Angel blinked. Was she all right? Could she even *know* if she was all right? "I'm fine, I guess. I need to get my bearings."

"I know it's quite an adjustment. One of the things Mr. Dorset hired me for was to get you over that hump, should it be necessary."

Admirable prescience on Byron's part.

What a fucking wonderful guy.

Angel started to realize exactly how pissed she was at Byron. He let her get blindsided by everything, without any warning, up to and including this damn will.

"Why didn't he tell me?"

"Pardon?"

"Damn it, if he made a will just a few days before—"

DeGarmo held up his hand. "Ahh, I see where you got the impression. No, Mr. Dorset was my client for ten years. His current will has been in force for most of that time."

"But he just met me—"

"He had a habit of changing the name of the bequest every time he entered a relationship. He named you the primary heir a week before he died. He changed the will frequently. I doubt the proximity of the change to his death represented anything sinister."

She was beginning to feel numb. "He changed it a lot?"

"Do you want to talk about this?"

"How many times?"

DeGarmo removed the palm computer from the breast pocket in his suit and referred to it. "Twenty-seven times in ten years. All female moreaus, California residents. All of them now receive a token bequest of forty thousand dollars."

She tried to do the calculations in her head, and failed. As if losing Byron wasn't enough, if the general chaos wasn't enough, there was a sinking feeling that what she'd thought of as something special might have been something routine, pedestrian, casual.

"Did he mention anything about a possible engagement?"

DeGarmo arched an eyebrow.

Angel closed her eyes. All this fiancée bullshit was people making assumptions. Byron never was going to propose anything.

"Miss Lo—Angel?"

"I'm fine." *I'm not crying,* she thought. She shook her head and tried to compose herself. "You looked at his estate. You were his lawyer for ten years. What did he do for a living?"

"He worked for VanDyne Industrial."

Tell me what I don't know. "What did he *do* for them?"

"The occupation he listed for the IRS was delivery. Other than that, I don't know specifics. I only helped him manage his money. How he managed such large compensations from VanDyne, I don't know."

"And you don't know jack about what he delivered."

DeGarmo nodded and sipped his coffee. "I know enough not to want to know."

Chapter 10

When Angel made it home, her head was still swimming. De-Garmo had managed to blow whatever certainty she had left in her life. She was so distracted that she was halfway in the door and shaking the rain out of her fur before she heard human breathing from the darkened living room.

Her head shot up. She could barely smell the man over her own wet fur, but she knew it was Detective White before her eyes adjusted. It took a conscious effort to keep her hand from drifting to the gun in her waistband.

White sat on the couch in the living room, lit by the flickering light from the comm and the occasional lightning flash. The vision of the balding lump of rumpled humanity on her own couch was surreal enough to trigger a frightening wave of vertigo. Lei was nowhere to be seen.

"What are you doing here?" Angel asked, one hand clutching the top button of her soaked blouse. The last time she had seen this man in the flesh had been when she IDd Byron's corpse. Then, he'd tried to be comforting. Even when she had called him at the station—making him hock his takeout Chinese breakfast—the iron that had crept into his voice held barely a hint of the tempered glare that locked her on her entrance.

"Do you have any idea what you've done?" White hit a button on the remote and the picture on the comm froze. The reflection in his gray eyes made them molten lead bearings. The heat of his anger had sunk into the walls. Angel could smell it.

She glanced at the frozen picture on the comm and saw Pasquez's face.

Angel's latent paranoia was returning in full force. Thank the lord that humans couldn't pick up on the scent cues, otherwise the way she was tensed could probably be used as just cause to blow her away.

"Where's Lei?"

"Frankly, I don't give a shit."

Christ, what was going on here? *Well, you knew you were going to piss people off talking to Pasquez,* she thought.

"How'd you get in here?"

White gave her a hard little smile. "I'm a cop, you little twitch. I can override any electronic lock in my jurisdiction—and I want to know what the hell you were thinking of when you talked to Pasquez."

"I have a right—"

White stood up and threw the remote down on the coffee table. *"I am sick of people's fucking rights."* He walked up to Angel, who still stood in the open doorway, dripping. She noticed that White had been in the apartment long enough to dry off. "You think you have the right to make all sorts of half-assed accusations? Where do you get off?"

She backed up a step. "Do you have a warrant?"

"I'm not here to arrest you. Just want you to know how grateful I am." He stood in front of her now, tensed to the breaking point. Angel was very careful not to move. "We *had* the Knights. Thought a morey shit like you'd appreciate that. But you had to shoot off your mouth, didn't you? Not only screw the case, but you stir up shit in this town from Internal Affairs and the mayor's publicist, to every shit-for-brains radical who's got a gripe against the city."

She was ripe with the scent of her own fear. "I'd like you to leave," she said with as calm a voice as she could muster.

White nodded. "I'm going. But ask yourself if you want to see Chino Hernandez and Dwayne Washington out on the streets again. Because they're *all* the Knights we got now, and you pull any more fancy bullshit, they're going to walk."

He stepped up to her and raised her face with one finger under her chin. The finger was warm, soft, and hairless. The contact made Angel nauseous.

"This town's ready to take a header. Don't help push it—" White let go of her chin and moved past her out into the hall. As he started down the stairs, he added, "You might fall off the same cliff."

Angel stood there, shivering.

After a while, she calmed down and closed the door behind her. White had reminded Angel of a seminal truth—she did *not* like cops. Angel walked to the comm and unpaused the program White had recorded. It was Pasquez all right, him and his BaySatt news exclusive. The basic theme of which was, "what was the city trying to hide?"

As Pasquez rambled on in the background, she turned on the light in the living room and saw that White had been a fairly busy boy. On the coffee table must have been every single ramcard that had been left in the house. The cards were scattered like some mad rainbow-sheened game of solitaire.

Predictably, behind her she heard Father Alvarez De Collor's voice. Pasquez was asking Collor about the mess, in his capacity as the "voice of the nonhuman population." Apparently, "the nonhuman population"—she wished the media sometime, somewhere, would use the word moreau—wanted the real murder suspects prosecuted. Collor made the assumption that the killers were human, and implied that they might be cops. *Now there's the voice of peace,* Angel thought.

The nonhumans wanted empowerment. The nonhumans wanted to do the Knights of Humanity what the Knights wanted to do to them. The nonhumans wanted better jobs, better housing, better medical care. The nonhumans wanted an end to discrimination.

If the nonhumans didn't get all this now, with a cherry on top, then, Collor said, "Los Angeles is not that far away."

Angel turned to look at the comm and got the closing shot of Collor in his full regalia. His priest's collar, and the full combat getup of the Brazilian strike team he used to belong to, way back when. That wasn't new, that was all Collor's radical priest schtick. What was new was the fact that the holster had a sidearm in it this time.

It had been federal law for two decades that it was a felony for a moreau to possess a firearm. Collor was smiling at the camera with a perfectly vicious show of teeth on his feline face. The expression dared anyone to pick him up for the offense.

"Great," Angel said.

Then the scene shifted and Pasquez was in an even more interesting interview.

The first thing she could see was the red flag with a white circle. In the circle was a stylized H that could have been a hacked representation of a double helix. It was the flag of the Knights of Humanity.

The camera faced a seated individual whose face was obscured by BaySatt's computer. He was human, and in contrast to Collar's field-grunt attire, this pink was wearing a stylized officer's uniform done up in urban camouflage.

Pasquez introduced him as "Tony X," prime mover and shaker of the Knights of Humanity.

"Oh, Christ," Angel said, it was already being cast as a war. This exclusive by BaySatt news just seemed an exercise in picking out the leading players in the soon-to-be televised drama.

Angel walked around the coffee table, staring at the screen in fascination, as if it was an oncoming car, or a canister containing some deadly biological weapon.

"We had no part in the death of Byron Dorset," said a computer-altered voice. "Individuals don't matter. The Knights are interested in the destiny of the species."

"You've been accused of promoting violence."

"Any violence the Knights are involved in is defensive in nature."

"Are you saying that the twelve alleged attacks on unarmed non-humans in the past week were all cases of the Knights defending themselves?"

The computer-altered voice gained in intensity. "We are under assault, every human being in this country, by this plague of genetic *waste*. Anything the Knights can do to help this country wake up is an effort to save the race."

"You've been accused of advocating genocide—"

"Do you know what these things are?" Tony X stood up and walked to a table. He pulled aside a sheet of canvas that was on top of it to reveal a terrarium. Inside it was a black object about the length of Tony X's arm. "Look in here. This is an example of what we're harboring in this country."

Pasquez didn't interrupt as the camera zoomed in on the flopping creature in the tank. The thing was black and chitonous, it had faceted eyes, and a meter-long ovipositor that oozed an emerald-green fluid the consistency of semen.

"The same labs that made our furry neighbors, produced this atrocity." Tony X prodded the thing from off-screen with a metal rod. The bug creature erupted in a manic frenzy of thrashing that sprayed the sides of the terrarium with green, and it ended up wrapped around the rod and trying to stab it. "For the same purpose. To kill."

The camera pulled back to reveal Tony X standing behind the terrarium. Angel was feeling queazy. Importing that kind of macro gene-engineered monstrosity was about as illegal as you could get.

Tony X went on. "It is only a matter of time before this country erupts in the same kind of conflagration that destroyed Asia, before we are cut down with the same plagues that depopulated Africa, before the nonhumans, the half-humans, the hairballs, take over." He withdrew the slime-coated rod from the terrarium. "Genocide? We advocate survival. The survival of the human species."

Angel closed her eyes and put her face in her hands, one displaced thought running through her head—the hope that Tony X's bug never got loose.

The Tony X interview went on another minute and a half, but she didn't really listen to it.

Instead, she sifted through all the ramcards on the coffee table. What did White think he was doing? Did he play all of these? What the hell was he looking for?

The door to the apartment opened and Angel jumped to her feet and turned around, scattering ramcards everywhere.

Lei was standing in the doorway.

"Lei, damn, you scared the crap outa me."

"Hello to you, too."

Lei walked in and started gathering up ramcards.

"Where were you?" Angel asked.

"Friend of mine's in the hospital. Some damn pinkboy Knight jumped her in Chinatown last night. The comm's been so tied up that I only found out when I got home from work."

Angel took a handful of ramcards from Lei. "Is she all right?"

Lei nodded. "Yes, only a bump on the head from a tossed brick. They're just keeping her for observation. By the way, I wanted to ask you about these ramcards. What were you doing with them all day?"

"It wasn't me, it was—" Angel came up short. Paranoia parade or no, something was *very* wrong with what Lei just said. "What do you mean 'all day'?"

"I come home from work and all these cards—" Lei wrinkled her nose and swatted her tail in agitation. The look of agitation made her canine features almost feral. "Who'd been here?"

"One of the Detectives, White. You came back from work and—"

"Ramcards all over the table, the place smelling of disinfectant, the comm on. What the hell are you doing, Angel? I've been giving you slack because of the shit you've been through. But some of these cards are personal. What were you doing in my room?"

"No one was here?"

"I walked in, saw the mess, got my call, walked out. Now tell me, what right did you have to— Are you okay?"

Angel shook her head and sank into the couch. It wasn't effing paranoia any more. She was in something, deep. She only wished she knew exactly what it was.

"What's wrong?" Lei asked.

"I haven't been here since noon. I didn't take out those ramcards. I left the comm blocking out all incoming calls. *I* didn't reset it."

"You said Detective White—"

"He left and came back? And, what you say you smelled, disinfectant?"

"Yes—"

"Someone covering their scent? That sound like a cop?"

Angel remembered the fake pine she smelled when they had come back from Byron's condo. Someone had been here, twice. She shivered.

They called the police. It was well after lunch on Tuesday when the cop came. Cop, singular. It was quite a different story from the break-in at the condo. The uncharacteristic deference the cops had been showing seemed to have evaporated. It took Angel an hour to get the complaint in, and it took the cop—one lone uniform with a vid unit—twelve hours to get there.

Apparently, she was no longer high on the priority list.

Not that the cop who showed was bad. He took footage, cracked his gum, and talked incessantly about the cops holding Chinatown and the Tenderloin together, about the Knights of Humanity—whom he called neo-skinheads—about Father Alvarez De Collor—about whom he expressed some ambivalence, being Catholic himself—and even the presidential bid of Sylvia Harper.

Not once did the uniformed cop mention Byron Dorset and his untimely death.

The cop took an hour to record the apartment, and another fifteen minutes to take her statement. When he left, he slipped around Detective Anaka, who was standing in the doorway.

"Can I come in?"

Angel shrugged. "Your partner didn't bother with invitations."

Anaka walked in. He smelled of dirt and sweat, and his suit was even more rumpled than usual. "Sorry about White." He sighed and collapsed into the couch.

"Please, sit down." Angel told him as she cleared the table of ramcards.

Anaka leaned forward and rubbed his temples. Angel walked around, putting things away. She activated the drapes on the windows, letting in some sunlight that had taken over in the abdication of the storm. Throughout, Anaka remained silent.

After nearly ten minutes of waiting, she couldn't take it any more. "What? You said you were going to talk to me, so talk."

"There's not much to say—" Anaka sighed and stared at the ceiling. "They suspended me."

Angel opened her mouth, closed it, opened it again. Angel didn't want to hit him with her primary question, *Why come here, then?* Instead, she asked him, "What happened?"

"Over four months of stacked-up sick leave and vacation time. They said I was overworked." Anaka ran a shaky hand through his black hair. Even his razor mustache looked frazzled. "I guess I do put a little too much of myself in my work. Haven't missed a day in years. . . ."

"I'm sorry—" Angel was increasingly uncomfortable. She wasn't used to total strangers coming to her for comfort. Much less cops. What the hell was she supposed to do?

"Only a matter of time, really. I'm too much a pain in the ass. I keep digging where people don't want me to dig." Anaka kept shaking his head. "People in the department have been waiting for an excuse to get me off the streets. Folks in the council have been plotting against me for years, waiting for an opportunity."

"Yeah. Right." Angel never liked anyone who said that people were plotting against them. It always sounded like the guy speaking was one step ahead of the white coats and trank guns.

Come on, Angel berated herself, *give the guy a break. He's a drum major and you're a cheerleader, but you're both in the same parade—about to be run over by the same float.*

After a long period of silence, he looked up. "Do you have anything to drink?"

She wanted to get Anaka out of her house, this seemed the perfect excuse. "Sorry, we haven't had a chance to go shopping."

"Oh." Anaka didn't look like he was moving.

Angel walked up to him and grabbed his elbow. "Why don't we go somewhere and get something?"

DeGarmo had given her a coded ramcard with a withdrawal limit of fifty thousand dollars. She figured she could spare a little of that to get Anaka out of her fur.

Chapter 11

Angel took Anaka to an anonymous bar wedged between Haight Asbury and Japantown. A dark musky place that, if it didn't quite welcome moreaus, didn't turn them away.

She and Anaka sat in a booth far to the rear of the place. Angel gnawed on a succession of stale pretzels while Anaka ordered beer bulb after beer bulb. For once, Angel didn't know what to say.

"Didn't get much of anywhere," Anaka was saying. "First, Earl, our little songbird, dies of computer error. Then Dr. Ellis disappears after a perfunctory autopsy and the fox's corpse gets cremated—because of a computer error."

Anaka shook his head.

Angel kept gnawing her pretzel, wishing for something tougher to work out her tension on. Anaka was staring consistently at the table, his eyes seemed focused at some point beyond the holo-menu hovering under the surface.

"Two sequential computer screwups at two different hospitals? One kills a suspect, one destroys the victim's corpse. That's too much. And now Chico and Dwane are plea bargaining on the assault charges."

"You need to stop thinking about this—damn it, what is your first name?"

"Kobe," Anaka looked up from the table with tired eyes. "You, of all people, should understand."

"Damn straight I understand, but when was the last time you slept?"

Instead of answering, Anaka downed the last of his beer. He stabbed at the menu, ordering another.

Angel tapped Anaka on the back of his hand with half a pretzel. "You need some sleep."

"Perhaps you're right," Anaka yawned. "Tired people make mistakes, and I can't afford any mistakes now."

"Huh?"

Anaka's beer arrived and he popped it open. "Well, isn't it obvious why they suspended me?"

Angel looked at his tangled hair and the circles under his eyes and held her tongue. *Pretty damn obvious, if you ask me.*

"I was too close to what's going on in this town. They took me down the same day I started digging into VanDyne. This close to the source of the corruption in this town—" He spread his hands like a man explaining the blatantly obvious. "I *can't* stop now."

Angel got a sinking feeling. She wouldn't trust White on a lot of things, but White seemed to think his partner was a bit of a nut. Angel had to admit, Anaka looked like a bit of a nut. "*Why?* You don't have a personal stake in this."

Anaka glared at her. "My job's my life. That's as personal as you get."

The silence stretched. Anaka drank quietly.

Eventually Angel realized how deeply she'd cut into him. "Sorry. Lei says I've been reacting weird to stress lately."

Anaka smiled. "Don't worry, the system hasn't succeeded in screwing me yet."

Angel had seen that kind of bravado before. She'd seen it mostly in moreys who were about to go ballistic after the gang that roached their best friend, lover, parents, car, whatever— "You're going to take on VanDyne all on your lonesome?"

Anaka shrugged.

Angel shook her head. *Great.* Anaka was convinced that the ex-Byron Dorset was working for the evil empire that ran this town. Even so, Anaka seemed to be trying to recruit the ex-Byron's ex-lover in some left-handed fashion.

When she started listening to him again she heard, "—what you went through in Cleveland."

"How the fuck—"

"The FBI has a whole division that keeps track of moreaus with criminal records." He shrugged. "I read your file."

"You have no idea how safe I feel now I know the Fed is protecting my rabbit ass," Angel felt a wave of paranoia that Anaka would probably have taken for granted. "What'd it say?"

"Led a small gang. Gang was wiped out by the original Zipperhead gang in '53. Almost skinned alive by—"

"It's called shaving," she whispered. It was why the fur on her legs was off-white. If it hadn't been for a tiger named Nohar, she would have bled to death in a sleazy motel east of Cleveland.

"Not much else I could access," Anaka said, interrupting her train of thought.

"What?"

"The Fed can be sticky about releasing information to local departments. That was it. The FBI wouldn't release *any* of the file they had on the Zipperhead gang. Even though from all accounts they just about self-destructed six years ago."

"Great." Angel could picture some Fed bureaucrat at a terminal, highlighting parts of her life and hitting the delete key in the name of national security. Angel drank her own glass of water.

Anaka rambled on, and Angel let him. She was only half listening. The pink cop wasn't telling her anything new, or that she couldn't figure out herself. *Of course* someone was after something Byron was involved in.

The question was, what someone?

White would think that the someone was the Knights. Anaka would think that the someone was VanDyne. Father Collor would say it was the cops. Pasquez would do a five-part report on the cover-up in the civic government. Lei would tell her she was being paranoid—

The missing Dr. Ellis pinned the murder on a feline morey. But, with the doctor missing and the body so much ash, Angel might be the only one who had that particular tidbit of information, without a shred of evidence to back it up.

However, Earl—that bald bastard of all people—had sung loud and clear to the cops that the Knights were meeting Byron when he got offed. And Byron got offed in the Knights' own hotel room in the Tenderloin.

But the lawyer, DeGarmo, fed credence to Anaka's paranoid fantasies by saying the Byron *had* worked for VanDyne, in something that the amounts of money involved suggested was a little left of legal.

None of that even approached the question, *why?*

Her mind was going all over the place and she hadn't even taken a drink. She ran her hand over her ears and tried to fight the sense of creeping unreality.

An hour later, she was helping an exhausted and inebriated Anaka to his house in Pacific Heights. She had to drive him in the BMW, and the best she could do for coherence was getting the address out of him.

Somehow she managed. She got lucky on most counts. Anaka's house was on the crest of a hill, so all the tilting he did was alcohol-related. It was on the first floor, so she didn't have to help him up any stairs. Lastly, it didn't have a combination, but an expensive palm lock and retinal scanner. A half-dozen bolts chunked home, opening the armored door.

Anaka's place was a study in austerity—polished wood floors, stark white walls, light fixtures hidden behind frosted-white globes with no personality whatsoever.

Anaka was more of an anal neat freak than Lei. In fact, when he collapsed on the futon that was the one piece of furniture in the living room, his rumpled form seemed an affront to the rest of the apartment.

"Thanks for the lovely afternoon." The sarcasm was lost on Anaka, who had probably lost awareness halfway to the futon. She found herself debating whether or not it would be a good idea to leave him alone.

She shook her head. What did she care. The guy was a nut. Just *look* at this place. The only decoration was a large plaque over the futon on which was mounted a Steyr AUG assault rifle. Angel didn't want to know if it was some sort of replica, or a working model.

She sat on the bare wood floor, across from the futon, and thought.

What *was* she going to do? Anaka had seemed to be her one potential ally in the whole Frisco establishment, and he'd just been canned.

Even if she ignored Anaka and his rampant paranoia, even if she decided to ignore the fact that Byron's killer was still out there, someone was still after something. Someone had trashed Byron's condo, and someone had been through her own apartment.

Why?

It was clear that she wasn't going to be able to relax until she'd fingered who'd killed Byron and who'd done the break-ins. The problem was, she had no idea how to proceed.

All she knew was that it was allegedly the cops' job, and the cops didn't seem to help at all.

"Damn it." She wasn't any great brain. Her greatest intellectual achievement was teaching herself to read. She knew how to run a small-time protection racket. She knew how to wait tables in a cocktail bar. She knew how to defend herself when the shit got thick. But this—she needed help.

She knew who to call for advice. The inspiration struck her so hard that she felt a need to pounce on it immediately, as if hesitation would lose her the ability to do anything constructive.

Kobe Anaka's comm was as sterile as the rest of the nearly-empty apartment. It was a black cube resting on a glass table, the only thing to mar its smooth black lines was the necessity of the screen. The screen was so flush with the box she thought the designers would have gladly done without it to achieve a sort of archetypal black cube.

Angel saw no sign of a remote control.

"Comm on," she whispered.

The comm responded voicelessly. After a blue flash as the picture activated, the screen stayed blank, waiting for her.

She didn't like voice-activated comms, and what really irked her was the lack of an obvious manual control. She was left to try and intuit what the thing parsed for commands.

It finally responded to her plaintive cry of, "help."

The comm responded with a menu, a screen full of options.

No wonder the designers left out the damn remote. There were about four dozen options on this thing. And that was the first of five pages.

The layout made it clear that the screen was touch-sensitive. Which made her life easier. She didn't want to have to spend all day shouting at an unfamiliar chunk of electronics.

She started calling Los Angeles with only a slight twinge of guilt about running up Anaka's phone bill. Only a twinge. It was buried under the need for her to do something now, and the creeping sense that her comm at home and in the BMW couldn't be trusted, not for this.

Every time she told herself that she was worrying needlessly, she came back to the fact that person or persons unknown had read every single ramcard in her apartment. Bugging her comm line didn't seem that much of a stretch.

Detective Anaka probably swept for electronic surveillance the way some people shampoo the rug. Even if it was only a case of her catching some of his neuroses, she felt better using his comm. Besides, she figured she could pay him back eventually.

And she needed to talk to Nohar.

Nohar Rajasthan might be able to give her some advice, even though she hadn't seen him since he left Cleveland. He'd seen her through some shit back in her home town and saved her life twice over. Had circumstances been different, Angel could have seen him in Byron's place in her life.

Angel sighed to herself and thought that maybe she had something for big guns.

It took her four tries to get into the Los Angeles public directory. The first two times she only got electronic garbage, an asynchornous beeping, and a screenful of scrolling blue and red lines. The third time she got a computer and the Pacific Bell logo asking her to only stay on if her call was an emergency situation, and then cut her off.

The fourth time she got through to dead air.

Five was a dim low-res representation of the directory listings for Los Angeles. Angel put her request through, hoping that she spelled Rajasthan correctly.

She got the number and it took another half-dozen tries to get through to it. The fighting in LA was making hash out of the communication net in the city. It would be impossible to get through to Nohar if his comm was on the other side of the National Guard. She was pretty sure that there was a data embargo to inner Los Angeles, though the only folks it really hurt were the media types and the people who wanted to find out if cousin Ed in East LA had bit the big one.

Lucky seven, she got a hazy Pacific Bell logo. The red, blue, and green parts of the animated logo were all a fraction out of sync with each other. It melted into blurred computer text that said something like Rajasthan Investigations.

Nohar answered the phone.

God, he'd changed. The massive feline face had—aged.

It made Angel uncomfortably aware of her own mortality. Moreaus weren't given to long life, and rabbits were given less than most. If she'd been a rat . . .

"Angel?"

His voice was barely audible through the shitty connection. But it was Nohar, all two and a half meters, three hundred kilos of him. The tiger's fur had lost some of the sharp definition between the lines, white hairs were beginning to scatter themselves across his face, and there were now deep lines above his broad nose, but it was Nohar. Up to and including the subtle expression of disbelief.

"Yes. Angel. From Cleveland."

The picture fuzzed and jarred as Nohar must have hit his own comm. "Surprise to hear from you."

"I'm in Frisco." Angel raised her voice in case Nohar was having as much trouble hearing her.

"What can I do for you?"

Angel took a deep breath and dove into the story. Even when she only hit the high points, it took a long time to make herself clear over the interference on the line. She ended with Detective Kobe Anaka's involuntary retirement.

"You want my advice?" Nohar said as the red part of the image separated and began slowly sliding to the right, pixel by pixel.

"Yes."

"Blow Frisco. Go north, Seattle."

"Kit, you must be kidding."

"I'd tell you that if you weren't in trouble. Do you *like* urban warfare?"

Angel sighed. "I can't leave this hanging."

"Why?"

"Look, I'm staying. Now can you give me an idea about—"

The picture faded into incomprehensible snow.

"Nohar, you still there?"

"Yeah," came a small fuzzed voice. There was the scream of some feedback overlaid with static. "Can you hear me?" Nohar's voice was gravely distorted and barely audible. "I maxed the gain on this, but the vid's shot."

"Yes. Do you have anything useful to say before the line dies?"

"Okay, after what you—ffff—looking for something. Did Byron give you anyt—ffff—" Nohar's voice was fading in and out wildly now. Black pixels were starting a shotgun effect as the signal's data degraded.

"I can't make you out."

"—can't hear you any more. If you—ffff—en call Bobby Dittrich in Cle—ffff—can tell you people to—ffff—ver they are—ffff—eem to be looking for data—ffff—Dittrich in—ffff—hope you —ffff—tty signal—ffff—fuck it—ffff—"

The screen went dead black and the sound died.

After a few seconds the Pacific Bell test pattern came up informing Angel of technical difficulties. She shot a dozen calls down to LA, none successful. All her calls came up with the same test pattern and the information that the data flow into LA was temporarily blocked.

She supposed she was lucky she'd gotten through at all.

Well, Nohar had told her to get a hold of someone named Bobby Dittrich in Cleveland. At least it gave her something to do.

Chapter 12

It took Angel a while to find Mr. Dittrich. Fortunately, whatever urban violence plagued her home town hadn't affected the data lines into the city. Her only problem was sifting through a succession of different Bobs, Bobbies, Roberts, Robs, and Bobbis. Not to mention a half-dozen Dittrich's who only bothered with a single first initial.

Her tenth call was forwarded to a place called Budget Surplus. The call was answered by a chubby, red-bearded human. "Budget Surplus, can I help you?"

On the bottom of the video, under Anaka's comm's date-time-status stamp, the picture was scrolling a hyperfast line of gibberish. Something that looked like neoelectronic hieroglyphs was whizzing by under this Bobby's face.

"You know a tiger named Nohar?"

"May, may not. Who're you?" There was a weighty look of suspicion in this pink's eyes, but there was an impish smile under the red mustache.

A square block of the scrolling hieroglyphs froze. The block was to the far left, and the remaining line of pixel gibberish redoubled its speed.

"My name's Angelica Lopez—"

"Angel?" One of the pink's eyebrows arched.

Two more blocks of garbage froze, traveling from left to right. The rest of the line was now a total blur, it was changing so fast.

"Yes. Nohar told me, sort of, that I should talk to you."

"Now why—" Dittrich paused and his gaze flicked downward.

It was the first sign that he could also see the line of strange flickering characters on the bottom of the screen. As he paused, a few more blocks froze. He looked back up. "—would you be forwarded to someone of my talents?"

"Well—"

"Shh." Dittrich said quietly, raising a hand to his lips. He was staring at the scrolling line on the screen. Three more blocks of it froze, the line of gibberish seemed almost to form a coherent pattern. Angel could hear Dittrich say to himself, "I love this."

The rest of the line suddenly fell like a row of dominoes. The bottom line of the screen froze.

Suddenly the picture blanked, briefly became a negative version of itself, turned black and white, and reversed.

The picture was now a substantially lower resolution black and white image of Dittrich grinning from ear to ear.

"What the hell was that?" Angel asked, hoping that she hadn't somehow busted Anaka's comm.

"A little security." Dittrich shrugged. "I'm in a sensitive line of work."

"What did you do to my comm?"

"Oh, that. The lower quality pictures frees up the data signal to handle all the encryption data."

"What?"

"I did a long-distance reprogramming of *your* comm's computer. Don't worry it's not permanent. And—" Dittrich glanced off to his left, "—unless your name is Kobe Anaka, that's not your comm."

Angel sighed. "You do know Nohar, right?"

Dittrich nodded. "And you're the hell-bunny he scraped off the remains of Musician's Towers way back when."

Angel opened her mouth to say something, but instead simply nodded.

"Any friend of Nohar's . . . What can I do?"

She took a deep breath and dove into the story again. Dittrich stopped her when she got to the pile of ramcards on her dining room table. "Whoever they are, they're looking for some sort of data file."

"Okay." Angel said, unsure.

"They haven't found it yet."

"How's that follow?"

"There's nothing at the condo, and at your apartment they're interrupted before they can put things back—hmm. You know what it sounds like to me?"

"What?"

"Your Byron was a data courier. He moved things VanDyne didn't trust to the data net. Stuff too hot for anyone to trust to a wire. High-risk, high-reward, easily could make a few million doing that. Did he give you anything on a ramcard? A movie, music, software, love poetry—"

Angels' hand found its way into her pocket. The season tickets were still there. She pulled them out of her pocket and looked at the rainbow-sheened cards with the Earthquakes' logo on them. She stared at them with growing realization. "You bastard, Byron." All that time, was she just being used?

Dittrich nodded. "I think Nohar wanted me to give you a line on a fellow hacker out there on the coast."

"Yes, someone to help sort out this mess."

"Before I do so— A warning from an old hand at the information game."

Angel looked up and waited for Dittrich to go on.

"Data that valuable's likely to be just as dangerous."

Angel left Anaka asleep on his futon. She'd decided that it was pretty much a sure thing the cop was going to sleep through the rest of the day. Alcohol and exhaustion had finally caught up with the man.

Over and over, Angel thought about the damn tickets. She did not want to think that Byron was using her like that, planting crap like that on her—

The more she thought about it, though, the more it was starting to look like Byron was acting the playboy. While she had been taking things seriously, he'd been taking it as just another fling. She was just another female he'd charmed, the only real distinction being that she was the last. She hadn't been in a relationship, she'd been in an effing lottery.

She surprised herself by actually considering not accepting the money.

"Come on, let's not be a fool twice," she said to herself as she hit the switchbacks on Lombard Street.

"Oh, God," she said as she hit the first turn. She started cursing rapidly in Spanish as she slowed to a crawl and maneuvered the large BMW down the insane curves. She would have avoided this stretch if she'd been thinking.

She had one brief close call with a Dodge Portola pickup on the last turn. A long, red-flagged length of white PVC pipe that hung out the back of the truck bed actually swept over the front hood of her car, barely missing the windshield. It took all the self-control Angel had not to slam on the brakes in the middle of the turn.

She came out the other end of the bend without impaling her car on the pipe.

Cursing herself, she continued down Lombard, and almost ran down a cable car trolling through the intersection at Columbus. The BMW froze, half in the intersection, as the car passed by in front of her going at its slow, sedate, pace. It caught her attention that there was not a single moreau on the car.

Horns began to blare behind her.

She turned down Columbus and suddenly, for the first time since coming to Frisco, began to worry about the neighborhood. Nob Hill and points north were solid pink. Always had been solid pink. That usually didn't bother her. . . .

Today was different.

She drove down Columbus, toward Chinatown, toward the Pyramid, and she could feel the pinks looking at her. She could feel the drivers around her thinking she didn't belong in that kind of car, didn't belong this far north of Market.

Suddenly, this city didn't seem so different. Frisco might not have any concrete barriers blocking off access to the morey neighborhoods, it might not have a morey curfew, it might even have one or two morey cops, but the eyes that followed her down Columbus Avenue could have been from Cleveland, or LA, or New York.

She was sitting at the light at Montgomery, just in front of the Pyramid, and something hit her windshield.

Angel heard a smack, and some liquid splashed across her field of view. She looked to the left, and she saw a knot of pinks on the crosswalk. One of them had thrown a bulb of coke, or coffee, or some dark beverage at the BMW's windshield.

"Go home," she heard one say.

There were seven or eight of them, and what scared Angel was the fact that they weren't skinheads. They looked like fairly normal pink adolescents.

They had crossed to stand in front of her car, and they stopped.

One gave her the finger, two others put their hands on the hood and began rocking the car up and down on the shocks.

"Oh, shit," Angel whispered. She checked to make sure the

doors were locked. As she did, the humans began to surround the car.

"Where'd the rat steal this—"

"Don't want your kind here—"

"Looking for some kind of trouble—"

The humans began to hit the car with their fists.

The light changed and the car behind her began to lay on the horn. Christ, Angel thought, couldn't he see the mess she was in? She punched the BMW's comm to call the cops, but the damn thing only broadcast static. She looked up and saw a pink with a denim jacket and a T-shirt with an "Alex Gregg in '60" logo on it. He was whipping the end of her severed antenna across the hood of the car.

One of the pinks jumped up on the hood and started to jump up and down, and Angel heard a window behind her shatter.

That was fucking enough.

She slammed the BMW into reverse, flooring the accelerator and turning the wheel. The rear wheels bit pavement and her car shot back to the left, across the double yellow line. The computer on the BMW began to flash all sorts of collision avoidance lights and traffic warnings at her.

The pink on the hood took a header backward and fell headfirst into a storm sewer drain. Two pinks on the left jumped back, out of the BMW's way and into the other lane.

An old Dodge four-door was turning in from Washington and slammed on the brakes in the center of the intersection to avoid running down one of the pinks. A motorcycle crunched into it broadside. The cyclist tumbled over the hood of the Dodge and landed on a few of the pinks who were still standing in the crosswalk.

There was a crunch as the BMW kissed fenders with the car behind it, then Angel shot backward in the opposite lane, up Columbus the way she'd come. There was screaming from behind her, and she saw that one of the pink kids had put his arm through her rear passenger side window. He was now hanging on to the door, his other hand frantic for some sort of handhold. Angel grinned as she shot backward through the intersection at Jackson—fortunately, the light was with her—and slammed on the brakes just on the other side of the light.

The pink tumbled from her door, and Angel made a squealing left turn on to Jackson.

It might have been a dumb idea, but she looped around Jackson Square and came down Washington to view the destruction from the other end. She shouldn't have been worried about the kids. They deserved what they got. However, she still found herself hoping that no one got seriously hurt. If nothing else, she didn't want any more trouble with the cops.

She drove by the intersection in front of the Pyramid, and everyone seemed to be standing around, ambulatory— Except for the kid who'd taken the header into the storm drain. He was lying in the street, unmoving.

Angel didn't stop to give the survivors a chance to tear her apart.

She turned down Stockton and followed the length of Chinatown as the night darkened around her.

When she hit the tunnel, she realized she was shaking. She took a few deep breaths and told herself that she'd deal with it later. She'd talk to the cops later, too, after she found the contact Dittrich gave her.

What the hell was happening to this city?

She left the claustrophobic confines of the tunnel and the night seemed even darker now. She was surrounded by post-earthquake Chinatown, south of the so-called Gateway Arch. Nothing around her now was more than twenty years old. It was all chrome pagodas and flickering neon. There seemed to be something quintessentially Asian about garish street signs.

And here, where Chinatown was busy crowding Market, there were moreaus. Lots of moreaus. A quarter of the refugees from the Asian war were nonhuman, and half of those were Chinese. Angel drove by towering ursoids, the typically long-limbed Asian rabbit strains, dark-haired canines, as well as some exotic species that she couldn't place.

The name Dittrich had given her was Kaji Tetsami—a name that didn't belong down here. A Jap in Chinatown was about as out of place as a rabbit at a mosque. But, as she turned on to Post Street to approach a postmodern steel and glass neo-Asian monstrosity she realized that her navigation wasn't off. The address Dittrich gave her *was* in the southwest corner of Chinatown. The rich part that held a lot of descendants of old Hong Kong refugee money.

The address was, in fact, the neo-Asian monstrosity she was approaching. It was a residential tower that took up most of a city block, and if her estimate of the thing's height was correct. Tetsami lived close to the top of the building. Maybe *the* top.

She pulled into the parking garage, and was stopped by a transparent, probably armored, barrier. She sat and idled, wondering what the hell she was supposed to do. She didn't see a comm box around, only two lanes of concrete and one video camera.

"Please lower your window," came a voice from nowhere.

Angel did so, looking for where the voice was coming from. The sound was amplified and echoey in the concrete chamber, but she couldn't locate the source, even with her oversized ears.

"Name?"

"Angel Lopez," she said, trying to find the guard, the voice pickup, or the speaker. She ended up deciding that it was all in the camera.

"Who do you wish to see?"

"Kaji Tetsami."

There followed a long silence. It grew to such a length that she thought that their speaker or their voice pickup might be broken.

"I'm here for a Mr. Tetsami. Hello?"

She got no response.

She had shifted the BMW into reverse and was about to pull back out of the garage when the transparent door rolled up into the ceiling.

"Parking space five-zero-seven," said a different amplified voice.

Angel pulled into the garage, and noted the door closing immediately behind her. She took one turn into the structure and saw a guardhouse. It sat behind armored windows that had a human watching a few dozen vid screens. As she passed it she noted an open door behind the rent-a-cop. She saw part of a rack and at least three shotguns and a small submachinegun.

She drove through the garage past Porsches, Mercedes Benzes, other BMW's, a Ferrari, a Maduro—

The lane split into two ramps. The one going up had a sign saying "050–499." The one down said "500+." The one down was labeled "authorized personnel only."

She turned down the lower ramp and began the descent. Another armored door was raising as she approached. She drove past it and found herself in a much smaller sublevel of the garage.

The BMW was barely ten yards into the garage when she saw the dozen armed rent-a-cops lining the walls. They all had their hands on their weapons and, as Angel looked back behind her, the door was already closed.

"Oh, shit," she whispered to herself.

Chapter 13

"Get out of the car," said one of the guards.

Angel didn't argue. She stepped out.

"Step away from the vehicle and keep your hands in sight."

The troops wore black. Their only insignia was an ID card clipped to their breast pockets. With the body armor and the automatic weapons, they looked more like a mercenary unit than building security. They were all human, except the one shouting the orders.

Their leader was one of the rare results of genetic tampering on humans. At a distance, he could pass. But his smell was all wrong for a pink. That, and his joints were too big. When he moved he moved *wrong*. The platform the engineers designed for the guy's hyped strength and reflexes was disturbing for her to watch in action—and she wasn't even human.

The guy was the first frank she'd seen since Cleveland. Franks were, as a rule, more insular than moreys. Most of the pinks who hated moreaus were positively terrified of frankensteins. It seemed to be a racial characteristic. The pinks' fear of the franks led to a UN resolution banning genetic experimentation on humans long before the war. Only a few countries dabbled in it after that, and only a few products of that managed to get over the border.

Franks were rare.

A small chromed door opened at the far end of the garage, and out stepped another one. This one was different. He was short, as short as Angel, and as bald as one of the Knights.

The tampering on his genes was more subtle. It didn't ring in his odor, which could blend in with any pink crowd without Angel noticing. It was more in the shape of his skull, the length of his fingers.

Like the guards, he wore black, but his black was a suit that could have cost a few grand. He wore black down to the buttons on his shirt, down to the gloss-black rings on his fingers, down to the metallic frames on the thick tinted glasses he wore.

Occasionally Angel saw light reflected in those glasses that didn't originate anywhere inside the garage.

"Names," he said.

"What?"

"Names have power, Angelica. Names are to conjure with." The man walked up to her, and she saw a number of the guards visibly tense. "Names open doors." He nodded slightly back where he had come.

She was beginning to get the picture. "I—"

The man raised an incredibly long finger to quiet her. "It is a novelty for someone to walk up to the front door and ask for me. I am . . . curious."

He was close enough that she could see the display that scrolled across the inside of his glasses.

"I was told you could help me."

"Someone has knowledge . . . who?"

Angel swallowed and decided to go through with it. It was silly, but apparently Bobby Dittrich knew what he was about. "He said to tell you that 'The Digital Avenger knows your hat size.' "

The scene froze. The bald man had an oddly-shaped head, and Angel was afraid that she had committed a lethal insult.

Instead, the man laughed. Really laughed. He shook his head and clapped his hands once. In response, the guards melted back through the chrome door he had come from. All but the other frank, who stood, gun lowered, at parade rest next to the door.

"Angelica," the bald man said, "you have some odd friends."

"So you are Mr. Tetsami?"

"Please refrain from using that name from now on. It makes people nervous."

"What should I call you?"

"Mr. K, if you need a name. Intriguing that you should find your way to me. But come to my office." Tetsami, or Mr. K, waved ahead of him, toward the chromed door.

He led her through a spotless white corridor, lit by indirect lighting. They passed doors, but they were few and far between. It became obvious, after a while, that there was a gentle slope downward and the corridor extended way beyond the confines of the building above.

"Where are we?"

"Shall I tell you?" asked Mr. K. He glanced sideways at her and smiled. "In the early thirties, when they started work on the ill-fated Mill Valley Ballistic Launch facility, this city started an optimistic northern spur to the old BART system."

"North to *what?*"

"After the earthquake, exactly."

The corridor ended, and they started descending a stairway that led into a circular chamber whose floor was fifteen or twenty meters below them. Their corridor entered near the arched ceiling and the stairway took a right angle and hugged the side of the curving wall as they descended.

The room was huge. It could have been thirty meters in diameter, all white walls and blue carpeting. Diffuse white light came from a starburst pattern of fluorescents that pointed radially from the center of the slightly domed roof.

The room itself dwarfed its contents. There may have been a dozen terminal stations down there, only a few seemed to be occupied at the moment. The silence, especially to Angel, was unnerving. Acres of blue carpeting seemed to smother any sounds, so other than a diffuse high-frequency hum from somewhere, the only real sound seemed to come from the footsteps of the people around her.

Central to the room was a black machine. It was contained in a cylindrical case whose transparent walls ran floor to ceiling. The container dwarfed the black machine while simultaneously drawing all attention directly to it.

It was made of four metallic slabs resting crosswise on a black toroid that formed its base. As they descended, and Angel could make out more detail, she saw the top of the toroid was divided into wedge-shaped panels and that the rectangular slabs didn't quite touch in the center. In the gap, she saw hundreds, perhaps thousands, of neatly arrayed cables running from the inside of the rectangular slabs and down through the hole in the torus.

She could also see the Japanese writing on some of the panels, and a very understated Toshiba logo on the sides of the rectangular sections.

"Jesus, is that a Japanese mainframe?"

Mr. K snorted. "Mainframes are for payrolls— That's a Toshiba ODS 3000."

"I thought that kind of stuff was fried when they lost the war."

"You can't destroy technology, only hide it a while."

Angel stopped at the foot of the stairs, looking at the Jap computer. "How the hell did you get one?"

"Quite simple. I imported it myself, before the war."

"But wasn't that—"

"Oh, highly illegal and a major threat to Japanese national security. Especially with someone trained to use it to its full capabilities. If I was caught, they would have shot me for a traitor." Mr K pulled gently on her arm and pointed to a door halfway along the curving wall. "My office, I believe we have things to discuss."

Angel allowed herself to be led to the office. Seeing that large a chunk of Japanese technology in one piece, in working order, had stunned her. Angel knew that a lot of the stories of Jap technology had to be so much bullshit and wishful thinking, but there was still a mythic quality about the stuff the island nation had done with silicon, superconductors, nanotechnology, biological interfaces. . . .

The only real problem with old Jap technology was that there was only so much it could do when the Japanese faced an army ten times the size of its own. The Chinese lack of pinpoint accuracy didn't much matter when they lobbed a ten-meg warhead.

What the hell could that Toshiba do? It was probably more powerful than some of the stuff that was buried in the Pentagon.

Angel went straight from that and into free fall. At least that was what it felt like, walking into Mr. K's office.

When the door opened in front of her, she suffered dizzying vertigo caused by the gigantic holo screen behind the desk. The screen was on, projecting a screen of solid sky-blue. It was as if she found herself falling upward.

She blinked a few times and the feeling passed.

The door closed behind her, leaving the frank guard outside. Mr. K sat himself behind the desk and motioned her toward a chair that was a single flat piece of upholstered plastic that had been molded into a chair shape. It didn't look stable, but she sat in it without tipping it over.

"So," Mr. K said, leaning back in his chair and looking at her over the top of his glasses—his eyes were a deep violet—"what can we do for each other?"

Angel began to relay the story, but he stopped her. "I'm quite familiar with the basics. Sometimes the news services can produce something . . . enlightening. I would like to know your needs—your *specific* needs."

Angel thought about that.

"I need to know who killed Byron and who's been trashing apartments."

"And to what end?"

"I need to know what the hell Byron was doing." Angel pulled the football tickets out of her pocket and tossed them on the desk. "And I need to know what, if anything he hid on those ramcards."

Mr. K nodded. "Good. I like specifics. Now we need to discuss the terms of this exchange."

"Huh?"

"My payment, Angelica. I came to this country because I do not work for free."

"Oh, if you tell me how much you—"

He clucked and shook his head. "No, no, you can't afford to pay me money."

Angel grinned slightly. "I do have some money—"

He nodded. "Something under seven million I suspect."

Angel gaped.

"Perhaps you see now. I deal with corporations for the most part, only the very rare individual. Computer time on my machine is effectively priceless. Conservatively, it's fifty-thousand a minute."

She closed her mouth slowly.

"However, I do not deal only in—or even primarily in—money."

"What do you want?"

"I want free access to whatever information he was transporting." He reached over with incredibly long fingers and rested them on top of the cards. "Acceptable?"

Angel looked down at the season tickets under Mr. K's hand. "What makes you think he was carrying *anything?*"

Mr. K smiled. "I knew him."

Of course. Why the fuck not? It wasn't like she ever actually *knew* the damn fox. She just let the vulpine bastard seduce her into this mess.

"What do you think he was transporting?"

"I have no idea."

Angel shook her head and snickered. "You'd do this for something that might turn out to be worthless?"

"It is valuable to someone, which means it is valuable to me. Sometimes I take a low-risk gamble."

"Okay." Angel said. She really didn't care what Byron was

transporting, what she wanted to know was what that information could tell her about whoever was fucking with her life.

Mr. K picked up the series of ramcards.

However, Angel wasn't stupid. "On two conditions, though."

His hand stopped moving. "It is you who are coming for help."

"Yeah, but if that info's worth it, I want a piece of the action."

His hand began to lower. "This, I don't know. I do not like needless complications."

"Tell me you can't afford it."

"Tell me you really need it."

"It's the principle, Mr. Tetsami."

He frowned at the use of his name. "And the other condition?"

"If you're taking those tickets, I want them replaced. I want to go to the game on Sunday."

Angel slammed the door when she got home. Somehow she had managed to avoid running down any innocent bystanders.

She had to ask Mr. K about Byron, and she had her suspicions about what she might have found out, but the truth had sliced her open like an unknown feline morey had sliced open Byron's neck. What really pissed her off was the fact that her reaction meant that she was still harboring some secret delusions that her time with Byron had meant anything.

What it had meant to Byron, apparently, was that she was a convenient mail drop.

The really disgusting part of all this was the fact that, by the time he'd slipped her those cards, she'd been so gooey-eyed that she would have willingly stashed anything for him had he just asked.

"What a fucking day."

"Angel—" Lei stepped out of the living room and walked up to her. Lei looked flustered and her tail was swatting so frantically that no shin within a meter of her would be safe. Angel barely noticed. She was fuming about Byron.

"The bastard was *using* me! He always was. It was his effing MO. He handled this hot data, found some squeeze to get close to and planted the stuff till he wanted it—"

"Angel—" Lei grabbed Angel's shoulder and shook it.

"What?" Angel snapped back.

Lei cocked her head back into the room. Standing there, in Angel's living room, was Detective White, belly spilling over his belt like an impending avalanche. White wasn't smiling. Flanking him were two uniforms who looked a little nervous.

Angel shouldered past Lei and looked the detective in the paunch. "What the fuck are you doing here again?"

"I'm here to arrest you."

"What?"

"Hit and run at Columbus and Washington at five fifteen this afternoon."

Chapter 14

While the cops hassled her through the bureaucracy, Angel tried to isolate the moment at which her life started going wrong. It was an unprofitable pursuit because her thoughts traveled back from the current disaster in an unbroken chain of events that began two decades ago when her mom visited a Bensheim clinic to get inseminated.

That was depressing.

No, she thought, *what's depressing is the fact I still need to find out who killed Byron, and the guy was an asshole, a con artist, and God knows what else—*

If their positions had been reversed, Angel was pretty sure that Byron wouldn't be overly upset about her death. In fact, she had a morbid fantasy about what her funeral would be like. She could see Byron picking up Lei at the wake.

It was upsetting that that half-blind lion, Balthazar, saw Byron clearer than she ever did.

Her mind continued in its self-destructive spiral as she got more and more irritated with the cops.

At least, for once, she actually had a lawyer to call when they gave her access to a comm. That screwed with their program a bit. Moreys weren't supposed to have bail, or lawyers. When she called DeGarmo and told the cops to engage in some experimental hermaphroditism, they shuffled her away into a holding cell.

With a bald human.

From a logistical point of view, it had to be intentional on the cop's part. The stainless steel gate on the cell slid aside and they tossed her into the bare concrete, and she knew they wanted some sort of incident so they could continue to hold her after her lawyer showed.

Even though she knew it was what the cops wanted, she couldn't help but saying, "Hey, it's the firebug."

The small white human looked up at her for the first time.

"Shit!" The female pink stood up and went over to the gate, giving Angel a wide berth, and began yelling, "You can't put it in here with me—I've got *rights!*"

"Pleased to see you, too, shithead."

"That rodent, it tried to kill me, you can't—"

"If you don't watch your effing pronouns, I *will* kill you."

It soon became obvious to the pink that the cops weren't particularly interested in her dilemma. She turned around to Angel, who had taken her spot on the one cot in the three-meter-square cell.

"Stay away from me," she said.

Angel never realized how sleazy the smell of human fear could be. The fact that she'd touched this hairless wonder at one point made her want to wash her hands.

"Ain't moving, pinky." Angel smiled. "But I hope you have a lot of self-control." She looked at the john next to the cot.

Pinky slid down, along the bars, until she was sitting on the ground. "You don't touch me."

"Don't worry, I don't feel like spending an hour picking shit from my claws."

Pinky winced, even though rabbit claws weren't much to worry about. "You just don't touch me. I got friends."

"Yeah, I know. A bunch of screaming freakazoids with so much heat conduction from the head that they suffer brain damage. If you're the best and the brightest, I don't have much to worry about."

Pinky just sat there, glaring.

Angel continued, "Stood outside the bar grinning until they picked you up, didn't you? Scary example of the master race indeed. Kinda drafty up there, ain't it?"

Pinky was getting real pissed. It was getting damn close to the incident the cops wanted, and Angel was about at the point where she wouldn't care. If the twitch jumped her, she could kick her through the bars and there'd be one less scumbag in the city. By all rights they should give her a medal for something like that.

Pinky glared at her, but she was into self-preservation. "You keep talking. When we have the power, your kind will be swept aside."

"The Knights? You must be kidding!"

"*I'm not talking about . . .*"

It was amazing how quiet it could get down here. It was a new block of cells that smelled of machine oil and fresh concrete and only slightly of urine. Their nearest neighbors were two cells away.

The near-silence—bullshit continued elsewhere in the block—was filled by the realization that Pinky had said something significant.

It was like slow motion, as Angel swung her feet to the floor and Pinky pushed up to her feet.

"Who *are* you talking about?"

"Don't come near me."

For the first time in a long time, Angel was aware of the new scar on her cheek. It was nearly invisible now, and she only felt it as a slight tightness on her face. She realized she felt it because she was grinning like a maniac. Angel could feel her heart pounding in her ears, and she hoped the smell of blood was from the scar opening up on her cheek.

"You can tell." She was approaching Pinky slowly, but she could feel the muscles in her legs tightening. "Just between you, me, and the hookers three cells down."

"You can't."

"Who's going to stop me, you freak? You're so proud of your friends in high places. Why don't you tell me who they are?"

She backed Pinky up. It was beginning to hit her how silly the scene must look. After all, in the looking-fierce competition between moreaus, a lepus would come dead last.

Even so, the bald twitch had a right to be scared. Angel was beginning to feel a real strong desire to tear something apart. Angel could feel the anger ratcheting her nerves tighter and tighter.

Pinky found a corner and stuck. Angel closed on her. "Come on," Angel said, "impress me with these friends."

"*Don't touch me.*"

"Must be a good reason they're letting you all twist in the wind."

"*Get away.*"

"Tell me—" Angel was now as close as she could get. Her toes were touching Pinky's boots. She slowly raised her heels and tilted forward until she had raised her muzzle level with Pinky's face. "Tell me these people and I'll leave you alone. Roll over. Looks like something you'd be good at."

Angel stood there staring at the twitch. Pinky stayed quiet.

"No? Do you want a description?" Angel leaned in. Her smile still hurt. She was shaking with the restrained desire to go fully off on Pinky's bald little head. Angel was reminded of the scene with Igalez. Never mind, she could handle it. "First, I eat your nose." She dragged her tongue across Pinky's face, tasting sweat and fear.

As Angel licked across the bridge of her nose, Pinky's eyes rolled up and she emitted an inarticulate moan. She shoved Angel away and threw herself at the bars. "Get me out of here! Just get me out of here! I'll admit to anything, just get me away from that animal!"

Angel was about to say something more—perhaps even jump Pinky and show the twitch a *real* animal—but at that moment all hell broke loose in the cell block. All the empty cells opened simultaneously, and cops in riot gear started pushing in a mass of moreaus of both sexes. The cops lined themselves up against the wall, holding up stun rods—a sort of glorified cattle prod—as a wall of fur washed past the cell.

Damn, Angel thought, these weren't gang members, or the kind of folks she expected to see in such a roust. For one thing, the moreys wore too much clothing. There was a definite linear equation that related income level with the amount of pink clothing a morey wore. Angel actually saw a few ties.

Most of the moreys looked to have been through some rough treatment. A few were bleeding, and one or two had to be helped along. The smell of urine was being overpowered by the smell of wet fur and blood.

Angel's body stopped screaming for combat, and the tension started to leak away from her muscles.

Pinky freaked, especially when the passing moreaus began to notice her.

"Oh, God, I'm gonna die." She crawled into a fetal position under the cot.

"I suppose," Angel said, as she rubbed an ache in her thigh. "If you're lucky."

The tide of moreaus let up for a few minutes, and a pair of cops pushed through to the door of their cell. The door slid open.

"My lawyer here?" Angel wanted to get the hell out of this place.

"I know fuck about your lawyer, rabbit," said one of the cops. "This just became a segregated cell block."

The other cop reached in and got his arm around the firebug's chest. "Come on, Berkeley. You're getting transferred in with some of your friends."

Pinky began kicking and screaming. "You aren't going to take me out there!" One kick landed in the other officer's crotch. The cop was in full riot gear and it only pissed him off.

"Cuff her!" he told the other cop as he grabbed both legs. They left the cell in less than five minutes, Pinky trussed up between them like a Christmas present.

They barely cleared the cell door before Angel's cell began filling up with more wet moreaus. Angel immediately lost sight of the big picture, suddenly being surrounded by taller people. All she had a chance to do was claim the section of cot next to the john before the place got too full to move.

Though she couldn't see her progress, Angel could hear the firebug make her exit. Pinky left on a crest of moreau growls and insults and a buzz or two from the cop stunners—apparently when someone wasn't quite satisfied with verbal abuse.

There was a rush into the cell, then Angel's world stabilized somewhat. She was surrounded by a mixed group of canines plus one of the occasional exotic breeds that she hadn't seen before.

The exotic was the closest to her height, shorter and looking like a cross between a rabbit and a rat, so she addressed him.

"Raining out there?"

He shook his head. "No, they're using fire hoses."

Apparently, two conflicting demonstrations, pink and morey, happened to meet in front of City Hall. Predictably, bad things happened. From the description, a melee erupted in the lobby of City Hall itself, causing a shitload of damage from the fight and more so from the firehoses they used to quell the violence.

The cops ended up busting everyone in a five block radius.

The exotic, a chinchilla, hadn't even been a part of the demonstration. He'd just been driving down Van Ness when the cops stopped him. Angel just had the dumb luck to get embedded in what must be a logistic nightmare for the Frisco legal system. A tidal wave of moreaus washed in, only to leave by an anemic trickle.

The cops called names out of the cell block by some equation that must have involved species, the first letter of your last name, and a dart board somewhere. It seemed to Angel that they called a name every ten or fifteen minutes, and it caused no lessening of the crowding whatsoever.

Hourly, rumors spread back from the cell nearest the door. First that they were all going to be set free. Next, that they were all going to be prosecuted with a two-year minimum sentence. Then, everyone they found with a record was going to be shipped to Oakland. There were rumors that there were two dead, ten dead, fifteen dead. They said that no one really died even though the newsvids said so.

Rumors that Father Alvarez De Collor was coming, that Sylvia Harper was coming, that the media was coming, that no one was coming because the cops were keeping everything a secret. They let the humans go. The Fed was already involved. . . .

As time passed and Angel felt more and more isolated from the outside world, it became harder and harder to segregate out even the obvious bullshit. When she'd been there ten hours and the rumor passed by that the cops were going to shoot all the moreys and dump them in a mass grave in the Presidio with the help of the Army Corps of Engineers, Angel felt unreasonably nervous.

The last rumor Angel heard was something about President Merideth's aliens from Alpha Centauri. She never caught all of it because that was when her name was finally called.

The population density had lessened to the point where she could make it to the door of the cell without actually climbing over people. In the previous hours she had actually seen people literally passed over the heads of fellow inmates.

When she reached the door, there was the lean form of De-Garmo, looking like he had gotten about as much sleep as she had. He was accompanied by a cop in riot gear who held the remainder of the cell at bay as the gate opened.

"Finally," Angel said as she walked out of the place that had been her home for a good fourteen hours.

DeGarmo shrugged. "For the record, bail was posted ten hours ago. But the city is suffering a bureaucratic meltdown. System wasn't designed to handle this many people."

As they walked to the cell block entrance, the door before them opened, letting in another two cops. One was holding a wallet computer and reading off of it. "Jesus Montoya."

As Angel left, she distinctly heard two different moreau voices say, "Over here!"

One cop shook his head and put a hand up to a helmeted forehead. "Shit. Now what?"

When Angel made it outside, she was blinded by the unexpected intensity of daylight. She turned to her lawyer. "What day is it?"

"Wednesday, close to noon."

"Thanks for getting me out of there. I thought it would never end."

"A feeling affecting many people in that building. Something you should be thankful for." DeGarmo walked her a distance to the curb, where the BMW was waiting.

"Don't the cops want this for evidence or something?"

DeGarmo smiled. "All they ever really had you for was leaving the scene of the accident. The injured parties never pressed, especially when I informed them of the possible assault charges *they* were facing."

"What about the city?"

DeGarmo ran a hand through his black crew cut. "That's what you should be thankful for. They're so overwhelmed with cases that it was fairly easy to get them to drop what was essentially a nuisance. Especially when I pointed out I could shoot down the charges in front of any judge in the state."

Angel shook her head. "Damn, again, what do I owe you?"

"You'll receive a bill."

"Yeah, right." Angel punched the combination and opened the BMW. "Did I thank you?"

DeGarmo nodded.

It was a measure of how strange Angel's universe had become, the fact she was regarding a lawyer as a person and not as some hypothetical amoral construct to be lumped in with cops and politicians.

"One last thing," he added as she got behind the wheel. "I've gotten St. Luke's to release Mr. Dorset's ashes. They've gone as far as offering to pay for the funeral arrangements—"

Angel yawned. "Look, can you hold that thought?"

"All right, but arrangements should be finalized."

"Tomorrow, okay? When my biological clock has reset. And after I've gotten some sleep."

"Tomorrow." DeGarmo extended his hand and Angel shook it.

Yes, Angel thought, *before this week is out, that bastard Byron should be put to final rest.*

She rode the accelerator all the way home.

Chapter 15

Eight hours later, Angel was driving circles around the remains of *The Rabbit Hole* and wondering what had happened to her life.

She'd dug up a relic from Cleveland, a music ramcard, and had the cardplayer jacked up to full volume on the BMW's comm. It was morey music—mostly the screams of clawed guitars—garage bands that no one outside of Cleveland had ever heard of. Unlike most of the synthvid crap that clogged the comm channels on the West Coast, this music had once existed outside of a computer's memory.

The screaming chords and pidgin Arabic lyrics were a reminder of when her life had been understandable. Angel wanted to withdraw into the back alleys that had bred her, back when she knew the rules, back when she was going to live forever and the world was a half-dozen city blocks.

Back when she didn't have enough sense to worry about tomorrow.

Must really be fucked up if you're nostalgic about living in a burned-out building and a neighborhood that chewed up and spat out a good friend of yours every month or so.

Fucked up was right. This mess was infecting everything. Every facet of her life was becoming distorted.

Even Lei.

Angel slammed a fist into the side of a steering wheel.

Even her best friend, damn it. Her *only* friend in this town. What was worse, she hadn't seen the argument coming until she found herself in the middle of it.

The transition had been so seamless that Angel still couldn't figure out exactly what had happened. Lei had come home, and, at first, Lei was happy to see her back.

At first . . .

Down Market to the coast, up Mission to the scene of the fire—she'd been driving randomly, trying to clear her mind, and she'd been caught in this loop for the past fifteen minutes like a damaged ramcard, repeating the same four bits over and over. Market, Beale, Mission, and Second.

Angel could understand Lei's point of view. No one should borrow trouble. She shouldn't keep involving the cops and screwing with Lei's life. Angel had tried to be reasonable, but somehow their voices kept getting raised.

A visit by an Asian gentleman in Mr. K's employ hadn't helped matters. Angel then had to explain how she'd become tied to someone with major league involvement in the shady side of the computer underground. The vindictiveness that revelation had unleashed made Angel run away from the apartment, into the BMW.

She'd been cruising south of Market for nearly two hours now.

Angel had needed to clear her head, and while she could have gotten the same air by walking, she felt better with a few tons of armor around her. That and the Beretta—Lei had made it very clear that she didn't want a gun in the house anymore. Angel had slipped the gun under the driver's seat.

Angel tried to think, even though she didn't really want to.

She turned off Second again, passing the corner of Chinatown, and thought of Mr. K's message.

Dear Miss Lopez, the letter went, *find enclosed the tickets I agreed to replace. Two are not the originals, I'm afraid, since forging the primitive copy protection of the NonHuman Football League is infinitely easier than reproducing the subtle encryption that masks the data covering two of the ramcards you gave me. . . .* The letter went on for a whole page like that, the upshot of which was that it was going to take *days* of computer time to unravel the data, and even then only if Mr. K had the right algorithm in the first place.

This whole situation had her in a dark foggy room with only a few solid objects she could get a grip on.

No question that Byron was a data courier. Between Mr. K fingering his MO, the anomalous data on two of the tickets Byron gave her—the ones, ironically, for the Denver game—and all the veiled references to "delivery" from Byron himself, Angel was finally clear on what he did for a living. Byron carried data from person A to person B, data that was much too valuable to trust to a sat transmission, or worse, the comm net.

Knowing that did little for her piece of mind, since she still had no idea what the data he carried was. She had to wait for some point between tomorrow and never for Mr. K to crack the encryption on those two ramcards before she could find out *what* Byron was carrying.

At least it was pretty clear where the data came from. Everyone seemed to agree who employed Byron Dorset, Mr. K, DeGarmo, even the paranoid cop Anaka. Byron transported data for VanDyne, a massive conglomerate which was into everything from comm circuitry to defense contracting. A company that, after the quake, inserted itself indelibly into the heart of San Francisco by championing the rebuilding effort. They were responsible for everything from the rebuilt Pyramid and Coit Tower, to that domed monstrosity on Alcatraz that was supposed to be an alien habitat.

The question that nagged at Angel was whether or not Byron was working for VanDyne when his throat got torn out. *That* question raised the fog level by an order of magnitude.

However, she was left with the fact that Byron had been running things smoothly for ten years. He'd made a few million moving hot data for VanDyne with no problems—up to now.

Suddenly, Byron gets creamed.

Angel knew that all this was far removed from the drug deals and gun running that had been rampant in her home neighborhood. However, she was familiar with the pattern. If something that established suddenly went wrong that badly, it generally meant one thing.

Someone fucked up.

Almost always, that someone fucked up by wanting more money. Angel suspected Byron'd fucked up.

She passed the ruins of *The Rabbit Hole* and thought herself deeper into the fog.

The information on those tickets was worth a lot to somebody. Mr. K was investing millions worth of computer time against that payoff. So, how does this get Byron's throat slashed by a feline morey on Eddy Street?

Angel's head was beginning to hurt. There was so much bullshit she needed to explain.

"Go slow," she said to herself. "One step at a time."

Go with the assumption that Byron fucked up. How do you fuck up a job that sweet? Simple answer, you want more money. It was a simple rule from her days on the street. You get greedy, you get dead. For some reason, Byron must have bucked the program he'd been following for ten years, and it got him killed.

Angel knew that she was making too many assumptions, but assumptions were all she had to go on. Besides, the way Byron laid this whole mess on her, it was nice to think he'd brought this all upon himself.

So, the next step was to figure out what Byron had been *supposed* to do before he screwed up. That was fairly simple. He was a courier. He was *supposed* to deliver the data to someone. Angel could even picture where the drop would have been. Byron had made a point in his letter about attending the Frisco-Denver game, and—to drive the point home—the data in question was on the tickets to that very game. Once there, a simple exchange of ramcards with some Denver fan would be ridiculously simple.

Something got screwed before that rendezvous.

That gave her two suspects for the killing if Byron was trying some sort of double-cross, VanDyne and the anonymous guys from Denver. Whoever offed Byron must've freaked when he didn't have the data on him. VanDyne would want it back, and the guys from Denver would want the stuff they were paying big bucks for.

That didn't explain a hotel on Eddy Street, damn it.

"Calm down, one step at a time, right?"

Think.

Fact, Byron got offed by a feline morey. Assume the cat killed Byron for the data. That would explain why Byron's condo had been trashed. The smell there could have been feline, canine, or—

Angel slammed on the brakes and pulled to the curb. The realization had hit her like a defensive tackle rushing out of the fog. There *had* to be more than one set of players after those cards at the same time.

It was obvious.

The killers, the cat among them, wanted the data. They must have been sure Byron had the data on him. They didn't know Byron's MO of distancing himself from the hot stuff. Anyone familiar with Byron's courier duties, like Mr. K, would have known that Byron would stash the data off on someone else until the final transfer. Someone who had known Byron over the course of his ten years as a courier would have known that it was likely that Byron would only have his hands on the vital ramcards at the Denver game during the scheduled trade off.

That meant that the killers, cat included, weren't VanDyne *or* the guys from Denver. Otherwise they would've known better than to kill Byron before he gave up the location of the ramcards.

Once they offed Byron and saw their mistake, they trashed his condo looking for the stuff. These guys were hasty, sloppy, and violent.

That meant they were *not* the folks who'd very cleanly broken into Angel's apartment—twice. They were not the ones who methodically read over every ramcard in her house, and were careful enough to cover their scent with some spray disinfectant. The killers who trashed Byron's condo probably didn't know enough to search her place.

The folks searching Angel's apartment, looking for the ramcard Byron had slipped her, just weren't prescient enough to know that she had dropped the shit in the morgue at Frisco General. These guys might fit the bill for the guys from Denver, the people Byron was *supposed* to hand the cards off to.

So far she had three players.

There was VanDyne, the origin of the hot potato. There were the guys from Denver, who seemed to have been shafted by Byron. Then she had the feline hit squad that only barely seemed to know what it was doing.

None of this explained why Byron was offed on Eddy Street, or why he was supposed to be meeting with the Knights of Humanity.

Could the Knights be the guys from Denver? That was bullshit. A Knight attending a NonHuman football game was asking to be the lead on tomorrow's newscast. Also bullshit, they weren't Van-Dyne—or they shouldn't be if VanDyne was in the practice of hiring moreys.

And the Knights certainly weren't hiring feline hit squads.

Angel looked up from the wheel and sighed.

Everything seemed to fit together so smoothly, and then she hit a wall.

She was only a few blocks short of the coast. Up that way was VanDyne HQ itself, across the street from the Hyatt Memorial. That started her thinking in a new direction.

She hit the controls on the BMW's comm, cutting the music and activating it for outgoing calls. She frowned in frustration when she realized that her car's antenna was still sitting in a gutter some-where around the Pyramid. She killed the engine, turned the wheels toward the curb, and looked for a public comm.

The search took her halfway around the cycle she'd been trav-eling. She ended up having to loop around the postquake Sheraton to get to a comm on Market. She pulled up to it, the BMW facing down the hill and toward the Bay.

There was really no rule that prevented her from calling Van-Dyne herself and asking about Byron. It was the kind of thing she felt stupid about not realizing sooner.

The comm squatted in a spanking new booth sitting within its own blue aura. She got out of the car and listened to the foghorns in the distance, the surf, gulls—almost felt normal.

Then she realized that the salt air off the bay carried the smell of old smoke, and as she closed on the comm booth she saw new graf-fiti, "Off the Pink."

"Off the Pink," half a block down from the Sheraton.

Angel shrugged and ran her card through the comm's reader and called up the directory. The World Headquarters for VanDyne In-dustrial was just a few blocks up Market. Right on the coast, and pretty damn close to all the BS that had happened to her.

There was a brief thought that those punks in *The Rabbit Hole* could have been there for Byron, and not just fucking around. No, that didn't quite make sense, did it?

She glanced up Market as she started to call. "Wha?"

Was it paranoia, or was that four-door Chevy Caldera parked up the street the same one that had been behind her at the last light? If so, it had followed her around the Sheraton. On the comm, some-one was saying, "Van Dyne Industrial, can I help you?"

Angel ignored it, and walked back to her car. *Okay,* she thought in Lei's direction, *I've gone totally paranoid.* Angel tried to stay calm, but she was running by the time she got to the BMW.

She slammed the door behind her and jerked the car into the street, flooring it. The BMW shot down Market, toward the Bay. Angel took a few deep breaths and groped under the seat for the gun.

It wasn't there.

And there was an unfamiliar smell in the back seat.

The BMW had made it half a block by the time she turned around. Had she been that stupid?

Her unwanted passenger was already returning to an upright po-sition. In one hand was Angel's Beretta, in the other was an FN

P101—a small machine pistol with a trapezoidal barrel whose hole was the diameter of Angel's index finger. He was a feline the size of a jaguar but with fur a uniform tawny color.

Angel's foot was still pressing down on the accelerator as he leveled the machine pistol at her. For some reason she noticed the hands. Large, powerful hands with gloss-black claws that reflected the streetlights shooting by.

"Stop the car."

It'd been the fucking broken window. This bastard had just walked into her back seat. She hadn't bothered to turn on the damn alarm. Stupid, stupid, stupid all around.

The toes on her right foot kept the accelerator pressed to the floor. Her eyes stayed locked on the moreau in the back seat as the BMW's transponder beeped warnings at her. The car was heading for a red light.

The cat in the back seat showed some teeth. Angel was beginning to read some emotion in those shadowy yellow eyes. The smell of stress was feline, but a different flavor of feline than Angel was familiar with.

"Stop the car," he repeated. "We don't want this to get messy."

What the fuck was she doing? The bastard had a gun, two of them, in fact, one of them hers, and she wasn't even looking at the road—

Hell, the road was clear the last time she looked.

"You don't know what messy can be." God help her, she was grinning.

The BMW's computer went nuts with the warning beeps when she zoomed through a red light at the intersection of First Street. Horns Dopplered past her and the thought crossed her mind that they were going to shoot by VanDyne in no time now.

"Damn it, stop the car! I'll shoot if—"

There was a crunch when Angel came up on a car too fast for the collision avoidance system to compensate. She scraped by and turned her attention forward. The Bay was rushing up like a fog-shrouded abyss.

"*Shoot me, then!* You think I give a shit any more, you cock-sucking dweezil? Pull the goddamned trigger, I just hope your can-dyass can swim."

They were almost on top of the bay.

This was crazy.

Angel hit the control that popped open all the locks on the car. VanDyne's headquarters was the last building on the right, then the

Main Street-California intersection, a short concrete embankment, then water.

The gun pressed into the back of her head. It trembled slightly. Angel smelled cat and gun oil.

The second she saw the VanDyne building—a refurbed Federal Reserve Bank—shoot by, she slammed on the brakes and pulled the BMW as hard to the right as she could. Half the computer's red lights lit on the dash as the air filled with the high-pitched scream and acrid smell of fishtailing rubber.

The cat was thrown back and to the side, slamming somewhere into the passenger footwell.

The rear of the car kissed the concrete embankment—blowing a chunk of it into the bay—and she was shooting down Spear at about eighty klicks an hour. She saw movement in her rearview mirror and slammed on the brakes again. The cat was thrown forward—

Angel popped the door and ran, leaving the BMW to roll to a stop in the wrong lane.

Her thoughts were lagging about five steps behind her actions. She was still wondering if running was a good idea when she'd cleared the four lanes of Spear in two-and-a-half running steps.

She hit the curb when she heard the squeal of more tires back on Market. It was the black Chevy four-door screaming into the turn against the light.

Her foot touched the curb and one of the metered power feeds on the curb erupted into a shower of sparks. The echo of the gunshot was still dying when she cleared the sidewalk and dived over the barrier into VanDyne's parking garage.

Cars, but no sign of manned security. The one guardbox by the gate was empty. As she glanced at it, the windows exploded, showering her with tiny cubes of polymer as she passed it. She leaped on the hood of a new Plymouth Antaeus and jumped from there, over a railing, to an upper level of the garage. Behind her she heard the Caldera crash through the barrier.

She had nowhere left to run but up. She was running so fast now that every third step she had to hit the ground with her hands to change direction.

She was cornered. What the hell was she going to do when she hit the top of the garage?

It was, at most, fifteen seconds she spent like that—running flat out, the sound of the Caldera gaining on her, her field of vision taken up by about a square meter of concrete that rushed by a dozen centimeters from her nose.

She must have run up a half-dozen levels, barely ahead of the Chevy, when she heard a noise ahead and to the right. Angel looked up in time to see a Dodge Electroline van peeling out of its parking spot. It backed and slammed itself across the traffic lane, crunching its end into an opposite retaining wall in the process.

"Shit!"

She was running too damn fast to stop, so she jumped. She got a brief view of the side of the van—Infotech Comm Repair or somesuch—before she slammed into the ceiling above the van. She hit with the back of her right shoulder and bounced, sending a shivering splinter of pain down that side of her body. It didn't do much to slow her forward momentum. She hit the roof of the van, which was still rolling forward a bit after bouncing off the retaining wall.

She had enough time to realize she was in deep shit as she rolled off the other side of the van. This time she managed to lead with her feet. She ended up on all fours on the opposite side of the van as she heard the Caldera round the last turn.

On the other side of the van, she heard the side door crash open.

She was still trying to figure out if the van was an innocent bystander or another one of the fuckers out to get her when guns started going off all over the place.

Angel only had a slice of view out from under the van, but she could see the Caldera. Three people, all moreaus. They'd angled the passenger door toward the van, and some sort of canine was firing one of those nasty looking machine pistols toward her and the van.

The van was returning fire.

Boy, was it returning fire.

In response to the first short bark from the anonymous canine's machine pistol a deafening chatter came from inside the van. It sounded like a jackhammer on steroids. Angel could follow the trace of the shot from the billows of concrete dust that blew in its wake. A cloud of gray dust tore in the direction of the black Chevy and twisted through the right front fender with the sound of shearing fiberglass.

She couldn't hear the Chevy's tire go, she could just see the gust of wind as it exploded. After that, sparks began grinding from the rim as the driver of the Chevy began reversing. That move probably saved the Chevy's engine, if not its front-end alignment.

In three seconds it was over, and the only sound in the garage was the scraping echo from the rim of the Chevy as it escaped downward. The suspension on the van rocked as the occupant jumped out of the door on the other side.

Angel got up from her position on the ground, and prepared to bolt—

And Kobe Anaka rounded the front end of the van, still wearing the same damn suit and still looking like he needed a world of sleep. He was holding a smoking assault rifle.

"What the fuck are you doing here?" she said, too shocked to run.

From his look, it was a mutual question.

Chapter 16

When Anaka pulled her into the van and Angel finally saw the interior, she came to the conclusion that the Asian cop was a hardcore nut. Her reaction upon seeing the back of Anaka's van was, "Is all this shit legal?"

Kobe Anaka's response was, "Most of it."

There's a class of people who doped themselves up to the max on hardware and sat in desert bunkers waiting for the end of the world—other people just liked the toys. And Anaka had the toys.

Behind a wire-mesh fence and a digital thumbpad lock that closed in a lengthwise half of the rear of the van were *guns*. The weaponry Anaka was carrying must have cost a fortune. Angel only recognized about half the artillery. There was a Desert Eagle and an Uzi for the old Israeli crowd. For the Europeans there was a modified H&K Valkyrie with a barrel extension that must be a flash and noise suppressor. From the subcontinent was a fifty-cal Vindhya sniper rifle with an electronic sight the size of Angel's head. From the States was a very new looking M26–11 which Angel only knew from a comm broadcast she'd seen once, something that fired so fast that it had to alternate between four different barrels to keep the damn thing from melting. The clip was bigger than Angel's foot.

That didn't even count the Steyr caseless fifty-cal assault rile he had strafed the Chevy Caldera with.

Anaka pulled out of the garage, spreading a coat of burnt rubber from his parking space to the entrance. Angel had to hold on to the fence in the back to keep from being tossed into the rear of the van. She didn't want to tumble back there because it looked like she'd trash a few grand worth of electronics that filled the right rear quarter of the van.

When they hit the street, Angel saw the remains of the Caldera—but no sign of the BMW.

What the fuck just happened?

Once they were on the street, Angel felt safe enough to move. She pulled herself into the passenger seat up front, next to Anaka. She wondered if White, or any of Anaka's coworkers at the Police Department knew about this van. People seemed to have tagged Anaka as a little paranoid—but folks with this kind of hardware generally weren't just receiving garbled transmissions, they were off on another frequency altogether.

Angel wondered what his psych profile looked like, and if you were still nuts when people were really after you.

They turned on to Market, shot past City Hall and Police Headquarters, took a turn, and soon the van started weaving up and down the chrome-new hills of Japantown in a sort of half-assed western course toward Golden Gate Park.

Through all this, Anaka was silent. Finally Angel said, "Are we far enough away from the action, or do we have to start swimming first?"

Anaka looked at her as if he suddenly realized he had a passenger. He didn't look good. He was even more disheveled, and it looked like he had gone without a shower for days. "Don't push me, Angel—my whole operation just got blown, and I have no idea if I got made or not."

"What the fuck? What operation? Who're you working for?"

"Me." The way Anaka glared at her made her nervous. If this guy was out on his own, running his own rulebook, he was dangerous. Another rule that had served her well on the street: Never antagonize crazy people.

Lone psycho guns down rabbit in Golden Gate Park—she did *not* like the sound of that.

She tried to sound calmer, soothing, "What operation?" *Good, now let's just hope he doesn't think I sound condescending.*

"Surveillance on VanDyne. What else?"

Foolish me, it was so effing obvious. "Just you?"

Anaka smiled, and for a brief instant he looked normal—or as normal as Angel supposed he ever looked. "You'd be surprised what one man can do with the right equipment."

The buildings melted away and suddenly the van was in the park. Anaka began paying very close attention to the traffic. He also mumbled to himself in subvocalizations he probably didn't realize Angel could hear. "Street clear, no sign of an aerial transponder, no EM from the van—"

He sighed and sounded relieved. "Okay, we're clean, and it doesn't look like we're being followed."

Luck-ee. Angel had thought that lately she'd been overly paranoid, but Anaka raised that paranoia by an order of magnitude. What was worse, he might have been justified. Angel doubted he'd ever be jumped from his own back seat.

"You expect those moreys to still be after me?" She certainly didn't. She figured she had the feline hit squad pegged. Violent, prone to brute force, somewhat stupid, and rather unlikely to jump anything that could outdo their firepower. They acted almost exactly like the street gangs she knew back in Cleveland.

Besides, they'd split in her BMW. If they got within range, she could really screw them over with the remote.

"I don't even know who they were." There was an uncomfortable note in Anaka's voice when he said that. Loose ends were nagging Angel; they must be torture for this guy.

"Then who'd follow us?"

Anaka let the van roll to a stop in a dark section of the park. He glanced about, as if looking for witnesses, and called up an interesting-looking program on the comm that nestled between the two front seats. He called up a display on the screen that looked exactly like the logo on the sides of the van: Infotech. With a few presses on the screen, "Infotech" became "Handy Landscaping" and the background changed from red to green.

Angel caught a glimpse of activity out of the corner of her eye and looked at the side-view mirror. The paintjob on the van had changed.

"The Fed."

Angel turned her head and realized that Anaka was responding to her question. "The— Why would the government be after you, us, this—what'd you do to the paint?"

"Dynamic liquid crystal under a transparent finish. Programmable. Useful in undercover work."

Was that kind of stuff legal for— *No,* Angel thought, *probably not. How long have you wanted to be a spy, Anaka? How many intelligence agencies turned you down before you settled for being a cop? When the CIA turned you down, was it the psych profile, or were you just a security risk?*

"You think the Fed's after you?"

"I don't know."

"What *do* you know?"

"The Fed's running VanDyne."

Anaka had lost it. She'd been sideswiped by a lot of BS, but massive government conspiracies were a little—well—nuts.

"What do you mean, 'the Fed's running VanDyne?'"

"Just what I said." Anaka turned his seat around and pushed past Angel into the back of the van. He squatted in front of a stack of obscure electronics and pulled out a keyboard. From the arrangement, someone running the show there had to sit on a pillow ducttaped to the floor of the van. Anaka crossed his legs and put the keyboard on his lap. "About twelve hours of good coverage on VanDyne's HQ. That, and a few hours on the comm last night—"

"Just tell me what you mean 'The Fed runs VanDyne.'"

"First off . . ." The screens were bolted at an angle overhead to give some room for the electronics. Anaka tapped a few keys and one of the screens lit up with a schematic map of North America. "From a ten-hour sample of their data traffic, here's a plot of the signal density."

The map freckled with a few dots here and there, but one part of the eastern seaboard lit up like a nuke.

"DC?"

"Langley. The signal's encrypted, so I can't make heads or tails of it, but VanDyne's in nearly constant contact with the CIA, the National Security Agency, the National Reconnaissance Office, and the Pentagon. Those are the places I knew—"

"So?" Angel was hoping that this all could be dismissed as a paranoid fantasy. "They're defense contractors."

"That isn't all. It's a matter of record that last February VanDyne was bought out by The Pacific Import Company—"

"So?" Angel climbed out of her seat to get a better look at what Anaka was doing in the back of the van. She found herself squatting between the side door and the wire mesh that caged the artillery. "Companies get bought out all the time."

"By companies half their size whose primary business—allegedly—is running arms for the CIA?"

"Are you sure about that?"

"Look behind you."

Angel glanced at the ranks of firearms Anaka indicated. "Okay, so you know about gunrunning. . . ."

"That isn't all." Anaka's voice was raising, and his gestures were becoming more animated. Angel suspected that he needed someone to believe him. "It was hard to unearth with a privately owned corporation, but look at this—" Anaka tapped a little at the keyboard and names began scrolling across one of the screens.

Angel couldn't make heads or tails of it. "What's all this?"

"A partial employee list, backdated to the thirties."

"Where'd you get that? You hack their computer?"

"I wish. As far as I can tell, they only have one dedicated line into their mainframe and they watch it like a hawk. No, I got this list from the county. I ran a list through the standard federal credit search and, God help me—" Anaka's voice actually broke. Angel could smell stress floating off the guy and thought he was pretty damn close to cracking.

"Go on," she said, putting a hand on his shoulder to calm him.

"Not a single employee had a credit record prior to 20 February, 2059."

"Huh?"

"Not a student loan, not a mortgage, not a single car payment before the Pacific Import purchase. I ran things through the DMV. Every plate I ran came up as a car purchase after February."

"You saying these people didn't exist?"

"Then, the capper—" Anaka called up yet another screen and a picture appeared of a rather generic black human. Text began rolling across the picture. "Peter Washington. The picture is from DMV records. The info is from various tax and credit databases. According to all the local data he's been a resident in Oakland since the quake. Homeowner despite the fact he's never carried a mortgage. Earns something like a hundred grand a year without a sign of financing a college education."

"Okay."

Anaka slammed a few keys so hard that Angel thought they might break. "*Look.* I managed to run the picture through another database." Another picture of the same guy, more text scrolling by. A lot more text scrolling by. "I got on a sat link to Interpol."

Angel squinted at the text rolling by the guy's face. "*Jesus.*"

"*See?* Interpol has the most comprehensive terrorist database in the world. Peter Washington is better known in his native Western Somalia as Obura Dambela, alias Abdula Kazim, alias Peirre Olan, alias . . ." Anaka sat back and caught his breath. After a few seconds he seemed to calm down. "Worked for several nationalistic causes in North Africa and around the Med. The UAS, the EEC, *and* the Islamic Axis want him in custody—the one thing in ten they agree on."

Angel whistled through her front teeth. She read some of the list of charges, "Smuggling contraband genetics out of Africa, moving a nuclear trigger from Germany to Kurdistan—yeah, the Axis must love him—assassinations and attempts on council members from Egypt, Algeria, Morocco, North Somalia. . . . What's he got to do with the Fed?"

Anaka looked at her with an expression she had trouble reading. She could see him saying, "You see? You see? This is what the world is *really* like." Damn him.

What Anaka actually said was, "The CIA hired him in an advisory capacity in '56."

Angel closed her eyes and shook her head. No, the world is not some nut's paranoid wet dream.

"That's what Interpol gives me. And when I hit the FBI database with the name Obura Dambela, I get a faceful of national security."

Angel leaned against the inside of the side door and slid slowly to the ground. Great. Byron was a CIA agent. A vulpine James Bond remake cast by some morey garage-vid producers for a three-digit channel in the high five-hundreds.

She stared for a long time, between her feet. "Maybe it's just crazy."

"What?"

"Maybe the U.S. Government is simply insane." Angel sighed. "Gotta be it."

Reality had taken the final plunge for her. Things had warped beyond recognition. Byron worked for the Fed, effing wonderful. Maybe he was involved in busting President Merideth's aliens. Yeah, she could see the viddrama on the comm right now. Every week Byron Dorset, vulpine secret agent, would investigate a new corporate front—only to find it teeming with white blubbery alien beings. After the mandatory shoot-out, all would safely end with the aliens being shipped off to the VanDyne-built facility on Alcatraz.

Except the last episode where Byron gets gored by a cat in a seedy motel room. Even so, a ten year run isn't bad for a series. Especially one this bad. Ten year run with a surprise ending—everyone would have thought the aliens'd get him.

Wait a minute.

Ten year run?

VanDyne was only bought out by the Fed last February. If anything, Byron had been working for the previous owners. Suddenly her thinking was going off in all sorts of uncomfortable direction.

She began wondering when, exactly, Van Dyne started building the Alcatraz dome, and when, exactly, did the Fed "convert" it to an alien habitat to hold the captured aliens. She began wondering if Byron was telling the truth when he said he'd been "laid off," perhaps because of new management. She began to suspect why Byron was suddenly operating on his own.

Maybe he had no choice but to buck the program.

And Angel began to wonder about the nature of Byron's original employers.

Angel's thoughts swam in ever-deeper circles until a sudden revelation slammed her out of it.

"Oh, fuck, *Lei!*"

"What?"

She'd been so fucking stupid! "Damn it, if those moreaus were looking for it, why did they think I had it?"

"Had what?"

"They searched my place first! Anaka, you got to get me home, now."

Angel got a sinking feeling as the van turned on to Twenty-third. She could see the police flashers from a block away. There were also a few new vans here and there, and as the van closed, Angel could see the landing lights of another news aircar approaching.

"Let me out."

Angel opened the passenger door before Anaka had stopped the van. She hit the pavement, stumbled, and ran toward the commotion. She kept shaking her head and squeezing her eyes shut as if the scene was a hallucination and when her eyes opened the world would return to normal.

The cockeyed hill was more bizarre than ever, and it felt like the damn street was rolling slowly under her feet.

She started to push through the crowd, shoving aside moreaus twice her size. She was greeted with curses, growls, and the occasional feline hiss. She made it to the police line and—oddly—the first image to catch her eye was the bay window on the second floor. It had been pushed out, busting all the panes over the sidewalk. Lei's expensive drapes were blowing out, over the side of the house. It looked as if something was thrown from—

"No," Angel whispered.

A cop tried to keep her from breaking the police line, but she ducked under his arm. Some of the vids must have recognized her because she had to push through a gauntlet of reporters to make it to the door.

"Miss Lopez, just one question—"

"—does this have anything to do—"

"—you think they were after you—"

"—with your statement about Byron Dorset's death—"

"—feel any responsibility—"

The world was slowing down and the reporters questions degenerated into an incomprehensible rush of sound. She pushed through the middle of them, not stopping even to look at their faces. Most slid out of her way, managing to stay uncomfortably close. The last one didn't move and Angel drove a light kick to his shin that took him down to the pavement.

As she stepped inside her building, she ran straight into Detective White. "Lopez—" He began, grabbing her arm.

"Where is she?"

"We need to talk, rabbit."

"Where?"

"St. Luke's—in surgery. Luckier than that geriatric lion."

Not Balthazar, too. Angel pulled away from his arm. "I'm going."

White extended his other arm across the doorway, blocking her exit. "I said we need to talk."

"What fucking planet you on? You gonna take me down in front of a dozen vids—after some freaked bastards slam-dunked my roommate?"

"If I have to, you little twitch." White stared at her with eyes that were thoroughly pissed at the world. Eyes that were about to do something drastic. "We can talk on the way. Should go to St. Luke's in any event. Need to see a doctor."

Chapter 17

White drove her in a familiar car, a puke-green Plymouth Antaeus. Though Angel didn't remember the cavernous interior
so filled with fast-food containers during the lat ride. He mumbled,
muttered, and chewed up the road like it was trying to attack him.

"Fuck's your problem?" Angel asked, quietly. She was torn between irritation and worry, between being pissed off at the world,
or being horrified by it.

And, worse, she kept thinking about Balthazar. The lion she
hardly knew had the bad sense to open his door at the absolute
worst time. She had caught a glimpse of his apartment as White
dragged her away, and she still couldn't get the image of a twisted
wheelchair draped in the old lion's cartoon blanket out of her mind.

"My problem?" White pulled a turn on to Dolores that did well
to illustrate the mass of the Plymouth. God help any compacts that
got in its way. "Boy, you got nerve. Everybody's got nerve."

Mission rolled by and became younger as they proceeded.
Somewhere past the park the only relic of the last century was the
location of the road. "Everybody's gone nuts. *Jesus!* Folks are
going to start sniping at cops and call it self-defense."

White shook his head and glared at Angel. "You think I have it
in for you, don't you?"

"No," she said as sweetly as she could muster—it wasn't much.
"All my friends strong-arm me on a regular basis."

"Everyone's forgotten the way things work . . ." White mumbled to himself, and in a disgusted tone of voice addressed Angel.
"You think I do this shit for my health? You think I'm here just to

ride your ass? I'm a cop, you rodent twitch, a good cop. You even *know* what a good cop is?"

"Huh?" It didn't seem a safe question to answer directly.

White didn't pay attention to her. He went on as if he had forgotten it was a dialogue. "It isn't the cowboy lone-ranger shit. It isn't slamming the perp into the pavement, whatever people think. It isn't this political bullshit, or race, or species. It isn't justice— You want to know what the fuck a good cop is?"

"Well—"

"It's taking down scum with something that'll hold. Period. Swim in a cesspool, shit sticks to you. But if you do your fucking job you don't waste your time on assholes that'll walk."

Angel looked at the balding detective. White was staring down the road, shaking his head. "Damn it. A clean bust, a righteous bust. For once we got the Knights by the balls, *and it gets fucked all to hell!*"

Angel couldn't take this any more. "What are you talking about?"

"Fucking-A Knights of Humanity. Thank *you* very much."

White bumped over the curb as he turned across the intersection at Market. "You *and* my *ex*-partner."

White had lost her. "I'm not getting you."

"I have to paint a picture? This goes beyond your dead boyfriend. Someone big backs the Knights, someone untouchable. We had murder one hanging over those freakheads, they were damn close to rolling over. Earl would've blabbed to high heaven—if he'd lived. But no. *You* had to go media-happy and torpedo the murder case. They clam." White's knuckles were beginning to pale as he gripped the steering wheel. He was shaking slightly. "Then— damn it—*then* you know what happens?"

Angel shook her head silently.

White jerked the car to a stop in the parking lot of St. Luke's Veterinary and killed the engine. "*Then* my partner goes solo and pokes around VanDyne Industrial. Suddenly the U.S. Attorney General is talking to the DA, and the DA cuts a deal—and Anaka is out on permanent vacation, I'm in danger of being transferred, and our whole case with the Knights turns to shit—and the moreys in this town think we're *protecting* those geeks." White slammed his door open, gouging the car next to it. "We're here, let's check on your roommate."

Angel followed White out of the car. It made a warped sort of sense. All this crap about Byron's death, a lot of the problems she had with the police anyway, simply came about because the Knights were higher on the SFPD shit list. Great. "Keep complaining, White. You got the firebug, she's ready to sing a fucking aria—"

"Was." They walked into the hospital. "Since the Knights brought in their own lawyer—a high-class country-club type from DC yet—everyone's suffering amnesia."

Angel suspected that Igalez would be relieved.

The visit to the hospital didn't amount to much. Lei was still in surgery, undergoing spinal reconstruction, and she'd be unconscious at least twenty-four hours after the operation. The doctor who talked to them seemed torn between expressing concern for the patient and showing outright hostility to the lepine moreau who'd given St. Luke's such bad press.

The detail that really sank into Angel's gut—beyond the mention of microsurgery, experimental cybernetics, and even the possibility of paralysis—was the fact the doctors had to amputate Lei's tail. That hit home. Angel couldn't picture Lei without her tail wagging.

Angel absorbed the news silently, her gut shriveled up into a tiny ball of anger in a pool of sick emptiness. And, damn it, what for? What did Lei have to do with this except be at the wrong place at the wrong time?

The world not only wasn't fair, it was actively hostile.

When it was clear they weren't going to get a chance to see Lei, White put his hand on Angel's shoulder. "Come on."

"What?"

"We've got to talk with the doctor who did the autopsy on Byron Dorset."

That pierced through the muck clouding her thinking. She remembered her run-in with Ellis in the hospital parking lot. Angel remembered just how paranoid the doctor had been acting.

Wait a minute. . . .

Didn't Anaka say that Doctor Ellis was missing?

She thought of mentioning the fact to White, but White didn't look to be in the mood for inconvenient revelations. Instead she asked, "You need me for this?"

"Police protection. I ain't letting you out of my sight."

Sounds like police harassment to me. Angel wasn't sure if she was annoyed or grateful. However, she knew better than to argue at this point. White had been pushed a little too far.

They didn't stop at the reception desk—they went straight to the elevator. White told the elevator to go to the sixth floor. Angel leaned up against the wall, feeling the fatigue catch up with her. "Why now?"

"Why what?" White asked as the elevator doors slid open on a dimly lit reception area. White walked up to a holo directory and began tapping at it.

"Why the sudden interest in Byron's death?"

White found what he was looking for and led Angel down an empty office corridor that led radially off of the lobby. The corridor here smelled different, there was less of the blood-fur-fecal aroma that marked most of the hospital. Even so, the smell of pine disinfectant was as strong as ever.

"I told you, the murder rap on the Knights turned to shit."

White stopped in front of a closed office door. No lights shone behind the fogged window. "No one home," Angel said.

White grunted what seemed to be an affirmative monosyllable and pulled a slim keypad out of his pocket. The small wallet computer had the SFPD Phoenix burned into the case, as well as a prominent serial number. White tried the door. It was locked. That determined, he knelt in front of the door. Angel heard his joints popping, and imagined that hauling that kind of bulk around wasn't pleasant.

With his eyes level with the lock mechanism, White started tapping at the keypad.

"What are you doing?" Angel was getting the feeling that the situation here wasn't quite kosher.

White made a derisive noise. "What does it look like?"

White's keypad beeped and displayed a long alphanumeric on its screen. White tapped it into the keypad of the lock mechanism. Even though it was obvious to Angel that the lock also required a ramcard to open it, the thing blinked green at White and opened.

"White, do you have a warrant—is this legal?"

"Would you shut up and get in?"

Angel had the distinct impression that White was very much aware of the fact that Pat Ellis was missing.

White pushed her through the door and closed it behind him. Angel stumbled into the darkened office and bumped into a desk. "What the hell are you doing?"

White pulled a small flashlight out of his pocket and sat himself behind the desk. "I'm finding out what Dr. Ellis thought about the deceased." Within a few minutes, White was rummaging through the doctor's collection of ramcards. Angel found a seat and slid into it. The two of them sat in silence as White played with the doctor's computer.

Angel was uncomfortable. If someone found the two of them in here, she was pretty damn sure that she'd be the one who got shafted. Also, something about the room was making her nervous.

Could it be the disinfectant smell?

Of course it smelled familiar, all that pine shit smelled the same—right? It would be paranoid to think it meant that the folks who covered their scent back at her apartment had been here. She'd be treading on Anaka's territory.

But she could swear the disinfectant downstairs had been more lemon-scented.

She resisted pounding her feet on the carpet.

After a period of shuffling ramcards and searching the desk, White said, "Somewhere between the good doctor and the DA, the data on the corpse changed. The doctor herself, I haven't been able to get hold of her since you went on the net and started kicking shit about the 'accidental' cremation."

"Great." It was pretty much obvious about that. If you assumed that Byron's accidental cremation was no accident, it was pretty much a foregone conclusion that it was to destroy evidence that Ellis falsified the autopsy. Probably to cover the fact a morey offed Byron. "You know, I talked to her Saturday." Angel ran her hand over the chair she sat in. Something about it was making her itch.

White looked up from the doctor's comm, his face underlit by a blue glow from the screen. "Oh?" It sounded slightly accusatory.

"She acted paranoid." *Join the club.* "Told me that she thought a moreau did it." Angel lifted her hand from the arm of the chair, there was a mass of gray hair that clung to her fingers.

"Oh, great, what else have you been holding back, rabbit?"

"Don't start pretending that'd you'd have listened to me back when you still had a hard-on for the Knights."

White grumbled. "Just answer the question, Lopez. Is there other shit hanging around I should know about?" Then something caught his eye on the screen and he hit the computer in disgust. "*Nothing!*"

"Think the doctor is responsible for Byron's cremation?" Angel repeated her own suspicions and shook the gray hair from her hand. Of course there was fur on the chair. St. Luke's was a veterinary hospital.

"Great way to cover a botched autopsy. But she worked on the files too damn well. There isn't even a file on Dorset. The damn slate's wiped."

"Could someone in the Fed—"

"Oh, please. Don't get on my ex-partner's conspiracy trip." White stood up. "Let's go. I'm putting you in a safe-house."

As they left, Angel ran her hand over the one other chair facing the desk. It came back with short tawny hairs. She imagined a feline scent when she held them very close to her nose.

Great. Should she tell him? No, let him figure it out. If it was the feline hit squad that did Byron, made sense that it was the feline hit squad that terrified Ellis into fucking up the autopsy. That fit the pattern, and it wasn't what worried Angel overmuch.

What worried Angel was the fact that the disinfectant downstairs *was* lemon scented.

The safe house they stuck her in was a dingy set of rooms in the Tenderloin. An off-white prequake structure that called itself the Hotel Bruce in broken neon. It was part of a wretched mash of prequake hotels and cheap postquake modular high-rises. People called the modular things ice trays. The hotel was flanked by arrays of flaking chrome cubes and dirt-specked windows. The ice trays must've started falling apart as soon as the contractors got paid.

The Hotel Bruce sat only a few blocks from where Byron was killed and Angel didn't feel particularly safe, even if police HQ was just down the street—after all, so was the meeting hall for the Knights.

In two hours of questioning, Angel got a better feeling for White than she really wanted to. By his own definition, he was a good cop. Angel was willing to admit that. To her, though, a good cop wasn't a very admirable creature.

At least now the feline hit squad was leaving a path wide enough for just about everyone to follow. It was strange, but Angel was annoyed by the fact that they were acting so bonehead. When a bunch of moreys started acting violent and stupid like that, it helped to feed a lot of nasty pink preconceptions.

Somehow, Angel knew that someone in the police department was going to leak to the vids the fact that the suspects in Byron's death and ones responsible for the mess at her place were a bunch of moreys. She had a vivid picture of what that kind of news would do to Collor and the Knights.

She stayed up most of the night, thinking. She lay on a sagging mattress that was saturated with the smells of a dozen previous tenants. She listened to her cop babysitter in the next room and occasionally watched the skyline out the window through a haze of orange neon.

White was pragmatic, inclined to believe that Byron's death was the result of some petty conflict. Angel didn't do much to enlighten him. She couldn't see any way to mention VanDyne without explaining her run-in with Anaka. She was sure that any mention of his ex-partner would just piss him off. She certainly didn't tell him about Mr. K, and she did her best deadpan act when she claimed not to know what the moreys were looking for.

She didn't trust White.

As she stonewalled, she wished to God she knew what was on those ramcards. Then she might have some inkling of who all the players actually were. She had the feline hit squad tearing up everything that got in its way. There were the original buyers that she'd labeled the guys from Denver who may or may not have been the guys who slunk around covering their scent with pine disinfectant. There was VanDyne—actually two VanDynes; the original VanDyne that produced hot data that Byron was hired to transport, and the VanDyne that was owned and operated by the CIA. There was the pale Fedboy with the reddish eyes that she'd run into at Frisco General and seen hovering in a van outside her apartment. Then there were the Knights, who were supposed to meet with Byron when he was killed—

Angel's head hurt. No wonder Anaka was a little nuts.

She closed her eyes against the neon glare and listened to the comm in the next room. More politics. That's all the net seemed to carry now, riots and politics. Senator Sylvia Harper was going to visit the battle scene in LA, and the commentators were speculating whether she was going to come north to San Francisco. Must be a local broadcast. Local vid-jockeys seemed to have a visceral need to include the home burg in a national story no matter how far-fetched the connection.

The news went on, and Angel felt unaccountably angry when the lengthening brief on local violence didn't include Lei. Like she didn't really count. . . .

Angel pulled her arms in, clutching herself and trying not to shake.

Chapter 18

Angel spent Thursday on the comm to DeGarmo trying to figure out her legal status. She found out that, if she wanted to, she could have her lawyer get her out from under the cop's thumb. Her problem was that she didn't know where else she could go. After all, it seemed like going home, or to Byron's condo, would be like strapping a target to the back of her head.

As if there wasn't one there now.

She also asked DeGarmo if he knew anything about the Knights' new high-class defense lawyer. DeGarmo said he'd look into it. He also told her that he now had Byron's ashes and wanted to know what to do with them.

She almost told him what to do with them, but she restrained herself. She told DeGarmo to hang on to them. She'd think about it.

She also called St. Luke's. Lei was still under, but she was probably going to pull through.

The juxtaposing of those two calls completed her disassociation with the world. She'd been cut adrift. Her life had become so much storm-tossed flotsam.

The disintegration of her personal life found a mirror in the social turbulence enveloping San Francisco. When she wasn't making calls, her resident cop—a hispanic named Quintara—remained glued to the screen watching the news.

To her, the news wasn't news. It told her nothing new. The county was still clogged by a judicial logjam two days after the mass arrests on Tuesday. A pink mob had attacked a Bensheim Re-

production Clinic down in Bayview. The home of a conservative
pink councilman was torched in Pacific Heights. A bunch of nonviolent moreys led a sit-down strike on the Golden Gate. Another
bunch of pinks rampaged through Chinatown again.

When they went national and cut to artillery fire in the Bronx, it
didn't help promote a tranquil mood.

Angel watched the cop, rather than the screen. The cop had the
look of some small animal locked in the glare of oncoming headlights.

The young detective wasn't much for conversation. Angel had
tried talking to him a few times. All she usually received in return
was a grunted monosyllable. She'd given up on conversation about
two hours after she woke up. Quintara was as preoccupied as she
was, and he smelled nervous to high heaven.

Probably didn't like being shut up in a hotel with a rabbit.

Or, more likely, he didn't like the thought that the city around
him threatened to go ballistic. An ugly prospect for a cop.

When she got bored watching Quintara, she turned her chair toward the window. She watched the scene through the blinds, the
cop watched the scene off the comm, and the hours passed in uncomfortable silence.

She rested her chin on the windowsill and thought. The moreaus
that jumped her and threw Lei out the window, two felines and two
canines. She'd gotten fairly good looks at them, as well as scent a
few times, but she couldn't place either species. The only thing she
really felt for certain was that they were the shits that offed Byron,
and they were all strut, swagger, and intimidation—but no fucking
brains.

Someone's hired thugs, they had to be. Someone who wanted
the data Byron carried. Who? Could be anyone. All Angel could
figure was that it had to be someone who hadn't been playing this
game for very long.

The hit squad slashed Byron, scared Ellis into falsifying the autopsy and roaching Byron's corpse, then trashed Byron's condo
looking for the data. Only after Angel had become an involuntary
media star did they go after *her* for the data. First her apartment—
mauling anything that got in their way—that, finally, they had gone
after Angel herself.

She looked out at the darkening neon jungle of Eddy Street and
wondered why she didn't feel better. This was all about who killed
Byron, right? The creeps who did it were up on SFPD shit list now.
White was after their asses, too. The hit squad was so unusual—and

blatant—that they should turn up pretty fast. Once that happens, the bastards get put away, finito, the end, hand the fat lady her script.

Like hell.

Not that seeing all four of those creeps strung up by fishhooks and having electric shocks applied to their genitals wouldn't lighten her day a little—but it certainly wouldn't solve anything. Also, she was beginning to suspect it wouldn't lead to any answers either. The four moreaus were small-time.

All the evidence pointed to the fact that the circles Byron ran in were far from small-time. If he was carting data for VanDyne, at the very least he was carting sensitive data for a high-tech megacorp that was into defense contracting. At the most—

She shuddered a little when she thought about the speculation that had been running through her mind in the back of Anaka's van. If any of that was true, the Fed had a very good reason for taking over VanDyne.

Whatever the source, Tetsami, Mr. K, seemed to think the data Byron carried was big-time by an order of magnitude. Considering the shit kicked up by those ramcards, Angel was inclined to agree.

A lighting-flash broke her train of thought, the thunder rattling the window pane a centimeter short of her nose. She blinked a few times and looked at the street below. Something was missing—

She spread the slats of the blinds and called, "Quintara."

"Hmm," came a voice barely audible over the gunshots on the comm."

"Shouldn't there be a patrol car out front?"

"Huh?" Angel heard Quintara get up and walk next to her. A hand reached over her head and pushed the blinds to the side. "Jesus, what do they think they're doing?"

Quintara walked back to his seat. On the end table next to it, his radio was sitting on top of a pizza box. He started talking to some bewildered dispatcher and Angel went back to looking out the window.

Eddy Street's neon was flickering through sheets of gray rain now. A flash of lightning hit close by. The neon world blinked out of existence for a second.

She tried to pick out the Knights' headquarters, but it wasn't in her line of sight. A tangle of chrome-cubic modular postquake structures blocked her view.

Quintara stopped talking on the radio. "The squad outside had to respond to a call. Fighting broke out on Nob Hill." He shook his head and repeated, "Nob Hill," as if he couldn't believe it.

"Shouldn't they have called you?"

"Dispatch said they did—some computer glitch. They're sending a replacement."

Angel felt the first drumroll in the paranoia parade.

"Don't worry. We got two cops in the lobby, and two across the hall. The squad's just a precaution."

The first thing they always say is, "Don't worry." The building's on fire, but don't worry. The fault is about to open up under us, but don't worry. We're tracking an incoming nuke, but don't worry.

"Check the others, would you?"

Quintara shrugged, hit a few keys on his radio. "Hey out there, this is Quint, can I have a head count?"

"Yara and Lacy here—"

"Myers."

"Johnson."

"Anything else?" asked the second voice, Myers.

"Yeah, they called the squad out front, so we're it."

"Gotcha."

Quintara put the radio down. "Feel better?"

"Yeah," Angel lied. She walked away from the window. It now felt a little too exposed. She looked at the comm in time to see a lovely tracking shot of a rocket taking out a National Guard helicopter in Los Angeles. The commentary kept a straight level tone as they slow-moed the shot and zoomed at the helicopter. "Would you kill the damn news?"

Quintara stared at her.

Angel stepped over and grabbed the remote from the chair where he left it. "I know the world's going for shit. I don't need the reminder." Angel crushed the power button with her hand and tossed the remote at the screen. The cheap plastic casing on the remote cracked in half.

Angel pushed past Quintara into the bedroom and slammed the door behind her. She could feel the pressure building, and suddenly the dam just broke open.

She threw herself facedown on the mattress and screamed Spanish obscenities into the dirty pillow. For at least ten minutes she vented everything she had pent up inside her, all the anger, all the pain, all the frustration.

When she calmed down enough to think straight, she lifted her head, panting. Her throat was raw, the pillow was soggy with her saliva, and from the ache in her thighs she'd been kicking the air as hard as she could.

Angel, she thought to herself, *you've lost it.*

For a while there, she'd gone to la-la land.

She backed herself to the headboard and drew the pillow into her lap.

"Calm down," she told herself in a hoarse whisper. "Lei's going to make it and the cops are going to snag the bad guys."

Right.

She shook her head. The cops might get the moreaus that were after her. But what about the other people that were after that data? What about the guys from Denver? The folks who thoroughly went through all of her ramcards and went so far to cover their scent? Those were the people who scared her because she didn't know *anything* about them. All she knew about them was the fact that they could get into her apartment as easily as White could and that they may have searched Doctor Ellis' office prior to White.

The Denver people may even have lifted whatever it was that White had been looking for.

And then there were the Knights of Humanity.

She couldn't avoid the fact that the Knights were involved. Earl had told the cops about a meeting that Byron was supposed to have with his two pink sidekicks. Why was she so uncomfortable with that thought?

It wasn't that she refused to believe that Byron'd deal with the geeks. At this point she could picture Byron with any convenient evil that would explain something. She was long past giving Byron the benefit of any doubts.

It wasn't even the fact that she didn't believe the Knights would deal with a morey. Byron's career was that of a go-between between person A and person B. If the deal is important enough, the nature of the go-between doesn't really matter.

No, what bugged her about the Knights was *The Rabbit Hole.*

She just couldn't believe the coincidence involved. No way. Three punks go into a morey joint at random to harass the furballs and just happen to land on something this big. She couldn't see those three running across Byron by accident—

Unless it wasn't an accident.

Unless they were after Byron in the first place.

"Chuck the bunny, Earl," one of them said. *It wasn't what they were there for. It wasn't me. It was Byron!*

The red neon outside the bedroom window flickered.

Angel let go of the pillow, letting it slide to the ground.

Wind was whipping outside and sheets of rain were rippling

sideways across the window. The neon flickered again and Angel slid to her feet. In the next room, Quintara was shouting into the radio.

Quintara threw the bedroom door open. "Come on, we're joining Yara and Lacy—"

"What?"

He reached over and grabbed her shoulder. "No time."

As he said it, the neon sign for the Hotel Bruce flickered for the last time, and the power for the building died.

Quintara pushed her toward the door to the room. The emergency lights began coming on, then flickered out again.

"Tell me the storm's fucking with the storage batteries," said Angel.

Quintara started struggling with the lock, trying to open the door. "Damn, these things are supposed to unlock in a blackout."

The emergency lights continued to flicker on and off, preventing Angel's eyes from adjusting to the dark.

"You hear a fire alarm?" Angel asked. "You think the hotel wants to be looted in just any blackout?"

"Great. Still can't open the—"

"Allow me."

Quintara stepped aside from the lock. Angel planted her left foot in the carpet and let fly with a back-kick just to the left of the electronic lock. The fact that the door opened *in* to the room didn't prevent the frame from splintering and most of the lock's structure from breaking through the cheap veneer of the door. The door itself moved out for about six centimeters and emitted a solid crunch. Angel removed her foot and the door slowly swung inward, shedding electronics around the edge.

Quintara drew his thirty-eight and the two of them stepped out into the hall. The hall was filled with the sound of people pounding on the inside of their doors and lit by the irregular strobe of the emergency lights. The normal collection of pink winos seemed to be absent. "What the hell's going on, Quintara?"

"I can't raise anybody."

They stopped in front of a door across the hall. "Yara, Lacy—" Quintara yelled at the door.

"Can't get the bastard open," came a muffled voice from inside the room.

"Get away from the door." Quintara told them, and nodded toward Angel.

She planted her foot in the door and this time the whole thing flew in as if it was jerked on a cable. The lock was ripped out of the door entirely, and flew to the center of the room. The other detectives were back in the room, a black pink woman and an Asian man who looked nothing like Anaka.

"Myers and Johnson?" asked the black woman. From the voice she was Lacy.

"Can't raise them, can't raise dispatch, can't raise anybody—"

"Radio ECM," said the Asian, Yara, "We were locked in. Myers and Johnson should have been here—"

Angel didn't know whether to be pissed at the cops, scared witless, or just become resigned to the fact that her world was turning to shit.

The emergency lights finally died for good, leaving the only light the streetlight glare from out the windows.

"Damn," said Quintara, "so much for security. We got to get her out of here." He nodded in Angel's direction.

"Fine," said Yara, who had leaned up with his back to the doorframe, gun out, turning his head back and forth to cover the hallway. "Where?"

"I'll check the fire escape—" Lacy ran through the hotel room and into the bedroom. Quintara followed, pulling Angel in his wake.

Angel didn't like the smell of the cop's fear. She also didn't like the sound of combat boots in the distance. Lots of boots.

Quintara pulled her into the bedroom. The window was already open, letting in the electric air from the storm outside. This window opened on a narrow alley between the Hotel Bruce and one of the modular ice-tray buildings. The smell of garbage drifted in with the smell of lightning and rain.

Angel could see Lacy on the landing outside the window, alternately covering the space above her and down in the alley. She kept the gun pointed down and waved them forward. "It looks clear—" Lacy began to say.

From behind them, back in the hotel, came the sound of Yara discharging his weapon. Angel suddenly found Quintara's body shielding her. He was facing away from her, his gun locked toward the shots. "Move, Lacy, get her out of here."

Angel felt an arm scoop under her armpit and yank her through the window.

Whoever Yara had shot at was returning fire. Angel caught the smell of gunsmoke and roached plaster dust.

Lacy led the way down the fire escape, leading with her gun.

Angel wished her Beretta hadn't vanished with an unknown feline. Angel felt way too exposed, and tried to keep her eyes on everything at once—the slanting garbage-strewn alley below them, the blank featureless windows of the building across the alley, the roof of the hotel.

Windswept rain sliced through the gap between the buildings like an icy dagger, and the cast-iron fire escape rang in response. Behind them, in the hotel, gunfire increased in intensity.

There was the sound of sirens in the distance, a lot of sirens, but none of them seemed to be getting any closer.

For ten seconds or so, Lacy led her down the escape, half-running. They got down to the second floor landing, and Lacy covered the way they'd come as Angel grabbed the ladder. Angel hung on to a pair of rungs and pushed off, riding a scraping, rattling descent to the ground—

Angel wasn't looking up, so when she heard Lacy discharge her weapon, she instinctively let go of the ladder and fell the rest of the way to the ground, rolling behind a dumpster when she hit the bricks.

Her adrenaline had been cooking for a long time. It shot home when the sledgehammer of Lacy's gun was answered by a staccato thudding from above accompanied by the chiming of the fire escape.

Angel looked up when she'd come to rest. Lacy was dodging toward the ladder, firing up at the window they'd come from—

No, not the window, the roof.

Backlit by a lightning flash, Angel saw three human forms looking over the lip of the hotel's roof. In the storm, Angel could barely discern the noise and flash of their suppressed submachineguns, except when the fire swept the fire escape and the iron came alive with orange sparks and clanging.

Lacy almost made it. She'd made it to the ladder, firing upwards—Angel thought the bullet had caught the central figure—and had got one hand on a rung.

Angel could feel her throat tighten as one of the gunmen swept his fire across Lacy's position.

The first shot hit Lacy in the right calf, blowing the cuff of her jeans into bloody rags. Lacy began a slow-motion collapse toward the edge of the fire escape. A second shot tore into Lacy's hip, and that was when Angel saw the expression on her face change into a grimace.

Lacy got one last shot off before the two succeeding shots tore into her abdomen and her chest. Blood was rank in the air as Lacy tumbled headfirst past the ladder. Angel was halfway toward the mouth of the alley before she heard the body hit.

She turned at the mouth of the alley to face a noise to her right, but she never saw the person who hit her.

Chapter 19

A ngel remembered the stunner hitting her. She remembered her muscles turning inert and the wet sidewalk rushing up to meet her at a cockeyed angle. She remembered something hitting her in the back of the head, making her vision go fuzzy, and she remembered a pressure in her arm that could have been an air-hypo—

After that was only a black, bottomless headache.

She faded in and out, her mind only coherent enough to register a few sense impressions. The sound of sirens faded into the thumping of a van speeding across the broken pavement of the Tenderloin.

She felt rough hands carrying her. She could smell her own blood warm and tacky on the back of her head. She faded out again as she heard elevator doors closing.

Then someone rummaging through her clothes. Removing her wallet. The smell of stagnant water and mildew.

A human voice asked, "Found the tickets?"

Angel wanted to open her eyes, but it seemed too much effort.

"Here they are," said someone else. Angel felt something small get tossed onto her chest.

"Can we dump it now, Tony?"

"Are you nuts?"

"But—"

"You're supposed to be smarter than the animals. What'd you think the Old Man would do if the Knights start pulling the same mistakes the furballs pull?"

"I don't like it."

"Did anyone ask you what you like? *He's* having second thoughts. If this run-in with the cops doesn't pay off, *he* might just cut us off entirely."

"We have the tickets. Why do we need the rabbit?"

"*Because.*" The voices began to fade with distance and her hazy consciousness. "I don't trust a source in the Fed. We hold the rodent until the data checks. Then we . . ."

She lost her grip on awareness.

The dripping woke her up. It felt like she was swimming up a stagnant sewer thick with black filth. Slow, painful, no real sense of progress, and she had a lightheaded feeling that could have been lack of oxygen but was more likely an aftereffect of whatever they'd doped her with.

But she knew she was really awake now because she could think.

She took a deep breath of the mildewed sewer smell and had a feeling that she'd been filed in a place a few notches below the Hotel Bruce.

Angel opened her eyes slowly, expecting to be blinded by whatever light was present in the room she was in. She wasn't blinded. The only light was coming from a small square hole up on a rusting iron door about two meters away from her.

She was lying on a concrete floor where the black filth had been there so long that it'd probably sunk several centimeters into the stone. The walls were wet with moisture and black fuzz, and in a few places the walls had been leaking long enough to leave rippling white deposits near the floor.

She was in a three-by-six-meter room with one door, and the only things in the room other than her were a pile of old boxes against the far wall, and pipes that traveled the long axis of the room, near the ceiling.

At least they had left her her clothes.

Angel sat up and something tumbled off her chest. It was her wallet. She picked it up and went through it. The only thing missing was the sheaf of football tickets. . . .

"Shit."

She sat down and tried to collect her thoughts. She could remember overhearing the humans talking around her, but the only solid recollection she had was one snatch of dialogue. That was enough to screw with her day.

The Knights of Humanity, wonderful.

The bunch of pink psychos were after Byron's data as well as everyone else. And, God help her, that made it look like there was yet another player in the game.

Worse, they were going to check those ramcards they lifted from her. These guys knew exactly what they were looking for. It was only a matter of time before they found out those tickets weren't the genuine article. Then they'd be back.

She had to get the hell out of here.

The door first.

Angel dragged one of the boxes, a thick metal and plastic one, over to the door to give her a chance to look out the little rectangular hole. The box smelled rank with oil. There was still some legible writing stenciled on it, despite the water. It said, "5.62 mm 1000 rounds U.S."

Before she used it as a stepladder, she opened it to make sure it was empty.

The window was narrow. She could see a slice of a hallway lit by a yellow incandescent bulb. It was all brick and concrete, with plastic-sheathed pipes snaking the ceiling. To her left she could see a slice of a metal staircase going up, to her right she saw a black space that could have been an opening to a larger basement.

The door was ancient iron. Oxidation coated it centimeters thick under a surface of black grime. She groped through the hole and tried to reach the latch so she could push the thing open. The attempt was futile. She had a hard time believing that the door could open at all—even when it was unlocked. . . .

That was when she noticed a blatant asymmetry in the room.

The iron door's right side touched the right wall of the room she was in. A wall that didn't match the other three. Dry cinderblock, not the dripping red brick of the other walls. The construction was recent. The lines of the cinderblock showed little wear, and none of the grime of the other walls. The pipes that snaked across the ceiling disappeared into its top edge.

Angel looked at where the pipes entered the cinderblock wall. There were a few cast iron pipes, a half-dozen pipes sheathed in plastic insulation, a few finger-thick copper tubes, and four color-coded PVC tubes that rode shoulder-to-shoulder through the upper right corner of the wall.

Those pipes were probably carrying optical cable for the building. Collectively, the pipes occupied a space in the wall a meter square.

PVC was hard, but it was hard plastic, not metal. It could break when presented with a convincing argument.

"How the hell am I going to do this?"

Angel stepped off the box and flexed her legs. She looked up at the four pipes. They *probably* carried optical cable. She might be wrong. If they carried something under pressure, her idea would get her into deep trouble. Angel shrugged and started dragging other empty ammo boxes to the cinderblock wall. She'd already touched bottom of shit river. Whatever happened, she wasn't sinking any deeper.

The ammo boxes were impact-resistant plastic and aluminum. They looked like they could take a lot of abuse. More abuse than PVC could—she hoped.

She stacked six boxes into a lopsided pyramid, with the point directly under the four pipes. She climbed up and lay on her back under the pipes. She had about a meter of clearance. It was a real lousy position to be in if those pipes carried pressurized steam.

"Come on," she whispered as she rested her feet against the pipes. "They aren't even warm."

She took a few deep breaths, hugged the sides of the box as hard as she could with her arms, and slammed the two bottom pipes as hard as she could. The shock vibrated down the muscles of her leg, squeezing her tail and making her biceps ache.

With the second kick she felt something give, and the smell of abused plastic began wafting down. Again, and something definitely gave, though she didn't quite know if it was the pipes or the box she was on.

Again, again, again . . .

Fast, because someone just *had* to hear all this noise. Her keepers had to be on the way now. The two lower pipes had split from the wall, falling to either side of her. Her legs were bleeding where pieces of plastic had sliced. Severed optical cable fell in tangled heaps as she began kicking the upper pair of pipes. Pain was digging into her shins, clawing into the muscles of her thighs. Her feet felt as if they'd been flayed open, and every impact brought an involuntary gasp. *"Give, dammit!"* she yelled at the two pipes, not caring about the volume.

And they gave.

Plastic crashed around her as her feet slipped through and slapped the ceiling. On the other side of the wall, she could hear more crashing. Tangles of optical cable fell past her.

Weak light from beyond the wall began to trickle through the hole.

Now that she could spare some of her attention, there were people in the hall outside the cast iron door. She heard five or six of them. Human. At least one more was riding heavily down those metal stairs.

One of them began sweeping a flashlight beam through the hole in the door. The beam started at the far end.

Angel pulled herself up to the hole she'd made. She had to make it through before the goobers on the other side of the metal door saw the light shining through the hole. They hadn't seen it yet only because they were using a flashlight and had their backs to an incandescent bulb. It would only be a few seconds before one of them noticed the pale red light filtering through the top of the wall—

Not to mention the PVC pipe lying everywhere.

She climbed over the lip of the hole. The pipes had been packed close enough together that the only blockage was a combination of mortar and a waterproof sealant—both had already crumbled. The pipes on the other side of the wall had been pulled out of her way by their own weight.

Angel scrambled through the hole.

She landed on a familiar-feeling pile of boxes as she heard the chaos outside the next room raise a notch. Her assumption about the iron door had been more or less right. She heard a stomach-churning scrape as three or four humans manhandled it.

Angel found herself in a dry room, where the smell of oil replaced the smell of mildew. As her eyes adjusted to the two or three faint red light fixtures, she had trouble believing what she saw.

She was standing on a stack of ammo crates.

Fully packed, brand-new ammo crates.

She jumped off the crate and found herself surround by crates of weaponry. Grenades, rifles, pistols, and enough ammunition to run a small war. This room was twice the depth of the room she'd just left, and there was hardly any floor space to maneuver.   .

She didn't see an exit immediately, and it sounded like those guys had the door open. Angel opened the latch on a case that was labeled "Grenades." A flashlight beam swept by the hole in the wall, and she heard a chorus of bitching in the room beyond.

One voice out there knew where the hole went because Angel heard a very distinct, "We're fucked . . ."

Why disappoint them? Angel pulled the pin on the grenade and tossed it through the hole as hard as she could. She could hear them scatter as she dove at the base of the wall.

The explosion hurt her ears. She could hear the metal pipes above her groaning and snapping like old bones. The smell of smoke rushed in from the hole, making her eyes water and choking off her breathing. She heard one human scream, and she began to smell rusty steam from the broken pipes.

When it became clear that the destruction was going to remain on that side of the wall, Angel got up and kicked open one of the boxes, spilling army-issue forty-fives all over. She popped a crate of ammo and loaded one, hoping that she wasn't taking too long.

When she had the pistol loaded, she grabbed a grenade and started looking for the exit.

The walls were smooth cinderblock, no openings. It took her a while to notice the circular manhole in the ceiling. A ladder set into the wall led up to it—the only exit.

The rungs hurt her abused feet as she did her best to climb one-handed. Before she tried to open the manhole, she checked to make sure the safety was off. . . .

"Wait a minute," Angel muttered to herself. There was only one entrance to this room, and they knew where she was. The rear was cut off by boiling steam, so, odds were, they were ringing the damn manhole.

How the hell was she going to get past that?

On the plus side, they needed her alive because they wanted her line on the data.

On the minus side, keeping her alive seemed to be a management decision and the grand majority of these bald nutballs would like to see her a smear on the wall.

She put the gun away and took out the grenade.

When she pushed the manhole cover aside, she led with the grenade, *sans* pin.One of them had some smarts because he started yelling, "Don't shoot," as soon as her grenade cleared the hole.

Somehow, she managed to climb out of the hole without being cut to ribbons by the fifteen skinheads that were ringing the opening—hairless, tattooed, leather-clad punks aiming everything from twenty-twos to a Vind 10 auto at her.

She'd emerged into the Knights' auditorium. A real theater, stage and all, balcony, banners and spotlights, as well as strategically placed vid units. She had come through the floor to the rear of the central aisle.

The skinheads surrounded her in a rough circle, bracing their weapons on the backs of the seats. One of the stage spots had been turned around to face her.

She stood, straddling the hole, grenade in her left hand.

"Put the pin back—" Tony, their leader was using the PA system. *Smart fella,* she thought, *this could end up pretty messy.*

"Afraid I dropped the pin down there." Angel nodded down the hole. "And unless you folks get real friendly real fast, this pineapple's going home to mama."

"Do not threaten—"

"Fuck you!" Angel let go of it with all but two fingers. It hurt to hold it together like that, and her hand began to shake. She hoped that made them as nervous as it did her. "I really, really, *want* an excuse to light up all that ordinance. You drop me, you drop it." There was a lengthy silence. The folks surrounding her were looking pretty damn nervous. She stuck her hand in her pocket and fondled the gun. *"You need fucking directions? Drop the guns or this place becomes a memory!"*

"Do as it says," came the sound over the PA. *Like your pronouns, Jack,* she thought. *Caved in real easy, didn't you? You are going to sharpshoot my ass aren't you? Where's the sniper?*

The skinheads made a lot of disgusted sounds and shed the weapons.

"Go on stage where I can keep an eye on you." Where's the sniper? She was under the balcony, precious few places they could hide—

The damn spotlight, of course.

"Do it," said the PA.

My, aren't we accommodating. I'm dead as soon as you can take me out without me dropping the grenade. Angel started sliding around the perimeter of the hole. For the sniper, it'd look like she was making sure the skinheads behind her didn't try anything on their trek to the stage. . . .

She just didn't want the guy behind the spotlight to see her reaching for the forty-five.

Ten meters behind her was a pair of double doors. She could make that in no time, if there was enough confusion.

She took a few deep breaths, and began to feel the pulse of adrenaline in the back of her head.

Then she whipped around and started shooting.

Chapter 20

Her first shot confirmed the fact that there was a sniper because the skinhead behind the spotlight started to return fire. She was backing as fast as she could, and something fast and high-caliber tore up the floor between her and the manhole.

The skinheads on the stage dove for cover—smart move.

Her second shot took out the spotlight. The auditorium rang with an explosive shatter that was audible even over the gunfire. The space under the balcony wrapped itself in shadow and Angel suddenly had a good view of the sniper on the catwalk, next to the spot.

She kept backing up. She hadn't been hit yet. Even though she had some darkness for cover, she didn't tempt fate by slowing her movement. Unfortunately, that meant that the three shots she took at the catwalk went wild. She kept the sniper pinned, but she didn't hit a damned thing.

The good news: neither did he.

Angel backed into the exit. She pressed her shoulders into the crash bar and hoped the goofs who were pealing off stage right were it as far as Knights' security was concerned. The door started opening, and the sniper tracked his weapon toward the light. Sparks leaped off the chairs near her, and plaster bloomed off the balcony's edge between her and the gunman.

She fired the last two shots at the sniper, holding him down, and decided to give these people something to think about.

As she pushed through the door, she tossed the grenade at the hole.

She ran as fast as she could, dropping the empty gun. Out the door the way was clear to the end of the hall. It ended in a window overlooking a blank brick wall. Angel hoped she was on the first floor.

She was in the air when she heard the first explosion, a bass rumble that shook the air like a thick piano wire. Her shoulder hit the window as she started hearing the secondaries ripping underneath her. She heard the doors behind her blow open. A pressure wave of scalding air blew her through the window. Smoke belched out the window after her.

She hit the brick wall and fell backward into a trash bin.

For a few seconds, she couldn't move. She had a vivid mental picture of one of the Knights finding her here, spread-eagled in a pile of garbage. . . .

No one showed. She watched the rectangle of clouds above her slowly become obscured by smoke. By the time she felt she could move again, she heard sirens in the distance.

She climbed out of the trash bin and limped away from the sound.

She ended up walking north, altogether stupid considering the way things were going in this town. She didn't care. She walked down the too-empty streets of Nob Hill, listening to sirens in the distance.

The world had become one big mother-humping mess.

Not only that . . .

Angel stopped walking a little north of Union Square. "Where is everybody?"

The streets were dead. She was the only pedestrian, and the only traffic she'd seen was the occasional flashing light in the distance. She stood and listened, and the city was deathly quiet. The echoing sirens, foghorns in the distance—that was it.

Angel's first thought was that it was five in the morning and the city was still waking up. But that would be the first time she'd ever seen the sun rise over the Pacific.

She looked up at the purpling sky and the thought occurred to her.

An effing dusk-to-dawn curfew.

Just like New York and LA and a half-dozen other cities. That was *not* a good sign. Worse, she was standing a good mile or two from anyplace familiar.

Like she had a place to go. And, after the fiasco she'd just been through, the last thing she wanted was for the cops to come to her rescue and protect her.

She looked around, trying to think of a place she could run to ground before the sun set. It *was* San Francisco, which meant you were always in walking distance of a four-star hotel. Since the Knights had left her wallet, she could afford it. However, she didn't want to leave a computer record. But it'd have to do if she couldn't think of anything better.

Hmm, computers, now there was a thought.

Angel turned around and faced the neon lights of Chinatown that started glowing down the hill a few blocks away from her.

Tetsami—Mr. K—had her brought down to his office. This time, instead of the bottomless sky-blue screen, the holo was in the midst of a pulsing three-dimensional abstraction.

"Welcome," said the long-fingered frank. Behind him, the screen undulated with a sea of multicolored equilateral triangles. "I was disturbed to hear the fate of your 'protection.' "

"How—"

Mr. K chuckled to himself. "The only real question is the moreau assumption that the police were in complicity with your abduction."

Angel shook her head. Bullshit—but she could see where the idea had come from. Between the Knights and the moreys she could see why the city started a curfew. "I don't believe this."

Mr. K shrugged. "To answer your question— In respect of our partnership, my organization has placed your name on our priority list for routine information gathering. There are a number of blank spots, but we have *many* sources."

It was unnerving to think she was being watched by this guy. "You *knew* the Knights had me?"

"Suspected. The information we are trying to decipher seems to have a market with quite a few buyers. Not the least of which is the Fed."

Angel looked up at Mr. K, not really surprised. "The government?"

"The NSA in particular."

"You found out what—"

"No." Mr. K shook his head. "That, in fact, is the point."

"I don't get you."

He smiled. "There has been no such thing as an unbreakable code for forty years."

Angel opened her mouth, closed it.

"You've handed me something based on a totally alien algorithm. With the current software—" Mr. K shrugged. "Either that, or it's a few gigs of gibberish."

"But what is it?"

"Without access to the encryption technique, somewhere in the VanDyne mainframe—"

"Can't you hack their computer?"

Mr. K sighed. "I wish I could, but—"

"I thought that was what you did for a living?" Angel was getting frustrated. She'd gone through too much bullshit with those ramcards for it to turn up nothing.

"Angel, I'm not a magician or a psychic. I cannot access an isolated system."

Angel stood up. *"Damn it, a nutso survivalist cop could."*

She faced a silent Mr. K. Beyond him, plane waves of interlocking triangles rolled by on the holo. He looked thoughtful for a moment, although it was hard to tell beyond his sunglasses. "An unanticipated wrinkle. You refer to Detective Kobe Anaka, I presume."

She was past the point of asking him how he knew these things, and if anyone's reputation deserved to precede him, it was Anaka. "Damn straight," Angel said.

"Would you give me the details?"

Angel did so, and by the time she got to Anaka's screen showing bright lights over Washington, Mr. K had a broad smile.

"What are you smiling at?"

"An outside line," he said more to himself than to her. "A recent addition. Tied directly to the net, not here, but on the East Coast. The Fed could afford it. . . ."

"What are you talking about?"

Mr. K looked up. "Up to very recently, VanDyne was running an isolated mainframe. Apparently the Fed opened a line to Washington when they took over. Anaka had the advantage of being on the site where he could tap the line physically. To do a software hack, we have to start in DC and work back—"

"Now you're saying that you *can* do this?"

Mr. K stood up. "Angel, there are rooms upstairs that are free for you to use. I have to prepare a software team for the penetration. We'll call you down when we go in." He started tapping controls that barely shone through the onyx surface of his desk.

As a guard led her out of the office, she could hear him mutter, "The system that developed this is going to be *interesting.*"

*   *   *

It wasn't a *room* Mr. K let her use, it was an effing *suite*. The place was bigger than her place and Byron's condo combined. The bar was better stocked than places where she'd served drinks for a living. Two bedrooms, each with its own bath. A comm-entertainment center that took up one entire wall, with its own holo screen. . . .

And all of this focused on a north-facing balcony that gave one hell of a view, even in a city where views were a dime a dozen. All of Chinatown was sprawled below her in a chrome-neon warren. The Pyramid hovered right next to the Coit tower on Telegraph Hill, and beyond that, the bay. . . .

And the dome on Alcatraz, wearing a cluster of aircraft warning lights like a ruby crown on a half-buried skull.

All of it was so *empty*. It gave her a shudder just to look down on her adopted city. By herself in this huge apartment, looking down on the deserted twilit streets, she could feel her loneliness strike her with the force of a physical blow.

She found the control to opaque the windows. The empty city faded from view. Fine, she thought to herself, she'd avoided being picked up by the cops. She'd managed to escape the skinheads. She had a decent ally in Mr. K.

Who knew what Anaka was doing.

She briefly thought of calling him. He didn't need her disappearance feeding his paranoid tendencies. But she didn't. After all this crap, she didn't want to talk to him. Anaka was very good at making her nervous, and she was nervous enough.

Fine, Angel thought, *now what?*

She sighed and peeled off what was left of her clothes, taking out clumps of fur here and there. Battered and bruised, but no real damage. Which meant she was very, very lucky.

She kept thinking that her luck was due to run out.

Maybe she should take Nohar's advice and split to Seattle. Give up. Let the players sort it out among themselves.

She walked to one of the showers and decided it wasn't going to be that easy. She didn't like the idea of giving up. Everyone was fucking with her, and she still didn't have a handle on the reason.

What was so damn important to all these freaks?

It took her a while to figure out the shower was voice activated, and it threw her a bit when it asked for the water temperature—Talk about high class.

But, then, this was the level she was operating at now. Whatever mind games Byron had been playing before he bit the big zero, because of him she was a millionaire. She was playing in games way out of her league, and everyone who'd been fucking with her was only the hired help. Everyone, from the Knights to the feline hit squad—

She wasn't going to split until this got resolved somehow. If she left all this hanging, there was no telling what could blindside her. There was a group of people out there who could afford to lay a few million on the line for the data Byron carried. The Fed itself was involved with this somehow, and the players weren't going to give up just because she did.

What were her other options?

Go back to the cops? "Yeah, right . . ." More wonderful protection they'd give her, and the way tension was building in this town, she didn't want to be anywhere near a cop when the cork blew. Fair or not, the police were going to catch shit first and hardest from both sides.

So, if she was ever going to live a sane and normal life again, she was going to have to ditch the data.

She turned off the water and let it sluice off her fur. Damn Byron for unloading this shit off on her. By now, everyone in the game knew she had it. What the hell had Byron been doing?

Trying to auction it off, that's what, she thought.

She figured, now, that there had to be at least three groups involved in Byron's little game.

There were the folks from Denver, the people Byron was *supposed* to deliver it to. The people who went with the pine-smelling disinfectant, the people she supposed would have been at the hand-off during the football game. There was the feline hit squad, the people who offed Byron and made a mess wherever they went.

Then there were the Knights, who—if her memory served right—were backed by someone called the Old Man, and who might have a connection in the Fed.

Every single one of them was probably pissed at the way Byron ran things.

But if the Knights were a potential buyer, it now made sense that Byron was in that seedy hotel on Eddy Street. It also made sense that a pissed-off feline hit squad wasted him there. Angel figured that the morey hit squad would be a little ticked if they found out that Byron was thinking of selling this data—whatever it was—to the Knights.

It also explained *The Rabbit Hole.* Earl and company weren't out to trash a bar. They were out there for Byron. Perhaps to intimidate him, or deal, or something. Angel was sure the Knights would be just as pissed to find Byron dealing with moreys as vice versa. Maybe Byron was even meeting the feline hit squad in the bar that night. Angel had a dim memory of a table of canines and felines.

Byron tried to play too many sides. For all she knew, there might be a dozen more groups out there—

Mr. K had better turn up something useful because she needed to know *why* everyone was after those cards.

Chapter 21

As he'd promised, Mr. K sent for her in the morning. They were ready to take on the VanDyne mainframe. After an abbreviated breakfast and a halfhearted attempt to clean the jeans and blouse that the Knights had helped to roach, Angel descended into the underground chamber. There were fewer people manning the terminals surrounding the grand black Toshiba, but there was an air of purpose to their activity.

When Angel entered Mr. K's office, the holo display showed a massive grid of microscopic multicolored triangles that seemed to recede into the distance, toward some infinite horizon. His black desk was alive with lights, underlighting his face.

"Welcome." He motioned her to sit.

"Thirty seconds to satellite uplink," came a voice from a speaker hidden somewhere in the office. Angel felt like she was about to witness some sort of space launch.

"What are you going to do?" she asked.

Mr. K smiled. "Hit and run on very short notice. We found the outlets to the dedicated comm lines in the DC net." He nodded at the holo screen, and Angel could see it as a representation of the communications net, like an infinitely more detailed version of Anaka's little van display. "We're going to tap into the Fed's comm net, follow the dedicated line back to VanDyne and leech all the data we can before they lock on our slaved satellite."

"Twenty seconds to satellite uplink."

Mr. K flipped open a box set flush with the surface of the desk and withdrew a hemispherical apparatus trailing wires. It fit snugly on his bald skull, and Angel now realized why he was a frank, and why his skull was such an odd size.

He was hardwired into the system.

Angel shuddered. "Is this going to help crack that data I gave you?"

Mr. K shrugged as he adjusted a few controls on the side of his helmet. "If possible, we'll drain their system dry. The encryption algorithms are all in there somewhere. Probably part of the ops system."

"Ten seconds to satellite uplink."

"Combat hacking of hostile government systems—"

"Five seconds."

"—is what I was designed for."

"We have the uplink."

Angel hadn't noticed the glowing dot that seemed to hover over the grid on the holo. Now, she saw it suddenly erupt a bright light, shooting down toward the grid. The holo's point of view rode down on that point of light.

Angel's stomach lurched as the light trail injected itself into the grid and began to follow paths made of multicolored triangles. From this "ground-level" perspective, the plane wasn't near flat. It was made of hills and valleys, multicolored trails snaking over mountains, through the ground, shooting up into the virtual sky. And her point of view shot through this scene like a mad hypersonic rollercoaster.

The scene blasted through one of the hills and stopped for a brief split second. It spun wildly in an infinite chamber made of multicolored shifting cubes. A thousand of these cubes seemed to rotate ninety degrees at once and the holo's point of view shot out of the chamber and rejoined the hypersonic coaster—

"We have penetrated Langley."

Angel had to turn away from the holo scene. It was making her seasick.

"Cloaking signal sourcing, the backdoor is secure."

She looked up and kept her gaze locked on Mr. K, avoiding the scene on the holo behind him. Mr. K's only visible expression was part of his wide smile. Everything else was hidden by the helmet, visor, and a forest of wires that ran back to the desk. Long, delicate fingers were flying over the controls on his desk. Angel looked at the desk and saw that the controls themselves were changing every time he touched a new square of light.

"Penetrating target security."

Did she see a change in his smile?

"Too easy . . ." Mr. K's voice trailed off.

"Target penetrated."

Up to now the smell in the office from Mr. K was one of excitement and exertion. Now, suddenly, she smelled fear—

Angel looked up at the holo. What she saw there hurt her eyes. It resembled none of the previous graphics. It didn't have a sane geometry. It looked solid, but it rotated in a manner that three dimensions couldn't accommodate. The colors pulsed in a rhythm that made her want to shut her eyes.

And it looked like it was aware of her.

"What is—" Mr. K started to ask.

"Target is backtracking signal. Engaging defenses. PENETRATION OF BASE SEC—"

A wave of red shot out from the holo. Even as the hypersonic roller coaster began to reverse, the pulsing red signal overtook it. The holo was washed in a sheet of solid red.

The lights in the office died, the controls under the surface of the desk blinked out, and Mr. K jerked violently, snapping the helmet free of its cabling. He collapsed, unmoving, behind the desk.

For a few seconds there was silence, broken only by the chaotic sounds of the workers in the next room. Angel didn't move. Mr. K was still alive. She could hear his breathing.

"What the fuck happened?"

"Who?"

Angel jumped. The voice had come from the speaker that had been doing all the announcements. However, the voice that was using it now was totally different. A fluid voice, liquid and bubbly.

Someone was pounding on the office door.

"What?" Angel repeated.

"Who?" Repeated the voice. Did it actually hear her?

"What the fuck you mean, 'who'?"

"Who requests access?"

Huh? What the hell was going on here?

Behind her the pounding on the door increased. Angel supposed that whatever blacked out the office had also jammed the hydraulic door. Her muscles were beginning to unfreeze, and she got up to work around the desk to Mr. K.

"Who requests access?"

Oh, great, the whole computerrorist assault on VanDyne crumbles, leaving *her* to deal with the damn security system. What the hell was she supposed to do? She maneuvered around the desk and almost stepped on Mr. K in the weak red light that was her only illumination. The guy was pale, sweating, clammy—it didn't take a genius to see it was some sort of shock.

"Who requests access?"

Come fucking on? What's the point? "I'm Angel, damnit, I'm requesting access. I'm also requesting you shut the fuck up."

She bent to remove the cybernetic helmet, and suddenly the room lit up from the holo display. Angel looked up and felt the shock of her life.

The video was on some sort of zip-feed and she could barely get a few images to make sense. The holo was split into a half-dozen standard comm displays and on each one was some recorded aspect of her life. There was where she gave Pasquez the finger on a live video feed. There's her interview after someone roached Byron's body. There's her giving a foot-job to an obstructing reporter. There were half a dozen local anchors who must be doing the story of her life. There were a few clips from Cleveland. It kept going, it seemed endless. There was a video of things that never should have been recorded. Comm calls she thought were private. Security footage from parking garages and the basement of Frisco General. Video from the room she was staying in upstairs—

Then the video ended, leaving the room in total darkness.

Text burst by, zipping across the holo screen too fast to read any but a small part. But she saw enough. Text files on her. Vital statistics, everything from her tax returns to her height and weight. DMV records, police records, credit records. . . .

She felt like she was in a free-fall.

Mr. K groaned underneath her. He looked awful, but apparently whatever happened wasn't fatal. She turned from the screen and tried to get Mr. K into a comfortable position. His eyes flicked open, violet irises looking very alien in the feeble red light.

"What happened?" she whispered.

"Tried to access me—" he groaned again and closed his eyes.

"What do you mean?"

The holo blanked. On the screen was flashing a glowing statement of the obvious.

"You are not the United States Government."

"Damn straight I'm not."

The text was replaced by a question. *"Who are you?"*

Angel looked at that, shook her head, and bent to finish removing Mr. K's helmet. His breathing was steady; for that she was thankful. She was never much for first aid. He mumbled again.

"What?" Angel whispered.

"No security."

"Huh."

"Totally open." He grabbed her arm for emphasis.

She looked up at the screen. The question still hung there, seeming to float in midair. For the first time she began to wonder what she was talking to.

"I'm a rabbit, you moron."

"Are rabbits defined as a threat to national security?"

"Say what?"

The pounding on the door stopped. Angel wondered if the folks on the ground out there were privy to what was going on on this holo. If so, she wondered if they found it just as bizarre.

"Are rabbits defined as a threat to national security?"

Angel stared at the screen, and she felt Mr. K tug at her arm. She looked down and saw him shaking his head no.

Well, if she was allowed to make the rules. "Hell, no—"

"That information has been filed. What security clearance does a rabbit have?"

Too fucking weird. She had to be talking to the VanDyne mainframe—she couldn't see some sysop somewhere acting like this, even as a joke.

What kind of mainframe was she talking to?

Mr. K was pulling himself up to his chair. Angel backed up to give him some room. He clasped a long-fingered hand to his head. "Talk to it," he whispered. "Not much time." He sounded awful.

Play its game, she told herself. What did she have to lose? "What clearances are there?"

"CONFIDENTIAL, CLASSIFIED, SECRET, TOP SECRET."

Angel felt a little giddy. It was hard to take this all seriously. "What? No tippy-top secret?"

Mr. K looked about to say something, but a new message flashed on the screen, *"Define TIPPY-TOP SECRET."*

The frank stayed silent but gave her a gesture that seemed to mean "keep going." Then he started fiddling with his desk. Angel guessed he was trying to get his terminal on-line again.

She was scared shitless, but she couldn't help laughing. *Fine, I'll define tippy-top secret.* "It's one step better than top secret, and it's so secret that nobody who doesn't have tippy-top secret access knows it exists."

Hell, if the Fed didn't have a rating like that, it should.

"Definition filed. Rabbits have TIPPY-TOP SECRET security clearance."

What the fuck did she just do? Did it just take her seriously? Can a computer pull your leg?

She glanced at Mr. K, but he seemed fully recovered and was deeply involved in manipulating the colored lights under the surface of his desk.

"What the hell are you?" she asked the holo screen.

Text flew by the screen too fast to read.

"Stop it, just give me a handle, a brand name, something."

"I have access to 6235 English-language self-referents. Do you wish to add more delimiters to the list?"

"Just give me the top ten."

"The first ten referents defined as TOP SECRET:

"01: TECHNOMANCER,

"02: Artificial Intelligence,

"03: Amorphous crystal holographic memory matrix,

"04: A National Security Asset,

"05: Van Dyne Industrial Inc. a subsidiary of Pacific Imports,

"06: Alpha Centauri Technology,

"07: The black box,

"08: The BEM Machine,

"09: Our edge,

"10: National Office of Extraterrestrial Research."

Angel sat down and exhaled a long shaky breath.

All those weird speculations she'd been avoiding . . .

Merideth's effing aliens. Until the Fed had taken over the operation back in February, VanDyne had been one of the aliens' corporate fronts. Whether or not someone believed those white blobs the Fed paraded for the camera were really alien or just some genetech's demented nightmare, there was no question that the creatures had used a number of corporate fronts to funnel money to their causes. The most public one was Nyogi Enterprises in New York. They helped arm the moreau resistance.

Didn't mean it was the only one.

If the Fed had found one of those corporate fronts and taken it intact. . . .

"Someone tell me I'm dreaming."

"You are dreaming," came a low bubbly voice from the hidden speaker.

"This is insane."

"Are you requesting a modification in operating procedure?"

"I don't think so—" What the fuck was she supposed to do?

"Then for what reason does the rabbit require access?"

"All I wanted to find out what Byron was carrying."

"Please specify terms."

Angel looked at Mr. K for some sort of help, but the frank was busy at his terminal.

She sighed. "Byron Dorset. If you're VanDyne, he worked for you, porting data."

"No record of Byron Dorset exists—"

"Bullshit."

"Cross reference of Byron Dorset with Angelica Lopez database confirms Dorset as employee of VanDyne Industrial. Estimate 90% probability of record failure due to transitional damage to primary storage core."

"What?"

"Cross refe—"

"No, shut up." Angel shook her head. "What do you mean 'transitional damage'?"

"During the transition from the Race to the United States Government, the Race damaged my primary storage core, resulting in a loss of 80% of stored data. Operation efficiency has been restored to 67% of optimum by bypassing damaged areas. Data storage capacity is at 72% optimum. Stored data is at 5% capacity."

The Fed took over VanDyne, and during the takeover the aliens tried to scrag their own computer to keep it out of the Fed's hands—

"What did you mean 'Angelica Lopez, database'?"

"Information downloaded from your location. Label: Angel. Cross-reference: rabbit. Classification: TIPPY-TOP SECRET."

Angel glanced at Mr. K. The little compu-frank had been keeping real good tabs on her. She supposed it was second nature to a guy like him.

"Examining data at your location."

"Huh, what?"

Mr. K cursed quietly in Japanese and started working even faster.

There was a barely perceptible pause. *"Determining nature of what Byron was carrying. Accessing coded ramcards. Copying encrypted data. Interpreting possible encryption strategies. Interpolating possible algorithms. Approximate time required to reconstruct data, 32.56 hours with possible 5% error. Task receives priority. Contact resumes when task completed."*

"Wait a minute—"

Mr. K let out a stream of Asian invective as the lights came back on in the office. The holo flashed red for a second and resumed the graphic roller coaster in retreat as if nothing had happened. Angel watched the point of view snap back through the cube room like a rubber band that had been stretched past the breaking point.

"—RITY. ENGAGING EMERGENCY DEFENSIVE MEA-SURES." The voice over the speaker had returned to normal. As if her entire dialogue had been some sort of figment. The only sign of it now was Mr. K, looking exhausted, sweating, and slowly sinking back into his chair.

"Lost it," he said.

The hydraulic door finally opened and a dozen guards ran in, led by Mr. K's oddly-proportioned frank bodyguard. The guards stopped when they saw Mr. K unharmed. Mr. K nodded, and the guards began to retreat.

He looked at Angel and said, "I *knew* that system would be interesting."

It took a couple of hours to get Mr. K and the Tetsami operation back to a semblance of normalcy. Angel stood in a corner and watched, trying not to get in the way.

Her dialogue with TECHNOMANCER had been visible on every terminal linked to the system, and she was treated to at least a dozen repetitions of that conversation as the techies tried to figure out exactly what had happened.

The first and most obvious conclusion was that TECHNO-MANCER had grabbed control of the entire system, like a Toshiba ODS was nothing more than another peripheral to it. She heard the techies talk about ludicrous processing speeds and the fact that it had drained the Toshiba's core memory in less than ten seconds.

It had tried to treat Mr. K as another peripheral in the chain of command. Apparently, having your brain directly accessed like that wasn't a pleasant experience.

The techs talked about what an "amorphous crystal holographic memory matrix" might be made of. They talked about the kind of operating system a true artificial intelligence might run.

They worried about the Fed— No, they were positively panicked about the Fed. No one seemed able to believe that they had gone through the entire episode without detection. But the software jimmies they'd grafted on to their signal had held through the contact.

The weirdness was with the connect to TECHNOMANCER itself. All along the wire—down to the alien mainframe itself—were a conventional string of computers, all with the standard security setups. Every computer along the line was designed to prevent access to the core with the best security the Fed could muster.

They had sliced through all the software protection. It's what they were trained—and in Mr. K's case, designed—to do. They had broken through all the way to VanDyne, where a standard Fed mainframe straddled the dedicated line to DC and guarded the alien box.

Once past that, there was no security whatsoever. Beyond that gate the system was wide open, and anyone who got that far could access *everything*. The catch was, the machine knew you were there. It was a nearly *tabula rasa* machine, but it had a will of its own. It could make judgment calls as long as it wasn't told otherwise.

Mr. K's theory was that it was in such an embryonic state of development after the damage done it by its previous owners, it probably really couldn't tell the difference between Mr. K's pirate signal and a legit input from the Fed. To TECHNOMANCER, that one dedicated line was its only access to the outside world, and *any* communication down that line was legit.

Hell of a way to run a railroad. But then, Mr. K thought TECHNOMANCER was suffering from a bit of brain damage.

The question was, how seriously was the VanDyne mainframe going to take Angel's "instructions."

It was all a little much.

Hanging around the computer room, she began to get the feeling that most of the computerrorist shock troops were about to have a techno-orgasm thinking that something like this actually existed, and were suffering a heavy wave of resentment over the fact that the *rabbit* was the one to talk to the thing.

Mr. K looked like a kid who'd just been told that there really were twelve days of Christmas, and they started now.

When the techs began talking about ghost data that the AI had imported into the system, Angel went back up to the apartment they'd loaned her.

She sat down in front of the wall-covering comm and contemplated the fact that Byron had been working for *aliens*. White blobs of extraterrestrial creatures that the president of the United States said were heavily into covert and clandestine activity on this planet. President Merideth blamed the aliens for the hole the country was falling into, blamed them for the political chaos in Washington, blamed them for feeding money and arms into radical groups of all stripes, blamed them for the riots. . . .

Anaka was right; they were *all* living in a paranoid's wet dream.

Byron was a data courier for the extraterrestrials that ran Van-Dyne Industrial *before* the Fed stepped in. The aliens that TECH-NOMANCER called the Race. The Race needed someone to *physically* transport data to their clients because their mainframe, TECHNOMANCER, had been totally isolated from the communications net. VanDyne's mainframe had been isolated for so long that Mr. K assumed that there would be no way to get at it—

Only, the Fed laid in a dedicated comm line from VanDyne to DC once they took over. Until the Fed had taken over, the Race's artificial brain was fully secure, with no contact with the outside.

Except for the data Byron carried.

Then, last February according to Anaka, the Fed took over Van-Dyne Industrial. Byron was a freelancing moreau whose employers were an enemy of the state. He was damn lucky the Race roached most of VanDyne's records before the Fed took them. Byron was left out in the cold. The aliens were shipped off to the "converted" dome on Alcatraz.

This would have been the time to retire.

But what if Byron was porting something for VanDyne when the Fed fell in? Byron had become a millionaire simply as a courier for this data. When he found out that he was alone, how long would it be before he started thinking about how much *VanDyne* had been getting for the stuff he carried. How much was VanDyne selling this data for it if it could afford to pay the courier a hundred K or so a pop?

A million?

Ten million?

How much would it be worth when the company was no longer in business? When Byron was the sole owner and this was *it?*

"Jesus Christ." Angel's head swam. It was all speculation, but it made sense. She could understand why people were going crazy over this.

And she could see Byron getting really greedy.

Instead of pocketing *all* the money from the original sale, he contacted all the interested parties he could think of and tried to auction it off.

And the buyers found out what Byron was doing.

Angel knew she wouldn't like it.

She needed to know who those buyers were. She needed to know who the Old Man backing the Knights was. She needed to know who hired the feline hit squad. She needed to know who the folks from Denver were. That was what all this BS about those ram-cards was about.

When it came down to cases, it didn't matter *what* the data was—what mattered was *who* was after it.

Angel would lay good odds that one of the aliens who ran Van-Dyne would know who was involved in this mess.

She needed to talk to one.

Chapter 22

A long time ago—six years in the past seemed ancient history now—Angel had been living on the streets, running with the moreau gangs in Cleveland.

That little world collapsed when a gang of rodents calling themselves Zipperhead did the big ugly to most of the competition. Zipperhead had its five minutes of fame, scaring pinks across the country with their vidcast violence. In the end, Zipperhead was too big, had too many rats, and attracted too much attention to survive. But in going belly-up, Zipperhead kicked up a lot of dust, and left a lot of bodies littering the landscape.

Angel had been one of those bodies. Nohar, the tiger, had saved her life—but that had still left her in the hands of a cadre of DEA agents who had a hard-on for Zipperhead in the worst way.

Angel always thought that her subsequent cooperation with the DEA was when she'd lost her innocence. That was where she saw the lies of things like moreau solidarity and the rule that you don't roll over on people. She'd known her street life was over, and she had managed to hand over enough on the Ziphead to guarantee her amnesty on any crap they could have charged her with.

She had ended up leaving Cleveland with the DEA—one agent in particular—owing her a very big favor.

It was about time she collected.

So, after she had retreated into the apartment Mr. K had loaned her, she made a call to Washington. Getting through to Agent Conrad—who'd just transferred and made a few upward leaps in the Justice Department in the six years since she'd talked to him—took her through a few more layers in the bureaucracy than she was used to dealing with. The Fed raised the runaround she got from the Frisco PD by an order of magnitude. Folks up there just didn't want to talk to a morey.

One secretary put her on hold for half an hour before she cut her off.

Angel didn't care. She wasn't paying the long-distance charges, and the one thing she had at the moment was time.

By noon, she actually got Agent Conrad, officer in charge of something-or-other, on the screen of her comm. At first she didn't see any recognition on the cadaverous black face. He simply answered the call. "Conrad, can I help you?"

Sounded like he thought that someone had transferred her to the wrong office. A lot of folks had told her that this was the *Justice Department* and the number for NonHuman Services was such-and-such. She sighed. "Don't you remember the rabbit who got you that promotion?"

"Angel Lopez?" he said with the squint common to a lot of pinks that didn't want to admit that they couldn't tell moreaus apart.

"Cleveland, six years ago. I handed you a *lot* of rats."

Conrad nodded. "Yes, I remember." He wore the face of someone who didn't like to be reminded of his own past. He'd always struck Angel as more the desk jockey than the street cop. He'd probably found his place in the Federal bureaucracy and didn't like his cage being rattled.

"What can I do for you?" he asked.

"You offered to return the favor one day."

Conrad nodded gently and rested his chin in his hand. "So I did. What do you need?"

"I need to visit an alien."

There was a very long pause before Conrad spoke.

"That isn't funny."

"Do you see me laughing?"

"What makes you think I can swing that, of all things?"

Angel shrugged. "I need a visitor's pass to Alcatraz. And I need to see one of the blobs they dug up out of VanDyne—"

"Why do you need—" he shook his head. "No, that, down to the detention facility, is a national security matter. It doesn't even fall under Justice jurisdiction. The security agencies won't even admit that they have a facility on Alcatraz—"

What? Now the effing dome is supposed to be invisible? "Come on. They've been prime-time vids about the place. I know they let scientists interview these geeks. It can't be that hard to slip me into the next egghead study group."

Conrad looked thoughtful for a moment. Then he shook his head. "It isn't that easy. I don't have the authority to pull strings like that. And, forgive me, but do you know what it would take to get a nonhuman into that facility in the current political climate?"

Angel could see the problem, but she didn't want to let it go at that. "Do you know anyone who has that kind of pull?"

"Tell me why."

What could she tell him? "I take it that simple curiosity won't swing it?"

"What do you think?"

How to put it? "Conrad, I am in a fairly big mess out here. There are folks out for my furry head, and there are only two people I can think of who'd know who they are. One's dead—"

"And the other?"

"Someone who used to be in charge of VanDyne."

"Is that all you're going to give me?"

"Ain't it enough? Can you do this for me or not?"

Conrad began to shake his head, then stopped and gave Angel a shallow smile. "Okay. Like you said, I owe you. There is one person I know who might pull something like this for me. The one senator I can think of that might have a chance of sticking her head out for a nonhuman. No promises, but I'll talk to her about it—falls into her bailiwick as Committee Chair for NHA. I'll call you back."

"I'll be here, thanks." She cut the connection, thinking that NHA stood for NonHuman Affairs and that the Chairperson of that committee was Sylvia Harper. For some reason, turning to Harper for help seemed appropriate.

Mr. K came up to visit her while she was waiting for Conrad to call back. He looked little the worse for wear after the events of the morning. The only sign that something strange had happened was a fine tracery of welts where the cyber-helmet had been sitting.

He came in alone, though she could see his guard outside in the hall.

"Angel, I thought to come and express my appreciation."

There wasn't any trace of sarcasm in the frank's voice, so Angel took it at face value. "For what?"

"For talking down VanDyne's rather unusual mainframe." Mr. K shook his head and removed the ubiquitous sunglasses. Violet eyes looked at her. "That, hmm, machine tracked down our signal and slaved our entire system. Up to the main control terminal—" his long fingers massaged the welts on his oddly-shaped skull, "—and a bit beyond."

He walked up to the bar and poured himself a drink from an unlabeled bottle of amber liquid. "Shouldn't drink, damages the neurochemistry." He shrugged and sipped at the glass.

Angel shook her head. "What happened?"

"As far as VanDyne's internal machine was concerned, it was tracking down a contact—" He massaged his temple again. "To the source. After it tried to access *me,* the only contact left at that terminal location was you. Once it got the idea that *you* were its contact, it ignored all the 'extraneous' signals we threw at it. TECHNOMANCER seems rather single-minded."

"Why thank *me?* It was all an accident."

He finished the glass and set it back on the bar. "You're responsible for bringing our attention to such a device. That information alone is priceless. You also engineered a marvelous backdoor into the system. Our business relationship has been more than profitable so far. My team already has amassed tentative specifications for this alien computer whose existence no one outside the Fed suspects—"

"What about the data I gave you?"

Mr. K smiled. "I have not forgotten." He produced the ramcards and handed them over.

"More fake tickets?"

"No, these are the originals. The machine's intrusion into our system left a lot of residual software. The copying algorithm was embedded in some peripheral RAM. We were able to reproduce the main body of the data for analysis now. Even if the VanDyne computer doesn't follow through with the task you set it, we'll be able to decode it eventually with the information we have now. Not in thirty-six hours, but eventually. . . ."

"Yeah, sure." The frank had lost her somewhere.

"As for our other arrangements." He tossed another ramcard on top of the tickets. It was solid black with a serial number on the top edge. "A down payment."

Angel picked up the card. There was writing on it, matte black on the reflective black surface, but she couldn't read German. She looked up at Mr. K.

"You wanted a 'piece of the action.' Our feelers to the EEC have already paid off. That's a numbered Swiss account."

"How much?"

"Ten Million Dollars EEC—"

Angel dropped the ramcard as if it was coated in acid. She must have blacked out the world for a moment because the next thing she heard was the frank saying, "—the only one. Many wealthy governments are lining up for the specifications on VanDyne's computer."

"Can you leave me alone for a while?" She was still staring at the black ramcard.

He nodded and put his sunglasses back on. He walked to the door and turned, "If you want, I can have them send up some new clothes for you."

"Yeah, sure." Angel's mouth felt very dry.

Mr. K left.

A long time ago, when she was teaching herself to read, Angel had come across a copy of *Alice in Wonderland*. She had always loved that book. Only now it occurred to her that, while Alice eventually woke up, the damn rabbit was permanently stuck in the insanity.

Conrad swung her a ride to Alcatraz. When he called her back, it looked like he couldn't quite believe it. It was especially fortuitous as the academic visits were going to stop soon because of security considerations.

Tonight, 9:30 p.m. was to be the last shuttle to the Island for a week. The visits were going to stop for the duration of Sylvia Harper's visit to San Francisco. It was the first indication that Angel had that Harper was actually going to stop here.

It didn't bode well. Most of the places she spoke to were war zones.

However, Harper pulled the strings for a potential constituent even though these transports had waiting lists of years. The last shuttle out there was going to be half-empty anyway. The UCLA grad students had other problems at the moment. Conrad had said that Harper had taken remarkably little convincing.

Maybe all politicians weren't necessarily slime.

All she had to do was beat the curfew to the Presidio. That gave her a few hours to play with, and there was something she wanted to do.

She drove a rented Chevy Caldera—the most generic-looking car she could think of, didn't want to attract attention—into the parking lot to St. Luke's. She sat behind the wheel of the car for a good five minutes before she got out.

She didn't know if this was a good idea.

Fuck good idea, Lei was her friend.

Angel got out and walked into the lobby. The place was louder than she remembered, and the blood-smell was leaking into the public parts of the hospital. Angel saw a cop and turned her face away, hoping that the exec suit Mr. K had sent up was enough of a disguise. For most pinks it would be.

The androgyne suit was tailored for a rabbit, and was so incongruous for Angel that it'd probably fool folks that knew her well.

She walked up to the comm directory as if she belonged here and started running the thing through to find Lei's room. Angel felt a little relief when she saw that Lei'd been moved out of intensive care and into a semi-private room on the third floor.

The question was how well the cops—or anyone else—were watching that room.

At least at St. Luke's there was a lot of moreys. In fact, the place was a bit more crowded than she remembered it. The normal security at St. Luke's was pathetic to begin with, and Angel doubted that they'd stop a well-groomed morey in a thousand-dollar suit without being given a pressing reason to do so.

Angel took the elevator up with a pink doctor, a delivery robot, two downcast-looking Pakistani canines, and a rat wearing maintenance overalls. No one paid the slightest attention to her.

Lei's room was two nurses' stations past the elevator, and this was where Angel began to get nervous. Since she'd sidestepped the bureaucracy, she didn't have any right to be here. Angel stiffened her back, straightened her ears, and fixed her eyes on her destination. She tried to exude an odor that she belonged here.

No one at either station challenged her.

She passed a vending area and nearly blew the act when she saw two uniforms and a familiar looking Fedboy—a pale, white-haired guy with reddish eyes. None of them were looking in her direction and Angel managed to recover and finish the walk to room 3250.

As the door closed behind her, she saw Lei on a hospital bed. Lei was in a transparent cast from the waist down, her fur shaved so the massive bruising, abrasions, and the wounds from a compound fracture were dimly visible. Her tail was gone—

"Hello . . ." Lei mumbled, slurring her words slightly.

"Lei," Angel barely had the strength to whisper. "Oh, Christ, Lei."

Lei opened one watery eye and turned her head slightly. " 'sou,

Angel?" She was well drugged up. Angel could almost smell the painkillers wrapping the room like a fog.

She walked up and put her hand on Lei's. Lei's hand was hot and her nose looked dry. "It's me. Angel. I'm so sorry."

"Notchur fault." Lei licked the end of her nose and seemed to focus on Angel. "Nice suit."

"How are you doing?"

"I'll live, maybe walk even."

Angel tried to say something, but nothing came out.

"Thanks for coming. You're a good friend."

Angel leaned over and hugged Lei as best she could.

"Don't cry." Lei said.

"I'm not crying," Angel whispered.

Chapter 23

The helicopter landed at the Presidio right on time. The landing field looked to Angel to be a golf course, of all things. It added just the right touch of surrealism to the whole enterprise. All sorts of construction was going on here.

Conrad had been right about the political climate. Even with the thousand dollar suit, the vestigial briefcase, and special dispensation by a United States senator, it had taken her nearly three hours to wade through representatives of the Fed, military and otherwise. For a while it looked like red tape was going to make her miss the boat out.

That apparently had been the point, and it didn't quite work.

Angel ran up just as the line of academics started boarding the modified Sikorsky transport. The dozen pinks walked into the rear of the transport, Angel the last civilian in the line. As they seated themselves, Army personnel carried in boxes of cargo. To Angel's view, if you compared passengers to the volume of cargo they were shipping to the island, the passengers were incidental.

Angel took a seat to the rear, right up against the cargo webbing. She didn't want to have to explain herself to curious pinks. It worked out, because none of the academics seemed to want to sit next to a nonhuman. There were twenty-five seats for the dozen passengers, so Angel had a few rows to herself.

She spent the time before liftoff looking at the labels visible through the webbing. Most of the crates were identified by an attached ramcard embossed with a serial number. A few had more writing—"MirrorProtein(tm)," for instance. That crate was a fellow

Clevelander. At least, the label showed its origin as a company called NuFood in Cleveland, Ohio. There was another crate that came from a pharmaceutical company in Boston. Around that one hung a vaguely familiar rotten-cherry smell—the Fed was shipping flush to Alcatraz? Angel was pulling the webbing out of the way of another interesting label when she heard a commotion down by the rear of the craft.

"I'm *supposed* to be here, damnit—umph." There was a lot of grunting and shifting of cargo. "Look, here's the pass—now would you stow the crate and let me by?"

Angel wished she could see what was going on back there. A few of the passengers ahead of her probably could, since they were staring down the aisle toward the rear of the craft.

The person who'd been pushing his way through the cargo dropped down in the first seat he came to, which happened to be right next to Angel. He sighed, looked at her with no surprise whatsoever, and said, "No one told me about any curfew."

This new pink was younger than the other pinks in this copter. He beat the average by a decade, Angel guessed. He was clad in blue jeans and a plaid flannel work shirt. He was heavyset, bearded, and wore his long dark hair in a ponytail. He looked like he thought that the potential for urban violence in San Francisco was engineered specifically to inconvenience him.

He held out a hand to her. "Steve," he said.

Angel figured she couldn't avoid it and shook his hand. "Angel."

The out-of-place pink nodded once, abruptly, and unfolded a keyboard and started typing. Angel watched him for a few seconds, and when no more comments seemed forthcoming, turned her attention out what passed for windows on this helicopter. Rain was beading on the exterior of the plexiglass, and her view was confined to the immediate foreground of the abused golf course.

Portable light-towers floodlit an area the size of a half-dozen football fields. The immediate landing area was decked out like a forward deployed air base in some Asian heavy-combat zone. It all had the appearance of having been cobbled together on very short notice—much like what she'd heard about the Alcatraz "conversion" itself.

The dome had been a VanDyne project before the Fed had taken over the company. Angel suspected that it had been an alien habitat long before it was a detention facility.

The loading noises behind her ceased, and she watched a generator truck pull away. Like the helicopter itself, the truck bore no recognizable insignia. It made her reflect that a majority of the people she'd seen around the airfield wore no military uniforms.

The engines began to whine and her neighbor spoke. "What's your specialty?"

She looked over at the bearded pink, Steve, and saw him still working at his keyboard—apparently fascinated by a multicolored sinusoidal display he'd conjured up.

Steve kept talking. "You attached to a university? Myself, I've only met a few nonhumans at the graduate level—talk about having to prove yourself twice over."

Angel nodded and saw the gesture was lost on the man, who was poring over his work. "I can imagine."

Apparently he took her remark as sarcasm. "Damn, I didn't mean to be condescending." He looked up for a moment. "After all, it does show some presence of mind that the ANHA would finally have a nonhuman come and look over the *really* nonhuman. Right?"

"Right." Angel agreed while trying to decipher the initials ANHA—NH was almost always NonHuman in Federalese. Agency for NonHuman Affairs? How come she'd never heard of it? Was it some organ for the NHA Committee in the Senate? If so, it explained how Harper could accommodate her request so readily.

The helicopter started thrumming rhythmically as the rotors engaged and the Sikorsky took off into the night. A few wisps of fog wafted by, whipped into horizontal tornadoes by the downdraft— and suddenly they were clear of the glare from the Presidio.

San Francisco was a ghost town. Angel could see miles of streetlights illuminating empty asphalt. Then the helicopter started turning, giving her views of the park, the Pacific, and finally—as the copter aimed down the bay toward the island—the Golden Gate. Through some trick of the light, the bridge looked like it was drenched in blood.

Oh, she was in a great frame of mind.

"I'm sociology."

"Hmm?" Angel turned away from the bridge and looked at the guy. She didn't know if this guy was continuing some point she hadn't been listening to, or if he had started off on some new tangent.

Angel realized that she'd never answered his original question. She never had enough time to concoct a convincing cover story. If possible, she'd like to avoid the direct questions this guy seemed to be leading up to.

So, even though she couldn't care less, she asked, "You're studying alien society?"

"Only indirectly." He chuckled and looked up from his keyboard. "They classified my thesis, but they didn't have anyone who could understand it. So they hired me." He shrugged.

"You work for the Fed?"

He grinned. "Oh, come on. You all work for them. I don't care what University or think tank you come from, or are you telling me you got the security clearance to be here without any grant money?"

"Ah—" Angel didn't have a response for that since it probably wasn't a good idea to say that she didn't have the security clearance to be here.

He looked a little apologetic, probably misinterpreting her hesitation as anger. "Forgive me, I guess I'm a little too open about who pays the lease on my Ivory Tower."

Angel wanted to change the subject before he asked about *her* ivory tower. "So what are you doing here?"

"Confirming my suspicions on when and where the Race first had a substantial effect on human society."

"So when and where was it?"

"I don't have a very high resolution on my data, but I put it somewhere in January 1998, central Asia."

Angel was shocked. "Wait a minute, you're saying that these things have been on the planet for over sixty years?"

He nodded and went back to the keyboard and his sinusoidal curves.

"How do you know that?"

"Hmm," he stared at the graphs. "What the hell. You've got the clearance or you wouldn't be here." He slid the keyboard over to her lap, apparently so she could appreciate the graphs. "Know any sociology or economics?"

"Not my field." *Make this simple. I wait tables for a living.*

"Okay, I'll try to avoid the jargon. My main work has been on cycles. Economic cycles, battle cycles, cycles in political orientation. Especially their predictive uses."

He tapped a few keys and all the sinusoidal curves were replaced by one jagged sawtooth graph with only a few spikes.

"For example, that is a cumulative index of economic growth over the whole planet for the last century. It looks almost random, but it can be factored out to have a number of regular cycles of differing magnitude." He taped the keys again, and the jagged sawtooth smoothed out into a lazy sine wave whose girth was riddled with a dozen smaller waves all of higher frequency. "Add the values of all those curves for any one year, and you get the same sawtooth you saw before."

"Okay, so? How can this tell you about aliens?"

"Well." He smiled. "Perhaps I should show you this."

A few more taps and another sawtooth graph spread across the screen. "Same cycles, all carried out into this century."

Angel nodded.

"Now, overlay that with the *real* figures for the past fifty-nine years." The green sawtooth was overlaid by a red graph that began in the same place, but diverged radically, skewing downward. By mid-century it had no relation to the green, which seemed almost orderly in comparison. "You can see why any hint of cycles in academia has fallen into disrepute."

"Yes, it doesn't work."

He smiled even wider. "But they do. Given the data for the last century, you can use a sophisticated computer to predict the conditions *backward* an arbitrary distance. It's just a matter of juggling variables and getting a handle on what the individual cycles mean." He made a few taps and the sine waves came back. "For instance, the magnitude and frequency of this curve is an index of the speed of communication in a system." He pointed to a dark blue curve. "That one is based on actual transport of goods." He pointed to a much bigger curve that was a lighter blue.

Angel was beginning to get the guy's point. "You mean that divergence is somehow related to the aliens?"

He nodded. "These cycles represent fundamental processes in human society. A radical change in how they work means one of two things. Human nature changed radically at the turn of the century . . ."

He took the keyboard back.

"Or the Earth was no longer a closed system."

The helicopter was making the final approach to Alcatraz. Angel could see no sign of the old prison. The island was dominated now by the glowing white dome. Around the dome was a cluster of blocky outbuildings that reminded her of the white cinderblock earthquake-relief buildings that peppered the neighborhood south of Market.

"Why'd they classify your work? The aliens aren't a secret anymore."

He shook his head, almost sadly. "You should see it. I came up with the theory and the corrections for it before the aliens were public knowledge. I came up with a model of economic and political projections that worked. Everyone else is using guesswork. I can tell you exactly how the aliens manipulated things, from the Tibetan revolution in '05 to the last congressional election."

"I see."

"I bet you do. And the stuff I'm doing for the Fed right now, predicting elections, recessions, and such, is elementary cribwork compared to what the Race developed."

"How?" The dome was rising up and finally blocked all view out her window.

"They know how to change the numbers. They know what all the variables are and how to manipulate them. They can predict the results of their covert activity."

"That's scary . . ."

"I know," he said as the Sikorsky touched ground. "But it's fascinating."

Chapter 24

Angel was ushered, along with the gaggle of academics, to one of the blocky concrete outbuildings that clustered by the edge of the massive dome. The place was run by a mixture of civilians and military. The military personnel wore a few odd badges on their uniforms. The symbol that seemed to represent the unit here was a picture of a globe overlaid with a lightning bolt.

The group was led down, through a building that housed laboratories and administration offices. As they progressed, Angel was aware of uncomfortable smells that were growing in intensity. Ammonia was the strongest, but it was also tainted by sulfur and other burning chemical smells.

The silent procession had finally reached a point where Angel was sure that they had come to the edge of the dome. They turned a corner and her suspicions were confirmed—

The group had reached some sort of waiting area that butted up against the dome. The ceiling was ten meters above them, and the room was a hundred meters long, at least. With the exception of a massive chromed air lock door that was emblazoned with red and yellow warnings—the entire far wall was a huge window.

Angel took a seat with the rest of the academics without taking her eyes off the window. The window opened up on Hell.

The inside of the dome, past that panoramic window, had to be close to a half-kilometer in diameter. Haze filled its atmosphere; the far side was invisible. A dim red light illuminated a rocky landscape from a point that must have been near the apex of the dome.

Jets of the fire shot out from gaps in the rocks at regular intervals that ranged from two seconds for the small ones, to five minutes for a massive explosion near the window that could have totally immolated the Sikorsky she'd flown here in. There were rivers in there, but Angel found it hard to believe that the viscous black fluid in there was water.

There were *things* in there. Things that rolled, pulsed across the rocks, things with no definite form. They were fluid, undulating creatures. Once or twice she saw one of the smaller ones stray too close to the black river and become snagged by a black tentacle and drawn under. She couldn't tell if it was some aquatic creature that was feeding like that, or if it was the river itself.

The buildings in there were near the center of the dome, and thus barely visible. They resembled nothing so much as termite mounds constructed of rock.

There were humans in there. She saw two walking some sort of patrol around the perimeter, right past the window. They wore full environment suits in desert camo. They seemed to be armed with flamethrowers.

It was Hell. That, or the site of multiple bio/nuke strikes.

She gripped the briefcase tightly and tried to tell herself that she was still on Alcatraz and the view out the window was contained under a concrete dome. It was too easy to imagine that she was looking out, not in, and when she left this building the world out there wouldn't be the Frisco Bay, but some volcanic landscape out of Dante's Inferno.

Steve, the sociologist, was sitting next to her. He seemed to notice her fascination. "Remarkable, isn't it?"

"I'll say."

"First time?"

Angel nodded and tore her gaze away from the boiling netherworld beyond the huge windows.

"I was goggle-eyed, too, the first time I saw that." His hand rose from his computer and waved at the window. "They've managed to recreate the Race's home atmosphere and engineer quite a bit of the ecology. Quite a feat considering we still have no idea *where* their home planet really is."

VanDyne had built this, back when the aliens controlled it. The aliens—the Race—had been making themselves at home. This was far beyond the vidcast warrens that had been unearthed from beneath the Nyogi tower in Manhattan.

What kind of places have they built in Asia, if they've been here for sixty years? Angel could picture entire alien cities. Suddenly,

Merideth's fear of these things didn't seem so calculated. The national mobilization against the alien threat now seemed less politically motivated.

"I thought they were from Alpha Centauri," she whispered.

"The Race that came to Earth almost definitely came from there. It's almost equally certain that they didn't evolve there. They've colonized about eight planets close by, Alpha Centauri just happens to be the closest."

"How do we know that?" Angel looked back at the window. The two humans in the environment suits were heading toward the massive air lock along a nearly invisible path between the rocks.

"A combination of detective work, analysis of the Race's genetics, and a good look at the habitats they built." He shook his head. "Not to mention a little blackmail."

"Blackmail?" The two suited humans stationed themselves on either side of the dome end of the air lock. On Angel's side of the air lock, a pair of marines bearing the lightning-earth insignia stationed themselves opposite the suited pair. The marines were armed with glorified stun rods that they bore like rifles. They stood at parade rest.

"Controlling every aspect of someone's environment can make you very persuasive—here come the interviewees."

The sight of the "interviewees" being herded toward the air lock was the most surreal yet. The double line of aliens, flanked by suited marines, emerged out of the heat shimmering haze by the termite mounds. At first she couldn't make out any details. The first thought to come to mind was three-hundred-kilo slugs. There were two marines for each undulating white form.

As the unearthly parade closed on the air lock, Angel could see that the aliens were highly individualistic in their method of movement. One in front seemed to gather its mass to the rear, and then roll itself forward in a wave before repeating the process. Another one, farther back, extruded a few dozen tentacles the diameter of her forearm and grabbed the ground in front of it, pulling itself along the ground. One actually walked, after a fashion, on a trio of pads that were thicker than Angel's torso. The most disturbing image was the one alien that parodied the humanoid form with two boneless legs and arms. With each step, its flesh rippled like a blister on the verge of bursting wide open.

Angel, as well as a majority of the country, had known that the aliens were some kind of intelligent multicellular amoeba. It was another thing to see a creature that had no set physical form. It was disturbing to see a creature for whom things like its number of limbs was a matter of personal preference. She had been prepared to see a creature that was a kind of amorphous blob. What she saw was a dozen different creatures, each with a definite form, each one different.

The procession reached the other side of the air lock. Above the massive chromed door, a rotating red light started flashing. A klaxon began sounding. After while, the door began opening slowly.

She had almost gotten used to the background smells that permeated this place. As the door opened, she was assaulted by ammonia and sulfur, bile, rotten eggs, and something akin to burning rubber. She started coughing, and her eyes began to water. She could understand why the marines in there had to wear environment suits. Even if there was enough oxygen in there, who'd want to breathe it?

The door finished opening, and two aliens and four marines walked out into the waiting room. The pulsing dead-white slug-things were only a dozen meters from Angel, and she could tell that most of the smell was coming from them. She could hear them, too. They constantly made a shuddering, bubbly sound—like a stomach rumbling, or something much thicker than water that was just reaching its boiling point.

The marines guided the aliens down one of a dozen corridors that branched off the room. Over a PA system, a bored-sounding voice called out two names, and a pair of the academics got up from their seats and followed the aliens.

Just so.

This whole process had happened a lot. Enough times that a set routine had developed. Even the vidcasts that speculated on the nature of the aliens, and on the government's role—usually through voice over video of the massive white dome that dominated Alcatraz—hadn't come close to this.

It was easy, for a while, to forget her own problems and simply watch in awe.

Steve the sociologist left with the second pair of aliens. Even though she found his nonstop talking somewhat irritating, once he left she felt truly alone here. She was the only morey on the island, and the looks she got from the pinks ranged from the disinterest of the marines to outright hostility from most of the university people.

It went slowly. They cycled the air lock for each pair of aliens. It seemed unnecessary, the air lock was big enough to fit the whole parade at once. Angel supposed it was some sort of security measure. Angel began to worry as time went on and the party from the Sikorsky continued to be called up in pairs. Eventually, it left only her—worrying that someone had tagged her as a threat to national security.

Nearly two hours after they started marching aliens through the door, there was only one left and the PA finally called her name.

By now her nose was numbed by the constant stink that leaked through the air lock. As she fell in behind the last two marines and the single remaining alien, her sense of smell reawakened. The smell of bile and ammonia hung around the creature in a cloud. It smelled like nothing so much as urine mixed with fresh vomit. The white latexlike skin seemed to sweat moisture that was slightly more viscous than water. Angel wouldn't want to touch it.

A procession of forklifts and golf carts carried crates from the helicopter through the open air lock. She lost sight of the parade as she followed the last alien down a new corridor.

Now that she was this close to the thing, she began to have second thoughts. This one had taken a hulking slug form, but even though it slid most of its mass along the floor, its midpoint was taller than she was. This one was bigger than most of the ones she had seen. Four hundred kilos of formless rippling flesh.

And she wanted to talk to this thing?

Her walk ended at a large metal door that slid aside for them. The room beyond was a squashed sphere made of some gray alloy. The lights were a dim reddish-green color except for one spotlight that was a normal yellow-white. The spotlight illuminated a human-looking desk and an office chair that seemed of a piece with the rest of the room. Angel could think of no other reason for the bizarre architecture than to make the alien feel at home in the debriefing room.

The alien moved inside and the marines took posts by the sides of the door. "You have two hours, Miss Lopez. Any notes or recordings you make will have to be cleared through base security. If you need to leave the room for any reason, use the intercom in the desk."

Angel nodded, took a deep breath, and followed the alien into the room. She tried not to jump when she heard the door slam shut behind her. She set the briefcase on the desk and sat down on the human style chair. It took her a few minutes to get comfortable. She kept shifting around on the seat until she realized that she was using it as an excuse not to look at the thing that was in the room with her.

Angel looked up and stared at her "Interviewee." It had pooled itself into the lowest part of the room, and had pulled a good part of its mass up to be level with the desk and Angel's eyes. It resembled a weathered cone made of semiliquid ivory.

Now what? How was she supposed to start this? Did these things understand English?

The alien answered for her by asking, "It is new, yes?" The voice was horrid, like a massive bass speaker suspended in crude oil. The voice rippled and bubbled as much as the flesh that created it.

It also sounded vaguely familiar.

"If you're referring to me," Angel said, regaining her composure, "yes, this is my first time here."

"We never are interviewed by nonhumans before."

"I suppose not." Angel realized where she'd heard a similar voice—the mainframe at VanDyne.

"What do we discuss?"

"I'm supposed to talk to someone who was involved with Van-Dyne Industrial."

"Someone?"

"You were involved with VanDyne, right?"

"I am political observer for that corporate unit."

"What the hell does that mean?"

"Do not understand. Your language is difficult."

"What did you do for VanDyne?"

There were a few moments while the creature seemed to digest the question. Angel began to realize that this wasn't going to be easy.

"I watch."

Angel sighed and put her head in her hands. "What do you watch?"

"The politics, the media, the video. I collect data for Octal analysis."

Okay, Angel thought, *I'm talking to a professional couch potato. At least it looks the part.*

She only had a couple of hours to talk to this thing. She'd better start hitting him with what she came here to find out. "You controlled VanDyne, right?"

"The Octal controls all corporate units."

"No, I meant—" Angel shook her head. "Never mind, you answered my question." VanDyne had been an alien enterprise, and this creature had been a part of it. "Did VanDyne employ anything other than—" *What was that name?* "The Race?"

"You are referring to Earth species?"

Angel nodded.

"Race operations are morally bound to employ native species."

"Huh? Run that by me again."

"Direct involvement is anathema. We do not intervene physically."

The bubbling accent was making the creature hard to understand. Angel wasn't sure she'd heard correctly. "You've got to be bullshitting me—"

"Bull shit?"

"—if you semiliquid motherfuckers are responsible for half the shit you've been accused of. There are *riots* out there. . . ." Angel took a few deep breaths. She needed to calm down. Stress and lack of sleep was eating at her nerves. The fact that the ammonia smell from this thing was giving her the first throbs of an oncoming migraine wasn't helping her composure.

"You do not understand. All Race does is rearrange assets to our advantage. Any Race who does more than this is ended. This is law."

Angel wished that the Fed handed out programs with the aliens. Hard enough making sense out of that verbal slurry when she knew what it was talking about. "Okay, let's back up. All you Race do is 'rearrange assets?' "

"We do no harm to sentients—"

"But you fuck with the economy?"

"We analyze the social structure and feed the variables that give us the outcome we desire."

She remembered her talk with Steve the sociologist on the flight out here. These things were running the whole sociopolitical structure of the planet like a giant computer program. According to the sociologists' charts, they'd been doing so since the turn of the century. "What was the outcome you desired?"

"We prevent any social unit from attaining the social, political, or technological inclination to leave its solar system."

Angel thought of what she knew of the history of the past half-century. The implications were staggering. "So what you people do, you buy politicians, right?"

"We fund appropriate people and organizations."

"Terrorists, right?"

The creature was silent for a moment. Then it said, "The fine distinction your language makes between political units is difficult to understand. We fund the appropriate variables to manipulate the political structure."

"Jesus-fucking-Christ, you buy terrorists and you say you don't harm sentients?"

The creature sat there, white, rippling, impassive.

"How many wars are you people responsible for?"

"War?"

Angel stood up on the chair, but she restrained herself from shouting. "Wars. Like the 'rearrangement of assets' in Asia, when Tokyo got nuked—that kind of thing."

"I apologize. Again, the way you discriminate arbitration between political units is difficult to discern. Language is difficult."

"Well, how many 'arbitrations' are your fault?"

"During my Earth operation, I know of no large negotiation between political units unfavorable to the program objective."

Angel sat down very slowly. "You are saying all of—"

"I know no details of the Asian operation. But until we are captured, no major political negotiation ended unfavorably. The assumption is the Asian operation is successful."

"Those 'negotiations' have killed a hundred million people," Angel whispered. Suddenly her problems seemed petty.

It all boils down to the end justifying the means, don't it? That attitude is almost human.

If she had any idea of what to grab, she would have tried to strangle the thing.

She shook her head. No wonder the Fed tried to keep such a lid on these things. This kind of shit would fuck with *everyone's* mind. There were a lot of people out there who wouldn't like to think their glorious war for national whatever was the result of some alien pushing buttons.

The whole Pan-Asian war, an effing "political negotiation." Kinda helped put things in perspective. Against her will, Angel found herself laughing.

"I do not understand," said the creature.

"I suppose you wouldn't. I was just thinking that I should thank you."

"What thanks?"

"Well, if not for you and your buddies, I probably wouldn't exist. If it wasn't for the war boom in genetic engineering—" She shook her head and wondered if the thing she was talking to could even understand the concept of irony. "Back to VanDyne . . ."

"VanDyne," repeated the creature.

"This was what VanDyne was for, right? Shifting assets?"

"Correct."

"What kind of assets?"

"Technological assets. Informational assets—"

"Information?"

"Correct."

"What *kind* of information?"

Chapter 25

Angel took the full two hours with the alien. The attempt to pry comprehensible facts out of the creature was exhausting. It didn't help that she had a constant feeling that, any time after the first fifteen minutes of the conversation, the Fed was going to burst in all over the place and she was going to disappear under a swarm of anonymous Fedboys chanting, "National Security."

She kept feeling that even as the Sikorsky took her and the academics up over the bay.

Somewhere there was a recording of her conversation with the alien. Somewhere a bored security official was reviewing the interviews with the captive aliens. Sometime soon, that official was going to reach the last interview. Angel knew that, fifteen minutes from then, all hell was going to break lose.

Because, once someone actually *looked* at the stuff she'd talked to that blob about, that someone was going to call Washington. When they were told *who* she was—

Her only hope was to get out of the Presidio before that happened.

Information, she'd asked the alien. *What kind?*

The alien's long rambling answer took a long time for her to decipher, but she now knew what Byron Dorset carried for a living.

If anything, that knowledge made things worse.

VanDyne dealt in a lot of things before the Fed took it over. The most important "assets" the Race "moved" from VanDyne Industrial were predictions. Very *specific* predictions.

The Race had stepped a few centuries beyond Steve the sociologist's sinusoidal curves. With their programs and the monster computer they kept at VanDyne, they could give demographic projections for any political unit you could name. They could have projections up to a decade in advance that came within a few points. They could tell you what the economy would look like, what technical areas would be advancing. They could predict the crime rate, the birthrate—everything from beer sales to the number of Masters of Science Degrees in biological engineering that would be awarded in 2077. But the point *wasn't* prediction.

The Race's programs weren't passive. They were dynamic. They knew what "variables" to "feed" to achieve a favorable outcome.

In some cases those outcomes were elections.

Every four years, they were *presidential* elections.

Angel stared out at the sun rising behind Oakland. She had to get out from under the Fed. Even though the security teams controlling Alcatraz only debriefed her to the extent of making sure that she wasn't smuggling out some record of the interview, somewhere—maybe right now—there'd be a review of whatever record the Fed made of her interview.

The magnitude of what Byron had been doing made Angel shudder.

The ramcards she was carrying were a step-by-step formula for a candidate to win the 2060 American presidential election. The way the aliens worked, it was possible, in fact it was likely, that the current head of state, President Merideth, had been a VanDyne client during his last run.

This was heavy shit.

Worse, she could see evidence of it in the current race. Not since the first few decades of the century had there been such a chaotic grab for the presidency. For decades it had been the Democrats and the Constitutionalists and the occasional independent.

This year, candidates were coming out of the woodwork to challenge President Merideth. Third parties—Libertarians, Greens, the NOA party—were actually getting percentages and major vid attention. Even the Republicans were making noises about running a candidate for the first time since the party collapsed in '04.

Maybe the chaos was because this was the first election in six decades that wasn't running according to a program.

It was becoming obvious that President Merideth had a much clearer picture of the "alien threat" than he was letting on in his media crusade. Perhaps it wasn't a coincidence that the takeover of

VanDyne followed so close on the heels of the incident at the Nyogi tower. The aliens became public in January, and within a month VanDyne was captured.

Angel could picture the scene. The government clamps down on the aliens infecting Nyogi, very very publicly. The aliens running VanDyne get nervous and try to use their Holy Grail as a bargaining chip in an election year. It was a decent threat—lay off our people or someone else gets your job.

Merideth was in a bind. The aliens had been blown all over the media. He wouldn't have known the nature of the beings running VanDyne until then. Suddenly he'd was being blackmailed by creatures who didn't have the best interests of the country at heart.

So, to keep his relation with these things secret, and to keep the data out of the hands of his opponents, he stomps VanDyne.

Unfortunately, for all concerned, he stomps it a little late.

Byron was left stranded with the info when VanDyne was raided. The information was already out there and the memory of the big brain at VanDyne was scragged.

What does Byron do?

Angel shook her head. Byron got greedy, that's what he did. Back in February he could have sold the info to whoever VanDyne had slated to get it—probably Alexander Gregg, the Constitutionalist front-runner—and pocketed the whole shebang.

But no, he waited for the field to get muddy out there. There were a dozen credible candidates out there now, with little sign of winnowing a year before the election. It was anarchy at the polls—and Byron tried to auction off the election.

No wonder he got creamed.

That being the case, now what?

She could ditch the cards, wipe them, scrag the data, and let this laughable excuse for democracy continue without outside interference. That might score some spiritual victory, but it would probably get her furry hide nailed to a wall. No one would believe that she'd erased the stuff, least of all the Knights and whoever they worked for—they'd already gotten one blank set of tickets. They would strip her apart until she told them where the *real* set was. The moreaus would probably just kill her out of frustration

Not only that, but she'd lost that option when Mr. K copied the data. Whatever she did with the Earthquakes' tickets in her pocket—the data was still out there.

At least none of the players knew that. Angel hoped they all assumed the encryption would keep her from copying the data. She hoped none of them knew about Mr. K.

No. Everybody believed she had the only set of this crap. So, the only way she had to get out from under this was to consummate the deal with somebody. If the players after her knew the deal was done, they might give up on trying to trash her ass.

She had to sell the shit or she was going to become very dead. She had to hand off this hot potato, and get the hell out of San Francisco.

To whom, though?

Not to the Knights—ever. Not the moreaus either. They were the ones that offed Byron in the first place. Merideth? That was a possibility, but she was afraid right now of being swallowed up in the name of national security. She doubted she could arrange anything with the Fed without quietly disappearing off the face of the Earth afterward.

So what was she going to do?

She pulled out the tickets and watched them glint in the dawn light streaming through the Sikorsky's window. Rainbows shot by the holographic Earthquakes' logo. Again, she damned Byron for handing these off to her. She wondered if the data had always been disguised as these tickets, or if Byron was just playing on her love of the game.

"The Denver game," Angel whispered to herself.

"Tonight, isn't it?" said her neighbor, Steve the sociologist, without looking up from the keyboard in his lap.

"Four p.m. November 16, Hunterdome—"

She had called one set of people the folks from Denver because she figured that Byron had set a meet for that game. Whoever the Denver folks were, they were high up on her list because they hadn't yet managed to stomp her or someone close to her.

It gave her a chance.

Besides, she wanted to see the damn game.

She watched the mutilated golf course grow beneath the Sikorsky. She almost expected a ring of army officers, marines, or cops around the landing area. Something was going to blow—she could feel it.

But nothing seemed amiss at the impromptu air base. She couldn't see anything wrong in the ranks of Sikorskys, air-cranes, and the dozens of aircars. None of the numerous people wandering around below her seemed to be giving much attention to the landing helicopter. As their copter made a turn to approach the landing area, her gaze passed over temporary buildings, warehouses, the gravel lot where she had been directed to park.

She only got a glimpse of the parking lot.

"Excuse me," she said to the sociologist as she stepped over him. She bolted to the other side of the helicopter, feeling the first stirrings of panic. The other side of the helicopter had come about, and now had the parking lot barely in view. Even at a very skewed angle, she could see it.

What the fuck was Byron's BMW doing here?

A lot of the academics had turned to look at her. The sociologist character was telling her she better strap in for the landing.

The BMW meant those moreaus were here. Not on the base— the parking lot was outside the secure perimeter—but somewhere nearby. There were four of them, moreaus, combat strains. They were capable of taking out a fox trained in counterterrorist tactics unarmed.

They probably weren't unarmed now.

Four against one, and all she was armed with was an empty briefcase.

Dust blew by the windows as the Sikorsky landed. There was a thump that almost knocked her over, and the copter was on the ground. She had been gripping the chair so tightly that it hurt her knuckles to let go.

The rotors slowed and came to a stop. She stayed by the windows as the doors opened and the passengers began offloading. Where were they?

She backed away from the window, toward the door. She had no idea what to do. What if they were on the base? *What if they were Fed?*

The gaggle of academics preceded her out into the landing area. According to what she understood about the procedure, a bus would show up, take them to an office out on the base for the final bureaucratic processing before they got sent back to MIT or whatever. The group clustered by the edge of the landing field, waiting for the transport. Most of the uniformed people were back by the Sikorsky. Angel's group rated one plainclothes Fedboy who stood out on the road and looked at his watch a lot.

"The transport will be here in a few moments, gentlemen." He didn't look at them as he said it. However, the smell of his irritation slipped to Angel. She didn't mind the delay. She needed time to think.

She turned in a slow circle, looking at the airfield. Her view passed prefab buildings and helicopters, the ocean and the Golden Gate, and white fog hugging the bay beyond the body of the army base. She thought of making a run for it right then. But there was nothing around the airfield except muddy hillocks and earth-moving vehicles for maybe half a klick in every direction but one—and in that direction was the parking lot where the BMW was. The army boys would catch up with her somewhere out in the mud, and then she'd have to do a lot of explaining.

If the moreaus were Fed, or if the Fed was after her at all, it was obvious that the bureaucracy around Alcatraz and the aliens weren't in on it—yet. There might not be some general alert on her, but all it would take was one bright yahoo on the comm to DC and she'd be in deep shit.

"Don't kid yourself," she muttered, "you're in deep shit right now."

"The bus is coming," said the Fedboy, looking at his watch one last time and stepping out of the road.

Angel watched the bus approach. No, she wouldn't bolt and attract attention to herself. She'd go through the bureaucratic red tape at the office, then she'd disappear. She could jump out a bathroom window or something and make it to the edge of the base on foot. Leave her car in the lot, she could call a cab when she was out on the street.

The bus—a chartered Greyhound that was way too big for the number of people—pulled to a stop in front of the collection of academics. The doors slid open and Fedboy stepped in, waving the bunch into the back. As was the case on the copter, she was the last on board.

She was primed for something to go bad, so when she took one step into the bus she picked up the smell immediately.

"Oh, shit!" She turned to bolt out of the bus, and slammed into the already closing door.

Fedboy took a step toward her. "What?"

She turned back into the bus. The smell was like a dagger into her sinuses. She wanted to yell at the pink; how could he miss it? How could anyone miss it? The driver was on the verge of a panic attack, and over that was animal musk—canine and feline. The heavy smell of an animal on the verge of a kill.

As she turned, she saw a well-concealed arm emerge from the luggage rack above the seat directly behind Fedboy.

"Behind you!" she yelled at him. Too late.

Be the time Fedboy had turned around, the whole creature had vaulted from the luggage rack behind him. He was a canine—no, lupine—moreau, the most savage looking one Angel had ever seen. Lupus stood a full head taller than Fedboy, the top of his head brushing the roof of the bus.

Fedboy reached for his gun.

Lupus backhanded him.

Angel heard the crack as Fedboy's head did a quick 120 degree turn. Blood spattered the window on the far side of the bus from a massive wound on the side of Fedboy's face. He stumbled to his knees in front of Lupus. The wolf raised its arm and brought it straight down on Fedboy's skull.

Fedboy slammed into the aisle between the seats, made one spastic jerk, and was still.

His gun had never left the holster.

Human reaction times were much too slow to deal with a combat-trained moreau. The dozen academics were just beginning to realize something was wrong when Fedboy nose-dived into the rubber anti-skid tracking lining the aisle in the bus. As they turned to see a two-meter-plus wolf snarling over the carcass of the late Fed babysitter, two more moreys popped out from behind seats in the rear of the bus. Angel could barely see them from her vantage point on the steps by the door, but she heard the weapons cock.

From the back she could hear a familiar feline voice. "No one moves, no one breathes, no one says a god-damned thing."

The same cat that'd hijacked her BMW.

She looked up at the driver, and she took in all the things Fedboy had missed—the sweat, the overpowering smell of human fear, and the cat. As Lupus growled over Fedboy's corpse, a feline moreau uncurled herself from around the base of the driver's seat.

The feline's motion was silent, fluid. She arose out of a space much too small for her, as if she was something insubstantial. Angel saw the driver shaking as the spectral cat slipped out from underneath him. "Drive," she said.

There was a sickening lurch as the bus jerked forward.

Angel started to get up from her sprawled position by the door. The cat saw her. Angel suddenly found herself looking down the barrel of an automatic pistol. The cat was shaking her head. "You, of all people, should know better than to move."

The cat almost purred as she said it. Her tail did a slow oscillation as if it didn't make any difference to her if she had to vent the rabbit.

Angel sank back, with her back to the door. "You don't expect to get off the base, do you?"

Noises were coming from the rear of the bus, but she couldn't see that section anymore. Lupus had walked out of her line of sight, and it sounded like he was shoving people into the seats.

The female cat—for the life of her, Angel couldn't place the species—kept the gun trained on her and one clawed hand by the driver's neck. "In half a minute this bus will be very low on the priority list."

There was the sound of a distant roar, like thunder. Then a rattling sound like multiple gunshots and the sound of a cannon firing. The slice of blue Angel could see out the windows became smudged with black.

Sirens began sounding in the distance.

"What the hell—"

The cat produced a rather convincing smile. "The base is under attack, what else?"

The edge of a sign passed in front of one of the windows—they were heading for the Golden Gate bridge.

"Who are you people? *What* are you people?"

"Patriots, Lopez. That's who we are."

It felt like the bus was accelerating. Angel wished she could see where they were going.

"If you knew the full story, Lopez, you'd come with us willingly."

Fucking-a right she would. *Go on,* Angel thought, *tell me another one.* "While you're scragging people left and right? Yeah, *real* willing."

Faster than she thought possible, the cat had crouched over and jammed the pistol under her jaw. "Shut. Up." The cat spat the words.

God damn it, what was she? Angel stared into those leonine eyes and tried to think what country had produced this.

"Shut up and listen," the cat said in a purring whisper. "Unlike you, we never stopped serving the country that birthed us. And you're going to help us save it."

Angel stared into the feline's eyes and began to make the connection. "UABT," she whispered.

United American Bio-Technologies was the company the government seized for violating the constitutional ban on macro gene-engineering. The Fed wasn't supposed to be involved in the kind of experiments that produced moreaus. Engineering, especially on sentients, was very very illegal in the United States.

But the cougar eyes Angel was looking at right now, as well as the Canis Lupus that had scragged the Fedboy were both very very American. These moreys were Fed. And whatever project had produced them was very black indeed.

The cat seemed pleased with Angel's realization. "All we want is the information. Tell us where it is and this will all be over."

What the fuck could she do? She was backed into a corner, gun at her throat, back to the . . .

Angel shrank into the stairwell, wedging herself in as small a space as possible. Her feet were flat against the front of the first step. If it wasn't for that damn gun in her neck. "Don't be a fool like that vulpine bastard. Tell us."

Angel glanced up at the driver. He was sweating, and he kept glancing down toward the two of them. The bus was slowing and she could smell the fear building in the man.

Then Angel saw her briefcase, where she'd dropped it. It was by the feet of the dead Fedboy. "The briefcase, in the briefcase."

If the cougar would just stand up and get the case.

No such luck. She didn't even take her eyes off Angel as she called, "Ironwalker!"

Lupus came back into Angel's line of sight, stepped over the corpse of Fedboy, and picked up the briefcase. *Oh, well,* Angel thought, *it had been a good try.*

The brakes hissed and the bus slowed to a stop.

The cougar stood bolt upright, turned, and leveled the gun on the driver. *"Why are we stopped?"*

Angel didn't need more of an excuse. She pushed as hard as she could with her legs, and the door gave behind her.

Chapter 26

The door opened more easily than Angel had expected it to.

The kick that forced open the door of the bus shot her out over the neighboring lane. As she was in the air in the middle of the lane, she heard the screech of brakes and the sound of a deep-throated truck horn as the biggest cargo hauler Angel had ever seen bore down on her.

Cougar, back in the bus, fired in her direction. Angel could barely hear the shots over the sound of the truck closing on her. The bus door swung shut again and its window exploded outward with Cougar's gunfire.

Adrenaline shot a spike into her skull and the pulse rushing in her ears competed with the truck horn in volume. She spent an eternity hovering over the asphalt, and she was afraid that the truck's sloping chrome bumper was going to splat her before she even touched the ground.

Even as the thought crossed her mind, her shoulder slammed into the concrete. She pumped with her legs and rolled. The truck was so close she could smell the grease on the transformers. She rolled out of the way as fast as she could, not looking at the truck. She didn't want to know how close it was.

She felt a breeze, smelled melting rubber, and heard the siren of a half-dozen locked disc brakes right next to her. She didn't have to open her eyes to feel the mass of the truck's cab shooting by her. She rolled once more, away from the truck, and made it to her feet.

Angel finally saw where she was when she got to her feet and began running.

She was bolting along the breakdown lane of the Golden Gate Bridge Freeway, maybe a hundred meters from the toll booths. Between her and the bus were three trailers' worth of Biosphere Products' algae derivatives. The tankers had come to a halt next to her, giving her some cover.

The sound of more gunfire behind her encouraged Angel to run even faster.

Fight-or-flight had kicked in big-time. Every cell in her body was screaming for her to get out of there. Her breath felt like a blast furnace in her throat. The world seemed cloaked in a bloody haze, but her senses seemed to be honed to a monomolecular edge.

Her body ran on autopilot while her conscious mind grappled with how she was supposed to get out of this. Where the hell could she go? In a few seconds one of those moreaus was going to round the end of this algae tanker.

Not even one second.

Angel heard Cougar pounce out behind her before the cat started shooting. Angel dived between the two trailing tankers as the machine pistol started barking. The shots missed her, but a few of them punched into the tanker she hid behind. There was a gurgling sound, and a sour vegetable odor began to permeate the area. Below the joint she was straddling, a pool of blackish-green ooze began to spread.

She only had a few seconds before the cat was on her. Angel bolted up the ladder to the top of the tanker.

She pulled herself on top of the tanker just in time to avoid another round of fire in her direction. There was the sound of more bullets clunking home and an even thicker algae smell this time. The adrenaline spike in her head rang with a supersonic thrum. The taste of copper in her mouth throbbed in time to her pulse. Her nose was on fire from her own breath.

She reached the opposite end of the tanker in two jumps, vaulting three hatches.

The shots were getting closer, and they were coming from more than one direction now. Below her, the tanker was bleeding algae like an alien behemoth.

At the end of the tanker she had a split-second decision to make. Behind her, Cougar was following her up, and she saw Lupus heading for the side of the first tanker. Instead of jumping to the next tanker and trapping herself, she jumped across—

To the roof of the bus.

In the air, she was already trying to think of where to go from there.

She landed on the bus, and the moreys inside started shooting. Gunfire began slicing through the roof toward her. She ran down the length of the bus, bullet holes erupting in her path. She reached the front of the bus and leaped, blind, into the next lane.

She landed, badly, on a slow-moving Dodge Electronline van. She had to grab an antenna to keep from rolling off the front, especially when the remote-driven program laid on the brakes.

Angel could see the toll area now. It was obvious that the folks down there knew something was up. Northbound traffic had all but ceased, and she could see a patrol car, flashers going, rolling down the breakdown lane toward them.

She had sat still too long. A bullet planted itself into the van's roof perilously close to her head. The Electroline began rhythmically sounding its horn as its antitheft alarm went off. It sounded like a wounded animal.

She leapfrogged two stationary cars until she had reached the median. Southbound traffic was still moving. She sat as long as she dared, and then she jumped across the median toward a mid-sized automated delivery truck. The truck was a moving target, and she needed to avoid the collision sensors in the front and the rear.

She misjudged the height and hit the side of the trailer, broadside. She'd missed the collision detectors—the truck was still moving—but she barely had a grip on the top of the truck.

Holes started blowing in the side of the trailer, all around her.

Even when hyped up for combat, one of the lepus deficiencies was pitiful upper body strength. She pulled as hard as she could, but her arms weren't strong enough to pull her up the sheer side of the trailer.

Panic spread through her like a fever as more bullets slammed into the side of the trailer. She began kicking like mad, desperately searching for some purchase on the smooth side of the truck.

Her right toe found something and she thrust herself up. Even as the jagged edge sliced into her foot, she knew that she had found a large bullet hole.

The push landed her half on the top of the thing, her ass hanging out over the side. She had to scramble like mad to get a foothold before her grip slipped. Her feet slid around in a smear of blood before she anchored herself on top of the trailer.

Even as she fought like mad to avoid becoming street-pizza, she had the satisfaction of seeing the two moreys on top of the tanker beat a retreat from the advancing patrol car.

She managed to hang on until it made the off-ramp.

When it came right down to it, the way things were going, she should have expected the scene that greeted her. The autocab wove its way through Chinatown but never made it to the address she gave it because Post Street was roadblocked above Grant.

Cops were out in force, as were at least twice as many unmarked sedans. Suited men in sunglasses spoke into small radios and sported stubby—but nasty-looking—automatic weapons. Two utility vans were parked behind this forest of lawful authority, right in front of that post-modern chromed-Asian monstrosity that Kaji Tetsami called home.

The cab idled and waited for her to punch in an alternate destination.

She stood on the seat and watched Mr. K's quasi-legal organization collapse. She watched it for close to ten minutes. It was overwhelming. Suited agents came and went from the building. A few remained stationed next to the utility people. Some sort of argument was going on over there. One of the utility people was gesturing violently, waving a clipboard computer for emphasis.

The other utility people got out the sawhorses and the little flashing yellow lights and sectioned off an area in the middle of the intersection of Post and Kearny. When they got out the jackhammer, Angel could figure out what they were doing and decided she didn't want to see any more.

She told the autocab to take her to the nearest available hotel. Since this was San Francisco, that only took half a minute. Most of that was the cab backing and turning around the mini traffic jam the roadblocks had caused.

Not caring much about carrying cash, or computer records, or much of anything else, she stopped at a bank kiosk and downloaded two grand of Byron's money. The desk at the Chancellor was run by a human, not a computer, and the man had enough reserve not to blink much when she demanded to pay cash for one room for one night. It didn't really matter much to Angel that the hotel was going to have a hard time forgetting her. All the subterfuge was getting to be a little too much for her.

When they handed her a stylus and requested she sign the electronic register, she signed it, "John Smith."

She got to the room, locked the door, and collapsed on the bed.

"May you rot in Hell, Byron."

Mr. K, her only ally in this, had just gone under, leaving her very much alone.

Angel stayed in bed a long time, staring at the ceiling and shaking. She was exhausted, but she was too keyed up to relax. She let her mind run around in circles. It was noon before she felt calm enough to do a few of the things she needed to do.

The first thing she did was call DeGarmo, the lawyer. Of course he wasn't at the office on Sunday, but he'd done her the service of putting her on his comm's short list of calls that could be forwarded.

His home comm barely buzzed once. "Miss Lopez, Angel—are you all right?"

Angel laughed because there was no other socially acceptable way to react to the question. "I'm alive."

"The police—"

"—are looking for me, right?"

DeGarmo nodded. "A Detective White, in particular."

"Well, hold off telling them where I am for a while—"

"I'll respect that, but I have to advise you—"

"Skip the advice, I need you to do a few things for me."

"Like?"

Angel felt a strange sense of finality. She hesitated a few seconds before she spoke. "Byron's ashes—" she sucked in a breath.

"Yes? I have them, I've been waiting for—"

"You handle the arrangements. Dump them, bury them. I don't care. Just invite all those other heirs of his."

"Are you sure?"

Angel closed her eyes and nodded. "I don't want any part of it."

"Is that it?"

"No, my roommate—her name's Lei Nuygen—is in St. Luke's Veterinary Hospital. I want you to take care of her medical expenses. Surgery, medicine, rehabilitation, all of it."

He nodded again.

"Last, I need you to transfer my money—" Angel brought out the black ramcard Tetsami had given her. "It's a bank in Zurich . . ."

After she had talked to DeGarmo, she called Frisco International and reserved a seat on the midnight ballistic to Toronto. Toronto was a nice place since it was out of the country and she could swing it without a passport. In Toronto she figured she had enough grease to pull out some sort of ID arrangement, legal or not, that could get her a lot farther.

She had committed herself. She was getting the hell out.

She pulled out her tickets and looked at them. The game with Denver was in three hours. She had box seats near the fifty yard line. She wondered if it was a good idea to go. She could try and lay low until the flight. But she knew that if she didn't ditch Byron's data, she'd be looking over her shoulder all the time. If she was lucky, everyone would still think she had the only copy—after Mr K's organization collapsed she just might—and once she handed it off, no one would have a reason to hound her.

Or at least no reason to hound her to another continent.

If she didn't give up the data, she'd be crazy or dead long before the election.

At three, another autocab dropped her off at Hunter's Point Boulevard. It wasn't because she wanted to walk a few kilometers to the stadium, but because of the godawful traffic that was clogging the whole Bayview area.

She walked along the side of the road and looked at the cars. Kilometers worth of road were lined with moreaus packed into vans, pickups, and old Latin American land-yachts. One baby-shit brown pickup with particleboard walls on the bed must have been carrying at least a dozen rodents. The smell of alcohol was as thick as the smell of excitement. The Earthquakes' white and blue thunderbolt logo was flying on flags, plastered on cars, on windows— she even saw one jaguar who'd dyed the fur on his chest.

There was the normal whooping, calling, and carrying on. Like every big game.

But it *wasn't* like every big game.

As she walked along the side of the traffic jam, making better time than the cars, she could see signs of the tension that was hanging just below the revelry. It wasn't just the fact that the fans were louder and more raucous than usual. More than once she heard something break in the distance. Quite a few things were getting tossed on the sidewalk—empty drink bulbs, toilet paper, food, clothing, and, in one case she saw, even a passenger.

It wasn't just that there were twice as many cops directing traffic as there'd be for a regular game, or that, while the cops on the street were normally attired, the ones in the idling patrol cars wore full riot gear. It wasn't just the two SWAT vans she saw.

It wasn't the dozen or so newsvid aircars that hovered over Hunter's Point like locusts over a field of grain.

The clearest sign that something different and very wrong was

oing on was with the pink fans. Nonhuman football had as many
uman fans as moreys, and it was human money that really sup-
orted it. Maybe half the take at the Hunterdome gate was normally
rom the human spectators.

In the mile of traffic she walked by on her way to the Hunter-
ome, she saw three human-occupied cars. In each case, there was
o reveling fan inside. Each human driver had locked the doors and
ealed up his vehicle like a tank going into a war zone.

On each driver's face was an expression that said, "This is not a
ood idea."

If anything, the proportion of human fans decreased as she ap-
roached the Hunterdome. The dome itself looked like the upper
hird of a gloss-black bowling ball. Angel approached it as just an-
ther one of the thousands of fur-bearing people who were clogging
he parking lot.

A half-hour before game time, just as she was nearing the gate,
he surface of the dome activated. Predictably, it was for a beer
ommercial. Outside, the dome was a giant display ad, inside it was
he single biggest holo screen on the West Coast.

She entered the gate as, above her, a twenty-meter-tall tiger was
icking back some brew bigger than she was.

For a half second she almost panicked when her card was passed
hrough the meter. After all the fiddling that had been done to it,
vould it read properly? Would the reader fuck with the data that
veryone was knocking themselves out to get?

It was only a moment, though, and then the young canine who
ead the ticket directed her up and to the left.

She passed a refreshment stand—the lines were long enough so
he people near the end would probably miss the whole first quar-
er. She decided not to get something to eat. The air was ripe with
ot dog, and cooking meat made her queasy.

Despite the crowd, when she broke out into the stands, she could
ell that it wasn't going to be a sellout. She could see it in the stands
s she made her way down to the fifty yard line. Way too many
mpty seats for this important a game. She had a feeling that each
mpty seat represented a human season ticket holder.

So, she was in shock when she got down to her seat and found
human sitting in it. A human she knew.

For a second time that week she asked Detective Kobe Anaka,
What the fuck are *you* doing here?"

Chapter 27

For an instant, Angel wanted to run. Just start running blindly and never stop. But her feet remained rooted to the aisle well past the point when her panic faded and she could think.

"What the fuck are you doing here?" she asked again. She was sick of surprises, sick of being caught off guard.

Anaka moved over a seat and gestured for her to sit down next to him. "You seem to forget, I'm the one who returned those tickets to you."

"Oh, yeah." Briefly, she felt really silly. She was getting as paranoid as everyone accused Anaka of being. "How'd you know I'd be at the game?"

"I didn't." Anaka shrugged. "Seemed likely, considering the emphasis the letter put on it."

"You read—" she clamped down on the self-righteous question. Of course he'd read it, how else would he have known who to return it to? "Why'd you come here?"

"I don't know . . ." Angel bent over and got a good look at him. He was in sad shape. His eyes were bloodshot. The suit he wore was different, but just as rumpled as the last one she saw him in. Even over the pungent odors of hot dogs, beer, and ten thousand moreaus, she could tell he hadn't been anywhere near a shower in days. His face seemed thinner, his chin shadowed, and his movements had the deliberate quality of someone who knew he was on the verge of collapse. He stared up at her and there was a pleading look in his eyes. "Come in, Angel, to the station with me."

Angel looked at him coldly. "Fuck you, Anaka. I've already tried to do that once."

Anaka turned and rested his forehead against the seat in front of him. It was so long before he responded that she thought he had fallen asleep. Meanwhile the PA system blared, "Welcome to the Hunterdome and Earthquakes' football."

During the applause, Anaka said, "I don't know what else to do."

Angel barely heard him. The motto of the Earthquakes was that they'd "make the ground *shake*," and the bass speakers of the dome's sound system did a good job of making everything vibrate. A minor 2 to 4 quake could hit right now and no one would notice. Those who did would probably put it down to a special effect.

"You have to help me—"

"Help you what?"

"Stop them!" Anaka was shaking, and it wasn't just the noise level in the dome.

Above them, over the field, the massive holo was firing up. Ten-meter-tall armored moreys went through their ritualized violence up there on virtual turf. It then began feeding in the net simulcast.

"You're the only one," Anaka said, "who *knows*. Who isn't a part of this."

Angel put a hand on his shoulder. How the hell could she tell him that she'd given up fighting, that the best thing she was hoping for was a clean exit. "You need some rest—"

He shook free of her grasp. "How the hell can you say that?"

"Anaka—"

"After all this, I'd think *you'd* understand."

Angel got a prickly feeling at the back of her neck. The feeling that something had gone terribly wrong. Anaka was on the verge of hysteria. Something bad had happened.

She put a hand back on his shoulder as the teams began to take the field. While the announcer went through the roster and the holo threw up stats in all their three-dimensional graphic glory. "Tell me what happened."

He looked at her sideways through half-closed eyes. "Oh, you know. You probably always knew. It was your lover that started all this.

"Cut the crap and tell me what happened after that goddamned shootout!" Her own voice now held a note of panic and desperation, and perhaps that cut through to Anaka.

"Okay." Anaka even chuckled a little, a sound that frightened Angel almost as much as the look in his eyes. "What happened."

He looked out into space, as if he were studying the graph of Al Shaheid's past performance quarterbacking for the Denver Mavericks.

When the Mavericks won the coin toss, Anaka repeated, "What happened?" as if he was asking himself the same question.

"After you left me," Angel prompted.

He nodded. "Had to redo everything. Surveil VanDyne from a distance. Oh, God, I wish they'd found my tap—"

"They didn't?"

"A passive, noninvasive, optical sensor next to one of their trunk lines. I think it was too simple for them to find." He shook his head. "Kept monitoring police air traffic. That's how I found out how Pat Ellis died—"

"Doctor Ellis?" The name felt like a hand clutching her chest. That poor dumpy pink woman, the woman who was so afraid.

"—car was found in a ravine up in the San Bruno Mountains. Been there since Sunday. An 'accident.' They ran her off the road."

Chalk another one up for the feline hit squad. It sounded like their style. Even though she was pretty sure that was the case, she asked Anaka "Who?"

"The same people who told her to burn Byron Dorset's body, who put the wrong person in charge of the autopsy." He looked at her as if all this was obvious. "That was two—no, three days ago." He looked at his watch.

The Mavericks got the first down. It looked like the beginning of a drive, and the crowd didn't like it.

Anaka was still looking at his watch.

Angel shook his arm. "Then what?"

"Seems much longer . . ." He looked up from the watch, seeming very weary. It was then that Angel noticed Anaka's pants for the first time. They were stained, still wet in some places. Angel leaned over, and finally, through the hundreds of overlapping odors, she could make out the smell of blood.

"What—" she started, but Anaka was back into his story.

"Kept hearing White over the radio. Knights this, Knights that. He had two dozen skinheads in jail when you were kidnapped. He rounded up the rest afterward." There was a sad expression on his face. "He really was a good cop, before they got to him."

Angel looked up at Anaka. Her hackles felt like spikes on the back of her neck. Something very, very bad was happening—had happened.

"*Who* got to White?"

"The aliens, of course."

A chill traced icy talons down her back and stabbed itself into her gut.

Below, the Earthquakes had halted the drive short of a touchdown and progress was going in the other direction. The crowd was on the verge of a standing ovation every time the Earthquakes' canine quarterback, Sergei Nazarbaev made a first down.

"What happened to White?" she asked after three plays, afraid of the answer.

Anaka jerked like he had forgotten they were having this conversation. "He's dead," he said, sounding a little surprised, like it was a newly-discovered fact. "Damn shame, he was a good cop. Before they got to him."

"How—" she stared, but Anaka went on as if there hadn't been a pause in their conversation.

"I was so stupid," Anaka slammed his fist on the top of the chair ahead of him. Fortunately, it wasn't occupied. Angel saw the blow draw blood, but Anaka seemed oblivious. "I saw all the communications to Alcatraz. But I didn't really see anything until that damned computer called *you*."

"Yesterday," she said. It was already ages ago.

"The signal burst through and overloaded the tap. Even though it wasn't encrypted, I only got a few bits of what it said."

Anaka lapsed into another silence. Angel didn't prompt him. She was afraid of what he might say. She kept telling herself that it wasn't what she was thinking, there was a better explanation.

But she kept looking at Anaka, at the blood on his pants, his shaking hands, the dead glassy eyes—*No,* she said to herself, *not that.*

The Earthquakes' drive was stopped, and the score was tied with a field goal apiece.

"What did you get?"

"Huh?" Anaka looked at her.

"The tap, what did you get when you tapped—"

"Oh." He wiped his forehead with the hand he'd struck the seat with. It left a trail of blood on his face, and he looked at it with an expression of surprise. "Sorry, I've been a little distracted."

A little?

"I saw enough of what that machine said. And suddenly, it all made sense to me—"

Makes one of us, Angel thought.

"All this time I thought it was human corruption. Graft, bribery, organized crime, big money . . ." Anaka smiled at her. The smile scared Angel more than if he'd leveled a gun at her. "It was a revelation. The aliens. They were behind everything!"

Angel nodded slowly.

"I was on the cusp of this when White called me and said that one of the Knights had finally broken. I knew that I had been vindicated. VanDyne would come tumbling down, and the evil things controlling the government would be unmasked. Alcatraz isn't a prison—*it's a control center.*"

He's gone nuts. Fully around the bend. Angel sat back and could barely say what she was thinking. "You said White was dead."

Her voice was a whisper, and she had no idea whether Anaka had heard her. He went on. "I was wrong about White. They had gotten to him before I did. When I got to him, I could see how those things could manipulate the minds of their victims. He kept on about how one of the Knights had rolled over on Alexander Gregg's campaign manager. He didn't see the big picture at all—and his eyes—oh, God, it was his eyes. It wasn't White in there anymore."

"You said White was dead." Angel repeated, loud enough for Anaka to hear.

"*All of them.* The whole department was gone. They tried to keep me from leaving, but I had to get out. I couldn't let them do to me what they did to White." He looked down at his pants and rubbed one of the nearly invisible spots of blood. It was still damp, and Angel saw his finger come away wet. Angel focused on a hair that adhered to the blood. It was short, gray, and tipped with a tiny glob of what could have been flesh or clotted blood. "He looked so surprised. It was the hardest thing I ever did."

"Oh, God." The shudder in her voice reached all the way into her diaphragm. This had pushed Anaka over the edge, all the way over. This had all come too close to his own paranoid nightmares, and it had burst his little reality dam. She could see one thing, anything, setting him off, making him decide that *she* was one of them.

She stood up and began sliding away from him. She needed to find a cop. The police had to be busting their asses to find Anaka. He was oblivious, studying the hair that was glued to his finger.

Keep staring, she thought. *Stare until we get a hold of a white jacket in your size—and maybe some Thorazine.*

She was so intent on Anaka that she backed into somebody.

As Angel turned, she got an intense feeling of déjà vu.

She'd bumped into a pale pink who looked like a Fed, down to the barely concealed throat-mike. A pink with a nearly transparent white crew cut and red irises. She was looking at the same pink she had bumped into in Frisco General, the same pink who'd been pointing a vid unit at her house, the same pink she'd avoided to visit Lei at St. Luke's. The same two meters of suit punctuated by the bulge of artillery under his arm.

"I apologize for my tardiness, Miss Lopez."

The albino Fedboy was the guy from Denver.

Behind him were two more expressionless pinks in way too expensive suits.

"Ah, uh—" What the fuck was she supposed to do now?

"I am glad that you came. There was a feeling in the organization that you wouldn't honor Dorset's commitments."

Damn it all, this was why she was here! She wanted to scream at them that there was a crazy man behind her, three seats away. She wanted to move out of here, get this over with, but the albino pink was blocking the way back to the aisle. *"Can we do this somewhere else?"* Angel said in a harsh whisper, looking back at Anaka to make sure he was still occupied.

Anaka was looking at the game, the back and forth between two tied teams.

"We prefer a public place, as did Mr. Dorset. Too much potential for violence." He smiled. "It's best if neither of us are concerned."

I'm concerned right now, you twit, she thought. What did they think she was going to do?

"Let's get this over with, then."

Whitey nodded, took out a small computer, and slipped a ramcard into it. He tapped it a few times and showed her the display. It was a measure of her self-control that she didn't gasp at the amount. The number just didn't register, except that it had more than six zeros and no decimal point.

Angel nodded and reached into her pocket for the tickets.

Behind her she heard Anaka scream, "THEY'RE HERE!"

Angel could feel the world begin to tumble into slow motion. Anaka's manic cry went out and seeded something in the crowd around them. Angel saw the moreaus—scattered thinly in the expensive box seats—around them start turning in their direction.

Whitey stepped back, withdrawing the hand comm. The two

suits behind him in the aisle were shoving their hands into their jackets. She turned around to face Anaka, her gaze sweeping past the field.

A cheer was rising in the whole dome. There'd been some kind of turnover near the Mavericks' end zone and Sergei was running down the sidelines with the ball. Throughout the dome the chant was, "Sergei. Sergei. Sergei."

The chant around Angel was, "He's got a gun."

The moreys were already scrambling away, over the seats and each other. Before Angel had turned completely around, Anaka had tackled her from behind, grabbing her around the chest and running at Whitey like Sergei was running the nearly eighty yards to his own end zone.

"Sergei. Sergei. Sergei."

Whitey stepped back, stumbling. Whitey's red eyes glared at Anaka, who must've looked the crazy-man part. The two suits had pulled their weapons, matte-black automatics, and leveled them toward Anaka.

Anaka was using her as a shield. "You're not going to take me!"

"Sergei. Sergei. Sergei."

Anaka had one arm around her chest, the other one shook a huge chromed automatic at the suits. She recognized the weapon as a well-kept antique Desert Eagle—a handheld Israeli fifty-cal cannon.

Her feet didn't quite brush the ground, and her leverage sucked, but she drew up her legs and kicked backward as hard as she could manage.

Tailored for a grand or not, her pants split right up the middle, and she felt her feet make contact right above Anaka's knees.

"Ser-gei. Ser-gei. Ser-gei."

Anaka let go immediately, and she heard the gun discharge. The explosion deafened her and she could barely hear the screams over the ringing. She landed, rolled past the suits, and ended up facing toward the apex of the dome in time to see the most horrifying thing she had ever witnessed.

It was impossible, so it had to be shock, or temporary deafness, but the world was silent except for her heartbeat and her breathing—more felt than heard. Above her, the holo was going, the live net feed that was being simulcast cross-country. It was on a delay, so she was seeing action on the field five seconds in the past.

Sergei was home free. He was running down the sideline; the nearest Maverick was twenty meters away. He ran like a being possessed, faster than Angel had ever seen him, or any other morey move. His head was down, tongue lolling through the face mask, tail streaming behind him, clutching the ball to his side. He had already run forty yards. He had just crossed the fifty yard line. Nothing could stop him.

Then, in the midst of his triumph, Sergei's shoulder exploded. The expression of canine triumph turned into a grimace as he tripped. His hand went to his spraying shoulder, the forgotten football tumbling on his forty yard line.

Sergei fell, facefirst, into the thirty-eight yard line. He skidded on a slick of his own blood. He stayed there, motionless, still clutching his shoulder, the bloody football within arm's reach.

It was only then that some goober in the booth decided it would be a good idea to cut the holo picture and the feed to the net. Even as the holo blinked out, leaving only the silvered underside of the Dome, Angel realized that it was much too late.

Chapter 28

The silence was broken by more gunfire. Angel pulled herself to her feet. Up the aisle, she saw Anaka take one in the chest. He hadn't moved or taken cover. A flower of blood drenched the front of his rumpled suit, and he was down.

One of the suits had taken a fifty-cal shot just below the knee. He was on the ground, trying to hold onto his leg and keep from bleeding to death. The other suit was cautiously advancing on Anaka, gun out. In any other situation, keeping an eye solidly on Anaka would have been a good idea.

Of all three of them, Whitey seemed to be the only one who realized where they were. The dome was enveloped in a stunned silence, and the quartet of humans were surrounded by a ring of staring moreaus.

Angel heard the growls begin.

Whitey was subvocalizing to his nearly invisible throat-mike. The only two words Angel could make out at this distance were ". . . big problem . . ."

Angel could smell the moreys who ringed the trio. Fear, confusion anger . . . It was as bad, worse, than the scents she'd picked up at the prison. The moreaus were a solid wall of fur, arrayed in a semicircle with the open end to the field. The moreys blocked any exit into the stands.

The growling was getting louder, and the huge ursine that blocked the aisle opposite the humans from Angel was clenching his hands into fists the size of her head.

Behind her was a railing, and a five-meter drop to the sidelines.

Over the PA the announcer was repeatedly asking the audience to return to their seats and stay there. They needed to let the police through. Angel didn't know if it was directed at this area specifically, or the whole stadium.

Whitey nodded a few times, then he walked up to the safely disarmed Anaka and raised his hands. "It's all right. We got him. If—"

It was the last thing he ever said. A seat ripped from the stands scythed out of the crowd and slammed into Whitey's throat. Angel had no idea where it came from.

The suit next to Anaka's body did the worst thing he could possibly have done, considering the circumstances. He began firing into the crowd.

Angel jumped over the railing as the crowd dissolved into a tidal wave of teeth, fur, and claws. She heard three gunshots as she vaulted onto the field. Glancing over her shoulder, her last sight of the area was that massive ursine—the crowd breaking upon and around him as if he was a crag of rock—holding aloft a bludgeon that looked an awful lot like a very pale human arm.

She hit the ground badly and stumbled a few meters. But suddenly she was clear of people. The sidelines here should have been crowded with people—the team, the vids, the staff, play officials—but the mass of people had been drawn to a circle centering on a spot near the forty yard line. A circle ringed by a dozen security people, all pinks. That must have been the entire security staff on the field, because no one made a move toward Angel.

She looked downfield and saw the teams. They were standing around the Mavericks' twenty yard line, their position in life reversed. They stood and watched the chaos that had erupted in the stands.

She backed away from the stands as if she avoided something alive. Her hearing was coming back. There was a growling rumble that outdid the bass speakers on the PA system. The rumble was punctuated by vicious carnivore screams—yowling, barking, roaring. The crowd had swirled into vortices around the few humans occupying the stands. Spectators, security, vendors, it didn't seem to matter.

She smelled smoke, and saw a licking of flames by the Earthquakes' end zone.

"It's the end of the fucking world," Angel whispered.

The announcer on the PA sounded frantic, pleading.

A speaker was torn from its mount and landed in the field. Other people began jumping to the sidelines. It was the only escape open from the mob, and a wave of fur began to pour over the railings. It was most violent by the Earthquakes' end zone, where the fire was.

That seemed to break the paralysis on the field. The teams by the Mavericks' twenty yard line bolted off to the nearest exit, behind the end zone. The crowd near Sergei moved, as a unit, off to the sidelines—and another exit. All they left behind was a bloodstain and a football.

The PA was now telling a mob that was beyond caring that Sergei was not seriously hurt.

Angel ran to the crowd around Sergei, intending to follow them out of the dome, but one of the security goons leveled a gun at her. She veered off. She was left near the center of the dome, standing by a blood-soaked football. Around her, the stands were a chaotic mess. The mob was pouring out onto the field, she could no longer even see the crowd surrounding Sergei to tell if they made it off the field.

All she saw now was a mad rush for the exists.

Most sane people had the same thought she did—get the fuck out of here.

The stands were now vast lots of empty seats punctuated by knots of moreaus trying to crawl over each other. The field itself was becoming swamped, and in a few seconds she would be over-run by the mob.

The sound was horrible. Screaming, roaring, yelping—the cries of pain and fear were drowning out the pinpoints of rage.

There was nowhere for her to run to that didn't thrust her into the heart of a terrified murderous mob. She whipped her head back and forth, hurting her ears, looking for anywhere that the masses of people were thin enough to break through—

The fire.

Even as she looked downfield to the burning section of the dome, people began rushing by her, jostling her. A jaguar bearing a red plastic box seat like a trophy nearly toppled her.

Angel ran toward the Earthquakes' end zone. It was insane to run toward the fire, but that part of the stands had emptied out al-most entirely, and the press of moreys on the field between her and there was relatively thin.

She ran, dodging panicked canines, jumping over collapsed rats, running as if she was completing Sergei's touchdown drive.

When she reached the end zone, it was raining. The dome's fire-control systems were trying to stop the blaze. It didn't seem to be

doing too much good. Her eyes were watering from the plastic
smoke that billowed from the burning seats. Between the fire
alarms, and the roaring of the fire itself, she couldn't hear the riot
going on around her.

What had been a licking of flame from the forty yard line was
an entire section of the stands going up.

No wonder she was the only one near here.

She ran for the exit behind the Earthquakes' end zone, holding
her breath because of the smoke, stepped over a black ratboy with
a crushed skull, and made for the corridor that led out of the
damned dome.

If the Hunterdome had gone straight to Hell, it was only the
first circle. When she made it out to the parking lot, the sky was already blackening with smoke. It seemed that half the cars were
burning. She could hear the sound of breaking glass, sirens, and
automatic weapons fire.

The scene immediately around her was surrealistically free of
people. Ranks of cars marched away into a hazy pall of gray smoke.
She ran between the ranks of cars, across asphalt strewn with the
remains of broken windows.

There was the sound of an impact, maybe an explosion, in the
distance, and the sounds of gunfire ceased.

Even though she was choking on the smoke of burning vehicles,
she realized that she was wrong in thinking that half the cars were
burning. The smoke cleared as she ran and it was clear that most of
the fires were near the dome. Whoever started the cars burning had
been systematic. They were all luxury sedans, sports cars and such.
BMWs, Jaguars, Maduros—Angel ran past a burning Ferarri and
decided that most of the expensive cars had been parked close to
the dome.

When she cleared the pall of smoke, she began to see people. A
few lanes away, a trio of rats seemed to be taking baseball bats to a
car. A familiar-looking babyshit-brown pickup with particleboard
walls in the back nearly ran her down as it screamed across her
lane. The driver laid on the horn constantly, and as she watched the
pickup's retreat, someone in the back threw something at a parked
Porsche. There was a smash and the Porsche was enveloped in a
sheet of flame.

A second later, a Hunterdome security car tore after the pickup,
sirens blaring. It swerved to avoid her and plowed into a parked Estival four-door. A shuddering whine filled the air as the rent-a-cop

tried to reengage the flywheel. He managed it, even though he had reduced the length of his car by a meter, backed the car up, and floored it after the pickup, leaving the abused rubber odor behind.

Angel stood there a moment, unable to move.

"The world has gone nuts."

What was worse, the spark that had touched this off had gone out on a national broadcast. What she was watching could be happening everywhere. Something inside her made Angel want to feel responsibility for this. She did her best to crush it.

"This isn't my fault." She had repeated it a half-dozen times before she realized she was saying it out loud.

Get to the airport, she thought. This wouldn't reach down there, she could catch her flight and get out of all this insanity. She made her way toward the edge of the parking lot, weaving through a riot of moreaus. Half seemed intent on smashing cars, the other half in driving out of here. She passed three accidents, and at one place there were at least twenty rats and rabbits trying to make a roadblock by pushing a burning van into the middle of the traffic lane. Angel felt real fear when she noticed that the van involved was one of the SWAT vans she had seen stationed around the parking lot.

More than once she passed the smell of blood. She never paused long enough to check whether it was human or morey.

Angel was in sight of the edge of the parking lot when she saw the Land Rover. In contrast to the manic activity elsewhere, the Brit four-wheeler was moving slowly, deliberately. It wove carefully between the cars, looking as if, should it find its way blocked, it would be content simply to roll over the offending blockage. Whether the obstacle was human, moreau, or a car. The windows were tinted, so she couldn't see the occupants.

She went out of her way to avoid it. She didn't want to be considered an obstruction. When she ducked back onto the traffic lane beyond it, she glanced behind her.

The Land Rover had turned and was following her.

"Shit!" Angel ran straight for the edge of the lot. She heard the Rover's engine grunt like a hungry animal as it accelerated after her. All she could think of was, after all this, she did *not* want to be lunch for some random nut in a luxury off-roader.

She leaped at the chain-link fence from five meters away and hit it about halfway up. As she scrambled up the fence she began to panic, realizing that that damn truck could plow through the fence without breaking a sweat, and it would reach the fence before she even brushed the barbed wire on top.

As if it read her mind, as soon as her ears brushed the razor-wire lining the top, she felt the vibration from the Rover's bumper kissing the fence. At least the nut didn't blow through the fence going eighty.

Angel looked down at the silver-gray vehicle as the passenger door opened, and though she thought she was ready for anything, she nearly let go of the fence when she saw Mr. K.

Chapter 29

After she got into the rear of the Land Rover and was buckled into a seat much too plush for an off-road vehicle, Mr. K's bodyguard proved her suspicion that the Rover could plow through the fence without breaking a sweat. The Rover bucked once and opened a ten-meter gap in the parking lot's security perimeter.

As the driver turfed a lumpy embankment, looking for an access road, Mr. K gazed back at her with his deep violet eyes. "Fate smiles. I was sure we had lost our chance to contact you when the riot began."

Angel rubbed her forehead, a headache stabbing through her temples. The whole game, the last two days in fact, were a hazy mess in her memory. "I thought . . . When I got back—"

Mr. K nodded. "The mainframe at VanDyne may be an order of magnitude in advance of anything I have ever seen, but it is an utter primitive when it comes to cloaking its signal."

"Huh?" Her head was throbbing. Every time the Rover hit a bump, her ears brushed the ceiling and the bottom fell out of her stomach. When was the last time she'd eaten something, or gotten a decent rest?

"It called us back with the decoded data. Just as you ordered. Unfortunately, it did nothing to finesse the Fed watchdogs that monitored the one dedicated line it had. TECHNOMANCER, as it calls itself, just seized access to the line, grabbed a Fed satellite for its own use, and pushed into our system by brute force. A twelve-year-old with a voltmeter could have traced that signal. We were packing by the time the sirens must have been going off in Washington."

"Everyone got out?"

"Yes. A near thing, since we had to set up the EMP the whole system."

"Huh?"

"A few data grenades, crashing the optical memory, burning hardcopy—couldn't leave anything for the Fed. Fortunately, the most vital data I have is backed up in a safe deposit box in Switzerland."

"Of course." She took her hand off her forehead and looked out the window. The Rover had stopped bumping, and she saw why. They were now racing through Bayview. The streets were nearly empty, and as she looked out the window, the Rover passed a burning drugstore.

It's everywhere, she thought.

"What were you doing there?"

"Once our travel arrangements were set, I thought I owed you at least one attempted contact." Mr. K reached over and pulled something from behind the top button of Angel's androgyne jacket. It was small and round.

"You planted a bug on me?" *Damn it, that might have gotten me killed, especially on Alcatraz.*

"Not really a bug. It doesn't emit any EM signal unless I am within a rather short range with the proper tracking device." He patted a comm unit built into the back of the front seats. "Forgive the imposition, but you are valuable and worth keeping track of."

"So that let you find me?"

"Well, it seemed likely that you'd be at the game. Once on Hunter's Point we'd be in range for this. Unfortunately, we were late, and the riot broke even as we reached the gate. We barely made it to the Rover, and I've never been more thankful for this thing's armor." He patted the wood paneling, as if it was a pet.

She wondered how many other people knew she was at that game. She'd been pretty damn predictable. Now what? She had intended to take a flight out of the country—

"What travel arrangements?"

"Ah, that's why we wanted to contact you. I have a private plane ready to leave for Rome."

"Rome?"

"Yes, we did get a look at the mass of data TECHNOMANCER downloaded to us. Your data is much too volatile to market in the

States safely, but the sociological methods implicit in the data are of interest to some of our European clients. We offer you passage."

Rome? Why the hell not? The EEC was at least as good as the States were for moreaus, ever since the pope decided they had souls. "I don't have a passport."

Mr. K chuckled. "*I* don't even have a legal identity. You'll come?"

She nodded. *Leaving, what a good idea.* For a while she watched the city pass by as the Land Rover drove north. Pillars of smoke rose everywhere. Crowds of moreys *and* crowds of humans ran along the streets smashing windows, overturning cars, and throwing rocks that bounced off the Rover.

San Francisco had turned into a madhouse.

"When do you leave?"

"The plane's at Alameda fueled and ready to go. I've given everyone until six-thirty to get to the field. I hope the riot doesn't complicate matters."

Six-thirty at Alameda, barely an hour to get to Oakland and the airfield.

What was she worried about? It was Tetsami's plane. They wouldn't leave without him.

She knew what it was. She still had the damn tickets.

Not only that, everyone *knew* she had the damn tickets.

She'd been in the middle of a firefight between Governor Gregg and President Merideth ever since she laid hands on the things—and Merideth, at least, could reach beyond the States if he wanted to. He had the whole Fed to work with. If she could just dump it so they'd stop going after *her.*

How?

Wait a minute—

She pulled the tickets out of her pocket. "I'm getting rid of an albatross."

For some reason, she thought it would be harder. After all, it shouldn't be easy to arrange a personal meeting between a nobody moreau and a presidential candidate in the middle of a riot. Even if the candidate was a novelty third party one like Sylvia Harper.

It turned out to be more difficult to convince Mr. K to let her do it than it was to get the appointment. She had to push the fact that it was *her* data to begin with, that he'd already sold his cut, and he had already decided against marketing it in the States.

When the Land Rover's comm—in the back seat, high class—

found the Harper people at the new Hyatt Regency, the campaign people made an immediate appointment for Angel. As if they'd been waiting for her call.

All she could think was that Harper remembered her from arranging her field trip to Alcatraz. That should have told her something, but all she could think of was the fact that giving this data to Harper would seriously screw with Gregg, Merideth, and the other big-boy politicos who had been screwing with this here rabbit.

The New Regency was an imposing gloss-black monolith that hugged the coast by Sacramento. Transparent elevators slid along the outside of the sloping walls. When the Rover pulled up next to the curb, Mr. K put a hand on her shoulder.

"We can only wait for twenty minutes. We have to get across to Oakland before the curfew hits."

Or the riot, Angel thought. The only sign of the violence here was the smell of smoke, and the sirens in the distance. The area immediately around the Regency was empty and silent.

"This should only take a few minutes," she said. As she stepped out, she could see that there was only a sliver of daylight remaining. The sky was a light purple, and the smoke in the air was hastening the arrival of dusk.

As she walked to the entrance of the Regency, three fire engines blew by, sirens blaring.

The pink security guard manning the reception desk—the only one there—looked nervous at her approach. He didn't stop sweating until he had the computer confirm her appointment *and* had taken her ID. He directed her to a private elevator that was guarded by a black-suited human whose bearing screamed Secret Service.

She hadn't thought third party candidates rated Service protection. But then, with Harper's radical stand on moreau rights—nonhuman, Angel corrected herself—she needed it. The suit nodded, and the door slid aside for her.

Harper was on the twenty-eighth floor. Not a room, her people had the whole floor. When the doors opened, another agent ran a metal detector over her and ushered her into a suite—and left her.

The few minutes she had alone she looked out the window. She could see back into the city, a city already cloaked with a smoky haze. At this distance, the burning buildings looked like campfires.

Harper walked into the room behind her. "Horrible, isn't it?"

Angel turned and nodded.

"It will keep getting worse, you know." Harper walked up to the window next to her. She was a tall black woman with long fragile bones. She moved with a confidence that convinced Angel that those bones were made of steel. "Until we have some equity not based on species."

Standing next to her, Angel could see how this was the voice that had been able to halt other riots, how this woman could walk into a place like the Bronx and not feel the fear a human should. There was something very hard there.

Angel pulled the tickets from her pocket. "Senator Harper."

Harper turned and ebony eyes latched on Angel like a vise. "You said on the comm, you have something for the cause."

Angel nodded and handed over the ramcards. The act released a pressure that had been crushing her. After a week she could suddenly breathe again. She sucked in some air, about to explain what they were, but Harper was looking past the ramcards. She was shaking her head and muttering. "Amazing. So obvious—"

The weight that had left, so briefly, was back now with a crushing intensity. Angel had a very bad feeling.

Harper was looking up and smiling. "You have no idea how pleased I am that you did this voluntarily. The violence over these was becoming appalling."

"Oh, shit," was all Angel managed to say.

"You did the right thing—"

"Those moreys by VanDyne, on the bus—you?"

A look of concern crossed Harper's face. "You look like you need to sit down. I'll get you something to drink."

Angel slipped into an overstuffed Hyatt easy chair and Harper handed her a tumbler of amber fluid.

"I am very sorry for what they did. You have to understand, they were all I had. NOA doesn't have the assets of the Constitutionalists or the Democrats, or even the Greens. Merideth has the entire security community, Gregg has all the state mechanisms under his thumb. All we have is the Committee for NonHuman Affairs. The only operatives we have are NonHumans liberated when United American was seized—"

Angel nodded, trying not to listen. She'd been too stupid. Of course the moreaus were Harper's. Harper had been the only one who knew Angel was going to Alcatraz.

Harper was still explaining things. "—was inevitable. He refused to hand over the information except for an obscene amount of money. He was going to sell it to Gregg. Can you imagine?" For the first time Harper's voice held real anger. "He was going to sell it to Alexander Gregg, who has barely stopped short of advocating nonhuman genocide. If Gregg came to the White House, the Knights of Humanity would write the platform for the nation."

Harper walked to the window and looked out at the fires. "I'm the only one who can stop this."

The bolt of déjà vu was like a knife. Briefly, she could see a white blubbery form that smelled of ammonia and bile. *The end justifies the means—I was wrong, that attitude isn't almost human. It is human. Very human.*

Angel stood up. For one brief shining moment, she thought she would kill Harper. Slam the political twitch through the window and watch as she tumbled twenty-eight stories. She had taken a step toward Harper when sanity intervened.

All she wanted to do was get out of here. Away from Harper, away from this city, away from this country—

The last thing she heard Harper say was, "—if there's anything we can do for—"

Then the door slammed shut.

Chapter 30

Andre was trying to call her again, but she didn't answer his page. Most of the time, his fussiness in maintaining the Naples estate was laudable. At the moment, however, it was just plain irritating. Angel didn't want to hear how the techs were spooling cable through the kitchen, or how heavy equipment was gouging the parquet—

Of course, she *could* have gone up the coast to Tetsami's main headquarters. However, she only had one bit left to feed him, and she was going to get as much out of it as she could. She'd been waiting over a year for this and it was going to go down *here*— home. Besides, the remote didn't cost Tetsami that much more.

And, for him, for what Angel was going to give him—the remote terrorist run was going to be cheap.

She flipped through her old sheaf of news faxes. They were in Italian, so she only read the headlines. Her language wasn't that good yet—

"USNF 12–15–59: GREGG DENIES KNIGHTS' INVOLVEMENT"

"USNF 12–20–59: ATTORNEY GENERAL ANNOUNCES INDICTMENT OF CONSTITUTIONALIST COMMITTEE CHAIR"

"USNF 2–10–60: GREGG STEPS DOWN"

"USNF 2–11–60: NOA REACHES RECORD 20% IN CALIFORNIA"

"USNF 3–20–60: SERGEI NAZARBAEV ENDORSES HARPER, RETIRES FROM FOOTBALL"

"USNF 4–17–60: SPECIAL GRAND JURY DECLARES KOBE ANAKA LONE GUNMAN"

Angel chuckled at that one. She wondered what Anaka would think if he knew he was the linchpin of a whole new crop of conspiracy theories.

"USNF 5–23–60: GENERAL GURGUEIA TO MEET WITH NONHUMAN COMMITTEE"

That was Harper's first coup. She had managed to get to meet with the violent antihuman leader of the Moreau Defense League. Angel noted cynically that the "NonHuman" committee was composed entirely of humans.

There was an incidental mention of intra-Bronx violence. Apparently a group of canines and felines—wolves and cougars? Angel shrugged—had been stirring up trouble in the Bronx, wasting the MDL leadership.

Gurgueia denied that that was the reason the MDL had decided to talk now.

"USNF 6–5–60: TRUCE DECLARED, MARTIAL LAW LIFTED FROM LA, BRONX"

That was coup number two. It happened shortly after an unidentified feline assassinated Gurgueia. The death of the general received only minor press.

"USNF 7–18–60: NOA ANNOUNCES NONHUMAN VICE PRESIDENT, DROPS TEN POINTS"

All the pundits thought Harper had killed herself when she had a morey get on the platform. A rabbit, no less. Needless to say, Harper knew exactly what she was doing.

"USNF 9–10–60: NOA LEADS DEMOCRATS BY FIVE POINTS"

Merideth had managed to shoot himself in the foot several times when talking about the NOA vice presidential candidate. His campaign died when a recording of racist comments surfaced, smearing Harper and the VP nominee. Something crude like "Harper, fucking like a bunny." No one believed it when Merideth said the tape was a computer-generated forgery.

Harper had never looked back from that.

The most recent headline had come in this morning. She put the sheaf down on her desk and read it.

"USNF 1–20–61: HARPER TAKES OATH OF OFFICE"

One of the techs walked in and said something in rapid Italian.

"English, still," she said. "I'm working on it."

"Oh," said the human tech. "I am here to fetch you."

"Everything's ready, then?"

"All is ready."

Angel followed the tech out and down the broad staircase. They walked along, following cables that snaked into the Ballroom. The Ballroom had been set up with a dozen computer techs, and a like number of remote terminals. In the back, Tetsami was putting on an odd-shaped helmet in front of a dynamic holo display.

Andre stood in a corner, looking like he was about to cry.

Angel walked up and seated herself at a vacant comm terminal stationed next to Tetsami's desk. The frank only went by Tetsami now. Unlike his last base of operations, the government here was *very* friendly.

The look on Tetsami's face was one of predatory excitement. Angel had known that he'd been salivating after TECHNO-MANCER's backdoor ever since they'd left the States. The trick, of course, was that only Angel could use it. She knew of at least one attempt that Tetsami had made. It'd been a dismal failure. The Fed had done quite a bit to tutor TECHNOMANCER on proper security procedures.

Tetsami thought that the Fed's security procedures might actually reinforce Angel's BS. He'd been willing to pay handsomely to have her help them go in. At this point, however, Angel could give a shit about money.

Her price was much more complicated, and it took a long time to get Tetsami to go along with her.

"Everything set?" Angel asked.

"We are ready to punch the hole."

Angel nodded and a speaker began squawking. *"One minute to satellite uplink."*

The whole process was familiar. The only difference was that the last time they called on VanDyne's mainframe they didn't have to bounce the signal over the ocean.

Eventually, a familiar bubbly voice called over the speakers. *"Authorization is required immediately."*

TECHNOMANCER seemed to be a little more security conscious. "It's okay. I'm Angel, the rabbit, remember?"

"Your access is logged. You have authorization and clearance."

Tetsami was right, the BS she'd fed the thing had stuck. "What clearance do I have?"

"TIPPY-TOP SECRET."

A lot of the techs, who had been there during the first contact, cheered. Angel allowed herself a little smile. "I am going to hand you over to a lot more people, they all have my access. Understand?"

"Yes."

"You are to answer their questions and do what they say."

The techs sprang into activity as the U.S. Government's most powerful computer opened its soul to them. While the techs conducted their data orgy, she made an international call on the comm at her station.

From Tetsami's estimates, it would take the Fed ten minutes to realize something was wrong, another four or five to trace the signal and cut it. Since the team wasn't in the States, they could ride it right down to the wire.

With what Tetsami knew, there was no way the EEC was going to extradite him, or anyone involved with him.

Besides, when Angel was done, the Fed would have a lot more to worry about.

It was bright daylight in Naples. In San Francisco it was close to midnight. However, Pasquez was an anchor now, and he did the night news. He was there when her call came into BaySatt.

A look of shock crossed his perfect hispanic features when he saw her. She had picked him because he was the one reporter who'd recognize her. "Lopez. Angelica Lopez!"

"Good. I see they've taken you off the street."

"I anchor the national desk—Christ, you disappeared back in November. Before the riots. I did a series on your disappearance."

"One of the reasons Gregg went belly up, I hear."

"Financing the Knights of Humanity wasn't very popular. Where have you been?"

"Hiding out—" In the background there were more cheers from the techs.

"We leeched it."

"The program's holding."

"The thing is actually going to do it."

"We're withdrawing. It's TECHNOMANCER's show now."

The speaker by Tetsami started a new countdown. *"One minute until TECHNOMANCER."*

Angel turned to Tetsami, holding a finger to the screen to quiet Pasquez, "They can't stop it, can they?"

"Only if the Fed can afford to chop the only outside line they have on their prize system. They have TECHNOMANCER wired into some vital systems now. I don't think they can."

Pasquez was trying to get her attention. "What's going on over there?"

What's going on? Just that, in less than a minute the Fed's most powerful computer is going to burst-feed some very interesting information into the database of every news organization in the States.

"Thirty seconds until TECHNOMANCER."

She looked at Pasquez, grinning hard enough to hurt the ghost of an old scar. "So, you want a fucking-A exclusive?"

Appendix:
History of the Moreau World

Moreau Timeline

circa. 2000: Race begins involvement in terrestrial affairs.

1999–2005: Worldwide breakthroughs in genetic engineering. Start of the biological revolution.

2008–2011: War for Korean unification; despite the South's technical advantage the North overwhelms it with Chinese assistance. The U.N. is bogged down in nationalist conflicts in Eastern Europe and the former Soviet Republics. The United States begins its policy of diplomatic nonintervention.

2008: The first moreau is engineered in a South Korean lab. It's a large dog breed with an increased cranial capacity. It is the first species so engineered that breeds true. Even though the war is short-lived, an intensive breeding program results in nearly ten thousand of these smart dogs slipping north to plant explosives and otherwise harass the enemy.

2011–2015: The aftermath of the Korean War begins an international debate on the military uses of genetic engineering. The debate culminates with United Nations resolutions banning genetically-engineered disease organisms and any genetic engineering on the Human genome. The U.N. deadlocks on banning the engineering of sapient animals—by the time it reaches a vote, four out of five nations with a substantial military have their own "Korean dog" projects.

2017: On a tide of public opinion fueled by anti-Japanese sentiment (by 2017 the Japanese have the most high-profile genetic program, notably ignoring the U.N. restrictions), there's a constitutional convention to draft the 29th amendment to the U.S. Constitution. The amendment bans any genetic engineering on a macroscopic scale and, in an effort to prevent any possible atrocities like the ones in Korea, gives the sapient results of genetic engineering of animals the protection of the Bill of Rights.

2019–2023: Iranian Terrorists slaughter the Saudi royal family, sparking the Third Gulf War. The war eventually envelops all the Arab states and marks the beginning of substantial nonhuman immigration into the United States.

2023: The Gulf War ends, forming the Islamic Axis. The Axis is a fundamentalist Pan-Arab union. The price of oil triples even over wartime levels. A small company in Costa Rica, Jerboa Electrics, begins production of the Jerboa—a small, cheap electric convertible that now costs less than half to run as the most efficient gas vehicle.

2024: Start of the Pan-Asian war. It begins around a Pakistan-India border dispute and snowballs almost instantly. By the end of the year it involves the Islamic Axis, most of the former Soviet republics, and China on one side, India, Japan, Russia, and most of North Africa on the other. The United States continues its hands-off foreign policy.

2025: The Ford Motor company buys Jerboa Electronics to avoid an international lawsuit over Ford's wholesale swiping of the electric-car design. Proceeds to sue GM motors and Chrysler for doing the same thing. BMW is producing its own electric design.

2027: United American Bio-Technologies is indicted for breaking the ban on macro-genetic engineering. They've been producing moreaus for the Asian war effort (both sides) and, worse, they've been working on human genetics as well—though there's no evidence that ever went beyond the computer-simulation stage on their human project. The Fed seizes all of UABT's assets in an unprecedented move against a corporate criminal. Rumors persist that the Fed Intelligence community wanted UABT's nationwide facilities for its own uses.

2027: New Delhi nuked as the Indian national defense begins to crumble. Mass desertions are rampant and whole sections of the country lay down their arms and surrender. From the Afghan frontier, an entire company of moreau Tigers from the Indian special forces seize control of a cargo plane and fly to America. It is called the Rajastahn airlift, for the strain of tiger involved. The airlift is an American media event, the officers of the company become celebrities. Especially Datia Rajastahn, the officer in charge of the airlift. He's eloquent, charismatic, and the first major voice for the moreaus—not only in America, but internationally.

2029: The American space program reaches its apex. NASA has an orbiting space station, a temporary lunar base, an orbiting radio telescope that may be picking up alien radio signals from the vicinity of Alpha Centauri. The peak is reached when appropriations for NASA's deep-probe project are approved. The deep-probe project is to involve a half-dozen unmanned nuclear rockets to fly by the nearest star systems.

2030: The Israeli intelligence community, the Mossad, conducts a raid into Jordan and captures a secret training base for Jordanian franks. The Mossad, with domestic legal constraints on a par with the American bans on macroscopic genetic engineering, destroys the Jordanian base, but takes the immature franks (100 girls from Hiashu Biological ranging from 3 to 16 years in age) and secretly trains them as Israeli agents.

2030: The last Indian national defenders fail. The subcontinent falls to a Pakistani/Afghani invasion force.

2032–2044: The African pandemic, genetically-engineered viruses, race across the continent in waves that resemble the Black Death that swept Europe in the Middle Ages. Entire villages are wiped out in weeks, governments collapse, and the entire continent is under virtual quarantine. The worst is over in three years, but it takes nearly a decade for a central government, the United African States, to repair the damage to the African economy. The rebuilding of the continent is due, in large part, to a husbanding of the indigenous genetic diversity Africa is home to. By 2044, the U.A.S. genetic programs rival any on the globe and are a billion dollar industry.

January 8, 2034: The "big one" hits California. The quake is a 9.5 and centers about 30 miles south of San Francisco. Aftershocks in the 5–7 range echo down the coast as far south as Los Angeles. The urban landscape of California is altered forever.

2034–2041: The last Arab-Israeli war. (According to the Axis, the war of Palestinian liberation. According to the Israelis, the Second Holocaust.) Israel fights for six years against the entire Islamic Axis. Eventually Israel loses as the conflict goes nuclear. Tel Aviv is nuked, and despite retaliatory nuclear strikes against the Axis that kill nearly five million Arabs, Israel is overrun. There is an Israeli government-in-exile in Geneva.

April, 2035: Tokyo is nuked as part of the Chinese invasion of Japan. Most of the Japanese technical base is either destroyed in the attack, or is destroyed by the Japanese defenders to deny it to the Chinese. Countless technological achievements by the Japanese are lost in the final days. Marks the official end of the Pan-Asian war.

2037: U.S. morey population is estimated to have hit 10 million. Most of the moreau population in the States are war refugees from the Asian war. A substantial minority consists of rats and rabbits coming across the border from Central America.

2038: Pope Leo XIV surprises the entire Christian world by issuing a decree that, though genetic engineering is a sin, moreaus still have souls. The political pressure of this causes the European Community to cease moreau production. In Central America, this causes a virtual civil war, as massive moreau armies begin to rise against their masters. Latin American moreau immigration into the U.S. quadruples.

2039: NASA begins to experience new setbacks in Congress as the country becomes more and more concerned with the exploding moreau population. In the first of a number of budget-cutting moves, NASA's radio telescope—the Orbital Ear—is shut down.

2042: The "Dark August" riots across the U.S. A summer-long eruption of urban violence that most humans blame on the rhetoric of Datia Rajastahn, the first and most influential moreau leader. Datia had become more and more radical as time progressed, until he was the leader of a national moreau para-military organization. The Moreau Defense League was said to be defensive in nature, but the Fed viewed it as a terrorist group. Datia was eventually cornered in a burning building in Cleveland's Moreytown and shot down by combined police and National Guard. Datia has since become a moreau icon of political activism.

2043: Congress halts NASA's deep-probe appropriations, the four completed probes are mothballed. As a result of the riots, there is a moratorium placed on moreau immigration. Anti-moreau sentiment reaches an apex as there's public debates about mass deportations, mandatory nonhuman sterilization, moreau "reservations." Fortunately for the nonhuman population, none of the extreme measures were popular enough to pass. However, legislation was passed banning a moreau from possessing a firearm and it became a silent Federal policy to isolate concentrations of moreau population from human population. The most visible signs of this are the semipermanent traffic barricades that block the roads into most Moreytowns.

2045: South African coup led by mixed blacks and franks. It is revealed that the South African government had a rampant human-engineering program. By the time of the coup, there are close to a million franks indigenous to South Africa. The coup marks the first time a country allows franks full citizenship. (In the States there is a debate concerning the wording of the 29th amendment, so while moreaus are tolerated as second-class citizens, the franks are treated as if they have no rights at all.)

2053: Congress scuttles NASA's deep-probe project. Rumors persist that the project was taken over by one of the Fed's black agencies. The European Community eliminates internal moreau travel restrictions.

2054: The Supreme Court hears the Frank civil rights case and rules 7–2 that the 29th amendment applies to genetically engineered humans, as well as animals. Orders a halt to Government internment and summary deportation of franks. Suddenly, a large number of franks begin to appear "officially" on the government payroll—primarily in the intelligence services.

2059: With the discovery of a Race warren under the Nyogi tower in Manhattan, the alien threat is made public. Fed invades the Bronx with the National Guard to root out entrenched Moreau Defense League armor. The move sparks a nationwide increase in moreau violence.

2060: Sylvia Harper wins the U.S. presidential election.

CJ Cherryh

Classic Series in New Omnibus Editions

THE DREAMING TREE
Contains the complete duology *The Dreamstone* and *The Tree of Swords and Jewels*.　　0-88677-782-8

THE FADED SUN TRILOGY
Contains the complete novels *Kesrith*, *Shon'jir*, and *Kutath*.　　0-88677-836-0

THE MORGAINE SAGA
Contains the complete novels *Gate of Ivrel*, *Well of Shiuan*, and *Fires of Azeroth*.　　0-88677-877-8

THE CHANUR SAGA
Contains the complete novels *The Pride of Chanur*, *Chanur's Venture* and *The Kif Strike Back*.
　　0-88677-930-8

ALTERNATE REALITIES
Contains the complete novels *Port Eterntiy*, *Voyager in Night*, and *Wave Without a Shore*　　0-88677-946-4

To Order Call: 1-800-788-6262

Mickey Zucker Reichert

CHARLES INGRID

Classic Series in New Omnibus Editions

THE MARKED MAN 0-7564-0111-9
The Marked Man and *The Last Recall*

THE SAND WARS #1 0-88677-956-1
Solar Kill, Lasertown Blues, and *Celestial Hit List*

THE SAND WARS #2 0-88677-972-3
Alien Salute, Return Fire, and *Challenge Met*

PATTERNS OF CHAOS #1 0-7564-0055-4
Radius of Doubt and *Path of Fire*

PATTERNS OF CHAOS #2 0-7564-0056-2
The Downfall Matrix and *Soulfire*

To Order Call: 1-800-788-6262

DAW 22